THE SHADOW OF SAGANAMI

DAVID WEBER

THE SHADOW OF SAGANAMI

This is a work of fiction. All the characters and events portrayed in this book are fictional, and any resemblance to real people or incidents is purely coincidental.

A Baen Books Original

Baen Publishing Enterprises
P.O. Box 1403
Riverdale, NY 10471
www.baen.com

ISBN-13: 978-1-4165-0929-5
ISBN-10: 1-4165-0929-1

Cover art by David Mattingly
Map by Randy Asplund

First paperback printing, October 2005

Library of Congress Cataloging-in-Publication Number 2004015087

Distributed by Simon & Schuster
1230 Avenue of the Americas
New York, NY 10020

Production & design by Windhaven Press (www.windhaven.com)
Printed in the United States of America

THE HUNTERS . . .
ABOUT TO BECOME THE HUNTED

"Sir, we're being hailed by the bogeys. It's voice-only."

Terekhov turned his chair to face Lieutenant Commander Nagchaudhuri and cocked one eyebrow. "Put it on speaker, please."

"Aye, aye, Sir."

"Freighter *Nijmegen*, this is Captain Daumier of the heavy cruiser *Anhur*. Cut your accel immediately and stand by for rendezvous!" The voice was harsh, hard-edged, with the flat accent of the slums of Noveau Paris. There was a chill menace to it.

"Odd, wouldn't you say, Ansten?" Terekhov murmured, and the executive officer nodded.

"In a lot of ways, Skipper. That's a Peep talking, all right. But why voice-only? And why not identify *Anhur* as a Havenite vessel?"

"Maybe she's pretending to be a 'regular' pirate, Skipper," Ginger Lewis offered from her own quadrant of Terekhov's com screen, and he made a small gesture, inviting her to amplify her thought.

"On my first deployment to Silesia, the Peeps had organized a commerce-raiding operation designed to look as much as possible like regular pirate attacks on our merchant traffic," she said. "Could this be more of the same?"

"Excuse me, Sir," Nagchaudhuri interrupted. "*Anhur*'s repeating her message."

"Missile Launch!" one of Kaplan's ratings announced suddenly. "I have a single missile launch from Bogey One!"

Kaplan's eyes flashed back to her plot. A single inbound missile showed on it as a red triangle, apex pointed directly at *Hexapuma* while it moved steadily across the display.

Terekhov leaned comfortably back in his command chair and crossed his legs, his expression serene, with the confident assurance expected of the commander of one of Her Majesty's starships. And if there was a hidden, fiery core of anticipation behind those blue eyes, that was no one's business but his.

Baen Books by David Weber:

Honor Harrington:
On Basilisk Station
The Honor of the Queen
The Short Victorious War
Field of Dishonor
Flag in Exile
Honor Among Enemies
In Enemy Hands
Echoes of Honor
Ashes of Victory
War of Honor
At All Costs (forthcoming)

edited by David Weber:
More Than Honor
Worlds of Honor
Changer of Worlds
The Service of the Sword

Honorverse:
Crown of Slaves
(with Eric Flint)
The Shadow of Saganami

Mutineers' Moon
The Armageddon Inheritance
Heirs of Empire
Empire from the Ashes

Path of the Fury

The Apocalypse Troll

The Excalibur Alternative

Old Soldiers

Bolo!

Oath of Swords
The War God's Own
Wind Rider's Oath

with Steve White:
Crusade
In Death Ground
The Stars at War
Insurrection
The Shiva Option
The Stars at War II

with John Ringo:
March Upcountry
March to the Sea
March to the Stars
We Few

with Eric Flint:
1633

For Anne McCaffrey,
because ideas, like dragons, fly,
and you helped give mine wings.

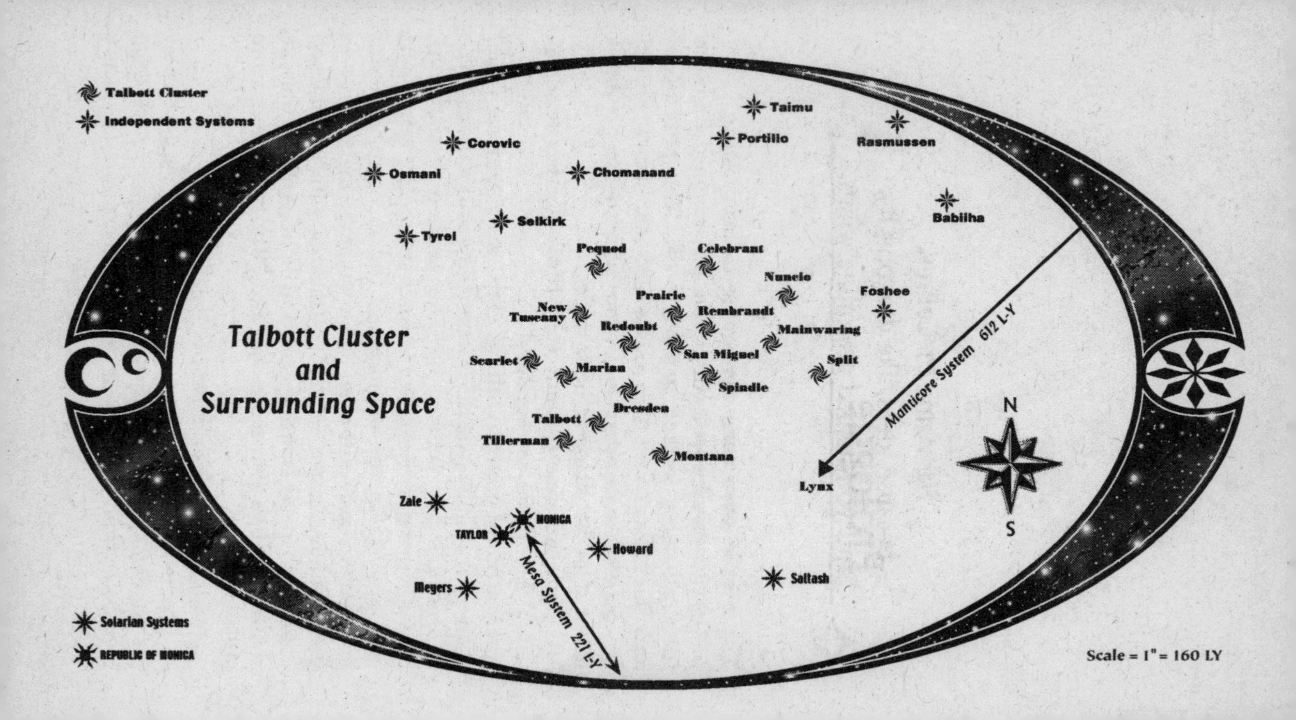
Talbott Cluster
Independent Systems
Talbott Cluster
and
Surrounding Space
Taimu
Corovic
Portilio
Rasmussen
Osmani
Chomanand
Babiiha
Selkirk
Tyrel
Pequod
Celebrant
Nuncio
Foshee
Prairie
New
Tuscany
Rembrandt
Redoubt
Mainwaring
San Miguel
Scarlet
Marian
Split
Spindle
Dresden
Talbott
Tillerman
Montana
Manticore System 612 L-Y
Lynx
N
S
Zale
MONICA
TAYLOR
Howard
Mesa System 221 L-Y
Saltash
Megers
Solarian Systems
REPUBLIC OF MONICA
Scale = 1" = 160 LY

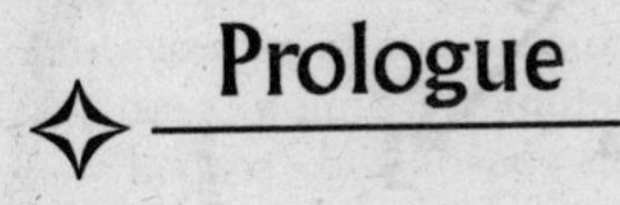

Prologue

The missile salvo came screaming in from astern.

Counter-missiles took out eleven. The crippled starboard tethered decoy sucked two more off. The port decoy had been destroyed two salvos ago—or was it three? He couldn't remember, and there was no time to think about it as he snapped helm orders.

"Starboard ninety! Hard skew turn—get her nose up, Chief! Stand her on her toes!"

"Starboard ninety, rolling ship, aye!" Senior Chief Mangrum acknowledged, pulling the joystick hard back.

Defiant's bow pitched up. She writhed to starboard, clawing upward, trying to wrench her vulnerable port side away from the enemy, and the incoming missiles tracked viciously after her. The wounded light cruiser's point defense lasers swivelled, tracking with unpanicked electronic speed, spitting coherent light. Another missile shattered, then two more—a third. But the others were still coming.

"*Valiant*'s lost her forward ring, Sir! She's—"

His head snapped around towards the visual display just as *Defiant*'s sister ship took another complete missile broadside from the nearest Peep battlecruiser. The heavy laser heads detonated virtually simultaneously less than five thousand kilometers off *Valiant*'s port bow. The deadly bomb-pumped lasers slashed out, stabbing through her fluctuating sidewall like white-hot needles through soft butter. Light armor shattered, impeller nodes flashed and exploded like prespace flashbulbs, atmosphere belched outward, and then the entire forward third of her hull shattered. It didn't explode, it simply . . . shattered. The brutally mutilated hull began to tumble madly, and then her fusion bottle failed and she *did* explode.

"*Handley* and *Plasma Stream* are crossing the Alpha wall, Sir!" Franklin shouted from Communications, and he knew he ought to feel something. Triumph, perhaps. But the fact that two ships of his convoy had escaped was cold and bitter ashes on his tongue. The other merchies hadn't, *Valiant* and *Resolute* had already died, and now it was *Defiant*'s turn.

Point defense stopped one, final missile—then the other six detonated.

Defiant bucked and heaved indescribably. Damage alarms shrieked, and he felt the concussive shocks of failing structural members as the lasers' transfer energy blasted into her hull.

"Missile Seventeen, Nineteen, and Twenty destroyed! Alpha Fourteen, Beta Twenty-Nine and Thirty destroyed! Heavy damage, Frames Six-Niner-Seven aft! Point Defense Twenty-Five through Thirty destroyed! Magazine Four breached! Lasers Seventeen and Nineteen destroyed! Heavy casualties Engineering and—"

The frantic litany of his ship's horrendous wounds rolled on and on, but he had no time to listen to it. Other people would have to deal with that the best they could, and his universe narrowed to the helm and his tactical repeater plot.

"Prep and launch Mike-Lima decoys, all forward tubes! Roll port! Evasion pattern Uniform-X-ray!"

Senior Chief Mangrum did his best. *Defiant* twisted back around to her left, doubling back on her course, turning her bow towards the oncoming missile storm. The decoy drones—not Ghost Rider birds, because those were all gone; weaker and less sophisticated than the tethered system, but the best she had left—streaked out in front of her, spreading out, calling to the sensors of the missiles trying to kill her. He could smell smoke, the stench of burning insulation and circuitry—and flesh—and the back of his brain heard someone shrieking in agony over an open com circuit.

"Point defense fire plan Horatius!" he snapped, and what was left of his Tactical Department started throwing canisters of counter-missiles out of the bow tubes. The canisters were seldom used, especially by a ship as small as a light cruiser, but this was exactly the situation for which they were designed. *Defiant* had lost over half her counter-missile tubes. The canisters used standard missile tubes to put additional clusters of defensive birds into space, and despite her vicious damage, the ship still had three-quarters of her counter-missile uplinks, which gave her control channels to spare.

At least two-thirds of the incoming salvos lost track, twisting off into the depths of space after the decoy drones. More of them disappeared as the light cruiser's counter-missiles' impeller wedges swept a cone in front of her. *Defiant*'s defensive fire bored a tunnel through the middle of the dense swarm of attacking missiles, and she roared down it, her surviving laser clusters in desperate continuous fire against the laser heads on her flanks. Bomb-pumped lasers lashed at her, but they wasted themselves on her impenetrable impeller wedge, for her hairpin turn had taken their onboard computers by surprise, and the surviving laser heads had no time to maneuver into firing positions.

And well they should have been surprised, a fragment of his brain thought grimly. His bleeding ship was headed directly into the teeth of the overwhelming enemy task force, now, not away, and the heavy spinal grasers of her forward chase armament locked onto a *Mars*-class heavy cruiser.

They opened fire. The range was long for any energy

weapon, even the massive chasers, but the Peep had strayed ahead of her consorts and the more massive battlecruisers as she raced eagerly for the kill, and *Defiant*'s gunnery had always been good. Her target staggered as the deadly blast of energy, dozens of times more powerful than even a ship of the wall's laser heads, sledgehammered into her. It was as if she had run into a rock in space. The chasers went to rapid, continuous fire, sucking every erg Engineering and their own capacitor rings could feed them. Audible warning alarms added their shrillness to the cacophony of damage signals, combat chatter, and beeping priority signals as the grasers overheated catastrophically, but there was no point cutting back, and he knew it.

So did the grasers' on-mount crews. They didn't even try to reduce power. They simply threw everything they had, for as long as they had it, and their target exploded into wreckage, shattering into jagged splinters, life pods, and vac-suited bodies. The tide of destruction swept aft, tearing her apart frame by frame, and then she vanished in a sun-bright fireball . . . two seconds before Chaser Two's abused circuitry exploded.

There was no time to feel exultation, or even grim satisfaction. The brief respite his desperate maneuver had won ended as the Peeps adjusted. The dead cruiser's squadron mates rolled, presenting their broadsides. They poured out fire in torrents, hurling their hate at their sister's killer. More missiles were shrieking in from every firing bearing, joining the holocaust of the *Mars*-class ships' fire, and there was no way to avoid them all. No more tricks. No more clever maneuvers.

There was only time to look at the plot, to see the incoming death sentence of his ship and all his people and to curse his own decision to fight. And then—

"Wake up, Aivars!"

His blue eyes snapped open, almost instantly. Almost . . . but not instantly enough to fool Sinead. He turned his head on the pillow, looking at her, his breathing almost normal, and she nestled against him. He felt her warmth, her softness, through the soft, silken fabric of her nightgown, and the short, feathery crop of dark red hair shifted on his shoulder—his right shoulder—like an equally silken kiss.

"It's over," she said softly, green eyes glinting like emeralds in the bedside light. *She must've turned it on when she heard the nightmare*, he thought.

"I know," he said, equally softly, and her mouth twisted in a sad, loving smile.

"Liar!" she whispered, reaching up, touching his neatly trimmed beard gently with a slender hand.

"No," he disagreed, feeling the sweat of remembered terror, remembered grief and guilt, cooling on his forehead. "It may not be as over as you'd like, Love. It's just as 'over' as it's going to get."

"Oh, Aivars!" She put her arms around him, laying her head across his chest, feeling the hard beat of his heart against her cheek, and tried not to weep. Tried not to show her fierce, bitter anger at the orders which were taking him away from her once more. Tried not to feel anger at the Admiralty for issuing them, or at *him* for accepting them.

"I love you very much, you know," she said quietly, not a trace of anger or resentment or fear in her voice.

"I know," he whispered, holding her tightly. "Believe me, I know."

"And I don't want you to go," she went on, closing her eyes. "You've done enough—more than enough. And I almost lost you once. I thought I *had* lost you, and the thought of losing you again, for good, terrifies me."

"I know," he whispered yet again, arms tightening about her with a welcome pain. But he didn't say "I won't go," and she fought down another spike of anger. Because he couldn't say it. He could never say it and be the man she loved. Hyacinth had wounded him in so many, many ways, yet the man she had always known was in there still. She knew it, and she clung to the knowledge, for it was her rock.

"I don't want you to go," she repeated, pressing her

face into his chest. "Even though I know you have to. But you come back to me, Aivars Terekhov. *You come back to me!"*

"I will," he promised, and felt a single, scalding tear on his chest. He hugged her more tightly still, and neither of them spoke again for a long, long time. There was no need, for in all the forty-three T-years of their marriage, he had never broken a promise to her. Nor would he break this one . . . if the choice was his.

Chapter One

Admiral of the Red Lady Dame Honor Harrington, Steadholder and Duchess Harrington, sat beside Vice Admiral of the Red Dame Beatrice McDermott, Baroness Alb, and watched silently as the comfortable amphitheater seating of the huge holographic simulator filled up. It was an orderly audience. It was also quite a bit smaller than it would have been a few years earlier. There were fewer non-Manticoran uniforms out there, as well, and the vast majority of the foreign ones which remained were the blue-on-blue of the Grayson Space Navy. Several of the Star Kingdom's smaller allies had cut back sharply on the midshipmen they sent to Saganami Island, and there were no Erewhonese uniforms at all. Dame Honor managed—somehow—to maintain her serene expression as she remembered the tight-faced midshipmen who had withdrawn from their classes in a body when their government denounced its long-standing alliance with the Star Kingdom of Manticore.

She didn't blame the young men and women, many of whom had been her students during her own time on the Island, despite her personal sense of betrayal. Nor could she really blame their government. Part of her wished she could, but Dame Honor believed in being honest with herself, and it had not been Erewhon which betrayed the Star Kingdom's trust. It had been Manticore's own government.

She watched the final midshipman take his place with a military precision fit to satisfy even a Saganami Marine. Then Dame Beatrice rose from the chair beside hers and walked with brisk yet measured strides to the traditional podium.

"Atttten—SHUN!"

Command Sergeant Major Sullivan's harsh voice filled even the vastness of the simulator with a projection the finest opera singer would have been hard-pressed to match, and a perfectly synchronized, thunderous "*Bang!*" answered as eleven thousand brilliantly polished boots slammed together in instant response. Fifty-five hundred midshipmen and midshipwomen came to attention, eyes front, shoulders square, spines ramrod straight, thumbs on trouser seams, and she looked back at them unblinkingly.

They were graduating early. Not as early as some of their predecessors had before Eighth Fleet's decisive offensive under Earl White Haven. But much earlier than their *immediate* predecessors had, now that Eighth Fleet's triumph had been thrown away like so much garbage. And they were headed not to the deployments of peacetime midshipman cruises, but directly into the cauldron of a new war.

A losing war, Dame Beatrice thought harshly, wondering how many of those youthful faces would die in the next few desperate months. How many of the minds behind those faces truly understood the monumental betrayal which was about to send them straight into the furnace?

She gazed at them, a master swordsmith contemplating the burnished brightness of her new-forged blades, searching for hidden flaws under the glittering sharpness. Wondering if their whetted steel was equal to the hurricane of combat which awaited them even as she prepared their final tempering.

"Stand easy, Ladies and Gentlemen."

The Academy Commandant's voice was even, a melodious contralto that flowed into the waiting silence, filling the stillness with its own quiet strength.

A vast, sibilant scuffing of boots answered her as the thousands of midshipmen assumed the parade rest position, and she gazed at them for several more seconds, meeting their eyes levelly.

"You are here," she told them, "for one final meeting before you begin your midshipman cruises. This represents a custom, a final sharing of what naval service truly is, and what it can cost, which has been a part of Saganami Island for over two centuries. By tradition, the Commandant of the Academy addresses her students at this time, but there have been exceptions. Admiral Ellen D'Orville was one such exception. And so was Admiral Quentin Saint-James.

"This year is another such exception, for we are honored and privileged to have Admiral Lady Dame Honor Harrington present. She will be on Manticore for only three days before returning to Eighth Fleet to complete its reactivation and take up her command once more. Many of you have had the privilege of studying under her as underclassmen. All of you could not do better than to hold her example before you as you take up your own careers. If any woman in the Queen's uniform today truly understands the tradition which brings us all together this day, it is she."

The silence was utter, and Honor felt her cheekbones heat as she rose from her chair in turn. The cream and gray treecat on her shoulder sat stock still, proud and tall, and the two of them tasted the emotions sweeping through the assembled midshipmen. Emotions which were focused on her, true, but only partially. For today, she truly was only a part, a spokeswoman, for something greater than any one woman, whatever her accomplishments. The silent midshipmen might not fully understand that, yet they sensed it, and their silent, hovering anticipation was like a slumbering volcano under a cool, white mantle of snow.

Dame Beatrice turned to face her and came to attention. She saluted sharply, and Honor's hand flashed up in answer, as sharp and precise as the day of her own Last View. Then their hands came down and they stood facing one another.

"Your Grace," Dame Beatrice said simply, and stepped aside.

Honor drew a deep breath, then walked crisply to the lectern Dame Beatrice had yielded to her. She took her place behind it, standing tall and straight with Nimitz statue-still upon her shoulder, and gazed out over that shining sea of youthful eyes. She remembered Last View. Remembered being one of the midshipwomen behind those eyes. Remembered Nimitz on her shoulder that day, too, looking up at Commandant Hartley, feeling the mystic fusion between her and him, with all the other middies, with every officer who had worn the Star Kingdom's black and gold before her. And now it was her turn to stand before a new arsenal of bright, burnished blades, to see their youth and promise . . . and mortality. And to truly sense, because this time she could physically taste it, the hushed yet humming expectancy and union which possessed them all.

"In a few days," she said finally into their silence, "you will be reporting for your first true shipboard deployments. It is my hope that your instructors have properly prepared you for that experience. You are our best and brightest, the newest link in a chain of responsibility, duty, and sacrifice which has been forged and hammered on the anvil of five centuries of service. It is a heavy burden to assume, one which can—and will—end for some of you in death."

She paused, listening to the silence, feeling its weight.

"Your instructors have done their best, here at the Island, to prepare you for that burden, that reality. Yet the truth is, Ladies and Gentlemen, that no one can truly prepare you for it. We can teach you, train you, share our institutional experience with you, but no one can be with you in the furnace. The chain of command, your superiors, the men and women under your orders . . . all of them will be there. And yet, in that moment when you truly confront duty and mortality, you *will* be alone. And that, Ladies and Gentlemen, is a moment no training and no teacher can truly prepare you to face.

"In that moment, you will have only four things to support you. Your training, which we have made as complete, as demanding, and as rigorous as we possibly could. Your courage, which can come only from within. Your loyalty to the men and women with whom you serve. And the tradition of Saganami. Some of you, most of you, will rise to the challenge of that moment. Some will try with all that is within you, and discover that all the training and courage in the universe do not make you immortal. And some, hopefully only a very few, will break."

The sound of a single indrawn breath would have been deafening as every eye looked back at her.

"The task to which you have been called, the burden you have volunteered to bear for your Queen and your Kingdom, for your Protector and your Planet, for whatever people you serve, is the most terrifying, dangerous, and honorable one in the universe. You have chosen, of your own free will, to place yourselves and your lives between the people and star nations you love and their enemies. To fight to defend them; to die to protect them. It is a burden others have taken up before you, and if no one can truly teach you the reality of all it means and costs until you have experienced it for yourself, there remains still much you can learn from those who have gone before. And that, Ladies and Gentlemen, is the reason you are here today, where every senior class of midshipmen has stood on the eve of its midshipman cruise for the last two hundred and forty-three T-years."

She pressed a button on the podium before her, and the lights dimmed. For an instant, there was nothing but dense, velvet darkness, broken only by the pinprick glitter of the LEDs on her podium's control panel, burning in the blackness like lost and lonely stars.

Then, suddenly, there was another light. One that glowed in the depths of the simulator.

It was the light-sculpted image of a man. There was nothing extraordinary about his appearance. He was of somewhat less than average height, with a dark complexion, a strong nose, and dark brown, slightly receding hair, and his dark eyes had a pronounced epicanthic fold. He wore an antique uniform, two T-centuries and more out of date, and the visored cap which the Royal Manticoran Navy had replaced with berets a hundred and seventy T-years before was clasped under his left arm.

"Your Majesty," he said, and like his uniform, his recorded accent was antique, crisp and understandable, but still an echo from another time. A ghost, preserved in an electronic shroud. And yet, despite all the dusty years which had swept past since that man breathed and slept and dreamed, there was something about him. Some not quite definable spark that burned even now.

"I beg to report," he continued, "that the forces under my command have engaged the enemy. Although I deeply regret that I must inform you of the loss of HMS *Triumph* and HMS *Defiant* in action against the piratical vessels based at Trautman's Star, I must also inform you that we were victorious. We have confirmed the destruction of thirteen hostile cruisers, light cruisers, and destroyers, and all basing infrastructure in the system. In addition, we have captured one destroyer, one light and two heavy cruisers, and two battlecruisers. Several of these units appear to have been of recent Solarian construction, with substantially heavier armaments than most 'pirates' carry. Our own casualties and damage were severe, and I have been forced to detach HMS *Victorious*, *Swiftsure*, *Mars*, and *Agamemnon* for repairs. I have transferred sufficient of their personnel to the other units of my command to fully crew each of my remaining vessels, and I have instructed Captain Timmerman, *Swiftsure*'s commander, as the detachment's senior officer, to return to the Star Kingdom, escorting our prize ships.

"In light of our casualties, and the reduction in my

squadron's strength, it will be necessary to temporarily suspend our offensive operations against the pirate bases we have identified. I regret to inform you that we have captured additional corroborating evidence, including the quality of the enemy's warships, of the involvement of both Manpower, Incorporated, and individuals at the highest level of the Silesian government with the so-called 'pirates' operating here in the Confederacy. Under the circumstances, I do not believe we can rely upon the Confederacy Navy to protect our commerce. Indeed, the collusion of senior members of the government with those *attacking* our commerce undoubtedly explains the ineffectiveness of Confederacy naval units assigned as convoy escorts.

"Given this new evidence, and my own depleted numbers, I see no option but to disperse my striking force to provide escorts in the areas of greatest risk. I regret the factors which compel me to temporarily abandon offensive action, but I fully intend to resume larger scale operations once I receive the reinforcements currently *en route* to Silesia.

"I have prepared a detailed report for the Admiralty, and I append a copy of it to this dispatch. Your Majesty, I have the honor to remain your most loyal and obedient subject.

"Saganami, clear."

He bowed, ever so slightly but with immense dignity, and his recorded image faded away.

There was another moment of darkness, one that left the watching audience alone with the memory of his message. His final message to Queen Adrienne, the monarch who had sent his squadron to Silesia. And then, the holo display came back to life.

This time there were two images, both command decks. One was the command deck of a freighter; the other, the bridge of a warship.

The freighter's command crew sat at their stations, their shoulders taut, their faces stiff, even terrified. The merchantship's skipper looked just as anxious as any of his officers, but he stood beside his command chair, not seated in it, looking into the communications screen which linked him to the second ship.

The warship's bridge was quaint and cramped by modern standards, that of a "battlecruiser" smaller than many modern heavy cruisers, with displays and weapons consoles that were hopelessly out of date. The same almond-eyed officer stood on the command deck, his old-style vac suit far clumsier and bulkier than a modern skinsuit. Battle boards blazed crimson at his ship's Tactical station, and the flow and rush of his bridge personnel's disciplined combat chatter rippled under the surface of his voice when he spoke.

"My orders aren't open to discussion, Captain Hargood," he said flatly. "The convoy will disperse immediately and proceed across the hyper limit on least-time courses. *Now*, Captain."

"I'm not refusing your orders, damn it!" Captain Hargood shot back, his voice harsh. "I'm only trying to keep you from throwing away your own ship and the lives of every man and woman aboard her!"

"The effort is appreciated," Commodore Saganami said with a thin smile. "I'm afraid it's wasted, however. Now get your ship turned around and get out of here."

"God damn it to Hell, Eddy!" Hargood exploded. "There are *six* of the bastards, including two *battlecruisers*! Just what the fuck do you think you're going to accomplish? Unlike us, you've got the legs to stay away from them, so *do* it, damn it!"

"There won't be six when we're done," Saganami said grimly, "and every one we destroy, or just cripple badly enough, is one that won't be chasing you or another unit of the convoy. And now, I'm done arguing with you, James. Take your ship, and your people, and get your ass home to that wife and those kids of yours. Saganami, clear."

Captain Hargood's display blanked, and his holographic image's shoulders slumped. He stared at the featureless screen for perhaps a half-dozen breaths, then shook himself and turned to his astrogator.

"You heard him," he said heavily, his face decades older than it had been mere moments before. "Get us out of here."

"Yes, Sir," the astrogator said quietly.

The simulator's imagery changed once more as the recording of the exchange between Hargood and Saganami ended. It was replaced by a huge tactical display, one so old its symbology had been tagged with newer, more modern icons a present-day tactician could read. A ship's name strobed in a light bar at the base of the display: RMMS *Prince Harold*, Captain James Hargood's ship.

The display's imagery wasn't very detailed, despite all computer enhancement could do. The range was long, and the sensors which drove it had been built by a technology that was crude and limited by modern standards. And even if neither of those things had been true, *Prince Harold* had been a merchant vessel, not a warship. But the display was detailed enough.

A single green icon, tagged with the name "*Nike*," drove ahead, accelerating hard towards six other icons that glared the fresh-blood color of hostile units. Two of the hostiles were identified as battlecruisers. Another was a heavy cruiser. The other three were "only" destroyers. The range looked absurdly low, but no one had fired yet. The weapons of the day were too crude, too short-legged. But that was about to change, for the range fell steadily as *Nike* moved to intercept her enemies.

The first missiles launched, roaring out of their tubes, and *Prince Harold*'s sensor imagery was suddenly hashed by jagged strobes of jamming. The icons all but vanished completely in the electronic hash, but only for a moment. Then multiple layers of enhancement smoothed away the interference, replacing it with a glassy clarity. The dearth of data gave away how badly *Prince Harold*'s sensors had been affected, yet what data there was was crystal clear . . . and brutal.

It lasted over forty minutes, that battle, despite the horrendous odds. Forty minutes in which there was not a sound, not a whisper, in all that vast auditorium while fifty-five hundred midshipmen's eyes watched that display. Watched that single, defiant green bead of light drive straight into more than four times its own firepower. Watched it concentrate its fire with a cold precision which had already discounted its own survival. It opened fire not on the opposing battlecruisers, but on the escorting destroyers. It hammered them with the thermonuclear thunder of old-fashioned contact warheads. And as the range closed, it clawed at them with the coherent light of broadside lasers.

Not a single member of the audience misunderstood what they were seeing. Commodore Saganami wasn't fighting to live. He was fighting to destroy or cripple as many pirate vessels as he could. It didn't matter to a slow, unarmed merchantman whether the pirate that overhauled it was a destroyer or a superdreadnought. *Any* pirate could destroy *any* merchantman, and there were as many pirates as there were ships in Saganami's convoy. Each ship he killed was one merchantship which would live . . . and he could kill destroyers more easily than he could battlecruisers.

Nike bored in, corkscrewing around her base vector and rolling ship madly to interpose her impeller wedge against incoming fire, snapping back upright to send an entire broadside of lasers blasting through the fragile sidewall of a destroyer. Her target reeled aside, belching atmosphere, trailing debris. Its wedge fluctuated, then died, and *Nike* dispatched it to whatever hell awaited its crew with a single missile even as she writhed around to savage one of its consorts.

The green icon twisted and wove, spiraling through its enemies, closing to a range which was suicidal even for the cruder, shorter-ranged weapons of her own day. There was an elegance to *Nike*'s maneuvers, a cleanness. She drove headlong towards her own destruction, yet she danced. She embraced her own immolation, and the hand which guided her shaped her course with a master's touch.

Yet elegance was not armor, nor grace immortality.

Another ship would have died far sooner than she, would have been raked by enemy fire, would have stumbled into the path of a killing salvo. But not even she could avoid all of the hurricane of destruction her enemies hurled to meet her, and damage codes flashed beside her icon as hit after hit slammed home.

A second destroyer blew up. Then the third staggered aside, her forward impeller ring a broken, shattered ruin, and *Nike* turned upon the heavy cruiser. Her missiles ripped into it, damaging its impellers, laming it so that even a lumbering merchantship could outpace it.

Her icon was haloed in a scarlet shroud that indicated escaping atmosphere. Her acceleration dropped steadily as alpha and beta nodes were blown out of her impeller rings. The weight of her fire dwindled as lasers and missile tubes—and the men and women who crewed them—were shattered one by one. Dame Honor and Nimitz had seen the horrors of battle, seen friends torn apart, splendid ships shattered and broken. Unlike Dame Beatrice's watching midshipmen, they *knew* what it must have been like aboard *Nike*'s bridge, in the ship's passages, in the armored pods where her weapons crews fought and cursed . . . and died. But those watching midshipmen knew they lacked Dame Honor's experience, knew they were witnessing something beyond their experience and comprehension. And that that same something might someday come for them, as it had come for Edward Saganami and the crew of HMS *Nike* so many years before.

The brutally wounded battlecruiser rolled up at point-blank range, barely eight thousand kilometers from her target, and fired every surviving weapon in her port broadside into one of the enemy battlecruisers. The pirate heaved sideways as transfer energy shattered armor and blasted deep, deep into her hull. She coasted onward for a few moments, and then vanished in a titanic explosion.

But *Nike* paid for that victory. As she rolled to take the shot, the second, undamaged pirate battlecruiser finally found a firing bearing of her own. One that was no longer obstructed by *Nike*'s skillfully interposed wedge.

Her energy weapons lashed out, as powerful as *Nike*'s own. Saganami's ship was more heavily armored than any cruiser or destroyer, but she wasn't a battleship or a dreadnought. She was only a battlecruiser. Her armor splintered, atmosphere gushed from her ruptured hull, and her forward impeller ring flashed and died.

She staggered, trying to twist back away from her opponent, and the heavy cruiser she had already lamed sent a full salvo of missiles into her. Point defense stopped some, but four exploded against her wavering sidewall, and more damage codes flashed as some of their fury overpowered the straining generators and blasted into her side. And then the hostile battlecruiser fired again. The green icon lurched, circled with the flashing red band of critical damage, and a window opened in the tactical display.

It was a com screen. *Prince Harold*'s name blinked in the date/time hack in the lower right hand corner, identifying the recipient of the recorded transmission, and more than one midshipman flinched physically as he found himself staring into the vestibule of Hell.

Nike's bridge was hazed with thin smoke, eddying towards the holed bulkheads and the bottomless hunger of vacuum beyond. Electrical fires blazed unchecked, Astrogation was so much blasted wreckage, and bodies littered the deck. Edward Saganami's face was streaked with blood as he faced the pickup, and more blood coated his vac suit's right side as it pulsed from a deep wound in his shoulder. The tactical display was still up behind him. Its icons and damage sidebars and the lurid damage codes on the damage control schematic flickered and wavered as its power fluctuated. But they were still there, still showed the other battlecruiser maneuvering for the final, fatal shot *Nike* could no longer avoid.

"We're done, James," Saganami said. His voice was hoarse, harsh with pain and the exhaustion of blood loss, yet his expression was almost calm. "Tell the Queen. Tell her what my people did. And tell her I'm sor—"

The simulator went black. There was utter silence in

the lightless auditorium. And then, slowly, one final image appeared. It was the golden cross and starburst of the Parliamentary Medal of Valor on its blue, white, and red ribbon. The same colors gleamed among the ribbons on Dame Honor's chest, but this Medal of Valor was different. It was the very first PMV ever awarded, and it hung before them for perhaps twenty seconds.

And then the lights came up once more, and Lady Dame Honor Harrington, Commanding Officer of the newly reactivated Eighth Fleet, Manticoran Alliance, looked out over the Royal Manticoran Naval Academy's four hundred and eleventh senior class. They looked back at her, and she inhaled deeply.

"Ladies and Gentlemen," she said, her soprano voice ringing out clear and strong, *"the tradition lives!"*

Sixty more seconds passed in ringing silence, and then—

"Dismissed, Ladies and Gentlemen," she said very quietly.

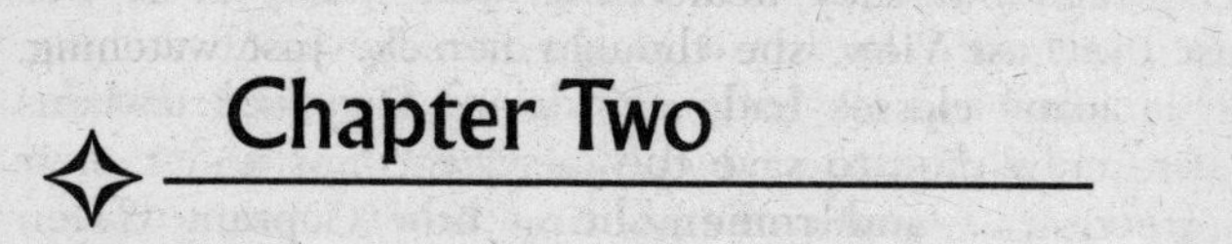

Chapter Two

She took one last look around her dorm room.

It was an absolute given that she'd forgotten something. She always did. The only question was how inconvenient/embarrassing it was going to be when she discovered what she'd forgotten this time.

She snorted at the thought, grinning as she imagined how Berry would have teased her about it. Berry insisted that Helen was the only person in the galaxy who carried her own pocket universe around with her. That was the only way she could possibly lose some of the things she managed to . . . misplace. Of course, Berry was almost compulsively neat in her own life, although no one ever would have guessed it from how sloppily she usually dressed. But that was only the current teenage style, Helen supposed. And, her expression sobered, it wasn't one Berry was going to be following any longer.

She shrugged, shoulders hunching as if she could somehow shake away her worry over her adopted sister. More like an adopted daughter, really, in many ways. It was silly, and she knew it. Yet somehow she'd thought she would always be the protector of the brutalized waif she'd rescued from the warrens of Old Chicago, and now . . . she wouldn't.

But there were always things that wouldn't happen, she told herself. Like her mother, who should have been at her graduation . . . and wouldn't be. She felt a familiar stab of pain and loss, and dashed away a tear. Silly that. She hadn't wept over her mother's death in years. Not because she no longer cared, but because even the most bitter wounds healed, if you lived. They left scars, but they healed and you went on. It was just the Last View, she thought fiercely. Just watching, as so many classes had, as Edward Saganami and his entire crew died to save the merchantships under their protection . . . and remembering how Captain Helen Zilwicki had done the same.

But that had been years ago, when Helen herself was only a child. And despite the deep, never to entirely fade anguish of it, her life truly had gone on, with other losses and other joys. If she'd lost her mother, she still had the bedrock love of her father, and now she had Berry, and Lars, and Catherine Montaigne. In a universe where it was the people you loved that really mattered, that was saying a lot. *One hell of a lot*, she thought fiercely.

She drew a deep breath, shook her head, and decided there was no point standing here trying to guess what she'd forgotten, or lost, or misplaced. If she'd been able to figure it out, it wouldn't have been forgotten—or lost, or misplaced—in the first place.

She snapped down her locker's lid, set the combination, and brought the built-in counter-grav on-line. The locker rose smoothly, floating at the end of its tether, and she settled her beret perfectly on her head, turned, and marched out of her dormitory room forever.

"Helen! Hey—Helen!"

She looked over her shoulder as the familiar voice called out her name. A small, dark-haired, dark-eyed midshipman bounced through the crowd headed for the Alpha-Three Shuttle Concourse like a billiard ball with wicked side spin.

Helen had never understood how Midshipman Kagiyama got away with that. Of course, he was over ten centimeters shorter than she was, and wiry. Helen's physique might favor her dead mother's side of the family more than it favored her massively built father, but she was still a considerably more . . . substantial proposition than Aikawa. His smaller size let him squeeze into openings she could never have fitted through, but it was more than that. Maybe it was just that he was brasher than she was. He certainly, she thought, watching him move past—or possibly through—a gesticulating herd of civilian businessmen, had much more energetic elbows than she did.

He skidded to a stop beside her with a grin, and she shook her head as the daggered glares of the affronted businessmen unaccountably failed to reduce him to a fine heap of smoldering ashes.

"I swear, Aikawa," she said severely. "One of these days, somebody's going to flatten you."

"Nah," he disagreed, still grinning. "I'm too cute."

"Cute," she informed him, "is one thing you definitely aren't, Aikawa Kagiyama."

"Sure I am. You just don't appreciate cute when you see it."

"Maybe not, but I'd advise you not to count on your OCTO to see it, either."

"Not at first, maybe. But I'm sure he'll come to love me," Aikawa said cheerfully.

"Not once she gets to know you," Helen said deflatingly.

"You cut me to the quick." Aikawa pressed a hand to his heart, and looked at her soulfully. She only snorted, and he shrugged. "Worth a try, anyway," he said.

"Yeah, you can be *very* trying," she said.

"Well, in that case, maybe I can hide from the OCTO behind you," he said hopefully.

"Hide behind me?" Helen arched an eyebrow.

"Sure!" His eyes glinted with barely suppressed delight. "Unless . . . Is it *possible*? Nah, couldn't be! Don't tell me you didn't know we're both assigned to *Hexapuma*!"

"We are?" Helen blinked. "I thought you told me last night that you had orders to *Intransigent*."

"That was last night. Today is today." Aikawa shrugged.

"Why the change?" she asked.

"Darned if I know," he admitted. "Maybe somebody decided you needed a good example to live up to." He elevated his nose with a superior expression.

"Bullshit," she said tartly. "If anybody decided anything, it was that you needed someone to step on you for your own good whenever that big head of yours gets ready to get you into trouble. Again."

"Gets *me* into trouble?" He shook his head at her. "And which one of us was it, again, that got us caught sneaking back onto campus at a quarter after Comp?"

"Which was the *only* time I got us caught, Mr. I've-Got-the-Record-in-Black-Marks-Cornered. You, on the other hand—"

"Dwelling on the past is the mark of a small mind," he informed her.

"Yeah, sure it is!" She snorted again, then tugged her locker back into motion, following the guide strip through the crowded concourse.

Aikawa trotted along beside her, towing his own locker, and she did her best to look unmoved by his presence. Not that she was fooling anyone, especially him. He was probably her best friend in the entire universe, although neither of them was prepared to express it quite that way in so many words. There was nothing remotely sexual about their friendship. Not because either of them had anything against sexual relationships. It was just that neither was really the other's type, and neither of them was prepared to risk their friendship by trying to turn it into anything else.

"So who else caught *Hexapuma*?" he asked.

"What?" She looked at him with mock amazement. "The Great Kagiyama, Master of Grapevines, doesn't know who else is assigned to *his* ship?"

"I know exactly who's assigned to *Intransigent*. And

until this morning, that was my ship. What I don't know is who's assigned to *your* ship."

"Well, I'm not entirely sure, myself," Helen admitted. "I do know Ragnhild is, though. She's ticketed for the same shuttle to *Hephaestus* as I am—well, both of us, now, I guess."

"Really? Outstanding!" Aikawa beamed. "I wonder what possessed them to put all three of the Three Musketeers on the same ship?"

"An oversight, I'm sure," Helen said dryly. "Of course, from the way you're talking, they didn't have all three of us assigned to *Hexapuma* initially, now did they?"

"A point. Definitely a point. So Ragnhild is the only other one you know about?"

"No, Leopold Stottmeister caught the morning shuttle up because he was going to have lunch with his parents at Dempsey's before he reported aboard. I know about him and Ragnhild for certain. But there may be one or two more."

"Stottmeister . . ." Aikawa frowned. "The soccer jock?"

"Yeah. I had a couple of classes with him, and he's a pretty sharp cookie. In the Engineering track, though."

"Oh." Aikawa looked up at her and their eyes met with the same expression. Both of them were in the Tactical track, traditionally the surest way to starship command. There was nothing *wrong* with someone who was more interested in hardware than maneuvers, of course. And God knew someone had to keep the works wound up and running. But neither of them could quite understand why someone would deliberately *choose* to be a glorified mechanic.

"So," Aikawa said after moment, his lips pursed, "with you and me, that makes four in Snotty Row? Two each of the male and female persuasions?"

"Yeah," Helen said again, but she was frowning slightly. "I think there's one more, though. I didn't recognize the name—Rizzo or d'Arezzo." She shrugged. "Something like that."

"Paulo d'Arezzo? Little guy, only four or five centimeters taller'n I am?"

"Don't know. Far as I know, I've never even met him."

"I think I have, once," Aikawa said as the two of them turned down another hallway and the crowd got even denser, packing tighter together as the corridor narrowed. "If he's who I think he is, he's an electronics weenie. Pretty good one, too." Helen looked a question at him, and shrugged. "I only met him in passing, but Jeff Timberlake worked a tactical problem in the final sims last term with d'Arezzo as his EW officer. Jeff said he was a damned good EWO."

"Sounds promising," Helen said judiciously.

"So that's it? Five of us?

"Counting you," she agreed as they squeezed their way along. "And as far as I know. But the assignment list wasn't complete when I got my orders. They told me there'd be at least one more snotty, but they didn't know who at that point. I guess that's the slot they dropped you into. Speaking of which, how *did* you get your assignment changed?"

"Hey, I was telling the truth for once!" he protested. "All I know is that Herschiser called me into her office this morning and told me my orders had been changed. I think they actually swapped me out with someone else who was assigned to *Hexapuma*."

"Oh?" She cocked her head at him. "And do you happen to have any idea who 'someone else' was? I hope it wasn't Ragnhild!"

"As a matter of fact, I do know. And it wasn't Ragnhild," Aikawa said, and she looked down at him sharply. His voice sounded much less amused than it had, and he shrugged as she frowned a silent question at him. "That's why I was asking who else was assigned," he said. "'Cause I didn't bounce anybody you just mentioned. Unless my usual sources fail me, the guy I *did* bounce was Bashanova."

"Bashanova?" Helen grimaced, as much in irritation at herself for repeating Aikawa like some witless parrot as anything else, but she wasn't sure she cared for the implications of that name. Kenneth Bashanova wasn't exactly beloved by either her or Aikawa. Or, for that matter, by at least ninety-nine percent of the people unfortunate enough to know him. Not that he cared particularly. The fourth son of an earl and the grandson of a duke had no need to concern himself with all of the little people clustered about his ankles.

If Aikawa's last-minute reassignment to HMS *Hexapuma* had saved her from making her midshipwoman's cruise trapped aboard the same ship as Kenneth Bashanova, she was devoutly grateful. He was poisonous enough with anyone, but his sort of aristocrat despised Gryphon Highlanders—like Helen—as much as Highlanders despised them, and he'd gone out of his way to step on her . . . once.

But whatever she thought of him, and however grateful she might be for his departure, Bashanova wasn't the sort of person who was involved in *random* last-minute changes. If he'd been reassigned to another ship, it was because someone had pulled strings to make that happen. Which might explain why the midshipman assignments to *Hexapuma* had been "incomplete" last night. And it also posed an interesting question. Had he been shifted to *Intransigent* because of some special opportunity waiting for anyone fortunate enough to make her snotty cruise aboard her? Or had he been shifted to get him *away* from *Hexapuma*?

"You haven't heard anything about *Hexapuma* that I haven't, have you?" she asked after a moment, and Aikawa chuckled.

"Two great minds with but a single thought, I see." He shook his head. "Nope. First thing to cross my mind was why the Noble Rodent had wanted out of *Hexapuma*, so I asked around."

"And?"

"And I couldn't find out anything to explain it. Heck, for that matter, I'd think even Bashanova would have wanted to stay put!"

"Why?" Helen asked, and Aikawa.

"Don't you have *any* 'informed sources'?"

"Hey, I'm the one who knew who else was assigned aboard her, smartass! And just because the 'faxes broke the story about my old man, don't go around thinking *I'm* some kind of spook. One spy per family's enough, thank you. Although, come to think of it, Lars is showing some signs of interest. Berry and I certainly never did, though!"

"Then how come she wound up up to her . . . eyebrows in all that business on Erewhon and Congo?" he demanded.

"Torch, not Congo," she corrected. "Congo's the system name; the planet is Torch. And I still haven't figured out how all that worked. But I'll tell you this much—it wasn't because *Berry* was playing spy!" Her snort of disdain was little short of magnificent. "Berry's the sanest person in the entire Star Kingdom. Well, was, anyway. No way was she playing Junior Spook with Daddy—as if he'd've let her, even if she'd wanted to! I'm sure one of them will get around to explaining that whole business to me one of these days, but I already know that much."

Actually, she knew a good bit more, but a lot of what she knew was most definitely not for public distribution.

"None of which," she went on more pointedly, "has any particular bearing on whether I have or haven't cultivated the same band of sneaks and informants you have. So instead of looking exasperated, suppose you tell me what's so special about *Hexapuma* besides the fact that she's a brand-new ship."

"Nothing in particular, I suppose. Except, perhaps, for her captain, that is." His tone was so elaborately casual that she considered throttling him, but then he laughed. "All right, I'll come clean. It just happens, Helen, that *Hexapuma*'s newly assigned skipper is one Captain Aivars Terekhov. The Hyacinth Terekhov."

Helen's eyes widened. She didn't need Aikawa to tell her who Aivars Terekhov was. Everyone knew his record, just as everyone knew about the Manticore Cross he'd won for the Battle of Hyacinth.

"Wait a minute." She came to a complete stop, looking down at Aikawa with a perplexed expression. "Terekhov. Isn't he some sort of distant relative of Bashanova's?"

"Yeah, but just some kind of twelfth cousin or something. Worth remembering if you want something from him, but otherwise—?" Aikawa shrugged and grimaced. He was from the capital planet of Manticore, not Gryphon, but his attitude towards the more self-important (and self-absorbed) members of the Manticoran aristocracy was as contemptuous as any Highlander's.

"But if they're related, why in the world would Bashanova want to be reassigned out of *Hexapuma*? I'd think his family would *want* him to make his snotty cruise under a relative—especially one in command of a brand, shiny new heavy cruiser. It's the way their minds work."

"Unless there's been some sort of family falling out," Aikawa suggested. "If Terekhov's feuding with the rest of the family—and from what I know about the Noble Rodent's immediate relatives, I wouldn't be a bit surprised if someone like Terekhov couldn't stand them—maybe Daddy Rat would feel better keeping his adorable little son out of the line of fire. Or," he shrugged, "it may be that there's something special about *Intransigent* that I haven't been able to find out about—yet. It's just as possible the Noble Rodent's trying to cop an inside advantage as that he's trying to avoid some sort of problem, you know."

"I suppose," she said doubtfully, tugging her locker back into motion as she started off down the shuttle pad guideline once more. And Aikawa did have a point, she conceded. But even as she told herself that, she knew her metaphysical ears were straining for the sound of a falling shoe.

HMSS *Hephaestus* was always crowded, especially now. With the abrupt, disastrous resumption of the war with Haven, the largest single shipyard the Navy owned was running at well over a hundred percent of its designed capacity. The destruction of the Grendelsbane satellite yards—and all the partially built warships in them—only made *Hephaestus'* frenetic pace even more frenzied.

The concourses were an almost solid mass of humanity, with civilians employed by the various contractors piling in on top of the military personnel assigned to—or simply passing through—*Hephaestus*. Getting through the massive space station's main arteries in anything remotely resembling a hurry was effectively impossible.

Which, unfortunately, didn't keep some people from trying to, anyway.

One such person—a large, well fed, and obviously (in his own eyes, at least) important civilian—was forging through the press of human bodies like a superdreadnought through a squadron of old-style LACs. He might not have the superdreadnought's impeller wedge, but he was using his beefy shoulders and elbows as a suitable substitute. Since he stood right at a hundred and eighty-eight centimeters in height, most of those who weren't restrained from shoving back out of good manners were intimidated by his sheer size and obvious willingness to trample lesser mortals.

Most of them, anyway.

His bulldozer progress came to an abrupt halt as what he had confidently believed was an irresistible force ran into what was in fact an immovable object. In point of fact, it was a man in a blue and gray uniform he'd never seen before. A very *tall* man, the better part of twelve centimeters taller then he was. And a very *broad* man, who must have weighed at least two hundred kilos . . . none of it fat.

The civilian hit that hundred-and-sixty-five-centimeter chest and bounced. Literally. He ended up flat on the seat of his trousers, the wind knocked out of him, staring up at the ogre he'd just flattened himself against like a bug on a windshield. Mild brown eyes regarded him with vague interest, as if wondering whether or not he might have been the source of the insignificant impact which had drawn their owner's attention.

The beefy young man had already opened his mouth, his face taut with fury, but it snapped shut even more abruptly than it had opened as he truly saw the man he'd run into for the first time. The uniformed giant gazed down at him, still mildly, then stepped carefully around him, beckoned politely for two other pedestrians to precede him, and continued on his own way without so much as a backward glance.

The severely shaken civilian sat there for several more seconds before he pushed himself rather unsteadily to his feet and resumed his own progress . . . much more circumspectly. He kept an eye out for additional ogres, but he'd never even noticed the tallish, slender young junior-grade lieutenant following in the first ogre's wake. Probably because, despite her own height, for a woman, her head didn't even top her escort's massive shoulder.

"I saw that, Mateo," Lieutenant Abigail Hearns said quietly, gallantly attempting to put a repressive edge into her voice.

"Saw what, My Lady?" Mateo Gutierrez inquired innocently.

"You deliberately changed course to plow that . . . person under," she said severely.

"How can you possibly suggest such a thing, My Lady?" Gutierrez shook his head sadly, a man clearly accustomed to being misunderstood and maligned.

"Possibly because I know you," Abigail replied tartly. He only shook his head again, adding a sigh for good measure, and she managed not to laugh out loud.

It wasn't the first time she'd noticed that Gutierrez seemed to take special offense when he encountered someone who used physical size or strength to intimidate others. Mateo Gutierrez didn't care for bullies. Abigail had been a bit surprised by how little astonishment she'd felt on the day she realized that for all his toughness and amazing lethality, he was one of the gentlest people she knew. There was nothing "soft," or wishy-washy about Gutierrez, but although he went to considerable lengths to hide it, he was the sort of man who routinely adopted homeless kittens, lost puppies . . . and steadholder's daughters.

Her temptation to laugh vanished as she remembered how she and Gutierrez had met. She hadn't expected to survive the brutal, merciless encounter with the pirates raiding the planet of Refuge. And she wouldn't have, without Gutierrez. She knew, with no sense of false modesty, that she'd held up her own end of that exhausting, endless running battle, but it hadn't been her sort of fight. It had been Mateo Gutierrez's kind of fight, and he'd waged it magnificently. That was what a professional noncom in the Royal Manticoran Marine Corps did.

She understood that part. What she wasn't quite clear on was precisely how a Manty Marine platoon sergeant transmuted into a lieutenant in the Owens Steadholder's Guard. Oh, she was certain she detected her father's inimitable touch, and as a Grayson steadholder, Lord Owens clearly had the clout to "convince" the Royal Manticoran Marines to allow one of their sergeants to cross-transfer to the Owens Guard. What she couldn't figure out was how her father had convinced Gutierrez to accept the transfer in the first place.

At least she knew *why* he'd done it, if not how, and she felt a fresh spurt of affectionate irritation at the thought. As a mere daughter, she'd had no standing in the succession to Owens Steading when she initially left home to become the first Grayson midship*woman* ever to attend Saganami Island. As such, she'd managed to make the trip without the personal armsman which Grayson law required accompany any steadholder's heir or potential heir.

But that had been before the Conclave of Steadholders awakened to the full implications of Benjamin Mayhew's alterations to Grayson's laws of inheritance. Daughters were no longer precluded from inheriting steadholderships, so the Conclave had determined that they should no longer be excused from the consequences of standing in the succession.

Abigail had been furious when her father informed her

that henceforth *she* must be accompanied on any deployment by her personal armsman. At least she didn't have to put up with the complete security team which accompanied the older of her two brothers wherever he went, but surely a serving naval officer didn't need a personal bodyguard! But Lord Owens had been inflexible. As he'd pointed out to her, the law was clear. And when she'd tried to continue the argument, he'd made two other points. First, that Lady Harrington, who was certainly a "serving officer" by anyone's definition, had accepted that *she* had to be accompanied at all times by her personal armsmen. If she could, then so could Abigail. And, second, that since the law was clear, her only real choices were whether she would obey it or whether the Grayson Space Navy would withdraw her commission.

He'd meant it. However proud he might have been of her, however completely he'd accepted her choice of a career, he'd meant it. And it hadn't even been a simple matter of a father's intransigence. There were all too many prominent Graysons who remained horrified by the very notion of Grayson-born women in uniform. If she chose to reject the law's requirements, those same horrified men would demand that the Navy beach her. And the Navy, whether it liked it or not, would have no choice but to comply.

And so she'd accepted that she had no choice, and, somehow, Lord Owens had convinced Mateo Gutierrez to become his daughter's armsman. He'd found her the biggest, toughest, most dangerous guard dog he could lay his hands on, and he'd traded unscrupulously on the bonds between her and Gutierrez to convince her to accept him. She'd continued her protests long enough to be certain honor was satisfied, but both of them knew the truth. If she had to put up with a bodyguard at all, there was no one in the entire universe she would have trusted more than Mateo Gutierrez.

Of course, the fact that she'd just been reassigned to a Manticoran warship rather than to a Grayson vessel did tend to complicate things a bit, and she wondered why she had been. High Admiral Matthews had told her it was because they wanted her to gain all the experience—and seniority—she could in a navy which was used to female officers before she took up her duties aboard a Grayson vessel. And she believed him—mostly. But there was that nagging edge of doubt . . .

"This way, My Lady," Gutierrez said, and Abigail shook herself as she realized she'd been woolgathering while she walked along. She'd completely failed to notice when their guide line turned down a side passage towards a bank of lifts.

"I knew that," she said, smiling sideways up at her towering armsman.

"Of course you did, My Lady," he said soothingly.

"Well, I did!" she insisted. He only grinned, and she shook her head. "And that's another thing, Mateo. We're assigned to a Manticoran cruiser, not a Grayson ship. And I'm only a very junior tactical officer aboard her. I think it might not to be a bad idea to forget about the 'My Ladies' for a while."

"It's taken me months to get used to using them in the first place," he rumbled in exactly the sort of voice one might have expected out of that huge, resonant chest.

"Marines are adaptable," she replied. "They improvise and overcome when faced with unexpected obstacles. Just treat it like something minor—like storming a dug-in ceramacrete bunker armed with nothing but a butter knife clenched between your manly teeth—and I'm sure a tough, experienced Marine like you can pull it off."

"Hah! What kind of wuss Marine needs a *butter knife* to take one miserable bunker?" Gutierrez demanded with a resonant chuckle. "That's why God gave us teeth and fingernails!"

"Exactly." Abigail smiled up at him again, but she also shook her head. "Seriously, Mateo," she continued. "I know Daddy and Colonel Bottoms insisted on that whole 'My Lady' thing. And it probably makes sense, on Grayson, or in the GSN. But we're going to have enough trouble with people who think it's silly neobarb foolishness to assign a *bodyguard* to any officer as junior as I am. Let's not rub any noses in anything we don't have to rub them in."

"You've got a point, Ma'am," he agreed after a moment. They reached the lift, and he pressed the call button, then stood waiting beside her. Even here, his eyes flitted endlessly about, sweeping their surroundings in a constant cycle. He might have been trained originally as a Marine, not an armsman, but he'd taken to his new duties like a natural.

"Thank you," she said. "And while we're on the subject of not rubbing any noses—or putting any of them out of joint—did you and Commander FitzGerald come to an understanding?"

"Yes, Ma'am, we did. Although, truth to tell, it was Captain Kaczmarczyk I really needed to talk to. I told you it would be."

"And I believed you. All I said was that you needed to touch base with the XO before you talked to the detachment commander."

"You were right," he conceded. "Probably." He couldn't quite resist adding the qualifier, and she shook her head with a chuckle.

"You, Mateo Gutierrez," she said as the lift doors sighed open, "need a good, swift kick in the seat of the pants. And if I could get my foot that high without getting a nosebleed, I'd give it to you, too."

"Such constant threats of violence," he said mournfully, even as his eyes swept the interior of the lift car. "It's a good thing I know you don't mean it, Ma'am. That's the only thing that keeps me from breaking out in a cold sweat when you threaten me that way."

"*Sure* it is," she said, rolling her eyes as he waved her forward and she stepped past him into the lift. He followed her, taking his position between her and the doors and actually making it look casual. Then he punched the button to close the doors.

"Destination?" a computer-generated voice asked pleasantly.

"HMS *Hexapuma*," Gutierrez told it.

Chapter Three

"All right, People. Let's not block the gallery, shall we?"

The soft Grayson accent sounded more amused than anything else, but there was a definite edge of command in it. Helen looked over her shoulder quickly, and her eyebrows rose as she recognized the young woman behind her. So far as she was aware, there was only one native-born Grayson woman in the Grayson Space Navy. Even if there hadn't been, the face behind her had been splashed across just about every HD in the Star Kingdom a T-year ago, after the business in Tiberian.

Helen broke off her conversation with Ragnhild Pavletic and stepped swiftly out of the lieutenant's way. The towering giant in the blue and gray uniform walking at the lieutenant's shoulder considered all three midshipmen thoughtfully. His uniform might be that of a Grayson armsman, but he himself could only have been from San Martin, with the dark complexion, heavy-grav physique, and hawklike profile of so many of its inhabitants. And while there was no threat in his eyes, something about him suggested that it would be a good idea not to crowd him or his charge.

The other two middies made haste to follow Helen's example. The lieutenant's seniority would have been enough to produce that result under any circumstances; the quality of her personal guard dog only gave it a bit more alacrity, and her smile showed that she knew it.

"No need to be quite *that* accommodating," she assured them mildly, and turned to look through the thick armorplast of the space dock gallery herself.

The sleek, double-ended spindle of an *Edward Saganami*-class heavy cruiser floated to her mooring tractors in the crystalline vacuum, physically connected to the gallery observation deck by personnel tubes while parties of hard-suited yard dogs and their remotes swarmed over her after impeller ring. Technically, *Hexapuma* was a *Saganami-C*, an "improved" version of the original *Edward Saganami* design. Once upon a time, she would have been considered an entirely different class, but BuShips' nomenclature had become a bit more flexible under the previous Admiralty administration. By calling the design a *Saganami*, rather than admitting that it was an improved, completely new class, they'd actually gotten funding to continue its construction—albeit in very small numbers—as part of the Janacek Admiralty's concentration on building up the Navy's lighter combatants.

At 483,000 tons, *Hexapuma* was sixty-one percent larger than the *Star Knight*-class ships which had been the Navy's newest, latest—and largest—heavy cruisers before what people were beginning to call the First Havenite War. Yet despite the increase in tonnage, and a vast increase in firepower, her ship's company was tiny compared to a *Star Knight*'s. In fact, the way the decreased manpower and life support requirements had freed up mass was as much the reason for her increased combat power as the improvements in weapons technology.

Unlike the original *Saganami* design, *Hexapuma* was uncompromisingly optimized for missile combat. Although she actually mounted only forty tubes, fewer than the intermediate *Saganami-Bs*, she still had half again the missile broadside of a *Star Knight*. And the tubes she *did* mount were bigger than a *Saganami-B*'s, capable of handling larger and more powerful missiles, while her magazine space had been substantially increased over the preceding class. Her energy weapons were fewer in number—she mounted only eight in each broadside, plus her chase armament—but, taking a page from the pattern the Graysons had set, they were individually more powerful than most navies' battlecruisers mounted. She could hit fewer targets at energy range, but the hits she landed would be devastating. And the *Saganami-C*s had been the first cruiser class to receive the new, improved two-phase bow wall generators.

In short, given her choice of engagement ranges, *Hexapuma* could have engaged and destroyed any prewar battlecruiser—Manticoran, as well as Peep.

"Pretty, isn't she?" the Grayson lieutenant observed.

"Yes, Ma'am. She is . . . Lieutenant Hearns," Helen agreed. The other woman—she was no more than two or three T-years older than Helen herself—glanced at her speculatively. She was probably used to being recognized, at least by other Navy types, Helen realized. But she looked as if she were wondering why Helen had made the point that *she*'d recognized her, and Helen suddenly hoped it wasn't because Hearns thought she was trying to brownnose. She met the lieutenant's eyes steadily for a moment, then Hearns nodded slightly and returned her attention to *Hexapuma*.

"Our new snotties?" she asked after a moment, without looking at them.

"Yes, Ma'am."

"Well, I realize it's considered bad luck to welcome a middy aboard before she's officially reported," Hearns went on, her gaze still fixed on the floating cruiser, "so I'll continue to assume you people are just passing through and stopping off to admire the view. It would never do to violate traditions, after all."

"No, Ma'am," Helen agreed, still speaking for all of them.

"If I were you," Hearns continued with a slight smile, "I'd spend a few more minutes taking time to admire her properly. You won't see very much of her from the inside. And," her smile broadened, "you won't have much free time for admiring *anything* after you report aboard."

She chuckled, then nodded to them and continued on her way towards the forward personnel tube, a slender, graceful destroyer trailed by a lumbering superdreadnought.

The Marine sentry watched expressionlessly as the trio of midshipmen approached the end of *Hexapuma*'s main boarding tube. The corporal had to have seen them playing gawking tourist and watched their exchange with Lieutenant Hearns, but no one could have guessed that from his expression. From the hashmarks on his sleeve, he'd seen at least six Manticoran years—over ten T-years—of service. He'd probably also seen more midshipmen than he could have counted in that time, and he regarded this newest batch with professional impassivity as they walked towards him.

The snotties shook down into formation on the move without a word. Pavletic had graduated highest of them in their class, although she'd edged the other two (who'd ended in a dead heat) by less than two points. But what mattered was that Pavletic's class standing made her senior, and at the moment, Helen was just as glad that it did.

The delicately built honey-blond midshipwoman led the way to the gallery end of the tube, and the Marine came to attention and saluted. She returned the salute crisply.

"Midshipwoman Pavletic and party to join the ship's company, Corporal," she said. The others had passed her the record chips of their official orders, and she handed all three of them over to the sentry.

"Thank you, Ma'am," the Marine replied. He slotted the first chip into his memo board, keyed the display, and studied it for a second or two. Then he looked up at Ragnhild, obviously comparing her snub-nosed, freckle-dusted face to the imagery in her orders. He nodded, ejected the chip, and handed back to her. Then he plugged in the next one, checked the image, and looked up at Aikawa, who returned his regard steadily. The sentry nodded again, ejected the chip, passed it back to Ragnhild, and then checked Helen's face against her orders' imagery in turn. He didn't waste a lot of time on it, but it was obvious he'd really *looked* at the imagery. However routine his duties might be, he clearly didn't take anything for granted.

"Thank you, Ma'am," he said to Ragnhild. "You've been expected. I'm afraid the Executive Officer is out of the ship just now, though, Ma'am. I believe Commander Lewis, the Chief Engineer, is the senior officer on board."

"Thank you, Corporal," Ragnhild replied. He hadn't had to add the information that Lewis was the Engineer, and some Marines, she knew, wouldn't have. The function of a snotty cruise was at least in part to throw midshipmen into the deep end, and declining to provide helpful hints about who was who aboard their new ship was one of countless small ways of adding to that testing process.

"You're welcome, Ma'am," the Marine replied, and stood aside for the three midshipmen to enter the boarding tube's zero-gee.

They swam the tube in single file, each taking care to leave sufficient clearance for his or her next ahead's towed locker. Fortunately, they'd all done well in null-grav training, and there were no embarrassing gaffes as, one-by-one, they swung themselves into *Hexapuma*'s midships boat bay's one standard gravity.

A junior-grade lieutenant with the brassard of the boat bay officer of the deck on her left arm and the name "MacIntyre, Freda" on her nameplate was waiting with an expression of semi-polite impatience, and all three of the midshipmen saluted her.

"Permission to come aboard to join the ship's company, Ma'am?" Ragnhild requested crisply.

The lieutenant returned their salutes, and Ragnhild handed over the record chips again. The BBOD cycled them through her own memo board. It took a bit longer than it had for the sentry, but not a lot. It looked to Helen as if she'd actually read Ragnhild's orders—or skimmed them, at least—but only checked the visual imagery on the others. That seemed a little slack to Helen, but she reminded herself that she was only a snotty. By definition, no one aboard *Hexapuma* could be wetter behind the ears than she was, and perhaps the lieutenant had simply learned to recognize the Mickey Mouse crap and treat it accordingly.

"You seem to be running a little late, Ms. Pavletic," she observed as she passed the chips back. Ragnhild didn't respond, since there wasn't really much of a response she could make, and MacIntyre smiled thinly.

"Well, you're here now, which is the important thing, I suppose," she said after a moment. She turned her head and beckoned to an environmental tech. "Jankovich!"

"Yes, Lieutenant." Jankovich's pronounced Gryphon accent was like a breath of home to Helen, straight from the Highlands of her childhood. And there was something else she recognized in it—an edge of deep-seated dislike. There was nothing especially overt about it, but Highlanders were remarkably bad at hiding their true feelings . . . from other Highlanders. The rest of the Star Kingdom found everyone from Gryphon rough-edged enough that they seldom picked up on the subtle signs that were unmistakable to fellow Gryphons.

"Escort these snotties to their quarters," the lieutenant said briskly, obviously unaware of the subliminal vibrations Helen was receiving from the environmental tech.

"Aye, aye, Lieutenant," Jankovich replied, and looked at the midshipmen. "If the Ladies and Gentlemen would follow me?" he invited, and led off towards the boat bay's central bank of lifts.

The midshipmen managed not to crane their necks and gawk as Jankovich led them to the Midshipmen's Berthing Compartment. That was its official name on the ship's inboard schematic, but, like all such compartments aboard all vessels of the Royal Manticoran Navy, it rejoiced in the colloquial nickname "Snotty Row." *Hexapuma* was a new ship, about to embark on her very first commission. As such, and as befitted a cruiser of her tonnage (especially one with her manpower-reducing automation), her Snotty Row was considerably larger and more comfortable than anything which might have been found aboard older, smaller, more cramped vessels.

Which was not, by any stretch of the imagination, the same thing as "palatial." Each middy would have his or her own privacy-screened sleeping compartment, but those consisted of very little more than their individual, and none too large, bunks. Each bunk boasted a mounting bracket to which the bunk's occupant could affix his or her locker. There was a cramped "sitting room" area against the forward bulkhead, and a large commons table with a tough, nonskid surface. The table also contained a pop-up com unit and at least three computer terminals. The bulkheads were painted a surprisingly pleasant deep, pastel blue, and at least the compartment—like the entire ship—still had that "new air car" smell and feel.

There were two midshipmen already waiting for them when they arrived. All three newcomers already knew one of them—Leopold Stottmeister—with varying degrees of familiarity. He stood just under a hundred and eighty-eight centimeters in height, with auburn hair, dark eyes, and a physique built for speed and endurance, not brute strength. He and Helen had known one another for the better part of three T-years, which was longer than he'd known anyone else in the compartment, and he gave her a welcoming grin.

"Well if it isn't Zilwicki the Terrible!" he greeted her. "Wondered where you were."

"We poor tactical types can't find our way to the head unassisted without one of you brilliant engineers to show us the deck plan," she said, folding her hands piously and casting her eyes up at the deckhead.

"Yeah, sure," he said in his pleasant tenor, and waved at the other two new arrivals while Helen turned her attention to the fifth member of *Hexapuma*'s midshipman contingent.

The nameplate on his chest said "d'Arezzo, Paulo," and he was a good six centimeters shorter than she was, with fair hair and gray eyes. But what struck her most immediately about him was how incredibly handsome he was.

All sorts of internal alarms went off as she observed that classic, perfect profile, the high, thoughtful brow, the strong chin—with cleft, no less!—and firmly chiseled lips. If Central Casting had sent out for an actor to play a youthful Preston of the Spaceways, d'Arezzo was *exactly* who they would have gotten back. Especially with those narrow hips and broad shoulders to go with all the rest of the package.

Helen's experience with people who approached d'Arezzo's level of physical beauty (she didn't think she'd ever met anyone who actually *surpassed* it) had been less than happy. The kind of biosculpt it took to produce those looks was expensive, and the people who were willing to fork over the cash for it were either very spoiled, very rich, or both. Not exactly the sort of people a Gryphon Highlander was likely to find congenial.

He'd been sitting at one end of the table, reading from a book viewer, when the newcomers arrived. Another bad sign, she thought. He hadn't even bothered to try to strike up a conversation with Leo, who was one of the easiest going, friendliest people she'd ever met. At least he'd looked up when they entered the compartment, but there was a cool reserve behind those gray eyes. He made absolutely no effort to enter the conversation until Ragnhild and Aikawa had exchanged handclasps with Leo. Then those manly lips curved in a polite, distant smile.

"D'Arezzo, Paulo d'Arezzo," he introduced himself, and extended his hand to Helen, who happened to be closest.

"Helen Zilwicki," she replied, shaking it with as much enthusiasm as she could muster. Something flickered in the backs of his eyes, and she hid a mental grimace. Her accent was too pronounced to disguise even if she'd been inclined to try, and it seemed to have affected him very much as his too-beautiful face had affected her.

The other two newcomers introduced themselves in turn, and he greeted each of them with exactly the same, exactly correct, handshake. Then he nodded to Leo.

"You guys obviously already know each other," he observed, manifestly unnecessarily, "so I imagine Leo is better placed than I am to bring you up to speed."

He gave them another polite smile and withdrew back into his book.

Helen looked at Ragnhild and Aikawa, then raised her eyebrows at Leo. The auburn-haired midshipman twitched his shoulders in a very slight shrug, then waved at the bunks.

"If this is all of us, and I think it is, we've got three extra berths. Paulo and I have already staked out two of the bottom berths—first-come, first-served, and all that—" he gave them a toothy grin "—but you three just go right ahead and divvy up the remainder however you like. Try not to get any blood on the decksole, though."

"Some of us," Helen observed, "are capable of solving interpersonal disputes without violence." She sniffed audibly and looked at the other two new arrivals. "And in the name of settling any possible disputes amicably," she said, "I think it would be wise of you both to accept that one of the two remaining lower berths is mine."

"Settle them 'amicably,' indeed!" Ragnhild snorted. "You figure you'll get whatever you want just because you were an assistant unarmed combat instructor, and you know it."

"Me?" Helen looked at her innocently. "Have I issued a single threat? Have I suggested even for a moment that I might be willing to tie anyone else up into a pretzel?"

"As a matter of fact, yes," Aikawa replied. She looked at him, and he waved one hand. "Oh, not right this instant, perhaps, but all of us know you, by reputation, at least. We know what a brutal, intimidating person you can be,

Helen Zilwicki. And we aren't going to be intimidated any longer, are we?"

He looked appealingly at the other middies. Ragnhild looked up at the deckhead, whistling tunelessly, and Leo chuckled.

"Don't look at me," he said. "I played soccer. And I kept as far away from unarmed combat as the instructors would let me. I never sparred with Helen, but I've heard about her. And if you think I'm going to piss off someone who taught some of the *instructors*, you're out of your mind."

Everyone else laughed, including Helen, but there was a cold core of ugly memory under her laughter. She loved *Neue-Stil Handgemenge*, the judo derivative developed on New Berlin several centuries earlier, and she'd been fortunate enough during the time she and her father had spent on Old Earth to study under *sensei* Robert Tye, who was probably one of the galaxy's two or three most experienced practitioners of the *Neue-Stil*. She was intensely grateful for the discipline, physical and mental, and the sense of inner serenity the *Neue-Stil* had given her, and her workouts and training katas were like a soothing, graceful dance. But she had also used that same training to kill three men with her bare hands before she was fifteen T-years old, defending not simply herself, but also her adopted sister and brother.

"Well, since we've settled everything so democratically and all," Aikawa said to Ragnhild after the laughter had faded, "suppose you and I cut cards to see who gets the other lower berth?"

Helen had just finished unpacking her toiletries when the com terminal chimed softly. D'Arezzo, still reading his book, was closest to the unit and pressed the acceptance key quickly.

"Midshipmen's Berth, d'Arezzo speaking," he said crisply.

"Good afternoon, Mr. d'Arezzo," a soprano voice said as an attractive, red-haired woman's face appeared on the display. "I'm Commander Lewis. I understand all of your fellow midshipmen have now arrived. Is that correct?"

"I think so, Commander," d'Arezzo replied, just a bit cautiously. "There are five of us present, at any rate, Ma'am."

"Which is our complete complement," Commander Lewis said with a nod. "I've just heard from Commander FitzGerald that he's going to be delayed for another several hours. Under the circumstances, he's asked me to formally welcome all of you aboard. Would it be convenient for you to join me on the bridge?"

"Of course, Ma'am!" d'Arezzo replied instantly, without so much as glancing at his fellow midshipmen. It was the first thing about the too-pretty midshipman of which Helen unreservedly approved. A "request" from a full commander, however politely phrased, was a direct command from God as far as any midshipwoman was concerned.

"Very well." Lewis reached out, as if to switch off her com, then paused. "Excuse me, Mr. d'Arezzo," she said. "I'd forgotten for a moment that you've all just reported aboard *Hexapuma*. Should I send a guide, just until you learn your way about?"

"No, thank you, Ma'am," d'Arezzo said politely. "I'm sure we can find our way."

"Very well, then," Lewis repeated. "I'll see you on the bridge in fifteen minutes."

"Aye, aye, Ma'am."

This time, she did cut the circuit, and d'Arezzo looked up to see all four other middies looking at him rather intently. Something like a ghost of a smile twitched at his firmly formed lips, and he shrugged.

"What?" he asked.

"I hope you know what *we're* doing," Ragnhild said dryly. "Because I know *I* don't have a clue how to find the bridge from here."

"Oh, I feel confident we could find it even from a cold start, if we had to," he replied. "As it happens, however . . ."

He slid his book viewer out into the center of the table, and Ragnhild bent over it. Then she chuckled suddenly and turned the viewer so the others could see it. It was a schematic of *Hexapuma*, and Helen felt her own mouth twitch in an unwilling smile. She still didn't care too much for the way d'Arezzo had buried himself in the viewer, ignoring everyone else, but at least what he'd been perusing so intently made more sense than the novel she'd assumed he was reading.

"As you know," Commander Ginger Lewis said, sitting very upright in the chair at the head of the table in the captain's briefing room immediately off of *Hexapuma*'s bridge, "it's traditional for midshipmen and midshipwomen on their graduation cruises to be formally welcomed aboard their ships. Usually, that duty falls to either the executive officer or to the assistant tac officer, since she's normally the one who will serve as their officer candidate training officer for the deployment. Unfortunately, at the moment Commander FitzGerald, our XO, finds himself detained dealing with the yard dogs, and our ATO hasn't reported aboard yet. And so, Ladies and Gentlemen, you find yourselves stuck with me."

She smiled with a curious blend of impishness, sympathy, and cool command.

"I find myself at something of a disadvantage, in some ways," she continued, "because I never attended the Academy. I was directly commissioned, and they put me through OCS aboard *Vulcan*. As a result, I never made a snotty cruise, so this particular rite of passage is outside my direct personal experience."

Helen didn't move a single muscle, but she found herself studying Lewis much more intently. The commander looked young for her rank, even in a society with prolong. And now that Helen was paying attention to the medal ribbons on the breast of the Engineer's space-black tunic, she was impressed. They were headed by the Osterman Cross. The Osterman was about one notch below the Manticore Cross, and, like the MC, it could be awarded only for valor. Unlike the MC, however, it could be awarded only to enlisted personnel or noncommissioned officers. The Conspicuous Gallantry Medal kept the OC company, as did the red sleeve stripe which indicated the commander had been wounded in action and the additional stripe which indicated someone who had been mentioned in dispatches.

An impressive collection, Helen thought. And one which almost certainly helped explain Lewis' commission. The RMN had always had a higher percentage of "mustangs"—officers who'd been promoted from the enlisted ranks—than most navies, but it appeared Ginger Lewis was something out of the ordinary even for the Star Kingdom.

"Despite that," Lewis continued, "I do have a certain degree of secondhand knowledge of what you people are getting into. I've seen quite a few snotties come and go, even before I became a Queen's officer myself, and there are only a few points I'd like to make to you.

"The first is one all of you've already had made to you over and over again. But that's because it's an important one. This cruise, here aboard *Hexapuma*, is your true final exam. Every one of you will officially graduate from the Academy, regardless of the outcome of your cruise, on the basis of your academic record, barring the unlikely event of your committing some court-martial offense in the course of it. *But*," she let her green eyes sweep their faces, and there was no longer any smile in them, "if you screw up badly enough aboard *Hexapuma*, you will *not* receive a commission in Her Majesty's Navy. If you screw up less than totally, you might receive a commission, but it wouldn't be a line commission, and you would never hold command of any Queen's ship. Remember that, Ladies and Gentlemen. This is pass-fail, and it isn't a game. Not a test you can retake or make up. I know all of you are intelligent, motivated, and well educated. I expect you to do well. And I strongly recommend to you that you expect—and demand—the same superior performance out of yourselves.

"The second point I want to make to you is that this is going to be *hard*. It's supposed to be. In fact, it's designed to be harder than it really has to be. Some middies break on their snotty cruises, and that's always a tragedy. But far better that they break then, than break in action after they've received their commissions . . . or after they've actually received a command of their own. So there are going to be times, over the next several months, when you're going to feel harried and driven to the point of collapse. But afterward, when you've survived it, you'll know you *can* survive it, and, hopefully, you will have learned to have faith in your own capacity to rise to challenges.

"The third point I want to make is that although you hold temporary warrants as Queen's officers for this deployment, and although your positions in *Hexapuma*'s chain of command are very real, you have not yet even attained what a civilian might call 'an entry-level position.' In fact, Ladies and Gentlemen, a midshipwoman is what you might think of as the larval stage of an officer. Be aware of that. You face the difficult task of projecting authority over men and women much older than you are, with many T-years more experience than you possess. You must have confidence in yourself before you can expect those men and women to have confidence in you. And be assured that they will recognize any effort to bullshit them, just as they'll recognize petty tyrants in the making when they encounter them. But your self-confidence can't stop with the ability to make them obey you. It must extend to the point of being willing and able to learn *from* them without sacrificing your authority.

"And the fourth point is that unlike a great many other middies, you're making your snotty cruise in time of war. It's entirely possible *Hexapuma* will be called to action while you are on board. You may be wounded. You may be killed. And what is even worse, as I can tell you from personal experience, you may see those you care about—friends or those under your orders—killed or wounded. Accept that now, but don't allow it to prey upon your thoughts or to paralyze you if the moment actually comes. And remember that aboard this ship, you are Queen's officers. You may live, or you may die, but your actions—whatever they may be—will reflect not simply upon you, but upon every man and woman ever called upon to wear the uniform we all wear. See to it that any reflections you cast are the ones for which you want to be remembered . . . because you will be."

She paused, her eyes circling the table once more, and silence stretched out in the briefing room. She let it linger for several seconds, then smiled again, suddenly.

"And now that I've hopefully scared you all to death," she said in a much more cheerful tone, "I suppose I should also point out that it won't all be doom and gloom. You may find yourself feeling utterly exhausted from time to time, and you may even feel your superiors are taking a certain unholy glee in contributing to your exhaustion. You may even be right about that. But that doesn't mean you won't find the odd opportunity to enjoy yourselves. And while we expect a professional demeanor and deportment, you won't be on duty all the time. I expect you'll even discover that those same superior officers may be surprisingly approachable if you find yourself in need of advice. Remember, People, you're here to learn, as much as to be tested, and while it's part of our job to identify any potential weak links, it's also our job to help temper and polish the strong ones.

"And now," she pressed a button on the arm of her chair, and the briefing room hatch slid silently open. A brown-haired senior chief petty officer stepped through it. He was of little more than medium height, with a slender build, but impressively muscular, and his uniform was perfectly turned out as he came to attention.

"This, Ladies and Gentlemen," Commander Lewis informed them, "is Senior Chief Petty Officer Wanderman. Senior Chief Wanderman is going to take you on a little tour. Before you set out, however, I believe you might find it advisable to return to your quarters long enough to change out of those nice uniforms into something you can get a little grease on. The Senior Chief believes in, ah, a hands-on approach. Don't you, Senior Chief?"

She smiled at the tough-looking, impassive petty officer, and there might have been the tiniest flicker of shared amusement in his brown eyes, though one would have had to look very close to find it.

"As the Commander says, Ma'am," he said. Then he looked at the midshipmen. "It's now thirteen-twenty-five hours, Sirs and Ma'ams," he told them. "If it would be convenient for you, I thought we might begin the tour at thirteen-forty-five."

It was really quite remarkable, Helen reflected. Until that moment, she hadn't realized a noncommissioned officer's polite "request" could also be a direct decree from God.

Chapter Four

Commander Ansten FitzGerald stepped through the briefing room hatch with his memo board tucked under his arm.

"Sorry I'm late, Sir," he said to the tall, blond man in the white beret sitting at the head of the briefing room table. "I had to . . . straighten out Commander Bennington."

"Ah. The yard dogs are still arguing about the Engineering spares?" Captain Aivars Aleksovitch Terekhov leaned back in his chair, arctic blue eyes faintly amused.

"Yes, Sir." FitzGerald shrugged. "According to Bennington, we're twenty percent over establishment in almost every category."

"Shocking," Terekhov murmured. He quirked an eyebrow at his Chief Engineer. "Do you have any idea how this sad state of affairs could have come about, Commander Lewis?"

"Why, no, Sir," Ginger Lewis said. She shook her head, guileless green eyes wide.

"Lieutenant Duncan?" Terekhov looked at the short, attractive officer at the foot of the table. Lieutenant

Andrea Duncan was the most junior officer present, and she looked more than a bit uneasy. Although she was *Hexapuma*'s logistics officer, she wasn't a natural scrounger. She took her responsibilities seriously, but unlike Lewis, she appeared to be . . . uncomfortable whenever it came to going outside officially approved channels. And the fact that Terekhov had been aboard as *Hexapuma*'s CO for less than three weeks didn't exactly make her feel any more at ease with him.

It didn't make FitzGerald feel a lot more at ease, for that matter. Not that a good executive officer was about to let that show.

"Uh, no, Sir," Duncan said after a moment, glancing at Lewis' serene expression. "None at all."

"I thought not," Terekhov said, and pointed at FitzGerald's waiting chair. The executive officer settled into it, and the bearded captain let his own chair come back forward. "And how did your conversation with Commander Bennington go, XO? Is the Station Patrol likely to turn up to place us under arrest?"

"No, Sir," FitzGerald replied. "I pointed out that whatever the exact numbers of spares we might have on board, all of our materials requests had been properly submitted and approved. I informed him that if he wishes to submit the required paperwork to have our original requests disallowed, all of our onboard spares off-loaded, new requests drawn up, considered, and approved, and the new spares loaded, that's certainly his privilege. I also pointed out that I estimated it would take him a minimum of three weeks, and that we're under orders to depart *Hephaestus* in less than two."

The executive officer shrugged, and one or two of the officers seated around the table chuckled. Given the current situation at the front, no yard dog was going to risk Their Lordships' displeasure by delaying the departure of one of Her Majesty's starships.

"I take it the Commander didn't indicate he intended to accept your generous invitation."

"No, Sir." FitzGerald smiled slightly. "As a matter of

fact, Sir, Bennington isn't all that bad a sort. Oh, he's a bean-counter, but I think that when it comes right down to it, he'd prefer for us to have the spares we may need in an emergency, whether we're excess to establishment or not. He just thinks we were a little too successful in our midnight requisitions. All I really needed was to give him an excuse he can use if any of his superiors fault him for what we got away with."

"I can live with that, as long as we don't really end up with our departure delayed," Terekhov said, then moved his right hand in a little throwing away gesture. FitzGerald hadn't known Terekhov long, but he'd already learned to recognize the mannerism. That hand-flick was the captain's way of shifting from one mental focus to another, and the XO wondered if he'd always had it, or if it was one he'd developed since the hand was regenerated.

"How does our schedule look from your end, Commander Lewis?" Terekhov asked. "Is the yard going to be done with us on time?"

"It'll be close, Sir," Lewis replied, meeting his eyes squarely. "To be honest, I don't think the yard dogs have time to get everything done, so I've had them concentrating on Beta Thirty. *That* much, they should have done with at least a couple of days to spare. Most of the rest of our problems are relatively minor, actually. My people can take care of them underway out of our onboard resources. That was one reason I, ah, *acquired* so many spares." She shrugged. "Bottom line, Sir, this is a new ship. We passed our trials, and aside from that one beta node, everything on our list is really nothing more than squeaky hinges and parts that need wearing in."

Terekhov gazed at her for a moment, and she looked back steadily. More than one engineer would have sounded far less confident than Lewis. They would have insisted it was *Hephaestus'* job to repair every problem their own departments' surveys had identified instead of cheerfully accepting responsibility for them themselves. Especially given the way their commanding officers were liable to react if it turned out they couldn't deal with them themselves, after all.

FitzGerald waited to see how Terekhov would respond. Captain Sarcula had been assigned to command *Hexapuma* while she was still only a gleam in BuShips' eye. He'd supervised her construction from the keel plate out, and begun the assembly of a handpicked command team, starting with one Ansten FitzGerald and Commander Lewis. But Sarcula's assignment had been overtaken by events. His orders to assume command of the battlecruiser *Braveheart,* following her skipper's death in action, had been totally unexpected, and Terekhov's abrupt assignment to *Hexapuma*, for all intents and purposes straight out of Bassingford Medical Center, must have come as just as much of a surprise to him as Sarcula's sudden transfer had come to FitzGerald.

That sudden reshuffling of command assignments had, unfortunately, become less uncommon than it ought to have been. BuShips and BuPers were still fighting to regain their balance after the shocking losses inflicted by the Havenites' opening offensives. But even so, it couldn't have been easy for Terekhov. He'd missed *Hexapuma*'s builders' and acceptance trials and inherited another man's command team, composed of officers he'd never even met before. They didn't know him, and he hadn't been given very long to form an opinion of their competence, either. Which meant he had precious little upon which to base any evaluation of Ginger Lewis' judgment.

If that worried him at the moment, however, it didn't show.

"Very well," was all he said, and the right hand flicked again. His head moved, as well, as he turned his attention to Lieutenant Commander Tobias Wright, *Hexapuma*'s Astrogator. Wright was the youngest of Terekhov's senior officers, and the most reserved.

"Have you received all of the downloads you requested, Commander?" he asked.

"Yes, Sir," the sandy-haired lieutenant commander replied. Terekhov gazed at him a moment longer, as if waiting to see if he cared to add anything to that bald reply, but Wright only looked back at him.

"Good," the captain said after a few seconds, and turned his attention to Lieutenant Commander Amal Nagchaudhuri. "Have we received our communications downloads, Commander?"

"Not yet, Sir." Nagchaudhuri was very tall—over a hundred and ninety-three centimeters—with dark black hair and brown eyes that stood out in sharp contrast to a complexion that approached albinism. That complexion was a legacy of the planet Sandor, from which his parents had immigrated before he'd learned to walk.

"We've received some of them, Captain," he continued, "but we won't be receiving the full crypto download until forty-four hours before we depart. I'm also still waiting for the Trade Union's secure merchant codes, but I've been assured that we should have them within the next day or two. Other than that, we're ready to go."

There was something about his last sentence. Not anything anyone could have put a finger on, but there, and FitzGerald looked at him with an edge of warning. Nagchaudhuri was a cheerful, extroverted sort. Some people tended to underestimate the sharp brain hidden behind the pun-cracking jokester he preferred to present to the rest of the universe. But there was a very serious and dedicated naval officer behind that facade, as well, and one with all of the fervent patriotism of a naturalized citizen. Amal hadn't taken it very well when he was informed of the change in *Hexapuma*'s assigned station.

Neither had FitzGerald, for that matter. But orders were orders, and there was no point in making his disappointment too evident to their new captain. Especially not if they'd received their orders for the reasons FitzGerald suspected they had.

If Terekhov had noted the same slight edge FitzGerald had, he gave no sign of it. Instead, he simply nodded.

"I'm sure you'll have everything we need before we depart, Commander," he said. The right hand moved, and he turned to the petite, fine-boned officer seated to FitzGerald's left.

"Commander Kaplan."

"Yes, Sir." Lieutenant Commander Naomi Kaplan was the physical opposite of Amal Nagchaudhuri. She was forty centimeters shorter, and where he was so pale-skinned he'd had a permanent nanotech sun blocker installed, her complexion was almost as dark as Queen Elizabeth's own. Which only made her blond hair, so light it was almost—but not quite—platinum, stand out even more vividly. Her eyes were as dark as Nagchaudhuri's, but they were also far more intense. She reminded FitzGerald forcibly of their ship's hexapuma namesake—territorial, naturally aggressive, perpetually poised for mayhem, and very, very sharp-clawed.

"I'm afraid I have some potentially bad news for your department, Commander. Lieutenant Grigsby won't be reporting aboard, after all. It seems there was an air car accident." He shrugged. "And there's also the matter of your request for an assistant for Lieutenant Bagwell."

"Sir?" Kaplan glanced at the lieutenant seated to her left.

Guthrie Bagwell was a solidly built man, thirty centimeters taller than the tactical officer, but almost painfully nondescript. His features were eminently forgettable, his hair was an unremarkable brown, and his brain was quite possibly the sharpest of any of *Hexapuma*'s officers. As the heavy cruiser's electronics warfare officer, he was one of Kaplan's subordinates, but ever since the new hardware developed as part of Project Ghost Rider had reached the deployment stage, EW had become a specialist's job once again. Bagwell, for all of his undisputed brilliance in his own esoteric area, completely lacked the broad-based tactical background which Lieutenant Grigsby had been supposed to bring to *Hexapuma* as her junior tactical officer.

"The entire Navy is chronically short of EW officers," Terekhov said. FitzGerald, watching him closely and listening to his calm, reasonable tone wondered how much of what he was saying was his own opinion and how much was the rationale BuPers had used when it denied Kaplan's request.

"The units being committed to active operations against Haven have a higher priority for electronics warfare specialists than units being assigned to . . . other duties," Terekhov continued. "And, to be perfectly honest—and with no desire to inflate any egos—the fact is that Lieutenant Bagwell has absolutely top-notch efficiency reports. He's substantially better, both in terms of ability and training, than anyone most ships could reasonably hope to have assigned to them. In part because of that, BuPers feels *Hexapuma* is adequately covered, and that the scarce supply of qualified EW officers shouldn't be further depleted providing such a paragon with backup which will probably never be needed for this deployment, anyway."

No, FitzGerald thought. *He* doesn't *agree with the rationale. In fact, I'd say he's pissed as hell about it. Interesting that he shows so little sign of it.*

"With all due respect, Sir, and without—I hope!—any threat of ego-inflation," Lieutenant Bagwell said, "I really wish BuPers didn't have quite so high an opinion of my ability." He smiled, and Terekhov's lips twitched in what was almost an answering smile.

"I think I can safely say Commander Kaplan and I agree with you," the captain said after a moment. "Unfortunately, that's not going to change BuPers' position. If it were, the, ah, forcefulness with which I have expressed that opinion would already have borne fruit. Under the circumstances, I think we're all just going to have to figure out how to spread the load as much as possible. I understand at least one of our midshipmen showed outstanding promise in the Island's EW program."

FitzGerald managed not to blink, but he couldn't help wondering where Terekhov had gotten that particular tidbit of information. If it was in one of the midshipmen's personnel files, the exec hadn't found it himself yet.

"A *midshipman*, Sir?" Kaplan repeated in a very careful

tone, and this time Terekhov did smile. Not that there was a great deal of humor in the expression.

"I'm not proposing we slot someone quite that junior into the JEWO's position, Commander. But I am hopeful Lieutenant Bagwell might at least be able to use this particular snotty as an assistant. A snotty cruise is supposed to be a sort of an apprenticeship, after all."

"Well, that's true enough, I suppose, Sir," the tactical officer said, trying her best not to sound overtly doubtful.

"In the meantime," Terekhov said, right hand flicking again, "I've screened BuPers about the Grigsby replacement matter again. I pointed out that, since we're already sailing without a junior electronic-warfare officer, it would behoove them to at least find us a junior *tactical* officer. I'm afraid I waxed rather emphatic on the point, and they've promised to find us a replacement—*another* replacement, I should say—before our departure. However," this time his smile was downright wintry, "under the circumstances, and given how long it took them to scare Grigsby up in the first place, I wouldn't care to place any money on the probability that they will. So it looks as if we may be sailing shorthanded at Tactical in more ways than one."

"I see, Sir." Kaplan's dark eyes were hooded, and she frowned. "I can't say I'm delighted to hear it," she continued after a moment. "As you say, Captain, this is going to leave us shorthanded. With all due respect to Guthrie—I mean, Lieutenant Bagwell—I believe we're in a somewhat better position to get by without a JEWO than without an ATO. Lieutenant Hearns is very good, but she's also extremely junior for the ATO's slot aboard a heavy cruiser. She's more than won her spurs, and her Academy grades and efficiency reports since graduation are both top-notch. But her actual combat experience was limited to that dirt-side business on Refuge."

"I agree that she hasn't had the opportunity to demonstrate her competence in space under actual shipboard combat conditions," Terekhov said. "On the other hand, as you say, she has 'won her spurs' and demonstrated she's not prone to panic. And the fact that she made her snotty cruise with Michael Oversteegen is probably a fairly good sign, too, wouldn't you say?"

"As I say, Sir," Kaplan replied a bit stiffly, "Abigail—Lieutenant Hearns—is very good. I have no reservations whatsoever about her capability. My only concern is for the level of her experience."

"Well," Terekhov said, his tone absolutely devoid of expression, "given our deployment orders, she should have the opportunity to slip into her duties fairly gradually."

Kaplan had been about to say something more. Instead, she closed her mouth and simply nodded tightly.

"There is one other point about Lieutenant Hearns' qualifications as ATO, Captain," FitzGerald said carefully after a moment. The captain looked at him, and the executive officer raised his right hand, palm uppermost. "We have five midshipmen on board, Sir, and traditionally, it's the ATO's job to act as the ship's Officer Candidate Training Officer. Lieutenant Hearns is only a jay-gee, and no more than a couple of T-years older than the snotties."

"I see your point," Terekhov murmured. He tipped his chair back and rocked it gently from side to side, his lips pursed in thought. Then he shrugged.

"I see your point," he repeated, "and I agree that it's something we'll need to keep an eye on. At the same time, I've been quite impressed with Lieutenant Hearns' record. And don't forget she's a steadholder's daughter. I don't think exercising authority over people that close to her own age would be as difficult for someone from that background as it might be for someone else. And the experience could stand *her* in very good stead, as well." He shook his head. "No, in the unfortunately likely case of BuPers' failing to find us a replacement for Lieutenant Grigsby, I think we might give Lieutenant Hearns a shot at it. Obviously, we'll have to see how well she handles it, and we may need to rethink it if it doesn't seem to be working out."

FitzGerald nodded. He wasn't at all certain he agreed with Terekhov, despite the fact that his own impression of Abigail Hearns had been extremely favorable. But he'd voiced his concern over a possible problem, as a good executive officer was supposed to do. Now, as a good executive officer was also supposed to do, he would devote his efforts to making his commanding officer's decision a success.

Everyone in the briefing room looked up as Lieutenant Commander Nagchaudhuri chuckled suddenly.

"Something amuses you, Commander?" Terekhov's tone might have been cutting. Instead, it expressed only mild interest, and the com officer shook his head with just a hint of apology.

"Sorry, Sir. I was just thinking. Lieutenant Hearns is also Miss Owens."

"Yes, she is," Terekhov agreed. "I believe I just observed that she was a steadholder's daughter myself."

"I know you did, Sir. But what I was thinking is that that makes her the equivalent of a princess of the blood. Which might make her even more qualified as our OCTO." Terekhov crooked an eyebrow, and Nagchaudhuri chuckled again. "Well, Sir, one of our midshipwomen is Helen Zilwicki. Anton Zilwicki's daughter. Which means, after that business in Congo, that *she's* a princess of the blood, too. After a manner of speaking, of course. In fact, if I understand what I've read about the Torch Constitution properly, I think she's probably the legal heir apparent if something should happen to Queen Berry."

"You know," Terekhov said with a slight smile, "I hadn't really considered that." He chuckled. "For a ship which is sailing without a single member of the *Manticoran* peerage in Snotty Row, we would appear to have an abundance—one might almost say a super-abundance—of noble blood aboard."

He considered the situation for several more seconds, still with that same, faint smile. Then he shook himself.

"Well, it should be interesting to see how that works

out," he said. "In the meantime, however, we still have a few other details to attend too. Commander Orban," he turned to Surgeon Commander Lajos Orban, *Hexapuma*'s ship's doctor.

"Yes, Sir?"

"I've been looking at your requests for additional sick berth attendants. In light of the situation in the Cluster . . ."

"You wanted to see me, Sir Lucien?"

"Yes, I did, Terence. Come in—sit down."

Admiral of the Green Sir Lucien Cortez, Fifth Space Lord of the Royal Manticoran Admiralty, looked up and pointed at the chair on the other side of his desk. Captain Terence Shaw, his chief of staff, took the indicated seat and looked at him expectantly. Sir Lucien had been back in his old job for less than three months, and Admiral Draskovic, his immediate predecessor, had left a monumental mess in her wake. Not as bad as the disaster which had been left at BuShips or over at the Office of Naval Intelligence, perhaps, but bad enough. Especially in the face of a war which was going so badly at the moment.

"I've been thinking about Terekhov," Cortez said abruptly.

"Aivars Terekhov, Sir?" Shaw asked. He'd served as one of Cortez's aides during Sir Lucien's previous stint as Fifth Space Lord, and he was no longer amazed by his boss' ability to carry names and faces around in his memory. Impressed, yes. Even awed. But seeing Cortez perform the same feat so often had worn away the outright amazement.

"Yes." Cortez tipped back in his chair, frowning. "I'm just not entirely comfortable with his orders."

"With all due respect, Sir," Shaw said, "I think this may be exactly what he needs."

Some people might have thought it odd that the commander of the Bureau of Personnel and his chief of staff should be spending time discussing the assignment of a single senior-grade captain. Some people might even have called it "wasting" their time, given all of the other emergency decisions demanding their attention. But Sir Lucien Cortez had demonstrated a master's touch at nourishing the careers of outstanding officers too often for Shaw to wonder about it now.

"His combat record is too good," Cortez said. "And God knows we need all the proven combat commanders we can get!"

"I agree with you, Sir. But given what happened at Hyacinth . . ." He let his voice trail off, and Cortez grimaced.

"I know all about Hyacinth, Terence. And I also know all the medals in the universe won't make a man like Terekhov feel any better about losing his ship or the destruction of so much of his convoy. But BuMed's psychiatrists say he's fit for duty again."

"I've read their evaluation, Sir, and I'm certainly not attempting to dispute their conclusions. I'm just saying that whether he's fit for duty again or not, letting him slip back into active command someplace a bit quieter than Trevor's Star might be advisable. And another point to consider is his Foreign Office experience."

"Um." Cortez frowned, but he also nodded.

Aivars Terekhov had left active RMN service for almost thirty T-years to pursue a diplomatic career. He'd done well during his twenty-eight T-years with the Foreign Office, but he'd maintained his reserve commission. Promotions had been much slower in the reserve than among active-duty regulars, and he'd advanced only to the rank of lieutenant commander before—like many reservists—reporting for active duty after the Battle of Hancock. Also, as with a lot of "retreads," Cortez's own BuPers had spent longer than it should have recognizing his raw ability and steering him into the promotions and more demanding duties it had deserved.

Which had ultimately gotten him sent to Hyacinth and disaster, the admiral reminded himself grimly.

"You know Admiral Khumalo's going to need experienced,

smart captains, Sir," Shaw continued. "And I can't think of anyone we could send him who could match Terekhov's diplomatic experience. He could be invaluable to Baroness Medusa and the Admiral, especially with his demonstrated ability to think outside the box. And, speaking frankly, you know as well as I do how few officers with that ability Admiral Khumalo has."

"And how poor he is at it himself," Cortez said with another grimace. Shaw didn't say anything in response. However true Cortez's assessment might be, it wasn't a captain's place to pass judgment on a rear admiral of the green.

"Actually, what I'd really prefer would be to recall Khumalo," Cortez continued. "Unfortunately, that's a political decision as much as a military one. Besides, who would we send out to replace him? To be brutally honest, Talbott doesn't exactly have the same priority as the front. Or as Silesia, for that matter."

He leaned further back in his chair, pinching the bridge of his nose wearily.

"Too many fires," he muttered, mostly to himself. "Too many fires, and not enough people to piss on all of them."

He sat that way for several seconds, then let his chair come back upright.

"Maybe you're right, Terence," he sighed. "We've got to prioritize *somehow*, and Earl White Haven's been as clear about that as anyone could ask. First, the front and our main combat formations. Second, the integration of our share of Silesia into the Star Kingdom. Third, commerce protection. And Talbott comes fourth. Not because it's unimportant, but because it's *less* important—or at least less vital—than the others . . . and so much less likely to turn around and bite us on the ass. At least everyone there got to *vote* on their future!"

And, Terence Shaw added silently, *whether the Government wants to admit it publicly or not, Talbott isn't going to be a matter of life or death for the Star Kingdom, whatever happens there. I hope.*

Cortez sat drumming on his desk with his fingers for a moment, then shrugged.

"All right. I'm still not entirely happy about it, but someone has to draw the Talbott duty, and Lord knows they need at least a few modern ships on the station, whatever happens. And Khumalo does need someone with diplomatic experience who can also help him think unconventionally. And maybe you're right. Maybe Terekhov really does need—or deserve, at least—the opportunity to get back up on the horse on a fairly quiet station."

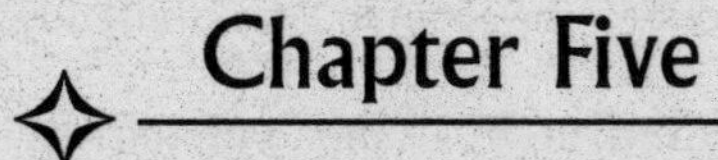

Chapter Five

Five men and three women sat in the luxurious conference room. Their clothing was perfectly suited to their surroundings, expensive and tailored in the latest Solarian styles, and their jewelry—understated, for the most part—was equally expensive. They were elegantly groomed, with the sort of sleek self-assurance that came with knowing they were masters of the worlds about them.

And, at the moment, they were not happy.

"Just who the fuck do these frigging neobarbs think they are?!" the man at the head of the table demanded. He was perhaps a bit overweight, but his face was normally quite handsome. At the moment, however, the anger blazing in his brown eyes and turning his jowls brick red made that easy to forget. "'The Star Kingdom of Manticore!' *Pfehhh!*" His lips worked, as if he were about to spit on the conference room's expensive carpet.

"I admit it's ridiculous, Commissioner Verrochio," one of the women said in a much calmer tone. Her gray eyes were just as angry as Verrochio's, but cold. Very cold. "Nonetheless, it's happening."

"Not while *I* can do anything about it, it isn't, Ms. Anisimovna!" Verrochio spat.

"The problem, Lorcan," one of the other men at the table said, "is that it's beginning to look as if there's not a great deal we *can* do. Openly, at least."

"That's ridiculous!" the commissioner snapped. "We're the Office of Frontier Security, and they're a jumped-up, Johnny-come-lately, neobarb 'kingdom' with delusions of grandeur! Hell, Old Sol alone has three or four times the population of their entire fucking 'star kingdom.' It's like a toenail threatening the entire rest of the body!"

"No, it isn't, Commissioner," the woman who'd already spoken said.

The commissioner glared at her, and Anisimovna shrugged. Her spectacularly beautiful face had profited from the finest biosculpt and genetic modifications money could buy, and at the moment, it was as calm and focused as Verrochio was choleric.

"It's not like that on two counts. The first is that the Manticorans aren't just any old 'neobarbs' as far as the League is concerned. Their home system is barely a week away from the Sol System itself, via the Beowulf terminus of their damned junction. And it's been settled for centuries—longer than some of the systems in the Old League itself. Certainly longer than several of the Shell systems! They get along fine with Beowulf and manage to stay on fairly good terms with Sol, unlike most neobarb kingdoms. They got hammered by the media during their first war with Haven, and most of the *other* systems of the League think of them as being isolated out on their little fringe of the explored galaxy, but they have remarkably good contacts on Old Earth. Which, of course, is the capital of the entire League. And they've had those contacts for over three T-centuries now, ever since the Manticore Junction was discovered and explored."

She shrugged, her voice and manner as calm as her expression, and paused, as if daring anyone to dispute what she'd just said. No one did, and she smiled ever so slightly.

"The second reason it's not like a toenail threatening the rest of the body is that, truthfully, the Manticorans haven't *threatened* anyone who's a citizen of the League," she pointed out. "And the way their ambassador is presenting matters to the Executive Council back on Old Earth, all they're doing here is accepting the results of a freely organized—*self*-organized—vote by the citizens of the Talbott Cluster. The results of the plebiscite were overwhelming, you know. Almost eighty percent in favor of requesting annexation by the Star Kingdom."

"And who cares about that, Aldona?" a very young, hazel-eyed man asked scornfully. "Plebiscites!" He snorted. "How many of them have *we* bought over the centuries?"

"Which, in many ways, is exactly what makes the current situation so . . . problematical, Mr. Kalokainos," the dark-haired woman seated beside Anisimovna pointed out. Her eyes were as cold as Anisimovna's, but their irises were a peculiar metallic silver, and her artfully skimpy (although hideously expensive) outfit of Telluridian worm-silk revealed some truly extravagant tattoos and body piercings. "You might say that it's a case of being hoist by our own petard." She grimaced. "I always did wonder where that particular cliche came from, but it's apt enough in this case. We've told the precious voters about so many of *our* plebiscites, that they're preconditioned to accept anybody's plebiscite as justification for annexation. And those close connections with Old Earth which Ms. Anisimovna just pointed out the Manties have include 'connections' with some of the best lobbyist firms on the planet. They know how to make the Manty plebiscite look very good, especially with those sorts of raw numbers."

She shrugged, and Anisimovna nodded firmly.

"Isabel is right, Commissioner Verrochio. However honest or fixed the vote may have been, it was overwhelming. Which means this isn't a situation where we can use the iron fist. The problem is figuring out what version of silk glove we need to use instead."

"And what sort of knuckleduster we can put inside it?" the man seated at Verrochio's right elbow murmured.

"Exactly, Junyan," Anisimovna agreed.

"Excuse me, Vice-Commissioner Hongbo," Kalokainos said, "but the last thing *I* think we need to do is to lend this naked territorial grab any semblance of credibility. We ought to be taking a clear public stance. Denounce this so-called plebiscite for a fraud and a travesty, proclaim Frontier Security's overriding responsibility to protect the true right of self-determination of Talbott's citizens, and whistle up an SLN task force to kick the frigging Manties back where they belong!"

Aldona Anisimovna managed not to roll her eyes in exasperation, but it was difficult, even for someone with her decades of experience in double-speak. Kalokainos actually managed to sound as if he meant his own rhetoric. Not that there was any chance he really did. Although, unfortunately, he probably did mean the last little bit.

"Perhaps, Volkhart, you aren't fully aware of just what the Manticoran Navy is capable of these days?" He gave her an angry glance, but she met it with the same icy self-control she'd shown Verrochio. "I assure you that *we* are," she added.

"It really doesn't matter what they're capable of," Kalokainos shot back. "They're pipsqueaks. Oh," he waved one hand irritably, "I'll grant that they're pipsqueaks with long, sharp teeth. But they wouldn't stand the chance of a snowflake in hell against the League Navy. We'd plow them under like pygmies, however good their tech may be, if only by throwing sheer numbers at them. And they're smart enough to know it, too. They wouldn't dare go toe-to-toe with us—especially not now that they're actively at war with the Peeps again!"

His words were directed to Anisimovna, but his *eyes*, she noticed, kept sliding towards Verrochio, and her lips tightened almost imperceptibly. She had her own suspicions about Kalokainos' personal agenda, and it was beginning to look as if those suspicions were correct.

"Trying to predict what the Star Kingdom of Manticore

will and won't do is a dangerous game, Volkhart. I speak from a certain painful personal experience, as you might care to recall." Unlike Kalokainos' eyes, hers stayed exactly where she told them to—on Kalokainos' face. But that didn't keep her from watching Verrochio's expression carefully. "Say what you will about the Manties, and I assure you that there are very few things we *haven't* said about them at Manpower over the centuries, they've already established that they're willing to run risks anyone else would consider insane in support of their precious 'principles.'" Her lips tightened with contempt, but she was too honest with herself to try to avoid the logical consequences of her own analysis. "If we push them too hard, there's no telling how they might respond. I certainly shouldn't have to remind *you* what sort of pressure they've chosen to exert in the past through their control of their damned wormhole junction."

Verrochio flinched. It was a tiny thing, little more than a half-seen tic at the corner of one eye, but it gave her a small spurt of satisfaction. Perhaps something was finally getting through the commissioner's self-important, self-centered rage.

"That was then, and this is now," Kalokainos retorted. "They've got their backs plastered to the wall this time. Their economy's running flat out, and they need every credit they can scare up. They're not going to risk a trade war with the Solarian League when they're desperately trying to build every warship they can!"

"I think you're wrong," she said flatly. "I'll remind you that their position was equally 'desperate' at the beginning of their first war with the Peeps, and they didn't hesitate to threaten to close the Manticoran Junction to all Solarian shipping then."

"Aldona has a point," Hongbo Junyan said, sliding smoothly back into the conversation with the skill he'd used to subtly direct his nominal superior for years. Kalokainos gave him an irritated glance. More importantly, as far as Anisimovna was concerned, Verrochio looked at him with automatic thoughtfulness.

"I'm not saying Mr. Kalokainos' argument isn't logical," the vice-commissioner continued. "The problem is that the Manties may not be feeling particularly logical. Hell," he allowed himself a snort and a grin, "if they were feeling *logical*, they never would've gotten themselves into a potential pissing match with Frontier Security at a time like this in the first place!

"But my point," his expression sobered, "is that they're probably forming their own estimate of the situation and the balance of power on a basis which includes their control of the Manticore Junction. And, I might point out, we'd find it very difficult to get at their home systems directly. Even if we managed to take Talbott entirely away from them with local forces, their fundamental territorial integrity—both at home and in Silesia—would be safe from us for months, at the very least. All they'd have to do would be to retreat back to the junction's central terminus, and we couldn't get at them at all. But they could certainly close the junction to all of our merchant shipping, at least until we managed to get a powerful fleet there through hyper. I'm sure that as the representative of Kalokainos Shipping, Mr. Kalokainos is actually in a better position than I am to estimate how many billions of credits that would cost League ship owners and corporations in the interval."

Verrochio was frowning intently now, and Kalokainos shrugged irritably.

"Of course they could hurt us economically if they were stupid enough," he said. "But if they did, even those idiots on the Executive Council would agree to full-scale military operations against them!"

Which, Anisimovna thought coldly, *is precisely what you and your cronies would just* love *to see, isn't it, Volkhart?*

"No doubt," Hongbo agreed, his dry tone in obvious agreement with Anisimovna's suspicions. "I doubt, however, that the Council would be particularly happy with the people who allowed that situation to arise in the first place."

"So do I," Verrochio said, his voice calmer and more thoughtful than it had been since the conference began. Kalokainos' grimace of anger wasn't quite as well concealed as he probably thought it was, but the commissioner was too intent on the horrific career consequences evoked by his assistant's last sentence to notice.

"No," he continued, shaking his head firmly. "I agree we have to respond—forcefully and effectively—to the Manties' intrusion into an area of the Verge where they have no business poking their noses. But we can't afford to let this escalate out of control. And much as I agree with you about the degree of insanity it would require for them to take on the entire Solarian League, Volkhart, Aldona and Junyan have made excellent points of their own. I'm not prepared to risk the possibility that Manticore is crazy enough to go to the mat with us."

"Obviously, it would be a suboptimal situation for all of us if they did," Kalokainos conceded almost gracefully.

"Which brings us back to the question of silk gloves," Anisimovna pointed out.

"Yes, it does," a fair-haired, blue-eyed man agreed. Kalokainos' expression showed a certain lack of surprise at the other's support for Anisimovna.

"And should we assume you have a suggestion, Mr. Ottweiler?" he asked.

"As a matter of fact, I do," Ottweiler replied coolly. Several of the others looked at him speculatively, and he hid a smile. Aside from Verrochio and Hongbo—and, of course, Brigadier General Francisca Yucel—he was the only person in the room who legally represented a star nation. It might be only a single-system polity, but the Mesa System had far more clout than any single system normally wielded.

"With all due respect, Valery," the other man who hadn't yet spoken, Izrok Levakonic, Technodyne Industries of Yildun's representative, said mildly, "Mesa hasn't exactly been going from triumph to triumph where . . . managing the Manties is concerned."

"No, we haven't." It was obvious Ottweiler didn't like

making the admission, but he did so without flinching. "I might point out, however, that Mesa, for several reasons," he carefully didn't look at Anisimovna or Isabel Bardasano, "is an openly declared enemy of the Star Kingdom. And however big and powerful the League may be, Mesa is only a single star system. We don't begin to have the advantage in resources which the League enjoys. And," he added, looking significantly at Verrochio and Hongbo, "in our last little fiasco at Verdant Vista, they had the backing of a sector governor. A *Frontier Security* sector governor, and the detachment of the SLN assigned to his sector."

"Don't blame *us* for that lunatic Barregos!" Verrochio snorted like an irate boar. "We'd have gotten rid of him in a heartbeat, if he hadn't made himself so politically unassailable over there in Maya."

"Of course you would have, Commissioner," Ottweiler agreed. "But that's actually part of my point. If you're not in a position to move openly against a governor in a sector which has been under OFS control for so long, then the degree of direct control we could reasonably expect you to exercise here in one of the Verge areas which hasn't yet received even protectorate status would have to be still lower."

Verrochio nodded gravely, and Anisimovna hid a mental chuckle of appreciation. Although Ottweiler officially served a duly elected government, everyone with an IQ higher than a rock's knew perfectly well that the "government" of Mesa was a wholly owned subsidiary of the interstellar corporations headquartered there. Which meant that, in a very real sense, Valery Ottweiler was Aldona Anisimovna and Isabel Bardasano's flunky. Nonetheless, the man had a natural knack she could never have matched when it came to managing career League bureaucrats like Verrochio.

I suppose I just don't have the patience to pretend they're anything except exceptionally large hogs swilling at the trough we *keep filled for them. Except, of course, that hogs are much more intelligent animals.*

"So what would you recommend, Valery?" Bardasano asked, exactly as if the three of them hadn't decided on that well before this meeting ever took place.

"I think this is a situation which will require careful management and preparation," he replied. "As I see it, our problem is that the Manticorans have managed to secure the higher moral ground, from a public relations viewpoint, because of their plebiscite. In addition, they actually have at least as much physical access to Old Sol as we do, as well as much better access to the Talbott Cluster."

"Oh, come now!" Kalokainos protested. "They may have contacts with Old Earth lobbying firms and media outlets, but nowhere near the contacts *we* have!"

"There was a reason I specified *physical* access, Mr. Kalolkainos," Ottweiler said calmly. "Of course they can't exert the same sort of leverage we can. They've chosen to stay well away from involvement in the League's political and bureaucratic structures, whereas we're intimately involved in both. And wealthy as they may be, they can't begin to match the resources which we, cumulatively, routinely devote to nurturing our relationships with the League's political leadership, media outlets, and civil service. They literally can't afford to, whereas we can't afford *not* to remain deeply and directly involved in our own economic and political system. All I said is that they have at least as much physical access as we do. We can't shut that access off, and we can't predict what they'll do with it—not with certainty. All of which implies that we have to do something to pull their political teeth before we make any open move to discredit the validity of their plebiscite.

"As far as Talbott is concerned," he continued in that same, reasonable tone, "they can move units back and forth to the Cluster almost instantly from their home system, whereas it would take us literally months to deploy any substantial additional fleet strength to the area. Assuming, of course, that we could convince the Navy to send us additional units in the first place. And on top of all of that, as we've just agreed, the Manticoran Wormhole Junction gives them a dangerous amount of economic leverage."

No one disagreed with his analysis. In fact, one or two people—noticeably Volkhart Kalokainos—nodded in obvious impatience at his recitation of well-worn facts.

"So," he continued, "it seems to me we have to find a way to offset as many of their advantages as possible. My own area of expertise is politics, so I'd like to address the problem from a political perspective. I'm sure some of the rest of you would be in a better position to comment on the strictly military and economic aspects of the situation."

He flashed a slight smile, and Verrochio nodded with an air of august approval.

"Obviously," Ottweiler continued, "as Isabel has already pointed out, we can't attack the plebiscite as a ploy on their part without some careful preparation, unless we're prepared to risk raising questions about our own use of plebiscites to legitimize Frontier Security's extension. No one would thank us for doing anything which would call the validity of our own previous plebiscites into dispute, after all.

"So any attack on the Manties' plebiscite has to be framed in terms of the honesty or dishonesty with which the votes were counted. In addition, it has to take into consideration the fact that the vote tallies have already been reported in the League 'faxes. The very fact that the totals have been reported at all is going to give the officially announced outcome a degree of legitimacy in the view of most League citizens. And unlike most neobarbs, the Manties can put their own talking heads onto Old Earth for the talk shows just as easily as we can, so we need to attack the results in a way which puts them firmly on the defensive from the outset."

"Agreed," Hongbo Junyan said when Ottweiler paused. "And just how do you propose to accomplish this notable feat?"

"Let's assume for the moment the votes actually were

counted honestly," Ottweiler said. In fact, as everyone in the conference room knew, the count *had* been honest. "Even so, it wasn't unanimous. Saying eighty percent of the registered voters voted in favor of seeking annexation is just another way of saying twenty percent of them voted *against* it, now isn't it?"

Heads nodded, and he shrugged.

"Well, I'd be extremely surprised if somewhere in that twenty percent there aren't quite a few radical loonies prepared to resist annexation. Possibly even by force."

You actually managed to make it sound as if we hadn't already done our research, Valery, Anisimovna thought admiringly.

"I think you could safely rely upon that, Mr. Ottweiler," Brigadier Yucel said. As the commander of the Solarian Gendarmerie assigned to Commissioner Verrochio, Yucel was charged with intelligence operations in and around his area of responsibility.

"Actually," she continued, "there are several groups which are already coalescing into potential resistance movements." She grimaced. The Gendarmerie had been keeping an eye on those same groups because they were the ones which would have been most likely to resist an *OFS* occupation of the Cluster.

"If—speaking purely hypothetically, you understand—" Ottweiler said with a conspiratorial smile, "*if* those groups were to rise up in heroic resistance to the Manticoran imperialists who shamelessly rigged the vote, thus depriving them of their sacred right of self-determination, surely the Office of Frontier Security's mandate would require it to carefully examine the legitimacy of the original vote, just as it rigorously examines the results of its own plebiscites.

"And," his smile turned into something any shark might have envied, "if media reports of the Talbott fighting were properly framed by journalists attuned to the grim realities of the freedom fighters' struggle to reclaim their stolen independence, it could, ah, offset much of the advantage the Beowulf Terminus' proximity to Sol gives the Manties. Talking heads may be impressive, but the League's public is sophisticated enough—one might almost say cynical enough—to know official representatives spin the truth to suit their own ends. And body bags, burning buildings, and bombing attacks, all absolutely genuine and captured on HD for the evening news, are more impressive than any talking head ever seen. If the Talbott freedom fighters figure out how to get that message out, the League's citizenry might well begin to recognize the difference between our own scrupulously fair and painstakingly honest plebiscites and the crooked, put-up affair the Manticorans have attempted to get away with."

"You know, I rather like that," Izrok Levakonic mused. The small, wiry man had a darkly sardonic face, and his smile held an edge of true whimsy. "It sounds so . . . noble of us."

"Indeed," Verrochio said a bit repressively. The OFS commissioner felt more comfortable scuttling about on the undersides of bureaucratic rocks. People willing to stand in the open and admit they were dedicated to gaming the system made him uneasy.

"Of course," Yucel said thoughtfully, her dark eyes intent, "for those selfless patriots to make their resistance effective, they'd require access to weapons. Possibly even financial support." She looked across the conference table at Anisimovna and Bardasano, and the Manpower representative smiled gravely.

"I'm sure they would," she said, and Yucel nodded ever so slightly.

"And what if the Manties stomp all over these 'freedom fighters' of yours?" Kalokainos demanded. Of all of those around the table, only his expression might have been called sour.

"That would be . . . difficult," Yucel said. "Not impossible, mind you, Mr. Kalokainos. But difficult. They'd have to have both the political will and the physical means to do so. I'm not sure they would have the will in the first place, since they'd discover fairly quickly that they couldn't do the job without a certain amount of bloodshed. My impression is that Manties are more tough-minded than your typical Solly, but they don't have much experience with the inevitable unpleasant consequences of imperial expansion. The Andermani would probably be prepared to handle whatever had to be handled; I'm not sure Manties would be.

"Even if they were, though, they'd need the *means*, and given all their other current military commitments, I'd have to question whether or not they could free up the ships and troops to deal quickly and effectively with this sort of resistance."

Anisimovna nodded, although she wasn't certain she was prepared to trust Yucel's analysis completely. The Gendarmerie brigadier was undoubtedly intelligent—more so than Verrochio, certainly, and probably more so than Hongbo. But she was also willfully brutal. Manpower's private reports strongly suggested Yucel had been transferred to Verrochio's backwater because her penchant for sadism had acquired just a bit too much notoriety in her last posting.

Whether or not that was true, there wasn't much question that her idea of how to suppress resistance involved the maximum application of force at the earliest possible point in order to provide examples which would terrify any potential resistors into submission. Or that she thought anyone who didn't share her own approach was weak-willed and contemptible.

"I think we can take it as a given that any resistance movements which acquired significant amounts of outside financial support and weapons would, at the very least, be expensive and bloody to suppress," Anisimovna said. "And all we'd really need to bring the legitimacy of the plebiscite into question would be enough violence to let us put the proper spin on our investigation."

"You may be right," Kalokainos conceded, manifestly against his will. "Even so, though, it would take something more than a mere guerrilla war to turn public opinion around. Especially given all those Manty contacts with Old Earth we've just been talking about."

"We don't have to completely turn it around," Ottweiler replied. "All we really need is to create enough skepticism to turn the Talbott Cluster into just one more batch of Verge neobarbs being taken over by *another* batch of neobarbs. The Manties may've been able to present a civilized facade, but that's already taken a major hit because of their confrontation with Haven. The media's been all over the Peeps'—excuse me, the *Havenites'* reform efforts. And those idiots in the High Ridge Government ignored Old Earth almost as completely as they did Haven itself. They made no effort to prevent the Havenite reformers from becoming very well regarded by the Solly public, and the *Alexander* Government has embarked on a clear policy of imperialist expansion in Silesia. The same thing's clearly happening in Talbott, obviously against the will of a significant percentage of the Cluster's citizens. Civilized facade or no, that sort of raw aggression against star systems too weak to defend themselves amply demonstrates Manticore itself is a neobarb nation. What else could you expect from an outright monarchy, after all?" He shrugged. "Once the situation is framed in those terms, Frontier Security would almost be *expected* to intervene."

"Which doesn't magically overcome the point you yourself made a few minutes ago about the Manties' military advantages," Kalokainos argued. "We may be able to create—I beg your pardon, *discover*—a situation which would let us justify military intervention in public relations terms. But getting the actual firepower to do it with, or convincing the Manties to back down, is another matter entirely."

Anisimovna quirked a sardonic eyebrow at him, and he flushed.

"I stand by my original analysis," he said defensively. "I still think it would be insane of the Manties to take on the League Navy. But certain other people at this conference have gone to some lengths to argue we can't count on their agreeing with me about that. So I'm simply pointing out that if we can't count on it, we still need to find a way to neutralize the possibility, however remote it might be."

"I think Valery's proposals would radically shift the parameters of the situation," Anisimovna replied in a reasonable voice. "And I think Brigadier Yucel's suggestion that the Star Kingdom's citizens might lack the stomach for what effective suppression of this sort of resistance would entail also has merit. But even if both of them are wrong and Manticore is prepared to deploy the warships and Marines required to crush the resistance *and* to forcibly resist any effort by Frontier Security to . . . stabilize the situation, what do we lose? How are we any worse off then, than we are right now? After all, there's no law of nature which would *force* us to push matters to an actual military confrontation if we chose not to."

Kalokainos started to say something, then paused, and Anisimovna could almost see the light click on behind his eyes.

Well, about time! she thought.

"I see," he said, instead of whatever he'd been about to say. "I hadn't fully considered the fact that the decision as to how far we want to push is completely in our own hands."

"Still," Verrochio said thoughtfully, "it wouldn't hurt to see about quietly requesting reinforcements to the Navy units assigned to me."

"I think we could probably justify asking for at least a few more destroyers, even without any upswing in violence in the Cluster, Sir," Hongbo agreed. "The mere fact that a star nation currently involved in a shooting war has suddenly turned up on our doorstep would probably justify that much."

"And as Mr. Ottweiler says, pointing out the way the Manties and Andermani have just cold-bloodedly divided Silesia between them wouldn't hurt, either," Kalokainos observed.

"No, it wouldn't. Not one bit," Anisimovna agreed. She looked around the conference table. "It sounds to me as if we have the beginnings of a strategy here," she said, and if it seemed odd that the representative of a mere multistellar corporation should be summing up the sense of their meeting rather than Commissioner Verrochio, no one remarked upon it. "Obviously, it's only a beginning, and I'm sure we can all offer suggestions to refine it. If I may, I'd suggest we adjourn for the moment. Let's discuss this informally among ourselves for a day or two, then sit down together again to see where we are."

"You were right about Kalokainos," Anisimovna said forty minutes later, as she accepted the tall, iced drink. She shook her head. "I have to admit, I had my doubts."

"That's because you're not in the shipping end of the business," Bardasano replied. She settled into one of the luxurious private suite's comfortable chairs with her own drink. Soft music played in the background, one wall was a slowly shifting mosaic of abstract light patterns, like sunlight through water, and a small counter-grav table held a tray of *sushi* at her right elbow. "We're more sensitive to what Kalokainos' unofficial little cartel is up to because it bears more directly on our operations," she added, picking up a pair of chopsticks.

Anisimovna nodded, then sipped thoughtfully while she watched Bardasano making selections from the tray. Although it was well known that Manpower and the Mesa-based Jessyk Combine worked closely together, most of the galaxy was unaware that Jessyk was actually wholly owned (through suitable cutouts and blinds) by Manpower. Partly as a result of how carefully the connections between the two interstellar giants were concealed, Anisimovna was less sensitively attuned to Jessyk's operations. Although she was a full member of the Manpower Board of Directors and Isabel was only a cadet, nonvoting member of Jessyk's Board, the younger woman had a much better grasp of the realities of interstellar shipping. And, Anisimovna admitted, of how those realities impacted on the problems—and opportunities—both Manpower and Jessyk confronted.

"So he and his father actually believe they can get the Manties involved in a shooting war with the League."

She shook her head. "That seems a bit ambitious, even in our circles."

"But you can see the beauty of the thing from their perspective," Ottweiler pointed out. There were no human servants present and the private hotel suite was protected by the best Solarian security hardware, so he saw no reason to pretend he wasn't speaking to two of the more powerful representatives of his actual employers.

"Think about it in their terms," he continued. "No matter how good the Manties are, they couldn't possibly stand off the entire League Navy. So any shooting war would have to end up with the Manties badly defeated—probably quickly. With any luck, it would mean the outright destruction of their entire 'Star Kingdom,' as well. In either case, the peace settlement would certainly include major concessions from them where the possession and use of the Junction is concerned."

"Personally," Bardasano said, a raw piece of some local fish poised in her chopsticks, "I'm betting Old Man Heinrich is thinking in terms of outright destruction. His son certainly is. Didn't you see him almost salivating over the possibility of a direct military confrontation between Verrochio's units and the Manties? He might as well have had a holo sign painted on his forehead! The possibility that it might slip over into outright war—or that his people could encourage it to 'slip over'—obviously gave his pleasure centers a good, hard jolt."

"I suppose both he and his father figure OFS would be put in charge of administering Manticore after a crushing military defeat," Anisimovna said.

"Exactly," Bardasano agreed. "And they figure their tame bureaucrats, like Verrochio—or Hongbo, I should say, since we all know who really pulls the strings—would be free to divvy up control of the Junction any way they wanted. And with enough money going into the right pockets . . ."

She shrugged, then smiled and tapped the elaborate stud in her left nostril with a fingertip before she popped the fish into her mouth.

"I wouldn't exactly be heartbroken if the Manties suffered a mischief." Anisimovna's tone's mildness fooled no one. "God knows they've been a big enough pain in the ass for as long as I can remember, even leaving aside our recent little misfortunes in Tiberian and Congo. But it's not as if the damned Peeps aren't just as a big a pain."

"For that matter, it was even more Haven than the Manties who engineered the Congo fuck-up," Bardasano said sourly, her smile of a moment before disappearing. The loss of the Congo Wormhole Junction before it could even be adequately surveyed had been almost as upsetting to the Jessyk Combine as the loss of Verdant Vista's slave-breeding facilities and pharmaceutical industry had been to Manpower.

"Agreed," Anisimovna said. "Which," she continued, fixing Ottweiler with her sharp gray eyes, "is why any solution to our present problems in Talbott which leaves Haven intact is second-best, in our view. We want both Manticore and Haven out of our lives for good. And we *don't* want any solution that takes out one of them but leaves the other. At least at the moment they're both too busy shooting at each other for either of them to turn their undivided attention to *us*."

"Of course," Ottweiler acknowledged. "At the same time, though, I'm sure all of us feel just a *little* anxious at the possibility that Manticore's maintaining a naval presence in Talbott. The Cluster is only a couple of light-centuries from Mesa—almost five hundred light-years closer than the Manticore home system."

"I doubt any of us are unaware of that, Valery," Anisimovna agreed dryly. "No one's arguing that we don't need to chop the Manticorans back down to size and get them the hell out of Talbott. I'm just not prepared to back any plan to provoke a full-scale war between Manticore and the League. Not at this point, at any rate."

"Still," Bardasano said thoughtfully, "Volkhart had a point, even if he didn't come right out and say it. If we succeed in pushing the Manties hard enough by supporting indigenous resistance movements, we could start a process which would slide out of control. Especially if someone like him was busy deliberately trying to provoke an incident serious enough to produce the general war he wants."

"Only if we let Verrochio and Yucel confront the Manties directly," Anisimovna said, and smiled unpleasantly. "I think it's time we suggested to our dear friend Junyan that it might be appropriate to have a word with Roberto Tyler."

"Junyan? Not Verrochio?" Ottweiler's tone was that of a man making certain he understood his directions, not of a man who questioned them.

"Junyan," Anisimovna confirmed, and Ottweiler nodded. Vice-commissioner Hongbo was far more deft at the sort of hands-on maneuvering any conversation with Tyler would entail.

"Understood." Ottweiler sipped at his own drink for a moment, his eyes unfocused as he contemplated possibilities. Then his gaze returned to the here and now and shifted to Anisimovna's face.

"I think I see where all of this is going," he said. "But even assuming Tyler's willing to play ball and Hongbo's prepared to give him—or, rather, get Verrochio to give him—the guarantees he'd want, the Monicans don't begin to have the firepower to confront Manticore."

"That's one reason why I have a private meeting with Izrok Levakonic scheduled for tomorrow," Anisimovna told him. "I think I can probably convince TIY to provide a small force augmentation for our friend Tyler."

"Even after what happened at Tiberian?" This time there was a trace of surprise, possibly even skepticism, in Ottweiler's voice.

"Trust me," Bardasano said before Anisimovna could respond. "Technodyne's Directors would sell their own mothers to Aldona for a crack at direct access to frontline Manty military hardware. In a lot of ways, I imagine Izrok would really be happier throwing in with Volkhart. They could steal a lot more tech if they actually took over the Manticore System's shipyards, after all. But I don't think they're very likely to get into a pissing contest with us. And they're too deep into the 'legitimate business community' of the League to act openly on their own." She shook her head. "No, they need someone to front for them. An 'outlaw' bunch like us . . . or like Tyler. So if we ask them, and especially if we're prepared to ante up the cash, they'll come through for the Monicans."

Chapter Six

"Bogey Three is altering course, Captain! She's coming around . . . another twelve degrees to port and climbing above us. Acceleration is increasing, too. Call it five-point-niner-eight KPS squared."

"Acknowledged." Helen Zilwicki gazed down at the repeater plot deployed from the pedestal of the captain's command chair at the center of *Hexapuma*'s auxiliary bridge. The display was smaller than the master plot at Tactical, but she could manipulate it as she chose, without disturbing the main plot. Now she tapped a command sequence into the keypad on the arm of her chair, and the repeater obediently recentered its display on the icon of Bogey Three.

The Havenite destroyer was indeed sweeping farther out to port, and another keypadded command projected her new vector. She was obviously trying to skirt *Hexapuma*'s missile envelope in order to get at the convoy beyond while her consorts maneuvered together to hold the Manticoran ship's attention. And she was accelerating at over six hundred gravities. Even with the newest generation of Havenite inertial compensators, that meant she was pulling over ninety percent of theoretical max. Assuming her maintenance people knew their jobs, she could risk cutting her safety margin that way, but it was a fair indication of how much importance the Peep force's commander attached to hitting the convoy.

"Status of Bogey One?" she demanded crisply.

"Maintaining profile at two-niner-six KPS squared, Captain," Paulo d'Arezzo replied from Tactical, his Sphinx accent equally crisp. "Her wedge is still fluctuating," he added.

"Acknowledged," Helen said again. She still didn't much care for d'Arezzo, and the fact that his voice was exactly the sort of musical bass that went with his Preston of the Spaceways face didn't help. But she had to admit Aikawa's friend had been right about the fair-haired midshipman's competence. She would have been happier to have him working the electronics warfare station, since he seemed to have some sort of arcane arrangement with the Demon Murphy where the ship's EW systems were concerned. The additional hours he'd been putting in since he'd been tapped as Lieutenant Bagwell's understudy were only refining what was obviously a powerful native talent.

And, she reflected, *at least the time he's been spending with Bagwell is keeping him out of* my *hair in Snotty Row.*

The thought was unfair, and she knew it, but knowing didn't change the way she felt. Or make the standoffish d'Arezzo any more convivial as a companion. Still, she would dearly have loved to be able to put his skills to work handling *Hexapuma*'s electronic warfare suite for this engagement. But Lieutenant Hearns had assigned Aikawa to EW, with Ragnhild (*not* Leo Stottmeister, of course) at Engineering. Intellectually, Helen understood why the acting OCTO was deliberately rotating their assignments for the simulations, but she didn't like the way it left her feeling subtly off-balance.

"Helm, come to zero-four-one by two-seven-five," she

said. "Roll ship fifteen degrees to port, and increase acceleration to six KPS squared."

That was considerably higher than the "eighty percent of maximum power" The Book called for under normal circumstances, but it still left an almost ten percent reserve against compensator failure.

"Coming to zero-four-one by two-seven-five, roll one-five degrees port, and increase to six KPS squared, aye, Ma'am," Senior Chief Waltham replied, and the cruiser altered course smoothly under his practiced touch.

"Aikawa, I want to knock back Bogey Three's sensors—especially for her missile defense," Helen said. "Suggestions?"

"Recommend an immediate salvo of Dazzlers," Aikawa said promptly. "Then fire a second salvo to precede the attack birds by, say, fifteen seconds. That should seriously degrade their sensor capabilities. Then seed half a dozen Dragon's Teeth into the broadside itself."

"I like it," Helen said with a wicked smile. Dazzlers were powerful jammer warheads which would tear holes in the destroyer's sensors but leave the targeting systems in *Hexapuma*'s missiles unaffected. Unlike the destroyer, they would know exactly what pattern the Dazzlers had been set for, and could be adjusted to "see" through the erratic windows the electronic warfare birds' programming provided. And if the destroyer's battered electronic eyes could see past the jamming at all, the Dragon's Teeth, each loaded with enough false emitters to appear as an entire salvo of attacking missiles, ought to do a pretty fair job of completely swamping their victim's tracking capability.

"Make it so, Tactical," she instructed d'Arezzo. "And set up a double broadside. I want to finish this tin can and get back to the main event."

"Aye, aye, Ma'am. Accepting EW download now. The birds are receipting. Ready to launch in another . . . twenty-seven seconds."

Helen nodded. It took a little longer to set up for a double broadside, using the off-bore launch capability the RMN had developed, but it would permit her to put almost forty missiles on the destroyer. That would undoubtedly be overkill, assuming Aikawa's EW suggestion worked half as well as she expected it to. Still, it was better to finish the target off—or at least cripple it thoroughly—in a single exchange so she could get back to the rest of the Peep attack force.

Hexapuma was individually bigger and more powerful than any of the attackers, and she'd also taken delivery of the new Mark 16 MDM. Nothing smaller (or older) than a *Saganami-C*-class ship would ever be able to handle them, but the *Saganami-Cs* had been designed around the new, larger Mark 9-c tubes. Even with the massive reduction in manpower represented by *Hexapuma*'s smaller crew, BuShips had been able to cram only twenty of them into each broadside, but the Mark 16 carried twin drives. That gave *Hexapuma* a powered missile envelope from rest of almost thirty million kilometers, which her present opponents couldn't possibly match.

But if she outclassed any of them enormously on a one-for-one basis, she was also outnumbered by five-to-one, and the op force commander had timed her ambush well. She'd been lying doggo in the poor long-range sensor conditions which were typical in hyper, with her ships' impeller wedges down, and caught *Hexapuma* and her convoy in hyper-space, transitioning between grav waves under impeller. And she'd waited until the last possible moment before bringing her nodes up, which had put her almost into her own missile range of *Hexapuma* before the Manticoran ship even saw her. If she'd been able to wait even fifteen minutes longer, *Hexapuma* would have been well inside that range, and probably dead meat, before she knew the enemy was there. Unfortunately for the Peep, the geometry hadn't been quite perfect. She'd had to power up when she did, or the convoy's vector would have prevented her from intercepting at all.

Still, she'd almost pulled it off. In fact, it was sheer good luck that the simulation's computers had decided *Hexapuma*'s initial broadside had gotten a critical piece of her heavy cruiser flagship's impeller drive. The damaged ship—one of the obsolete *Sword*-class ships, from her emissions signature—was still boring in, but slowly. The fluctuating impeller wedge d'Arezzo had spotted earlier was like an old wet-navy oil slick, trailing like blood as proof of the cruiser's laming wound. That left only the four destroyers, which were about to become *three* destroyers.

Helen's new heading turned *Hexapuma* almost directly away from the damaged Havenite flagship as she maneuvered against the overeager destroyer trying to swing around her. Apparently whoever was in command over there hadn't read the latest briefing on Manticoran missile ranges. The destroyer's bid to stay out of *Hexapuma*'s envelope was going to come up short—way short, like over twelve million kilometers short. In fact, it would have come up a couple of million klicks short even against the Mark 13 missiles of one of the RMN's older heavy cruisers. That was still far enough out to degrade *Hexapuma*'s accuracy—fire control was still trying to catch up with the extended ranges of the new missiles—but not badly enough to keep a forty-missile double broadside from blowing her out of space. Best of all, nothing on the Peeps' side had the range to engage *Hexapuma* in reply. The Peeps had multi-drive missiles of their own, but they hadn't managed to engineer that capability down into something a heavy cruiser mounted. Their capital ships and battlecruisers could match or exceed anything even *Hexapuma*'s new birds could do, but their cruisers still had barely a quarter of her extended reach.

Hexapuma completed her turn and raced towards the destroyer.

"Dazzler launch . . . *now*," d'Arezzo announced, and red lights flickered to green on his panel as the jammers streaked away. D'Arezzo watched a time display ticking downward on his panel for several seconds, then said, "Second Dazzler launch in five . . .four . . . three . . . two . . . one . . . *now!* Attack broadside launching in fifteen seconds."

Helen flipped her repeater plot back to a smaller scale, one that let her observe all the enemy units, including the crippled flagship. The tiny color-coded icons representing the staggered flights of Dazzlers moved slowly, even at their incredible acceleration, on such a tiny display, and she glanced at the flagship again. Once she'd dealt with the leading destroyer, she'd swing back to take the other three still coming in from the other side. And once all four of them had been swatted, she could deal with the *Sword*-class at her leisure.

All neat and tidy, she told herself. *Even that snoot-in-the-air prick d'Arezzo's done a bang-up job this time.*

Even as she thought the last sentence, she scolded herself for it. D'Arezzo obviously continued to prefer his own company to that of anyone else, but he seemed to possess enough ability and competence to offset it.

"Attack broadside launch *now*!" d'Arezzo announced, and the repeater plot was suddenly speckled with dozens of outgoing missile icons. Helen watched them with satisfaction. In another couple of minutes—

"Missile launch!" d'Arezzo barked abruptly. "*Multiple* hostile launches! Captain, Bogey One's launched at us!"

Helen's eyes darted away from the missiles she'd sent roaring towards the enemy destroyer. D'Arezzo was right. The enemy flagship had launched missiles at them, and not just a few birds. There were at least thirty in that incoming salvo, and even as she watched, the "fluctuating" impeller wedge firmed back up. Its acceleration shot upward, peaking at over four hundred and eighty gravities, and it spun on its axis. Nineteen seconds after that, a *second* massive salvo erupted from it as the spin brought its other broadside to bear.

And the second salvo had been fired with an even higher initial acceleration. It was already overtaking the first launch, and Helen knew exactly what was about to happen.

Suckered, goddamn it! she thought. *That's no heavy cruiser—it's a frigging battlecruiser* pretending *to be a heavy cruiser! Just like it was pretending to be damaged so I'd ignore it while I concentrated on swatting destroyers. And those are MDMs. MDMs launched with enough oomph on their first-stage drives to bring them all in as one, huge, time-on-target salvo.*

"Helm, hard skew port! Electronics, I want two November-Charlie decoys—deploy them to starboard and high! Tactical, redesignate Bogey One as primary target!"

She heard her voice snapping the orders. They came sharp and clear, almost instantly, despite the consternation and self-reproach boiling through her. But even as she issued them, she knew it was too late.

At the range at which the enemy had fired, *Hexapuma* had a hundred and fifty seconds to respond before the incoming laser heads reached attack range and detonated. If she'd had another two minutes, maybe even one, the decoys Helen had ordered deployed—*too damned late, damn it to hell!*—might have had time to suck some of the fire away from their mother ship. As it was, they didn't.

Helen watched her plot and swore as the two Peep broadsides merged . . . and their combined acceleration suddenly leapt upward. That TO over there knew her job, damn it. She had more than enough range to reach her target, so she'd set her birds' first-stage drives to terminate and their second-stage drives to kick in as soon as her separate broadsides had matched base vectors. They would burn out much more rapidly, but the new settings would get them to *Hexapuma* even more quickly than d'Arezzo—and Helen—had estimated. They'd be coming in faster, as well. And even if she burned out the second stage completely, she'd still have the third. There'd be plenty of time left on their clocks for terminal attack maneuvers.

And the bastards knew exactly what they were doing when they timed it, too, she thought viciously. *We have to cut the downlinks to our attack birds to free up the tracking and datalinks to deal with the damned battlecruiser!*

The offensive missiles would continue to home on the

targeted destroyer, but without guidance from *Hexapuma*'s onboard sensors and computers, the odds of any of them attaining a hard lock went down drastically, especially at such an extended range. Which meant the destroyer was probably going to survive, as well.

"Third enemy launch!" d'Arezzo announced, as the still-rolling enemy battlecruiser continued to pump missiles towards *Hexapuma*, and Helen punched the arm of her command chair in frustration. *Hexapuma* was going to be hurt badly, even if she survived the opening double broadside. With battle damage hammering her capabilities back, those follow-up salvos were going to be deadly.

D'Arezzo's counter-missiles zipped out, racing to meet the initial attack. There'd be time for only two defensive launches against it, and Helen bit her lip, watching the midshipman's fingers dance and fly. He was hunched slightly forward in his bridge chair with totally focused intensity, and she saw the light codes for his initial counter launch blinking from strobing amber to blood-red as the individual counter-missiles' internal seekers locked onto their designated targets. As each of his birds "saw" its own target, it dropped out of *Hexapuma*'s shipboard control queue, freeing additional tracking capacity and control downlinks for the counter-missiles in his second-tier launch.

He was good, she acknowledged. Not quite as good as she or Aikawa were, perhaps. But then, both of them had known before they ever reached the Island that they wanted to be tactical officers, generalists, whereas d'Arezzo's emphasis had been on the new EW systems. For an electronics snot, he was doing damned well.

Too bad it wasn't going to be well enough.

Peep missiles didn't carry as much ECM as Manticoran. Despite all the improvements in their technology since the last war, Haven was still playing catch-up in a lot of areas. But the ECM they did have was much better than it once had been, and d'Arezzo's plot jumped in the electronic equivalent of a gibbering fit as a complex orchestration of countermeasure emitters activated at the last possible moment.

Two-thirds of d'Arezzo's counter-missiles lost lock as the blizzard of jamming lashed at them. Again, it was all a matter of timing. If they'd had more time, the defensive missiles might have been able to adjust and reacquire. If the range at launch had been longer, the attacking missiles would have been forced to bring up their ECM sooner, because they would have been intercepted farther out. That would have given d'Arezzo's onboard systems and more powerful computers a longer look at the emitters' patterns. Would have allowed him to analyze them and refine his counter-missiles' solutions against them while they were still accepting downlinked control data from *Hexapuma*. Would have allowed him a third-tier launch.

But none of those things were going to happen, and the Havenite missiles broke past the first-tier counter-missiles almost completely unscathed. The second-tier birds did better, taking out fourteen of the attack missiles. But that left sixty-six still incoming. Some of them had to be dedicated ECM platforms, with no laser heads, and CIC had identified half a dozen of them and designated them to be ignored by defensive fire. There had to be more of them, but there was no time to sort them out; every one of the other missiles had to be considered an attack bird, and *Hexapuma*'s last-ditch point defense lasers began to fire with computer-controlled desperation.

She nailed another thirty-two missiles in the fleeting seconds she had to engage them. Another eleven laser heads wasted their fury on the impenetrable roof or floor of her impeller wedge. Of the fifteen remaining potential attack missiles, seven turned out to be ECM platforms.

Eight weren't.

The universe heaved about Helen as eight laser heads detonated as one, lashing her ship with deadly bomb-pumped fury. The computers running the simulation had tied Auxiliary Control's grav plates into the sim.

Now the midshipmen's senses insisted that AuxCon was twisting and bucking, that *Hexapuma*'s entire massive hull was *flexing*, as transfer energy blasted into her. The cruiser's protective sidewalls had bent and blunted most of the incoming lasers, and the ship's armor absorbed still more damage. But those missiles had come from a battlecruiser, not another cruiser. They were capital ship missiles, and Peep warheads were bigger and more powerful than Manticoran warheads as compensation for their less capable ECM and EW. No cruiser sidewall in the galaxy could have actually *stopped* them.

"Hits on Beta Three, Beta Five, and Alpha Two!" Ragnhild announced from Engineering, even as alarms shrilled. "Heavy casualties in Impeller One! We've lost Sidewall Two, Four, and Six! Radar Two and Lidar Two down! Direct hits on Graser Four and Graser Eight, and Missile Four, Six, and Ten are out of the net! Magazine Three is open to space! Heavy damage between Frame Three-Niner and Frame Six-Six!"

Hexapuma's acceleration fell as enemy fire hammered her forward alpha and beta nodes. Her starboard sidewall fluctuated as more hits smashed the forward generators. Then it came back up—at greatly reduced strength—as Ragnhild spread the capacity of the surviving generators to cover the deadly gap. If not for the skew turn Helen had ordered, which had twisted *Hexapuma* up on her side relative to the Peep battlecruiser, interposing her impeller wedge on the direct attack bearing, it would have been even worse.

Not that what they had wasn't bad enough.

"Evasion pattern Delta-Québec-Seven!" she snapped. "Half-roll us inverted, Helm!"

"Delta-Québec-Seven, aye!" Senior Chief Waltham responded. "Rolling ship now!"

The maneuver whipped *Hexapuma*'s wounded starboard side away from the enemy. It turned her impeller wedge away from the maximum protective angle, but it brought her undamaged port broadside to bear and put the weakened sidewall farther away, made it a harder target. The decoys were fully on-line now, too. That might make a difference. . . .

And, Helen thought grimly, *our starboard sensors have been shot to shit. At least this way we can* see *the bastards!*

D'Arezzo sent a double broadside of his own roaring off towards the enemy. It crossed the enemy's *second* broadside seconds after launch, and the plot was a seething confusion of incoming and outgoing missile wedges cutting holes in *Hexapuma*'s sensor coverage like old-fashioned gunsmoke, more counter-missiles stabbing into the Peep's massive attack wave, laser clusters firing furiously, and then—

AuxCon heaved madly one last time, and every light went out.

The absolute blackness lingered for the prescribed fifteen seconds. Then the master plot came back up, and two blood-red words floated in the darkness before them like a disembodied curse.

"SIMULATION OVER," they said.

"Be seated, Ladies and Gentlemen," Abigail Hearns said, and the midshipmen sat back down in the briefing room chairs from which they'd risen as she entered the compartment.

She walked briskly across to the head of the table and took her own seat, then keyed her terminal on-line. She glanced once at the notes it displayed, then looked up with a faint smile.

"That could have gone better," she observed, and Helen writhed mentally at the stupendous understatement of that mild sentence. She hadn't been hammered that brutally in a simulation since her second form. An ignoble part of her wanted to blame her command team. Especially, she realized with a flicker of guilt, her tactical officer. But however tempting that might be, it would have been a lie.

"Ms. Zilwicki," Abigail said, looking at her calmly, "would you care to comment on what you think went wrong?"

The younger woman visibly squared her shoulders, but that was the only outward sign she allowed of the intense frustration Abigail knew she must be feeling at this moment.

"I made a poor initial tactical assessment, Ma'am," she said crisply. "I failed to properly appreciate the actual composition of the opposition force and based my tactics on my incorrect understanding of the enemy's capabilities. I also failed to realize the enemy flagship was only simulating impeller damage. Worse, I allowed my initial errors to affect my interpretation of the enemy's actual intentions."

"I see." Abigail considered her for a moment, then looked at Midshipman d'Arezzo. "Would you concur, Mr. d'Arezzo?" she asked.

"The initial assessment was certainly inaccurate, Ma'am," d'Arezzo replied. "However, I should point out that as Tactical Officer, *I* was the one who initially evaluated the Peep flagship as a heavy cruiser, just as I also classified her as damaged by our fire. Ms. Zilwicki formulated her tactics based upon my erroneous classifications."

Zilwicki's eyes flicked sideways to the midshipman's profile as he spoke, and Abigail thought she detected a trace of surprise in them. *Good,* she thought. *I still haven't figured out exactly what her problem with d'Arezzo is, but it's time she got over it, whatever it may be.*

"Ms. Zilwicki?" she invited.

"Uh." Helen gave herself a mental shake, embarrassed by her own hesitation. But she hadn't been able to help it. The last thing she'd expected was for self-absorbed Paulo d'Arezzo to voluntarily assume a share of the guilt for such a monumental fiasco.

"Mr. d'Arezzo may have misidentified the enemy flagship and the extent of its damage, Ma'am," she said after a heartbeat, shoving her surprise aside, "but I don't believe that was his fault. In retrospect, it's obvious the Peeps were using their EW to spoof our sensors into thinking Bogey One was a heavy cruiser—and an old, obsolete unit, at that. Moreover, CIC made the same identification. And whatever his assessments might have been, I fully concurred with them."

Abigail nodded. D'Arezzo was right to point out his ID errors, but Zilwicki was equally right to bring up CIC's matching mistake. The Combat Information Center's primary responsibility, after all, was to process sensor data, analyze it, plot it, and display the necessary information for the ship's bridge crew. But the tactical officer had access to the raw data herself, and it was one of *her* responsibilities to assess—or at least demand a CIC recheck of—any ship ID or damage state which struck her as questionable. And if d'Arezzo had looked carefully enough at the "heavy cruiser's" emissions signature, he probably would have noticed the tiny discrepancies Abigail had carefully built into the Havenite's false image when she tweaked Lieutenant Commander Kaplan's original scenario.

"That's true enough, Ms. Zilwicki," she said after a moment. "As were Mr. d'Arezzo's comments. However, I believe both of you are missing a significant point."

She paused, considering whether or not to call on one of the other midshipmen. From Kagiyama's expression she suspected he knew where she was headed, and having the point made by one of their fellows would probably give it more emphasis—and underscore the fact that they should have thought of it themselves at the time. But it could also lead to resentment, a sense of having been put down by one of their own.

"I'd like all of you to consider," she said after a moment, instead of calling on Kagiyama, "that you failed to make full use of the sensor capabilities available to you. Yes, at the moment the enemy brought up their impellers, they were already within your shipboard sensor envelope. But they were far enough out, especially given that sensor conditions in hyper are never as good as in n-space, that relying solely on shipboard capabilities gave away sensor reach. If you'd deployed a remote array, you would almost certainly have had sufficient time to get it close enough to the 'heavy cruiser' to burn through its

EW before it managed to draw you so badly off balance and out of position."

She saw consternation—and self-recrimination—flicker through Zilwicki's eyes. Clearly, the sturdily built midshipwoman was unaccustomed to losing. Equally clearly, she disliked the sensation . . .especially when she thought it was her own fault.

"Now," Abigail continued, satisfied there was no need to dwell on her point, "conceding that the initial misidentification and failure to realize the enemy flagship was only simulating damage were the primary causes of what happened, there were also a few other missteps. For example, when the flanking destroyer began to pull out to swing around you, you changed heading to close the range. Was that an optimal decision . . . Ms. Pavletic?"

"In retrospect, no, Ma'am," Ragnhild replied. "At the time, and given what we all believed the situation to be, I would have done exactly the same thing. But looking back, I think it would have been better to maintain our original course even if our misinterpretations had been accurate."

"Why?" Abigail asked.

"The tin can wasn't going to get outside the *Kitty*'s missle env—"

The midshipwoman chopped herself off abruptly, and her face turned an interesting shade of deep, alarming red. Abigail felt her lips quiver, but somehow—thank Tester!—she managed to keep from chuckling, or even smiling, and completing Pavletic's destruction. A stricken silence filled the compartment, and she felt every middy's eyes upon her, awaiting the thunderbolt of doom certain to incinerate their late, lamented colleague for her deadly impiety.

"Outside the, ah, who's what, Ms. Pavletic?" Abigail asked calmly, as soon as she felt reasonably certain she had control of herself.

"I'm sorry, Ma'am," Ragnhild said miserably. "I meant *Hexapuma*. Outside *Hexapuma*'s missile envelope."

"I gathered you were referring to the ship, Ms. Pavletic.

But I'm afraid I still haven't quite caught the name by which you called her," Abigail said pleasantly, eyes holding the honey-blond midshipwoman steadily.

"I called her the *Kitty*, Ma'am," Ragnhild admitted finally. "That's, ah, sort of our unofficial nickname for her. Just among ourselves, I mean. We haven't used it with anyone else."

"You call a heavy cruiser the '*Kitty*,'" Abigail said, repeating the name very carefully.

"Um, actually, Ma'am," Leo Stottmeister said, speaking up manfully in Ragnhild's defense—or at least to draw fire from her, "we call her the *Nasty Kitty*. It's . . . really meant as a compliment. Sort of a reference to how new and powerful she is, and, well . . ."

His voice trailed off, and Abigail gazed at him as levelly as she had at Pavletic. Several seconds of tense silence stretched out, and then she smiled.

"Most crews end up bestowing nicknames on their ships," she said. "Usually it's a sign of affection. Sometimes it isn't. And some are better than others. A friend of mine once served in a ship—*William Hastings*, a Grayson heavy cruiser—which ended up called *Shivering Billy* because of a nasty harmonic she picked up in two of her forward impeller nodes one fine day. Then there's HMS *Retaliation*, known to her crew as HMS *Ration Tin*, for reasons no one seems to remember. Or HMS *Ad Astra*, a perfectly respectable dreadnought which was known as *Fat Astor* when she was still in commission. Given the alternatives, I suppose '*Nasty Kitty*' isn't all that bad." She saw them beginning to relax and smiled sweetly. "Of course," she added, "*I'm* not the Captain."

The newborn relaxation vanished instantly, and she smothered another stillborn chuckle. Then she shook her head and pointed at Pavletic again.

"Before we were interrupted, I believe you were going to explain why turning towards the destroyer wasn't, after all, the best available option, Ms. Pavletic?"

"Uh, yes, Ma'am," the midshipwoman said. "I was saying that she wasn't going to be able to get outside our missile envelope, whatever she did. Not with Mark 16s in the tubes. If she'd tried to swing wide enough for that, she'd have taken herself out of any position to attack the convoy, and she literally didn't have the time and accel to pull it off whatever she tried to do. So if we'd maintained our course, we could still have engaged her without turning our backs on the Peep flagship."

"Which would also have kept our forward sensors oriented on the 'heavy cruiser,'" Helen added, and Abigail nodded with a slight smile of approval.

"Yes, it would," she agreed. The forward sensors aboard most warships, including *Hexapuma*, were significantly more capable than their broadside sensors, because they were more likely to be the ones their crews relied upon when pursuing a fleeing enemy. Given the "bow wave" of charged particles which built up on the forward particle shielding of any vessel as it approached relativistic velocities, the sensors designed to see through it had to be more capable. Which meant they would have been more likely than *Hexapuma*'s broadside sensors to see through the enemy's EW.

"Once the decision to close on and engage Bogey Three had been made," she continued, "there was the question of fire distribution. While ensuring the prompt destruction of your target was appropriate, a full double broadside represented a considerable margin of overkill. Given that, it might have been wiser to throw at least a few more birds at the 'heavy cruiser' at the same time. If nothing else, that would have required her to defend herself, in which case it might have become evident she had a lot more point defense and counter-missile tubes than a heavy cruiser ought to have. In addition, if she really had been the heavy cruiser she was pretending to be, and if you actually had inflicted the damage she was pretending you had, her defenses might have been sufficiently compromised for you to land additional hits with only a portion of your full missile power. That, however, could definitely be argued either way. Concentration of fire's a cardinal principle of successful tactics, and although the destroyer wasn't yet in range to threaten the convoy, she *was* the closer threat. And, of course, if the 'heavy cruiser' had actually suffered the impeller damage you believed she had—and if she'd been unable to *repair* it—you'd have had plenty of time to deal with her."

She paused again, watching her students—although it still felt peculiar to consider people so close to her own age "students"—digest what she'd just said. She gave them a few seconds to consider it, then turned back to Ragnhild Pavletic.

"Now, Ms. Pavletic," she said with a pleasant smile. "About your damage control response to the initial damage. Had you considered, when Sidewall Two was destroyed, the possibility of rerouting . . ."

Chapter Seven

"I feel like an idiot," the young woman half-snarled. Her dark-brown eyes flashed angrily, but the two men sitting across the private table from her in the busy, dimly lit restaurant bar didn't worry about that. Or, rather, they weren't worried that the anger was directed at them. Agnes Nordbrandt was furious about a lot of things lately. Which, after all, was what had brought them together.

"Better to feel like an idiot than to get snapped up by the graybacks," one of the men replied. The nickname referred to the Kornatian National Police's charcoal gray tunics.

"Maybe." Nordbrandt tugged irritably at the blond wig covering her own black hair. One of the others quirked an eyebrow, and she snorted. "Getting arrested might just give me a more visible platform!"

"For a day or two," the other man said. He was obviously the senior of the two, and his physical appearance—medium brown hair, medium brown eyes, average features, medium complexion—was so eminently forgettable that Nordbrandt felt irritably certain he'd never bothered with a disguise in his life. "Possibly even for a few weeks. Hell, let's be generous and give it three months. Then they'll sentence you, send you off to do your time, and you'll vanish from the political equation. Is that what you really want?"

"Of course it isn't." Nordbrandt's eyes darted around the dim room.

A large part of her current irritation, as she was perfectly well aware, stemmed from her dislike for having a conversation like this in a public place. On the other hand, the man she knew only as "Firebrand" was probably right. Given the paucity of modern technology in the Talbott Cluster, the other patrons' background noise probably provided all the cover they needed. And there was something to be said for hiding in plain sight to avoid suspicion in the first place.

"I didn't think so," Firebrand said. "But if you have any inclinations that way, I'd really like to know now. Speaking for myself, I have no desire to see the inside of anybody's jail, whether it's right here on Kornati or in some Manty prison far, far away. Which means I'm not especially interested in working with anyone who might want a firsthand penology tour just so she can make a political statement."

"Don't worry," Nordbrandt grunted. "You're right. Letting them lock me up would be worse than pointless."

"I'm glad we agree. And do we agree on anything else?"

Nordbrandt looked at him across the steins of beer on the table between them, studying his expression as intently as the poor light permitted. Unlike many people living in the Verge—that vast, irregular belt of marginal worlds beyond the Solarian League's official borders—she was a prolong recipient. But she really was almost as young as she looked. Only the cruder, less effective first-generation prolong therapies were available here on Kornati. They halted the apparent aging process at a considerably later point in a recipient's life than the more recently developed second- and third-generation therapies. At thirty-three, Nordbrandt was a whippet-thin, dark-complexioned woman who seemed to vibrate with the unending internal tension of youth, anger, intensity, and commitment.

Even so, she hesitated. Then she gave her false golden curls a shake and took the plunge with a nod.

"Yes, we do," she said flatly. "I didn't spend my life fighting to keep those Frontier Security *ljigavci* off my world just to turn it over to someone else."

"We obviously agree with you, or we wouldn't be here," Firebrand's companion said. "But to give the Devil his due, there actually is a difference between OFS and the Manties."

"Not to me there isn't." Nordbrandt's voice was even flatter, and her eyes flashed. "Nobody's ever been interested in trading with us, or treating us like equals. And now that the galaxy's found out about the Lynx Terminus and all the money it represents to whoever controls it, you want me to think we suddenly have both the frigging Sollies and oh-so-noble Manticorans lining up to embrace us solely out of the goodness of their hearts?"

Her lips worked, as if she wanted to spit on the tabletop, and the man who'd spoken shrugged.

"That's true enough, but the Manties didn't even suggest we join them. It was our friends and neighbors' idea to *ask* them to annex us."

"I know all about the annexation vote," Nordbrandt replied bitterly. "*And* how my so-called 'political allies' deserted in droves when Tonkovic and that unmitigated bastard Van Dort started waving around promises of how rich we'd all be as good little Manty helots." She shook her head fiercely. "Those rich bastards figure they'll make out well enough, but the rest of us will just find ourselves screwed over by another layer of money-gouging overlords. So don't tell *me* about the vote! The fact that a bunch of stupid sheep voluntarily walk into a wolf's lair behind a Judas goat doesn't make the wolf any less of a carnivore."

"And you're prepared to back your views with more than just words and get-out-the-vote projects?" Firebrand asked quietly.

"Yes, I am. And not just me. As I'm sure you realized before you ever contacted me."

The man known as "Firebrand" nodded, and reminded himself not to let Nordbrandt's intensity and narrow focus fool him into underestimating her intelligence.

It was his turn to study her thoughtfully. Agnes Nordbrandt had been one of the youngest members of the planetary parliament of Kornati, the sole inhabited world of the Split System, before the discovery of the Lynx Terminus had brought the Star Kingdom of Manticore into contact with Split. She'd won that position as the founder of the Kornatian National Redemption Party, whose extremist nationalist politics had resonated with the large percentage of Kornati's population which feared the eventual arrival of the Office of Frontier Security in Split. But those not unjustified fears couldn't explain her success by themselves. Although she'd been adopted as an infant and raised by a childless couple who'd been among the junior ranks of Kornati's oligarchical elite, she'd also reached out to the disenfranchised, the all-too-large Kornatian underclass who struggled daily to put food on the table and shoes on their children's feet.

Many of her political opponents had sneered at her for that. They'd mocked the National Redemption Party as a mismatched hodgepodge with no coherent platform. As for trying to build a political machine out of the underclass, the very idea was ridiculous! Ninety percent of them hadn't even registered to vote, so what sort of political base could *they* provide?

But Nordbrandt been a shrewder political animal than they'd recognized. She'd maneuvered with the best of them, building alliances between her NRP and less extreme politicians and political parties, like Vuk Rajkovic's Reconciliation Party. Perhaps the marginalized urban poor who supported her most enthusiastically didn't vote, but there'd been enough middle class voters whose fear of the Sollies had combined with their recognition that economic reform was essential to give her a surprising strength at the ballot box.

Until the temptation to stampede into Manticore's arms as a way to escape generations of debt peonage exploitation by Solly commercial interests under the auspices of OFS had reached Kornati, at least.

The Manticoran standard of living, despite over a decade of bitter warfare with the People's Republic of Haven, was one of the highest in the explored galaxy. The Star Kingdom might be small, but it was incredibly wealthy, and the extent of its wealth had lost nothing in the telling. Half of Kornati's people seemed to have believed that simply acquiring Manticoran citizenship would somehow make *them* instantly and incredibly wealthy, as well. Most of them had known better deep down inside, and, to their credit, the Manticorans never made any such promises. But any illusions the Kornatians might have cherished about Manticore hadn't changed the fact that they'd known *exactly* what to expect from OFS. Faced with the decision, seventy-eight percent of them had decided *anything* was better than that, and that permanently binding themselves to Manticore was the one way to avoid it.

Nordbrandt had disagreed, and she'd mounted a bitter, no-holds-barred political campaign to resist the annexation vote. But that decision had shattered the National Redemption Party. It had quickly become apparent that many of the NRP's erstwhile supporters' resistance to being gobbled up by Frontier Security had been fueled far more by fear than by the fiery nationalistic socialism which had inspired Nordbrandt. Her support base had crumbled quickly, and as it had, her rhetoric had become steadily more extreme. And now it appeared she was, indeed, prepared to take the next logical step.

"How many other people agree with you?" Firebrand asked bluntly after a moment.

"I'm not prepared to discuss specific numbers at this point," she replied, and leaned back slightly in her chair with a thin smile. "We hardly even know one another, and I'm not in the habit of getting intimate on a first date."

Firebrand chuckled appreciatively, although his smile barely touched his eyes.

"I don't blame you for being cautious," he said. "In fact, I'd be far less likely to risk any association with someone who *wasn't* cautious. But by the same token, you need to convince me that what you have to offer is sufficient to justify my willingness to risk trusting you."

"I understand that," she said. "And I agree. To be brutally frank, I wouldn't be risking contact with you unless I believed *you* could offer *us* something sufficiently valuable to justify taking some chances."

"I'm glad we understand one another. But my point still stands. What *do* you have to offer?"

"A real Kornatian," she said bluntly, and smiled at the involuntary flare of surprise—and alarm—in Firebrand's eyes.

"Your accent's quite good, actually," she told him. "Unfortunately for you, linguistics have always been something of a hobby of mine. I suppose it has something to do with a politician's ear. I always found it useful to be able to talk like a 'good old girl' when it came to politicking at the grass-roots level. And, as we say here on Kornati, 'You're not from around here, are you?' "

"That's a very dangerous conclusion, Ms. Nordbrandt," Firebrand said, his eyes narrow. His companion's hand had disappeared into the unsealed opening of his jacket, and Nordbrandt smiled.

"I trust neither of you thinks I came here by myself," she said gently. "I'm sure your friend here could kill me any time he wanted to, Mr. Firebrand. In that case, however, neither of you would get out of this bar alive afterward. Of course, I'm also sure all three of us would like to avoid that . . . messy outcome. Wouldn't we?"

"*I* certainly would," Firebrand agreed with a tight smile. His intent gaze never left Nordbrandt's face. It was possible she was lying, but he didn't think so. Not from what he saw in her eyes.

"Good." She picked up her beer stein and sipped appreciatively, then put it down again. "I had my suspicions the first time you and I spoke," she said, "but I wasn't positive until this meeting. You really are very good. Either you've made an intensive study of our version of Standard English, or else you've had a lot of contact with us. But in response to your question about what I have to offer, I think the fact that I've recognized you as an off-worlder and taken appropriate steps to cover myself before meeting you says something about my capabilities. And leaving all of that aside, it's obvious to me that you're looking for a Kornatian ally. Well—"

She gave a little shrug and raised her left hand in a palm-up gesture of presentation.

Firebrand picked up his own beer and drank from the stein. It was only a time-buying gesture, and he knew she knew it as well as he did. After a moment, he lowered the beer and cocked his head at her.

"You're right," he admitted. "I'm not from Kornati. But that doesn't mean I don't have the Split System's best interests at heart. After all, Split is part of the Cluster. If the Manty occupation goes down smoothly here, it's going to affect how all the rest of the Cluster reacts. And I am here looking for Kornatian allies."

"I thought so." Her voice was calm, but despite what Firebrand had come to realize was an even more impressive degree of self-control than he'd first thought, there was a flicker of eagerness in her eyes.

"Forgive me," he said, "but in light of your well known . . . patriotism, I have to be a little wary. After all, your position during the plebiscite debate was pretty clear. 'Kornati for Kornatians,' I believe you said."

"And I meant it," she told him, her voice level. "In fact, I want you to remember it. Because the first instant that I begin to suspect *you* have designs on Kornati, I'll turn on you in a heartbeat. But that doesn't mean I'm stupid enough to think I don't need allies of my own, at least as badly as you appear to.

"Oh," she waved her left hand between them, like someone fanning away smoke, "I can make things hard for the Manties and their rich-pig collaborationists here in Split. I can cause all kinds of trouble, at least in the short term. It's even theoretically possible I could topple Tonkovic and her cronies, which would put the Manties in an interesting quandary. If I were Planetary President, would they live up to all their promises about self-determination, or would they show their true colors and send in their Marines?

"But, realistically speaking, there's not much possibility of my followers and me being able to throw Tonkovic out using our own unassisted resources. And even if we succeeded, it would be much easier for the Manties to decide to resort to forcible suppression against a single 'outlaw' star system. No," she shook her head, "I'm prepared to fight them with only my own supporters, if that's the only alternative open to me. But the odds of actually achieving something would go up enormously if Split weren't the only system which rose up to throw the Manties out. And even if we can't manage the outright overthrow of the collaborationists, I think there's an excellent chance a unified, Cluster-wide resistance movement could convince the Manties they'd poked their noses into the wrong hornet nest. They're already at war. If we make it too expensive and difficult to hold us all down, they're likely to decide they have more important fish to fry closer to home."

Firebrand took another, longer sip of beer. Then he set the stein aside with a decisive air.

"You're right," he said simply. "Whatever you or I might like, the truth is that we're on the short end of the balance of political and military power at the moment. There's no way, realistically speaking, we could hope for wholesale changes of government throughout the Cluster. But you're also right that if we make the game too unpleasant, the price too high, the Manties probably will decide to take their marbles and go home. They can't afford to do anything else. And if we can manage to send them packing, we may just be able to convert the prestige and momentum of that into the ability to run the collaborationists out of town, after all."

He nodded slowly, his expression somber.

"I'll be honest with you, Ms. Nordbrandt. You aren't the only person here on Kornati we've considered contacting. There's Belostenic and Glavinic, for example. Or Dekleva. But I'm impressed. The combination of perceptiveness and pragmatism you've just demonstrated is exactly what I came looking for. I don't need dewy-eyed idealists, and I don't want raging fanatics. I want someone who can differentiate between fantasy and what's possible. But I still need to know how far you're prepared to go. Raging fanatics are one thing; people who aren't willing to do what's necessary are just as bad. So are you an ivory tower analyst, able to theorize with the best but unwilling to get your hands dirty . . . or bloody?"

"I'm prepared to go as far as it takes," she told him flatly, her wiry body coiled about its tension as she met his eyes steadily. "I'm not in love with the concept of violence, if that's what you mean by 'raging fanatics.' But I'm not afraid of it, either. Politics and political power are all upheld by force and the readiness to shed blood, in the final analysis, and the independence of my star system is important enough to justify anything I have to do to protect it."

"Good," Firebrand said softly. "Very good. At the moment, it's still a matter of putting the pieces into place. Just as I'm here on Kornati, I have colleagues having similar conversations on other planets across the entire Cluster. Within a few weeks, a couple of months at the outside, we should be in a position to begin making concrete plans."

"So all of this, all your talk about what 'I need,' is only a hypothetical exercise?" Nordbrandt's eyes were suddenly cold, but Firebrand only shook his head calmly.

"Not in the least. It's just still at a very early stage. Do you really think I'm in a position to make spur-of-the-moment decisions for my entire organization, solely on the basis of a single firsthand conversation? Would you want to have anything to do with me if you thought that was the case?"

He held her eyes until she shook her head slowly, then shrugged.

"I'll take my report back to our central committee. I'll recommend strongly that we establish a formal alliance with you and your people here on Kornati. And as we find similar allies on other planets, we'll either coordinate operations for you, or possibly even put you into direct contact with one another, as well as with us. In the end, what we hope to accomplish is the creation of a central coordinating body—one on which you would almost certainly hold a voting seat—to organize and support a Cluster-wide resistance movement. But building that, especially if we want to prevent the local authorities, like your President Tonkovic, from infiltrating us and taking us out before we can accomplish anything, is going to take some time."

She nodded, obviously unwillingly. Her eyes were hot with disappointment, with the frustrated desire to do something *now*, but there was discipline behind the frustration. And an awareness that what he'd said made sense.

"In the meantime," he continued, "I *may* be in a position to begin providing a strictly limited amount of financial and material support. Eventually, obviously, my people hope to provide more substantial assistance, including access to weapons and intelligence. If we manage to create the central coordinating structure we're trying to put into place, we ought to be in a position to receive intelligence from all of our planetary members without jeopardizing the security of any of them. We'll be able to put all the pieces anyone gives us together into a single, coherent whole which ought to allow all of us to formulate more effective strategies. And we also hope to pool our financial resources. Speaking of which, I hope you realize it may be necessary for us to do some things none of us would really like to do in order to finance our operations?"

"That's understood." Nordbrandt's voice carried more than a touch of distaste, but, once again, her eyes were unflinching. "I'm not looking forward to it, but resistance movements can't exactly send out Revenue Service agents to collect income tax."

"I'm glad you understand that," Firebrand said gravely. "To begin with, though, it looks as if we're going to be able to secure at least the seed money we need through a little judicious electronic manipulation."

"Oh?" Nordbrandt perked up visibly.

"Oh, yes," Firebrand said with a nasty smile. "I'm obviously not at liberty to give you any details. For that matter, I don't have many details to give, at this point. But come the end of the current fiscal quarter, Bernardus Van Dort is going to discover that the Trade Union is running an unanticipated deficit."

Nordbrandt clapped a hand over her mouth to smother a delighted peal of laughter, and her brown eyes danced devilishly. Firebrand grinned back like a little boy who'd just gotten away with cutting an entire week of school without being caught. He'd thought she'd like the notion of pilfering from the coffers of the powerful, theoretically nonpolitical trade organization which had taken the lead in organizing the annexation plebiscite in the first place.

"There *is* a certain poetic justice involved, isn't there?" he said after a moment, and she nodded enthusiastically.

"As I say, I don't know any details," he continued, "but if the operation comes off half as well as I've been led to expect, we ought to be able to begin providing some discreet additional funding to you and your organization in the next couple of months. Possibly even a bit sooner, though I don't think you should count on that. Of course, before we can do that, we're going to have to have some idea of just how large and how active your own organization is likely to be.

"I'm not going to ask for any details," he went on quickly, one hand waving the thought aside. "But obviously we're going to have to have some idea of the relative needs and capabilities of the various organizations we hope to bring together if we're going to make the best use of what are inevitably going to be limited resources."

"I can see that," she agreed. "But I'm obviously going to have to discuss this with my people before I can commit them to anything."

"Naturally." Firebrand grinned again. "I'm sure it's going to seem like it's taking forever for us to get this up and running. But I truly believe that once we have it in place, it's going to make the difference between success or failure for the entire Cluster."

"Then let's hope we do get it organized," Agnes Nordbrandt said, and raised her beer stein in salute to her new allies.

"Are you out of your mind?!" "Firebrand's" companion demanded quietly as the two of them strolled down the sidewalk together twenty minutes later. Any casual observer would undoubtedly have dismissed them as no more than two friends, making their way home from an evening of conviviality and looking forward to a night's rest before facing another day of work.

"I don't think so," Firebrand replied, then chuckled. "Of course, if I were out of my mind, I probably wouldn't realize it, would I?"

"No? Well Eichbauer never authorized us to go that far, and you know it. For God's sake, Damien, you all but promised that lunatic funds!"

"Yes, I did, didn't I?" Captain Damien Harahap, known to Agnes Nordbrandt as "Firebrand," chuckled. "I thought my explanation for their origin was downright inspired. *She* certainly liked it, didn't she?"

"Goddamn it, *will* you be serious?" His fellow's exasperation was obvious to Harahap, although it wouldn't have been to that putative casual observer, and the senior agent sighed. He'd worked with the other man before—not often, but two or three times—and he supposed he ought to be accustomed to his partner's stodginess. But it was rather sad that he had so little sense of how the Great Game was played.

"I *am* being serious, in my own perhaps peculiar fashion," he said after several seconds. "And I might remind you that I've worked with Ulrike—I mean, Major Eichbauer—a lot longer than *you* have."

"I'm aware of that. But this was supposed to be an *exploratory* probe. We were looking for information, not setting up goddamned conduits! You're so far outside our instructions it isn't even funny."

"It's called 'initiative,' Tommy," Harahap said, and this time there was a faintly discernible edge of contempt in his smile. "Do you really think Eichbauer would have sent us to gather this kind of information if there wasn't at least a potential operation floating around?"

He shook his head, and the other man grimaced.

"You're senior, and Talbott's your so-called area of expertise, so it's your ass hanging out there to be kicked. I still think she's going to rip you a new one as soon as she reads your report, though."

"She may. I doubt it, though. Worst case, 'Mr. Firebrand' just never gets around to revisiting Kornati. Nordbrandt will never see me again, and all she'll have are some unanswered questions and useless speculation." Harahap shrugged. "She may decide I was just pulling her chain, or she may figure I was quietly arrested and disposed of. But if Ulrike *is* up to something, establishing credible contact with someone like Nordbrandt could be very useful. And I'm sure we could scare up enough funding to make my little fable about looting the RTU stand up without ever going beyond Ulrike's discretionary funds."

"But why?" the other man asked. "The woman isn't too tightly wrapped, and you know it. And she's smart. That's a bad combination."

"That depends on what you're trying to accomplish, doesn't it?" Harahap shot back. "I agree she seems a couple of canisters short of a full load. If I wanted to keep Frontier Security off *my* planet, I'd jump on the opportunity to join Manticore in a heartbeat. So would anyone else whose mind spent its time in the real universe. But I think Nordbrandt genuinely believes she can orchestrate a resistance movement which could not only convince Manticore to go elsewhere, but do the same thing to OFS and probably even overturn Kornati's entire economic system, as well."

"Like I said—a lunatic."

"Not entirely," Harahap disagreed. The other man looked at him incredulously, and he chuckled again. "Oh, she's dreaming if she thinks Frontier Security would lose an instant's sleep over turning her and all her loyal followers into so much dogmeat. OFS has had too much experience swatting people like her. But she could just have a point where *Manticore* is concerned. And if Major Eichbauer, or her esteemed superiors, are actually contemplating any sort of operation here in Talbott, just who do you think it's going to be directed against?"

"I suppose that's a reasonable point," the other man said unwillingly.

"Of course it is. And it's also the reason—well, one reason—I'm going to recommend we make good on that funding offer of mine. And that we cultivate Westman, as well."

"Westman?" The other man looked at him sharply. "I'd think he was more dangerous even than Nordbrandt."

"From our perspective?" Harahap nodded. "Certainly he is. Nordbrandt simply figures there's no real difference between OFS and Manticore. *Any* outside power mucking around in Talbott is the enemy, as far she's concerned. Hard to blame her, really, even if she is a bit of a fanatic about it."

For a moment, a few fleeting instants, his expression tightened, his eyes bleak with the memory of a boy's childhood on another planet not unlike Kornati. Then it disappeared, and he chuckled yet again.

"The point is, though, that she's so focused on resisting *anyone's* 'imperialist designs' on her home world that she's constitutionally incapable of recognizing how much better terms she could expect from Manticore than from Frontier Security.

"Westman's a whole different case. Nordbrandt hates Van Dort and the Trade Union because of the role they played in inviting Manticore in; Westman hates *Manticore* because inviting it in was Van Dort's idea. He's hated and distrusted the Rembrandt Trade Union ever since it was created. He's spent so long worrying about its mercantile imperialism that he's automatically opposed to *anything* the RTU thinks is a good idea. But when you come right down to it, he really doesn't *know* anything more about the Manticorans than Nordbrandt does. At the moment he's seeing them strictly through a prism that's still focused on the way things were before Manticore suddenly acquired a wormhole terminus here. He's more organized and better financed than I think Nordbrandt is, and his family name gives him enormous influence on Montana. But if he gets himself educated about the difference between Manticore and Frontier Security, he's just likely to decide there might be something in this 'Star Kingdom' business for the Montana System, after all."

"And you're still going to recommend we cultivate him?"

"Of course I am. What's that old saying about keeping your friends close, but your enemies closer?" Harahap snorted. "If we can convince him of our sincerity—and if we can get Nordbrandt on board to act as local protective camouflage, we'll stand a better chance of doing that—we'll be in a much more promising position when it comes to controlling him. Or, at least, to containing him."

He walked along in silence for another minute, then shrugged.

"Don't ever forget what we're really doing here, Tommy. I'm convinced Eichbauer is setting up an operation, or at least scouting the terrain to be ready if she's ordered to mount one. And in that case, the object has to be preventing Manticore's annexation of the Cluster. Both Nordbrandt and Westman could be very useful for that sort of maneuver. Getting our hooks into them so we can 'encourage' them and direct them as effectively as possible would be worthwhile in its own right. But the bottom line is that if we manage to keep Manticore out, it's only going to be so we can move in ourselves. And in that case, it's even more important to have good, solid communications with people like Nordbrandt and Westman."

He looked at his companion, and this time his smile was icy cold.

"It's always so much easier to round up the local opposition for disposal if they think you're their friends."

Chapter Eight

Ansten FitzGerald looked up at the sound of a cleared throat. Naomi Kaplan stood in the opened hatch of his small shipboard office.

"Chief Ashton said you wanted to see me?" she said.

"Yes, I did. Come on in. Take a seat." He pointed to the chair on the far side of his desk, and she crossed the decksole and sat down, smoothing her long blond hair with one hand. "Thanks for getting here so promptly," he continued, "but it really wasn't quite that urgent."

"I was on my way stationward when Ashton caught me," she said. "I've got a dinner date at Dempsey's with Alf in about—" she looked at her chrono "—two hours, and I wanted to do a little shopping first." She grinned, her dark-brown eyes glinting. "I'd still like to get the shopping in if I can, but to be perfectly honest, I'd rather have the free time to stay out *after* dinner, Daddy. So I thought I'd come see you ASAP."

"I see." FitzGerald smiled back at her. The petite, attractive tactical officer reminded him of a hexapuma for more than just her ferocity in combat. He didn't know whether he envied Alf Sanfilippo, or whether he sympathized with him, but he knew the other man wasn't going to be bored that evening.

"I think you can probably count on having the free time you want," he told her, and then his smile faded. "But you may not have much more than that." She cocked her head, looking a question at him, and he shrugged. "How do you think Lieutenant Hearns is working out?" he asked.

Kaplan blinked at the sudden apparent *non sequitur*. Then her eyes narrowed.

"Are you asking my opinion of her as my assistant tactical officer, or as *Hexapuma*'s OCTO?"

"Both," FitzGerald replied simply, tipping back in his chair and watching her expression.

"Well," Kaplan said slowly, "I haven't really had the opportunity to see her in action, you understand." FitzGerald nodded. For someone who had absolutely no trace of hesitation when the fecal matter hit the rotary air impeller in combat, Kaplan had a pronounced tendency to throw out sheet anchors in *non*-combat situations.

"Having said that," Kaplan continued, "I'd have to say that so far she's worked out quite well as the ATO. I've worked with her in the simulator, along with our entire Tac team, and she's very, very good. As I would have expected from her Academy grades and her evaluation from Captain Oversteegen." She snorted suddenly. "Actually, it would be a goddamned miracle if she *weren't* a superior tactician after studying under Duchess Harrington at the Island and then going to finishing school under Oversteegen!"

"I imagine some people could manage to remain blissfully incompetent, no matter who they studied under," FitzGerald said dryly.

"Maybe they could, but I guarantee you they couldn't do it without getting hammered in their evaluations by the Salamander and Oversteegen."

"Um." FitzGerald considered for a moment—it didn't take any longer than that—then nodded. "Point taken," he conceded.

"As I say," Kaplan went on, "she's performed very well in simulated combat. Given the degree of composure she showed dirt-side during that business on Refuge, I'm not worried about her losing her nerve or panicking when the missiles are flying for real, either. I haven't had as much opportunity to evaluate her on the administrative side, though. Everything I've seen suggests that she sees keeping up with her paperwork and staying current with the department's details as being almost as important as solving tactical problems—which is rare enough for officers with twice her experience. But we've only been working together for a bit over one week. Over all—" she shrugged "—I think she could hold down the slot if she had to."

That, FitzGerald reflected, was probably about as unequivocal a statement as he could expect out of her at this point. It wasn't that Kaplan was one of those compulsive ass-coverers. She was perfectly willing to stand up and take responsibility for the consequences of her decisions or recommendations. But if she had no fear of consequences for herself, she did have her own peculiar version of a moral fear of consequences for *others*. Of making the wrong decision through hastiness and letting down those who had the right to rely upon her judgment. He wondered what episode in her past accounted for that tendency, but he doubted he would ever know.

"And her performance as OCTO?" he asked.

"So far, excellent," Kaplan replied with a promptness which surprised him. "I actually had more reservations about that aspect of her duties than I did about her performance on the bridge," the TO said. "The main thing that worried me was the same thing you pointed out to the Captain: how young she is. I figured she might have trouble maintaining the necessary distance because of how close to her age the snotties are. But it hasn't worked out that way. I've been monitoring her sims with them, for example, including her post-action critiques. She not only manages to maintain her authority without ever having to use a hammer, but for someone her age, she's also shown an amazing sensitivity to their social dynamics."

"Really?" FitzGerald hoped he didn't sound as surprised as he felt. Kaplan's comments amounted to the closest thing to an unconditional endorsement he believed he'd ever heard from her.

"Really," the tactical officer affirmed. "Matter of fact, she's better at the dynamics thing than I ever was. I can appreciate someone who does it well, but it's never really been my strong suit. I can *do* it; it just doesn't come naturally to me, and I think it does come that way for Abigail. For example, I know there's something going on between Zilwicki and d'Arezzo. I don't know what it is, and I don't think Abigail knows, either, but there's some source of friction that seems to be coming from Zilwicki."

"Is there something I should be stepping on as XO?" FitzGerald asked, and Kaplan shook her head quickly.

"No, it's nothing like that. She just doesn't *like* him very much, for some reason. It's probably exacerbated by the fact that he's the closest thing to a genuine outsider in Snotty Row. The others all shared classes at the Island, but he doesn't seem to have caught any of the same class schedules they did. On top of that, he has a pronounced tendency to keep to himself. He's the closest thing to a true loner I've seen in a snotty in a long time. And, to be honest, the way we've tapped him to work with Guthrie isn't helping. It's pulling him outside the normal snotty parameters and only underscoring that 'outsider' status of his."

She shrugged.

"It's not that Zilwicki or any of the others are actively riding him, or getting on his case. For one thing, they're all good kids. For another, they all take their responsibility to function as junior officers seriously. They're not going to piss in each other's beers over any minor crap. But Zilwicki's as much of a natural leader as he is a loner, and her attitude affects those of the other snotties. She's not deliberately hammering d'Arezzo, but the fact that she doesn't much care for him is helping to *keep* him an outsider. So Abigail's been deliberately assigning the two of them to work together in situations which require them to cooperate to solve problems. Sooner or later, that's going to get them past whatever it is Zilwicki's got stuck up that stiff-necked, Highlander nose of hers. Either that, or bring it out into the open where *Abigail* can deal with it once and for all."

FitzGerald gazed at her for a moment, smiling quizzically, then shook his head.

"'Stiff-necked, Highlander *nose*.'" He shook his head again. "Do you have any idea how scrambled a metaphor that is, Naomi?"

"So sue me." She made a face at him. "Doesn't mean it's not accurate, now does it?"

"No, I don't suppose it does." He rocked his chair from side to side for several seconds, his lips pursed in thought. "So, from what you're saying, you're satisfied with her performance?"

"Yes, I am," Kaplan said, coming up to scratch with unusual firmness. Then she grinned suddenly. "By the way, did I tell you what she says the snotties are calling the ship?"

"The snotties?" FitzGerald cocked an eyebrow at her.

"Yep. Sounds like the official nickname's probably been bestowed—the *Nasty Kitty*."

"*Nasty Kitty*." FitzGerald rolled the name on his tongue, then chuckled. "Well, I've heard worse. *Served* on ships with worse, for that matter. Any idea who came up with it?"

"None. Abigail says Pavletic used it first—and damned near died when she realized she'd let it slip. And, of course, Abigail took the opportunity to twist all of their tails just a bit. In a gentle, kindly fashion, of course."

"Oh, of course!" FitzGerald agreed. He considered the name again and decided it would probably stick, unless something catchier had already come out of the enlisted quarters. And as he'd said, he'd heard worse. Much worse.

"Well, it's a good thing she's got her new name all issued and ready to go," he said. "And it's an even better thing that you're satisfied with Abigail's performance," he added, and smiled sourly as it was her turn for both eyebrows to arch. "It seems Captain Terekhov was correct. We're not going to get a more senior ATO assigned before our departure date. Especially since said departure date has just been moved up by forty-five hours."

Kaplan sat back in her chair, her expression suddenly thoughtful. Forty-five hours was two Manticoran planetary days.

"May I ask if we were given any reason for expediting our departure?"

"No, we weren't. Of course, there could be any number of reasons. Including the fact that *Hephaestus* obviously needs our slip. We've got ships with combat damage coming back from the front. I wouldn't blame the yard dogs a bit if they wanted to see our back just because they've got somebody else with a higher priority waiting in line behind us. And, of course, it could also be that Admiral Khumalo needs us in Talbott more badly than we'd thought."

"He's certainly got his hands full," Kaplan agreed. "Although, from the intelligence summaries I've been reading, the situation in Talbott's a lot less tense than the situation in Silesia right now."

"Admiral Sarnow is 'living in interesting times' in Silesia, all right," FitzGerald agreed. "On the other hand, he's got a lot more ships than Khumalo does, too. But whatever our Lords and Masters' logic, what matters to us is that we're pulling out in three days, not five."

"Agreed." Kaplan's expression was pensive, and she drummed on the arms of her chair. Then she glanced at FitzGerald and opened her mouth, only to hesitate and then close it again. He gazed at her, his own face expressionless. Knowing her as well as he did, he knew just how concerned she must be to have come that close to voicing the unthinkable question.

Do you think the Captain is past it?

No serving officer could ask a superior that. Especially not when the superior in question was the ship's executive officer. The captain's alter ego. The subordinate charged with maintaining both the ship and the ship's company as a perfectly honed weapon, in instant readiness for their commanding officer's hand.

Yet it was a question which had preyed upon FitzGerald's own mind ever since he'd learned who would be replacing Captain Sarcula.

He didn't like that. He didn't like it for a lot of reasons, beginning with the fact that no sane person wanted an officer commanding a Queen's ship if there was any question about his ability to command *himself*. And then there was the fact that Ansten FitzGerald was an intensely loyal man by nature. It was one of the qualities which made him an outstanding executive officer. But he wanted—needed—for the focus of that loyalty to deserve it. To be able to do *his* job if FitzGerald performed his own properly. And to be worthy of the sacrifices which might be demanded of their ship and people at any time.

There was no one in the Queen's uniform who had more amply proven his courage and skill than Aivars Aleksovitch Terekhov. Forced into action under disastrous conditions which were none of his fault, he'd fought his ship until she and her entire division were literally hammered into scrap. Until three-quarters of his crew were dead or wounded. Until he himself had been so mangled by the fire that wrecked his bridge that the Peep doctors had been forced to amputate his right arm and leg and regenerate them from scratch.

And after that, he'd survived almost a full T-year as a POW in the Peeps' hands until the general prisoner exchange the High Ridge Government had engineered. And he'd returned to the Star Kingdom as the single officer whose command had been overwhelmed, destroyed to the last ship, however gallant and determined its resistance, at the same time Eighth Fleet, in the full floodtide of victory, had been smashing Peep fleet after Peep fleet.

FitzGerald had never met Terekhov before he was assigned to *Hexapuma*. But one of his Academy classmates had. And that classmate's opinion was that Terekhov had changed. Well, of course he had. *Anyone* would have, after enduring all that. But the Terekhov his classmate recalled was a warm, often impulsive man with an active sense of humor. One who was deeply involved with his ship's officers. One who routinely invited those same officers to dine with him, and who was fond of practical jokes.

Which was a very different proposition from the cool, detached man Ansten FitzGerald had met. He still saw traces of that sense of humor. And Terekhov was never too busy to discuss any issue related to the ship or to her people with his executive officer. And for all his detachment, he had an uncanny awareness of what was happening aboard *Hexapuma*. Like the way he'd singled out d'Arezzo as a potential assistant to Bagwell.

Yet the question remained, buzzing in the back of FitzGerald's brain like an irritating insect. *Was* the Captain past it? Was that new detachment, that cool watchfulness, simply an inevitable reaction to the ship and people he'd lost, the wounds he'd suffered, the endless therapy and the time he'd spent recuperating? Or did it cover a weakness? A chink in Terekhov's defenses? If it came to it, did the Captain have it in him to place *another* ship, another crew, squarely in the path of the storm as he had done in Hyacinth?

Ansten FitzGerald was a Queen's officer. He was past the age where glory seemed all important, but he was a man who believed in duty. He didn't ask for guarantees of his personal survival, but he did demand the knowledge that his commanding officer would do whatever duty demanded of them without flinching. And that if he died—if his *ship* died—they would die facing the enemy, not running away.

I suppose I'm still a sucker for the "Saganami tradition."

And when you come right down to it, that's not so bad a thing.

But, of course, he couldn't say any of that any more than Kaplan could have asked the question in the first place. And so, he simply said, "Go enjoy your dinner with Alf, Naomi. But I'd like you back aboard by zero-eight-thirty hours. I'm scheduling an all-department heads meeting for eleven-hundred hours."

"Yes, Sir." She rose, her shuttered eyes proof she knew what had been going through his mind as well as he knew what had gone through hers. "I'll be there," she said, nodded, and walked out of his office.

"We have preliminary clearance from Junction Central, Sir," Lieutenant Commander Nagchaudhuri announced. "We're number nineteen for transit."

"Thank you, Commander," Captain Terekhov replied calmly, never taking his blue eyes from the navigating plot deployed from his command chair. *Hexapuma*'s icon decelerated smoothly towards a stop on the plot, exactly on the departure line for the Lynx Terminus transit queue. As he watched, a scarlet number "19" appeared beneath her light code, and he nodded almost imperceptibly in approval.

It had taken them a long time to get here. The trip could have been made in minutes in hyper-space, but a ship couldn't use hyper to get from the vicinity of the star associated with a junction terminus to the terminus itself. The gravity well of the star stressed the volume of hyper-space between it and the junction in ways which made h-space navigation through it extraordinarily difficult and highly dangerous, so the trip had to be made the long, slow way through normal-space.

Helen Zilwicki sat at Lieutenant Commander Wright's elbow, assigned to Astrogation for this evolution. Astrogation was far from her favorite duty in the universe, but just this once she preferred her present assignment to Ragnhild's. The blond, freckled midshipwoman was seated beside Lieutenant Commander Kaplan, which was usually the position Helen most coveted. But that was usually, when the astrogation plot and the visual display didn't show the Central Terminus of the Manticoran Wormhole Junction.

The Manticore System's G0 primary was dim, scarcely visible seven light-hours behind them, and its G2 companion was still farther away and dimmer. Yet the space about *Hexapuma* was far from empty. A sizable chunk of Home Fleet was deployed out here, ready to dash through the Junction to reinforce Third Fleet at Trevor's Star at need, or to cover the Basilisk System against a repeat of the attack which had devastated it in the previous war. And, of course, to protect the Junction itself.

Once that protection would have been the responsibility of the Junction forts. But the decommissioning of those fortresses had been completed under the Janacek Admiralty as one more cost-saving measure. To be fair, the process had been begun before the High Ridge Government ever assumed office, for with Trevor's Star firmly in Manticoran hands, the danger of a sudden attack through the Junction had virtually disappeared. Perhaps even more important, decommissioning the manpower-intensive fortresses had freed up the enormous numbers of trained spacers to man the new construction which had taken the war so successfully to the People's Republic.

But now Manticore, and the diminished Manticoran Alliance, was once again upon the defensive, and threats to the home system—and to the Junction—need not come *through* the Junction. Yet there was no question of recommissioning the fortresses. Their technology was obsolete, they'd never been refitted to utilize the new generations of missiles, their EW systems were at least three generations out of date, and BuPers was scrambling as desperately for trained manpower as it ever had before. Which meant Home Fleet had to assume the responsibility, despite the fact that any capital ship deployed to cover the Junction was over nineteen hours—almost twenty-one and a half hours, at the standard eighty percent of maximum acceleration the Navy allowed—from Manticore orbit. No one liked hanging that big a percentage of the Fleet that far from the capital planet, but at least the home system swarmed with LACs. Any Light Attack Craft might be a pygmy compared to a proper ship of the wall, but there were literally thousands of *Shrikes* and *Ferrets* deployed to protect the Star Kingdom's planets. They ought to be able to give any attackers pause long enough for Home Fleet to rendezvous and deal with them.

Ought to, Helen thought. That was the operative phrase.

Almost stranger than seeing so many ships of the wall assigned to ride herd on the Junction, was seeing so many of them squawking Andermani transponder codes. For the entire history of the Star Kingdom—for even longer than there'd *been* a Star Kingdom—Manticoran home space had been protected by Manticoran ships. But not any longer. Almost half of the superdreadnoughts on Ragnhild's tactical plot belonged to the Star Kingdom's Grayson and Andermani allies, and relieved though Helen was to see them, the fact that the Star Kingdom needed them made her feel . . . uncomfortable.

The number code under *Hexapuma*'s icon had continued to tick steadily downward while Helen brooded. Now it flashed over from "11" to "10," and Lieutenant Commander Nagchaudhuri spoke again.

"We have immediate readiness clearance, Sir," he said.

"Thank you, Commander," Terekhov repeated, and glanced at *Hexapuma*'s helmswoman. "Put us in the outbound lane, Senior Master Chief."

"Aye, aye, Sir," Senior Master Chief Jeanette Clary responded crisply. "Coming to outbound heading."

Her hands moved gently, confidently, and *Hexapuma* responded like the thoroughbred she was. She nudged gently forward, accelerating at a bare fifteen gravities as Clary aligned her precisely on the invisible line stretching into the Junction's heart. Helen watched the heavy cruiser's icon settle down on the plot's green streak of light and knew Clary wasn't doing anything she herself couldn't have done . . . with another thirty or forty T-years of experience.

"In the lane, Captain," Clary reported four minutes later.

"Thank you, Senior Master Chief. That was handsomely done," Terekhov responded, and Helen looked back up at the visual display.

The Junction was a sphere in space, a light-second in diameter. That was an enormous volume, but it seemed considerably smaller when it was threaded through with ships moving under Warshawski sail. And there were seven secondary termini now, each with its own separate but closely related inbound and outbound lanes. Even in time of war, the Junction's use rate had continued to do nothing but climb. Fifteen years ago, the traffic controllers had handled one transit every three minutes. Now they were up to over a thousand inbound and outbound transits a T-day—one transit every eighty-five seconds along one of the fourteen lanes—and an astonishing amount of that increase moved along the Manticore-Lynx lane.

As she watched, a six-million-ton freighter came through the central terminus from Lynx, rumbling down the inbound lane. One instant there was nothing—the next, a leviathan erupted out of nowhere into here. Her Warshawski sails were perfect disks, three hundred kilometers in diameter, radiating the blue glory of transit energy like blazing mirrors. Then the energy bled quickly away into nothingness, and the freighter folded her wings. Her sails reconfigured into impeller bands, and she gathered way in n-space as she accelerated out of the nexus. She was headed away from the Manticore System, for the Lynx holding area, which meant she was only passing through—like the vast majority of Junction shipping—and was probably already requesting insertion into another outbound queue.

Hexapuma moved steadily forward, and Helen watched in fascination as the azure fireflies of Warshawski sails flashed and blinked like summer lightning, pinpricks scattered across the vast sooty depths of the Junction. The nearest ones, from ships inbound from Lynx, were close enough for her to see details. The most distant ones, from ships inbound from the Gregor System, were so tiny that, even with the display's magnification, they were only a handful of extra stars. Yet she felt the vibrant, throbbing intensity of the Junction, beating like the Star Kingdom's very heart. Her father had explained to her when she was very young that the Junction was both the core of the Star Kingdom's vast wealth, and the dagger against the Star Kingdom's throat. Not so much because of the possibility of invasion through the Junction, as because of the temptation it posed to greedy neighbors. And as she looked at that unending stream of merchantships, each of them massing millions of tons, each of them paying its own share of transit duties, and probably at least a third of them carrying Manticoran transponder codes, she understood what he'd meant.

Senior Master Chief Clary held *Hexapuma*'s place in the queue without additional orders, and as the number under her icon dropped to "3," Terekhov glanced down into the com screen connecting him to Engineering. Ginger Lewis looked back at him, her green eyes calm.

"Commander Lewis," he said, with a tiny nod. "Stand by to reconfigure to Warshawski sail on my command, if you please."

"Aye, aye, Sir. Standing by to reconfigure to sail." Terekhov nodded again, then gave Senior Master Chief Clary's maneuvering plot a quick check. The number on it had dropped from "3" to "2" while he was speaking to Lewis, and his eyes switched briefly to the visual display as the Solarian freighter ahead of *Hexapuma* drifted farther forward, hesitated for just an instant, and then blinked into nothingness. The number on Clary's plot dropped to "1," and the captain turned to cock an eyebrow at Lieutenant Commander Nagchaudhuri.

"We're cleared to transit, Sir," the com officer reported after a moment.

"Very good, Commander. Extend our thanks to Junction

Central," Terekhov said, and turned his chair slightly back towards Clary.

"Take us in, Helm."

"Aye, aye, Sir."

Hexapuma accelerated very slightly, moving forward under just over twenty-five gravities' acceleration as she slid flawlessly down the invisible rails of her outbound lane. Her light code flashed bright green as she settled into exact position, and Terekhov looked back at Lewis.

"Rig foresail for transit."

"Rig foresail, aye, Sir," she replied. "Rigging foresail—now."

No observer would have noticed any visible change, but the bridge displays told the tale as *Hexapuma*'s impeller wedge dropped abruptly to half-strength. Her forward nodes were no longer generating their part of the wedge's n-space stress bands. Instead, her beta nodes had shut down, and her alpha nodes had reconfigured to produce a Warshawski sail, a circular disk of focused gravitation that extended for over a hundred and fifty kilometers in every direction.

"Stand by to rig aftersail on my mark," Terekhov said quietly, his eyes focused on his own maneuvering plot as *Hexapuma* continued to creep forward under the power of her after impellers alone. A new window opened in a corner of the plot, framing numerals that flickered and changed, dancing steadily upward as the foresail moved deeper into the Junction. The Junction was like the eye of a hyper-space hurricane, an enormous gravity wave, twisting forever between widely separated normal-space locations, and the Warshawski sail caught at that unending, coiled power. It eased *Hexapuma* gently into its heart, through the interface where grav shear would have splintered an unprotected hull.

The dancing numbers whirled upward, and Helen felt herself tensing internally. There was a safety margin of almost fifteen seconds on either side of the critical threshold, but her imagination insisted upon dwelling on the gruesome consequences which would ensue if that window of safety were missed.

The numbers crossed the threshold. The foresail was now drawing sufficient power from the tortured grav wave spiraling endlessly through the Junction to provide movement, and Terekhov nodded slightly in satisfaction.

"Rig aftersail now, Commander Lewis," he said calmly.

"Aye, aye, Sir. Rigging aftersail now," she replied, and *Hexapuma* twitched. Her impeller wedge disappeared entirely, a second Warshawski sail sprang to life at the far end of her hull from the first, and a wave of queasiness assailed her entire crew.

Helen was no stranger to interstellar flight, but no one ever really adjusted to the indescribable sensation of crossing the wall between n-space and h-space, and it was worse in a junction transit, because the gradient was so much steeper. But the gradient was steeper on *both* sides, which at least meant it was over much more quickly.

The maneuvering display blinked again, and for an instant no one had ever been able to measure, HMS *Hexapuma* ceased to exist. One moment she was seven light-hours from the Star Kingdom's capital planet; the next moment, she was four light-years from a G2 star named Lynx . . . and just over seven light-*centuries* from Manticore.

"Transit complete," Senior Master Chief Clary announced.

"Thank you, Helm," Terekhov acknowledged. "That was well executed." The captain's attention was back on the sail interface readout, watching the numbers plummet even more rapidly than they had risen. "Engineering, reconfigure to impeller," he said.

"Aye, aye, Sir. Reconfiguring to impeller now."

Hexapuma's sails folded back into a standard impeller wedge as she moved forward, accelerating steadily down the Lynx inbound lane, and Helen permitted herself a mental nod of satisfaction. The maneuver had been routine, but "routine" didn't mean "not dangerous," and

Captain Terekhov had hit the transit window dead center. If he'd been off as much as a full second, either way, *she* hadn't noticed it, and she'd been sitting right at Lieutenant Commander Wright's elbow, with the astrogator's detailed readouts directly in front of her.

But now that transit had been completed, she found herself beginning to envy Ragnhild after all. Astrogation's maneuvering plot wasn't as good as Tactical's for displaying information on other ships, and there were a *lot* of other ships out there.

This terminus of the Junction was less conveniently placed than most of the others in at least one respect. The closest star, a little over five and a half light-hours from the terminus, was a planetless M8 red dwarf, useless for colonization or for providing the support base a wormhole junction terminus required. Every bit of the necessary infrastructure had to be shipped in, either direct from Manticore or from the Lynx System—sixteen hours of flight for a warship in the Zeta bands, and thirty-two hours for a merchantship in the Delta bands. That wasn't very far, as interstellar voyages went, but it was far enough that it would be difficult for anyone to make a day-trip for a few hours' visit at a planet suited to human life.

Moreover, Lynx was a Verge system, with very limited industrial infrastructure and even less modern technology. There was a distinct limit on anything except raw materials and foodstuffs which it could provide, and its labor force would have to be entirely retrained on modern hardware before it could make any significant contribution to the development and operation of the terminus.

Which didn't mean there wasn't a great deal going on, anyway. Even with the limitations of her astrogation display, as opposed to the tactical plot, Helen could see that.

Although the Star Kingdom had opted not to reactivate the fortresses around the Junction's central terminus, there were at least a dozen of them under construction at the Lynx Terminus. They wouldn't be as big as the

Junction forts, but they were being shipped in in prefabricated chunks, and unlike the Junction forts, they were being built with the latest in weapons, sensors, and EW systems. And they were also being built using the same manpower-reducing automation which was a feature of the most recent Manticoran and Grayson warship designs. When finished, each would mass about ten million tons, significantly larger than any superdreadnought, and with far less internal volume devoted to impeller rooms. Bristling with missile tubes and LAC service bays, they would constitute a most emphatic statement of the Star Kingdom's ownership of the wormhole terminus.

Purely civilian installations were also under construction at a frantic rate. The mere existence of the terminus, especially in light of all of the other termini of the Manticoran Wormhole Junction, was acting on merchant shipping less like a magnet than a black hole. The Lynx Terminus cut distances—and thus time—between, say, New Tuscany and Sol from over five hundred light-years to less than two hundred and fifty. That was a savings of over twelve *T-weeks* for a typical freighter, and the interlocking network of the Manticoran Junction and a handful of smaller ones allowed similar time savings around almost three-quarters of the Solarian League's huge perimeter. And, Helen thought grimly, when the annexation was completed, that terminus would also move the Star Kingdom's border far around the Solarian frontier and five hundred light-years closer to places like Mesa.

As she gazed at the display, she could see construction crews working on freight terminals, repair facilities, crew hostels, and all the dozens of other service platforms the wormhole's through-traffic was going to require. And she could see the long line of ships, waiting patiently for their turns to transit to Manticore, just as she could see the merchant vessels which had preceded *Hexapuma* moving steadily away from the terminus. Most of them appeared to be headed away from the Talbott Cluster, towards busier, wealthier, more important planets deeper into the Shell systems of the League. Some of them, however, were obviously bound for Talbott, and she wondered how much of that traffic would have been here if the terminus hadn't effectively reduced shipping distances so drastically.

She was still gazing at the display, listening with one ear as Lieutenant Commander Nagchaudhuri reported their arrival to the control ship serving as temporary home for Manticoran Astro Control's Lynx detachment, when something else occurred to her.

The forts were under construction, the civilian infrastructure was growing almost literally as she watched, and hordes of merchies were streaming through the terminus . . . and the Royal Manticoran Navy's total presence—aside from *Hexapuma*, who was only visiting—were two relatively modern destroyers and one elderly light cruiser.

Well, she thought, *I suppose Home Fleet* is *on call at the central terminus, but still . . .*

The sight of that grossly understrength picket—almost as weak as the one the first Janacek Admiralty had assigned to Basilisk Station before the First Battle of Basilisk—made her feel even queasier than the wormhole transit had. She knew the Navy couldn't be strong everywhere, but she also knew the Talbott Station task force was far more numerous than anything she saw here. Surely, Rear Admiral Khumalo could have spared *something* more to watch over the billions of dollars worth of fortresses and service platforms under construction. Not to mention the *trillions* of dollars worth of merchantships and cargo passing through the terminus itself every single day.

But I'm only a snotty, she reminded herself. If *Earl White Haven wants my opinion on his deployment policies, he knows where to send the e-mail.*

Her mouth quirked wryly at the thought.

"Ms. Zilwicki."

Helen twitched in her chair, all temptation towards humor vanishing as Captain Terekhov's calm, cool voice addressed her.

"Yes, Sir!" At least she managed to avoid sounding

as if she'd been daydreaming, despite the fact that she had been, but she felt her cheekbones heat as she heard the trace of breathless scared rabbit in her own voice. Fortunately, the naturally dark complexion she'd inherited from her father wasn't one that showed blushes easily.

"Plot us a least-time course to the Spindle System, if you please, Ms. Zilwicki," Terekhov requested courteously, and Helen swallowed hard. She'd calculated endless courses to all sorts of destinations . . . under classroom conditions.

"Aye, aye, Sir!" she said quickly, giving the only possible answer, and began punching data requests into her console.

Lieutenant Commander Wright sat back, elbows propped on his chair's arm rests, with a mildly interested expression. Part of her resented his presence, but most of her was deeply relieved he was there. He might not intervene to save her from herself if he saw her making a mistake during her calculations. But at least she could count on him to stop her at the end if she'd plotted a course to put them inside a star somewhere on the far side of the League.

The computers began obediently spewing out information, and she plotted the endpoints of the necessary course, feeling grateful that *Hexapuma* was already outside the local star's hyper limit. At least she didn't have to crank *that* into her calculations!

Next she punched in a search order, directing the computer to overlay her rough course with the strongest h-space gravity waves and to isolate the wave patterns which would carry them towards Spindle. She also remembered to allow for velocity loss on downward hyper translations to follow a given grav wave. She'd forgotten to do that once in an Academy astrogation problem and wound up adding over sixty hours to the total voyage time she was calculating.

She felt a small trickle of satisfaction as she realized the same thing would have happened here, if she'd simply asked the computers to plot a course along the most powerful gravity waves, because one strong section of them never rose above the Gamma bands, which would have required at least three downward translations. That would not only have cost them over sixty percent of their base velocity at each downward translation, but *Hexapuma*'s maximum apparent velocity would have been far lower in the lower bands, as well.

She punched in waypoints along the blinking green line of her rough course as the computer refined the best options for gravity waves and the necessary impeller drive transitions between them. The blinking line stopped blinking, burning a steady green, as the waypoints marched along it. Helen knew it was taking her longer than it would have taken Lieutenant Commander Wright. Still, she decided, she didn't have much to feel embarrassed about when the numbers finally came together.

"I have the course, Captain," she announced, looking up from her console at last.

"Very good, Ms. Zilwicki." Terekhov smiled slightly, and waved one hand in Senior Master Chief Clary's direction.

"Helm," Helen said, "come to one-one-niner by zero-four-six at five hundred and eighty gravities, translation gradient of eight-point-six-two to h-band Zeta-one-seven. I'm uploading the waypoints now."

"Aye, aye, Ma'am," Clary replied. "Coming to one-one-niner by zero-four-six, acceleration five-eight-zero gravities, translation gradient eight-point-six-two, leveling at Zeta-one-seven."

Helen listened carefully as the senior master chief repeated her instructions. Under any conceivable normal circumstances, there was no way a petty officer of Clary's seniority was going to get them wrong. Even if she did, she almost certainly would have caught any error when she checked her actual helm settings against the course data Helen had loaded to her computers. But even improbable accidents happened, which was why the Navy insisted orders be repeated back verbally. And just as it was Clary's duty to repeat her orders, it was Helen's duty to be certain they'd been repeated correctly.

Hexapuma turned to starboard, climbing relative to the plane of the ecliptic of the local star, and moved ahead with ever gathering velocity as she accelerated at her maximum normal power settings.

"Thank you, Ms. Zilwicki," Terekhov said gravely, then he looked at Commander FitzGerald. "I believe we can secure from transit stations, XO. Set the normal watch schedule, if you please."

"Aye, aye, Sir." The executive officer turned to Lieutenant Commander Wright. "Commander Wright, you have the watch."

"Aye, aye, Sir. I have the watch," Wright agreed. "Third Watch personnel, man your stations," he continued. "All other watches, dismiss."

There was an orderly stir as the other three watches' bridge crew, including Helen and Ragnhild, but not Aikawa, turned their stations over to the Third Watch. As they did, Wright seated himself in the command chair at the center of the bridge which Captain Terekhov had just surrendered to him. He pressed the stud on the arm rest which activated the ship-wide intercom.

"Now hear this," he said. "This is the Officer of the Watch. Third Watch personnel, man your stations; all other watches, dismiss."

He settled himself more comfortably in the chair and leaned back as HMS *Hexapuma* bored steadily onward into the Talbott Cluster.

Chapter Nine

Abigail Hearns watched Chief Steward Joanna Agnelli remove the dinner plates. The meal had been first rate, and so was the wine, although if the Captain had chosen it himself, his palate didn't quite match that of Captain Oversteegen or Lady Harrington. But whatever his qualifications as a wine expert, he—or someone—had certainly shown excellent taste when it came to furnishing his quarters.

The decksole was covered with gorgeous, handwoven mats of velvety-soft, superbly dyed silk-sisal from her own home world—probably from Esterhaus Steading, judging by their stylized lizard-hawk motif. She doubted anyone else in *Hexapuma*'s company had the knowledge to realize just how rare and expensive those mats were. Abigail did, because her nursery back home had been floored in them when she'd been a child, and just looking at their rich-toned patterns made her want to kick off her boots and run barefoot across them.

The bulkheads bore a few paintings. All of them, from what she could see, were excellent. Most were holo-portraits, although there was one breathtaking original neo-oil of a red-haired woman with laughing green eyes. In some ways, she reminded Abigail of Commander Lewis, although this woman was probably older (always difficult to be certain in a prolong society), with a rounder face. It was an extraordinarily attractive face, too. Not beautiful, but brimming with life and character . . . and wisdom. Abigail thought she would have liked her.

The rest of the day cabin carried that same combination of taste, quality, and comfort—from the crystal decanters on the sideboard to the hand-rubbed polish of the ferran wood table and chairs. But despite its air of welcoming graciousness, there was also an edge of rawness. Newness. None of the furnishings had been with the Captain long enough to slot comfortably into the spaces of his life, she thought.

Probably because everything he'd surrounded himself with before had been destroyed with HMS *Defiant* at the Battle of Hyacinth. She wondered how that must feel, when he looked at the new paintings, the new furniture.

Abigail wasn't certain what to make of the dinner itself, either. Terekhov wasn't one of the RMN officers who followed the tradition of dining regularly with his officers. In Abigail's native Grayson Space Navy, *every* captain was expected to follow that practice, a legacy of Lady Harrington's indelible imprint upon their service, and Abigail had to admit it was the tradition she preferred. But *Hexapuma*'s Junction transit lay over two T-weeks behind them, and this was the first time Captain Terekhov had invited anyone—aside from Commander FitzGerald and Commander Lewis—to dine with him.

When she'd learned of the dinner, and that she was on the guest list, Abigail had more than half-dreaded a boring evening, an ordeal to be suffered through while a captain who disliked parties pretended he didn't. But Terekhov had fooled her. It might be true he didn't care for parties, and he might not have been entirely comfortable at this one. But if that were the case, no one could have guessed it from watching him or listening to him. He'd remained the cool, slightly distant man he'd been from the beginning, yet he'd managed somehow to make every guest feel individually welcome. He'd been just as pleasant to Midshipman Kagiyama and Midshipwoman Pavletic as to Commander FitzGerald or Surgeon Commander Orban, even as he had maintained precisely the right distance from each of his juniors. In many respects, it had been a genuine *tour de force*, and yet that inner barrier, that sense of being one step removed from everyone about him, remained.

Abigail couldn't help wondering what hid behind that barrier. Strength, or weakness? Part of her was tempted to assume the former, yet she remembered only too well how drastically she had misjudged her own first captain. And so she remained undecided, feeling as if there were a shoe poised to drop somewhere just out of sight.

All of the toasts had been drunk. Aikawa, as the junior officer present, had gotten through the loyalty toast to the Queen with admirable composure, and the Captain himself had called for the Protector's Toast from Abigail. She'd appreciated that, just as she'd appreciated and admired the fashion in which he'd discharged all of his host's responsibilities, and now she watched him lean towards Lieutenant Commander Kaplan at his left elbow. Abigail couldn't hear what they were saying from her own place at almost exactly the other end of the table, but Kaplan grinned suddenly, then actually laughed out loud. Terekhov straightened back up with a small smile of his own, but then his expression sobered, and he picked up his knife and rapped gently on the side of his wineglass with the back of the blade.

The musical chime cut through the buzz of low-voiced after-dinner conversation, and all eyes turned towards him.

"First, Ladies and Gentlemen," he said, "allow me to thank you all for joining me tonight. It's been an even more pleasant evening than I'd anticipated."

A low, inarticulate murmur answered him, and he smiled, ever so slightly. No doubt he was thinking exactly what Abigail was—that only a complete lunatic would even contemplate trying to turn down a dinner invitation from her commanding officer.

"And secondly," Terekhov continued, "I must confess I had at least a minor ulterior motive in inviting you. Commander FitzGerald and I have discussed our orders at some length, and I have no doubt the ship's grapevine has been buzzing with more or less garbled versions of those orders for weeks now. Since we'll be arriving in the Spindle System in less than three T-days, I thought it would be as well to take this opportunity to give all of you the official version of our mission."

Abigail straightened in her chair, and a quiet stir flowed up either side of the long table as every other officer present did the same thing. Terekhov saw it, and his smile grew a bit broader.

"There are no real mysteries here, Ladies and Gentlemen. I'd be surprised if the grapevine version of our orders isn't at least mostly accurate. Basically, the *Nasty Kitty* has been assigned to Talbott Station, under the command of Rear Admiral Khumalo."

Abigail saw Ragnhild Pavletic and Aikawa Kagiyama go absolutely rigid. Their eyes were suddenly huge, and she rather thought they'd both forgotten to breathe. The Captain seemed totally unaware of their reaction, but Abigail saw the faint twinkle in his eyes and recognized Naomi Kaplan's frantic effort not to erupt into laughter all over again. So *that* was what he'd been saying to the Tac Officer!

Most of the others at the table seemed to take it in stride. Commander FitzGerald's mouth twitched ever so slightly, and Commander Lewis grinned broadly. Most of the rest at least smiled, and Abigail felt herself doing the same as she realized the nickname had just been rendered official.

"Admiral Khumalo's primary mission," the Captain continued, still without so much as a glance at the paralyzed snotties, "is to assist Baroness Medusa, Her Majesty's Provisional Governor for Talbott, in overseeing the smooth integration of the Cluster into the Star Kingdom."

Then his smile faded, and his expression became very serious.

"I know many of our people, including, no doubt, some of the officers in this room, have been disappointed by our assignment to Talbott. They believe, with reason, that every Queen's ship is needed at the front. They believe that in some involuntary fashion we are shirking our duty to our Queen and the Star Kingdom by being assigned to a mere flag-showing mission six hundred light-years from home.

"I understand why some of them—some of you—may feel that way. However, you are wrong if you think our mission here is unimportant to the future of the Star Kingdom. It is very important. Whether we like it or not, the Star Kingdom most of us have known and served all of our lives is changing. It's growing. In the face of the renewed Havenite threat, Queen Elizabeth and Prime Minister Alexander, with the strong concurrence of Parliament, have determined that we have no choice but to expand. In Silesia, that expansion, sanctioned by treaty agreement with the Andermani Empire and approved by the sitting government of Silesia, will ultimately permit us to put an end to the pirate threat which has cost so many Manticoran ships and lives, including that of Commodore Edward Saganami, over the centuries. It will allow us to drastically reduce our anti-piracy efforts in that region, thus allowing us to retain a higher percentage of our ship strength for frontline deployments. And it will also bring an end to the ceaseless cycle of violence which has afflicted the people living on the planets of the Confederacy for far too long.

"Some will disapprove of our annexation of Silesian territory, regardless of the reasons. Undoubtedly, some of those who disapprove will be Silesians who suddenly find themselves living under Manticoran rule. Others will be outsiders—some from the region, and some from outside it—who will resent or fear the expansion of our borders and, ultimately, the strength of our Star Kingdom.

"The situation in Talbott is somewhat different. The decision to annex Silesia was made on the basis of military necessity, more than any other factor. The decision to annex

Talbott stemmed from the spontaneously expressed will of the citizens of the Cluster. I don't believe anyone ever anticipated that the discovery of the Junction's seventh terminus would result in the admission of a multisystem cluster to the Star Kingdom. And aside from our obvious security concerns for the Lynx Terminus, there's no pressing military need for us to acquire territory here. But when a locally organized plebiscite votes by such a wide majority to request annexation, Her Majesty has no choice but to consider that petition very carefully."

He paused to take a sip of water, then continued.

"Ultimately, the Cluster will undoubtedly become of great economic and military importance to the Star Kingdom. Its population is many times the Star Kingdom's prewar population, and its star systems are for all intents and purposes undeveloped. There will be a huge internal market for our goods and services, not to mention vast opportunities for investment, and the mere existence of the Lynx Terminus can only continue to attract even more shipping both to Talbott and, via the Junction, to Manticore itself.

"Yet all that lies in the future. What concerns us at this moment isn't the potential advantages our Star Kingdom may reap from the annexation, but our responsibility to the people of these star systems and planets, who are in the process of voluntarily making themselves our fellow citizens and Her Majesty's subjects. That is why Admiral Khumalo is here, and the reason *Hexapuma* was assigned here.

"And," his smile had completely disappeared, and his expression was grim, "it is a mission which is fraught with peril."

Abigail felt one or two people stir, as if in disbelief or disagreement, but she herself felt no inclination to join them. Perhaps it was the Church of Humanity Unchained in her, her belief in the doctrine of the Test, but she'd never expected for a moment that the incorporation of Talbott into the Star Kingdom would go as smoothly as the optimists had predicted so confidently.

"If there are those who resent and would, if they could, oppose our expansion into Silesia," Terekhov continued, "there are many more who will resent—and who *will* oppose—our annexation of Talbott. I scarcely need to remind any of you of the existence of the Office of Frontier Security, or of the Mesa System, or of the many Solarian shipping lines which deeply resent our domination of the carrying trade around the periphery of the League. All of those elements will be most unhappy at the mere thought of finding a lobe of the Star Kingdom on the League's very doorstep.

"At the moment, Admiral Khumalo has made the Spindle System the central base for Talbott Station. Although Spindle may not be . . . ideally placed for the protection of the Lynx Terminus, it is the site of the Talbott Constitutional Convention, where delegates from every system are assembled to hammer out the constitutional provisions which will govern the admission of the Cluster to the Star Kingdom. As such, the security of that system must be assured.

"But there are other security considerations, other systems which may be exposed to external threats, or even to the possibility of internal, domestic unrest. Such unrest is probably inevitable, no matter how great the majority in favor of annexation may have been, and it's entirely possible we'll find ourselves involved in suppressing outbursts of outright violence. If that should be the case, I want every man and woman in *Hexapuma*'s company to remember that the people reacting violently to our presence *live* here. They have been citizens of these star systems and these worlds all of their lives, and if they fear or resent the submergence of their systems and their worlds in the Star Kingdom, they have every right to do so. They may not have the right to resort to violence, but that's another thing entirely. I will not have any of our people making the situation worse by using one iota more of force than is absolutely necessary to the accomplishment of our mission."

He looked around the dining cabin, his gaze sweeping

slowly across the face of every officer seated around the table. Then he nodded ever so slightly, as if satisfied by what he'd found in their expressions.

"As to any external threat to the security of the lives and property of the citizens of Talbott or to the interests and obligations of the Star Kingdom and Her Majesty's Government, we will deal with those as they arise. Once again, tensions will be running high, especially among those economic and political interests who most resent our presence here. I will not tolerate any action or behavior likely to provoke an unnecessary incident, but neither do I intend for this ship or any member of her crew to back down in the face of threats. We have a job to do, Ladies and Gentlemen, and we cannot do it if we are unable or unwilling to act resolutely and swiftly to counter any threat to the Cluster, to the Star Kingdom, or to our ship."

He paused once again, and his smile reappeared once more.

"I don't automatically assume we'll face a struggle to the death," he told them wryly. "If we should encounter such a threat, I fully intend to see that any deaths will be suffered by the other side. But that doesn't mean I'm *anticipating* the worst, and it's my earnest hope this deployment will end up being just as boring and just as uneventful as those of us who feel guilty for not being at the front fear it will. Because if it is, Ladies and Gentlemen, it will mean we have accomplished the mission for which Her Majesty sent us here. And now—"

He picked up his wineglass, raising it until the deckhead lights turned its contents into a glowing ruby globe.

"Ladies and Gentlemen of *Hexapuma*," he said, "I give you duty, loyalty, and Sir Edward Saganami. The tradition lives!"

"The tradition lives!" The response rumbled back as other glasses rose in answer.

"Well, what do *you* think?" Aikawa asked.

"About what?" Helen shot back. "About the *Nasty Kitty* thing?"

They sat around the table in the Snotty Row commons area, nursing their beverages of choice—Helen was enjoying a stein of Crown's Own, one of the better Gryphon dark beers—while Helen and Leo grilled Aikawa and Ragnhild. Those two had seemed to be in a state of semi-shock over the Captain's casual use of their privately bestowed nickname, but they seemed to be bouncing back. Finally.

That's twice for Ragnhild, Helen thought around a bubble of mental laughter as she looked at the petite midshipwoman. *She must have been ready to crawl under the table on the spot!*

"Not that," Aikawa said with a grimace that was half a smile. Then his expression sobered. "What do you think about that line the Captain was handing out about how important it is that we're assigned out here at the ass-end of nowhere."

"I don't think it was 'a line,' Aikawa," Ragnhild said, shaking off her own lingering echoes of the Captain's smiling ambush and looking up with a frown of her own. "I think he meant every word of it. You don't?"

"Hunnf." Aikawa pursed his lips and gazed up at the deckhead. Then he shrugged. "I'm not sure I do," he admitted. "Oh," he waved one hand in the air, "I don't think he was *lying* to us, and there wasn't a single thing he said I could really disagree with. I just can't help wondering how much of the emphasis he was putting on it was because he *has* to believe it's important we be assigned out here. I don't mind telling you guys," he looked around, his expression slightly troubled, "that I've had the occasional guilt attack ever since I found out where we were going. I mean, think of everyone we knew at the Island who wound up being sent straight to the front, or even Silesia, where there are real pirates to worry about. And here we are, assigned to 'protect' a bunch of people who've voluntarily *asked* to join the Star Kingdom!"

He shook his head, his expression an odd mixture of emotions, including both guilt and frustration and more than a touch of relief.

"Well, I wasn't there," Leo Stottmeister said slowly, "but every single word he said about how close we are to the League, and about Mesa, and about the shipping which is already moving through Lynx is absolutely true. And I may never have dealt with Frontier Security myself, but my Uncle Stefan's ship pissed off an OFS paper-shuffler, once. They didn't do anything wrong, but by the time the dust settled, that Solly bastard had condemned and confiscated their entire ship and its cargo. Uncle Stefan always figured the son of a bitch got a cut of the ship's value, but he said the profit was just icing on the cake for him. Their ship's real crime was that they'd snagged a profitable cargo out from under the nose of a Solly shipping line that had a sweetheart deal with Frontier Security."

The tall midshipman shrugged, his face unwontedly serious.

"I know Ragnhild has relatives in the shipping industry, but I don't know about any of the rest of you. I can tell you this, though—Uncle Stefan isn't the only person I've heard talk about how much some of the Solly freight lines hate us. And Frontier Security thinks of us as a bunch of neobarbs with delusions of grandeur. You mix that all up into a single ball of snakes, and God knows what you'll get out of it! Just don't expect it to be good."

"Leo's got a point," Ragnhild said, her expression more worried than it had been. "We're used to thinking of the Star Kingdom as a star nation, a military and economic power, and it is. But compared to the League, we're *tiny*. It wouldn't take much for some overconfident, greedy, bigoted Solly—wouldn't even necessarily have to be an OFS stooge, either—to do something outstandingly stupid."

"And if that happens," Paulo d'Arezzo put in quietly, "it's likely to have all sorts of ramifications."

All of them turned to look at him in surprise. After more than two months aboard, he was still the aloof, keep-to-himself denizen of Snotty Row. The fact that he'd been released from at least a part of the normal duties associated with a snotty cruise because of Lieutenant Bagwell's need for an understudy had actually increased his isolation, and they were surprised to hear him speaking up now. But he only looked back at them and shook his head slowly.

"If you were the captain of a Queen's ship in Silesia, and a Manticoran merchant or merchant skipper told you he'd been robbed, or cheated, or mistreated, or threatened by a Confederate Navy captain, how would you react?"

"But—" Aikawa began, only to be cut off by Helen.

"Paulo's right," she said, although it irritated her to admit it. "The situations probably wouldn't be at all the same, but that's exactly the way it would seem to an SLN skipper. Because Leo's right about how the Sollies think of us. I've been to Old Earth and seen it myself. In some ways, it's even worse than for the 'neobarbs' who don't have such close contact with Sol." She grimaced. "You know my dad was still in uniform when we were there, right?"

Heads nodded, and her grimace turned even sourer.

"Well, we were at a party one night, and I overheard this woman—I found out later she was a Solly assemblywoman, no less—pointing Daddy out to one of her friends and saying 'Look at that. He looks just like he belongs to a *real* navy, doesn't he?' "

"You're shitting us," Aikawa protested.

"I wish I were," she told him. "We just aren't real to most of them, even people who damned well ought to know better. And Leo's shipping lines and OFS flunkies aren't all we have to worry about out here. Don't forget how much closer we are to Mesa, because I'll guarantee you *they* aren't going to!"

"You may be right," Aikawa said, obviously unwillingly. But then he gave his head a little toss and grinned at her. "And while we're on the subject of Mesa and your esteemed parent, Ms. Midshipwoman Princess Helen, suppose you finally tell all of us just what went down at Congo?"

"Yes!" Leo agreed instantly. He jabbed an irate finger at Aikawa and Ragnhold. "I bet you *already* told your loyal henchmen all about it."

"Not *all* about it," Ragnhild protested with a chuckle, "or Aikawa wouldn't be asking." She turned to look at Helen herself. "Actually, I'd like to hear all of it."

"There's not really all that much to tell—" Helen began, but Aikawa laughed.

"*Sure* there isn't!" he said. "Now give!"

She looked around the compartment for a second, wondering exactly how to respond, and felt their eyes on her. All of them were obviously intensely curious—even d'Arezzo—and she knew she was going to have to satisfy that curiosity eventually, whatever she wanted. On the other hand, there were some aspects of that entire business she didn't fully understand herself, and others she did understand which were going to stay on a strictly Need to Know basis for a long, long time. On the other hand . . .

"Okay," she said finally. "First, a couple of ground rules. There are some things I can't tell anyone, not even you guys. So you're going to have to settle for what I figure I can give you. No probing questions, and no little tricks to try and get more out of me. Agreed?"

They looked back at her, their expressions slightly sobered, and then Aikawa nodded.

"Agreed," he said.

"All right, here's the short version. Back last Seventeenth Month, about six T-months before the shooting started back up with the Peeps, my dad—you know, Mr. Super Spook—and my sister Berry got tapped by the Queen to be her representatives at the Stein funeral on Erewhon. High Ridge and his stooges weren't sending anyone, and Her Majesty was a bit irritated with them about that. I don't think she really likes the Renaissance Association all that much, but they are the closest thing to a grassroots reform party in the League, so she figured *someone* from the Star Kingdom should attend its leader's funeral. Anyway, she decided to send her niece, Princess Ruth, as her *personal* representative, and she asked Daddy to go along, both to ride herd on the Princess and also because of his relationship with Cathy Montaigne and the Anti-slavery League. She figured that would make the point that she was putting her thumb into High Ridge's eye even more strongly."

And, she thought, *because the Queen and Ruth decided between them that the House of Winton needed a resident spook of its own, and they wanted the best teacher for Ruth they could find. Which happened to be my own dear Daddy.*

"Everything seemed to be going pretty much to plan, when Daddy got called away to Smoking Frog."

She saw a sudden additional curiosity in several of her listeners' eyes, but she had no intention of explaining what *that* particular bit of business had been about. The Star Kingdom was still buzzing with speculation about the mysterious disappearance of Countess North Hollow, and she intended for it to stay that way.

"While he was gone, as I'm sure you all know from the 'faxes, a bunch of Masadan lunatics tried to abduct the Princess when she was aboard the main Erewhonese civilian space station."

Where she was disguised as Berry, while Berry was disguised as her, *which is how they got the wrong person, which is how the entire* ridiculous *situation came about in the first place.*

"They managed to get her, but her security detachment killed most of the terrorists before they went down, and the surviving terrorists got themselves pinned down aboard the space station."

Which is almost accurate. We'll just leave out any mention of Havenite secret agents, Ballroom terrorist gunmen, and Solarian League Marine officers.

"Not all the Masadans had been involved in the actual abduction; another batch of them had managed to hijack a Jessyk Combine transport that happened to have an entire consignment of genetic slaves on board, and they threatened to blow up the freighter, with those thousands of slaves, unless their surviving buddies and the Princess were delivered to them. Unfortunately, by that time all of their buddies were already dead, although they didn't know that. So the Princess—" *meaning my* sister, *the little idiot!* "—decided it was her responsibility to hand herself over to them. Which she did."

Accompanied only by what sounds like the scariest son of a bitch in the entire Havenite secret service.

"But it was actually all a trick. While the surviving terrorists were congratulating themselves on getting their hands on Princess Ruth, a boarding party—" *and let's not even get started on where* it *came from* "—got aboard the transport undetected. They managed to take out the terrorists, and handed the ship over to the slaves.

"But by that time, someone had come up with the bright idea of using the ship—which everyone else thought was still in the terrorists' possession—as a sort of Trojan horse against Congo. Which was probably the only thing in the universe we, the Erewhonese, and the Sollies—" *and the Havenite secret service* "—could possibly have agreed upon at that point, given how our relations with Erewhon had gone into the crapper. By the time Daddy got back from Smoking Frog and found out everything that had been going on while he was away, most of the decisions had already been taken. And somehow Berry got involved as a sort of liaison between the slaves and everybody else. Probably—" *we'll just brush through this part as quickly as we can* "—because for all practical purposes we're both Lady Montaigne's daughters (even if she and Daddy've never bothered to get married), and that made her someone the ASL and the Ballroom felt they could trust.

"Anyway, Princess Ruth got Captain Oversteegen and the *Gauntlet* involved, and, along with some Solly Navy types who had their own axes to grind, got the transport to Congo, along with an assault force made up mainly out of the liberated slaves and some Ballroom 'terrorists' Daddy just happened to know how to find, which boarded Manpower's space station and captured it."

She shrugged, her face suddenly grim.

"Without the space station to back them up with orbital fire support, the Manpower goons and the slave overseers on the planet didn't stand a chance. It was . . . pretty ugly. Lots of atrocities and lots of payback. And it would've been a lot worse without Berry. She managed to put the brakes on the worst of the massacres, and along the way, somehow, and I still don't understand exactly how it all worked, she got drafted to be their Queen."

She shrugged again, this time helplessly, and raised her hands, palms uppermost. She really *didn't* understand how it had all worked, even though Berry had done her best to explain it in her letters. All she knew was that the brutalized waif she'd rescued from the subterranean labyrinths of Old Chicago had become the reigning monarch of the planet Torch and a kingdom full of liberated slaves fanatically devoted to the destruction of Manpower and all things Mesan. With an ex-Solarian Marine lieutenant as her military commander in chief, a princess of Manticore as her chief of intelligence, the local Havenite intelligence service's chief of station as her conduit to the Republic of Haven, and a precarious balance of support from both Manticore *and* the Republic which seemed to be standing up despite the resumption of hostilities. And, of course, her very own wormhole junction.

With termini whose locations none of her people, so far, knew the least thing about, since Manpower either hadn't explored them itself or had managed to destroy the data before it lost Congo.

She shook off the familiar thought with a grimace, and looked up to see five sets of eyes looking at her in various stages of bogglement.

"Anyway," she said again, "that's the simple version of it."

"Excuse me," d'Arezzo gave her one of his rare smiles, yet there was something in his eyes that she couldn't quite identify, "but if that's the simple version, I'm glad I missed the *complicated* one!"

"You and me both," Leo agreed, nodding emphatically.

Ragnhild only looked at Helen thoughtfully, but Aikawa leaned back and folded his arms.

"I know we all agreed not to try to drag any more out of you, so I'll just content myself with pointing out that your little explanation left quite a few loose ends floating around." She met his gaze with her best innocent expression, and he snorted. "Leaving aside any more questions about how the change in management was engineered, can you tell us if there's any truth to the rumors your sister's new planet has officially declared war on Manpower and Mesa?"

"Oh, sure. *That's* no secret," Helen replied. "What did you expect a planet inhabited almost exclusively by freed genetic slaves to do?"

"And they're using those frigates your father and mother—I mean, your father and Lady Montaigne—had built for the ASL for their fleet?" d'Arezzo asked, his expression intent.

"As the nucleus for it. At the same time, I understand they're negotiating with both us and the Peeps for heavier ships. Even 'obsolete' Allied designs are as good as anything Mesa or Manpower might have. And everyone on Torch figures it's only a matter of time until Manpower decides it's found a way to regain possession of Congo somehow. So building up a big enough fleet to discourage temptations is pretty high on the priority lists of 'Queen Berry's' senior advisers."

"I can see why it might be," Leo said dryly. "But, tell me, how does your dad think Mesa feels about the Star Kingdom's part in what happened to Congo?"

"He thinks Mesa's probably pissed off as hell," Helen said with a smile. "After all, Oversteegen and *Gauntlet* escorted the 'hijacked' Trojan horse to Congo in the first place. By now, they have to know Princess Ruth—the Queen's own niece—was involved in the entire thing up to her ears, too. Then there's the fact that it was Oversteegen who initially faced down the Mesan task group sent in to retake the system. Not to mention the fact that we've basically been at war with Manpower ourselves for the better part of four hundred T-years."

"And, like the Captain said," Leo murmured slowly, "the Cluster's only a couple of hundred light-years from Mesa."

"Exactly," d'Arezzo said. "We're one of the few Navies that actually enforce the Cherwell Convention like we mean it, and the Star Kingdom and Mesa have been locking horns for centuries now. Even when we were the better part of a thousand light-years apart."

"Damn straight." Ragnhild nodded. "Manpower's going to be pretty unhappy to suddenly find *us* with secure fleet bases that close to its home system. Which is why I think the Captain has a definite point about just how nasty things could turn. We've always had a tendency back home in the Star Kingdom to think of Manpower and Mesa as two separate entities—sort of like the Star Kingdom and the Hauptman Cartel, or Grayson and Sky Domes. But it doesn't really work that way. Manpower and a handful of other huge companies *own* Mesa, and Mesa has its own navy. Not too big compared to *our* Navy, maybe, but nothing to sneeze at, and equipped with modern Solly designs. Plus most of the companies headquartered there have at least some armed ships of their own. With us as distracted by Silesia and the front as we are, they'd almost have to be tempted to use that military capability in an effort to destabilize our annexation of the Cluster."

"And Frontier Security would be just absolutely *delighted* to help them do it," Leo agreed grimly.

"You know," Aikawa said thoughtfully, "this deployment may not turn out to be quite so boring as I figured it would."

Chapter Ten

"You there, Steve?"

Stephen Westman, of the Buffalo Valley Westmans, grimaced and shoved his hat back on his head. It was of a style which had once been called a "Stetson" on humanity's homeworld, and a decorative band of hammered silver and amethyst winked as he shook his head in exasperation. There was such a thing as operational security, but so far most of his people seemed to have trouble remembering that.

At least I managed to get my hands on commercial market Solly crypto software. The Manties can probably break it once they get here in force, but as long as we're only up against our own locally produced crap, we should be okay.

"Freedom Three, this is *Freedom One*," he said into his own com in a patiently pointed tone. "Yes, I'm here."

"Aw, hell, Ste—I mean, Freedom One." Jeff Hollister sounded sheepish. "Sorry 'bout that. I forgot."

"Forget about it . . . this time," Westman said. "What is it?"

"Those fellows you wanted us to keep an eye on? They're headed up the Schuyler. Looks like they figure to put down for the night somewhere around Big Rock Dome."

"They do, do they?" Westman pursed his lips thoughtfully. "Why, that's mighty interesting, Freedom Three."

"Thought you might think so." Hollister's tone was satisfied.

"Thanks for passing it along," Westman said. "I'll see you around."

"Later," Hollister agreed laconically, and cut the circuit.

Westman folded up his own com and shoved it back into his pocket while he considered the information.

He was a tallish man, a shade under a hundred and eighty-eight centimeters in height, with broad, powerful shoulders. He was also strikingly handsome, with sun-bleached blond hair, blue eyes, and a bronzed face first-generation prolong kept reasonably young, but which sixty-one T-years of experience, weather, and humor had etched with crow's-feet. At the moment that face wore a thoughtful expression.

Well, he mused, *it's about time I get this show on the road, if I'm really serious. And I am.*

He considered for a moment or two longer, standing in the dappled shade of the Terran aspens which had been introduced to Montana over three T-centuries before. He listened to the rustle of wind in the golden leaves and looked up, checking the sun's position out of automatic habit as deep as instinct. Then he nodded in decision, turned, and walked through what appeared to be a solid wall of stone into a large cavern.

Like the crypto software he'd purchased for his people's communicators, the holo generator which produced the illusion of solid stone was of Solarian manufacture. It galled Westman to use Solly technology, given the fact that the Solarian League and the never-to-be-sufficiently-damned Office of Frontier Security had been The Enemy much longer than the Manties. But he was a practical man, and he wasn't about to handicap himself or his followers by using anything but the best hardware available.

Besides, there's something . . . appropriate about using Solly equipment against another fucking bunch of carrioncat outsiders. And those bastards on Rembrandt are even worse. If that son of a bitch Van Dort thinks he's going to waltz Montana off and fuck us over again, he's in for a painful surprise.

"Luis!" he called as he walked deeper into the cavern. Much of it was natural, but he and his people had enlarged it considerably. The New Swan Range was lousy with iron ore, and enough of that still made the best natural concealment available. He didn't really like putting so many eggs in a single basket, even one this well hidden, but he hadn't had a lot of choice when he first decided to go underground—literally. Hopefully, if things went the way he planned, he'd be able to expand into an entire network of satellite bases that would lessen his vulnerability by spreading out his assets and his organization.

"Luis!" he called again, and this time, there was an answer.

"Yes, Boss?" Luis Palacios called back as he came clattering up the poured concrete steps from the lower level of caverns.

Palacios had been Westman's foreman—effectively, the field manager for a ranching and farming empire which had netted profits on the order of ninety million Solarian credits a year—just as he'd been for Westman's father. He was lean, dark, and almost a full centimeter taller even than Westman, and the left side of his face carried three deep scars as a legacy from one of Montana's near-cougars. He was also the one man on Montana—or, for that matter, in the entire Talbott Cluster—whom Westman trusted without reservation or qualification.

"Jeff Hollister just called in," Westman told him now. "Those Manty surveyors and that jackass Haven are headed up the Schuyler to Big Rock. What say you and I and some of the boys go extend a proper Montana welcome?"

"Why, I think that'd be right neighborly of us, Boss,"

Palacios said with a grin. "Just how warmly do you figure to welcome them?"

"Well, I don't see any reason to get carried away," Westman replied. "This'll be our first party, after all."

"Understood." Palacios nodded. "You want me to pick the boys?"

"Go ahead," Westman agreed. "Be sure to include at least three of the ones we're considering for cell leaders, though."

"No sweat, Boss. Bennington, Travers, and Ciraki are all on call."

"Good!" Westman smiled in approval. "Tell them I figure to drop in on our off-world guests tomorrow morning, but we've got a ways to go. So I want to move out within the next four or five hours."

Oscar Johansen checked his GPS display with a certain sense of satisfaction. He'd been pleased to discover that Montana at least had a comprehensive network of navigation satellites. He could have asked HMS *Ericsson* or *Volcano*—the support ships the RMN had stationed here—to provide him with the same data, but he really preferred working with the existing local infrastructure . . . whenever he could.

You never knew what you were going to find on a planet in the Verge. Some of them were little better than prespace Old Earth, while others were even further advanced than Grayson had been before it signed on to the Manticoran Alliance. Montana fell somewhere between the two extremes. It was too dirt-poor to afford a really solid tech base, but it had made innovative use of what it could afford. Its navigation satellites were a case in point. They were at least a couple of centuries out of date by Manticoran standards, but they did the job just fine. And they also pulled double duty as weather satellites, air traffic control radar arrays, law enforcement surveillance platforms, *and* traffic control points for any freighters which called here.

And there's no reason why the place has *to be so*

poor, he thought as he tagged the GPS coordinates to the electronic map in his memo board. *The beef they raise here would command top prices back home, and with the Lynx Terminus, they can ship it fresh direct to Beowulf or even Old Earth.* He shook his head, thinking of the astronomical prices Montanan beef or nearbuffalo could bring on the mother world. *And there are dozens of other opportunities for anyone with just a little bit of startup capital.*

Which, after all, was the reason Johansen was here. The Alexander Government had made it clear that Her Majesty had no intention of allowing her new subjects in Talbott to be turfed out of the development of their own star systems by sharp Manticoran operators. The government had announced it would carry out its own surveys of the Cluster, in conjunction with local governments, to confirm all existing titles of ownership. Those titles would be fully protected, and to ensure local participation in any development projects, the Chancellor of the Exchequer had announced that, for its first ten T-years of operation, any new startup endeavor in the Cluster would enjoy a reduction in taxation equal to the percentage of ownership held by citizens of the Cluster. After ten T-years, the tax break would reduce by five percent per T-year for another ten T-years, then terminate completely in the twenty-first T-year. Given where the Star Kingdom's wartime tax rates stood, that provision alone was guaranteed to ensure the massive representation of local interests.

Johansen looked up at the sun blazing in a wash of crimson and gold coals on the western horizon. Montana's primary—also called Montana—was a bit cooler than Manticore-A. And Montana was almost one full light-minute farther from its primary than the capital planet of the Star Kingdom was from Manticore-A, too. With evening coming on rapidly, that coolness was especially noticeable, and he looked over to where the expedition was pitching its tents for the night. They were going up with the efficiency of well-organized practice, and his eyes strayed to the rippling, steel-colored sheet of water rushing over the rocks and gravel of the Schuyler River. Local trees, interspersed with Terran oak and aspen, grew right down to the riverbank, casting their shadows over the crystal-clear water, and temptation stirred. There had to be some deep pools out there, he thought, and he'd already encountered the planet's nearbass.

It's usually a good idea to maintain a certain separation between the chief and his Indians, he thought with a lurking smile, *so I probably shouldn't disturb them now that they've gotten into the swing of things over there. And if I get busy fast enough, I might even hook enough fish to give us a little variety for dinner. Even if I don't, I can always* claim *that was what I was trying to do!*

He headed for his personal air car and his tackle box.

The sun rose slowly over the eastern rampart of the Schuyler River Valley. Light frost glittered on the higher slopes to the north, and long fingers of shadow—crisp and cool in the mountain morning—reached out across the sleeping surveyors' camp.

Stephen Westman watched the sun edging higher, then checked his chrono. It was time, and he rose from his seat on the fallen tree trunk, lifted his pulse rifle from where it had leaned against the trunk beside him, and started down the slope.

Oscar Johansen rolled over and stretched luxuriantly. His wife had always been perplexed by the way his sleeping habits flip-flopped whenever he was in the field. At home, he was a night owl, staying up until all hours and sleeping as late as he could get away with. But in the field, he loved the early hours of sunrise. There was something special, almost holy, about those still, clear, crystalline minutes while sunlight flowed slowly, slowly back into a world. Every planet habitable by man had its analogues of birds, and Johansen had never yet been on a world where one of them hadn't greeted the dawn.

The songs or calls might vary wildly, but there was always that first, single note in the orchestra. That moment when the first singer roused, tested its voice, and then sounded the flourish that formalized the ending of night and the beginning of yet another day.

His Manticoran-manufactured tent's smart fabric had maintained his preferred overnight temperature of twenty degrees—sixty-eight degrees on the ancient Fahrenheit scale Montana's original, deliberately archaic settlers had brought with them—and he picked up the remote. He tapped in the command, and the eastern side of the tent obediently transformed itself into a one-way window. He lay there on the comfortable memory-plastic cot, enjoying the warmth of his bedroll, and watched the morning shadows and the misty tendrils of vapor hovering above the river, as if the water were breathing.

He was still admiring the sunrise when, suddenly, the fly of his tent flew open. He shot upright in his cot, more in surprise than anything else, then froze as he found himself staring into the business end of a pulse rifle.

"Morning, friend," the weathered-looking man behind the rifle said pleasantly. "I expect you're a mite surprised to see me."

"God*damn* it, Steve!"

Les Haven sounded more irritated than anything else, Johansen decided. The Land Registry Office inspector obviously knew the tall, blond-haired leader of the thirty or forty armed, masked men who'd invaded their encampment. The Manticoran wondered whether that was a good sign, or a bad one.

"Looks like you've fallen into bad company, Les," the leader replied. He jerked his head at Johansen. "You procuring for off-world pimps these days?"

"Steve Westman, if you had the sense God gave a neoturkey, you'd know this was just goddamn silliness!" Johansen decided he would have been happier if Haven had been just a *bit* less emphatic. But the Montanan had the bit well and truly between his teeth. "Damn it,

Steve—we voted in favor of annexation by over seventy-two percent. *Seventy-two percent*, Steve! Are you gonna tell that many of your neighbors they're idiots?"

"Reckon I am, if they are," the blond-haired man agreed amiably enough. He and four of his men were holding the survey party at gunpoint while the rest of his followers busily took down the tents and loaded them into the surveyors' vehicles.

"And they are," Westman added. "Idiots, I mean," he explained helpfully when Haven glared at him.

"Well, you had your chance to convince them you were right during the vote, and you didn't, did you?"

"Reckon not. 'Course, this whole planet's always been pretty stubborn, hasn't it?" Westman grinned, the skin crinkling around his blue eyes, and despite himself, Johansen felt the man's sheer presence.

"Yes, it has," Haven agreed. "And you're about to get seventy-two percent of the people on it mighty riled up!"

"Done it before," Westman said with a shrug, and the Land Registry Office inspector exhaled noisily. His shoulders seemed to slump, and he shook his head almost sadly.

"Steve, I know you've never trusted Van Dort or his Trade Union people any more than you've trusted those Frontier Security bastards. And I know you're convinced Manticore's no better than Mesa. But I'm here to tell you that you are out of your ever-loving mind. There's a whole *universe* of difference between what the Star Kingdom's offering us and what Frontier Security would do to us."

"Sure there is . . . until they've got their claws into us." Westman shook his head. "Van Dort's already got his fangs in deep enough, Les. He's not opening the door for another bunch of bloodsuckers if I have anything to say about it. The only way we're going to stay masters of our own house is to kick every damned outsider out of it. If the rest of the Cluster wants to stick its head into the noose, that's fine with me. More power to them.

But nobody's handing *my* planet over to anybody but the people who live here. And if the other folks on Montana are too stubborn, or too blind, to see what they're doing to themselves, then I guess I'll just have to get along without them."

"The Westmans have been respected on this planet ever since Landfall," Haven said more quietly. "And even the folks who didn't agree with you during the annexation debate, they still respected you, Steve. But if you push this, that's going to change. The First Families've always carried a lot of weight, but you know we've never been the kind to roll over and play dead just because the big ranchers told us to. The folks who voted in favor of annexation aren't going to take it very kindly when you try to tell them they don't have the right to decide for themselves what they want to do."

"Well, you see, Les, that's the problem," Westman said. "It's not so much I want to tell them they don't have the right to decide for themselves. It's just that I don't figure they've got the right to decide for *me*. This planet, and this star system, have a Constitution. And, you know, I just finished rereading it last night, and there's not a single word in it about anybody having the legal right—or power—to sell off our sovereignty."

"Nobody's violating the Constitution," Haven said stiffly. "That's why the annexation vote was handled the way it was. You know as well as I do that the Constitution *does* provide for constitutional conventions with the right to amend the Constitution any way they choose, and that's exactly what the annexation vote was. A convention, called exactly the way the Constitution required, exercising the powers the Constitution granted to its delegates."

"'Amend' isn't the same thing as 'throw in the trash,'" Westman retorted. It was obvious he felt strongly, Johansen decided, but he was still calm and collected. However deeply his emotions might be engaged, he wasn't allowing that to drive him into a rage.

For which Oscar Johansen was devoutly grateful.

"Steve—" Haven began again, but Westman shook his head.

"Les, we're not going to agree on this," he said patiently. "It may be you're right. I don't think so, you understand, but I suppose it's possible. But whether you are or not, I've already decided where I stand, and how far I'm ready to go. And, I've got to tell you, Les, that I don't think you're going to much like what it is I have in mind. So I'd like to take this opportunity to apologize, right up front, for the indignity I'm about to inflict."

Haven's expression became suddenly much more wary, and Westman gave him an almost mischievous smile. Then he turned his attention to Mary Seavers and Aoriana Constantin, the two female members of Johansen's ten-person survey team.

"Ladies," he said, "somehow I hadn't quite figured on there being any women along this morning. And while I realize we here on Montana are a mite backward, compared to someplace like Manticore, it just goes against the grain with me to show disrespect for a lady. So if the two of you would just sort of move over there to the left?"

Seavers and Constantin gave Johansen an anxious look, but he only nodded, never taking his eyes from Westman. The two women obeyed the order, and Westman smiled at Johansen.

"Thank you, Mr. . . . Johansen, isn't it?"

Johansen nodded again.

"Well, Mr. Johansen, I hope you haven't taken my somewhat strongly expressed opinion of your Star Kingdom personally. For all I know, you're a perfectly fine fellow, and I'm going to assume that's the case. However, I think it's important for me to get my message across to your superiors, and to Les' bosses, as well.

"Now, this morning's in the nature of a warmup exercise. Sort of a demonstration of capabilities, you might say. And because that's all it is, I'd just as soon no one get hurt. I trust that meets with your approval?"

"I think you can safely assume it does," Johansen told him when he paused.

"Good." Westman beamed at him, but then the Montanan's smile faded. "At the same time," he continued, his voice flatter, "if it comes to it, it's possible a whole lot of people're going to get hurt before this is over. I want you to tell your superiors that. This one is a free—well, *almost* free—warning. I'm not going to be issuing very many more of them. So tell your superiors that, too."

"I'll tell them exactly what you've said," Johansen assured him when he paused expectantly once more.

"Good," Westman repeated. "And now, Mr. Johansen, if you and all your men—and you, too, Alvin—would be so good as to strip to your skivvies."

"I beg your pardon?" Johansen looked at the Montanan, startled into asking the question, and Westman gave him an oddly sympathetic smile.

"I said that I'd appreciate it if you'd strip to your underwear," he said, then nodded towards the two women. "A true Montana gentlemen would never inflict that indignity upon a lady, which is why *these* two ladies have been excused. You gentlemen, however, are another case."

He smiled pleasantly, but there was absolutely no give in his expression, and his henchmen were obviously ready to enforce his demand if it proved necessary.

Johansen looked at him for another few moments, then turned to his subordinates.

"You heard the man," he said resignedly. "I don't think we have much choice, so we might as well get started."

Johansen's survey crew, aside from the two women, and all of their local colleagues stood barefoot in their briefs and watched their vehicles and all of their equipment heading off deeper into the mountains. Westman and two of his men waited beside the final air car. The leader watched the last of his other men depart, then turned back to his prisoners.

"Now," he said, "Les here knows the way to Bridgeman's

Crossing. You gentlemen just head off that way. I'll be sending a message to your boss, Les, telling him you're coming, but it may take me a few hours to get it to him without giving him any hints about where to find us."

"Steve," Haven said very quietly and seriously, "you've made your statement. God only knows how much trouble you've gotten yourself into already. But we've known each other a long time, and I like to think we've been friends. And because we have, I'm telling you now. Give this up. Give it up before someone does get hurt."

"Can't do it, Les," Westman said with genuine regret. "And you'd best be remembering what I've said. We have been friends, and it would grieve me to shoot a friend. But if you keep helping these people steal my planet, I'll do it. You know I mean what I say, so I'd suggest you convince President Suttles that I do. I expect Trevor Bannister knows it already, but from what I've seen, keen intelligence isn't exactly Suttles' strong suit, so Trevor may need a mite of help getting through to him. And, Mr. Johansen, I'd suggest you convince your Baroness Medusa of the same thing."

He held their eyes a few more moments, and then he and his last followers climbed into the air car and it lifted off into the cool morning.

"I don't like what I'm hearing. I don't like it at all," Henri Krietzmann said harshly.

His tone and expression contrasted strongly with the deliciously cool breeze blowing across the penthouse terrace. The primary component of the distant binary system known as Spindle was a G0 star, but the planet Flax was thirteen light-minutes from it, and it was spring in the planet's northern hemisphere. Spectacular thunderheads—blinding white on top and ominous black across their anvil bottoms—drifted steadily in from the west across the Humboldt Ocean, but it would be hours before they arrived. For the moment, the three men on the terrace could enjoy the brilliant spring sunshine and the windborne perfume of spring blossoms from the terrace's bounteous planter boxes as they gazed out over the capital city of Thimble on the west coast of the improbably named continent of Gossypium.

It was a beautiful city, especially for a planet in the Verge. Its buildings were low, close to the ground, without the mountainous towers of modern counter-grav cities. That was because when most of Thimble was being built, the people doing the building hadn't *had* counter-grav. But if they'd been limited to primitive technologies, they'd obviously taken great pains when they designed their new capital. The huge central square, built around a lovingly landscaped park of flowering green and intricate water features, was clearly visible from the penthouse terrace. So were the main avenues, radiating out from the square like the spokes of a vast wheel. Most of the city buildings were constructed of native stone, a blue granite that glittered when the sun struck it, and more water features and green spaces had been carefully integrated into the city plan.

It wasn't until one got beyond the center of the city on the landward side, away from the ocean, that one began to encounter the ugly, crowded slums which were the legacy of poverty in almost any of the Verge systems.

"None of us particularly likes it, Henri," Bernardus Van Dort said mildly. Van Dort was fair-haired and blue-eyed. He stood well over a hundred and ninety-five centimeters in height, and he sat with the confidence of a man who was accustomed to succeeding. "But we can hardly pretend it was unexpected, now can we?"

"Of course it wasn't unexpected," the third man, Joachim Alquezar, put in, his lips twisting wryly. "After all, stupidity's endemic to the human condition."

Although very few people would ever have described Van Dort as short, Alquezar made him look that way. The red-haired native of the planet San Miguel was two hundred and three centimeters tall. San Miguel's gravity—only eighty-four percent of Terran Standard—tended to produce tall, slender people, and Alquezar was no exception.

"'Stupidity' isn't really fair, Joachim," Van Dort reproved. "Ignorant, yes. Unaccustomed to thinking, yes, again. And prone to react emotionally, certainly. But that isn't the same thing as irredeemably stupid."

"Forgive me, Bernardus, if I fail to discern a practical difference." Alquezar leaned back, cradling a snifter of brandy in his right hand and waving a cigar gently with his left. "The consequences are identical."

"The *short term* consequences are identical," Van Dort replied. "But while there's not a great deal that can be done about genuine stupidity, ignorance can be educated, and the habit of thought can be acquired."

"It always amazes me," Alquezar said with the smile of an old friend rehashing a familiar argument, "that a hardheaded, hard-hearted, money-gouging Rembrandt capitalist can be so revoltingly *liberal* in his view of humanity."

"Oh?" Van Dort's blue eyes glinted as he smiled back. "I happen to know that 'liberal' only became a dirty word for you after Tonkovic pinched it for herself."

"Thereby confirming my lifelong suspicion—previously unvoiced, perhaps, but deep seated—that anyone who actually *believes* someone who claims to be a liberal suffers from terminal softheadedness."

"I hope the two of you are enjoying yourselves." Krietzmann's tone hovered just short of biting. At thirty-six T-years, he was the youngest man present. He was also the shortest, at a brown-haired, gray-eyed, solidly muscled hundred and seventy centimeters. But despite the fact that he was twenty T-years younger than Alquezar, and over forty younger than Van Dort, he looked older than either of them, for he was a citizen of Dresden.

"We're not enjoying ourselves, Henri," Van Dort said, after a very brief pause. "And we're not taking the situation lightly. But I think it's important to remember that people who disagree with us aren't necessarily monsters of depravity."

"Treason's close enough to depravity for me," Krietzmann said grimly.

"Actually," Alquezar said, looking steadily at Krietzmann while the breeze ruffled the fringe of the umbrella over their table and sent the Spindle System flag atop the hotel popping and snapping, "I think it would be wiser if you didn't use words like 'treason' even with Bernardus and me, Henri."

"Why not?" Krietzmann shot back. "I believe in calling things by their proper names. Eighty percent of the Cluster's total population voted to join the Star Kingdom. To my mind, that makes anyone who's prepared to resort to extralegal means of resisting the annexation guilty of treason."

Alquezar winced ever so slightly, and shook his head.

"I won't disagree with you, although I imagine the point could be argued either way, at least until we get a Constitution adopted that establishes exactly what is and is not legal on a Cluster-wide basis. But however accurate the term may be, there are certain political drawbacks to using it. One which springs immediately to mind is that throwing around terms like 'treason' and 'traitor' will actually help your opponents polarize public opinion."

Krietzmann glared, and Van Dort leaned forward to lay a hand on the younger man's forearm.

"Joachim is right, Henri," he said gently. "The people you're describing would love to provoke you into something—anything—they and their supporters can characterize as extremism."

Krietzmann glowered some more, then inhaled deeply and gave a choppy nod. His shoulders relaxed ever so slightly, and he reached for his own glass—not a brandy snifter like Alquezar's or a wineglass like Van Dort's, but a tall, moisture-beaded tankard of beer. He drank deeply, then lowered his glass.

"All right," he half-growled. "Point taken. And I'll try to sit on myself in public. But," his eyes flashed, "that doesn't change the way I feel about these bastards in private."

"I don't think anyone would expect it to," Van Dort murmured.

Not if they have any sense at all, at any rate, he thought. *Expect emotional detachment out of* Henri Krietzmann *on an issue like this? Ridiculous!*

He felt a familiar twinge of guilt at the thought. Dresden was ruinously poor, even for the Verge. Unlike his own Rembrandt, or Alquezar's San Miguel, which had managed to pull themselves up by their bootstraps to become fabulously wealthy—by Verge standards—Dresden's economy had never risen above the marginal level. The vast majority of Dresden's citizens, even today, were ill-educated, little more than unskilled labor, and modern industry had little use for the unskilled. The Dresden System's poverty had been so crushing for so long that only the most decrepit (or disreputable) of tramp freighters had called there, and no outside system—*including Rembrandt*, he admitted bleakly—had ever been attracted to invest there.

Which was why Dresden's medical capabilities had been as limited as its industrial capacity. Which was why Henri Krietzmann had seen his father and his mother die before they were sixty T-years old. Why two of his three siblings had died in early childhood. Why he himself was missing two fingers on his mangled left hand, the legacy of an industrial accident in an old-fashioned foundry on a planet without regen. And why Krietzmann had never received even the cheapest, simplest first-generation prolong therapies and could expect no more than another sixty to seventy years of life.

That was what fueled Henri Krietzmann's hatred of those attempting to derail the Constitutional Convention. It was what had driven him to educate himself, to claw his way out of the slums of the city of Oldenburg and into the rough and tumble of Dresden politics. The fire in his belly was his blinding hatred of the Solarian League, and of the Office of Frontier Security's pious platitudes about "uplifting the unfortunately retrograde" planets of the Verge. If OFS, or any of the Solly lobbying groups who claimed to be so concerned about the worlds it engulfed, had really cared, they could have brought modern medicine to Dresden over a century ago. For a fraction of what Frontier Security spent on its public relations budget in the Sol System alone, they could have provided Dresden with the sort of education system which would have permitted it to build up its *own* industrial and medical base.

Over the last twenty T-years, largely as a result of the efforts of men and women like Henri Krietzmann, that had begun to change. They had scratched and clawed their own way up out of the most abject poverty imaginable to an economy that was merely poor, no longer destitute. One which was finally beginning to provide something approaching decent health care—or something much closer to it—to its citizens. One whose school systems had managed, at ruinous expense, to import off-world teachers. One which had seen the possibilities for its own development when the Trade Union came calling and, instead of resisting "exploitation" by Rembrandt and its allies, had actually looked for ways to use it for its own advantage.

It had been a hard, bloody fight, and it had instilled a fiercely combative, fiercely independent spirit in the citizens of Dresden, matched with boundless contempt for the parasitic oligarchs of star systems like Split.

Oh, no. *Detachment* was not a quality much to be found in Dresden.

"Well," Alquezar's deliberately light tone told Van Dort his old friend had followed—and shared—his own reflections, "however Henri wants to describe them amongst ourselves, we still need to decide what to do about them."

"That's true enough," Van Dort agreed. "Although, I caution all of us—myself included—yet again that we must avoid creating an undue impression of collusion between us. More especially, between you and me, Joachim, and Henri."

"Oh, give it a break, Bernardus!" Krietzmann's grim expression was transfigured by a sudden grin, and he snorted a genuine laugh. "Every voter in the Cluster knows you and your Trade Union set up the annexation effort in the first part, unscrupulous and devious money grubbers that you are. Yes, and funded it, too! And I was the politician who led the effort on Dresden. And Joachim here is the head of the Constitutional Union Party—and just happens to be the senior Convention delegate from San Miguel, which just *happens* to be another member of the Trade Union . . . of which, he also *happens* to be a major shareholder. So just who, with the IQ of a *felsenlarve*, is going to believe we aren't in collusion *whatever* we do?"

"You're probably correct," Van Dort conceded with a slight smile of his own, "but there are still proprieties to observe. Particularly since you're currently the President of the Convention. It's perfectly reasonable and proper for you to consult with political leaders and backers, and you campaigned openly enough for the President's job on the basis of your determination to drive the annexation through. But it's still important to avoid the impression that we 'unscrupulous and devious money grubbers' have you in our vest pocket. If you're going to work effectively with *all* of the delegates to the Convention, that is."

"Probably something to that," Krietzmann agreed. "Still, I don't think someone like Tonkovic cherishes any illusions that I nurture warm and fuzzy feelings where she's concerned."

"Of course you don't," Alquezar agreed. "But let me be the one to lock horns with her openly. You need to remain above the fray. Practice polishing your disinterested statesman's halo and leave the down and dirty work to me." He grinned nastily. "Trust me, I'll be the one having all the fun."

"I'll avoid having myself tattooed into your lodge, Joachim," Krietzmann said. "But I'm not going to pretend I like Tonkovic."

"Actually, you know, Aleksandra isn't all *that* bad," Van Dort said mildly. The other two looked at him with varying degrees of incredulity, and he shrugged. "I don't say

I like her—because I don't—but I worked quite closely with her during the annexation vote campaign, and at least she's less slimy than Yvernau and his friends on New Tuscany. The woman's at least as ambitious as any politician I've ever known, and she and her political allies are as self-centered and greedy as anyone I've ever met, but she worked very effectively to support the plebiscite. She wants a degree of local autonomy she's never going to get, but I don't believe she has any intention of risking the chance that the annexation might actually fail."

"Whatever her intentions, she's fiddling while the house burns down," Krietzmann said bluntly.

"Not to mention encouraging the kind of resistance movements we're all worried about," Alquezar added.

Van Dort considered pointing out that Alquezar's own CUP's agenda probably did some encouraging—or at least provoking—of its own, but decided against it. There was no real point. Besides, Joachim understood that perfectly well, whether he chose to say so or not.

"Well, that's really neither here nor there right this moment," he said instead. "The real question is how we respond to the emergence of organized 'resistance movements.'"

"The best solution would be to drive the Convention through to a conclusion before they have the opportunity to really get their feet under them," Krietzmann said, and both his guests nodded in agreement. "That's why I'm so pissed off at Tonkovic," the Convention President continued. "She knows perfectly well that she's not going to get anywhere close to everything she's asking for, but she's perfectly content to string out the negotiating process as long as possible. The longer she can tie us up, the more concessions she can expect to extort out of us as her price for finally bringing a draft Constitution to a vote."

"She'd probably say the same about me," Alquezar pointed out.

"She *has* said it," Krietzmann snorted. "But the real difference between the two of you, Joachim, is that she sees the indefinite delay of a finalized Constitution as a completely legitimate tactic. She's so focused on securing her own platform to protect her own position in Split that she's ignoring the very real possibility that she could delay the Convention long enough for the entire effort to come unglued."

"She doesn't believe that will ever happen," Van Dort said. "She doesn't believe Manticore would permit it to."

"Then she needs to listen to what Baroness Medusa is saying," Krietzmann said grimly. "She's made herself plain enough to anyone who *will* listen. Queen Elizabeth and Prime Minister Alexander aren't about to force anyone to accept Manticoran sovereignty. Not here in the Cluster, at any rate. We're too close to the League for them to risk incidents with OFS or the SLN unless the local citizenry's support for the Star Kingdom is *solid*. And they don't really *need* any of us just to hang onto the Lynx Terminus. In fact, we actually complicate the equation, in a lot of ways. To put it bluntly, we're much too secondary to the Star Kingdom's survival needs at the moment for them to start pouring starships and Marines down a rat hole to suppress resistance to an involuntary conquest."

"Surely neither the Queen nor the Governor sees this as some sort of conquest!" Van Dort protested.

"No . . . not yet," Krietzmann agreed. "But until we decide the constitutional basis for our formal annexation and send it to Parliament for ratification, there's really nothing Alexander or even the Queen can do. And the longer we spend arguing about it, and the wider we allow our own internal divisions to become, the longer the delay in getting the damned thing drafted in the first place. And if the delay stretches out long enough, or if enough brainless wonders embrace the 'armed struggle' people like that lunatic Nordbrandt are calling for, then what looked like the smooth assimilation of eager new citizens starts to look like the forcible conquest of desperately resisting patriots. Which, I hardly need point out to you two, is exactly how OFS is already trying to spin this for the Solly media."

"Damn." Even that mild obscenity was unusual for Van Dort, and he shook his head. "Have you discussed this with Aleksandra?"

"I've tried to." Krietzmann shrugged. "She didn't seem impressed by my logic. Of course, I have to admit I'm a politician from a pretty bare-knuckled school, not a polished, cultured diplomat, and she and I have never liked each other a lot, anyway."

"What about you, Joachim?" Van Dort looked at his friend, and it was Alquezar's turn to shrug.

"If it's escaped your notice, Bernardus, Tonkovic and I aren't on speaking terms at the moment. If I say the sky is blue, she's going to insist it's chartreuse. And," he admitted grudgingly, after a moment, "*vice versa*, I suppose. It's called polarization."

Van Dort frowned down into his wineglass. He'd tried to stand as far in the background as he could once the Convention actually convened. There'd been no way he could do that during the annexation vote campaign, but he was well aware that his very visibility had helped to produce what resistance to the vote there'd been. The Rembrandt Trade Union consisted of the systems of Rembrandt, San Miguel, Redoubt, and Prairie, and the RTU had made plenty of enemies in the Cluster. In Van Dort's opinion, much of that enmity had resulted from envy, but he was honest enough to recognize that many of the Cluster's other worlds had more than a little justification for feeling that the RTU had used its economic clout to extort unfair concessions.

Quite a lot of justification, actually, he thought. *And I suppose that's my fault, too.*

However necessary it might have been to expand the Trade Union's reach and wealth, the legacy of distrust and hostility its tactics had aroused still lingered. People like Stephen Westman, on Montana, had made opposition to the "continued economic exploitation" of their worlds by Rembrandt and its Trade Union partners a keystone of their opposition to the annexation vote. Of course, Westman had his own, very personal reasons for hating anything Van Dort was associated with, but there was no doubt that a very large number of his fellow Montanans—and of the citizens of other planets in the Cluster—resented the RTU enormously, whatever they thought of the annexation itself. Which was why Van Dort had very deliberately stepped back from public participation in the Convention's actual deliberations here in Spindle. But now . . .

He sighed. "I suppose I'd better talk to her." Krietzmann and Alquezar both looked at him with "Well, at *last*!" expressions, and he grimaced. "I've still got a few markers with her," he conceded, "and so far, at least, we haven't developed the sort of antagonism you and she have, Joachim. But don't expect any miracles. Once she's got an idea or strategy into her head, knocking it back out again is all but impossible."

"Tell me about it!" Alquezar snorted. "But you've still got a better shot at it than I do."

"I suppose," Van Dort said glumly. "I suppose."

Chapter Eleven

"Welcome to Talbott Station, Captain Terekhov. Commander FitzGerald."

"Thank you, Admiral," Terekhov replied for them both as he shook the rear admiral's offered hand.

Rear Admiral of the Green Augustus Khumalo was three centimeters shorter than Terekhov, with a very dark complexion, dark eyes, and thinning dark hair. He was broad shouldered, with big, strong hands and a powerful chest, although he was becoming a bit on the portly side these days. He was also distantly related to the Queen, and there was something of the Winton look around his nose and chin.

"I sometimes think the Admiralty's forgotten where they put us," Khumalo went on, smiling broadly. "That's one reason I'm so glad to see you. Every time they slip up and send us a modern ship, it's a sign they remember."

He chuckled, and the captain responded with a polite smile. Khumalo waved him and FitzGerald into chairs, then gestured at the slender, strong-nosed junior-grade captain who'd been waiting with him when Terekhov and FitzGerald were shown into his day cabin.

"My chief of staff, Captain Loretta Shoupe," the station commander said.

"Captain," Terekhov acknowledged, with a courteous nod. FitzGerald nodded in turn, and the chief of staff smiled. Then Khumalo settled his own bulk into the comfortable chair behind his desk, facing Terekhov and FitzGerald across a deep-pile rug. Khumalo's flagship was HMS *Hercules*, an old *Samothrace*-class superdreadnought. Her impressive size was reflected in the spaciousness of her flag officer's quarters, but she was sadly obsolete. How she'd managed to avoid the breaker's yard this long was more than Terekhov would have been prepared to say, although if he'd had to guess, he would have bet she'd spent most of her lengthy career as a flagship assigned to minor fleet stations like this one. Certainly the fact that she was the only ship of the wall assigned to Talbott Station, and that she had to be almost as old as Terekhov himself was, said volumes about the force levels the Admiralty was prepared to assign to Talbott.

But old or not, she was still a ship of the wall, and he'd never seen a more luxuriously furnished cabin. Terekhov himself was more than modestly affluent, and Sinead had hammered at least a modicum of an appreciation for the finer things through his skull. But the vastness of Khumalo's personal wealth was obvious in the hand-loomed carpets, the holo tapestries, the nicknacks and crystal in the display cabinets, the antique trophy weapons on the bulkheads, and the rich, hand-rubbed patina of bookcases, coffee tables, and chairs. The portrait of Queen Elizabeth III on one bulkhead gazed out at the display of wealth with what seemed to be a slightly disapproving air, despite her smile.

"Obviously, your arrival is more than welcome, Captain," the Rear Admiral continued, "as is your news from home. I've already reviewed the dispatches the Admiralty sent out aboard *Hexapuma*. It sounds as if the situation at the front is stabilizing, at least."

"To some extent, Sir," Terekhov agreed. "Of course, I don't believe anyone's really too surprised. We took it on the chin in the opening engagements, but the Havenites got badly chewed up in Silesia themselves. And it doesn't look as if they had quite as many of the pod designs in commission when they pulled the trigger as ONI's worst-case estimates assumed. I doubt they expected the Andies to come in on our side, either, or that the Andies had developed pod designs of their own. So they've probably had some serious strategic rethinking to do. And the fact that they know they're up against Earl White Haven at the Admiralty, and that Admiral Caparelli is back as First Space Lord, with Duchess Harrington in command of the new Eighth Fleet, may be playing a small part in their thinking, too."

"No doubt." Khumalo's agreement was prompt but little more than polite, and a small flicker of distaste seemed to touch his eyes.

Terekhov gave no sign he'd noticed either of those things, but Ansten FitzGerald certainly saw them. *Hexapuma*'s executive officer added the rear admiral's lack of enthusiasm to rumors he'd heard about Khumalo's political connections to the Conservative Association and concealed a mental grimace of his own.

"More likely," Khumalo continued, "the Peeps are delaying further active operations while they digest the technological windfall they acquired when the damned Erewhonese turned their coats!"

"I'm sure that's playing a part," Terekhov agreed with no discernible expression at all.

"As I say," the rear admiral said after a moment, "I've viewed the dispatches. I haven't had time to digest the intelligence summaries, yet, of course. And it's been my experience that even the best recorded summaries aren't as informative as a first-hand briefing. May I assume you received such a briefing before being sent out, Captain?"

"I did, Sir," Terekhov replied.

"Then I'd appreciate it if you would share your impressions with Captain Shoupe and myself." Khumalo smiled tightly. "Never a bad idea to know what the current Admiralty *thinks* is going on in your command area, is it?"

"Of course not, Sir," Terekhov agreed. He sat back a bit further in his chair and crossed his legs. "Well, Admiral, to begin with, Admiral Givens made it clear our intelligence assets here in Talbott are still at a very early stage of development. Given that, she emphasized the need for all of Her Majesty's ships in Talbott to pursue the closest possible relations with the local authorities. In addition—"

The captain continued in the same competent, slightly detached voice FitzGerald had heard so often over the past month and a half as he quickly and concisely summarized several days of intelligence briefings. FitzGerald was impressed by both his memory and the easy skill with which he organized the relevant information. But even as the executive officer listened to his captain's voice, he was conscious of Khumalo's expression. The rear admiral was listening intently, yet it seemed to FitzGerald that he wasn't hearing what he'd wanted to.

"—so that's about the size of it, Admiral," Terekhov finished, the better part of forty minutes later. "Basically, ONI anticipates a gradual, inevitable backlash against the annexation from those who voted against it and lost. Whether that backlash will remain peaceful or express itself in acts of frustrated violence is, of course, impossible to predict at this point. But there's some concern about who might decide to go fishing here, if the waters get sufficiently troubled. And Admiral Givens stressed the importance of ensuring the Lynx Terminus' security."

FitzGerald's mental antenna tingled suddenly at the ever so slight change of emphasis in his captain's last sentence. He saw Captain Shoupe's eyebrows lower almost warningly, and Khumalo's face seemed to tighten.

"I'm sure she did." His tone hovered on the edge of petulance. "Of course, if the current Admiralty were prepared to deploy sufficient hulls to Talbott, I'd be in a far better position to do that, wouldn't I?"

Terekhov said nothing, only gazed calmly back at the

rear admiral, and Khumalo snorted. His mouth twitched in a smile of sorts, and he shook his head.

"I know. I know, Captain!" he said wryly. "Every station commander in history has wanted more ships than he actually got."

He sounded, FitzGerald thought, as if he regretted letting out that flash of resentment. Almost as if he thought he had to somehow placate Terekhov, which was an odd attitude for a senior rear admiral to adopt in conversation with a mere captain.

"But the truth is," Khumalo continued, "that in this instance, our low position on the current Admiralty's priority list means we genuinely don't have sufficient strength to be everywhere we need to be. It's the next best thing to two hundred and fifty light-years from Lynx to the Scarlet System, and the entire Cluster represents five and a half million cubic light-years—it's flattened quite a bit, not a true spherical volume, or it would be even bigger. That's almost nine times the volume of the *entire* Silesian Confederacy, but Admiral Sarnow has twelve times as many ships as we do, even though he's in a position to call on the Andermani for additional support in an emergency. And, I might add, he doesn't have a junction terminus to worry about."

He shrugged.

"I realize our available forces have to be prioritized, and that Silesia, especially in light of our alliance with the Andermani, has to have priority. For that matter, Silesia has several times the population—and industry—the Cluster does, despite its smaller volume. But however good the current Admiralty's reasons for the force levels they've assigned may be, I'm simply spread too thin to cover our area of responsibility in anything like the depth real security would require."

That's the fourth or fifth time he's referred to "the current Admiralty," FitzGerald thought. *I'm not too sure I like the sound of that. Especially not from someone whose political connections were so close to the High Ridge crowd.*

"I realized as soon as I read my orders that our forces were going to be spread unacceptably thin, Sir," Terekhov said calmly. "I don't think anyone back home likes the force level assigned to Talbott, and it was my impression—not simply from Admiral Givens' briefings, but from every other indication, as well—that the Admiralty is only too well aware of the difficulties you're facing out here."

"Hmph!" Khumalo snorted. "Be nice if that were true, Captain! But whether it is or not, I've still had to make some decisions—difficult decisions—about where to employ the units I do have under command. Which is why the Lynx picket is as understrength as you undoubtedly noticed when you passed through. That's the one spot in our entire command area where we can count on rapid reinforcement from the home system if it hits the fan."

"I can see the logic, Sir," Terekhov said. Which was not, FitzGerald observed, the same thing as saying he *agreed* with it.

"Yes, well," Khumalo said, sorting through a pile of document chips on his desk, as if looking for something for his hands to do. After a moment, he restacked them neatly and looked back up at his guests.

"Thank you for the briefing, Captain Terekhov," he said. "I appreciate its thoroughness, and both your ship and your proven capabilities will be welcome, most welcome, here in Talbott. I'm afraid I'll be working you and your people hard, but I have every confidence in your ability to meet any challenge which might arise."

"Thank you, Sir," Terekhov murmured as he and FitzGerald rose at the obvious indication that their arrival interview was at an end.

"Captain Shoupe will see you out, Captain," Khumalo continued, rising to offer his hand once again in a farewell handshake. He shook hands with FitzGerald, as well, and smiled pleasantly.

"System President Lababibi has invited me to a political banquet in Thimble tomorrow evening, Captain," he said, as if in afterthought as he walked them to his cabin hatch. "Most of the Constitutional Convention's senior delegates will be there, and Baroness Medusa will also be attending. She's suggested that I bring some of my senior staffers and captains along with me, and I feel it's important for the Navy to make a good showing at these affairs, especially given our responsibilities and the force levels we have to work with. I trust you and some of your own officers will be able to attend?"

"We'd be honored to, Sir," Terekhov assured him.

"Good. Good! I'll look forward to seeing you there," Khumalo said, beaming as the hatch opened and the Marine sentry stationed outside it came to attention. "And now," he continued, "I'll leave you in Captain Shoupe's care. Good day, Captain. Commander."

The hatch slid shut again before Terekhov could say anything else, and he and FitzGerald were suddenly alone in the passage with Shoupe and the carefully expressionless sentry.

"This way, please, Sir." The chief of staff had a pleasant soprano voice, and her hand moved gracefully as she gestured down the passage.

"Thank you, Captain," Terekhov said, and the three of them set off towards *Hercules'* boat bays.

"The Admiral seems to be even more shorthanded than I'd expected from my briefings and orders," Terekhov observed as they stepped into one of the superdreadnought's lifts and the door closed behind them. His tone was pleasantly impersonal, that of someone who could have been simply making idle conversation, except for the fact that he'd waited until there were no other ears at all to hear it.

"Yes, he is," Shoupe replied after an almost imperceptible pause. She looked up at Terekhov, brown eyes meeting blue. "And I'm afraid he isn't quite as confident as he'd like to appear that there aren't additional political factors involved in the priority accorded to Talbott."

"I see," Terekhov said with a slight nod.

"At the moment, we have an almost impossible number of balls to keep in the air simultaneously," the chief of staff continued, "and I'm afraid the Admiral is feeling the strain, just a bit."

"I'm sure anyone would be, in his position," Terekhov replied.

"Yes. That's one reason—" The lift car reached its destination, and Shoupe cut off whatever she'd been about to say. She gave Terekhov a small smile, and stood back courteously for him to leave the car first.

Too bad, FitzGerald thought, as he followed her out in turn. *She was about to say something interesting there. As in that old curse about living in "interesting" times.*

"All right," Aivars Terekhov said, several hours later, laying his white beret on the conference table in his bridge briefing room and looking around it. Ansten FitzGerald, Ginger Lewis, Naomi Kaplan, and Captain Tadislaw Kaczmarczyk, the CO of *Hexapuma*'s Marine detachment, looked back. Chief Agnelli had provided steaming cups of coffee or tea, as each guest preferred, and insulated carafes of both beverages sat on a tray in the center of the table.

"I've had the opportunity to review the intelligence packet from Commander Chandler, Admiral Khumalo's intelligence officer," Terekhov continued, "and also the Admiral's rules of engagement and general orders for the Station. Now I'd like to go over them briefly with you."

Heads nodded, and he tipped his chair back slightly, nursing his own coffee cup in both hands.

"I suppose things always look a bit different to the people actually on the spot from the way they look to the folks back at headquarters," he began. "Given the fact that Admiral Khumalo's been out here ever since the Talbott Station was created, he's clearly in a better position to be aware of local conditions than anyone could be back in Manticore.

"Our primary tasks, as laid down in his general instructions, are first to maintain peace on and between the Cluster's planets. Second, he's charged with assisting the Spindle System government and Baroness Medusa's available Marines—which amount to only a single understrength battalion—in maintaining the security of the

Constitutional Convention here on Flax. Our third priority is to suppress piracy and, of course, genetic slaving throughout the Cluster and to discourage . . . adventurism by any outside elements."

He paused for a moment, his eyes sweeping around the table, and there was no need for him to elaborate on just which "outside elements" Khumalo's general instructions might refer to.

"Fourth," he continued, "we're to assist local authorities in the suppression of any extralegal resistance to the annexation. Apparently the people who lost the vote are becoming increasingly vocal, and there are indications at least a few of them are about to step beyond mere verbal expressions of displeasure.

"Fifth, we already know our local charts are seriously inaccurate. The Admiral's assigned a high priority to updating our astrogation databases, both by collecting information from local pilots and merchant skippers and by conducting regular survey activities of our own.

"And, sixth and finally, we're to 'show the flag,' not simply inside the Cluster, but along its outer fringes, as well. Piracy here in the Cluster has never been as serious as in, say, Silesia, but there's always been some. The Admiral desires his ships to make their presence known along the arcs Nuncio-Celebrant-Pequod-Scarlet and Lynx-Montana-Tillerman, where he's set up standing patrol lines. On the one hand, we should serve as an advertisement of the advantages of membership in the Star Kingdom, and on the other, remind any larcenously inclined souls from outside it that Her Majesty would take their little pranks amiss."

He smiled thinly at their expressions.

"As you can see, this won't exactly be a relaxing pleasure cruise."

"That's one way to put it, Sir," Ginger Lewis observed after a moment. "Since you're discussing the Admiral's general instructions, may I assume we don't have any specific movement orders just yet?"

"You assume correctly, Ginger," Terekhov agreed with a

nod. "When we do receive orders, however, I imagine we'll find ourselves moving around quite a bit. Looking over the ship list, it's obvious *Hexapuma* is the most powerful modern unit assigned to the Station. I don't see any way the Admiral can afford not to work us hard."

"I can see that, Sir," FitzGerald put in. "Still, if you'll pardon my saying so, I didn't hear anything in that specifically about the security of the terminus."

"No, you didn't," Terekhov agreed. "We have two separate problems. One is the security of the terminus; the other is the security of the rest of the Cluster. The fact that the terminus is an eight-day trip from Split, the closest system in the Cluster proper, even for a warship, doesn't make reconciling those responsibilities any easier."

His tone was level, his expression calm, yet for just a moment, FitzGerald thought he saw something else behind those blue eyes. Whatever it was, it disappeared as quickly as it had come—assuming it had ever been there in the first place—and Terekhov continued in the same dispassionate voice.

"From the economic, astrographic, and military perspectives, Lynx is the real strategic chokepoint of the cluster, as far as the Star Kingdom is concerned. But from the immediate *political* perspective, Spindle, where the Constitutional Convention is meeting, is at least equally critical. And, the need to maintain a visible presence in the Cluster's inhabited star systems is yet another magnet drawing our available strength away from Lynx. Under the circumstances, and bearing in mind that Lynx can be reinforced on short notice by Home Fleet, Admiral Khumalo's decided his short-term emphasis must be placed on supporting the political processes of the Constitutional Convention and assisting the local planetary governments."

But what do you *think he should be doing?* FitzGerald wondered. Not that he even considered asking the question aloud.

"I can see why you wanted Naomi and Tad sitting in

on this, Sir," Lewis said after a moment. "I'm not too clear on why *I'm* here, though."

"First, because you're my senior officer, after Ansten," Terekhov replied. "And, second, because unless I miss my guess, we're going to be pushing the ship's systems hard, without much in the way of outside support. Admiral Khumalo has three depot ships—four, counting the one stationed here—to support all of his units. At the moment, the others are assigned to Prairie, Montana, and Scarlet, to provide the maximum coverage for his patrol units. There are also ammunition ships at Montana and Prairie. Aside from that, however, we'll be essentially on our own for both maintenance and general logistics.

"Naomi is obviously going to be deeply involved if—or perhaps I should say when—we encounter pirates or slavers. And Tadislaw's Marines are going to be at least as busy, even assuming we weren't going to run into any need to deploy planet-side detachments. Which, I might add, I'm quite certain we are going to find ourselves doing. But the bottom line is that everyone else aboard the ship depends on Engineering. If we suffer a major maintenance casualty, it's going to make a huge hole in Admiral Khumalo's available strength. So," he smiled suddenly, "I basically wanted you sitting in on this so I could tighten the screws on your sense of responsibility!"

"Gee, thanks, Sir," Lewis retorted with a smile of her own.

"Don't mention it. It's known as motivation enhancement." Several people chuckled, and Terekhov let his chair come fully back upright.

"It's obviously too early to be thinking in anything but the most general terms," he said in a more serious tone. "The one thing we can depend on is that Murphy will surprise us, no matter how much effort we put into preparing for his inevitable appearance. When that happens, our ability to cope with the surprise is going to depend on our agility and flexibility. That's one of the primary reasons I asked all of you to attend this meeting. I intend to conduct a general briefing for all department heads within the next day or so. But you people's departments are going to carry the largest share of the burden, so I wanted to give each of you an early heads-up and take the opportunity for all of us to try bouncing some preliminary ideas off of one another.

"For example, Major Kaczmarczyk, it's occurred to me that the nature of the developing political situation here in the Cluster is likely to require intervention by the Station's Marines. That means you and your people, as far as *Hexapuma* is concerned."

"Yes, Sir." Kaczmarczyk was a short, solid, compact man in his late thirties with brown, bristle-cut hair and a neatly groomed mustache. He seemed just a little detached from the naval officers seated around the table with him, but his oddly colored amber-green eyes were very direct as he looked back at his captain.

"I foresee a very broad spectrum of missions for you, Major," Terekhov continued, "and the nature of the political equation is going to require a certain deftness. There may very well be situations in which a hammer is what will be required, although I'm sure everyone would prefer to avoid that. But there will also be situations in which your people are going to be required to perform more as policemen than as combat troops. I realize it's difficult to switch back and forth between those roles, and that the training and mindsets they require are to some extent mutually contradictory. There's nothing we can do about that, unfortunately, so I want you to concentrate on prepping your people to operate in small, independent units at need. I'll try to avoid chopping you up into penny-packets, but I can't promise that you won't find yourself detaching individual squads."

"I've got good noncoms, Sir," Kaczmarczyk said. "But I don't have a whole lot of warm bodies, and some of those I do have are pretty green."

"Point taken," Terekhov agreed.

The renewed war and the sudden huge increase in the Star Kingdom's territory had combined with the Navy's new construction policies to force changes in the size of the Marine detachments which Manticoran warships embarked. Traditionally, the RMN had assigned companies to light cruisers, and full battalions—including their attached heavy weapons companies—to capital ships. Heavy cruisers and battlecruisers had embarked "short" battalions: regular battalions with the heavy weapons companies detached.

Other navies had embarked far smaller detachments, but prior to the Havenite Wars, the Manticoran Navy's primary responsibilities had been piracy suppression and peacekeeping operations. Blowing pirate cruisers out of space was a straightforward proposition, but the Navy had found that recapturing merchantmen which had been taken by pirates without killing off any surviving members of their original crews required something a bit more delicate than a laser head or a graser. The boarding parties tasked to go over and retake those ships were composed of Marines. So were the boarding parties sent to support Navy inspections of suspected slavers or smugglers. And so were the landing parties sent down in places like Silesia to deal with planet-side riots, attacks on Manticoran nationals, and natural disasters.

Unlike most other navies—including both the SLN and the Star Kingdom's own Grayson ally—Manticoran Marines were also integrated into damage control parties and assigned to man broadside weapons aboard the ships in which they served. Aboard *Hexapuma*, for example, Kaczmarczyk's personnel crewed half a dozen of the ship's grasers. RMN ships had been able to carry so many Marines because they weren't *displacing* naval ratings; they were performing the same functions *as* naval ratings.

But that practice required additional cross-training of the Marines. It took time to produce people who could proficiently perform the multiple tasks assigned to them, and it wasn't cheap. Which was one of the reasons even the RMN had been forced to rethink things a bit.

The increased automation which had allowed the Navy to drastically reduce its manpower (and life support) requirements and pack in additional firepower and defensive systems had been another. Maintaining the traditional size of the Marine detachments would have defeated much of that advantage. Which didn't even consider the fact that the Star Kingdom's sudden expansion required additional garrisons and peacekeeping forces which, particularly so close on the heels of major "peacetime" reductions in the roster strength of both the Navy and the Marines, had stretched the available supply of Marines to the breaking point. The troop strength of both the Marines and the Army was being increased as rapidly as possible, but manpower, not money or industrial capacity, had always been the Star Kingdom's Achilles' heel.

All of which explained why, instead of the four hundred and fifty-four men and women, in three companies, commanded by a major, assigned to a heavy cruiser under the "old" establishment, Captain Kaczmarczyk (who received the "courtesy promotion" to major aboard ship—since a warship could afford no confusion over who one meant when one said "Captain") had barely a hundred and forty in his single company. Even at that, they represented almost half of *Hexapuma*'s total complement of three hundred and fifty-five.

"We'll just have to do the best we can," Terekhov continued. "I'm hoping that, for the most part, the local governments will be able to deal with their own internal problems. For one thing, if we get involved, we run the risk, as 'imperialist outsiders,' of escalating whatever ill feeling produced the problem in the first place. If they need to call on us at all, I'm hoping it will be either for intelligence support, using our recon systems, or for quick, hard, in-and-out strikes on specific targets.

"In line with that, Major, I'd like you and your intelligence officer to go over these briefs from Commander Chandler." He handed over a slim folio of record chips. "They're planet-by-planet analyses, based on the most recent data available from local law enforcement types. Of course, a lot of that data is probably out of date by now, given transit times, but it's still the best information available. I'd especially like you to look for—"

"Well, Loretta. What do you think of him?"

"I beg your pardon, Sir?" Captain Shoupe looked up from the data chips she'd been sliding into slots in a folio. She and the rest of the staff had just finished their regular daily report on the station's status, and it was early afternoon, shipboard time. Rear Admiral Khumalo always preferred to catch a short nap before dinner, and the other staffers had already departed.

"I asked what you think of him," Khumalo replied. The rear admiral stood with his back to her, gazing into the cool, glowing depths of one of his holo tapestries. "Captain Terekhov, of course."

"I haven't really had the opportunity to form an opinion of him, Sir," she said after a moment. "He seems pleasant enough."

"Yes, he does, doesn't he?" Khumalo said in a rather distant tone. "Still, he's not quite what I'd expected."

Shoupe said nothing. She simply stood there, waiting patiently. She'd been with Khumalo ever since the rear admiral had been sent out to Talbott, and, almost despite herself, she'd actually grown fond of him. He could be frustrating, vacillating, and vain, and he was definitely one of the Navy's "political" admirals. But he also worked long hours—one of the reasons he liked to catch naps in the afternoon—and whatever his other faults, he was truly determined to bring the annexation of the Cluster to a successful conclusion.

"I've read the reports on the Battle of Hyacinth, you know," the rear admiral continued after a moment. "It must have been terrible." He turned to look at her. "Have you read the reports, Loretta?"

"No, Sir. I can't say I have."

"Hyacinth was supposed to be in our possession," Khumalo said, walking slowly back over to his desk and sitting behind it. "In fact, it *was* when Terekhov's convoy was dispatched there. It was supposed to be turned into one of Eighth Fleet's forward supply depots, but the picket force covering it was hit by a Peep counterattack. The picket didn't have any of the new ship types, and the Peeps were in overwhelming strength. The picket commander had no choice but to withdraw, and when Terekhov arrived, he sailed straight into an ambush."

The rear admiral paused for a moment, one hand toying with a richly ornamented dagger he used as a paperweight.

"The Peeps called on him to surrender, you know," he went on after a few seconds. "He refused. He didn't have any of the pod technology, but he did have all of the new electronics, including the latest generations of ECM and the FTL com, and the freighters in his convoy were loaded with all the latest technology, including spare parts and MDMs intended to reammunition Eighth Fleet. He couldn't let that fall into enemy hands, so he tried to fight his way out, at least get the merchantmen back out across the hyper limit.

"He did get two of them out. But he lost six, and his entire division of light cruisers, and three-quarters of his personnel. Most of the merchie crewmen survived, after they set their scuttling charges and took to the boats. But his own people were massacred."

He stared down at the jewel-hilted dagger and drew it from its sheath. Light glittered on its keenly honed edge, and he turned it slowly, watching the reflection.

"What would you have done in his place, Loretta?" he asked softly, and she stiffened. She said nothing for a moment, and he looked up.

"That's not a trick question," he said. "I suppose what I should have asked is what's your opinion of the decision he actually made."

"I think it took a lot of courage, Sir," she said after a moment, her tone still a bit stiff.

"Oh, there's no question of that," Khumalo agreed. "But is courage enough?" She looked a silent question at him, and he shrugged slightly. "The war was almost over, Loretta. By the time he was ambushed at Hyacinth, it was pretty clear nothing the Peeps had was going to stop Eighth Fleet whatever happened. So was it a case of good judgment, or bad? Should he have surrendered his ships, *let* the Peeps have the technology, knowing they wouldn't have time to take advantage of it?"

"Sir," Shoupe said in a very careful tone, "you're talking about cowardice in the face of the enemy."

"Am I?" He looked at her levelly. "Cowardice, or good sense?"

"Sir," Shoupe began, then paused. Khumalo's career had been primarily that of a military administrator. He'd commanded several fairly important bases and support stations, some quite close to the front in the First Havenite War, but he himself had never commanded in combat. Was it possible he felt threatened by Terekhov's reputation?

"Sir," she resumed after a moment, "neither you nor I were there. Anything we may think is a case of second-guessing the man who *was* there. I don't know what the best decision was. But I do know Captain Terekhov was the man who had to *make* the decision in a very narrow time window. And, with all due respect, Sir, I have to say it's far more obvious now that the Peeps were about to lose it all than it was at the time. And I suppose it's also fair to add that if he had surrendered, and if the Peeps *had* gotten their hands on his ships and the freighters, with their systems and cargoes intact, we'd probably be in even worse shape vis-a-vis the Peep navy than we are now."

"So you're saying you think he was right, at least given the limitations of what he knew at the time?"

"I suppose I am, Sir. I pray to God I'll never have to make a similar decision. And I'm sure Terekhov prays to God that he'll never have to make another one like it. But I think that, given the choices he had to select between, he probably picked the right one."

Khumalo looked troubled. He sheathed the dagger and laid it on his desk, then sat gazing down at it. For just a moment, his face looked worn and old, and

Shoupe felt a powerful pang of sympathy. She knew he wondered why he hadn't been recalled when the Janecek Admiralty collapsed, taking his patrons with it. Was it simply because no one had gotten around to it yet? Were his recall orders already on board a dispatch boat *en route* to Spindle? Or had someone decided to leave him here as a suitable scapegoat if something went wrong? It was like having a double-ended Sword of Damocles hanging over his head, and now, obviously, something about Terekhov bothered him deeply.

"Sir," she heard herself saying, "forgive me, but we've worked together closely for some time now. I can see that something about Captain Terekhov, or his decisions at Hyacinth, or both, concerns you. May I ask what it is?"

Khumalo's mouth twisted for just a moment, then he pushed the dagger to one side, squared his shoulders, and looked at her.

"Captain Terekhov, despite the recent date of his promotion to senior grade, is now the second most senior ship commander on this station, after Captain Saunders. After myself, he is, in fact, the third-ranking officer in Talbott. In addition to that, his ship is the most modern and, arguably, powerful unit we have. That makes him, and his judgment, far more significant than they might have been somewhere else, especially given the diplomatic aspects of the situation."

He paused, still looking at Shoupe, and the chief of staff nodded.

So that's at least part of it, she thought. *He's wondering if Terekhov's stint at the Foreign Office means he's here to help jab us into a greater "political sensitivity," or something like that. And the fact that the Admiral's such an uncomfortable fit for the current Government must make him worry about it even more.*

But if that was the case, Khumalo chose not to admit it.

"I have to ask myself whether his actions at Hyacinth reflect good judgment, as well as courage," the admiral said instead, "or if they reflect something else. With all of the hundreds of potential sparks floating around, I don't need someone whose first inclination is going to be to squirt extra hydrogen into the furnace."

"Sir, Captain Terekhov didn't strike me as a hothead," Shoupe said. "I haven't had any opportunity to form a real opinion of his judgment, but he seems levelheaded enough."

"I hope you're right, Loretta," Khumalo sighed. "I hope you're right."

Chapter Twelve

"Good evening, Madam Governor."

"Good evening, Madam President." Dame Estelle Matsuko, Baroness Medusa, and Provisional Crown Governor of the Talbott Cluster in the name of Queen Elizabeth III, bowed slightly, and Samiha Lababibi, President of the Spindle System, returned it. The two women were both dark complexioned and slender, although Lababibi had a more wiry, muscular build, courtesy of a lifetime passion for yachting and skin diving. At a hundred and sixty-five centimeters, she was also seven and a half centimeters taller than Dame Estelle. But both had black hair and brown eyes, although Dame Estelle's had a pronounced epicanthic fold. She was also several decades older than Lababibi, even if her second-generation prolong made her look younger, and she'd resigned the office of Home Secretary to accept her present assignment.

"I'm glad you were able to attend," the system president continued. "I was afraid you wouldn't have returned from Rembrandt in time."

"The timing was a bit closer than I'd anticipated," Medusa agreed. "I was in the middle of discussions with the Trade Union's executive council when the report of that business on Montana came in."

"Oh, *that*." Lababibi rolled her eyes with a grimace of disgust. "Little boys playing sophomoric tricks," she said.

"Little boys with pulse rifles, Madam President," Medusa replied. Lababibi looked at her, and the Provisional Governor smiled with very little humor. "We were lucky this time. Lucky this Mr. Westman was prepared to make his point without actually shooting anyone."

"Madam Governor," Lababibi said, "Stephen Westman—all those Montanans, even the women!—have far too much testosterone in their systems. They still believe all that First Landing frontiersman nonsense. Or claim they do, anyway. But I assure you, the vote there was almost as one-sided as here on Flax. Lunatics like Westman are only a tiny minority, even on Montana, and there's no way—"

"President Lababibi," Medusa interrupted pleasantly, "this is a social gathering. I really shouldn't have let myself sidetrack you into discussing Mr. Westman at all. I do think you may be . . . underestimating the potential seriousness of the situation, but please, don't distress yourself over it tonight. We'll have sufficient time to discuss it *officially* later."

"Of course." Lababibi smiled.

"Thank you." Medusa turned to scan the crowded ballroom of the Spindle System President's State Mansion. They actually called it that, she reflected, without any of the shorter, less pretentious titles which would have been used most places. Nor had they spared any expense on its interior decor. The outer wall was composed entirely of French doors, giving onto the immaculately groomed Presidential Gardens with their deliberately archaic gas-jet torches flaming in the cool spring night. The opposite wall consisted solely of floor-to-ceiling mirrors, which gave the already large room a sense of glassy vastness, and the end walls and ceiling were decorated with heroic *bas relief* frescoes, glittering with touches of gold leaf. The long line of tables set up beside the live orchestra was covered in snowy white linen and littered with expensive tableware and hand-blown glassware, and massive chandeliers, like cascades of crystal tears, hung from the vaulted ceiling.

In many ways it was all horridly overdone, and yet it worked. It blended together beautifully, a perfect frame for the richly dressed guests, in the formal styles of a dozen different planets. Yet even as Medusa admitted that to herself, it still bothered her a bit to see such a magnificently decorated room in the mansion of the chief executive of a star system as poor as Spindle was.

But, then, all *these systems are crushingly poor,* she thought. *Devastated economies in the midst of everything they need to be prosperous . . . except for that first boost up. All except Rembrandt and its trading partners, perhaps. But even the Trade Union's members are poverty stricken compared to Manticore, Sphinx, or Gryphon.*

She'd known that, intellectually, before she ever arrived here. But knowing and *understanding* were very different. And one thing that bothered her deeply was the vast gulf between the haves and have-nots in Talbott. Even the wealthiest Talbotter was scarcely even well-off compared to someone like Klaus Hauptman or Duchess Harrington. But on many of these worlds there *was* no middle class. Or, rather, what middle class they had was only a thin layer, without the numbers or strength to fuel the growth of a self-sustaining economy. And that was less because of the huge size of the lower classes than because of the vast over-concentration of wealth and property in the hands of a tiny, closed wealthy class. In terms of real buying power, and the ability to command the necessities of life, the gap between someone like Samiha Lababibi and someone from Thimble's slums was literally astronomical. And although the Lababibi family fortune might have constituted little more than pocket change for Klaus Hauptman, it, along with those of a handful of other families, represented a tremendous portion of the total available wealth of the Spindle System . . . and starved the economy as a whole of desperately needed investment capital.

And as for economic power, so for politics. Samiha Lababibi looked perfectly at home in this sumptuous ballroom because she was. Because hers was one of three or four families who passed the presidential mansion back and forth at election time, like some private possession. Medusa came from a star nation with an overt, official aristocracy; Lababibi came from a "democracy" in which the ranks of the governing class were far more closed and restricted than anything the Star Kingdom of Manticore had ever dreamed of.

Yet the Lababibis weren't pure parasites. Samiha was actually a flaming liberal, by Spindle standards. She was genuinely committed to her own understanding of the good of all of her star system's citizens, although Medusa suspected she spent more time emoting over the poor then she did actually *thinking* about them.

Hard for it to be any other way, really. She doesn't actually know *them at all. They might as well be living on another planet for all that her path is ever going to cross theirs. And just how much does that differ from a Liberal back home? Or*—Medusa grinned—*from the "Old Liberals."* Montaigne's *certainly spent enough time with the have-nots, and her version of the party's something else entirely.*

"I see Mr. Van Dort and Mr. Alquezar are here," she said aloud. "I haven't seen Ms. Tonkovic or Mr. Krietzmann yet, though."

"Henri is here somewhere," Lababibi replied. "Aleksandra screened me to apologize. She plans to attend, but some last-minute matter came up, and she's going to be a little late."

"I see," Medusa murmured. *Translated: she'll be here when she's good and ready, thus making it clear that she has no intention of becoming one more hanger-on of the Provisional Governor.*

She was about to say something more, when her eye caught sight of a cluster of black and gold uniforms.

"Excuse me, Madam President," she said, giving Lababibi a gracious smile, "but I just noticed the arrival of Admiral Khumalo and his officers. As Her Majesty's senior civilian representative here in Talbott, I really must go and pay my respects. If you'll forgive me?"

"Of course, Madam Governor." Lababibi, and Medusa went sweeping off across the ballroom floor.

"So, tell me, what do you think of the President's modest home?" Aikawa Kagiyama murmured into Helen's ear.

"A nice enough little hovel, in an unpretentious, understated sort of way," she replied judiciously, and Aikawa snorted a chuckle.

"I imagine Lady Montaigne—excuse me, *Ms.* Montaigne—could outdo her if she put her mind to it," he agreed.

"Oh, no! Cathy's taste is far too good to ever indulge in something like this. Although," she added in a more serious tone, "I *do* like the mirrors. I'd like them better if the air-conditioning were a little more efficient, of course. Or if they'd at least propped some of those glass doors open. When you pack this many bodies into one confined space, it gets a bit warmer than I really like."

"No shit." Aikawa nodded in agreement, then cocked his head as he saw a small, slender woman moving across the floor towards them. She wore the elegantly tailored trousers and jacket of formal Manticoran court dress, and the crowd of Spindalians and off-planet diplomats stepped aside to let her pass. It didn't look as if they even realized they were doing it; it was simply an inevitable law of nature.

"Is that who I think it is?" he asked quietly.

"Of course not. It's the Pope," she replied sarcastically from the corner of her mouth.

"Good evening, Admiral."

"Good evening, Madam Governor." Augustus Khumalo bowed gracefully to Dame Estelle. "As always, it's a pleasure to see you."

"And you, Admiral," Baroness Medusa replied. Then she looked past him at the commanding officer of his flagship. "And good evening to you, too, Captain Saunders."

"Madam Governor." Captain Victoria Saunders had been born a Sphinx yeoman. Despite three decades of naval service, her bow lacked the spontaneous, almost instinctive grace of her admiral's.

"May I present Captain Aivars Terekhov of the *Hexapuma*, Madam Governor," Khumalo said, indicating *Hexapuma*'s commander with an easy wave.

"Captain Terekhov," Medusa acknowledged.

"Madam Governor." Like all of Khumalo's subordinates, the tall, broad-shouldered officer in the white beret of a starship commander was in full mess dress, and he rested the heel of his left hand on the hilt of his dress sword as he bowed to her. Medusa's dark eyes regarded him intently for just a moment, and then she smiled.

"*Hexapuma*. She's a *Saganami-C* class, isn't she?" she said.

"Why, yes, Milady. She is," he confirmed, and her smile grew a bit broader as he managed to keep any surprise at her observation out of his voice and expression. Khumalo's face had gone completely expressionless momentarily, and Medusa suppressed an urge to chuckle.

"I thought I recognized the name," she said. "One of my nieces is a captain at BuShips. She mentioned to me that they were going to begin naming the later *Saganamis* after predators, and I can't think of anything much more predatory than a Sphinxian hexapuma. Can you?"

"Not really, no, Milady," Terekhov conceded after a moment.

"And are these your officers?" she asked, looking past him.

"Some of them," he replied. "Commander FitzGerald, my Executive Officer. Commander Lewis, my Chief Engineer. Lieutenant Commander Kaplan, my Tactical Officer. Lieutenant Bagwell, my Electronics Warfare Officer. Lieutenant Abigail Hearns, Commander Kaplan's assistant. Midshipwoman Zilwicki, and Midshipman Kagiyama."

Medusa nodded as each of Terekhov's subordinates bowed to her in turn. Her gaze sharpened slightly and slipped past Hearns to the towering man in the non-Manticoran uniform standing behind her as the Grayson lieutenant was introduced, and she shook her head ruefully when it was Helen Zilwicki's turn.

"My, what an interesting wardroom you have, to be sure, Captain," she murmured.

"We do have a somewhat . . . varied assortment," he agreed.

"So I see." She smiled at Helen. "Ms. Zilwicki, I hope you'll be kind enough to give Ms. Montaigne my greetings when next you see her. And, of course, I trust you'll present my respects to Queen Berry, as well."

"Uh, of course, Madam Governor," Helen managed, acutely aware of the sharp look Rear Admiral Khumalo was pointing in her direction.

"Thank you." Medusa smiled again, and then returned her attention to Khumalo.

"I recognize Captain Anders and Commander Hewlett, Admiral," she said, inclining her head to two more white-bereted officers. "But I don't believe I've met these other ladies and gentlemen."

"No, Madam Governor. This is Commander Hope, of the *Vigilant*, and her executive officer, Lieutenant Commander Diamond. And this is Lieutenant Commander Jeffers, of the *Javelin*, and his executive officer, Lieutenant Kulinac. And this is . . ."

"Tell me, Captain Terekhov. What's your impression of the Cluster?"

"In all honesty, President Lababibi, I haven't been here long enough to form any first-hand impressions," Terekhov said easily.

He stood with a delicate, fluted wineglass in one hand, smiling pleasantly, and if he was aware of Rear Admiral Khumalo's slightly flinty expression, he gave no sign of it. The cluster of Manticoran officers stood out sharply from the rest of the visually spectacular throng. The senior delegates to the Constitutional Convention had coalesced around them with the inevitability of gravity, and Terekhov's recent arrival and seniority made him a natural focus of attention.

"Come now, Captain!" the System President chided gently. "I'm sure you were thoroughly briefed before being sent out here. And you've voyaged all the way from Lynx to Spindle."

"Yes, Ma'am. But briefings scarcely qualify me to form first-hand impressions. As for the voyage from Lynx, it was spent entirely in hyper. I've actually seen virtually nothing of the Cluster."

"I see." She regarded him thoughtfully, and the extremely tall, red-haired man standing beside her chuckled.

"I'm sure the good captain will soon have far more opportunity than he ever wanted to get to know all of us, Samiha. Although, to be honest, I suspect that the people already living here—including most of the ones in this room—didn't really have any better impressions of our neighbors before the annexation vote than Captain Terekhov does."

"I think that's putting it just a bit too strongly, Joachim," Lababibi said tartly.

"But not by very much," a new voice said, and Terekhov turned his head to see a green-eyed, auburn-haired woman who hadn't previously been introduced.

"Ah, there you are, Aleksandra . . . at last," President Lababibi said. She smiled, not entirely pleasantly, and turned back to Terekhov. "Captain, permit me to introduce Ms. Aleksandra Tonkovic, President of Kornati and the Split System's senior delegate to the Constitutional Convention. Aleksandra, this is Captain Aivars Terekhov."

"Captain Terekhov." Tonkovic held out her right hand. Terekhov shook it, and she smiled at him. She was a strikingly handsome woman—not beautiful, in any conventional sense, but with strong, determined features and sharp, intelligent eyes. "I'm afraid my colleague Joachim is correct about our relative insularity prior to the annexation vote—if, perhaps, less correct about certain other issues."

"Since this is a social gathering, Aleksandra, I shall refrain from engaging you in philosophical combat and smiting you hip and thigh." Joachim Alquezar also smiled . . . although there was very little humor in his eyes.

"Good," President Lababibi said, with a certain emphasis. Almost despite himself, Terekhov crooked one eyebrow, and the Spindalian smiled crookedly at him. "I'm afraid Mr. Alquezar and Ms. Tonkovic aren't precisely on the best terms, politically speaking."

"Oh, yes," Terekhov said. "If I remember correctly, Mr. Alquezar heads the Constitutional Union Party while Ms. Tonkovic heads the Talbott Liberal Constitutional Party."

"Very good, Captain," Alquezar complimented. Rear Admiral Khumalo's expression was somewhat less congratulatory. He started to sidle sideways, but Baroness Medusa intercepted him in what appeared to be a completely innocent fashion.

"I'm a Queen's officer, Mr. Alquezar. And I have the honor to command one of her cruisers in what I'm sure everyone in this room recognizes is a . . . delicate situation." He shrugged with a pleasant smile. "Under the circumstances, I have a certain responsibility to do my homework."

"To be sure," Alquezar murmured. His eyes twitched briefly sideways in Khumalo's direction, and then he glanced at Tonkovic. Almost as one, they stepped closer to Terekhov.

"Tell me, Captain," Alquezar continued. "As a Queen's officer who's done his homework, what do you think of the . . . political dynamic here?"

Despite his conversation with Governor Medusa, Khumalo had managed to drift a few meters closer to Terekhov and the two Talbotter political leaders. If the captain noticed, no sign of it crossed his face.

"Mr. Alquezar," he said with a slight chuckle, "if I

haven't had an opportunity to form a first-hand opinion of the Cluster as a whole, what makes you think I've had the chance to form any meaningful opinion of the local political equation? And even if I had, I rather doubt, first, that any opinion of mine could be particularly reliable, on the basis of so little information, or, second, that it would be my place as a serving military officer to offer my interpretation to two of the leading political figures of the region. Presumptuous, if nothing else, I should think."

"Exactly so, Captain," Khumalo said heartily, moving close enough to graft himself onto the small conversational knot. "Naval officers in the Star Kingdom are executors of political policy, Mr. Alquezar. We're not supposed to involve ourselves in the formulation of that policy."

He'd at least used the verb "supposed," Alquezar noted, exchanging a brief, almost commiserating glance with Tonkovic.

"Agreed, Admiral," another voice said, and a flicker of something suspiciously like panic danced across Khumalo's face as Henri Krietzmann blended out of the crowd. "On the other hand," the Convention's president observed, "this is scarcely your normal political situation, now is it?"

"Ah, no. No, it isn't," Khumalo said after a moment. He darted an imploring look at Medusa, but the Provisional Governor only returned it blandly. She obviously had no intention of rescuing him. If he'd wanted to quash the conversation between Terekhov, Lababibi, Alquezar, and Tonkovic before the captain could say something the rear admiral didn't want said, he'd failed. Now he found himself standing there with the four most powerful political leaders of the entire Convention, and he looked as if he would have preferred standing in a cage full of hexapumas . . . with a raw steak in his hand.

"I think we can all agree with that, Henri." There was a distinct chill in Tonkovic's voice, and Krietzmann gave her a thin smile.

"I would certainly hope so. Although," he observed, "it's sometimes difficult to believe we do."

"Meaning what?" she demanded, a spark of anger dancing in her green eyes.

"Meaning that the Convention is an exercise in living politics, Aleksandra," Lababibi said before Krietzmann could respond.

"Which is always messy," Medusa agreed, and smiled impartially at the disputants. "Admiral Khumalo and I could tell you tales about politics back home in Manticore, couldn't we, Admiral?"

"Yes." If Khumalo was grateful for the Provisional Governor's intervention—or, at least, for the form that intervention had taken—it wasn't apparent in his expression. "Yes, Baroness, I suppose we could."

"Well," Krietzmann said, his eyes flicking ever so briefly to Alquezar and then to Lababibi, "I'm sure that's true. But I have to admit I feel more than a little concern over reports about things like that business on Montana or, if you'll forgive me, Aleksandra, this 'Freedom Alliance' Agnes Nordbrandt has proclaimed back on Kornati. I'm beginning to feel as if the house is on fire and we're too busy arguing about the color of the carpet to do anything about the flames."

"Really, Henri." Tonkovic's smile was scalpel-thin. "You're being unduly alarmist. People like Westman and Nordbrandt represent a lunatic fringe which will always be with us. I'm sure they have their equivalents back on Manticore."

"Of course we do," Khumalo said quickly. "Of course, the situation is different, and tempers seldom run quite so high as they are out here right this minute. And, of course—"

He broke off, and Medusa used her wineglass to hide a grimace of combined amusement and irritation. At least the pompous ass had stopped himself before he said *"Of course, we're* civilized *back home."*

"With all due respect, Admiral," she said in her best diplomat's tone, "tempers *do* run just as high back home." She smiled at the Talbotter political leaders. "As I'm sure all of you are well aware, the existing Star Kingdom is a political system with several centuries of experience and tradition behind it. As Mr. Alquezar and Ms. Tonkovic have just made clear, on the other hand, your people are still in the process of forging any Cluster-wide sense of true identity, so it's scarcely surprising your political processes should be striking more sparks, on every level. But don't make the mistake of assuming that bitter partisan political strife isn't very much alive and well back home. We've simply institutionalized its channels and managed to turn most of the bloodletting into nonphysical combat. Usually."

Khumalo's expression had tightened at her oblique reference to the collapse of the High Ridge Government, but he nodded.

"Precisely what I meant, Madam Governor, although I doubt I could ever have put it quite that well myself."

"I'm sure," Krietzmann said. "But that still leaves us with the problem of how to deal with our own crop of idiots."

"That's exactly what they are," Tonkovic said crisply. "Idiots. And there aren't enough of them to constitute any serious threat. They'll subside quickly enough once the draft Constitution is approved and all of this political angst is behind us."

"Assuming a draft ever *is* approved," Krietzmann said. He accompanied the remark with a smile, but his distinctive, saw-edged, lower-class Dresden accent was more pronounced than it had been.

"Of course it will be," she said impatiently. "Everyone at the Convention agrees we must have a Constitution, Henri," her voice had taken on a lecturing tone, the patience of a teacher explaining things to a slow student. She was probably completely unaware of it, but Krietzmann's mouth tightened dangerously. "All we're seeing is a lively, healthy debate over the exact terms of that Constitution."

"Excuse me, Aleksandra," Alquezar said, "but what we're seeing is a debate over what we expect the Star Kingdom to put up with. *We* asked to join *them*. As such, are we going to agree to abide by the Star Kingdom's existing domestic law and accept that it extends to every system, every planet, of the Cluster? Or are we going to demand that the Star Kingdom accept a hodgepodge of special system-by-system exemptions and privileges? Do we expect the Star Kingdom to be a healthy, well-integrated political unit in which every citizen, whatever his planet of birth or present residence, knows precisely what his legal rights, privileges, and obligations are? Or do we expect the Star Kingdom to be a ramshackle, shambling disaster like the Solarian League, where every system has local autonomy, every planet has veto power over any proposed legislation, the central government has no real control over its own house, and all actual authority lies in the hands of bureaucratic monsters like Frontier Security?"

He'd never raised his voice, but ripples of stillness spread out from the confrontation, and Tonkovic's eyes blazed with green fury.

"The people of the Talbott Cluster are the citizens of their own planets and their own star systems," she said in a cold, flinty voice. "We have our own histories, our own traditions, our own systems of belief and political structures. We've offered to join the Star Kingdom, to surrender our long-held sovereignties to a distant government which isn't presently ours, and in whose creation neither we nor any of our ancestors had any part. I believe it's not merely reasonable, but our overriding responsibility, as the representatives of our native planets, to ensure that our own unique identities don't simply disappear. And to ensure that the political rights we've managed to cling to aren't simply thrown away in the name of some vast, uniform code of laws which has never been any part of our own tradition."

"But—" Alquezar began, but Lababibi put a hand on his forearm.

"Joachim, Aleksandra—and you, too, Henri. This is a social gathering," she said in a calm, firm voice, unconsciously echoing what Medusa had said to her several hours earlier. "None of us is saying anything we haven't all said before, and that we won't all say again in the proper forum. But it's impolite to involve Admiral Khumalo and Captain Terekhov in our domestic, family quarrels. As your hostess, I'm going to have to request that we drop this topic for the evening."

Alquezar and Tonkovic turned to look at her in unison. Then they looked back at each other and both of them visibly inhaled deeply.

"You're quite correct, Samiha," Alquezar said after a heartbeat or two. "Aleksandra, we can duel one another into bloody submission another time. For the rest of this evening, I propose a truce."

"Accepted," Tonkovic replied, obviously making a genuine effort to infuse a little warmth into her own voice. The two of them nodded to each other, then to the others, and turned and walked away.

"*Whew!* That looked like it was going to turn nasty," Aikawa whispered in Helen's ear. The two of them stood to one side, taking unabashed advantage of the sumptuous buffet to stoke their metabolisms. And using the effective invisibility their extremely junior status bestowed upon them to eavesdrop shamelessly on their superiors.

"*Turn* nasty?" Helen murmured back under cover of munching on a canape. "Aikawa, those two—Tonkovic and Alquezar—must've been sticking daggers into each other for a long time. And that other guy, Krietzmann! He's one scary little bastard." She shook her head. "I sure wish *I'd* had the chance to read those political briefings the Captain was talking about."

"You and me both," Aikawa agreed. "But did you notice the Admiral?"

"You mean besides the fact that he didn't really want the Captain talking to any of them?"

"Yeah. It seemed to me he was on both sides at once."

"Meaning what?" she asked, turning to look at him.

"Well, he seemed to agree with what's-her-name—

Tonkovic—that whatever's going on on this Montana place isn't all that serious. Nothing to really worry about. But it looked to me as if he really agreed politically with the other two, Alquezar and Krietzmann."

"Of course he did. And so would I. Agree with the other two, I mean."

"Yeah," Aikawa said, but his expression was troubled, and she raised an eyebrow at him. "I just wish I knew what the Captain really thinks about all this," he said after a moment, answering the unspoken question.

Helen considered that for a few seconds, then nodded.

"Me, too," she said. "Me, too."

Chapter Thirteen

"You're late, Damien."

"I know I am, Ma'am," Damien Harahap, known to certain individuals in the Talbott Cluster as "Firebrand," said crisply, his uniform cap tucked under his left arm as he came to a respectful stance of attention. It was probably a bit of overkill, but the sharpness in Major Eichbauer's tone, coupled with her note's instruction to come in full uniform, suggested there were appearances to maintain this afternoon.

"There was an accident of some sort on the J-Line tramway," he continued, and she grimaced. "I never did find out exactly what it was, but it took me almost twenty minutes to find a jitney."

"Well, I don't suppose we can blame you for the vagaries of Estelle traffic," she said. "*Especially* not Estelle traffic." She waved for him to step the rest of the way into the anonymous-looking office.

There were a lot of offices like it here in Estelle, the capital city of the Republic of Monica, Harahap reflected. Monica specialized in anonymity as much as it did in bad civic engineering and the provision of mercenaries. Or volunteers for the Office of Frontier Security's intervention battalions . . . if there was a difference.

That thought carried him across the threshold, and then his brown eyes sharpened as he saw who else was sitting in the office, across the coffee table from Eichbauer's borrowed desk. He wasn't certain who the silver-eyed woman with the elaborate tattoos might be, but he recognized the beautiful, golden-haired woman sitting beside her from her file imagery. She wasn't the sort of person someone like him was likely to come into contact with, but he made it a habit to be familiar with as many of the truly big sharks as he could.

Now what, he wondered sardonically, *is a sitting member of Manpower's Board of Directors doing on a third-rate planet like Monica? And Ulrike wanted me in uniform. My, my, my.*

"Sit," Eichbauer told him, pointing at a comfortable if utilitarian chair beside her desk.

"Yes, Ma'am." He sat, settling his cap in his lap, and waited attentively.

"Damien, this is Ms. Aldona Anisimovna and Ms. Isabel Bardasano," Eichbauer said. "Ladies, Captain Damien Harahap, Solarian Gendarmerie."

"Ms. Anisimovna, Ms. Bardasano," Harahap acknowledged courteously. The fact that Eichbauer was using Anisimovna's real name surprised him a bit, but it probably also indicated that Bardasano was a real name, as well. Interesting.

Neither of the Mesans—at least, he assumed from her tattoos and piercings that Bardasano was also a Mesan—spoke, but both of them returned his acknowledgment with slight inclinations of their heads.

"Ms. Anisimovna," Eichbauer continued, "is here to discuss certain activities in the Talbott Cluster. She's already broached the matter with Brigadier Yucel, and the Brigadier has instructed me to cooperate with her fully. Which I am now instructing you to do, as well."

"Of course, Major," he said politely, while his mind raced. Eichbauer, he knew, despised Yucel. The tall, stocky major's strong features and sharp green eyes hinted only too accurately at the shrewd brain hiding behind them. She was intelligent, efficient, and none too squeamish when it came to the pragmatic realities of her job, but Yucel's taste for brutality was no part of her makeup.

That might account for the chill formality she was displaying, if whatever was going on was one of Yucel's brain children. But so might the fact that, like any Frontier Security officer with a brain, Eichbauer knew who OFS really worked for. It wasn't often a mere major had the opportunity to work directly under the eye of one of the movers and shakers of Mesa. It could be either a definite career-enhancing opportunity, or the slippery lip of oblivion, depending upon outcomes, and an effective display of professionalism could help determine which.

But why meet here? The Meyers System was only sixty light-years from Monica, barely a week's hyper travel for the sort of modified dispatch boat someone like Anisimovna would use as her personal transport. And Meyers, unlike Monica, was a Frontier Security protectorate. They could have met under conditions of maximum security there, so why come to Monica? And why were he and the major both in *uniform,* of all damned things? Their particular branch of the Gendarmerie seldom advertised.

"I need hardly explain to you, I'm sure, Damien, that Brigadier Yucel desires us to maintain the lowest possible profile," Eichbauer continued, which only made him wonder about the uniforms even more. "In fact, one of the primary considerations of this . . . operation is deniability. There must be no traceable connection between the Gendarmerie or OFS and Ms. Anisimovna and Ms. Bardasano."

He nodded his understanding (of at least part of what she'd just said), and she rewarded him with a small smile.

"Having said that, however, you're going to be working very closely with these ladies. In fact, for all intents and purposes, you'll be assigned full-time to this operation until its conclusion." Despite himself, he felt his eyebrows trying to rise and instructed them firmly to stay put.

"We understand we're putting you in something of an awkward position, Captain Harahap," Anisimovna said smoothly. "We regret that. And, of course, we'll make a strenuous effort to . . . compensate you for any inconvenience or risk this operation may require you to assume."

"That's very kind of you, Ma'am," he murmured while his inner avarice began ringing up credit signs. Having a Director of Manpower in one's debt, even if only slightly, wasn't the sort of thing that hurt a man's bank account. Especially not if one performed well enough to be remembered as a valuable resource for future needs, as well.

"Let me sketch out a hypothetical scenario for you, Damien," Eichbauer said, cocking her chair back slightly. He turned to look directly at her, watching the other two women unobtrusively out of the corner of a highly trained eye.

"As you know," she continued, "the Talbott Cluster has decided to dash headlong into the arms of the Star Kingdom of Manticore. Obviously, some of the people who live in the Cluster have decided they're in a position to cut some sort of favorable deal with Manticore. It's unfortunate that these self-interested manipulators are selfishly dragging their fellow citizens into the maw of a reactionary monarchy. Especially one which is currently engaged in a losing war that's entirely likely to drag the Cluster down in the event of its own defeat."

Harahap nodded, although he couldn't quite suppress a small flicker of distaste. He came from a protectorate planet himself. He wasn't going to shed any crocodile tears or pretend he hadn't known exactly what he was doing when he signed up with Frontier Security as his ticket out of that poverty-ridden pesthole. But that didn't make it any easier to forget how his parents had felt when OFS moved in to "protect" them from the horrible dangers of liberty.

"In addition to the dangers the Manties' war would pose to the Talbotters if this ill-considered annexation went through," Eichbauer went on, "there's the morally repugnant avarice and greed inherent in the Star Kingdom's naked grab for the Lynx Terminus of the so-called 'Manticore' Wormhole Junction. Should it succeed, it will give the Manties a lock on an even larger percentage of the League's shipping. Their shipping lines already carry far too much commerce which, for the League's own security, should be moving in League hulls, not foreign registry vessels, without adding Lynx to the equation. And if the Star Kingdom manages to secure a foothold here in Talbott, it will almost certainly extend its policy of harassing legitimate Solarian shipping and mercantile interests into this portion of the Verge. Obviously, then, it would be in the interests of neither the Talbotters nor the Solarian League for this so-called voluntary annexation to go through, yes?"

"I see your point, Ma'am," he said obediently when she paused. *Did you know this was coming when you sent me off to evaluate the various "resistance groups," Ulrike? Or was it just another case of preparing for all contingencies?*

"I'm glad you do, Captain," Anisimovna said, leaning forward in her chair with the slightest edge of a smile. "It was those concerns which first brought me into contact with Brigadier Yucel. Obviously, there's an element of self-interest in it for me and for my business colleagues, but in this instance our financial interests run in parallel with those of the League . . . and, of course, Frontier Security."

"The big problem, Damien," Eichbauer said a touch more briskly, as if to reassert control of what was clearly an operational briefing, "is that the Manties have managed to claim some sort of moral mandate on the basis of this supposed free vote in favor of annexation. It's untrue, of course, but their representatives on Old Earth have managed to talk fast enough to fool a lot of people into believing otherwise. Some of those people have access to significant political influence, and they've chosen to endorse the Manticoran version of events, which officially ties OFS' hands. But that doesn't mean we're blind to our responsibilities. So when Ms. Anisimovna and her colleagues approached us, we saw an opportunity to kill several birds with a single stone."

Harahap nodded. In some star nations, he knew, the sort of thing Eichbauer had just said would have constituted something very close to treason. In others, it would simply have led to an instant demand for her resignation. In the Solarian League, it was merely the way things were. The bureaucracies had been eluding civilian control for so long, in the name of keeping the system running, that the evasion of civilian oversight was as routine as brushing one's teeth. And as openly accepted among those who did the evading.

"We—meaning, specifically, you and I—have an intimate knowledge of the political and social dynamic of the Cluster," the major continued. "We know who the players are, and what their motivations and strengths and weaknesses are. Frontier Security cannot become officially involved in any effort to organize overt resistance to the annexation. Perhaps even more importantly, we can't involve ourselves in the funding, training, or equipping of any sort of guerrilla opposition."

"No, Ma'am. Of course not," he agreed obediently, despite the huge number of times OFS had done precisely that.

"Fortunately, private interests, represented in this instance by Ms. Anisimovna and Ms. Bardasano, have a greater freedom of action than we official representatives of the League. They're prepared to provide funds and weapons to those Talbotters who stand ready to use them to resist this calculated, naked Manticoran imperialism . . . *if* they can identify those who require their aid. Which is where we come in.

"As I say, Frontier Security can't be openly involved. Both for the reasons I've already mentioned and—" she looked directly into his eyes "—because of other, equally valid considerations. You, however, are sadly overdue for some leave. If you should happen to choose to take some of that accumulated leave in order to place your knowledge and contacts at the service of this completely unofficial effort to turn back Manticoran aggression, I would approve your request immediately."

"I understand, Major," he said, although he wasn't positive he actually did.

The basic parameters were clear enough. Eichbauer wanted him to act as the Mesans' contact and bagman with the lunatic fringe elements she'd had him evaluating for the past several months. He had few concerns about his ability to handle that part of the assignment. What he didn't quite see yet was how it was going to help anyone if he did. If Frontier Security was going to assume the sort of hands-off approach Eichbauer had taken such pains to sketch out, then simply creating unrest in the Cluster didn't seem to accomplish much. Talbotters like Nordbrandt, or even Westman, certainly weren't going to actually *defeat* both their own law enforcement agencies and the Star Kingdom. As he'd pointed out to his partner, they might be able to create a sufficiently nasty situation to convince the Manticorans to back off, but it was more likely simply to create the sort of bloodshed which could be used to *justify* intervention. That sort of induced anarchy had been Frontier Security's passport often enough in the past, but if OFS wasn't prepared to step in openly this time, then what was the point?

If Anisimovna had been an official representative of the Mesa System government, he might have believed Mesa was interested in moving in on the Cluster itself. But that sort of imperialistic expansion had never been part of the Mesan tradition. Simply destabilizing the area and getting Manticore, with its anti-slavery obsession, off Manpower's back would probably be worthwhile from the interstellar corporation's viewpoint. But that didn't explain what Frontier Security was doing in the middle of it all.

Unless there was a reason besides simple deniability and security for having this little meeting on Monica. . . .

"I understand," he repeated, "and you're right, Ma'am—I *am* overdue for a few months of leave. If in the process of taking it I can, purely coincidentally, of course, and strictly in my capacity as a private citizen, make myself useful to Ms. Anisimovna and the citizens of the Cluster, I'd be delighted to avail myself of the opportunity."

"I'm glad to hear it, Captain," Anisimovna purred. "And, since that's the case, might I suggest you return to your hotel, slip into something a bit less eye-catching than your uniform, and then check into the Estelle Arms? You'll find a reservation there in your name. It's quite a nice suite, just a few doors down from my own."

"Of course, Ma'am," he said, and looked back at Eichbauer. "With your permission, Major?" he murmured.

"It sounds like a fine idea to me, Damien," she said, with only the faintest trace of warning in her tone. "I'll handle the paperwork for your leave myself, as soon as I get back to the office. But you can consider yourself officially on leave, on my authority, from right now."

And you're on your own, so watch your ass, her green eyes added.

"Thank you, Ma'am," he replied. "I will."

Roberto Tyler, the duly elected President of the Republic of Monica (just as his father and grandfather had been), stood gazing out his office window at the city of Estelle. The G3 system primary burned down out of a cloud-spotted blue sky on the city's white and pastel ceramacrete towers. Its older, original buildings were much closer to the ground. Built out of native materials and old-fashioned concrete, they looked insignificant and toylike in the shadows of the looming towers which had become the norm since the planet finally reacquired counter-grav technology in the early years of his father's presidency. It was unfortunate, he reflected, that even today the construction of those towers was in the hands of out-system technicians, not Monica's own citizens. But there wasn't much choice about it, given the ongoing limitations of the Monican educational system.

He watched a native cloudcoaster, one of the furry, high-flying mammalian bird-analogues of Monica, sail past well below his two-hundred-and-tenth-floor office window. There were more private air cars in the capital's airspace than there'd been when he was younger, although still far fewer than there would have been in a city of the Shell, far less anywhere in the Old League. For that matter, there were fewer than in the skies of Vermeer, the capital of Rembrandt. He felt a familiar flicker of resentment at that thought, but that didn't make it untrue. Unfortunately, Rembrandt and Monica had rather different export commodities.

The admittance chime sounded, and he turned back towards his office door, folding his hands behind him. The door opened a moment later, and his secretary stepped through it.

"Mr. President," the well-groomed young man said, "Ms. Anisimovna is here."

The secretary stepped aside with a respectful bow, and perhaps the most beautiful woman Tyler had ever seen moved past him in a rustle of whispering silk. Tyler didn't recognize the style of Aldona Anisimovna's floor-length gown, but he approved of the way its filmy folds draped her spectacular figure. And of its deeply plunging neckline and the hip-high vent on its left side that displayed the perfection of her equally spectacular legs. As he was undoubtedly supposed to. No doubt Anisimovna had a full file on his own preferences and hobbies.

She was accompanied by three other people, all of whom Tyler recognized, although he'd actually met only one of them before. He knew the others' faces from the pre-meeting briefing conducted by Alfonso Higgins, his Chief of Intelligence, however, and he came forward, extending his hands to Anisimovna.

"Ms. Anisimovna!" he said with a broad smile. She held out her own right hand, and he shook it in both of his, still smiling. "This is a pleasure. A genuine pleasure," he told her.

"Why, thank you, Mr. President," she replied with a smile of her own which showed teeth as perfect as all the rest of her. Reasonably enough; her family had been availing itself of the advanced genetic manipulation techniques of Manpower for three or four generations now. It would have been shocking if her teeth hadn't been perfect.

"And, as always, it's a pleasure to see you, too, Junyan," Tyler continued, turning to Vice-Commissioner Hongbo.

"Mr. President," Hongbo Junyan murmured, bending his head in a polite bow as he shook the President's hand in turn. Tyler gripped it for another second, then turned to Anisimovna's other two companions with politely raised eyebrows, as if he had no idea who they might be.

"Mr. President," the Manpower board member said, "allow me to present Isabel Bardasano, of the Jessyk Combine, and Mr. Izrok Levakonic, of Technodyne Industries."

"Ms. Bardasano. Mr. Levakonic." Tyler shook two more hands, and his mind was busy.

Despite the amount of business Monica and Monican interests—including quite a few of the Tyler family's enterprises—did with Mesa, he personally knew very few Mesans. Nor was he particularly familiar with the internal dynamics of Mesan society. But Alfonso Higgins was another matter. According to him, Bardasano's spectacular tattoos, and the dramatically cut garments which displayed a degree of body piercing that made Tyler want to wince, marked her as a member of one of the Mesan "young lodges." There were at least a dozen "lodges," all in bitter competition with one another for dominance, and all at odds with the older Mesan tradition of inconspicuousness. Secure in the wealth and power of their corporate hierarchy, they deliberately flaunted who and what they were, rather than attempting to blend into the "respectable" Solly business community. Given the track record of the Audubon Ballroom, Tyler doubted that he would have been quite so eager to mark himself out as a target. Perhaps Bardasano simply had an unreasonable degree of faith in her personal security arrangements.

And perhaps, if she did, she had justification. One thing Higgins' did know about Bardasano was that, despite her relatively junior status as a mere cadet member of the Jessyk board, she was considered a dangerous, dangerous woman. She'd come up through the clandestine side of Jessyk's operations—the ones no one was supposed to know about. According to the rumors Higgins had picked up, she favored a hands-on style, very different from the remote spymaster approach, with multiple layers of cutouts, others in her line of work preferred. And according to those same rumors, people who blew operations for which Bardasano was responsible tended to come to abrupt and nasty ends.

As for Levakonic, even Higgins' people knew very little about him. But they knew a great deal about Technodyne Industries of Yildun, and it was unlikely Technodyne would have sent a low-level flunky this far from home, and in the company of someone like Anisimovna.

And, the president told himself, *Anisimovna is the spokeswoman, not Hongbo. That's interesting, too.*

"Please, be seated," he invited, waving at the comfortable powered chairs scattered about his spacious office. They accepted the invitation, settling down in the main conversational nook, and well-trained servants—scandalously expensive luxuries in the Old League, but easily come by here in the Verge—padded in with trays of refreshments.

Tyler accepted his own wineglass and leaned back in the office's largest and most impressive chair, allowing himself a moment to savor the extraordinarily expensive hand-painted oils on its walls, the handwoven carpet, and the original DeKuleyere sculpture beside his desk. The constantly, subtly shifting sonics radiating from the light sculpture were almost imperceptible, yet he felt them caressing him like a lover.

He knew nothing he could possibly do would make him anything except a Verge neobarb in his guests' eyes, however courteously they might conceal that. But his father had had him educated on Old Earth itself. The experience hadn't done anything to dull his contempt for the Old League's gooey, saccharin attachment to its cult of the individual, but it had at least left him with an educated palate and an appreciation for the finer things in life.

He waited until all his guests had been served and the servants had withdrawn. Then, resting his elbows on the arms of his chair and cupping his wineglass in both hands, he looked at Anisimovna and cocked one eyebrow.

"I was intrigued when your local representative screened my appointments secretary, Ms. Anisimovna. It isn't really customary for me to meet with people without at least some idea of why it is they want to see me. But in light of the business relationships between your corporation and so many of Monica's prominent citizens, I was certain whatever you wished to see me about would scarcely be a waste of my time. And now I see you accompanied by my good friend Vice-Commissioner Hongbo, and Mr. Levakonic. I must admit, it piques my curiosity."

"I rather hoped it would, Mr. President," she replied with a winsomely charming smile. He chuckled appreciatively, and she shrugged. "Actually, we're here because my colleagues and I see a situation in which all of us, including you and your republic, face a difficult problem. One which it may be possible not only to solve, but to transform into an extremely profitable *opportunity*, instead."

"Indeed?"

"Oh, yes. Indeed," she said. She leaned back, crossing her legs, and Tyler enjoyed the view as the clinging fabric molded itself to her trim, half-exposed thighs. It turned briefly invisible in intriguingly fleeting patches as it drew taut, too, he noted.

"The difficult problem to which I refer, Mr. President,"

she continued, "is the sudden, unwarranted and unwelcome intrusion of the Star Kingdom of Manticore into the Talbott Cluster."

Tyler's appreciation of the scenery faded abruptly, and his eyes narrowed. "Unwelcome" was an extremely inadequate way to describe Manticore's sudden arrival on his doorstep. The Cluster had never been particularly important to Monica (or anywhere else) before the Manties' discovery of their damned terminus. Even the label "Talbott Cluster" was thoroughly inaccurate; the body of stars it defined was neither a cluster nor centered on the Talbott System. It was only a convenient label Solarian astrographers had hung on it because the wretchedly poor Talbott System had been the site of Frontier Security's first observation post in the area. OFS had abandoned Talbott long since in favor of the much more valuable Meyers System once Meyers became an official League protectorate, but the name had stuck.

But the Star Kingdom was here now, and its reputation preceded it. He hardly expected his relationships with people like Anisimovna to find favor in Manticoran eyes, nor did he look forward to the effect the nearby example of Manticoran ideas of personal liberty—not to mention standards of living—was likely to have upon his own citizenry.

"I'll agree that I'd love to see the Manties' interference in Talbott swatted," he said, after a moment. "And, if you'll forgive me, I can well understand why Mesa and Manpower would also like to see them excluded from the region. I have to wonder, however, why you're discussing this with me, when it's apparent you've already discussed it with Mr. Hongbo. He, after all, represents the Solarian League and all its might; I'm simply the president of a single star-system."

"Yes, you are, Mr. President," Bardasano put in. "At the moment."

"At the moment?" he repeated, and she shrugged.

"Let me suggest a possible scenario," she said. "What would happen to your economy, and to your military power, if, instead of Manticore, Monica controlled the Lynx Terminus?"

"Are you serious?" He looked at her in disbelief, and she shrugged again.

"Assume for the moment that I am," she suggested. "I'm sure you've already observed the increased volume of shipping in the area. I'm something of a specialist in the area of the interstellar transportation of goods and people, Mr. President, and I can assure you, the volume will only grow with time. The new routing possibilities are still being worked out, and it will take a while for all of the hulls already in motion to settle down into the new patterns. And, of course, as the volume of the commerce increases, the need for transshipment points, warehouses, repair facilities, and all of the other paraphernalia associated with a wormhole terminus will increase along with it. As will the flow of transit fees, warehousing taxes, and so forth into the controlling power's treasury. I took the liberty of analyzing Monica's economic performance over the last ten T-years. By my most pessimistic estimate, possession of the Lynx Terminus would double your government's revenue stream within three T-years. By the time the terminus hit its full stride, your gross system product would have risen by a factor of six . . . at least. In addition to which, of course, your position as gatekeeper to the rest of the galaxy would make Monica the unquestioned dominant power in the Cluster."

"No doubt all of that is true, Ms. Bardasano," Tyler said, trying to hide the spike of sheer, unadulterated avarice her word picture had sent through him. "Unfortunately, as I understand it, the Manties have a short way with people who try to control the termini of their wormhole junction. I seem to recall they hold sovereignty even to the Sigma Draconis Terminus in the League itself."

"Not precisely correct, Mr. President," Hongbo said respectfully. "The Sigma Draconis Terminus lies outside the territorial limit of the star system. Nonetheless, the Manticorans were forced to make certain concessions to Sigma Draconis and the Beowulf planetary government.

The Sigma Draconis Terminus, for example, isn't fortified, and *Sigma Draconis*—not Manticore—is responsible for its security. In return for the protection afforded to the terminus by the Sigma Draconis System Defense Force, Beowulf receives a percentage of the use fees on that terminus. In addition, all Beowulf-registry freighters pay the same transit fees through all termini of the junction as *Manticoran*-registry ships. It would be more accurate to say, I think, that Manticore *shares* sovereignty over the terminus with Beowulf. And even that much is true only because Beowulf chose to accept the arrangement."

"Very well, Junyan," Tyler said just a bit testily. "Let's call it shared sovereignty, if you wish. Somehow, I don't think Manticore is particularly interested in sharing sovereignty over *this* terminus. And unlike Beowulf, Monica possesses neither the fleet strength to insist that it do so, nor the protection of the Solarian League Navy to hide behind if we irritate the Royal Manticoran Navy."

"We're aware of that, Mr. President," Anisimovna said, leaning forward to lay one hand lightly on his knee . . . and show him an impressive bit of decolletage. "And I assure you," she continued, "that we would never have asked to meet with you if we'd intended to put you at risk. Well," she allowed herself another small smile as she sat back in her chair once more, "perhaps that's not quite entirely accurate. There *will* be an element of risk. There always is when one plays for truly high stakes. But in this instance, the risk is both manageable and much smaller than it might appear at first sight."

"Really?" He put an edge of coolness into his voice. "It sounds to me as if you intend to invite me to unilaterally proclaim Monican sovereignty over the Lynx Terminus. I fail to see how that could constitute a 'manageable' risk, when my entire fleet consists of less than one light task force, compared to the RMN. And while my own intelligence sources aren't the equal of the SLN's—or even your own, I dare say—they're quite sufficient to tell me

Manticore's hardware is now much more dangerous than anything Monica has. Then, too, there's the minor matter that the entire Manticoran Home Fleet is just sitting at the other end of the terminus."

"Mr. President," Anisimovna said a bit reproachfully, "you're getting ahead of our . . . proposal. Yes," she raised one hand gracefully, "it's perfectly understandable that you should see the physical threat represented by the Manty navy. In fact, it's your responsibility as Monica's head of state and military commander in chief to see exactly that. However, please consider that there would be absolutely no advantage to us in sacrificing your navy or your star nation. We're prepared to make a substantial economic investment in your success in any operation or gambit we might suggest you undertake. As businesspeople, we would scarcely do such a thing unless we fully and confidently expected the venture to succeed."

Tyler considered her narrowly. The argument was logical enough, but he couldn't quite ignore the fact that she was talking about the possible loss of a *financial investment*, one he was certain no corporation like Manpower would ever assume in the first place if it couldn't afford to write it off in the event of disaster. He, on the other hand, would risk something just a bit more permanent than that.

Still . . .

"Very well," he said. "Explain just what it is you have in mind."

"It's actually not all that complicated, Mr. President," Anisimovna told him. "We—meaning my own business colleagues, not the League or Mr. Hongbo's Frontier Security—are prepared to provide your navy with a rather powerful reinforcement. At the moment, if my figures are correct, your fleet consists of five heavy cruisers, eight light cruisers, nineteen destroyers, and several dozen LACs. Which comes to just over four million tons. Is that substantially correct?"

"Yes, it is. I'm sure Admiral Bourmont could give you more complete figures, but four million tons will do," he said, still watching her intently, and refraining from pointing out that almost a half million tons of that consisted solely of sadly obsolete light attack craft. Or that the cruisers fell far short of cutting-edge technology themselves.

"Very well," she said. "We're prepared to supply you with fourteen Solarian *Indefatigable*-class battlecruisers, each of approximately eight hundred and fifty thousand tons. That comes to twelve million tons, or a three hundred percent increase in your navy's tonnage."

Roberto Tyler felt as if someone had just kicked him in the belly. His ears couldn't have heard what he thought they just had. But if she meant it. . . .

"While the *Indefatigables* are being replaced in Solarian service by the *Nevada*-class ships, Mr. President," Levakonic said, speaking up for the first time, "they served primarily with the frontier fleet elements. As I'm sure you're aware, that means they were kept much more rigorously updated with refits than is traditionally the case for Solarian ships of the wall or battlecruisers attached to the Central Reserve. These vessels represent very nearly the latest word in SLN weaponry and EW capabilities. Ms. Anisimovna has pointed out that they would effectively quadruple your existing tonnage. In terms of actual effective combat strength, your navy's capabilities would increase by a factor of well over a hundred."

"Yes. Yes, they would," Tyler admitted after a moment, and he could hear the raw greed in his voice himself. "I fail to understand, however, just how private businesspeople like you and Ms. Anisimovna might happen to have access to such ships." He resolutely refrained from looking at Hongbo.

"As I just pointed out," Levakonic said calmly, "the *Indefatigables* are being replaced by the *Nevadas*. The process is going to take years. It's also going to be expensive, and Technodyne is one of the primary builders for the new class. To help defray construction costs, the Navy is disposing of some of the *Indefatigables* slated to be replaced by transferring them to us for scrapping and reclamation. Obviously, they have on-site inspectors to ensure that the hulls are stripped and broken up. As it happens, however," his expression, Tyler noticed, remained completely innocent and bland, "some of those inspectors have developed a case of what used to be called myopia. A few of the older ships have somehow fallen through cracks and dropped off of the SLN tracking system. Under the right set of circumstances, fourteen of them could be here within, oh, about sixty T-days."

"I see." Tyler was getting his imagination back under control, and he smiled crookedly at the Technodyne representative. "I imagine, though, that it might be a bit difficult for your employers if those 'scrapped' ships turned up intact in someone else's navy."

"'A bit difficult' would be a fairly generous understatement, Mr. President," Levakonic agreed. The small, wiry man smiled with what Tyler suspected was the first genuine amusement any of his visitors had displayed. "That's why we'd have to insist that all of them be comprehensively refitted in your own yard here in Monica. We'd need more than just a simple change of transponder codes. We could reshape their emissions signatures significantly by changing out sidewall generators and the main active sensor arrays, but there are several other, smaller changes we'd want to make, as well. In combination, they should be more than enough to adequately disguise the ships' origins. It wouldn't stand up in the face of a physical boarding and examination, but that shouldn't really be a factor."

"I suppose not," Tyler said. But then he shook himself.

"This is all extremely fascinating . . . and very tempting," he said frankly. "But even with a reinforcement like that, the Monican Navy would disappear like water in a vacuum if the Manty Home Fleet came calling." He shook his head. "However much I might like the notion of controlling the Lynx Terminus, and of keeping the Manticorans as far away from Monica as possible, I'm not prepared to commit suicide by challenging them to open combat."

"It wouldn't work out that way," Anisimovna predicted with what Tyler privately thought was a ludicrous degree of assurance.

"Without wishing to seem discourteous, Ms. Anisimovna, I don't believe I feel quite as confident of that as you appear to."

"Honesty is always welcome, Mr. President, even at the risk of discourtesy. And I'm not surprised you don't share my confidence. The entire idea's come at you cold, without the opportunity to consider all the ramifications. But I assure you that *we* have considered them quite carefully. And although I recognize we're suggesting you assume a more immediate and larger degree of personal risk than we are, I might also point out that if this gambit fails, and your new battlecruisers are traced back to Mr. Levakonic or to myself, then the consequences for us and for our corporations will also be . . . extreme."

His eyes flared, and she smiled gently.

"I'm not trying to equate our degrees of risk, Mr. President. I'm simply trying to make the point that we wouldn't be recommending any such course of action to you if we didn't honestly and completely expect it to succeed."

And I can believe as much of that as I want to, he thought sardonically. *But, then again, my relationship with Manpower and Mesa is worth too much to jeopardize by being blunt. And it can't do any harm to at least* listen *to whatever insanity she wants to propose.*

"Very well," he said. "Explain just why you believe I could get away with anything like this, please."

"Let's consider this situation from the Manties' side," Anisimovna suggested reasonably. "Their intelligence on the Cluster can't have been very complete before they first located the Lynx Terminus. After all, Lynx is over six hundred light-years from Manticore; Monica is another two hundred and seventy light-years from Lynx; and the Star Kingdom had absolutely no strategic interests in the area.

"Things have changed, however, and I'm sure their

intelligence services have been working overtime to secure as much information as possible about the Cluster and its immediate neighbors—including Monica. And they've probably done an excellent job of analyzing the data they've been able to collect, especially now that Patricia Givens has returned to head their Office of Naval Intelligence.

"Because of that, they know exactly—or, at least, to within a fairly close margin—how powerful your navy is. We may as well all be honest here and admit that Monica's long-standing relationship with Frontier Security would make you of special interest to the Manties, so it's virtually certain they've devoted an additional effort to collecting, collating, and analyzing information about you."

She paused, and Tyler nodded.

"I'm sure you're right, at least about the bit about their having a special interest in us. That's why I'm confident their Admiralty must already have drawn up contingency plans for the unlikely event that we were foolish enough to get frisky and step on their toes."

"Of course. *But*," Anisimovna's gray eyes flashed with what certainly seemed to be genuine enthusiasm, "those plans are based on the ship strength they know you possess. If you were to suddenly appear before the terminus with no less than fourteen big, powerful, *modern* battlecruisers, they would have to realize there'd been some sort of sudden, radical change in the balance of military power in the Cluster. They won't know where you got those ships, or who you got them from. Nor will they know how many *other* ships you may have acquired. The possibility that you got them directly from the League, or at least with the League's official knowledge and approval, will have to cross their minds. And the fact that they're already at war with the Republic of Haven, which has them stretched extremely tightly, will be another factor in their thinking.

"I'm not going to suggest that anyone could guarantee they wouldn't eventually move against you, assuming they concluded you were acting solely on your own. But they'll hesitate, Mr. President. They have to. Given how close to desperate their military situation is right now, they can't possibly unhesitatingly divert the strength to deal with your newly discovered battlecruisers—*and whoever might be backing you*—until they've had time to analyze the situation."

"And if they respond out of knee-jerk reaction by sending, say, twenty or thirty of their own battlecruisers, or a single squadron of superdreadnoughts, through before they have time to realize all the reasons why they have to analyze the situation?" Tyler inquired.

"Should they be stupid enough to do that, Mr. President," Bardasano said, "I believe you'll be able to present them with an argument against pressing any launch buttons after they get here."

"Indeed?" He looked at her skeptically. "Such as?"

"After you've accepted the surrender of the Manty terminus picket, or blown it out of space, as the case may be," she said calmly, "a dozen or so Monican freighters will begin emplacing mines. Actually, courtesy of Mr. Levakonic, they'll be something new, something Technodyne developed out of the reverse flow of information from the previous Havenite regime."

Tyler looked at Levakonic, and the Technodyne rep smiled.

"We call them 'missile pods,' Mr. President," he said. "They have a great deal more standoff range than any conventional mine, and enough of them will blow any ship ever built out of space."

"And where do these 'Monican freighters' come from?"

"Oh, I imagine I know someone who could loan them to you," Bardasano said, gazing up at the ceiling.

"And the cost of all of this generosity—battlecruisers, freighters, missile pods . . . ? I may not be Admiral Bourmont, but I have a pretty shrewd notion that what you're talking about would cost considerably more than the next ten or fifteen years of our GSP."

"Certainly it would be expensive, Mr. President," Anisimovna agreed. "But not any more than could be readily repaid by someone who had possession of a junction terminus. You could undoubtedly work quite a bit of it out by simply granting transit fee exemptions to Jessyk Combine shipping passing through."

"So." Tyler let his gaze sweep over all of his visitors. "And how long are these missile pods good for? What's their endurance?"

"No more than two or three weeks," Levakonic admitted. "A month, at most. After that, they have to be taken off-line for service and maintenance."

"But they'd be your hole card against an immediate, ill-conceived response from Manticore," Anisimovna said quickly.

"And while your freighters were placing the mines," Bardasano said, "your navy would be sweeping up all of the merchantships which were present awaiting transit at the time of your arrival. And, of course, the additional ships coming in through hyper and unaware of the change in ownership. I'm sure you'd feel enormous remorse if you allowed any of those vessels to pass through the terminus before the situation with Manticore was fully resolved. After all, accidents happen, and it's entirely possible that a merchantship coming through from Lynx might be mistaken for a hostile warship and destroyed by the Manties before they realized their error. It would therefore be your responsibility to hold all of those ships under the close, protective escort of your own naval units."

"Where," Levakonic said softly, "any errors in targeting by attacking Manticoran warships might, regrettably, of course, kill hundreds of innocent merchant spacers. *Solarian* spacers, whose government would be . . . most unhappy over their deaths."

Tyler looked at them again, shaken by the ruthlessness they were prepared to employ.

"All right," he said finally. "I'll concede that everything you've said so far is at least possible. But it's all ultimately short term. Simply manning that many battlecruisers would stretch my trained manpower to the limit. I don't even know if it would be possible out of our current manpower. Even if it were, I don't have the trained technicians to provide the maintenance your missile pods are going to require, and I doubt very much that you could afford to provide me with enough of them. Not to mention the fact that even if you were able to do so, it would only make it painfully clear where 'my' ships and missile pods actually came from. And I can't hold dozens of merchantships indefinitely, either. The Solarian shipping lines would be screaming for my head within weeks, months at the outside, and then I'd find the SLN *and* the RMN coming after me."

"No, you wouldn't." It was the first time Hongbo had spoken in several minutes, and Tyler's eyes snapped over to the Frontier Security official.

"Why not?" he asked tautly.

"Because, Mr. President," Anisimovna said, "you will have contacted the Office of Frontier Security through its offices in the Meyers System *before* you dispatch your naval units to the Lynx Terminus. You'll explain to OFS that you can no longer sit by and watch the deteriorating situation in the Cluster. Obviously, the citizens of the Cluster's star systems are violently opposed to their annexation by the Star Kingdom of Manticore. You, as the head of state of the most powerful *local* star nation, with your *legitimate* interests—humanitarian, as well as those related to your own security—have seen no option but to intervene. And, as the first step in ending the bloodshed and restoring domestic tranquility and local self-government, you have seized control of the Lynx Terminus in order to avoid further destabilization by outside interests."

"'Deteriorating situation'? 'Bloodshed'?" Tyler shook his head. "*What* deteriorating situation?"

"I have it on the best of authority that violent resistance to the imposition of Manticoran rule is already brewing," Anisimovna said somberly. "The freedom-loving citizens of the Cluster are awakening to the cynical way in which the plebiscite vote was manipulated to create the appearance of an overwhelming mandate for annexation by the

Star Kingdom. And as they awake, they are preparing themselves for an armed struggle against the interlopers and their local collaborators."

Tyler felt his eyes trying to boggle. That was the most preposterous load of—

Wait, he thought. *Wait! That report from Alfonzo. Anisimovna and Bardasano met with Eichbauer and some Gendarmerie captain right here in Estelle. And Eichbauer and what's-his-name were in* uniform. *Which means Anisimovna wanted me to know about the meeting. But* Hongbo *hasn't said a thing about it. So there's something here that officially isn't happening but Hongbo knows about anyway, and they want me to know he does.*

"I see," he said, very slowly, after a moment. "And, of course, Frontier Security would share my concern over the bloodshed and unrest in the Cluster."

"We'd have no choice but to examine your allegations most carefully, Mr. President," Hongbo agreed gravely. "After all, our fundamental mandate is to prevent exactly this sort of imperialistic adventurism on the frontiers of the Solarian League. And, of course, to safeguard the personal liberties of the citizens living in the regions under our protection."

"And how—hypothetically speaking, of course—do you believe Frontier Security would eventually rule in this case?" Tyler asked, watching Hongbo's expression very carefully.

"Well, you understand, Mr. President, that anything I was to say at this point would have to be just that—hypothetical?" Hongbo looked at Tyler until the Monican nodded. "On that basis, then, I should think Commissioner Verrochio's first action would be to dispatch an SLN task force to stabilize the situation at Lynx. The task force's commander's orders would undoubtedly be to take control of the terminus in the League's name until such time as the competing claims to it could be adjudged. Your ships would, of course, be required to withdraw from the area, as would any Manticoran military units. Anyone who attempted to defy his instructions would find himself—briefly—at war with the Solarian League.

"Once that situation was stabilized, our investigation and verification teams would spread out through the Cluster. We'd interview all parties, including the freedom fighters, in order to make a determination on the true representativeness of the annexation vote.

"I must confess that I personally harbor some fairly profound personal reservations about the validity of that vote." He met Tyler's gaze levelly and allowed himself a thin, fleeting smile. "Obviously, though, we'd have to wait for our careful and painstaking investigation to confirm those reservations. If, however, they found what I suspect they might, I don't believe we'd have any choice but to set aside the sadly flawed initial annexation vote and hold a second plebiscite, under strict League supervision and poll monitoring, to determine the true desires of the Cluster's citizens."

"And if it should happen that this new plebiscite disavows the original vote?"

"In that case, Mr. President, one of the options which would be presented on the new plebiscite's ballot, I'm sure, would be a request for temporary Frontier Security protection while a constitution was drafted to unify the systems of the Talbott Cluster into a new, autonomous sector under the leadership of an enlightened *local* power. The . . . Monica Sector, perhaps."

"With, of course," Bardasano almost purred, "sovereignty over the junction terminus which would be the new sector's most valuable natural resource."

Roberto Tyler sat back in his chair, gazing at the glittering vista they had stretched out before him. He raised his wineglass and sipped, then lowered it again and smiled.

Chapter Fourteen

"Well, you can stop wondering about where we're being sent," Leo Stottmeister announced two days after the Thimble banquet.

"And why, might that be, O Font of Wisdom?" Ragnhild demanded suspiciously.

"Because I, by a mighty feat of deductive reasoning, have divined the answer." He grinned at the other midshipmen around the commons table. "I just finished helping Commander Wright download all available astro material from *Hercules* on Nuncio, Celebrant, Pequod, and New Tuscany. And I've got to tell you guys, it isn't all that great."

"Nuncio, eh?" Helen scratched an eyebrow and frowned. "So we're catching the Northern Patrol."

"Looks like," Leo agreed. "And I'm guessing we're going to spend a lot of our time doing survey work." The others looked at him, and he shrugged. "*Hercules*' astrogation department has been doing its best to update the various charts, but they really suck. We know about where to find the stars themselves, but we know damn-all about the system astrography, and even some of the grav wave data looks suspect."

"Not too surprising our charts're so bad, I guess," Aikawa said. "Before we found the Lynx Terminus, this wasn't an area we were particularly interested in. I guess I'm just a little surprised the locals don't have better information than you seem to be suggesting."

"Some of them may," Ragnhild said "There have to be at least some decent charts in the hands of local merchant skippers."

"Then why doesn't *Hercules* already have them?"

"I can think of two possible reasons," Leo suggested. "One, the flagship—" by which he meant "the Admiral," as all his listeners were aware "—hasn't assigned sufficient urgency to running the data down. Or, two, the locals who have the information aren't inclined to share it."

"There's a third possibility," Paulo d'Arezzo said diffidently. All eyes swiveled in his direction, and he smiled faintly. "The Cluster represents a pretty big volume," he pointed out. "It takes a while to get from one star to another, and the locals don't have a lot of dispatch boats. So any information that's moving out there is probably moving aboard regular merchies—which means slowly—and *Hercules* has to wait until whichever local skipper has the necessary data wanders by Spindle. It could just be a delay in the information loop."

"I suppose that's possible," Leo said after a moment, and Helen wondered if he felt as surprised by his agreement with d'Arezzo as she did. Although, a certain sour honesty made her admit, on the rare occasions when the overly handsome middy deigned to open his mouth, he had a pretty fair track record for making sense.

"Well, whatever the reason, the charts we've got have more holes in them than anything else," Leo continued. "If I were the Captain, I wouldn't trust any of them as far as I could spit. So, like I say, we're going to be spending a lot of our time surveying."

"Borrrrrrrring," Ragnhild sighed.

"Are we ready to proceed, Mr. Wright?" Aivars Terekhov asked.

"Yes, Sir," the Astrogator replied crisply.

"Very well. The con is yours, Commander."

"The con is mine, aye, Sir. Helm, come to zero-seven-niner by one-one-one. Make your acceleration four-zero-zero gravities."

"Aye, aye, Sir. Coming to zero-seven-niner by one-one-one, acceleration four-zero-zero gravities," Senior Chief Clary responded.

She moved her joystick, and *Hexapuma* rolled on her long axis and swung her bow towards the Spindle hyper limit. She went almost instantly to the specified acceleration, and loped off across the trackless waste of the system's ecliptic.

Terekhov leaned back in his command chair, watching his bridge crew as the ship moved smoothly towards her destination, sixty-plus light-years distant. The voyage would require eight and a half days, by the standards of the rest of the universe, although it would take only a little over five and a half by *Hexapuma*'s clocks.

It was impossible to tell from looking at him what he thought of his orders. At least they hadn't come as a surprise. And if he thought playing mapmaker in a poverty-stricken backwater while his Star Kingdom fought for its life elsewhere was less than the best possible employment for him or his ship, no sign of it showed in his pensive expression.

"Commander FitzGerald," he said, after a moment.

"Yes, Sir?"

"Set the normal watch schedule, if you please. Once we cross the Delta wall, we'll exercise Tracking and send the crew to Action Stations for weapons drill."

"Aye, aye, Sir." FitzGerald turned to Lieutenant Commander Kaplan. "Commander Kaplan, you have the watch."

"Aye, aye, Sir," Kaplan acknowledged. "I have the watch." She stood as the captain climbed out of his command chair, then she crossed to it, and settled herself into it in his place. "Dismiss the departure watch," she announced. "Second watch personnel, man your stations."

HMS *Hexapuma* accelerated steadily onward, oblivious to the comings and goings of the ephemeral beings on her bridge. Unlike her crew, she had no doubts, no questions. Only purpose.

Agnes Nordbrandt forced herself to amble along, lost in the flow of the crowds. It wasn't easy, yet she knew unhurried, apparently aimless movement was her best camouflage. It was purposeful movement, brisk movement, that drew the watchful eye, and she couldn't afford that on this, of all days.

She did allow herself to glance at her chrono. Twelve more minutes. It seemed like an eternity after all the hard work, the planning, the sweating. Now, in less than another fifteen minutes, it was all going to pay off, and the smug, smiling parasites who'd mocked her and her followers as an inconsequential "lunatic fringe" would discover just how wrong they'd been.

She moved out of the main pedestrian flow and into a park. It was a carefully selected park, and she strolled idly along its paths. She supposed there was no compelling reason she had to be this close to the Mall in person. Not really. In fact, it was a dangerous complication, with potentially deadly risks. But she also knew she couldn't possibly have stayed away. However tactically foolish it might have been of her, she *had* to be here, within visual range of the Nemanja Building, the home of the Kornatian Parliament.

She found the park bench she'd been looking for and settled down on it. As promised, the Nemanja Building, like an elaborate marble and granite wedding cake on its gentle hill, was clearly visible between the uppermost, blossom-laden boughs of the Terran cherry trees planted along the park's verge. The planetary flag flapping from the pole atop its tallest tower signified that Parliament was in session, and she took her book reader from her bag and laid it in her lap, before she glanced casually at her chrono yet again.

Now.

She looked up, and for one, fleeting moment her expression of casual boredom disappeared into a flare of savage satisfaction as a brilliant light flashed from the fifth floor. She watched the fifth-floor installment of the verandalike balcony which circled the Nemanja Building at each level disintegrate, fly outward, and then go spinning towards the ground in broken bits and pieces that tumbled with dreamlike slowness. A plume of dust and smoke jetted upward from the gaping wound in the parliament building's flank, and dust trails hung in midair, comet tails traced by the plummeting rubble.

The explosion's rumbling thunder reached her eighteen seconds after the flash, and she saw other people in the park looking up, crying out, pointing and shouting questions at one another. Birds—native Kornatian species, and Terran imports alike—erupted from the park's greenery, shrieking in terrified protest, and playing children froze, turning to stare uncomprehendingly at the towering jet of smoke.

And then, hard on the heels of the first explosion, the rumble of other explosions came washing over the capital. Not one more, or two, but ten. Ten more explosions, ten more charges of commercial blasting compound many times as powerful as the ancient chemical explosives of prespace days. They ripped through government office buildings, shopping malls, banks, and the Split Stock Exchange. Fire and smoke and the demonic howl of emergency sirens—and the screams and shrieks of the wounded and dying—followed close behind the explosions, and Agnes Nordbrandt bared her teeth, shivering in a strange ecstasy of mingled horror and triumph. She watched the dust and smoke billowing above the city of her birth, like funeral palls across the cloudless blue dome of the sky. She saw other people leaving the park, running towards the explosions, and she wondered whether they were going to gawk at the disaster or out of some instinct to help. Not that it mattered.

She sat on the bench, waiting, while ten more minutes

ticked into eternity . . . and then the second wave of explosions shook the city.

She watched the fresh smoke clawing at the skyline, and then she calmly slid her book reader back into her bag, stood, walked one hundred and six meters down a graveled path, and opened the unlocked hatch in the storm drain's ceramacrete cover. She swung down the ladder, closing the hatch and locking it carefully behind her. There was only a trickle of water down the very bottom of the drain channel, and she pulled out her hand light and strode briskly away.

Vuk Rajkovic, Vice President of the Republic of Kornati, stared in horrified disbelief at the smoldering wreckage. The bomb on the fifth floor of the Nemanja Building had been bad enough. It had killed eleven of Parliament's deputies and at least twenty members of their staffs. But the *second* bomb, the one planted on the third floor, directly under the first one . . .

He shook his head, feeling nausea swirl underneath the shock. The vicious calculation of that second bomb touched his horror with a sun-hot lick of hatred. That one had only gotten one more deputy—old Nicola Martinovic, who'd plunged back into the smoke and flames like the old warhorse he was. He'd carried two people out and gone back for a third just as the fresh fireball and the flying cloud of shrapnel which had once been stone walls, plaster, framed diplomas, and portraits of husbands and wives and children came screaming out of the rubble.

But Nicola hadn't been alone. The Nemanja Security Force had been there, the cops diving in, tearing at the flaming wreckage with bare hands. And the first of the Capital Fire Department rescue teams, flinging themselves into the flames and the leaning, groaning structural members, ready to fall. They'd been there, too. And the second explosion had slaughtered them, as well, as it spilled the entire western third of the building into the streets below.

And if I'd gotten around from the Chamber just a little bit faster, it would have slaughtered me, *right along with them*, he thought. A part of him almost wished it had.

"Mr. Vice President! *Mr. Vice President!*"

Rajkovic turned, blinking smoke-reddened eyes, as Darinka Djerdja, his executive assistant, clawed her way through the smoke towards him.

"Yes, Darinka?" *Too calm,* he thought. *I sound too calm. It must be shock.*

"Mr. Vice President, this wasn't—I mean," Darinka dragged in a deep breath, then coughed explosively as the smoke hit her lungs. He handed her his handkerchief, and she held it over her mouth and nose, coughing into it until she finally managed to catch her breath.

"Now, Darinka. Try again."

"Mr. Vice President," tears cut startlingly white tracks in the soot and grime on her pretty face, "these weren't the only bombs."

"What?" He stared at her. He couldn't have heard her correctly.

"All over the Mall, Mr. Vice President," she told him, reaching out in her distress to grip him by the upper arms and shake him. "The Stock Exchange. First Planetary Bank. The Sekarkic Square subway station. They're everywhere! We have hundreds of dead and wounded, Sir—*hundreds* of them!"

"All right, Darinka," he told her, although a part of him sneered that it would never be *all right* again. "All right, I understand. I'd better get over to Civil Defense. Do you have your official com?"

"Yes, Sir," she said with almost pathetic eagerness, grasping at anything useful she could do.

"All right. Listen, the regular civilian circuits are jammed, and I lost my com somewhere between here and the Chamber. So get on yours. Contact General Suka. Tell him that on my instructions he's to declare martial law. Do it now; I'll get the formal, signed proclamation to him as soon as I can. Then get hold of Colonel Basaricek, at Police HQ. Give her the same message. And tell both of them I'm going to Civil Defense, and that we'll use the com room there as our headquarters. And tell the General he'd better start bringing in emergency personnel from other cities. We're going to need them."

"Mr. Vice President, you'd better see this."

Rajkovic turned away from yet another hoarse-voiced, exhausted conference. Six hours had elapsed since the horrendous attack, and the news just kept getting worse. According to Brigita Basaricek, the commanding officer of the Kornatian National Police, the count of confirmed dead had already topped five hundred, with twice that many injured. The missing numbered in the thousands, but some of them—*most of them, please God!*—were probably simply lost in the confusion, not buried under the rubble.

Probably.

"What?" he snapped at the aide whose name he'd never learned. He regretted his tone the moment the words were out of his mouth, but the young man didn't even seem to notice.

"It's the HD, Sir. There's a message from someone claiming responsibility."

Rajkovic found himself back in the communications room without any conscious memory of having moved. The place was crowded, uniformed and civilian personnel standing motionless, staring at the HD in total, shocked silence. They didn't even notice he was there, until he started elbowing his way through the crowd like the aggressive soccer wing he'd once been.

They got out of his way when they finally realized who he was, and he found himself in the front row, staring up at the display with the rest of them. Staring at a face he knew well, someone who had once been a close political ally . . . and an even closer friend.

"—responsibility in the name of the Freedom Alliance of Kornati. We regret that we have been driven to this extremity, but we will not turn aside from the road we have chosen. The collaborationist regime of President

Tonkovic and her sycophants will not be allowed to sign away the sovereignty of our home world. The indecently wealthy traitors whose corruption and greed have inflicted so much poverty, so much suffering, upon so many Kornatians, will profit no further from their crimes. Their plan to sell our planet to the highest bidder to protect their own obscene fortunes will not succeed. And the off-worlders who seek to steal our souls along with our rightful wealth, our liberties, and our rights as freeborn citizens of the sovereign Planet of Kornati, will find only death on our soil. The Freedom Alliance is the avenging sword of the betrayed people of the Split System, and it will not be sheathed while a single traitor clings to power on our world! Let those who love freedom rally to us—and let those who worship slavery fear us!"

She stared out of the HD, dark eyes blazing with a messianic light, and her voice rang with absolute conviction and sincerity. It came to Vuk Rajković in that moment that she'd never before found her true place. Not in the electoral fray, not in efforts to reform a corrupt political system, not in the thrust and parry of parliamentary debate. Not even in the white-hot crucible of the annexation campaign. But she'd found it now. This was the struggle to which she could give all she was, all she believed in—all she possessed or would ever possess. He saw it blazing in her face as he looked at her, and he turned to Colonel Basaricek.

"Find that bitch, Brigita," he said harshly. "Find her . . . *and kill her*."

Chapter Fifteen

"—with the Honorable Delegate from Marian." The heavyset speaker stood at the podium, looking out over the assembled delegates of the Constitutional Convention and shook his head. "I have no doubt of her sincerity, nor do I question the probity of her motives," he continued gravely. "Yet the fact remains that she is proposing to barter away ancient, hard-won liberties in the name of political expediency. I cannot support such a proposal, and the delegation from New Tuscany regretfully votes in the negative."

Henri Krietzmann's expression gave no hint of his emotions. That sort of impassivity didn't come easily to him, but he'd had a crash course in it over the past endless weeks here on Flax. And he supposed Bernardus and Joachim were right. There was no point trying to hide what he felt when everyone here knew exactly why Dresden had sent him to the Convention, but it was a pragmatic necessity to appear impartial whenever he held the Convention's gavel. And, perhaps even more to the point, he had a moral responsibility to *be* impartial in the fashion in which he exercised his authority on the Convention's floor.

He watched Andrieaux Yvernau leave the microphone and return to his own seat, and a corner of his mind noted the rebellious expressions on a couple of the other New Tuscany delegates. It would appear the delegation's unanimity was less pronounced than Yvernau would have preferred. But it was still far more so than Krietzmann liked. Unlike Dresden, where hardscrabble poverty was the great unifying condition, New Tuscany had its own exorbitantly wealthy (by Verge standards) upperclass, like Spindle and at least half of the Cluster's other systems. Yvernau was probably almost as rich as Samiha Lababibi. As such, the delegation chief faced both enormous opportunity and great risk once the annexation went through, and he wanted all the safeguards he could get. A few of the other New Tuscan delegates, without his vast personal fortune to protect, were growing impatient with him. Unfortunately, the delegation, like the New Tuscan government itself, was overwhelmingly dominated by the local oligarchs. It was highly unlikely any of the others would openly break with Yvernau. In fact, they were under binding instructions to follow his directives, which had put New Tuscany firmly into Aleksandra Tonkovic's political pocket.

Krietzmann waited until Yvernau settled back into his chair, then looked at the Christmas tree of blinking attention lights on his display.

"The Chair recognizes the Honorable Delegate from Tillerman," he said, gesturing for the woman in question to take the microphone.

"Thank you, Mr. President," Yolanda Harper, the Tillerman System's chief delegate said, standing up but never moving away from her seat, "but I'll keep this brief, and I don't think I'll need a mike to make m'self understood." The lanky, brown-haired, weathered woman turned to face the other delegations and threw up one calloused, farmer's hand in disgust. "That last was just about the biggest load of shit I've heard or seen since the last fertilizer shuttle arrived at my place this spring," she said in her blunt, hard-syllabled voice.

"The Tillerman delegation unanimously endorses the resolution, and—"

The Chamber door flew open, and Krietzmann looked up in reflex outrage. The Convention's closed sessions weren't to be disturbed, and certainly not in such abrupt, unceremonious fashion! He opened his mouth to say something sharp, then paused. Maxwell Devereaux, the Convention Sergeant at Arms, wasn't trying to prevent the interruption; he was hurrying down the aisle from the open door in front of the haggard-faced, uniformed messenger, and his expression sent a sudden icy chill through Krietzmann's blood.

"I'm sorry, Henri—I mean, Mr. President," Devereaux said hoarsely. "I know we're not supposed to, but—" He drew a deep breath, and shook himself, like a man who'd just been punched in the gut. "This is Major Toboc. He just arrived with a dispatch from Split. I . . . think you'd better view it."

It was hard to tell which of the faces in the private conference room was most ashen.

Henri Krietzmann sat at the head of the table, with Samiha Lababibi at the opposite end. Joachim Alquezar sat to Krietzmann's left, facing Aleksandra Tonkovic across the tabletop, and silence was a cold, leaden weight, crushing down on them all. Finally, Krietzmann cleared his throat.

"Well," he said harshly, "I suppose we should all have seen this coming."

Tonkovic flinched, as if he'd slapped her. Then she stiffened in her chair, shoulders squaring, and glared at him.

"What do you mean by that crack?" she demanded sharply.

Krietzmann blinked at her in genuine surprise. For just a moment, he couldn't imagine what might have set her off. Then he realized, and his own anger flickered at the thought that she could be so petty as to think that at a moment like this—!

No, Henri, he told himself firmly. *This isn't the time. And whatever else may be going through her head, she* has *to be hurting right now. Of course she's looking for someone to take some of that anger and pain out on. But, Jesus, I wish Bernardus were here!*

"Contrary to what you may think, Aleksandra," he said, forcing his voice's harshness back into a tone of reason by sheer willpower, "that wasn't an attempt on my part to say 'I told you so.'"

"No?" She glowered at him. But then she scrubbed her eyes with the heels of her hands, and her shoulders slumped once more. "No, I guess it wasn't," she said wearily. "It's just—" Her voice trailed off, and she shook her head, slowly.

"Henri wasn't saying he'd told you so, Aleksandra," Alquezar said after a moment. "And neither am I. But it's probably going to feel like we are."

She looked up at him, green eyes flashing, and it was his turn to shake his head.

"Look, Aleksandra. All of us, including you, have been saying for months now that some degree of backlash was inevitable. And we've all been admitting there's at least a lunatic fringe—like Westman—that was likely to take things into its own hands. But I don't think anyone, including me or Henri, ever expected something like this. We should've at least allowed for the possibility, though, and there's going to be a lot of recriminations—and *self*-recrimination—while we cope with the reality. Some of it's going to hurt, and a lot of it's going to be ugly. But here in this room, the four of us—especially!—have to be able to talk to each other as frankly as we possibly can."

She glared at him for a few more seconds, then nodded, manifestly unwillingly.

"All right. I can see that."

"Thank you," he said softly. Then he drew a deep breath. "But having said all that, Aleksandra, this is *exactly* the sort of incident I've been most afraid of. Oh, I never expected something this bloody, this . . . vicious, or on such a scale, so quickly. But I've been predicting violent acts of some sort, and I have to reiterate my position. The longer we drag out this Convention, the worse it's going to get. And the worse it gets, the more likely the Star Kingdom is to rethink its willingness to accept the original plebiscite at all."

"Oh, nonsense!" Tonkovic said sharply. Yet it was evident she was throttling her own deep surge of anger and trying to maintain at least some detachment. "Of course this was a horrible, *horrible* act! I've always known Agnes Nordbrandt was an idiot, but I never guessed she was a lunatic, as well. The woman has to be insane—she and her entire NRP! Not that an insanity defense's going to help her when we apprehend her! But blaming her actions on the fact that the Convention hasn't reported out a draft Constitution yet is ludicrous!"

"I didn't blame her actions on the delays. What I said is—"

"A moment, Joachim, please," Lababibi interrupted gently, and he paused, looking at her.

"Of course you're not saying that somehow Aleksandra's refusal to abandon her position *created* Nordbrandt or this 'Freedom Alliance of Kornati' nightmare of hers. But you *are* arguing that the extended debate here in Thimble helped create the opportunity for her to commit this atrocity. And that any failure to embrace *your* party's platform will only make things worse. Not to mention your implication that if things do get worse, Manticore will *probably* decide to reject our annexation request, after all."

Alquezar's jaw muscles clenched, and he glowered at her, his brown eyes hard. But then he flipped one hand in a gesture of unwilling assent—or at least concession.

"All right," he acknowledged. "I suppose I am. But I also think that whether Aléksandra agrees with me or not, these are serious concerns which need to be addressed."

"I think Joachim has a point," Krietzmann said in his most noninflammatory tones. Despite his effort to avoid any appearance of additional provocation, Tonkovic glared at him. And, he noticed, Lababibi didn't look especially happy, either.

"First," Tonkovic said, "let's remember whose planet this happened on. I'm not just the Split System's chief of delegation here at the Convention. I'm also the Planetary President of Kornati. Vuk Rajkovic is the *acting* head of state—my deputy, while I'm here on Thimble. And those people who were killed in the Nemanja Building were colleagues of mine. They were my *friends*, damn it! People I've known for decades—some of them literally all my life! And even the people I never met were *my* citizens, *my* people. Don't you ever think, not for one fleeting second, that I don't want Agnes Nordbrandt and every one of her butchering lunatics arrested, tried, and *executed* for this atrocity. And when the time comes, I'll put my own name in the hat when the court draws the lots for the firing squad!

"But you've seen the reports. I'm assuming you've read them as carefully as I did, and there's nothing in any of them to indicate that this Freedom Alliance of hers is anything but a tiny, super-violent splinter group. Yes, they planted bombs all over the capital. And yes, they got away with it. But not because they have thousands of members lurking behind every hedge, every door, with bombs in their hands. They obviously planned this all very carefully, and before she went underground, Nordbrandt was a member of Parliament herself. She had access to all our security data, all our contingency plans. Of course she knew where the loopholes were—where we were vulnerable! We should have completely overhauled all of our security arrangements as soon as she dropped out of sight. I admit that. And the responsibility for our failure to do so rests squarely on my shoulders. But they did it with homemade weapons. With commercially available blasting compound, and with timers and detonators any *farmer* on Kornati would have in the electronics bins in his barn. They planned it meticulously; they placed their bombs to inflict the maximum possible casualties and psychological shock; and much as I hate them, they showed as much skill as ruthlessness in carrying it out. They're obviously a serious threat, one we have to take seriously. But they're not ten meters tall, and they can't pour themselves through keyholes like vampires, and they *damned* sure aren't werewolves we're going to need silver pulser darts to kill!"

She glowered around the conference table, her nostrils flared and her green eyes hard.

"And your point?" Lababibi asked very gently.

"My point is that I'm not going to let myself be panicked into doing exactly what Nordbrandt *wants* me to do. I was sent to this Convention by the voters of Kornati with a specific mandate. A mandate supported by a clear majority of those same voters. I'm not going to permit this madwoman and her insane followers to manipulate me into violating that mandate. I can think of nothing which would be more likely to produce exactly the sort of polarization she's looking for. And to be brutally cold-blooded and honest about it, what's happened doesn't change a thing vis-à-vis the political realities of this annexation proposal. Not unless we permit it to, and I refuse to do that."

Krietzmann stared at her, unable to keep his incredulity completely out of his expression, and she glared defiantly at him.

"Whatever it does domestically, in terms of the Cluster's 'political realities,'" Alquezar said after a moment, "its impact on the *Manticoran* political calculus is beyond our ability to affect by a sheer act of political will, Aleksandra. Queen Elizabeth's fighting a war for her Star Kingdom's survival. If a situation arises in the Cluster which causes her to believe she'd be forced to divert a significant military force here, to act in a morally repugnant suppressive role, she may very well decide that all she really needs is the Lynx Terminus. And if that happens, just how do you think Frontier Security is going to react to our efforts to avoid its embrace by courting Manticore?"

"I think you may be overstating the potential consequences, Joachim."

Alquezar's head snapped around in surprise, because the comment hadn't come from Tonkovic. It had come from Lababibi.

"I'm not saying you're creating threats out of whole cloth," the Spindle System President continued. Her voice and expression alike were troubled, as if she wasn't entirely happy with what she was saying, yet she went on without hesitation. "But what we're looking at at this moment is a single act of violence. Yes, a particularly—no, let's be honest; a *horrifically* atrocious act of violence. But it's only one incident, and Manticore isn't going to abandon the annexation process and risk the interstellar perception that it's broken faith with us without far more justification than that.

"Queen Elizabeth's appointed a provisional governor. She's authorized and sanctioned our Constitutional Convention. In fact, she's *insisted* we tell her the terms upon which we seek annexation. She's also made it clear that if the Star Kingdom's Parliament finds our terms unreasonable, or unacceptable, they'll be rejected. But those were the actions of a monarch who believes in the political process and who's committed to making this annexation work. So as long as we're confronted by the actions of what are obviously marginalized maniacs, frustrated by their irrelevance to mainstream political opinion, and as long as our own law enforcement agencies are rigorously pursuing both the investigation and the perpetrators, she isn't about to pull the plug."

Krietzmann's eyes narrowed ever so slightly at Lababibi's argument. Intellectually, he was certain, the Spindalian head of state felt far closer to his own and Alquezar's positions. But he'd always sensed a certain ambivalence in her support, and that ambivalence suddenly seemed far more pronounced.

It's the economic factor. The class *factor.* The thought came to him abruptly, sharply, with an almost audible click. *That bit in Nordbrandt's statement about "wealthy traitors" and selling the planet to the highest bidder and "obscene wealth." Lababibi's an oligarch. All of her friends and family, and all of her friends' families—hell, every significant member of the entire damned political establishment here on Flax!—are oligarchs. It's the reason she's always been so much more comfortable with Joachim than with wretched, lower-class me.*

But now Nordbrandt's put her view of the Cluster's economic inequity squarely on the table alongside everything else, and Lababibi suddenly finds all those precious liberal convictions of hers cold comfort. Or, even worse, she can refuse to admit that—can continue to embrace them and use them to justify switching her support openly to Tonkovic. After all, all she's really doing is defending the traditional rights and freedoms of everyone in her star system. If it just happens that warping the entire Constitution around to protect that also protects the status quo—and her family's wealth and power—well, these things happen. . . .

He'd started to open his mouth in instant, instinctive protest. But then he closed it and shot Alquezar a quick, warning glance, as well. He took a handful of seconds to organize his own thoughts, then let his gray eyes sweep coolly back and forth between Tonkovic and Lababibi.

"I think you're being overly optimistic, Samiha," he said in a calm, level voice. "It's possible, however, that my own convictions are overly *pessimistic* in that regard. I don't think so, but I'm willing to acknowledge the possibility. I hope, though, that you're willing to concede in turn that Joachim and I have a legitimate right to be concerned over the Manticoran reaction to this?"

"Of course you do," Lababibi said quickly, as if she was relieved that he, too, had obviously decided to help avoid any open breach. "My God, who *wouldn't* react strongly to something like this?! At the very least, public opinion in the Star Kingdom is going to wonder what sort of neobarbs we are to let it happen."

"Which is one more reason to resist Nordbrandt's

efforts to stampede us into some sort of extreme reaction," Tonkovic put in.

Alquezar stirred in his chair, but Krietzmann stepped on his toe under the table. It was rather ironic, the Convention President thought, that he, the hotheaded proletarian, was suddenly playing the role of sweet reason and restraining the "cold-blooded" capitalist.

"We may not be in total agreement about just who's stampeding where, Aleksandra," he said, allowing a tinge of coolness to color his voice, as well as his eyes. "But at this point, all we really have are the initial reports. I hope you'll keep the entire Convention apprised of the status of your investigations back on Kornati?"

"Of course we will! In fact, I think it would be a good idea for the Convention to appoint a liaison group and dispatch it to Kornati to ensure that the delegates get unbiased, complete reports on the exact extent of our progress."

"Thank you. I think that's an excellent idea. And I'm sure quite a few of the other delegations would be pleased if you made that proposal yourself at this afternoon's emergency session."

"I will," she promised.

"Thank you," he repeated. "And I'm also sure that if any of us can do anything at all to assist you, you have only to ask."

"At this point, we have no reason to believe this is anything except a purely domestic problem. If we turn up any evidence which even hints at the possibility of some sort of interstellar connection, we'll bring it to the Convention's attention and seek any appropriate coordination," Tonkovic said. "And while I don't agree with Joachim that Manticore is likely to back out of the annexation commitment, I intend to keep Baroness Medusa fully informed on our progress."

"I think that would also be an excellent idea," Krietzmann approved, and she actually smiled at him, however thinly.

"On that note," he continued, "perhaps we should

adjourn. I'm sure all of us are anxious to sit down with our own delegations. And I know all of us have to get this information, and the Convention's reactions to it, reported to our own governments."

Tonkovic and Lababibi nodded. Alquezar didn't, but neither did he protest, and Krietzmann slid back his chair and stood. They all shook hands, then Tonkovic and Lababibi went one way down the hall while Krietzmann and Alquezar went the other.

The Dresdener could feel the towering San Miguel delegate's frustration and bubbling anger, but at least Alquezar had kilotons of self-control. However furious he might be, he wasn't going to vent that fury in public.

In private, now, Krietzmann thought. *That's a different matter. But there's no point burning any additional bridges sooner than we have to. And if we push Lababibi and the other oligarchs too hard, drive them into forting up under Tonkovic's banner . . .*

He shook his head, his expression worried, and wished again that Van Dort were still on Flax.

"What kind of maniac *does* something like this?" Rear Admiral Augustus Khumalo was visibly shaken, his face drawn, as the visual imagery of the carnage in Kornati's capital flowed across the briefing room's display.

"The kind who thinks she doesn't have anything left to lose, Admiral," Dame Estelle Matsuko said harshly.

"And the kind, if you'll forgive me for pointing it out, Madam Governor," Gregor O'Shaughnessy said, "who wants to provoke an extreme reaction from her political opposition."

Khumalo gave Medusa's senior intelligence officer a cold look.

"I think *this*—" he jabbed an angry finger at the images of covered bodies, ambulances, fires, rubble, smoke, and ugly bloodstains that looked as if some lunatic had run amok with a bucket of red paint "—is about as 'extreme' as it gets, Mr. O'Shaughnessy! Those are dead civilians. Civilians who ought to already be citizens of the Star Kingdom!"

"No one's trying to minimize what happened, Admiral." O'Shaughnessy was ten centimeters shorter than the rear admiral, with thinning gray hair and a slight build. He'd come up through the civilian intelligence community, and there was a slight, almost imperceptible—*almost* imperceptible—edge of hostility between him and Medusa's military subordinates. To his credit, O'Shaughnessy was aware of it, and usually tried to contain it. Like now. His tone was reasonable, nonconfrontational, as he faced the far more physically imposing Khumalo.

"All I'm trying to say, Sir," he continued, "is that classic terrorist strategy—and let's not fool ourselves, this was clearly a terroristic act—is to create the maximum possible polarization. They want the authorities to appear oppressive, to appear to overreact. To clamp down hard enough to convince the undecided that the terrorists were right all along about the fundamental oppressiveness of the state."

"He's right, Admiral," Commander Ambrose Chandler put in. Chandler sat to Khumalo's left while Captain Shoupe sat on the rear admiral's other side. Khumalo's staff intelligence officer was a good five centimeters taller than the rear admiral, although he was considerably less broad shouldered. He was also twenty-five years younger, and—in O'Shaughnessy's opinion—he had a tendency to avoid irritating his boss, which sometimes undermined his own arguments. But he was generally conscientious about attempting to provide good analysis, and this time he shook his head, meeting Khumalo's glower squarely.

"At the moment, Sir," he continued, "the overwhelming reaction in Split has to be one of revulsion, outrage, and fury. Right now, the vast majority of Kornatians want nothing more than to see Nordbrandt and her accomplices arrested, tried, and convicted. And that reaction is going to persist, for a time at least. Would you agree, Gregor?"

"In the short term? Oh, certainly! In the longer term, however . . ." O'Shaughnessy raised his right hand, palm uppermost, and tipped it back and forth.

"How could anyone feel anything *but* outrage?" Khumalo demanded with harsh incredulity.

"There's probably at least a tiny minority which actually agrees with them," O'Shaughnessy said, obviously picking his words with care. "The majority, as Ambrose says, almost certainly don't, but the Kornatian economy's in worse shape than almost any of the Cluster's other economies. There really is serious poverty and economic hardship, and the people who've been stepped on hardest by the existing social structure are likely to feel at least some sympathy for her announced motives, however much they deplore her methods. And the majority that don't support her, the ones who're horrified by what's happened, are going to want two things, Sir. First, they'll want the perpetrators apprehended. Second, they'll want their government to do the apprehending without becoming some sort of police state."

He shrugged, his normally warm brown eyes cold and thoughtful.

"So the terrorists' objectives are going to be first, to remain un-apprehended, and, second, to provoke the Kornatian government into appearing extremist. At the very least, they want the government to appear ineffectual. At best, they want the government to appear both ineffectual and oppressive and corrupt."

"I simply can't believe that anything could overcome the repugnance and hatred for those responsible that something like this generates," Khumalo argued, shaking his head and waving his hand at the bloodsoaked imagery once again.

"Trust me, Admiral," Medusa said quietly. "Gregor's right about the Kornatian economy, and the political dynamic in a situation like this one is complicated and fluid enough for almost anything to happen. Especially if those in authority stumble and botch things. The Kornatians are going to want firm, decisive action, but they also have a tradition of the fierce defense of individual civil liberties. Whether Tonkovic's position here at the Convention is based on genuine principle or just a huge dose of self-interest, there are plenty of people in the Split System who do have firm political principles that would be outraged by any sort of police state mentality. So any action the government takes to crush Nordbrandt and her lunatics is going to be a potentially double-edged sword."

Khumalo shook his head again, his jaw clamped stubbornly. But he appeared unwilling to disagree openly with his civilian superior.

"One other thing of which we ought to be aware," O'Shaughnessy said. All eyes swiveled to him, and he smiled, with absolutely no humor. "According to my carefully cultivated sources, Henri Krietzmann is meeting at this very moment with Joachim Alquezar, Aleksandra Tonkovic, and Samiha."

"Do you have any prediction of what will come out of their meeting?" the provisional governor asked.

"No, Milady. There are far too many variables for me to even hazard guesses at this point. I hope to have at least some information about that for you by this evening, however."

"Good." Medusa grimaced. "Oh, how I *wish* Van Dort were still here on Flax! Drat the man's timing!"

"I wasn't aware he'd left, Milady," Khumalo said in some surprise.

"Oh, yes. He's been gone for almost a T-week. He left the day after *Hexapuma* sailed."

"Then I have to agree that his sense of timing was . . . unfortunate," the portly rear admiral said.

"Well, he obviously didn't know *this* was going to happen," Medusa sighed. "He was afraid his image as a 'moneygrubbing capitalist' hovering about the fringes of the debate like a vulture or a spider was exacerbating the situation. He told me he felt like the ghost at the banquet and said he wanted to get out of the spotlight because he thought his presence was hampering the Convention's deliberations."

"I suppose I can understand that," Khumalo agreed with a frown. "Like you, Milady, I wish he hadn't chosen this particular moment to disappear, though."

"He may return to Spindle when as he hears about this," Medusa said, then gave her head a little toss. "But whatever he may do, we have to decide what *we're* going to do."

"With all due respect, Milday," O'Shaughnessy said, "I think that's going to have to depend in large part on how the Talbotters react. At the moment, I'd say there's probably a seventy-thirty chance President Tonkovic is going to officially request assistance from us. I don't know if she'll *want* to, but if she hesitates, there'll be a lot of pressure on her from other delegates who want us involved."

"I'd be cautious there, Governor," Chandler said. She looked at him, and he shrugged. "At the moment, this is purely an internal affair of Kornati. We're involved, but only at one remove—as the supposed justification for the criminals' actions, not as an actual presence on the planet. And, as you just pointed out, they have that deeply ingrained civil libertarian tradition, crossed with a genuine sense of economic inequality from much of their lower class. So if we suddenly start landing Marines on the planet at the upper classes' request to kick down primarily *lower-class* doors, we run the risk of lending credibility to Nordbrandt's allegations. The fact that our assistance was requested by the legally elected local authorities won't be much protection once her adherents start twisting and spinning the story."

"Ambrose has a legitimate point, Dame Estelle," O'Shaughnessy said. He gave the commander a rare look of unqualified approval. "In fact, to be blunt, Nordbrandt *does* have some valid points about the political system. It's thoroughly skewed in the favor of a relatively tiny number of wealthy families . . . like Tonkovic's. Some of those families will want to keep us far, far away—or at least to minimalize our 'interference' on their world—lest we contaminate the situation with our off-world notions. But others are going to press for immediate, powerful intervention on our part. They're going to want us to come in and stamp out the flames for them right now, *immediately*, before they get burned any worse. So I'm afraid you may find you're going to have to walk a fine line between giving Tonkovic the assistance she asks for—assuming she does ask—and avoiding the appearance of sending in some sort of . . . imperial storm troopers."

"Oh, marvelous," Medusa muttered. Then she produced a wan but genuine smile. "Well, Her Majesty never promised me it was going to be easy!"

She drummed her fingers on the table, thinking hard for several seconds, then looked back up at Khumalo.

"Admiral, I want you and Captain Shoupe to begin contingency planning. We can't make any hard and fast decisions at this point, but I want to know exactly what our resources and capabilities are if, in fact, President Tonkovic does ask for help. I'd also like recommendations from you and Commander Chandler, Gregor, on what levels of support we *want* to offer if it's requested. I want the best appreciations the two of you can put together of the most effective kinds and levels of assistance we could offer. And I want your best estimates as to how the Kornatian public's liable to react to each of the different levels. And the same for the Kornatian political leadership. I know any 'estimate' you put together at the moment can't be more than a guesstimate. But get started now, and integrate any additional information as it comes in."

She paused, and her expression turned bleak and hard.

"Understand me, People," she said then, in a voice just as cold and focused as her expression. "I don't want to escalate anything that doesn't have to be escalated. And I certainly don't want us to look like—what did you call them, Gregor? Imperial storm troopers?" Her mouth twisted on the words, but she didn't flinch. "Our job isn't to support, or to give the appearance of supporting, repressive local regimes. But if the legitimate government of any star system in the Cluster requests our assistance, we *will* provide it. We may make our own judgments about the most effective way to do so, but we have a moral obligation to support the legally elected governments who've requested that we take them under the Queen's protection . . . and, especially, their *citizens*. And if it turns out we have to land Marines and kick down doors to do that, then we'll land Marines with great big *nasty* boots. Is that clear?"

She was the smallest person at the table by a considerable margin, but every head nodded very quickly indeed.

"Good," Dame Estelle Matsuko said quietly.

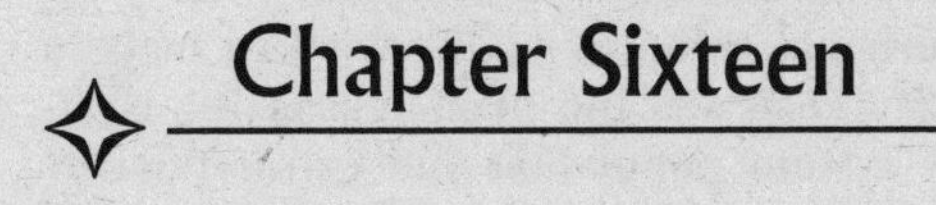

Chapter Sixteen

Nuncio was a poverty-stricken star system, even for the Verge. Which was particularly ironic, given the system's potential, Aivars Terekhov thought as *Hexapuma* decelerated smoothly towards her parking orbit and he listened to the soothing routine of his bridge.

The G0/K2 binary system boasted two remarkably Earth-like planets, thoroughly suitable for human occupation with only a little development. Basilica, the habitable world of the G0 primary component, orbited its star at a distance of twelve light-minutes, and boasted a planetary environment any resort world might have envied. With a planetary mass ninety-seven percent of Old Earth's, a hydrosphere of eighty percent, rugged mountains, gorgeous volcanic atolls, sandy beaches, endless rolling plains, and an axial inclination of less than three degrees, Basilica was as close to climatically idyllic as any home for humans outside man's original star system could hope to be. Unfortunately, the planet's successful colonization had called for a degree of subtle genetic manipulation of the terrestrial plants and food species to be introduced there. Had Nuncio been colonized today, or even as recently as the last couple of T-centuries, it would have been a snap.

Even at the time the system actually was settled, making the necessary alterations would have been relatively straightforward for a good Solarian genetic lab.

Unfortunately, the colonists' analysts had missed the data in the initial planetary survey which should have told them before they set out that the changes were needed. By the time they realized what they actually faced, all of the "good Solarian genetic labs" and their capabilities had been light-centuries behind them . . . which explained why it was Pontifex, the habitable planet of the *secondary* component which had actually been settled.

Not that the original colonists hadn't tried to make a go of Basilica first. That was the main reason for Nuncio's current tiny system population and extraordinarily backward infrastructure. Like the original inhabitants of Grayson, the Nuncians' ancestors had been religious emigres who'd deliberately sought a new home, far beyond the reach of their hopelessly secular fellow humans. That had made them the first colony expedition into what had since become the Talbott Cluster, just as the Graysons had settled their homeworld long before the starship *Jason* delivered the first colonists to a planet named Manticore.

Unfortunately for those first Nuncians, they had encountered a trap almost as deadly, although in quite a different way, as the one which had met Austin Grayson's followers, and they'd been operating on a considerably tighter budget when they organized their exodus. They hadn't shared the Church of Humanity Unchained's prejudice against technology, but they hadn't been able to afford as much of it as other, more successful colonizing expeditions, and what they'd managed to bring with them hadn't been up to managing the required genetic modifications. That simple fact had almost wiped them out when their crops failed and sixty-five percent of their food animals died within one generation. Somehow, they'd managed to retain enough space flight capability (barely) to transfer about half of their surviving population—and what remained of its food supplies—to Pontifex, a much colder, dryer world, six light-minutes from its cool primary and with far more extreme seasonal changes, but without Basilica's subtle genetic trap.

None of the people left behind on Basilica had survived, and over half of those they'd managed to transfer had died during their first winter on Pontifex. The half which survived—less than sixteen percent of their original expedition—had fought desperately to cling to the technology they still had, but it had been a long, bitter struggle, and the dreadful death toll of the colony's first few years had killed too many trained technicians, too many teachers. They'd regressed to an early steam-powered level before they managed to arrest the agonizing slide downward, and there they'd stayed for generations. Now, six centuries after mankind first landed on Pontifex, and two centuries after the Nuncians had been rediscovered by the rest of humanity, the planetary population was barely three hundred and fifty million, and its technological capabilities and educational system were far inferior to the ones Grayson had attained before joining the Manticoran Alliance.

And, Terekhov mused as *Hexapuma* settled into her assigned orbit around Pontifex, *they didn't exactly react to their difficulties the way the Graysons did. Planet names notwithstanding, according to Commander Chandler's intelligence package, these people are as aggressively atheistic as it's possible for human beings to be. Which is something I'd better remind all our people to keep in mind.*

"Incoming message, Sir," Lieutenant Jefferson Kobe, the com officer of the watch reported, and Terekhov turned his chair to face the communications section. "It's from their planetary president's office, Sir," Kobe said after a moment.

"Put it on my terminal, please, Mr. Kobe," Terekhov requested, tapping the key to deploy the larger of his two com screens.

"Aye, aye, Sir," Kobe acknowledged, and a moment later, Terekhov's screen blinked to life with the hawk-like face of a man who was probably in his mid-thirties, bearing in mind the primitive medical establishment of the planet.

"Greetings, Captain—?" The caller paused, and Terekhov smiled.

"Captain Aivars Terekhov, commanding Her Majesty's Starship *Hexapuma*, at your service, Mr.—?" It was his turn to pause interrogatively, and the hawklike face returned his smile.

"Alberto Wexler, at *your* service, Captain Terekhov," he said. "I'm President Adolfsson's personal assistant. He's requested me to welcome you to Nuncio and to invite you—and some of your officers, perhaps—to meet with him and Commodore Karlberg, the commander of our Space Force. He wondered if you might care to join the two of them for dinner this evening?"

"That's very kind of President Adolfsson," Terekhov replied, "and I certainly accept the invitation. With the President's permission, I'd like to bring my executive officer and one or two of my midshipmen along." He smiled again, much more broadly. "Commander FitzGerald would be there for business; the midshipmen would be along to practice being seen and not heard."

Wexler chuckled.

"I don't see any reason why the President—or Commodore Karlberg—should object, Captain. If eighteen o'clock local would be convenient for you, we'll expect you then. I'll double-check to confirm with President Adolfsson that your midshipmen will be welcome, and someone from my office will be in touch to confirm arrangements."

"Eighteen o'clock sounds fine, Mr. Wexler," Terekhov said, checking to be sure the ship's clocks had been recalibrated to the base time of the rest of the universe—and to the local planetary day—after *Hexapuma* dropped below relativistic velocities.

"Until dinner, then, Captain," Wexler said, and cut the circuit.

✧ ✧ ✧

Ragnhild Pavletic decided that there were times when catching the Captain's eye had its drawbacks. Like now. No doubt it was immensely flattering to be chosen for semipermanent assignment as her CO's personal pilot. It was a great honor for a mere middy to be picked over petty officer pilots who might have as much as fifty T-years worth of experience, or even more, and she knew it. The fact that Ragnhild had stood first in her class for flight training every term for her entire time on the Island had more than a little to do with it, and she knew that, too. She'd set the new standard for virtually every record except the time/distance glider record set by Duchess Harrington over forty T-years ago. That one seemed destined to stand for quite a while longer, although Ragnhild took considerable quiet pride in the fact that she'd broken two of the Duchess' other records.

Whatever the reasons, she'd been assigned permanently to Hawk-Papa-One, *Hexapuma*'s Pinnace Number One, which, in turn, was permanently assigned to "Hexapuma Alpha," Captain Terekhov himself. That meant she tended to stay current on what the Captain was up to and she could expect to end up attending a lot of dirt-side meetings and (possibly) soirees her fellow middies would not, which was good. But that very opportunity sometimes had its downside. Like tonight.

Of course it was flattering to be informed that she would be accompanying the Captain and the Exec to their very first meeting with the local planetary potentate. It also, unfortunately, made her highly visible, and unlike some of her fellow midshipmen, Ragnhild was of firmly yeoman ancestry. She'd had the social decorum expected of a Manticoran naval officer hammered ruthlessly into her at the Academy, but that wasn't enough to make her feel confident in rarefied social circles. She always secretly dreaded that she'd pick up the wrong fork, or drink out of the wrong glass, or commit some other unpardonable breach of etiquette which would undoubtedly spark an interstellar incident, if not an outright war.

That was all bad enough, but the fact that Pontifex

didn't possess even first-generation prolong made it far worse, because Ragnhild Pavletic was cute. It was the curse of her life. She wasn't beautiful, not pretty or handsome, but *cute*. She was petite, delicately built, with honey-blond hair, blue eyes, a snub nose, and even—God help her—freckles. Her hair was so naturally curly she had to keep it cut into a short-cropped mop less than five centimeters long if she was going to have any hope of managing it, and she, unfortunately, was a *third*-generation prolong recipient. Worse yet, she'd received the initial treatment even earlier than most, with the result that it had started slowing the physical maturation process proportionately sooner. Which meant that at a chronological age of twenty-one T-years, she looked like a pre-prolong thirteen-year-old. A *flat-chested* thirteen-year-old.

And the Captain was taking her down to meet the president of an entire planet full of pre-prolong people who were going to think she was exactly as old as she looked. To them.

She gritted her teeth and tried to smile pleasantly as she settled Hawk-Papa-One onto the apron of the old-fashioned airport outside Pontifex's capital city of Ollander Landing with polished precision. Paulo d'Arezzo had been selected to share her evening's ordeal, but he, unfortunately, was marginally junior to her. The Navy's protocol for boarding and disembarking from small craft was ironbound and inflexible: passengers boarded in ascending order of rank, from most junior to most senior, and disembarked in the reverse order. She'd hoped, initially, that as pilot she might be able to skip her assigned place in the queue, but Captain Terekhov seemed to possess ESP. He'd informed her that since she was to attend the dinner tonight, she could hand the pinnace over to its flight engineer as soon as they hit the ground in order to debark with the other guests.

That meant Captain Terekhov was the first person down the boarding ramp to the assembled honor guard standing beside the long, clunky-looking ground limousine and

Paulo was the last. Which meant that the midshipman's preposterous good looks didn't get a chance to distract any attention from her.

The honor guard snapped to the local version of attention and presented arms crisply, but Ragnhild saw more than one or two sets of eyes widen as they caught sight of her. Damn it, she was so *tired* of looking like someone's kid sister, even back home where people were accustomed to prolong!

She forced her expression to remain calm and collected as she followed Captain Terekhov and Commander FitzGerald and listened to the polite, formal greetings from President Adolfsson's representative. Despite the amount of attention she was devoting to looking like she was at least old enough for high school, she was aware that it was unusual for a planetary president to send his personal executive assistant to greet the mere captain of a visiting warship. Within his own domain of *Hexapuma*, Captain Terekhov was junior only to God, and even that precedence tended to get a bit blurred. But he was only the captain of a heavy cruiser, when all was said and done, and this Wexler was greeting him as if he were at least a senior flag officer.

The Captain took it all in stride, apparently effortlessly, and Ragnhild envied his composure and confidence. Of course, he was fifty-five T-years older than she was. He looked very much of an age with Wexler, and he was a senior-grade captain, to boot, but still . . .

"It's a pleasure to greet you in person, Captain," Wexler was saying. "It's just not the same, somehow, over a com link." His mouth twisted in a wry smile. "Of course, half of our local coms don't even have visual, so I suppose I shouldn't complain, since the President *does* have that capability on all of his lines."

Ragnhild stood behind the Captain, listening unobtrusively to the conversation, and wondered if Wexler was deliberately drawing attention to Pontifex's primitive technology. It happened, sometimes. Or that was what her instructors at the Academy had told her, anyway.

Sometimes the inhabitants of planets whose societies or technology bases had been hammered especially hard took a sort of aggressive, in-your-face reverse pride in their neobarbarian status.

"It's actually fairly amazing what a broad spectrum of technological capabilities societies can adjust themselves to," Captain Terekhov observed. "The capabilities change, but the interactions and the basic human motivations seem to remain surprisingly intact."

"Really?" Wexler said. "I often wish I'd had the opportunity to travel, myself, a chance to see how other planets have adapted themselves. I suppose that's probably the one thing I most envy about someone like you, Captain. A professional naval officer who spends his time visiting one world after another."

"Actually, Mr. Wexler," Terekhov said with a smile, "naval officers spend most of their time looking at displays and repeater plots—when they're not doing paperwork or looking at the bulkheads of their cabins. We do get to see quite a few different worlds, in peacetime, at least. But we spend a lot of time basically sitting around between planetfalls. In fact, I sometimes envy people who have the opportunity to sit in one place long enough to *really* understand a planet and its societies."

"Another case of the other man's grass always being greener, I suppose," Wexler murmured, then gave himself a little shake and gestured at the waiting ground car.

Planetary President George Adolfsson looked quite a bit like Alberto Wexler. He was older, possibly within ten T-years of Terekhov's own age, and the hawklike profile was leaner, more angular. But the dark hair (liberally laced with gray in his case) and dark eyes, with their odd little flecks of amber scattered around the iris, were the same, and so was the easy sense of humor.

"Thank you for joining us for dinner, Captain."

"Thank you for the invitation, Mr. President," Terekhov replied, shaking the offered hand firmly. "May I present

Commander FitzGerald, my executive officer, Midshipwoman Pavletic, and Midshipman d'Arezzo?"

"Indeed you may, Sir." Adolfsson shook each of the Manticorans' hands in turn. "And this," he indicated the tall, rawboned, sandy-haired man standing respectfully at his right shoulder, "is Commodore Emil Karlberg, the senior officer of the Nuncio Space Force."

"In all its magnificent glory," Karlberg said dryly, extending his own hand to Terekhov. All of the Nuncians' Standard English had a peculiar accent, with swallowed last syllables, flattened vowels, and a staccato rythym pronounced enough to make their speech actually a bit difficult to follow. Planetary variations from the norm were far from uncommon, but this one was much more noticeable than most. No doubt the planet's long isolation from the galactic mainstream, coupled with the loss of most of its recorded sound technology during the interval, helped account for it. But there were obviously purely local variations, as well, for Karlberg had a markedly different accent from Adolfsson or Wexler. It was sharper, more nasal.

"I've viewed the download you were kind enough to make available to us on your ship's capabilities," the commodore continued. He shook his head. "I realize *Hexapuma* is 'only' a heavy cruiser, but she seems like a superdreadnought to us, Captain. My 'Space Force' consists of exactly eleven light attack craft, and the biggest of them masses all of eighteen thousand tons. So the entire Nuncio fleet masses about a third as much as your single ship."

Ragnhild instructed her expression to remain one of simple polite interest, but Karlberg's statement stunned her. Intellectually, she'd known from the outset that none of the poverty-stricken governments in the Cluster had the economic and industrial capacity to build anything like an effective naval force. But that was pathetic. Less than a single LAC squadron to defend—or even effectively patrol—an entire star system? She wanted to glance at Paulo, to see how he'd reacted to it, but she knew better than to allow her attention to wander.

"Emil, don't get started talking shop so quickly!" President Adolfsson scolded with what was obviously a fond smile. "Captain Terekhov's been in-system for less than twelve hours. I think you might give him, oh, another thirty or forty minutes of amiable social chitchat before you dive headlong into all that *important* stuff."

"Oops." Karlberg shook his head again, this time with an expression strongly reminiscent of a small boy who'd just been told he was too bouncy for polite manners.

"Don't worry," the President assured him. "I won't have you beheaded just yet. It would delay dinner, and getting the gore out of the carpet is always such a pain."

Karlberg chuckled, and Terekhov and FitzGerald both smiled broadly. The midshipmen didn't, and Wexler surprised Ragnhild by smiling sympathetically at both of them. It wasn't the smile that surprised her; it was the fact that it was the sort of smile subordinate officers shared in the presence of their joint betters, and not the smile of a patronizing adult for a mere child. She was entirely too familiar with the difference between them.

Perhaps, she thought, as the President ushered his guests down a glass-sided hallway filled with the rich, golden sunset of Nuncio-B towards a spacious, woodpaneled dining room, this dinner wasn't going to be quite the ordeal she had dreaded.

"So that's about the size of it, Captain Terekhov," George Adolfsson said two hours later. He leaned back comfortably in his chair, nursing a glass of Pontifex's traditional plum brandy while he gazed across the table at his Manticoran visitors. "As far as everyone on Pontifex is concerned, the chance to join your Star Kingdom is the greatest opportunity to come along since the Founding Idiots landed their incompetent, superstitious posteriors on Basilica."

His tone was so dryly, bitingly humorous Ragnhild had to raise one hand to conceal her smile. The meal had been delicious, although she personally found the brandy far too rough edged for her taste. And President

Adolfsson had been a charming host. It turned out Wexler was the President's nephew, as well as his assistant, and she suspected that uncle and nephew had gone out of their way to charm their visitors. And done so very effectively, because, when it came right down to it, they were simply naturally charming.

But the President also had a dead serious side, and it showed as he met Terekhov's eyes very steadily.

"We've got considerably less than a half billion people in the entire Nuncio System, Captain," he said quietly, all traces of banter vanishing from his voice. "We don't have prolong, we don't have *any* sort of decent medical establishment, our educational system is a joke by modern standards, and our cutting-edge technology is probably at least two hundred T-years behind yours. But we do know all about the benefits Frontier Security brings. That's why over ninety-five percent of the voters here on Pontifex favored annexation by your kingdom, instead. And it's also the reason our delegation to the Constitutional Convention is working so closely with Joachim Alquezar."

"With all due respect, Mr. President," Karlberg said, "I'm still not comfortable about tying ourselves so closely to the Rembrandters."

"Emil," Adolfsson said patiently, "what happened to us here wasn't Bernardus Van Dort's fault. It wasn't even the Rembrandt Trade Union's fault. Damnation, man! There's only *been* a Trade Union for the last fifty T-years! Rembrandt and San Miguel certainly never 'looted' Pontifex's economy. It's past time we stopped being envious and started emulating them! Although," he added in the tone of someone making a grudging concession, "I suppose we won't have to be quite so . . . assertive in our business negotiations with our neighbors."

"*Assertive!*" Karlberg snorted. Ragnhild was still surprised by the comfortable, casual way the commodore addressed his President. She tried—and failed—to imagine *anyone* talking that way to Queen Elizabeth. Yet despite the comfort level, there was nothing disrespectful about Karlberg. It was almost as if his familiarity was an indication of the true depth of his respect for the President.

"I realize my ship and I are new to the Cluster, Commodore," Terekhov said. "But I've spent quite a few hours reading over the intelligence briefings Admiral Khumalo and Governor Medusa have made available. From what I can see, Mr. Van Dort must be a remarkable individual, and I understand he and Mr. Alquezar are close personal friends, as well as business and political associates."

"You understand correctly, Captain," Adolfsson replied. "Oh, he didn't organize the Trade Union solely out of selfless humanitarianism. But I've never subscribed to the theory that the entire RTU was conceived of simply as a means to fleece the other star systems in the area. And whatever else may be true, I'm convinced Van Dort—and Alquezar—are deeply committed to driving through this annexation."

"So am I, Uncle George," Wexler said. "But they could be fully committed to doing that simply because of all the opportunities they see to get even richer as part of the Star Kingdom. Altruistic concern for the rest of us may run pretty far second to that."

"No reason it shouldn't," Adolfsson said with a shrug. "'Rich' isn't a dirty word, Alberto. Especially not when the difference between rich and poor for a planet is also the difference between prolong and its absence, or the chance for a decent job and housing for all our citizens."

"Point taken, Mr. President," Karlberg said. "I guess it's just reflex. I've spent so long envying the Rembrandters every time one of their freighters came rumbling through that it's hard not to go right on doing it."

"The President is right, though, I think, Commodore," Terekhov said. "Even without the annexation, the Cluster's simple proximity to the Lynx Terminus would have tremendous economic implications for all your star systems. Assuming, of course, that somebody like Frontier Security didn't move in on you as soon as you became prosperous enough to be worth grabbing."

"I know," Karlberg agreed, nodding briskly. "And we've

already seen some signs of those economic implications of yours, Captain. Not that much so far, but we've had three freighters stop over here in Nuncio in just the last month and a half. That may not sound like much to someone from Manticore, and one of them only stopped on spec, to see if there was any reason the owners should make us a semi-regular stopover in the future. But that still represents a huge jump in local traffic for us, and I expect it to continue to increase. Unfortunately, it looks like there are some liabilities coming along with the good news."

"What sort of liabilities, Sir?" FitzGerald asked.

"We're in the outermost tier of the systems of our so-called 'Cluster,' Commander," Karlberg said. "We're more exposed than other systems—like Rembrandt and San Miguel—which are basically pretty much slap in the middle. I suspect we're also going to attract less of the new investment everyone is visualizing, unless the President's hopes of luring investors into sinking capital into developing the resort potential of Basilica bear fruit, of course. But even so, we're undoubtedly looking at a major increase in our prosperity and in the amount of merchant traffic in the area. Which is what concerns me most at the moment."

"Why, Commodore?" Terekhov asked, watching Karlberg intently.

"Because it's going to make us more of a target, especially given how exposed we are, and I don't have the available assets to encourage the ill-intentioned to stay the hell out of my star system," Karlberg said bluntly. "Especially not if they have modern vessels available."

"Modern vessels?" Terekhov leaned forward, and his eyes narrowed. So did FitzGerald's—and both midshipmen's, for that matter. The pirates operating out of the Verge in the Talbott Cluster's vicinity tended to be among the less technically capable of their ilk. In many ways, they were the equivalent of the rowboat-equipped pirates who'd haunted prespace Old Earth's shallow coastal seas, and they made the average Silesian pirate look like first-line naval units in comparison. Against that sort of opposition, even Karlberg's diminutive, obsolescent light attack craft should have made a good showing.

"Yes," the commodore said, and there was no longer any trace of levity in his voice or expression. "Someone's intruded into the system here at least three times in the last two weeks. Whoever it is isn't interested in introducing himself, and the only one of my LACs that's gotten close enough to try for a solid sensor sweep failed completely. Now, admittedly, our electronics are pretty much crap compared to yours, Captain, but we ought to be getting at least *some* useful data. We aren't, which suggests that whoever we're up against has considerably more modern electronics than we do. Which, in turn, suggests they're probably much more modern and capable generally than we are."

"You keep using the plural, Commodore," Terekhov observed. "You're fairly confident you're dealing with more than a single intruding vessel?"

"I'm ninety-five percent certain there are two of them," Karlberg said. "And, whatever they are, they're bigger and, presumably, tougher than anything I've got. And they're arrogant buggers, too. They're waltzing right into and through my star system because they know damned well that nothing I've got could hurt them, even if I could manage to track them accurately."

"I see," Terekhov said slowly. He glanced at Fitz-Gerald, and Ragnhild finally allowed herself to glance at Paulo, as well. She could see from his expression that he was thinking the same thing she was. If Karlberg was correct (and Ragnhild was impressed by the man's obvious capability) about how modern these intruders were, where had they come from? What were modern vessels doing playing pirate in such a poverty-riddled portion of the Verge? This was the sort of area that attracted chicken thieves, not the sort that could pay the operating costs of modern, powerful raiders.

"Well, Commodore, Mr. President," Terekhov said after a few moments of silent thought, "if you do have somebody wandering in and out of your system with less than honest motivations, then I suppose we ought to see what *Hexapuma* can do to discourage them." He smiled thinly. "As permanently as possible."

"Mr. Dekker?"

"Yes, Danny?"

"Mr. Dekker, I think you'd better see this." Daniel Santiago's Montana accent was more pronounced than usual, and his brown eyes looked worried.

"What is it?" Dekker pushed back his chair and rose, walking across to Santiago's desk.

"This e-mail just came in." Santiago pointed at his old-fashioned display. "The system says it comes from an address that doesn't exist."

"What?" Dekker bent over his subordinate's shoulder, peering at the screen.

"It used to exist," Santiago continued, "but this provider shut down over two T-years ago."

"That's ridiculous," Dekker said. "Somebody must be playing games with his mail origination."

"That's why I think you should take a look at it, Boss," Santiago said. He reached out and tapped the message subject header, and Dekker's eyes narrowed.

"Re: Reasons to evacuate . . . right now," it said.

"I do *not* believe this!" Oscar Johansen said. "What did I do? Kill one of this guy's relatives in a previous incarnation?"

"It's not really personal, Oscar," Les Haven said with a grimace. "It just seems that way."

"Yeah? Easy for *you* to say!" Johansen glared at his hardcopy printout of the mysterious e-mail. "You're not the one who's going to have to explain all of this to the Home Secretary!"

"Well, you aren't either, come to that," Haven replied. "My government's gonna have to do the explaining. And President Suttles and Chief Marshal Bannister are gonna purely hate it."

"And so is Chairwoman Vaandrager," Hieronymus Dekker put in with a heavy sigh.

The three of them stood behind a police cordon and a hastily erected wall of sandbags, gazing resignedly at the Rembrandt Trade Union's Montana office from a range of two kilometers. The building sat in a corner of the Brewster City Spaceport, backed up against the warehouse-surrounded trio of combined personnel and heavy-lift freight shuttle pads which customarily serviced RTU traffic on Montana. At the moment, they weren't servicing anything, and the office building itself had been evacuated within fifteen minutes of the e-mail's receipt.

"You think he's serious?" Johansen asked after a moment.

"Steve Westman?" Haven snorted. "Damn betcha, Oscar. Man may be a brick or two shy of a full load, but he *is* a determined sort of cuss. As you might have noted about three weeks ago."

"But this—!" Johansen said, waving helplessly at the deserted office building and shuttle pads.

"He probably thinks it's funny," Haven said. Johansen looked at him, and the Montanan shrugged. "The RTU more or less extorted this particular landing concession out of the planetary government 'bout twenty T-years ago," he said. "Matter of fact, today's the anniversary of the formal signing of the lease agreement."

"We didn't 'extort' anything out of anyone." Dekker's tone was stiff and a bit repressive.

"Didn't use guns or knives," Haven conceded. "And I don't recall anyone being outright threatened with dismemberment. But as I do recall, Hieronymus, Ineka Vaandrager—she wasn't Chairwoman then, Oscar; just the head of their Contract Negotiation Department—made it pretty clear that either we gave you folks the concession, or the RTU put its southern terminal on Tillerman. And slapped a fifteen-percent surcharge onto all Union shipments in or out of Montana, just to smack our wrists for being so ornery and disagreeable about it all." He squinted up at the taller, fair-haired Rembrandter. "'Scuse me if I seem a mite prejudiced, but that sounds kinda like extortion to me."

"I admit," Dekker said uncomfortably, avoiding the Montanan's eyes, "that it was a perhaps extreme tactic. Chairwoman Vaandrager hasn't always been noted for the . . . civility of her negotiating tactics. But to respond with threats of violence on this scale hardly seems a rational act."

"Oh, I dunno," Haven said. "Least he sent your employees a warning to get out of the way, didn't he? Hell, Hieronymus—for a feller like Steve, that's downright gentlemanly. And at least the whole shebang is far 'nough away from everything else he can blow the crap out of it 'thout damaging anything else or killing anybody."

"But surely your planetary authorities should have acted sooner if they knew all along that he was angry enough with us to do something like this—" Dekker began, looking far from mollified by Haven's observations, but the Montanan cut him off with a vigorous head shake.

"He was mighty pissed off, all right. But not enough for something like this. Not until Van Dort organized the entire annexation effort."

"Not even Mr. Van Dort could have 'organized' something on that scale if the proposal hadn't won the endorsement of the overwhelming majority of the Cluster's citizens!" Dekker protested.

"Didn't say he could have. Didn't say it was a bad idea, for that matter. I just said it was Van Dort who did the actual organizing," Haven replied. "And he did. Now, Steve doesn't much like Van Dort, for a lot of reasons, including the fact that he was original Chairman of the RTU's Board and he's still the biggest stockholder the RTU has. When he says 'frog' the RTU jumps, which means the plebiscite vote had the RTU Board's approval. Which probably means it had Vaandrager's, who may be the one person in the entire Cluster Steve likes less than he does Van Dort. And the fact that *she* approved it, far as a feller like Steve is concerned, automatically makes it just one more example of how she 'negotiates' for whatever it is she wants. Which brings him right back to this tidy little enclave of yours, and I've gotta tell you, Hieronymus—there aren't many Montanans who won't understand exactly how he's thinking. So if he's in the mood to be sending messages, this has to be just about the best exclamation point he could've come up with. 'Specially since the RTU managed to 'negotiate' that exclusive contract with Manticore to transport all the Star Kingdom's official freight, mail, and personnel here in the Cluster."

Johansen started to object that the RTU was the only local entity with the ability to meet all the Star Kingdom's shipping requirements. Despite what anyone else might think, that was the only reason it had been able to secure that exclusive contract, and the contract itself was only interim, until it was possible to invite other bidders to compete. But he kept his mouth closed, instead. Les Haven already knew all of that . . . whether he *believed* it or not, which was more than Johansen was prepared to say. And whatever Haven thought, now that Johansen had spent some time in the Cluster himself, he could well understand how anyone already suspicious of outside interference in the Cluster's affairs or angry over the Trade Union's economic muscle might easily conclude that the contract was a sweetheart deal from Manticore to repay the RTU for serving as the Star Kingdom's front man.

Not that understanding was any particular comfort as he looked at the shuttle pads and warehouses which contained, among other things, something in excess of fifty million Manticoran dollars worth of survey equipment, air cars, computers, communications systems, field desks, and camping equipment.

"I know how much of *our* stuff you have warehoused, Hieronymus," he said, after a moment. "How much else is in storage or on the pads?"

"Something in excess of one-point-three billion Rembrandt stellars," Dekker replied, quickly enough to show where his own unhappy thoughts had been. "On the order of five hundred million of your Manticoran dollars. Not to mention, of course, all of the base equipment and—"

Johansen never discovered whatever else the RTU's chief Montana factor had been about to say.

The first explosion was the brightest. The brilliant flash was literally blinding, and the Manticoran wondered how Westman had managed to get military-grade chemical explosives into the warehouse. The structure housed—*had* housed—low value, bulk cargo, so security had probably been at least a little laxer than on the other buildings, and for all its violence, the explosive device itself could probably have been hidden in something as small as a large suitcase. But even so—

His brain was still beginning to spin up to full speed with the awareness that Westman obviously hadn't been bluffing after all, when the other explosions began. At first, they weren't as violent as the initial one, but they'd obviously been placed with some forethought. The first explosion had torn open the central warehouse and scattered flaming debris over most of the compound. The second group of explosions was in the shuttle pads themselves. The first two didn't seem all that spectacular; but there was a personnel shuttle docked in Pad Three. A shuttle which had developed some technical glitch—a glitch which hindsight suggested to Johansen had been arranged with malice aforethought—that had immobilized it and prevented its removal when the e-mailed warning arrived. A shuttle whose hydrogen tanks and emergency thruster fuel reservoirs were almost full.

If the first explosion had seemed overpowering, this one was stupendous. The entire pad disintegrated in a towering, blue-white flower of dust-curdled fury, and Johansen instinctively flung himself flat on his belly behind the sandbags. The e-mail had warned everyone to keep well back, but he doubted anyone had anticipated anything like this. The blast front from the splintered shuttle raced outward in a ring of flame and dust that enveloped the shuttle pads on either side. It ran into the back of the RTU office block like a tsunami, smashing its way in through windows and doors, and the entire structure blew apart like a house of sticks in the path of a tornado. Warehouses and freight vehicle maintenance bays disappeared into the vortex to be chewed up and spat out in very, very tiny bits and pieces.

The chain of explosions blended into one, huge, overwhelming event, and Oscar Johansen felt like a gnat trapped between the swatting palms of an enraged fire giant as a mushroom cloud of smoke, dust, wreckage, and swirling flame towered high into the heavens.

This, he thought, looking up as the outward-speeding, ground-level ring of smoke and dust swept by overhead like a lateral hurricane, *is* not *going to look good on my resumé*.

Chapter Seventeen

Thank goodness I set up a secure contact point the last time I was here, Damien Harahap thought. *I just wish these goddamned romantics didn't have this damned horse fetish!*

He shifted uncomfortably in the saddle. The Montanans' ancestors had scarcely been unique in importing horses and other draft animals as part of their original colonizing expedition. If nothing else, animal transport provided an always useful and sometimes vital fallback. Machines could break, technology could fail or be lost. But horses, donkeys, and oxen—or camels, depending on local climatic conditions—could survive, and reproduce, almost anywhere mankind himself could manage to cling to life.

But the Montanans had taken the whole business rather farther than most. It was part of their romanticized lifestyle. And, Harahap grudgingly conceded, there were times and places where the stupid, four-footed, sharp-spined, *stubborn* creatures had their uses.

And the fact that they produce no detectable energy signature—aside from infrared—is a case in point, he admitted. Not that the Montana government had the sort of reconnaissance assets wealthier, more advanced star systems might have boasted. Still, the Montana Marshals Service, the local planetary police force, had an impressive record of successes. It wasn't especially huge, but its personnel were smart, well trained, and—unusually for police, in Harahap's experience—accustomed to thinking outside the box. It was only a matter of time before the Manties provided them with the technological upgrades to let them begin using their existing capability to good effect, so Westman's insistence on developing the proper mindset and techniques to evade the eventual spy satellites probably did make sense. Especially given how hot the hunt for him and his associates had turned in the four days since they'd pulled off their little bombing attack.

If I hadn't prearranged the message drop last time I was here, I'd never've been able to find him, and it's going to get worse. They're going to have to go further underground, so I guess I can't blame them for being just a bit . . . overly security conscious at the moment. However uncomfortable it is.

At least he and the blasted animal were almost to the agreed meeting site. He hauled out his GPS unit to double-check, and grimaced in approval. He'd thought that was the clump of trees Westman's messenger had described to him, but it was good to have confirmation.

His horse ambled up the trail, stubbornly moving at a speed *it* found good, and Harahap tried to look as if he thought it was a reasonable pace, as well. Eventually, he reached the designated spot and clambered down from the saddle with a profound gratitude flawed only by the knowledge that eventually he'd have to climb back on top of the unnatural beast for the trip back to what passed for civilization.

He tied the horse's reins around a native falseoak, gave it a sour look, and stood massaging his backside while he gazed out from the top of the cliff.

He could see why Westman's messenger had told him this was one of the planet's more popular scenic attractions. Of course, most sensible tourists settled for making the trip from the capital in a few minutes of comfortable air car travel. Only the genuine lunatics insisted on doing it in the "authentic Montana way," and Harahap was darkly certain that the livery stable operators who rented them horses for the trip probably hurt themselves laughing while they watched the off-planet idiots go riding off.

From his present height, Harahap could see for what had to be at least a hundred kilometers across the gorge of the New Missouri River, and despite his aching buttocks and thighs and the grim reality of the errand which brought him here, he felt more than a touch of outright awe. The New Missouri was the second-longest river on Montana, and over the eons, it had carved a path through the New Sapphire Mountains that dwarfed anything Harahap had ever seen. Westman's representative had informed him proudly that the New Missouri Gorge was almost twice the size of something called the Grand Canyon back on Old Earth, and it was certainly more than enough to make Damien Harahap feel small and ephemeral.

He pulled out a holo camera and began obediently taking pictures like any proper nature lover. The camera was part of his tourist's cover, but he'd already decided this was one set of pictures he was actually going to keep when he heard the rattle of stones from the higher slopes behind him. He lowered the camera and looked around casually as Stephen Westman rode down the slope on a tall, roan gelding.

"I must say," Harahap said as the Montanan drew up beside him and dismounted with the fluid grace of a lifetime's practice, "this is a much more spectacular backdrop than our previous meeting enjoyed."

"It is that," Westman agreed, blue eyes looking past his visitor to take in the spectacular view once more. It was a sight he never tired of, although sometimes it took the awe of an off-worlder's first glimpse of it to remind him just how wonderful it was.

"I'm not sure all this isolation was really necessary, though," Harahap continued. "And while I'd never want to sound critical, I might point out that standing here on the edge of this cliff makes us rather vulnerable to any directional microphones in the area."

"It does—or would, if there were any," Westman replied, and smiled thinly. "To be honest, Mr. 'Firebrand,' one reason I chose it was so I could be positive you'd come alone. And while I'd never want to sound ominous, I might point out that standing here on the edge of this cliff makes you a rather easy target for the fellows with pulse rifles sitting out there amongst the shrubbery to watch my back."

"I see." Harahap considered the Montanan's smiling face calmly, then nodded. "So it was less about security from the authorities' sensor systems than about getting me nicely out in the open."

"Yep," Westman acknowledged. "Not that I really think you're working for Suttles or the Manties. I know Chief Marshal Bannister pretty damned well, and this wouldn't be his style. And I don't think the Manties've had time to get around to sending their agents after me this way. But you *could* have been working for the Rembrandters. Not very likely, but it was possible. Matter of fact, you still could be."

"As an *agent provocateur*?" Harahap chuckled. "I approve of your caution. But if I were working for Vaandrager or Van Dort, the pulse cannon–armed air cars would already be sweeping down upon us."

"And crashing in the Gorge," Westman said with a smile. Harahap cocked an eyebrow at him, and the Montanan shrugged. "I invested quite a bit of money in the necessary tools before I went underground, Firebrand. Including some rather nice Solly shoulder-fired surface-to-air missiles. They may be a mite out of date, and I don't have many of them, but they work just fine, and I expect they should deal with anything short of a modern assault shuttle. I sort of figured this would be a good place to trot some of them out."

"Then it's fortunate for both of us that I don't work for the RTU." Harahap returned the other man's smile while he considered whether or not Westman was telling him the truth. On balance, and especially in light of how smoothly he'd carried out his strike on the Trade Union's spaceport enclave, Harahap was inclined to believe him.

"But if you're not working for the Rembrandters or the Manties," Westman observed, "that still leaves the question of exactly who you *are* working for."

"I told you the last time we spoke. Of course, we didn't have a name then, but we're the same people. And we've decided that calling ourselves the Central Liberation Committee has a nice ring to it."

Westman's lips quirked, mirroring the flash of amusement in his eyes, but Harahap wasn't fooled. This was an extremely intelligent man, whatever his prejudices, and he understood that anyone who chose to involve himself in this sort of game had to have motives of his own. Motives which might or might not have any particular correspondence to the motives he *said* he had.

"We've finally started getting ourselves effectively organized," the Gendarmerie captain continued, "and our scam to extract operating funds from the RTU worked out even better than we'd anticipated." As he'd hoped, Westman's smile grew a little broader at the reference to the supposed embezzlement from the Trade Union's coffers. The idea seemed to amuse him even more than it had Nordbrandt. "We've also managed to locate a moderately corruptible Solly source in the Meyers System for weapons and other hardware."

"You have," Westman said with no particular emphasis.

"We have. I'm not going to try to fool you, Mr. Westman. Like your SAMs, these aren't the very latest weapons available. In fact, they're probably from a planetary militia's armory somewhere. But they've been thoroughly reconditioned, and they're as good as or better than anything your government has. The communications and surveillance equipment is newer and better than that—the latest Solly civilian equipment. Probably still not quite as good as the Manty military will have, but light-years better than anything you could obtain locally."

"And you're prepared to make all of this available to me out of the goodness of your hearts, of course."

"Actually, to a large extent, that's exactly right," Harahap said, meeting the other man's searching gaze with the utter sincerity that was one of his most important professional assets. "Oh, we're not totally altruistic. Noble and generous, of course, but not *totally* altruistic."

Westman snorted in amusement, and Harahap smiled. Then he let his expression sober once more.

"Seriously, Mr. Westman. Probably eighty or ninety percent of the Central Committee's motivations are a combination of altruism and self-interest. The other ten percent come under the heading of *pure* self-interest, but, then, we could say the same about you, couldn't we?"

He held Westman's gaze until the other man nodded, then went on with a small shrug.

"We don't want to see this annexation go through any more than you do. Even if Tonkovic manages to hold out for every constitutional guarantee in the galaxy, there's no reason to believe a government as far away as the Manticore System would feel any particular obligation to honor them. Especially not once they've gotten their own military forces and domestic collaborators set up here at the local level. We don't much care for Rembrandt and the RTU, either, and you and I both know who's going to wind up skimming all the cream off the local economy if this thing goes through. So we've got plenty of reasons of our own to want to throw all the grit we can into the works. But having said that, I'd be less than honest if I didn't say that at least some of the Central Committee's members think they see an opportunity for their own star systems' investors and shippers to help themselves to a larger slice of the pie here in the Cluster if we can take the RTU down a peg."

"Which suggests that even if we get rid of the Manties *and* the Rembrandters, we're likely to see someone else trying to move in on the RTU's operation," Westman said sourly.

"It's an imperfect universe," Harahap pointed out gently. "And any political or economic system is dynamic, constantly changing. Look at it this way—you may not get a perfect resolution out of removing Manticore and the RTU from the equation, but you *will* have gotten rid of the two devils you know about. And whatever new changes someone else may try to impose, you'll be starting fresh, from a level playing field, if you want to keep them off of Montana."

Westman made a noncommittal sound. He stood gazing off over the Gorge, and Harahap let the silence linger for a minute or two. Then he cleared his throat. Westman looked at him, and he flipped his shoulders in a small shrug.

"The bottom line is that we all want at least some of the same things . . . and none of us are likely to get any of them operating on our own. At the moment, the Manties and the governments committed to the annexation have all the central organization, all the information sharing, and all the firepower. Your operation showed imagination, careful planning, and ability. Those are exactly the qualities in you which attracted our attention in the first place. But they're also the qualities which are going to make squashing you a priority for the Manties. The same thing will be true of anyone who proves he's an effective opponent, and they're far better off—organizationally, not simply in terms of manpower and weapons—than we are. So if we want any realistic chance of keeping control of our own star systems and our own souls, we're going to have to come up with some sort of countervailing coordination of our own. That's what the Central Committee is trying to provide."

"And just how widespread are your . . . call them 'local chapters'?" Westman asked after a moment.

"We're still setting them up," Harahap admitted. "In addition to our conversations with you, we've been in contact with people from New Tuscany to Split. Some of them—like Agnes Nordbrandt, in Split—have already signed on with us," he continued, bending the truth just a bit. It wasn't much of a lie, after all. He hadn't been in contact with Nordbrandt since their conversation on Kornati, but he felt confident she would jump at the official offer of assistance when he made it.

"Nordbrandt?" Westman's eyes sharpened with interest. "So she meant it when she said she was going underground, did she?"

"Oh, yes, she certainly did," Harahap said. "Of course, I've been moving around a lot lately, but I met with her personally a couple of months ago, and we discussed her plans in some detail." Another small exaggeration there, but one Westman couldn't check. And one which should polish Harahap's credibility just a bit brighter. "Why? Have you heard anything more recent about her?"

"It's over a hundred and twenty light-years from Montana to Split," Westman pointed out. "It takes even a dispatch boat two weeks to make the trip. The last I heard was over a month ago, when she resigned her parliamentary seat and announced she intended to oppose the annexation 'by other means.'" He shrugged. "If she's as serious as you're saying, I'm sure we'll be hearing more from her sometime soon."

"No doubt," Harahap agreed. "From the plans she discussed with me, she should be making quite a splash. Maybe not as spectacular as that little trick you pulled off last week, perhaps, but enough to make the Manties sit up and take notice.

"But the delay in the information loop that you just pointed out is one of the strongest arguments in favor of your accepting the Central Committee's assistance," he continued. "If all goes well, we'll be located in the Spindle System ourselves. That will put us right on top of the deliberations of the Constitutional Convention, and let us disseminate intelligence information as rapidly as it comes into our hands. And, let's face it, Spindle is probably where the Manties will set up their own administrative hub once they take over, so information is going to flow to the center much faster than it moves around the periphery."

Westman nodded, his expression thoughtful. He turned to gaze back out over the Gorge one more time, removing his hat and letting the brisk, cool breeze ruffle his blond hair. A Terran hawk passed overhead, outspread wings riding the Gorge's thermals, and Harahap heard its shrill, piercing cry as it stooped upon some small prey. Finally, Westman turned back to him and extended his hand.

"All right," he said. "Like you say, even if we all have our own individual motives, at least we all agree on the importance of smacking down Rembrandt and kicking the Manties' asses back out of the Cluster. I expect that's enough to go on with for now."

"I don't think you'll regret this," Harahap lied.

"If I do, it won't be the first thing in my life I've regretted," Westman said philosophically. The two of them shook hands firmly, and the Montanan put his Stetson back on his head. "And now that we're all such close friends," he continued, "I expect we need to be giving some thought to communications links." Harahap nodded, and Westman pursed his lips. "How long will you be on-planet?"

"I really need to leave again as soon as possible," Harahap said frankly. "We've got other representatives working the far side of the Cluster, but I'm the contact person most of the people here on the southern border actually know."

"I suppose that makes sense," the Montanan conceded. He thought some more, then shrugged. "I can have my communications people set up three or four separate secure channels by tomorrow morning," he said. "We're organized on a cell basis, and each channel will connect to a separate cell, so even if we lose one or two of them, you should still be able to contact me when you come back around."

"Sounds good," Harahap agreed, impressed by the amount of thought Westman had clearly put into this entire operation. "And we'll have to make some arrangements for the arms delivery."

"How soon can we expect them?"

"That's a bit hard to say, exactly," Harahap said. "I'd guess we're probably looking at something between two and three months. The weapons are already in the pipeline, but we have to have them delivered. And, to be honest, I wasn't positive you were going to agree to associate yourself with us, so you're not the first stop on our delivery schedule." He grimaced. "Pity. It would have made a lot more sense to drop your consignment off on the way into the Cluster from Meyers. As it is, we'll have to loop back and catch you on the way home."

"Well, I imagine we'll survive in the meantime," Westman said with a slow smile. "After all, I wasn't figuring on any outside support when I set things up. We'll be all right until your guns get here."

"Good," Harahap said with another of his patented sincere smiles. "I'm really looking forward to working with you."

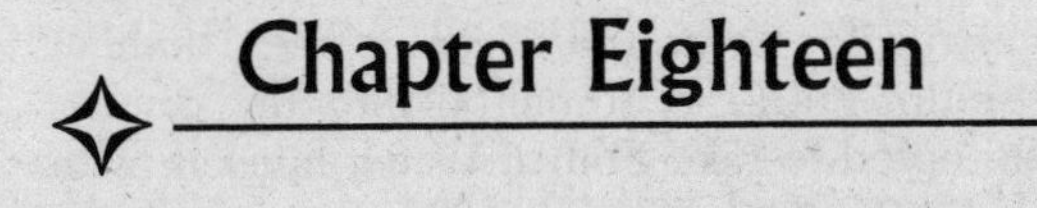

Chapter Eighteen

"I think we have something here, Sir."

Ansten FitzGerald sat up straight, pulling his attention away from the routine departmental reports he'd been scanning, and turned his command chair to face the tactical section.

It was late at night by *Hexapuma*'s internal clocks, and the Fourth Watch had the duty, which meant the assistant tactical officer ought by rights to be the officer of the watch. Normally, neither the captain nor the executive officer aboard a Manticoran warship stood a regularly scheduled watch, since, in theory, they were *always* on call. The communications officer, astrogator, tactical officer, and assistant tactical officer usually took the regularly scheduled watches, with Tactical getting the additional slot because of the Manticoran tradition that made Tactical the fast track to command. The theory was that if tactical officers were going to be promoted to command responsibilities faster than others, they needed the additional early experience.

But rank had its privileges, and usually the junior officer on the totem pole got the least desirable—latest (or earliest, depending upon one's perspective)—watch assignment. Unfortunately, in this case, the ship's assistant tactical officer was a mere junior-grade lieutenant, just a bit *too* junior to be routinely saddled with full responsibility for an entire heavy cruiser and her company. Lieutenant Guthrie Bagwell might have been able to take the slot, but EW was still the odd man out, and some people being assigned as EWOs didn't really have that much watch-standing experience of their own. Besides, Guthrie was so overworked—even with d'Arezzo helping out—that he was on the same sort of "always on call" status as the captain and the XO. And rather than pull the assistant astrogator or assistant com officer, both of whom were senior-grade lieutenants, into the queue, FitzGerald had opted to take Fourth Watch himself, with Abigail Hearns at Tactical.

He'd wondered at first if she was likely to take offense, to feel he didn't trust her competence. He'd also been prepared to live with her unhappiness if she had because, in the final analysis, he *didn't* trust her competence. Not because he doubted her ability or motivation, but because her actual experience remained so limited. The most capable officer in the universe still needed to be brought along carefully, needed the seasoning only experience could provide, if he was going to reach his full potential. And so Ansten FitzGerald had made a habit of bringing routine paperwork to the bridge with him and burying himself in it while Abigail quietly stood "his" watch, gaining the requisite seasoning with the reassuring knowledge a far more experienced officer was immediately available if something unexpected came up.

She seemed to understand what he was doing, although it was hard to be certain. She was such a self-possessed young woman that she probably wouldn't have allowed any resentment to show, even if she'd felt it. He sometimes wondered how much of that was because of her belief in the Doctrine of the Test which was so central to the Church of Humanity Unchained's theology, but whatever its origin, he'd quietly marked it down as yet another point in Lieutenant Hearns' favor.

Besides, he'd discovered, she was simply an immensely *likable* young woman.

"You think we have what, Lieutenant?" he asked now.

She was leaning forward, studying her plot intently, and he saw her reach out one hand and tap a complex series of commands into her touchpad without even looking at her fingers. His command chair was too far from her display for him to make out any fine details, but he could see data codes shifting as she refined them.

"I think we may have a reading on Commodore Karlberg's intruders, Sir," she said, still never looking away from her display. "I'm shunting the data to your repeater plot, Sir," she added, and he looked down as the small display deployed itself from the base of his chair.

Two of the trio of icons on the display strobed with the bright, quick amber-red-amber flash that CIC used to indicate questionable data, but it certainly *looked* like a pair of stealthily moving impeller wedges, creeping in above the system ecliptic. Much more interesting, however, in some ways, was the third icon—the one burning the steady red which indicated assurance on CIC's part. That one obviously belonged to a merchantman, although what a merchantship would be doing that far above the ecliptic—and that far outside the system hyper limit—was an interesting question. Especially since it seemed to be following in the strobing icons' wake.

He checked the range and bearing data, and his lips pursed in a silent whistle. They were even farther out than he'd thought. Nuncio-B's hyper limit lay 16.72 light-minutes from the star. At the moment, *Hexapuma*, in her parking orbit around Pontifex, was about ten light-minutes from the star, but the ship or ships Lieutenant Hearns was tracking were at least forty-five light-minutes out. There was absolutely no legitimate reason for any ship to be stooging around that far from any of the system's inhabited real estate.

"I wasn't aware we'd deployed our remote platforms that far out," he said conversationally.

"We haven't, really, Sir," she replied. He looked up to raise an eyebrow, and she colored slightly but met his gaze levelly. "All the remote arrays are operating inside the zones Captain Terekhov and Commander Kaplan specified," she said. "I just moved them to the outer edge of their assigned areas."

"I see." He tipped his chair back, resting his left elbow on the arm rest and his chin in his left palm while the fingers of his right hand drummed lightly on the other chair arm. "You're aware, Lieutenant," he continued after a moment, "that if you push the platforms that far out on a spherical front you virtually eliminate their lateral overlap?"

"Yes, Sir," she said crisply. "I thought about that, and if the Exec would look at the main plot?"

He glanced at the display. At the moment, it was configured in astrogation mode, and a complex pattern of vectors appeared on it. He studied them for a few moments, then snorted in understanding.

"Very clever, Lieutenant," he conceded in a neutral tone, watching the pattern evolve. She'd sent the remote platforms dancing through a carefully choreographed waltz that swept them back and forth across their zones. There were moments when they moved apart, widening the gap between them and weakening the coverage, but they always moved back towards one another again.

"What's the timing?" he asked.

"It's set up so that a ship would have to be traveling at at least point-five cee to cross the zone without being in detection range of at least two platforms for at least fifteen minutes, Sir. It seemed unlikely to me that anyone would try to sneak into the inner system at that high a velocity."

"I see," he said again. He frowned at the display for several more moments, then grunted. "It's obvious you put a lot of thought into designing this maneuver, Lieutenant. And, as I say, it's very clever. Moreover, I doubt very much that we would have picked these people up this soon if you hadn't done it. However, may

I suggest that in future you also put a little thought into clearing your ideas with the officer of the watch? It's considered the polite thing to do, since he's the one officially responsible if anything should happen to go wrong, and he tends to get his feelings hurt if he thinks people are ignoring him."

"Yes, Sir."

Self-possessed or not, he saw her blush this time. He considered giving the point one more lick, but it clearly wasn't necessary. And, perhaps even more to the point, initiative was one of the rarest and most valuable qualities in any officer. If she'd suffered her brainstorm and gotten her calculations for the remote arrays' courses wrong, she might have left a dangerous hole in *Hexapuma*'s sensor perimeter, and she'd needed to be whacked for taking it upon herself to assume she'd gotten them right. But the fact was that she had, and if she *had* requested permission to execute her plan, he would have granted it.

"Well, in that case," he said instead, "suppose you tell me what it is you think we've found?"

"Yes, Sir," she said. Then she paused for just a moment, as if marshaling her thoughts, and continued. "Obviously, Sir, the information we have on the two closer signatures is too vague to extrapolate any meaningful details. I've refined and backtracked from the datum the computers first recognized, and we can back plot their vectors for about twenty minutes before recognition, now that we know what to look for. On that basis, I can tell you they've been decelerating slowly but steadily. At the moment, all I'm prepared to say, besides that, is that one of them—the one I've designated Bogey One—is larger than the other one. Neither of them's larger than a cruiser, that much I'm sure of. But that leaves a lot of wiggle room.

"Bogey Three, the freighter, is actually more interesting at the moment. I think whoever they are, they figure they're far too far out-system for anything the Nuncians have to see them. I've only got them on passives, so I don't really have many details, even on the freighter, but

I think its presence alone is significant. The one thing these people aren't is any sort of bobtailed convoy—not coming in from that far out and above the ecliptic and decelerating at their observed rate—and the freighter isn't squawking a transponder code. So I think what we're looking at here is a pair of pirates accompanied by a prize they've already taken. If you'll notice, Commander, the freighter's decelerating harder than Bogey One and Two. She's killing velocity at a steady hundred and twenty gravities, and she's already down to just over seventy-eight hundred KPS, so she'll come to rest relative to the system primary in another hour and fifty-six minutes. Which will leave her forty-six-point-three light-minutes from the primary and approximately thirty-six light-minutes from the planet."

"And what do you think they're up to with her?"

"I think they just want to park her somewhere safe while they go sniffing further in-system, Sir," she said promptly. "They're coming in so slowly and cautiously that—"

She broke off, and her hand flicked over her keypad again.

"Status change, Sir!" she announced, and FitzGerald's eyes went to his repeater plot, then narrowed. The blinking icons had changed abruptly. They continued to blink, but they were fainter now, connected to a single steadily burning red crosshair. A slowly spreading, shaded cone of the same color radiated from the crosshair, its inmost edge moving in-system with the strobing icons.

"Either they've just killed their wedges, or their stealth just got a lot better, Sir. And that far out, I don't think it's likely they just brought that much more EW on-line."

"Then what do you think they're doing, Lieutenant?" FitzGerald asked in his best professorial manner.

"They were still moving at approximately eighty-six hundred KPS when we lost them," she said after a moment. "I'd guess they're planning on coming in ballistic from this point, with their impellers at standby. That velocity isn't very high, but that would make sense if they want to be as unobtrusive as possible—they wouldn't want to have to spill any more velocity if they end up needing to maneuver. At that low a speed, they can decelerate using minimum power wedges, so as to hold their signatures down, if they decide that's what they want to do. But they're coming in on a shortest-distance flight path towards Pontifex, so they obviously want a look at the traffic in the planet's vicinity. I'd say they figure that leaving the freighter out there, beyond the hyper limit, will keep anyone from spotting her, on the one hand, and put her in a position to escape into hyper before anyone could possibly intercept her, on the other. In the meantime, they can come in, take a look around the inner system, and find out whether or not there's anything here worth attacking. Commodore Karlberg was obviously right—they have to be more modern and powerful than anything he's got, given how they managed to futz up our sensor arrays—so they probably figure that even if somebody spots them, they can fight their way clear without too much trouble if they have to."

"I believe I agree with you, Ms. Hearns," FitzGerald said.

He tapped a few quick calculations into his own keypad and watched the results display themselves on the plot.

The shaded cone continued to grow steadily, indicating the volume into which the strobing icons might have moved at their last observed acceleration and velocity since the array had lost its hard lock, and he frowned. It was possible the bogeys' stealth systems actually had baffled the arrays. In that case, it was also possible they'd begun decelerating unseen, as a preliminary to moving away from the system. But that possibility wasn't even worth considering. There wasn't much *Hexapuma* could do about them if they were, and they weren't going to pose any immediate threat to Nuncio, but he didn't believe for a moment that they were doing any such thing—not with the freighter still decelerating steadily towards rest.

No, it was far more likely that Abigail's analysis was right on the money, in which case . . .

The result came up on his plot. At their last observed velocity, the two strobing icons would drift clear to Pontifex in just over twenty hours. And if they continued to coast in, running silent on ballistic courses, nobody with Nuncio's level of technology would see a thing before they actually crossed the planet's orbital shell. *Hexapuma*, on the other hand, armed with a hard datum on where they'd killed their wedges and knowing exactly what volume of space to watch, should be able to find them again with her heavily stealthed remote arrays' passive systems without their knowing a thing about it. It would be simple enough to steer the remotes into positions from which they could observe Bogey One and Bogey Two's predicted tracks closely enough to defeat the level of stealth they'd so far demonstrated, at any rate. The trick would be to do it using light-speed control links. It was unlikely the bogeys had picked up the arrays' FTL grav pulses yet, given how far away from the arrays they still were and how weak those pulses were, but *Hexapuma*'s transmissions to them would be far more easily detected. So the data *Hexapuma* had was going to get older, but would still be enormously better than anything the bogeys had. Or that they would believe Nuncio could have, which meant . . .

The XO sat back in the command chair, thinking hard. The freighter was the joker in the deck. Captain Terekhov and his senior officers had discussed several contingency plans built around the possibility that one or even two pirate cruisers might come calling, but none of those contingencies had considered the possibility that they would bring a captured prize with them. Taking out the pirates themselves would be a good day's work, but it was possible some or even all of the merchantship's original crew was still on board her.

The thought of leaving merchant spacers in pirate hands was anathema to any Queen's officer, but FitzGerald was damned if he saw any way to avoid it this time. However good *Hexapuma* and her crew might be, she could be in only one place at a time, and she was the only friendly vessel in-system which could realistically hope to engage the pirate cruisers and survive. Yet she was also the only hyper-capable friendly warship in Nuncio, which meant she was the only unit which could pursue the merchantship if her prize crew got into hyper-space.

No matter how he chewed at the unpalatable parameters of the tactical problem, Ansten FitzGerald could see no way to solve both halves of the equation, and just for a moment, he felt guiltily grateful that the responsibility for solving them lay on someone else's shoulders.

He reached out and tapped a com combination on his keypad. The screen lit with the image of *Hexapuma*'s snarling hexapuma-head crest which served as the com system's wallpaper, and a small data bar indicated that it had been diverted to a secondary terminal for screening. Then the data bar blinked to indicate an open circuit as the recipient accepted the call sound-only.

"Captain's steward's quarters, Chief Steward Agnelli," a female voice which couldn't possibly be as wide awake as it sounded said.

"Chief Agnelli, this is the Exec," FitzGerald said. "I hate to disturb the Captain this late, but something's come up. I'm afraid I'm going to have to ask you to wake him."

Aivars Terekhov took one more look at the immaculate officer in his cabin's mirror as Joanna Agnelli brushed a microscopic speck of lint from his shoulder. She looked up, brown eyes meeting his in the mirror, and her mouth twitched in a brief smile.

"Do I pass muster?" he asked, and her smile reappeared, broader.

"Oh, I suppose so, Sir."

He was still getting used to her Sphinxian accent. Dennis Frampton, his previous personal steward, had been born and raised in the Duchy of Madison on the planet Manticore, and his accent had been smooth, with rounded vowels quite unlike the sharp crispness of Sphinxians like

Agnelli. Dennis had been with him for over five T-years, long enough for him and Terekhov to have become thoroughly comfortable with one another. And it had been Dennis who'd convinced him that appearing in proper uniform at all times, and especially when it looked as if something . . . interesting might be going to happen, was one of a captain's most valuable techniques for exuding a proper sense of control and confidence. He'd always insisted on inspecting *his* Captain's appearance minutely before letting him out in public.

Just as he had at Hyacinth.

A shadow of memory and sharp-edged loss flickered in the ice-blue eyes looking back at him from the mirror. But it was only a shadow, he told himself firmly, and smiled back at Agnelli.

"My wife always said I should never be allowed out without a keeper," he said.

"Which, begging the Captain's pardon, shows she's a very smart lady," Agnelli replied tartly. She came from the old school, with an astringent personality and a firm sense of her responsibility to badger and pester her captain into taking proper care of himself. And she was also the only person aboard *Hexapuma* whose cabin intercom was left keyed open at night in case that same captain needed her.

Which meant she was the only person aboard the cruiser who knew about the gasping, sweating nightmares which still woke him from time to time.

"I've taken the liberty of putting on a fresh pot of coffee," she continued. "It should be ready shortly. With the Captain's permission, I'll bring it to the bridge in . . . fifteen minutes."

Her tone was rather pointed, and Terekhov nodded meekly.

"That will be fine, Joanna," he said.

"Very good, Sir," Chief Steward Agnelli said, without even a trace of triumph, and stepped back to let him go out and play.

✧ ✧ ✧

"Captain on the bridge!"

"As you were," Terekhov said as he strode briskly through the bridge hatch, before any of the seated watchstanders could rise to acknowledge his arrival. He crossed directly to FitzGerald, who stood looking over Abigail Hearns' shoulder at her display.

The exec turned to greet him, warned by the quartermaster's announcement, and felt a brief flicker of surprise. He knew he'd personally awakened the captain less than ten minutes ago, yet Terekhov was perfectly uniformed, bright-eyed and alert, without so much as a single hair out of place.

"What do we have here, Ansten?"

"It was Ms. Hearns who actually spotted it, Skipper," FitzGerald said, and squeezed the young Grayson lieutenant's shoulder. "Show him, Abigail."

"Yes, Sir," she replied, and indicated the display.

It took her only a very few sentences to lay out the situation, and Terekhov nodded. He also noticed that the remote arrays must have been right up against the extreme limit of their assigned deployment envelopes to have picked up the two lead bogeys before they closed down their impellers, and he knew *he* hadn't authorized the change. He scratched one eyebrow, then shrugged mentally. He felt confident that the XO had already attended to any reaming which had been required. After all, taking care of that sort of thing so his captain didn't have to was one of an executive officer's more important functions.

"Good work, Lieutenant Hearns," he said instead. "Very good. Now we only have to figure out what to do about them."

He smiled, radiating confidence, and folded his hands behind him as he walked slowly towards the chair at the center of the bridge. He seated himself and studied the deployed repeater plots, thinking hard.

FitzGerald watched the Captain cross his legs and lean comfortably back in the chair and wondered what was going on behind that thoughtful expression. It was impossible to tell, and the exec found that moderately maddening. Terekhov couldn't really be as calm as he looked, not with that freighter tagging along behind.

Terekhov sat for perhaps five minutes, stroking his left eyebrow with his left index finger, lips slightly pursed as he swung the command chair from side to side in a gentle arc. Then he nodded once, crisply, and pushed himself back up.

"Ms. Hearns, you have the watch," he said.

"Aye, aye, Sir. I have the watch," she acknowledged, but she remained where she was, and he gave a mental nod of approval. Technically, she should have moved to the command chair, but she could monitor the entire bridge from where she was, and she recognized that it was more important not to leave Tactical uncovered at the moment.

"Be so good as to contact Commander Kaplan and Lieutenant Bagwell, if you please," he continued. "My compliments, and I'd like them to join the Exec and me. We'll be in Briefing One; inform them that it will be acceptable for them to attend electronically."

"Yes, Sir."

"Very good." He twitched his head at FitzGerald, and then flipped his left hand towards the briefing room hatch.

"XO?" he invited.

"So that's about the size of it, Guns."

Aivars Terekhov gestured at the plot imagery relayed to the briefing room table's holo display, and FitzGerald wondered if he was aware he was addressing Naomi Kaplan with the traditional informal title for the first time since coming aboard. For that matter, FitzGerald had been just a bit surprised to hear himself calling Terekhov "Skipper" for the first time. Despite that, it felt surprisingly natural, and the executive officer wondered just when that had happened. He pondered the thought for a few seconds, then shook it off and refocused on the matter at hand.

Despite the late hour, Lieutenant Bagwell had opted to join his captain and the executive officer in the briefing room. From his appearance, it was obvious he'd been up anyway—probably working on another simulation for his EW section, FitzGerald suspected.

Kaplan, on the other hand, wasn't physically present, but she had the com terminal in her quarters configured for holographic mode. FitzGerald could see her in the corner of the briefing room's two-dimensional display, gazing intently at the same light sculpture that hovered above the conference table. She hadn't wasted time climbing into her uniform, since Terekhov had given her permission to attend electronically, and she wore an extremely attractive silk kimono which must have put her back a pretty penny.

"That freighter's going to be a stone bitch, Sir," the tac officer said after a moment. "Right off the top of my head, I don't see any way to retake her. Even if we let the shooters have free run of the inner system, she'd probably see us coming and slip away across the hyper wall before we ever got close enough to retake her."

She didn't point out that simply *destroying* the freighter would have been no challenge at all.

Unless the ship was sitting there with both its impeller nodes and its hyper generator carrying full loads—*not* a good idea for civilian-grade components—it was going to take a minimum of half an hour, by any realistic estimate, for the crew to fire up and make their escape. If Bogey Three's impeller nodes were hot, she could get under way in normal-space in as little as fifteen minutes, but it would take a good forty-five minutes to bring her nodes up if they weren't at standby. And bringing her hyper generator on-line in a cold start would require an absolute minimum of thirty minutes. Actually, the time requirement would more probably be forty or fifty minutes, given that they were talking about a merchant crew. And if they weren't, the understrength engineering crew the pirates had probably put on board would be hard-pressed to get the job done even that rapidly.

With the sensor suite a typical merchie carried, it was improbable to the point of impossibility that the prize ship—and Kaplan had no more doubt than the Captain or FitzGerald of what the lurking freighter was—could pick up *Hexapuma*, coming in under stealth, before she got well into the powered envelope of her multi-drive missiles. If she didn't, she couldn't possibly escape into hyper in the interval between the time *Hexapuma* fired and the time the attack birds arrived on target. And no merchie in the galaxy was going to survive a full missile broadside from an *Edward Saganami-C*-class cruiser.

Unfortunately, blowing her out of space wasn't exactly the best way to rescue any merchant spacers who might still be on board her.

"Letting One and Two operate freely would be unacceptable, even if it let us get all the way into energy range and take out the merchie's impellers before she could translate clear," Terekhov began mildly, then paused as the briefing room hatch slid open.

Joanna Agnelli walked through it, carrying a tray which bore three coffee cups, a plate of bran muffins, liberally stuffed with raisins and still steaming from the oven, and a covered butter dish. She crossed to the conference table, set down the tray, poured a cup of coffee and settled it on a saucer in front of Terekhov, and then poured cups for FitzGerald and Bagwell. Then she took the cover off the butter dish, handed each bemused officer a snow-white linen napkin, cast one final look around the briefing room, as if searching for something to straighten or dust, and withdrew . . . all without a single word.

Terekhov and his subordinates looked at one another for a moment. Then the exec grinned and shrugged, and all three of them picked up their coffee cups.

"As I say," Terekhov picked up his previous thought along with his cup, "pulling *Hexapuma* out of the inner system's unacceptable. There's no way we could expect Commodore Karlberg to take on two modern warships.

And, frankly, capturing or destroying those two ships has a far higher priority than retaking a single captured merchie."

"Agreed, Sir," Kaplan said, but her tone was sour. It cut across the grain for any naval officer to abandon possible survivors to pirates, and the naturally combative tactical officer found the notion even more repugnant than most.

"I don't especially like that either, Guns." Terekhov's tone was mild, but his expression wasn't, and Kaplan sat just a bit straighter in her quarters. "In this case, however, it's possible that what we're looking at aren't your regular, run-of-the-mill pirates."

He paused, holding the coffee cup in his left hand as he gazed back and forth between his subordinates with an oddly expectant light in his eyes, as if waiting for something.

"Sir?" FitzGerald said, and Terekhov made the right-handed throwing away gesture he used to punctuate his thought processes.

"Think about it, Ansten. We've got two warships here. So far, we don't know much about them, except that their stealth capabilities and EW were good enough to keep our sensor array from getting a hard read. Admittedly, we're only using passives, they're coming in under emcon, and the range is very long, but there's no way a typical pirate has that kind of capability. Especially not the sort who'd normally operate out here in the Verge. And while word of the Lynx Terminus must have spread pretty much through the League by now, along with the news that shipping is going to be picking up in the vicinity, we're quite a long way from Lynx at the moment. So just what's sufficiently important about a system as poverty stricken as Nuncio to attract pirates with relatively modern vessels?"

FitzGerald frowned. He'd been focused on the tactical aspects of the situation, and the Captain's question hadn't even occurred to him. It took him a few more seconds to work through the logic chain which Terekhov had obviously already considered, but Bagwell got there first. He looked at Terekhov, tilting his head to the side.

"Sir," he said slowly, "are you suggesting they weren't 'attracted' at all? That they were *sent*?"

"I think it's possible." Terekhov tilted his chair back and sipped coffee, gazing up at the holo display as if it were a seer's crystal ball. "I can't assess how *probable* it is, Guthrie, but I find those ships' presence here . . . disturbing. Not the fact that raiders are operating in the area." The right hand moved again. "Weakness always invites predators, even when the hunting isn't all that good. But I *am* disturbed by their evident capability. And if I were an outside power intent on destabilizing the area to hinder or prevent the annexation, I'd certainly consider subsidizing an increased level of pirate activity."

"That's not a happy thought, Skipper," FitzGerald said.

"No, it's not," Terekhov agreed. "And I'd say the odds are at least even that I'm being overly suspicious. It's entirely possible we have two genuine pirates here, and that they're simply taking the long view and scouting the area with an eye to future operations. In either case, taking them out has a higher priority than retaking the merchie. But the need to determine which they really are, if we can, lends weight to the desirability of taking at least one of them more or less intact."

"Yes, Sir," FitzGerald agreed, and Kaplan nodded.

"But that's going to mean getting them in a lot closer," the exec went on. "I think Abigail's right, and these people aren't any bigger than a pair of cruisers. In that case, taking them with missiles would be fairly straightforward. Unless they're Peeps with heavy pods on tow, of course, which is sort of unlikely this far from home."

Terekhov's lips twitched in a smile at FitzGerald's massive understatement, and the commander continued.

"Range advantage or no, though, we don't want to be throwing full broadsides at them unless we intend to go for quick kills and risk destroying them outright. And unlike their merchie, these people will have hot nodes and generators, despite the wear on the components. If they're outside the hyper limit, they'll probably have time to duck back across it before we can disable them with smaller salvos. So we need to let them in deep enough to give us some time to work on them before they can make a break over the hyper wall."

"At least." Terekhov nodded. "And, while taking out the actual pirates may have a higher priority than retaking the freighter, I fully intend to attempt both."

All three of his subordinates looked at him in surprise. Surprise, he noticed, which held more than a hint of incredulity, and he smiled again, thinly.

"No, I haven't taken leave of my senses. And I'm not at all sure we can pull off what I have in mind. But there's at least a chance, I think, if we play our cards properly. And if we can pull the preparations together fast enough."

He set down his coffee cup and let his chair come fully upright, and all three of his officers found themselves leaning forward in theirs.

"First," he said, "we have to deal with Bogey One and Bogey Two. As you say, Ansten, that's going to require getting them close enough to *Hexapuma* for us to work on them. If I were in their place, I wouldn't come inside the system hyper limit at all. If these ships are as modern and capable as their stealth capabilities seem to suggest, they probably have the sensor reach to get a good read on any active impeller signatures from at least twelve or thirteen light-minutes. So they could stop that far from Pontifex, which would leave them at least two light-minutes outside the limit, and easily spot any of Commodore Karlberg's LACs which happened to be under way. They probably wouldn't be able to pick up anything in a parking orbit with its impellers down, but if they're really modern units and they're prepared to expend the assets, they could punch recon drones past the planet. And they could feel fairly confident that nothing Nuncio has could intercept their drones even if they managed to detect them in time to try.

"At the moment, we know where they are with a fair degree of certainty. Moreover, we're pretty sure what course they intend to follow, and I think Lieutenant Hearns is right that they intend to coast in ballistic all the way. So it wouldn't be very difficult to accelerate out on an interception heading. We'd be able to localize them with our remote arrays, and they wouldn't be able to see us with their shipboard sensors until it was too late for them to avoid action. Unfortunately, that would mean we'd encounter them well outside the hyper limit, where they'd have the opportunity to escape after the first salvo, and we'd also have a high relative velocity at the point at which we overflew them if they didn't run. Our engagement window would be short, and we'd be right back with the options of either destroying them outright or letting them escape.

"The only other possibility is to entice them into coming to *us*. Which suggests that it's time we consider a Trojan Horse approach."

"Use our EW systems to convince them we're a freighter, Sir?" Bagwell asked.

"Exactly," Terekhov agreed.

"Pulling it off would depend on how stupid they are, Sir," Kaplan pointed out from his com display. Her diffident tone suggested she had her doubts about that, but her dark brown eyes were intent.

"I've had a few thoughts on that already, Guns," Terekhov said. "The biggest problem I see, actually, is that I want to hold our accel down to something that would be on the low side even for a merchie."

"How low were you thinking about, Skipper?" FitzGerald asked.

"I'd like to hold it to under a hundred and eighty gravities," Terekhov replied, and the exec frowned.

"That *is* on the low side," he said, rubbing his chin thoughtfully. "I'm assuming you want them to think we've panicked and we're trying to run away from them?" Terekhov nodded, and FitzGerald shook his head. "For us to be 'running' at that low an acceleration, we'd have to be up in the six- or seven-million-ton range. I don't see them believing a freighter that big would be here in Nuncio. Merchant traffic may be picking up in the area, but no shipping line I can think of would tie up a hull that size this far out in the sticks."

"Actually, Sir," Bagwell said, "I might have an idea there."

"I hoped you might," Terekhov said, turning to the EWO.

"There are a couple of ways we could approach it," Bagwell said. "We're going to have to get Commander Lewis involved in this, but taking some of the beta nodes out of the wedge and playing a few games with the frequency and power levels on the ones we leave in should let us produce an impeller wedge that's going to be pretty hard for anyone to tell apart from the wedge of, say, a three- or four-million-ton merchie. And if Commander Lewis is as good as I think she is, she ought to be able to induce an apparent frequency flutter into the alpha nodes, especially if she lets the betas carry the real load."

"You think these people's shipboard sensors would be able to pick up a flutter from far enough out to make that work, Guthrie?" Kaplan asked. The electronics warfare officer looked at her com image, and she shrugged. "If they can't see it with their shipboard arrays, then I think they'd be likely to go ahead and pop off one of those recon drones the Skipper was talking about a minute ago. That might pick up the flutter, all right, but it would also probably get close enough for a look at us using plain old-fashioned opticals. In which case, they'd recognize what we really are in a heartbeat."

"We'd need to discuss it with Commander Lewis," Bagwell agreed, "but this is something Paulo—I mean, Midshipman d'Arezzo—and I have been kicking around for a couple of weeks now. And—"

"A couple weeks?" Terekhov interrupted, with a quizzical smile, and Bagwell smiled back with a small shrug.

"Skipper, you told us one of our jobs out here was

anti-piracy work, and Paulo and I figured that sooner or later we'd have to deal with a problem pretty much like the one we're looking at here. So we started playing around with simulations. If Commander Lewis—and you, of course, Sir—are willing to put a little extra wear on the ship's alpha nodes, I think we can generate a pretty convincing normal-space flare. The sort of flare a *failing* beta node might produce. Nice and bright, and clearly visible to any modern warship at at least ten or twelve light-minutes. And just to put a cherry on top, we could simulate successive flares. The sort of thing you might see if an entire impeller ring that was in pretty shaky shape was overstressed so badly its nodes began failing in succession."

"I like it, Skipper," FitzGerald said. Terekhov looked at him, and the exec chuckled. "I'm sure Ginger won't be delighted about abusing her impeller rooms the way Guthrie's suggesting, but I'm willing to bet she could do it. And it would explain that low an acceleration rate out of a relatively small merchantship."

"And if it's visible from extreme range," Kaplan agreed with gathering enthusiasm, "the bad guys won't see any reason to expend a recon drone to check it out. They'll be too confident they already know what's going on to waste the assets."

"All well and good, Naomi." FitzGerald's smile faded a bit around the edges. "But they're still likely to be suspicious if we 'just happen' to leave orbit as they 'just happen' to come into sensor range of Pontifex. And if we're getting under way with what appears to be a seriously faulty impeller ring, that's even more likely to look suspicious to them."

"That's one of the things I was already thinking about," Terekhov said before the tac officer could reply. "Since it shouldn't be that difficult for us to track these people with our own arrays, it ought to be possible for us to coach a Nuncian LAC onto a course which will bring it close enough to the bogeys for it to have detected them. At which point, the LAC skipper would quite reasonably broadcast an omnidirectional general warning that stealthed ships were entering the inner system."

"It could get a bit rough on the LAC if she gets too close to the bogeys, Skipper," Kaplan pointed out.

"I think we could avoid that," Terekhov replied. "The fact that the LAC is broadcasting a warning at all should be pretty convincing evidence to the bogeys that she managed to detect them, regardless of how likely or unlikely that appears. If we bring the LAC in behind them, where she could get a look at their after aspect, the 'detection range' would go up pretty dramatically. And that would also allow us to put the LAC on a course which would make it impossible for her to intercept the bogeys, even if she wanted to. I don't see any reason for the bogeys to go out of their way and waste the time to bring a single obsolescent light attack craft into their engagement range when the damage has already been done. Especially if decelerating to do so would distract them from the pursuit of a lame-duck merchie.

"Actually, I'm more concerned about the bogeys' reaction to our decision to run deeper into the system rather than breaking for the hyper limit on a tangent. I'm hoping they'll figure we've panicked, or that we hope they're still not close enough to have us on shipboard sensors and that we can get out of sensor range fastest by heading directly away from them." He shrugged. "I like to think I wouldn't be stupid enough to assume either of those things myself, but I'm not at all sure I wouldn't be. God knows we've all seen enough merchant skippers do illogical things in the face of sudden, unanticipated threats. I think it's likely these people will assume we're doing the same."

"You're probably right, Skipper," FitzGerald said. "But do you really think Commodore Karlberg will agree to put one of his ships that close to these people?"

"Yes," Terekhov said firmly. "I think he wants them swatted badly enough to run a far greater risk than that. Especially after I explain to him how we're going to take a stab at retaking the merchie, as well."

"You mentioned something about that already, Skipper," FitzGerald said. "But I still don't see how we're going to pull it off."

"I can't guarantee we are," Terekhov conceded. "But I think we've got a pretty fair chance. A lot will depend on Bogey Three's exact design and several other factors beyond our control, but it ought to be possible. Here's what I have in mind . . ."

Chapter Nineteen

Abigail Hearns sat in the copilot's seat on the flight deck of the pinnace tractored to the hull of the Nuncian Space Force light attack craft. Although NNS *Wolverine*—named for a Pontifex species which bore remarkably little resemblance to the far smaller Terran predator of the same name—dwarfed the pinnace, she was tiny compared to any true starship. In fact, at barely fifteen thousand tons, she was less than five percent the size of *Hexapuma*, yet she was one of the more powerful units of Nuncio's fleet.

And, Abigail thought, remembering a night sky speckled with the brief, dying stars of deep-space nuclear explosions, *she's not that much smaller than the LACs we had when Lady Harrington took out* Thunder of God. *There's a certain symmetry there, I suppose . . . if this works out.*

Wolverine sat motionless in space relative to Nuncio-B, holding her position while Pontifex—and HMS *Hexapuma*—moved steadily away from her at an orbital velocity of just over thirty-two kilometers per second. Five other LACs sat with her, all that could reach her present position before she'd stopped in space, holding position on minimal power, and let her homeworld move away from her. They were packed to the limits of their life-support capacity with two companies of Nuncio Army troops who, Commodore Karlberg had assured Captain Terekhov, were fully qualified for boarding actions and vacuum work. She hoped Karlberg was right, although if everything went well, it probably wouldn't matter one way or the other.

The real teeth of the boarding force lay in the platoon of Captain Kaczmarczyk's Marines distributed—along with Abigail Hearns, Mateo Gutierrez, Midshipman Aikawa Kagiyama, and Midshipwoman Ragnhild Pavletic—between the two pinnaces under her command. She'd kept Ragnhild with her aboard Hawk-Papa-Two and put Aikawa aboard Hawk-Papa-Three with Lieutenant Bill Mann, Third Platoon's CO, and now she glanced at the midshipwoman's snub-nosed profile. The young woman looked tense, but if she was nervous, she gave remarkably little indication. She sat in the pilot's couch, the gloved hand resting on the helmet in her lap relaxed, fingers spread, and rather than sitting there staring at the time display, she was gazing raptly out the cockpit canopy at the Nuncian vessels.

Probably because she's never seen anything that antique outside of a historical holo drama, Abigail thought wryly.

She grinned, and then the smile faded as she caught sight of her ghostly reflection in the armorplast beyond Ragnhild. She looked much the same as ever . . . except for the hastily modified rank insignia on her skinsuit. Its sleeves still carried the single gold ring of a junior-grade lieutenant, but the single gold collar pip of the same rank had been replaced by the doubled pips of a *senior*-grade lieutenant. She was tempted to reach up and touch them, but she suppressed the urge firmly and returned her attention to the instrument console.

There's no way they'll let me keep them, whatever happens. But it was a nice gesture on the Skipper's part. And practical, too, I suppose.

Terekhov had surprised her with the appointment to the acting rank just before she left the *Hexapuma*. In theory, he had the authority to make the promotion permanent, but only pending a BuPers review. And given that Abigail had held her current rank for less than eight months before reporting aboard *Hexapuma*, she rather doubted BuPers would feel inclined to confirm it. In fact, her peculiar status as a Grayson currently in Manticoran service—and the only steadholder's *daughter* serving in either of her two navies—would probably make the Promotion Board even stickier than usual. But at least it made her technically superior to Mann in rank, which was handy, since the Captain had stressed that *she*, not the Marine, was in command. And it also gave her a leg up with Captain Einarsson, *Wolverine*'s commander and the senior NSF officer of the hastily organized little squadron.

Captain Magnus Einarsson was obviously one of the Nuncians who had trouble remembering that prolong meant the Manticorans with whom he was interacting were uniformly older than they appeared to Nuncian eyes. When he looked at Abigail, he saw a teenager, probably somewhere on the lower side of sixteen, and not a young woman almost ten T-years older than that. Worse, Nuncio was an uncompromisingly patriarchal culture. The bitter centuries of bare subsistence and miserable medical care had created a society which was forced to stoically endure a horrendous child mortality rate. For most of their planetary history, Nuncian women had been too busy bearing children—and dying of childbirth fever, as often as not, until the local medical establishment finally rediscovered the germ theory of disease—to do much of anything else. Only in the last two or three generations had the system's slowly climbing technology level made it possible to change that. And, human societies being human societies, cultural changes of that magnitude didn't happen overnight.

Yet another parallel with home, the Grayson lieutenant thought sardonically. *Although at least this atheistic bunch doesn't try to justify it on the basis of God's will! But without Lady Harrington, the Protector, and Reverend Hanks to kick them in the butt, they're going to be slower—and even more mulish—about accepting the change, anyway.*

Einarsson, at any rate, clearly had serious reservations (which he no doubt thought he'd concealed admirably) about accepting "recommendations" from even a senior-grade lieutenant who happened to be female. How he would have reacted if she'd turned up with her permanent rank was more than she cared to contemplate.

She looked down at the chrono once more and nodded as it came up on the five-hour mark since her remote arrays had detected the intruders. Five hours in which Pontifex had moved over half a million kilometers, taking *Hexapuma* with it. If the bogeys had managed to put one over on *Hexapuma* and get a recon drone into space headed to intercept the planet at the time they themselves would approach the hyper limit, its course would take it far enough from *Wolverine*'s present position to make anything as weak as a LAC's impeller signature invisible to them. And since Bogey One and Two themselves were still far beyond shipboard detection range of the planet—

"Stand by for acceleration in three minutes," Captain Einarsson's voice said in her earbug.

The three minutes ticked past into eternity, and then the six LACs and their pinnace parasites went instantly to five hundred gravities of acceleration.

Well, we'll find out whether or not the Skipper is a tactical genius in about ten and a half hours, Abigail thought.

Naomi Kaplan settled herself at Tactical, racked her helmet on the side of her bridge chair, and gave her console exactly the same quick but thorough examination she always did. It took several seconds, but then she made a small sound of approval and sat back, satisfied.

"I have the board," she said to the midshipwoman sitting

beside her, where she'd minded the store while Kaplan caught a belated breakfast. The ship was at Condition Bravo—not yet at General Quarters, but with her crew already skinsuited—and it was the RMN tradition to see that its people were well fed before battle. Kaplan had already seen all of her people fed . . . and been informed rather pointedly by Ansten FitzGerald that he wanted *her* fed, as well.

"You have the board, aye, Ma'am," Helen Zilwicki said, and Kaplan looked at her.

"Nervous?" she asked in a voice too low for anyone else on the bridge to overhear.

"Not really, Ma'am," Helen replied. Then paused. "Well, not if you mean *scared*," she said in a painstakingly honest voice. "I guess I probably am worried. About screwing up, more than anything else."

"That's as it should be," Kaplan told her. "Although you might want to reflect on the fact that just because we think we're bigger and nastier than they are, we're not necessarily right. And even if we are, we're still not invulnerable. Somebody can kill you just as dead by hitting you in the head with a rock as with a tribarrel, if she gets close enough and she's lucky."

"Yes, Ma'am," Helen said, remembering the breaking-stick feel of human necks in the shadows of Old Chicago's ancient sewers.

"But you're right to concentrate on the job," Kaplan continued, unaware of her middy's memories. "That's your responsibility right now, and responsibility is the best antidote to more mundane fears, like being blown into tiny pieces, that I can think of." She smiled at Helen's involuntary snort of amusement. "And, of course, if you *should* happen to screw something up, I assure you that you'll wish you *had* been blown into tiny pieces by the time I'm done with you."

She frowned ferociously, brows lowered, and Helen nodded.

"Yes, Ma'am. I'll remember," she promised.

"Good," Kaplan said, and turned back to her own plot.

Zilwicki was a good kid, she thought, although she'd had some reservations, given the midshipwoman's connection to Catherine Montaigne and the Anti-Slavery League. Not to mention her super-spook father's working association with the technically proscribed Audubon Ballroom. Unlike altogether too many officers, in her opinion, Kaplan didn't figure politics—hers or anyone else's—had any business in the Queen's Navy. Personally, she was a card-carrying Centrist, delighted that William Alexander had replaced that incompetent, corrupt, fucking *asshole* High Ridge, although she normally stayed out of the political discussions which seemed to fascinate her fellow officers. As a Centrist, she wasn't particularly fond of Montaigne's bare-knuckled political style, and she'd never cared for the Liberal Party, even before New Kiev sold out to High Ridge. But she had to admit that, whatever Montaigne's faults, there was absolutely no doubt of her iron fidelity to her own principles, be they ever so extreme.

Still, Kaplan had wondered if someone from such a politicized background would be able to put it aside, especially now that Zilwicki's kid sister had become a crowned head of state! But if there'd ever been a single instance of Zilwicki's political beliefs intruding into the performance of her duties, Kaplan hadn't seen it. And the girl was a fiendishly good tactician. Not as good as Abigail, but she had the touch. So if someone had to sub for Abigail, Zilwicki was an excellent choice.

But I don't want anyone *subbing for Abigail*, Kaplan thought, and felt a flicker of surprise at her own attitude. The youthful Grayson had a knack for inspiring trust, on a personal as well as a professional level, without ever crossing the line to excessive familiarity with superiors *or* subordinates. That was rare, and Kaplan finally admitted to herself that she was worried. That she disliked letting Abigail out of her sight, especially out amongst those primitive, sexist Nuncians.

Of course, she thought wryly, *she's probably had one*

helluva lot more experience dealing with primitive sexists than I *ever have! There's probably quite a few of them in her own family, for that matter.*

She snorted at her own reflections, and checked the time.

Nine hours since the remote arrays had first detected the intruders, and so far, everything was ticking along right on schedule.

"Ma'am, I think you should look at this," Helen said after rechecking her data twice, very carefully. It had come out stubbornly the same each time, however preposterous it seemed.

"What is it?" Lieutenant Commander Kaplan said.

"The Alpha-Twenty array just picked Bogey One back up, Ma'am. It got a good look at her, too, and I don't think she's exactly what anyone's been expecting."

Kaplan looked up from the missile attack profile she'd been reviewing and turned until she could see Helen's plot. She'd had Helen monitoring the sensor arrays—largely to give her something to do, Helen suspected. But now she looked at the data codes and the library entry sidebar CIC had thrown up on the plot at Helen's request, and her eyebrows rose.

"Well, Ms. Zilwicki," she said dryly, "I see you have a true Gryphon's gift for understatement."

She studied the display for another few moments, and Helen watched her as unobtrusively as possible.

The data had come in on a laser, not FTL, to insure that the bogeys didn't pick anything up, so it was several minutes old. But that didn't matter for ID purposes, and after a moment, the TO shook her head and reached for her com key. She pressed it and waited two or three seconds until a voice spoke in her own earbug.

"Captain speaking."

"Sir, it's Kaplan. We just got a positive relocation on Bogey One. She's right where we'd expected her to be, and the array got a pretty good look at her. Ms. Zilwicki—"

she gave Helen a quick smile and a wink that made her feel astonishingly good "—patched the data through to CIC, and we have a tentative identification."

"And?" Terekhov asked when she paused.

"Skipper, according to CIC, this is a *Mars*-class heavy cruiser."

"A Peep?"

There was something in the Captain's voice. A sharper edge, or a pause. A fleeting break, perhaps. Something. But Kaplan couldn't quite put her finger on it, whatever it was. And if she'd actually heard it at all, it had disappeared by his next sentence.

"CIC is confident of that?" he asked.

"Reasonably, Sir. They're still calling it tentative, but I think that's just ingrained caution. There is one weird thing about it, though, Skipper. The sensor array crossed astern of Bogey One, right through her stealth field's keyhole, and got a read on her emissions. That's how we were able to ID her. But according to CIC's analysis of the neutrino data, this ship appears to have the old Goshawk-Three fusion plants."

"Goshawk-*Three*?"

"Yes, Sir. And according to ONI, their yards upgraded to the Goshawk-*Four* at the construction stage with the third flight for the class, and they've systematically updated the surviving older members of the class—there aren't many of them left—since the armistice. There were some serious design flaws in the Goshawk-Three, and the Four not only corrected those but boosted output by over fifteen percent, so they've made a real effort to upgrade across the fleet. According to ONI, they shouldn't have any of the old Threes left."

"That's . . . very interesting, Guns." Terekhov's voice was slow and thoughtful. He was silent for a few moments, then said, "There's no indication that they picked up the array as it passed?"

"None that I can see, Sir. They're still just drifting along, exactly the way they were. That's a very stealthy array, Skipper, and we've got the grav-pulse transmitters locked down on all the platforms. I think it's extremely unlikely they've seen a thing yet."

"Agreed," he said. "All right, Guns. Thanks for the update."

"We strive to keep the customer satisfied, Skipper." Kaplan heard him chuckle as she cut the circuit, and she smiled herself, then looked back across at Helen.

"That was good work, Ms. Zilwicki. Very good work, indeed." *Which*, she didn't add aloud, *is why I made certain the Skipper knew who did it in the first place.*

"Thank you, Ma'am," Helen said. *And*, she didn't add aloud, *thanks for telling the Captain I did it.*

Aivars Terekhov's forced chuckle faded, and he returned his eyes to the book viewer, but he didn't really see it. His mind—and memories—were too busy. Too . . . chaotic.

A Peep. He remembered FitzGerald's earlier comment and shook his head. No Havenite warship should be this far from home. Not the next best thing to a thousand light-years from the Haven System.

He closed his eyes and rubbed them hard, trying to massage his brain into working, but it obstinately refused. It was trapped, caught in a hideous fragment of memory, watching the *Mars*-class cruisers rolling to present their broadsides. Watching that hurricane of death sweeping out towards HMS *Defiant*. His nostrils remembered the stench of blazing insulation and burning flesh, the screams of the wounded and dying, and a memory of maiming agony—a memory of the soul, deeper than bone and sinew—rolled through him. And the faces. The faces he'd known so well and condemned to the death *he'd* somehow cheated.

He inhaled deeply, fighting for control, and a soft soprano voice spoke suddenly.

"*It's over*," Sinead said. "*It's over*."

He exhaled explosively, blue eyes opening to gaze across the cabin at the bulkhead portrait. He felt her head on his shoulder, her breath in his ear, and the demon-memory retreated, banished by her presence.

A flush of shame burned dully over his face, and his right fist clenched on the book viewer. He hadn't realized his armor was that thin, hadn't dreamed it could hit him so hard, so suddenly. An icy stab of fear cut through the heat of his shame like a chill razor at the abrupt thought of what might have happened if it had slammed him that way in the middle of an engagement.

But it didn't, he told himself fiercely. *It didn't. And it won't. It was the surprise, the unexpectedness. I can handle it, now that I know what's coming.*

He stood up, laying the book viewer on the cushion of the huge, comfortable chair Sinead had picked out for him, and walked across to stand in front of her portrait, looking into her eyes.

I won't let that happen again, he promised her.

I know you won't, her green eyes said, and he nodded to her. Then he turned away, watching his right hand—his *regenerated* right hand—as he poured fresh coffee from the carafe Joanna had left on his desk. Almost to his surprise, that hand was rock steady, with no tremor to betray how badly he'd been shaken.

He took the coffee back to his chair, moved the book viewer, and sat back down.

His mind was beginning to work again, and he sipped the hot, comforting coffee while he replayed Naomi Kaplan's report mentally. She was right; it *was* "weird." Weird enough to find *any* Havenite warship way the hell and gone out here, but one with Goshawk-Three fusion plants?

His experiences at Hyacinth had left him with a fiery, burning need to know all there was to know about the ships which had slaughtered his division and his convoy. He'd haunted ONI, trading ruthlessly on his "war hero" status, until he'd learned the names of the task force commander and each of his squadron COs. He'd learned the enemy order of battle, which ships his people had destroyed, which they'd damaged. And in the process, he'd learned even more about the enemy's hardware than he'd known before the battle. Including the reason the Goshawk-Three had been retired with such indecent haste when the follow-on generation of fusion plants had become available.

The Goshawk-Three, like the heavy cruisers and battlecruisers in which it had originally been mounted, had been a typical product of the prewar Peep tech base: big, powerful, and crude. Unable to match the sophistication of the Star Kingdom, the People's Republic had relied on hardware designed for brute strength and far shorter intervals between overhauls, but the Goshawk-Three had been unusually crude, even for the Peeps. It had represented a transitional phase between their prewar hardware and the more sophisticated designs they'd managed to produce later, courtesy of Solarian tech transfers. It had been substantially more efficient than its predecessors, producing almost twice the output for a bare ten percent increase in size. But it had reduced the redundancy of its failsafes to save mass . . . and ended up with what turned out to be an extremely dangerous glitch in the containment bottle. At least two ships had suffered catastrophic containment failure in parking orbit under standby power levels. No one, the Peeps included, knew how many other ships had been killed by the combination of the same design fault and combat damage, but the number had undoubtedly been far higher than that.

So why should the Peeps send an obsolete ship, with notoriously unreliable power plants, a thousand light-years from home? Of all the people who might wish the Star Kingdom ill, the Republic of Haven had the least to gain from destabilizing the Talbott annexation. Of course, that very fact could explain why they might send an obsolete unit, whose combat power was no longer up to frontline standards and which would scarcely be missed from their order of battle. But why should they care enough to send *anyone*? And surely if they were going to hang some poor damned captain out at the end of a limb this long, they wouldn't have stuck him with Goshawk-Three fusion plants, on top of everything else!

Yet it appeared that they'd done precisely that, and try

as he might, Aivars Terekhov couldn't think of a single explanation for the decision that made any sense at all.

But even as he tried to think of one, another thought was running somewhere deep, deep in the secret hollow of his mind.

A *Mars*-class. Another *Mars*-class. And no light cruiser to kill it with, this time.

Oh no, not *this* time.

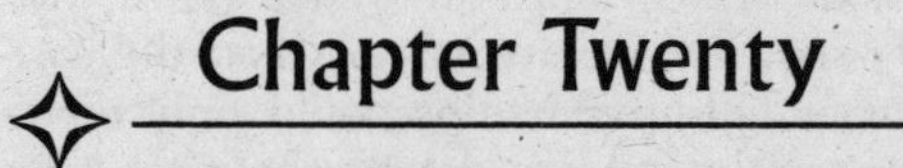

Chapter Twenty

"We're coming up on your specified mark, Ma'am," Midshipwoman Pavletic said politely.

Abigail Hearns looked up from the letter she'd been keyboarding into her memo pad and glanced at the time display. Ragnhild was right, and she saved and closed the letter and put the pad away.

She hit the button and her chair slid smoothly back into position.

"I have control," she announced.

"You have control, aye, Ma'am," Ragnhild acknowledged, surrendering the flight deck to her. Not that it made a great deal of difference with the pinnace still tractored to *Wolverine*'s hull, Abigail thought as she punched in the command to reconfigure the plot to tactical.

So far, it appeared the Captain's plan was working. Or, to be more accurate, nothing had gone actively wrong . . . yet. At the moment, *Wolverine*, her consorts, and the two piggybacking pinnaces, were over thirty-three light-minutes from Pontifex and a bit over two and a half light-minutes from Bogey Three. From the cockpit, Nuncio-B was little more than an especially brilliant star to the naked eye, and the planet wasn't visible at all. The pinnace's onboard sensors were much better than that, of course. In fact, they were as good as anything the far larger Nuncian LACs carried. Which didn't mean either the pinnaces or the LACs could see much of anything smaller than a star or a planet—well, perhaps a moon—at this range. Nor could they see much about a powered-down freighter at a hundred and fifty-one light-seconds.

Fortunately, Captain Terekhov had taken steps to provide Abigail with sharper, clearer eyes. One of *Hexapuma*'s sensor drones was tractored to *Wolverine*'s spine beside the pinnace. With the LAC's impeller wedge down, the drone's exquisitely sensitive passive sensors had the sort of reach most navies' all-up starships could only envy. Abigail still couldn't make out any details about the volume of space around the planet, but she had a perfect lock on the freighter, and the array was close enough to pick up even the minute emissions from things like hyper generators at standby.

The big ship—vast compared to a pinnace or a LAC, but actually on the small side for an interstellar freighter—was clearly IDed now as a four-million-ton, Solarian-built *Dromedary* class, and Abigail queried the pinnace's computers for information. As she'd hoped, there was quite a bit of it.

The storage capacity of computers wasn't unlimited, but when *Hexapuma*'s databases had been updated for her current deployment, they'd been loaded (among other deployment-specific information) with the specs and design schematics for the most common Solarian merchantship classes, since she was far more likely to be meeting Sollies than Manticoran vessels here in the Verge. She, in turn, had downloaded that information to her pinnaces, which would be conducting any examinations or searches of suspect merchantmen she might encounter. Now data scrolled across Abigail's display, cross-referenced to the full spectrum of Bogey Three's emissions.

The *Dromedary* class had been designed almost a hundred and fifty T-years ago, she noted, and aside from occasional updates in its electronics, it was virtually unchanged today. That was an eloquent testimonial to its suitability for the sort of general utility required of a smallish (relatively speaking) freighter working around the fringes of the League's merchant marine. It might be a bit much to call the *Dromedaries* "tramps," but it wouldn't be far off the mark, either.

Abigail watched the data come up and rubbed the tip of her nose thoughtfully. Normal complement was forty-two—large for a Manticoran ship of her tonnage, but manpower was at less of a premium in the League, and their merchant designs tended to use less comprehensive automation. Maximum theoretical acceleration for the class was two hundred and ten gravities, but that was with a zero safety margin on their compensators, and no sane merchant skipper was going to operate his ship at those levels. The standard ships of the class were designed for a hardwired five percent compensator safety margin, limiting them to a maximum of two hundred gees, although it was possible this ship's legitimate owners—or the pirates who'd captured it—might have removed the safety interlocks to give them a bit more acceleration. A dozen gravities either way wasn't going to make much difference, however.

The class's electronic profile followed, and her eyes narrowed as she compared it minutely to the sensor drone's readings. According to the drone data, the ship's single powerplant was operating at minimal levels, and the emissions signature of her impellers suggested the beta nodes were also at standby. It didn't look as if the alpha nodes were up at all, and there was no sign of the subtle gravitic stressing of a hyper generator at standby. That was good. Without the alpha nodes, her maximum acceleration would be reduced by well over thirty percent—call it a hundred and thirty gravities, barely a quarter of what a Nuncian LAC could turn out, and only about twenty percent of what the newest generation of Manticoran pinnaces could produce.

More importantly right now, however, it was going to take her at least a half hour to put her generator on-line and duck into hyper.

The class's hull schematic appeared next, and Abigail studied it carefully. Like almost any commercial freighter, a *Dromedary* consisted of a thin skin wrapped around the minimum necessary power plant, life-support, and impeller rooms and as much empty cargo space as possible. In the *Dromedaries'* case, the designers had placed the essential systems along the spine of the hull to provide the maximum possible unobstructed hold space. The holds themselves were designed to be quickly and easily reconfigured to make the best possible use of the available space, but tucking the power systems and life-support up out of the way provided the optimum degree of flexibility.

Yet that design philosophy had certain drawbacks. By pulling those systems up out of the core of the ship, the designers exposed them to potential damage. Manticoran civilian designers had a tendency to sacrifice some cargo-handling flexibility by moving things like fusion plants and hyper generators closer to the center of a ship, rather than leaving them exposed, but Solarian designers were less concerned, by and large, about such design features. A smaller percentage of the Solly merchant marine worked in high-risk environments like Silesia or deep into the Verge, and the Solarian philosophy was that any merchantship which found itself under fire should surrender and stop pretending it was a *war*ship before it got hurt.

Which could be a bit rough on the occasional crewman, but there were always more where he came from.

She pressed the com button on her chair arm.

"*Wolverine*, Einarsson," an accented voice said in her earbug.

"Sir," she said in her most formal tones, "this is Lieutenant Hearns. Our sensor data confirms identification as a *Dromedary* class. I'm downloading the hull schematic to you. As you'll see, Sir, she's a spinal design, and I've highlighted her hyper generator room's location. According to her emissions, her generator is off-line, and it looks like only her beta nodes are live at standby levels."

There was silence from the far end of the com link,

and she pictured Einarsson running through the same calculations she had.

"It looks as if we'll be going with one of the variants of the alpha plan after all," the Nuncian captain said after a moment.

"Yes, Sir," she replied respectfully, managing to sound as if she were accepting his direction rather than acknowledging a conclusion she'd already reached.

"Of course," Einarsson continued rather wryly, "whether or not we'll be able to use any variant of it depends upon what we hear from Captain Terekhov, doesn't it, Lieutenant?"

"Yes, Sir, it does."

"Very well. Let me know the moment you do hear something."

"Aye, aye, Sir."

"Einarsson, clear."

Abigail leaned back, eyes closed, and pondered the parameters of the tactical problem and Captain Terekhov's solution to it.

The small force of Nuncian vessels and their Manticoran parasites were moving towards the freighter at a relative velocity of just a hair over 17,650 KPS, and the LACs' maximum deceleration rate was five hundred gravities. It had taken them an hour of steady acceleration to reach their current velocity before shutting down their wedges to avoid detection, and it would take them another hour to kill their velocity, during which time they would cover another 31,771,000-plus kilometers. At the moment, they were about forty-two million klicks from the freighter, so to decelerate for a zero/zero intercept, they'd have to begin decelerating in no more than four minutes. The pinnaces, with their higher acceleration rate, had a bit more time to play with—they could achieve a zero/zero intercept if they began decelerating any time in the next fifteen minutes. If they didn't begin decelerating, they'd blow past Bogey Three at a range of about 67,500 kilometers and a velocity of over seventeen thousand KPS, in a shade over forty minutes.

But the instant any of them began decelerating, even a half-blind freighter with civilian-grade sensors was bound to spot them, and they would still be far out of energy weapon range. The small lasers mounted by *Hexapuma*'s pinnaces, without the more powerful gravitic lensing of their mothership's main battery weapons, would do well to inflict damage at any range over eighty thousand kilometers. The Nuncian LACs' lasers, although bigger, with more brute power, had far poorer fire control. They had the range to hit the freighter from a half million kilometers, but they'd have no effective control of *where* they hit it, and the sheer power of their weapons made any hit far more likely to inflict damage which might prove lethal instead of merely crippling.

So they'd have to overfly the freighter, disable her hyper generator in passing with the *pinnaces'* lasers, and then decelerate and come back. The fact that the *Dromedaries* were a spinal design would help—Abigail had been afraid they'd have to penetrate deeply into their target's hull to reach her generator, and Captain Terekhov had been forced to face the same possibility. That was the real reason *Wolverine* and the other LACs were along, because in the end, Terekhov was willing to risk destroying the freighter if that was the only way to stop it, and the Nuncian weapons were powerful enough to blast through to a deeply buried target.

Tester only knew how many things could have gone wrong if they'd had to do that, and Abigail would be just as happy if He never told her. As it was, they could probably disable the freighter's generator without tearing the ship apart outright. The problem would be that they couldn't be *positive* how much damage they'd done. It was possible they might do enough purely cosmetic damage to the ship's hull for it to look to their sensors as if they'd blown the generator completely apart, when they'd actually done only minor damage, or even—unlikely, but possible—missed it completely. In which case, as soon as the pinnaces and LACs had passed far enough by to lose the energy range, the pirates could simply bring the generator up and disappear into hyper.

By the same token, they might actually damage the generator, but not beyond the possibility of quick, jury-rigged repairs. In that case, the pirates might still be able to put the generator back on-line before anyone could decelerate and return to intercept them. So, ideally, Captain Einarsson's little force wanted to fire the instant they were certain of scoring the proper hit without blowing the ship apart, then decelerate at their maximum possible rate, so as to cut the pirates' available response time to a minimum. Since they were going to have to rely on the pinnaces for the shot, that meant closing to under a hundred thousand kilometers before even beginning to decelerate. Which meant, in turn, that even the pinnaces would be fifty minutes flight time and almost twenty-six and a half million kilometers down range from the freighter before they could decelerate to rest relative to its current position. And even then, it would take them another seventy minutes to actually return to it.

Two hours was a long time for the pirates to make repairs. Abigail was convinced the odds would be in their favor, not the pirates', but even if everything went perfectly from a timing perspective, Captain Terekhov was still running a grave risk. Even a pinnace's laser could fatally disembowel a merchantship if it hit just wrong. Even if it hit only the precisely desired target, there was still an excellent chance at least some of the freighter's original crew—assuming any were still alive aboard her—would be working in her impeller and hyper generator rooms under duress. In a worst-case scenario, they might do damage enough to kill a dozen innocent civilian spacers and still not enough to let them retake the ship before she vanished over the hyper wall.

Even in a best-case scenario, there was going to be bitter criticism of the Captain's plan from some quarters, because it didn't include any attempt to demand Bogey Three's surrender. Under the strict letter of interstellar law, a warship was always obligated to demand compliance with its instructions before firing into a merchantship, and a naval officer ignored that obligation at her peril. In this instance, however, there was no point making the effort. No doubt Bogey Three would happily have promised to stay exactly where it was if Abigal demanded that it do so. And it would have obeyed faithfully . . . just long enough for Abigail's velocity to take her safely out of weapons range.

No. In this case, the only real options were to cripple the target without warning, so that it couldn't hyper out whenever it wanted to, or else not even to attempt to retake it. The Captain had accepted that unflinchingly, and the fact that Abigail agreed with him a hundred percent didn't make her any happier about knowing that even under the best possible outcome, she was about to kill people.

But worse, in many ways, was the possibility that she might never have the chance to kill them. The Captain had made it clear that, badly as he wanted Bogey Three taken, and despite the grave risks he was prepared to run to accomplish that, taking out the armed vessels took precedence over retaking the freighter. So Abigail and Einarsson were specifically prohibited from firing on the *Dromedary* at all unless Terekhov was confident of engaging the armed vessels before any light-speed warning from the freighter could reach them.

The good news was that *Hexapuma* had the latest generation of FTL grav-pulse communicator. The pinnaces didn't have proper receivers, but the recon drone did. Its datalink channels to its mothership were perfectly capable of receiving messages and relaying them to Abigail's pinnace via com laser or—in this case—optical cable.

The bad news was that even people who couldn't read grav-pulses could detect them, and it was general knowledge by now that the RMN had that technology. So Captain Terekhov couldn't risk transmitting the release to attack until—or if—he'd sucked his own intended victims in close enough to be sure of engaging them.

All of which meant it was entirely possible the pinnaces

and LACs wouldn't be allowed to fire on the freighter as they went speeding past. Unless, of course, the freighter spotted them and began maneuvering to avoid them. In that case, there was no point in not firing, since her prize crew would certainly go ahead and warn its comrades. On the other hand, at their current velocity, the pinnaces would cross their engagement range of the freighter less than twelve seconds after entering it, so it would probably be impossible to tell whether or not the freighter had detected them until it was too late to act.

Well, she thought, *Father Church always says the Test can take many forms. I suppose I should be grateful that at least* I *don't have to make the decisions facing the Captain.*

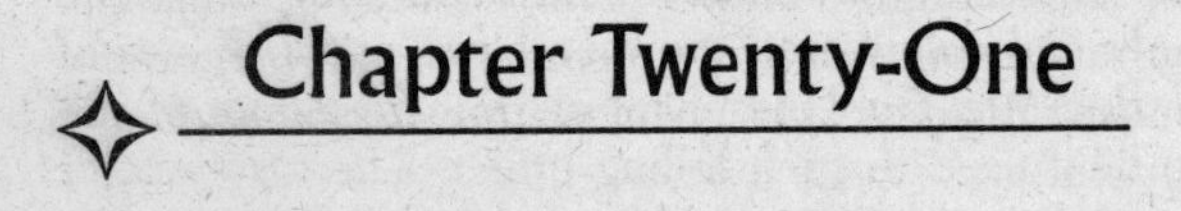

Chapter Twenty-One

Winter wrapped a cold, gray fist around the city of Vermeer. Heavy mist drifted above the broad, slow-flowing Schelde River, and woebegone native longfrond trees drooped over the gray-green water in their humid shroud. The sky was the color of old slate, shedding a handful of fat, lazy snowflakes, and the raw chill hovered barely above the freezing point.

In short, a depressingly typical winter's day on sunny Rembrandt, Bernardus Van Dort thought sardonically as he stood, gazing out the familiar window, hands clasped behind him. *Only a batch of loopy, Renaissance Revivalists like my esteemed over-educated, under-brained ancestors could pick a planet like this for their new home. Bunch of artistically obsessed nincompoops, the lot of them.*

The dreary scene was a far cry from the springtime warmth of Thimble. Then again, Rembrandt wasn't as nice a planet, in lots of ways, as Flax. He wondered sometimes if his homeworld's miserable climate helped explain the alacrity with which Rembrandters had abandoned the Founders' cultural pretensions. He didn't know about that, but he was quite certain it explained the emergence of the merchant marine—rare, for any system in the Verge—which had allowed Rembrandt to become a mercantile power.

A matter of anything that gets us off-world has to be a good idea, that's what it was. He smiled at the thought. *I know* I *always luxuriated shamelessly on visits to planets which actually see the sun between summer and late spring.*

The office door opened behind him, and he turned. The movement also brought him back to face the office's luxurious appointments. During the decades when it had been his office, the furnishings had been almost spartan, their only real ostentation the mementos and trophies of the grizzled Van Dort merchant skipper founders of the fortune he'd used to such telling effect. Their only color had been the mountain landscapes and rolling prairie scenes which had reminded his wife Suzanne of her own homeworld. They'd lurked among the grimmer, harsher Van Dort mementos like small, warm windows onto a slower, gentler life, and he felt a fresh pang of loss when he looked up and they were no longer there.

Now the office boasted expensive light sculptures, exquisite handcrafts from literally every world of the Cluster, exotically inlaid wood paneling from the rain forests of the Marian System, framed holos of its present occupant closing contract and trade treaty negotiations with magnates and heads of state. Its new, ankle-deep carpet, and polished display cabinets filled with glittering cut crystal, polished wood and beaten copper images, reeked of wealth and power, and he found the change . . . distasteful.

Fair enough, I suppose, he thought with a mental grimace, *given how distasteful I find the present occupant, as well.*

Ineka Vaandrager was a small, fair-haired woman, no more than a hundred and sixty centimeters tall, who moved with a sort of choreographed precision, like a machine programmed to get from one point to another by the shortest possible route. She was thirty T-years younger than Van Dort and, like him, a first-generation prolong recipient. But the therapy's sustained youthfulness made her hazel eyes no softer, and she had a mouth like a steel trap. She wasn't really unattractive in any physical sense, but there was a coldness—a hardness—about her which Van Dort had always found repellent.

Which didn't keep you from making use of her, did it, Bernardus?

He faced that admission squarely, accepting that the problem she represented was as much of his making as of anyone else's, even as he made himself nod to her, with a smile whose welcome she must know as well as he did was false. She smiled back with matching sincerity but declined to offer him her hand as she crossed to the huge desk sitting with its back to the office's outer wall of windows.

"I'm sorry I'm late, Bernardus," she said. "It was unavoidable, I'm afraid. I hope Erica saw to your needs while you waited?"

"Yes, she did," Van Dort replied, but he let a trace of hardness, at odds with his affable tone, show in his own blue eyes. Vaandrager saw it, and her mouth tightened as he silently called her bluff on the "unavoidable" nature of her tardiness. She really was a remarkably petty woman in so many ways, he reflected.

"Good," she said shortly, and waved for him to take one of the chairs facing her desk as she sat behind it. "Well, I'm sorry you were kept waiting." She waited while he seated himself and her own chair adjusted to her body, then smiled brightly, as if determined to get their meeting off on a fresh foot after an inauspicious beginning. "But we're both here now! So, what can I do for you, Bernardus?"

"I'm a bit concerned about some things I've been hearing." He came to the point with characteristic brevity. "Specifically, about new negotiations with Scarlet. I was under the impression we already had quite a favorable agreement in place with them—we certainly did when I left for the Convention—so I fail to understand why it's necessary to 'renegotiate' at this point. And I've heard about certain threats of retaliation in which our representatives seem to have indulged when President Standley proved . . . unreceptive to our 'requests.' "

"Did you come all the way home from Spindle over something that routine?" she asked, and shook her head in amused exasperation.

"It's scarcely 'routine,' " he said, his own expression anything but amused. "And, as I say, I fail to see any pressing reason for new trade negotiations at a time when we ought to be concentrating on . . . other matters, shall we say? I thought we were in agreement about that, Ineka."

He held her eyes across the desk, and she made an impatient, throwing away gesture.

"It's just business, Bernardus," she said impatiently. "Your Convention was supposed to report out a Constitution long before this. It hasn't, and the Trade Union's affairs can't simply be placed on indefinite hold, you know. Surely you don't expect the rest of the universe to stop dead in its tracks while you're off playing statesman!"

"It's not 'just business,' " he said flatly. "It's an attempt to pound Standley into submitting to demands even more unfavorable to his star system than the last package. It's also, in case you've failed to notice, a poster example of why so many other planets in the Cluster don't trust us as far as they can spit. And right this minute, especially in light of what's happened on Kornati, we can't afford to give them any more justification for distrusting us."

"Don't be absurd!" she scoffed. "Nothing we can do is going to make people who resent us suddenly start trusting us instead. Or do you think giving away all the trade advantages we've built up over the past fifty T-years is going to convince someone like that butcher Nordbrandt to make nice with us?"

"Did you actually bother to view the reports from Kornati at all?" Van Dort demanded. "Or has your brain just gone into total shutdown?"

"Yes, I viewed them," she said sharply. "And I don't care for your tone!"

"Well, that's too damned bad. I don't care for *your* stupidity."

Their eyes locked, mutual hostility like a palpable force between them.

"You're not Chairman of the Board any longer. *I* am," she gritted. Then she made her jaws relax, but her hard eyes never wavered as she went on in a flat, biting tone as flexible as hammered steel. "And as Chairwoman, I don't intend to let a group of insane, bloodthirsty malcontents dictate our trade policies! You can go back to Spindle and kowtow to them if you want—*we* have no intention of following suit."

"You know," he said in a far more conversational tone, leaning back and crossing his legs, "I never realized, back when I first tapped you for Negotiations, just how blunt an instrument you actually are. It may surprise you to discover this, Ineka, but not all problems are nails you can pound flat or boulders you can smash by simply reaching for a bigger hammer. I suppose it's my own fault for not recognizing your limitations at the time, but I thought we needed someone like you. I was in a hurry, more worried about results than any hostility we might generate, and there were . . . other things on my mind."

His eyes darkened briefly in memory of old, unhealed pain, but he shook it aside, and his eyes narrowed with hard, focused purpose.

"Truth to tell, I still believe we *did* need those results—then. But I've come to suspect I was wrong to think a hammer was the best way to get them. Especially a hammer as fundamentally stupid as you are."

Vaandrager's face darkened as his tone flayed her sense of self-importance. She opened her mouth to snap back, but he continued.

"That, however, is an error I intend to correct."

His voice was harder now, flatter, and she closed her own mouth as wariness flickered in her own eyes. Bernardus Van Dort might not be as abrasively confrontational by nature as she was. Indeed, he was essentially a collegial sort, who believed in negotiation and compromise, however ruthless his public image might be. But there was a will of iron under that normally affable exterior, and the Trade Union's corporate offices were littered with the corpses of careers whose once promising owners had provoked his ire.

"Look, Bernardus," she said after a moment, schooling her voice into something closer to normal, "I suppose I apologize for that last statement. Or, at least, its tone. But that doesn't make it untrue. And the fact that you're no longer Chairman—and that I *am* Chairwoman—means our viewpoints are bound to diverge. I have a responsibility to our stockholders and to everyone else who depends on the umbrella of the Union. It's always been our policy to press for progressively reduced import and export duties for our shipping and industries, because we *depend* on the removal of trade barriers for our goods and shipping, and you know it. I'm not going to abdicate that responsibility just because some mass murderers on a planet so poor it doesn't have a pot to piss in don't like us. And, I remind you, when you *were* Chairman, your own policies were rather more . . . aggressive than the ones you seem to be attempting to insist upon now."

"Yes, they were," he agreed in the patient tone of one addressing a small, spoiled child. "On the other hand, the plebiscite completely transformed the entire political and economic equation, and when the environment changes that radically, policies have to be adjusted."

"Business is business," she said flatly, "and politics are politics. Don't expect me—or our investors—to confuse them, or to abandon core policies and sacrifice hard-won gains for some quixotic quest of yours. There was a time when you understood that."

"There was a time when my options and tools were more circumscribed . . . as you ought to understand perfectly well. Or were you absent the day your corporate mentor explained exactly what it was the Trade Union was intended to to accomplish?"

"*Please!*" She rolled her eyes. "Do you really think anyone else ever believed that pious, moralistic 'mission statement'? Propaganda's all very well, and it obviously has its place, but don't make the mistake of believing anyone else ever took it seriously."

"I don't really care about 'anyone else.' *I* took it seriously when I drafted it. And I still do."

She started to laugh, then stopped as she finally recognized the true depth of the incandescent rage hidden behind the cold self-control in his icy blue eyes. The scornful amusement drained out of her expression, and he watched it go with grim satisfaction.

"You really don't want to cross swords with me, Ineka," he told her softly. "*I* created the Trade Union. It was my idea. I found the initial capital—most of it out of my own family's pockets. *I* talked a gaggle of other independent shipowners into associating themselves with me, and I sold the notion to old President Verstappen and Parliament. I talked San Miguel, Redoubt, and Prairie into joining as equal partners. And yes, *I* wrote our mission statement. And whatever you may think, I didn't do all of that just to put money in your credit accounts or cater to your own over-inflated ego."

"I—" she began hotly, but his voice rolled right over hers, still soft, but inexorable as Juggernaut.

"I did it because it was the only possible option I saw to avoid what Frontier Security's done to every other Verge system that attracted its attention. Because the only way I could think of to protect our citizens from the kind of debt peonage the Solly multistellars impose was to become a fat enough goose, with enough potential golden eggs, to be able to buy better treatment, like the Maya Sector did.

"Oh, I won't try to pretend the possibility of getting even wealthier didn't appeal to me as well, but money's only a tool, Ineka. You've never understood that. You seem to feel some compulsion to just keep piling it up, higher and deeper, as if it had some intrinsic value besides the things you can *do* with it. But neither of us could possibly spend the money we already have fast enough to keep our net worth from increasing hand over fist, so what's the point in squeezing the last drop of blood out of a turnip just to keep score or count coup?"

He paused, and she let her chair come forward, planting her elbows on her desktop and leaning towards him.

"You—and, I suppose, I—may be in that fortunate position, Bernardus. But we have shareholders and investors, the citizens of our member governments and our captain-partners, who aren't. People who expect us to show the maximum return on their investment, gain the most advantageous tariff and import duty terms we can, demolish trade barriers and gain favored-planet status any way we have to. To create and maintain the system that helps them build the sort of personal independence most people in the Verge can't even dream of. The level of economic security your dream and all the years of hard work you and others put into it made possible for them in the first place."

"Don't trot that argument out with me, Ineka," he said scornfully. "It's the most valid one you have, but it's not what punches *your* buttons. You could care less about the small shareholders, and independent captains, or the prosperity of member governments' citizens. You're too busy hobnobbing with the big financiers, the shipping line owners, and enjoying the power you have, the club you hold over entire planetary governments, when you get ready to 'demolish trade barriers.' In fact, what you remind me of most is a home-grown OFS. And when people like Nordbrandt resort to violence and use the specter of economic exploitation to justify their actions, *your* actions just keep pumping hydrogen into the fire."

"I resent that!"

"Resent it all you like," he told her flatly. "I came home for two reasons. One was to remove myself from the political debate, because some of the delegates were spending more time worrying about the RTU 'puppet-master' than about drafting a Constitution. But the other was to investigate reports I was getting about your policy directives. I didn't have any idea Nordbrandt was going to murder so many people, but the reports from Kornati only emphasize to me how right I was to be worried about *you*."

She glared at him, and he leaned forward in his own chair, looming over her even seated. Van Dort rarely relied upon his own imposing physical stature in negotiations, but he was far from unaware of the advantages it gave him. He used them ruthlessly now, intruding into her space, underlining the nonphysical dimensions of his threat.

"You aren't going to do anything to lend one gram of additional credence to the arguments of the Cluster's Agnes Nordbrandts and Stephen Westmans. The Union's member systems and shareholders already stand to make a fortune off our existing service contracts with the Star Kingdom. Once the annexation's completed, we'll still enjoy the inside position in the Cluster, because we're already up and running—the only organized local shipping cartel. But all those tariff and tax advantages you've extorted out of other systems, all the trade barriers you've busted, won't matter squat. We'll all belong to the same political unit, and aside from the junction use fees, the Star Kingdom's always pursued a policy of interstellar free trade. Do you think they'll do less for their *domestic* commerce? That the Queen of Manticore's going to let you keep your sweetheart deals? Or that you'll actually *need* them?"

He grimaced in disgust. Was she really so smallminded she didn't realize even that much? Couldn't see the huge edge the Union's existing connections and infrastructure would give it in the new, unified Cluster economy? They might no longer dominate it outright, but where was the need to do that when a smaller slice of such a hugely increased pie would be so vast?

"If you can't think of it any other way, think about this—the amounts of money you'll be able to pile up in your private accounts if the annexation goes through will dwarf anything you could ever have managed without it. But if enough people start agreeing with Nordbrandt, the annexation *won't* go through. And if it doesn't, OFS won't hesitate an instant. They'll move in on the Cluster like vultures, and we'll be just wealthy enough to be their priority target, and not wealthy enough to have any voice in the terms of our peonage. So forget about altruism, or the silly concept that human beings have any value that can't be quantified in terms of money, and think about what will happen to you—you personally, Ineka—when the Sollies move in."

She stared at him, her mouth taut with rage, and he suddenly realized that she didn't really believe it.

My God. She actually thinks she can cut a deal with OFS—that she's a big enough fish, got enough clout, to protect her personal position if she offers to throw in with them and bring her local contacts and knowledge with her. And she doesn't give a solitary damn *about anyone else. She'd be perfectly happy to play Judas goat if it let her hang onto her own precious, privileged position. Could it be she'd actually* prefer *OFS? Yes, it could be, in some ways, at least. Because if the annexation goes through and we integrate into the Star Kingdom's economy, she's suddenly going to be a much smaller fish. And one without the power to rattle the cages of planetary presidents. But as an OFS collaborator . . .*

He felt physically ill at the thought, but as he looked into those hard, flat hazel eyes, he could no longer deny the truth.

She really is exactly what Nordbrandt claims to be fighting.

The thought sent a chill through him, and, for just a moment, he felt inexpressibly weary. Was this what he and Suzanne had once dreamed of? What he'd spent fifty T-years of his life building?

He wanted to reach across the desk and throttle her. Yet, even then, he realized that in many ways, on a personal level, Vaandrager simply represented what he'd been trying to do on a star system's level.

"I'm not going to argue with you about this any longer, Ineka," he said. "I thought you might be reassuring to the Board when I resigned. That they'd see you as a promise that whatever else happened, we wouldn't simply abandon our current advantages until we were certain the annexation would make them unnecessary. That's why I didn't oppose your campaign for the Chairwomanship—because I wanted to avoid as much instability as we could while the Constitution was drafted. But I see now that that was a mistake."

"Are you threatening me?" she demanded tautly. "Because, if you are, you're making a *serious* error."

"You worked for me for thirty T-years," he told her levelly. "In all that time, did I ever make a threat I couldn't back up?"

He met her furious glare coldly, and something flickered at the backs of her hot eyes. Something like fear.

"You may believe," he continued, "that I've been unaware of your efforts to sew up proxies while I've been off-planet. If so, you're wrong. I know exactly how many votes you have in your pocket. Can you say the same about me?"

Her fists clenched on the desktop, and her expression was a mask.

"I spoke with Joachim at some length before I left Flax," he went on. "We were both . . . disturbed by reports we were receiving. Which was why I took the precaution of getting his signature on a request to convene a special meeting of the Board."

The color flowed out of her set face as he watched.

"As you may be aware, the Van Dort family—which is to say, me—controls forty-two percent of the Union's voting shares outright. The Alquezar family controls another twelve percent. There are no proxies involved, Ineka. Unlike you, Joachim and I control our votes directly, and I remind you that according to the bylaws, a special meeting must be convened upon the request of fifty-one percent of the voting stockholders. I'd hoped I might convince you to see reason. I see now that I can't. Fortunately, there are other remedies."

"Now, just a minute, Bernardus," she began. "I know tempers are running high. And you're right about how my ego sometimes gets involved in these things. But there's no need to destabilize the entire Union just because you and I disagree on policy and tactics."

"Spare me, Ineka," he said wearily. "You were my mistake. Now I'm going to fix it. Don't waste your time or mine pretending you and I can come to some sort of meeting of the minds. What's happening in Thimble right now is far more important than anything happening here, and I'm not going to have you standing in the way."

"You arrogant prick!" Vaandrager lurched to her feet, leaning both hands on the desk, her eyes flaming with hate. "You sanctimonious, holier-than-thou *bastard*! Who the *hell* d'you think you are to come into *my* office and lecture me on morality and social responsibility?!"

"I think I'm the one who gave you an opportunity to convince me to leave you in the Chairwomanship," he said softly.

She closed her mouth, and it was his turn to stand, looming over her with a height advantage of over thirty-five centimeters.

"You've never understood that with power comes responsibility," he told her. "Maybe I'm foolishly romantic—maybe I am sanctimonious—to believe that. But I do. That's why you'll be out of this office within six days, one way or the other. I'm posting the request for the special meeting this afternoon. If you choose to resign rather than force me to take it to the Board, I'll settle for that. If you choose to fight me, I'll make it my personal business to break you. When we lock horns, you'll lose, and not just the Chairwomanship. When the dust settles, you'll find yourself out on the street without—as you so quaintly put it—a pot to piss in, wondering what lorry just ran over you." He smiled thinly, without a single trace of humor. "Believe me, Ineka."

He held her gaze once more, and tension crackled between them like poisoned lightning.

Then he turned and walked out of the office which had once been his without another word.

Chapter Twenty-Two

"Sir, if the Nuncians and Lieutenant Hearns are still on profile and Bogey Three hasn't moved, they'll be coming up on crossover in approximately twenty-seven minutes."

Lieutenant Commander Kaplan's tone was crisply professional, and Aivars Terekhov nodded in acknowledgment of her warning. And also of what she hadn't said; assuming the conditions she'd described, Abigail Hearns' pinnaces were two minutes from the point of furthest advance at which they might have decelerated to a zero/zero intercept at Bogey Three's current position. The LACs, with their lower acceleration rate, were already past that point, and the joint force was about 2.86 million kilometers—a little over ninety-five light-seconds—from Bogey Three. Of course, they'd never really anticipated that the pinnaces would decelerate until after executing their attack run, but they were still getting dangerously close, against even a freighter's sensors, if Bogey Three's crew was on its toes. Theoretically, he could wait twenty-six minutes before transmitting the attack order, since the transmission time would be effectively zero for the grav-pulse com. Except for the minor problem that the moment

Hexapuma's FTL com opened up, Bogey One and Two were going to know about it.

He tilted his command chair back slightly, steepling his fingers under his chin, and contemplated the master tactical plot.

As he'd anticipated, Bogey One and Bogey Two had continued in-system at their creeping velocity of eighty-six hundred kilometers per second for thirteen hours and twenty-two minutes, headed straight for the position Pontifex would have occupied when they arrived. Given that absolutely undeviating approach, it had been even simpler than he'd expected for Kaplan and Midshipwoman Zilwicki to track them, and the Nuncian LAC *Grizzly* had been duly vectored into position to "detect" the intruders and sound the alert. The bogeys had responded by cracking on a few dozen gravities of acceleration, accelerating along the same heading and trying to get far enough from *Grizzly* to drop back off her sensors . . . again, just as he'd anticipated, and he conscientiously kept reminding himself not to get overconfident.

It wasn't an easy thing to remember, at least where the two lead bogeys were concerned. For the last hour and thirty-four minutes Bogey One and Bogey Two—now identified as a *Desforge*-class destroyer, one of the Havenites' older classes, but still a powerful unit for her type—had been chasing the terrified Rembrandt freighter *Nijmegen* (so identified by *Hexapuma*'s transponder code) which had broken from planetary orbit in a foolish, panicky bid to evade them. Only a totally terrified merchant skipper would have fled deeper into Nuncio-B's gravity well, especially starting with a velocity disadvantage of more than eighty-five hundred kilometers per second and a ship whose best possible acceleration was no more than a hundred and seventy KPS^2.

They'd reacted to their juicy, unanticipated target by going in pursuit at five hundred and thirty-one gravities. The recon drones he'd more than half-feared, despite Bagwell's inspiration, hadn't materialized. Probably because Commander Lewis had cooperated so completely with the

EWO's suggestions. No engineer was ever really happy about deliberately overstressing the systems under his care, but Ginger Lewis had seemed to find an unholy delight in the notion.

"Sucking pirates in where we can kill them, Skipper? And all you want me to do is take a few hours off the components?" The attractive engineering officer's smile had been decidedly predatory. "No sweat. And if these really are Peep commerce raiders, that's just extra icing on the cake! Remind me to tell you sometime about my first deployment. I'm in favor of killing as many of the bastards as we can catch!"

Terekhov had made a mental note to follow up and get the details about that first cruise of hers. But whatever had happened on it, she clearly harbored a pronounced distaste for any pirate, and she'd entered into Bagwell's ploy with a vengeance. She'd even added a few wrinkles of her own, including a brief, simulated total failure of the wedge while the bogeys were still too far out to actually see the ship herself.

Terekhov had had Kaplan deploy an additional remote array before Lewis' simulated failure so he could observe *Hexapuma*'s sensor image directly himself. His array had been a lot closer than the bogeys were, and probably more sophisticated, to boot. But for all that, had he been one of the pursuing pirates and seen what the array had, he would have bought the illusion completely. The heavy flare Lewis had produced by heterodyning two alpha nodes—strictly against The Book, and, despite her enthusiasm, more than a little dangerous, even for someone with her skills—had duplicated the spike of a blown beta node almost perfectly. It had also taken something like three hundred hours off the service life of the nodes in question, but if they nailed a pair of Peep warships operating in the Cluster, Terekhov expected the Admiralty to forgive him for that.

The wedge shutdown which had followed instantly on the heels of the flare had been even better—a true work of art. It had been exactly the right length for a frantic civilian engineer to shunt the blown node out of the circuit, reboot her systems, and bring the wedge back up. If Terekhov had been on Bogey One's bridge, he would have been thoroughly convinced *Hexapuma* was a limping, staggering, desperate fugitive, running because running was all that was left, not because she truly expected to escape.

The bogeys seemed to have bought it without question, at any rate. They'd been burning along after *Hexapuma* at that same, steady five hundred and thirty-one gravities' acceleration from the instant they detected his ship, and the range between them had fallen from twelve light-minutes to only seven and a third. "*Nijmegen*" was up to ninety-five hundred kilometers per second, but the bogeys were up to a base velocity of almost thirty-nine thousand. *Hexapuma* was just over one and a half light-minutes inside Pontifex's orbit, eight and a half light-minutes from Nuncio-B, which put the bogeys—at 15.8 light-minutes from the primary—almost exactly forty-eight light-seconds inside the system's hyper limit. Better yet, the acceleration they were turning out was fifty gravities lower than *Hexapuma*'s standard maximum, and a hundred and ninety-five less than she could turn out if she cut her compensator margin to zero.

The only sour note was that, despite the *Mars* class's obsolescent power plants, she clearly had at least a late pre-cease-fire compensator. The *Mars* ships were enormous for heavy cruisers—at 473,000 tons, Bogey One was barely ten thousand tons smaller than *Hexapuma*—and they paid for that extra mass with sluggish acceleration. Bogey One's observed acceleration already exceeded the max her class had been capable of when they were first laid down, but Peep acceleration rates had been creeping upward even before the High Ridge cease-fire. With the latest pre-cease-fire version, a ship of her size could have pulled a maximum acceleration of six hundred and ten, which would have meant she was currently pulling a bit less than eighty-seven percent of her maximum possible acceleration. If she had the *post*-cease-fire compensator, her max theoretical acceleration should be about six hundred and thirty gravities, in which case she was pulling a bit under eighty-five percent. The Peeps tended to cut their margins finer than the RMN, accepting the risk of catastrophic compensator failure as the cost of shaving away some of the Alliance's acceleration advantage, so it was possible this ship could have the older compensator.

But Terekhov had to assume he was up against a post-cease-fire compensator, which meant *Hexapuma*'s theoretical maximum acceleration was only ninety-six gravities higher than Bogey One's. Bogey Two, assuming equal generations of compensators, would have a slight acceleration advantage over *Hexapuma*, but not much of one. Like the *Mars*-class cruisers, the *Desforge*-class destroyers were big ships for their types, with correspondingly lower acceleration rates.

Yet even in a worst-case scenario, with the most modern compensators the Peeps had, there was no longer any way both bogeys could avoid action, given their overtake velocity and the current range.

They undoubtedly had at least a few gravities in reserve, but he couldn't know how many until they showed him, so he had to base his estimates on what he'd already seen. And assuming they'd already been operating at max, it would have taken them two hours and four minutes just to decelerate to zero relative to the system primary. At that point, they would have traveled to within 7.7 light-minutes of Nuncio-B, hopelessly inside the system's hyper limit. Even assuming post-cease-fire compensators, Bogey One would require an hour and forty minutes and be less than nine and a half light-minutes from the primary before she came to rest relative to it. In either case, neither of his targets could possibly escape back across the hyper limit before *Hexapuma* brought them to action. One of them might be able to avoid *close* action, if they split up quickly enough and both concentrated solely on running away from her. In that case, Aivars Terekhov knew exactly which ship he would run down and kill . . . and not just because a cruiser was a more valuable unit than a destroyer.

He put that shivery, hungry thought aside and made himself consider the possible scenarios.

Even assuming they did have the later compensators and went to maximum military power with a zero safety margin, if *Hexapuma* turned on them this instant and went to her own max deceleration, they would meet in seventy-one minutes. *Hexapuma*'s velocity relative to Nuncio-B would be over 20,550 KPS, directly away from the star, while the bogeys would still be traveling *towards* the primary at 12,523 KPS when their vectors crossed over at zero. They'd be down to a bit over nine and a half light-minutes from the primary, right in the heart of the system hyper limit, and given *Hexapuma*'s range advantage and the fact that she had a bow wall while the bogeys almost certainly did not, she should manage to blow both of them out of space (assuming that was her objective) long before their vectors ever intersected.

But the most likely scenario was that the bogeys would remain at their current compensator settings and begin decelerating within the next twenty-four or twenty-five minutes. If *Hexapuma* truly had been the crippled, fleeing freighter she'd taken such pains to portray, they'd have to begin decelerating within that time frame to achieve a zero/zero intercept with her if she continued to "flee." That would take them another ninety-odd minutes, depending on the exact point at which they decided to begin decelerating, and hunter and hunted alike would be traveling at somewhere around 20,200 KPS towards the primary at the moment their vectors merged. Ideally, Terekhov wanted to encourage the bogeys to pursue the "freighter" as long as possible. The shorter the range, and the closer to equalized their velocities, the more devastating his own sudden surprise attack would become.

The problem was how to tell Hearns and Einarsson within the next twenty-seven minutes that they were cleared to engage the freighter without dissuading the pirates from continuing to close. . . .

"Guns."

"Yes, Skipper?"

"How far out are the tertiary arrays?"

"They're approximately thirteen light-minutes outside the bogeys, Sir."

"Lieutenant Bagwell."

"Yes, Sir?"

"How likely would you say our bogeys would be to detect a directional grav pulse transmitted directly away from them by one of the stealthed arrays thirteen light-minutes astern of them?"

"That would depend on how good their sensor suites are, and how good the people using them are," Bagwell replied. "BuWeaps' R and D people evaluated and tested as much of their hardware as we could recover from the ships Duchess Harrington knocked out at Sidemore Station. On the basis of their tests, and assuming these people have well-trained, alert sensor crews," he was punching information into his console as he spoke, cross-indexing against the recorded test data, "I'd have to say they'd have somewhere around a . . . one-in-ten chance. That might be a little pessimistic, but I'd rather err on the side of overestimating their chances, rather than underestimating."

"Understood." Terekhov pursed his lips for a few moments, then looked back at his EWO. "On the other hand, you're evaluating their chances on the basis of current first-line equipment, correct?"

"Yes, Sir."

"Assume instead that they have what was first-line equipment as of Operation Buttercup." Despite himself, Bagwell's eyebrows rose, and Terekhov smiled thinly. "It's not as loony as it sounds, Commander. We know these people have Goshawk-Three fusion plants, and those should have been replaced even before the High Ridge cease-fire. They weren't. I'd say there's at least a fair chance that if they didn't replace something as dangerous as that, they also didn't waste any effort on upgrading Bogey One sensors. Mind you," his smile got a little broader, "I can't imagine why they didn't upgrade both, if they were going to keep the ship in inventory at all. But since we know they didn't change out the fusion plants—" He shrugged.

"Yes, Sir." Bagwell input additional data, then looked back up at his captain. "Assuming the parameters you've specified, Sir, even a well-trained and alert sensor watch would probably have no more than one chance in about two hundred."

"Thank you." Terekhov tipped his chair back once more and thought hard for perhaps ten seconds. Then he straightened up again.

"Commander Nagchaudhuri."

"Yes, Sir?"

"Assume we wanted to relay through one of the tertiary arrays to the array we deployed with Lieutenant Hearns. Would her array be able to receive a transmission from the FTL telemetry downlinks aboard the tertiary array?"

"Um." Nagchaudhuri squinted thoughtfully. "I can't see why not, Skipper, although that's actually more of a question for Commander Kaplan and Lieutenant Bagwell, in some ways. There's no reason the transmitters and receivers aboard the arrays couldn't manage it, but we'd have to remotely access the software to redirect the downlink to the pinnaces instead of CIC. I've got some familiarity with that, but not enough to feel comfortable estimating how complicated it might be."

"Guns?"

"No reason I can think of why we couldn't do it, Skipper," Kaplan said enthusiastically. "Lieutenant Hearns is already hardwired into the telemetry links from her array. We just have to convince the tertiary array to aim its pulses at her, instead of the inner system, and that's a snap. The systems were designed to allow single arrays to share data between distant recipients by rotating their downlink channels through more than one addressee. Of course," she cautioned, her expression sobering slightly, "there *is* at least a small chance Bogey One or Two will also pick them up. The transmitters are directional, and we've made a lot of progress since the first FTL coms came in, but we're still a long way from completely eliminating backscatter. There's going to be *something* to see. All in all, I'd say Guthrie's probability estimate is probably pretty close to on the money, but we could both be wrong."

"Very well. Commander Nagchaudhuri."

"Yes, Sir?"

"Commander Kaplan and Lieutenant Bagwell will put together the programming elements. Once they have, you'll immediately transmit them and release authorization to attack and retake Bogey Three to one of the tertiary arrays, via com laser, for relay to Lieutenant Hearns."

The light-speed transmission from *Hexapuma* to the selected array took twenty minutes and eighteen seconds. Implementation of the piggybacked reprogramming took another twenty-seven seconds. Transmission of the release order required all of sixteen seconds.

Twenty-one minutes and one second after its transmission from *Hexapuma* the release authorization appeared on Lieutenant Abigail Hearns' display . . . exactly forty-seven seconds before the point at which Captain Einarsson's little force must either commit to the attack or let the opportunity pass as they went streaking past Bogey Three.

"Assuming everything went according to plan, Skipper," Ansten FitzGerald said quietly in Terekhov's earbug, "Abigail just received the release order. And in about thirty seconds, she's going to start kicking the shit out of Bogey Three."

"I know." Terekhov had sent the ship to General Quarters, and FitzGerald, with Helen Zilwicki as his tactical officer and Paulo d'Arezzo as his electronic warfare officer, was in Auxiliary Control. AuxCon was a complete, duplicate command bridge located at the far end of *Hexapuma*'s core hull. If anything unfortunate should happen to Terekhov, Naomi Kaplan, and Guthrie Bagwell, it would be FitzGerald's job to complete the task at hand.

Terekhov frowned as that thought flicked through his brain. In many ways, it made sense to keep his most experienced officers here, where command would be exercised unless catastrophic damage smashed the bridge or managed somehow to cut it off from the rest of the ship. The odds against that happening were high, after all. But it was far from impossible, which was why there was an AuxCon to begin with, so perhaps it might also make sense to consider transferring either Bagwell or Kaplan to FitzGerald's alternate command crew. Because if something did happen to the regular bridge, *Hexapuma* was probably going to be in such deep shit that FitzGerald would need the very best command team he could get if the ship was going to survive.

The thought flashed through his mind in the space between one breath and the next, and he nodded to FitzGerald on the small com screen deployed by his right knee.

"At the moment, she's forty-six light-minutes from the primary—thirty-four-plus light-minutes from Bogey One. Allowing for light-speed limitations and how far Bogey One's going to move in the meantime, that gives us another thirty-six minutes, whatever happens out there."

"Yes, Sir," FitzGerald agreed, and they smiled at one another. "How much closer do you think they'll get before they finally figure out we've been screwing with their minds, Skip?" the exec asked after a moment.

"Hard to say." Terekhov shrugged. "They've been chasing us for two hours. After that long, they have to've gotten our identification as a merchie pretty firmly nailed into their brains. Even the best tac officers have a distinct tendency to go on seeing what they already 'know' is there, even after anomalies begin to crop up. The range is down to two hundred and seventy-three light-seconds, and they've been decelerating for just over two minutes, so their overtake velocity's over thirty-three thousand KPS. We've managed to get far enough above them for the geometry to keep them from getting a good look up the kilt of our wedge, so the sensor image they're getting from us is still essentially the one we *want* them to have. The fact that they aren't maneuvering more aggressively to try to get that look seems to me to be a further indication that they've bought our merchie imitation hook, line, and sinker. So I'd say we've got a pretty good chance of their coming all the way in before they realize they've been foxed."

"Unless Bogey Three does get a warning off," FitzGerald observed.

"If accelerations remain constant for another thirty minutes," Terekhov replied, "the range'll be down to less than seventy million kilometers, and their overtake velocity will be only a tad over twenty-four thousand KPS." His smile would have smitten any Old Earth shark with envy. "That's still outside even our missile envelope, but they'll be coming towards us, deeper into the gravity well, and we've got a higher base acceleration." He shook his head. "They're screwed, Ansten. And every minute that passes only makes it worse for them."

"Yes, Sir," FitzGerald agreed. "Of course, the closer they get, the deeper into *their* engagement envelope *we* get."

"True, but if we're headed toward them, we've got our bow wall, and a ship as old as Bogey One doesn't. There's no way they could've refitted a bow wall without completely gutting her forward impeller rooms, and that brings us back to those fusion rooms of hers. If they were going to invest the time and money to refit bow wall technology, they'd've refitted those power plants at the same time, so without the one, they don't have the other. Crank in our advantages in missile range, Ghost Rider, and our superior fire control, and you have to like our odds against both of them at almost any range."

FitzGerald nodded in agreement, but something about Terekhov's expression and tone bothered him. Those arctic-blue eyes were brighter than they had been, almost fevered, and the eagerness in the Captain's voice went beyond mere confidence. Terekhov had baited his trap brilliantly, and Ansten FitzGerald was prepared to wager that the rest of his plan would unfold as predicted. But, the fact remained that Terekhov was deliberately courting action with two hostile units, and the very plan intended to get them to relatively short range at relatively low relative velocities would also give the bogeys their best chance of getting into their own effective range of *Hexapuma*. In any missile engagement, the Peeps were almost certainly as completely outclassed as Terekhov had suggested. But even an obsolescent *Mars* class was a big, powerfully armed unit, and if they managed to get clear down to energy range before they were knocked out of action . . .

"I hope things are going as well for Abigail," he said.

"So do I, Ansten," Terekhov replied, his tone much more sober. "So do I."

Chapter Twenty-Three

"Very well, Lieutenant Hearns." The same attack release order from *Hexapuma* glowed on Captain Einarsson's com display aboard *Wolverine*, and the Nuncian wasn't waiting for Abigail to formally relay it to him. Despite possible reservations about female officers, he obviously had no more interest in wasting precious time than she did. "It looks like it's up to your people. Good luck, Einarsson clear."

"Thank you, Sir," Abigail acknowledged, then glanced at Ragnhild. Abigail was an excellent pilot, but she knew she wasn't in Ragnhild's league when it came to natural ability, and she was perfectly prepared to let the midshipwoman have the stick.

"Separate now," she said quietly.

"Aye, aye, Ma'am. Separating now," Ragnhild replied crisply, and Abigail felt the shudder as the tractors released and the maneuvering reaction thrusters began pushing them away from *Wolverine*.

She left that part of the operation to Ragnhild and punched the channel to the other pinnace.

"Hawk-Papa-Three, this is Hawk-Papa-Two. We are cleared for attack. I repeat, we are cleared for attack.

Separate now. I repeat, separate now and engage your wedge as soon as you clear your safety zone. Papa-Two has the alpha target: Papa-Three has the beta target. Confirm targeting and stand by to engage."

"Hawk-Papa-Two, Papa-Three is separating," Aikawa Kagiyama's voice came back through her earbug. "Confirm targets. Papa-Two will take the alpha target; Papa-Three will take the beta target."

"Very well, Papa-Three," Abigail said, and her eyes never wavered from the targeting display in front of her.

The two pinnaces had completed separation from their host LACs even while Aikawa was speaking. Now main reaction thrusters blazed to life, slamming them forward under almost a hundred gravities of acceleration. It wasn't much, compared to impeller drive, but it was an enormously higher acceleration than the thrusters normally generated. Their primary function was for final docking approaches or other circumstances which required the pinnaces to maneuver in close proximity to other spacecraft. A pinnace impeller wedge was minuscule compared to that of a starship, or even a LAC, but it was still lethal to any solid structure it encountered, and contact with a larger, more powerful wedge would burn out the pinnace's nodes as catastrophically as a direct hit from a capital ship graser. Which was why Hawk-Papa-Two and Papa-Three had to be at least ten kilometers clear of any of the LACs—or each other—before the safety interlocks would allow their nodes to come fully on-line.

Fortunately, the engineers who designed the RMN's small craft had grasped the point that emergencies sometimes happened and built the Navy's pinnaces with that in mind. The reaction thrusters were far more powerful than their normal operational envelope would ever require, although their endurance at such high power settings was relatively short. The bad news was that, without a wedge, the pinnaces had no inertial compensators, which left only the internal gravity plates. They did all they could, but on their best day, they couldn't match the performance of a compensator, and over fifteen gravities of apparent acceleration got through to the protoplasm of their crews.

It squeezed like the hand of an angry archangel. Abigail's harsh grunt was driven from her lungs, but she'd known it was coming, and her skinsuit tightened about her limbs and torso to force blood back into her brain. She ignored the physical discomfort while the pinnace vibrated like a living creature under the thrusters' power, and she watched the time display on her console through half grayed-out vision as it spun downward even as the range from *Wolverine* raced upward. Then her eyes flicked back to her targeting display.

The *Dromedary* sat rock steady on the display. It wasn't an actual optical image of the freighter, although it was now less than seventy thousand kilometers away. The pinnace's imaging systems could have showed the freighter easily enough at that range, but the tactical computers had been instructed to generate a wire-drawing of the ship, instead. The skeletal schematic allowed her a far better grasp of the actual targeting parameters, and the countdown to optimal firing range spun downward in its own window in the corner of the display.

She felt a deep, visceral urge to take the shot herself. To squeeze the stud on her control column when the countdown reached zero. But that was the primitive warrior part of her. The shot had already been locked into the computers, and the inhuman precision of emotionless cybernetics was far better suited than an acceleration-hammered human brain to a maneuver like this. The window was too tight for anything else.

The thrusters burned for seven endless seconds. Then, abruptly, between one labored breath and the next, the thunderous vibration ceased as the pinnaces moved far enough from the LACs to bring up their impellers. Even as Abigail gasped in relief, a corner of her brain pictured the sudden consternation on the freighter's command deck as the impeller sources blazed suddenly on the big ship's sensors at the deep-space equivalent of dagger range, rocketing towards her now at six hundred gravities' of acceleration.

She had another thirty-three seconds to envision it and wonder if the stunned pirates could overcome their shock quickly enough to get a signal off before her pinnaces reached their programmed attack range.

But then again, if Hexapuma*'s ID on One and Two is right, maybe "pirates" isn't exactly the right noun after all*, she thought, and then the countdown window reached zero.

The pinnaces had moved over thirty-eight hundred kilometers closer to Bogey Three in the thirty-nine seconds they'd spent under power, but the range was still just a shade over sixty-four thousand kilometers when the lasers fired. *Hexapuma* was one of the first ships to receive the new Mark 30 *Condor*-class pinnaces, and the *Condors'* sensor suites, EW, and fire control had all been improved in tandem with their upgraded compensators, while the previously standard nose-mounted two-centimeter laser had been upgraded to a five-centimeter weapon, with significantly improved gravitic lensing.

A proper warship's sidewalls would have brushed the best efforts of those weapons contemptuously aside, and if its sidewalls had been down, its armor would have absorbed the hits with little more than superficial damage. But warship armor was a carefully designed, multilayered combination of ablative and kinetic armors—complex metallic-ceramic alloys of almost inconceivable toughness—laid over a hull framed and skinned in battle steel.

Bogey Three was a merchantship. Her hull was unarmored, and formed not out of battle steel, but out of old-fashioned, titanium-based alloys, and when those lasers hit, the results were spectacular.

Despite the misconceptions which civilians, accustomed only to medical and commercial laser applications, somehow still managed to cling to, weapons grade lasers were *not* fusing weapons. The energy transfer was too sudden, too huge, for that. Plating struck by an incoming laser shattered, and that was precisely what happened to Bogey Three.

Atmosphere belched from the ragged wounds smashed with brutal suddenness through the freighter's skin. Small breaches, compared to those a full-sized warship's weapons would have torn, but the people on the other sides of those breaches had been given absolutely no warning. One instant, they were going about their normal routines in the normal, shirt-sleeve environment of a starship; the next, a shrieking demon of coherent energy exploded into their very midst. Splinters of their own ship slashed into them like buzz saws, and even as the wounded screamed, the atmosphere about them went howling into the voracious vacuum. Automated emergency systems slammed blast doors shut, sealing off the breached compartments . . . and denying those damned souls trapped in destruction's path any possibility of escape.

But the human carnage was secondary, just a side effect. Those precisely targeted stilettos of energy had other objectives, and Abigail's fire smashed deep into Bogey Three's hyper generator compartment. She couldn't tell how much damage she'd actually inflicted, but the pinnace's tactical computers estimated a seventy-two percent chance that it was sufficient to cripple the generator beyond immediate repair. In fact, the computers were pessimistic; what was left of that generator would have been useful only for raw materials.

Hawk-Papa-Three's shot went in effectively simultaneously, but much further aft, and its target was not Bogey Three's ability to enter or leave hyper, but rather its ability to maneuver in normal-space.

Commercial impeller wedges were unlike military ones. A warship generated a double stress band above and below its hull; a merchant vessel generated only a single band. The difference reflected the fact that it was theoretically possible for an enemy to analyze an impeller wedge sufficiently to adjust for the gravity differential's distorting effect on sensors. If he could do that, then he could "see" through it, which no one thought was a good idea applied to his own navy. Using a double wedge, in which the outer protected the inner from analysis, thwarted any such effort. And, of course, naval designers, by their very nature, worshiped the concept of redundancy as the way to survive battle damage. But merchant designers had other priorities, and civilian-grade impellers were fifty to sixty percent less massive, on a node-for-node basis, than military-grade installations. The military-grade systems were commensurately more expensive, and their design lifetimes were substantially shorter, all of which was highly undesirable from the viewpoint of designing a durable, low-maintenance, low-cost freight-hauling vessel.

But one of the consequences of the difference in design was that whereas a warship, like a pinnace, could generate a functioning impeller wedge with only one impeller ring, a freighter required both. And another consequence was that whereas warship impeller rooms were subdivided into mutiple armored, individually powered and manned compartments, a civilian impeller room was one large, open space, completely unarmored and without the multiply redundant power and control circuits—and manpower—of a military design.

Which was why Hawk-Papa-Three's shot inflicted such horrific damage.

The laser's entry wound itself was no more than a pinprick, a tiny puncture, against the vast dimensions of its target. Any one of the beta nodes in Bogey Three's after impeller ring massed dozens of times more than the attacking pinnace did. But size, as size, meant nothing. The laser blasted straight through the impeller room's thin skin and directly into Beta Twenty-Eight's primary generator. The generator exploded, throwing bits and pieces of its housing into the surrounding jungle of superconductor capacitors and control systems, and a brutal power spike blew back from it to Beta Twenty-Seven and Twenty-Nine. Without the internal armored bulkheads and cofferdams, the separate, parallel control runs, and redundant circuit breakers of military design, there was little to stop the train wreck of induced component failures, and a chain reaction of shorting, arcing superconductor rings raced through the compartment. The trapped lightning bolts crashed back and forth with the ferocity of enraged demons, taking one node after another completely off-line with catastrophic damage, and more frantic alarms screamed on the freighter's bridge.

Unlike the damage to the hyper generator, the effect of Hawk-Papa-Three's fire was immediately evident as the entire after impeller ring went from standby power to complete shutdown in less than two seconds. It had to be actual battle damage—no human's reaction time was fast enough to cut power that quickly. But, again, it was impossible for Abigail's sensors to confirm the *extent* of the damage in the flashing seconds her pinnaces took to scud past at over 17,600 KPS.

The fleet little vessels turned, keeping their noses aligned on Bogey Three, and went to maximum power, decelerating at six hundred gravities. Astern of them, the Nuncian LACs had also made turnover, but their deceleration rate was a hundred gravities lower than the pinnaces', and the range between the allied components of the small attack force opened quickly.

"Hawk-Papa-Two, this is Einarsson," Abigail's earbug said ninety seconds later. "Do you have a damage estimate, Lieutenant?"

"Not a definitive one, Sir." Part of Abigail wanted to add "of course," to that, but she reminded herself that even her pinnace's sensor capabilities must seem almost magical to the Nuncians. And at least Einarsson had waited until she'd had a chance to examine the available data before he asked the question.

"From what we could see during the firing pass," she continued, "we scored good hits on her after impeller room, at least. The ring's down, and a commercial design doesn't have much ability to come back from that kind of damage without outside assistance. Obviously, there's no way we can be certain that's the case here, but it seems likely.

"It's a lot more difficult to estimate what kind of damage we may have done to her hyper generator. It wasn't on-line to begin with, so we didn't have a standby power load to monitor or see go down. From the observed atmospheric venting, it looks like we definitely got deep enough to get a piece of the generator, and the computers estimate a seventy percent chance it was big enough. But we won't know for certain until we're actually aboard her."

She didn't offer any estimate on personnel casualties . . . and Einarsson didn't ask for one.

"No, we won't know until then," the Nuncian said, instead. "But it sounds like you hit them hard enough to give us a chance to get aboard. Which, to be honest," he admitted, "is more than I really expected. Without your pinnaces, we wouldn't even have had a shot at pulling this off. Well done, Lieutenant Hearns. Please accept my compliments and pass them on to the rest of your people."

"Thank you, Sir. I will," she said.

"And after you do that," Einarsson added grimly, "go back there and kick those people's a—butts up between their ears."

"Aye, aye, Sir," Lieutenant Abigail Hearns said, without even a trace of amusement for his self-correction. "I think you can count on that one."

Hawk-Papa Flight continued decelerating hard. The pinnaces' velocity fell by almost six kilometers per second every second, slowing their headlong plunge towards the Nuncio System's Oort Cloud and the endless interstellar deeps beyond. Their sensors continued to hold Bogey Three, and Abigail's grimly satisfied estimate that the freighter had been successfully lamed hardened into virtual certainty as the freighter's position and emissions signature alike remained unchanged.

"Excuse me, Ma'am."

She turned and looked at the midshipwoman in the pilot's seat. Ragnhild's expression was calm enough, but there was a shadow behind her blue eyes. Blue eyes which saw not merely her current mission commander or *Hexapuma*'s JTO when they looked at Abigail, but also her officer candidate training officer—her teacher and mentor.

"Yes, Ragnhild?" Abigail's tone was calm, unruffled, and she returned her own gaze to the console before her.

"May I ask a question?"

"Of course."

"How many people do you think we just killed?" Ragnhild asked softly.

"I don't know," Abigail replied, infusing just a hint of cool consideration into her tone. "If there was a standard station-keeping watch in both compartments, there would have been two or three people in the hyper generator room, and four or five in the after impeller room. Call it eight." She turned and looked the younger woman levelly in the eye. "I don't imagine any of them survived."

She held the midshipwoman's gaze for a three-count, then returned her attention once more to her displays.

"It's possible the number's higher than that," she continued. "That estimate assumed a station-keeping watch, but they may've had full watches in both compartments, especially if they were at standby for a quick escape. In that case, you can double the number. At least."

Ragnhild said nothing more, and Abigail watched her unobtrusively from the corner of one eye. The midshipwoman looked unhappy, but not surprised. Sad, perhaps. Her expression, Abigail thought, was that of someone who had just realized that she'd come much more completely to grips with the possibility of her own death in combat than with the possibility that she might kill someone else. It was a moment Abigail herself remembered only too well, from a cold day on the planet Refuge, two T-years past. The moment she'd squeezed the trigger of a dead Marine's pulse rifle and seen not the sanitized electronic imagery of distant destruction but the spray patterns of blood from shredded human flesh and pulverized human bone.

But you were in command then, just like now, she reminded herself. *And the people you killed were the ones who'd just killed one of* your *Marines . . . and fully intended to kill all of you. You had other responsibilities, other imperatives to concentrate on. Ragnhild doesn't—not right now, this instant, at least.*

"However many we've already killed," she continued into the midshipwoman's silence, "it's less than are going to die aboard Bogey Three one way or the other before this thing's done." She turned her head to look at Ragnhild again. "If they're smart, they'll surrender and open their hatches the instant we get back. But even if they do, the odds are at least some of them—possibly all of them—will die anyway."

"But if they're Peep raiders, they're covered by the Deneb Accords!" Ragnhild protested.

"*If* they're Peeps operating under the legal orders of their own government, yes," Abigail agreed. "Personally, I think that's unlikely."

"You do . . . Ma'am?" Ragnhild was obviously surprised, and Abigail shrugged. "But the Captain's message said we have to assume they are," the midshipwoman protested diffidently.

"I realize the other two bogeys have been identified as Havenite designs, and I'm not saying I have any intention of ignoring the Captain's instructions and acting on the assumption that their crews aren't also Havenite. But neither of those ships is new-build, and we're an awful long way away from any star system in which the Republic would have any legitimate strategic interest."

Ragnhild looked as if she wanted to protest, and Abigail smiled slightly. No doubt the midshipwoman felt trapped between her Captain's apparent certainty and the skepticism of her own OCTO. Who, she was undoubtedly remembering at this particular moment, was a very junior officer, herself.

"I don't know which assumption Captain Terekhov is operating under, Ragnhild," she admitted. "He may not have come to an actual conclusion himself yet. Or he may have access to information to which I'm not privy that provides an additional reason to believe these are official Havenite commerce raiders. In either case, he's got a responsibility to bear even unlikely possibilities in mind.

"But I do remember the ONI reports I saw aboard *Gauntlet* on my own snotty cruise. One of the possibilities Captain Oversteegen had to consider was that the pirates *we* were looking for in Tiberian might be StateSec holdouts from the Saint-Just Regime who'd taken their ships and gone rogue when he got himself shot. Admittedly, Tiberian was a lot closer to the Republic than the Talbott Cluster is. But if I were the commander of a shipload of StateSec goons who'd refused to surrender, I'd have wanted to get as far away from Thomas Theisman and Eloise Pritchart as I possibly could. On balance, I think it's more likely we're looking at something like that than that Theisman would consider sending two obsolescent ships the next best thing to a thousand light-years from his main combat zone to harass us in an area the Star Kingdom hasn't even formally annexed yet."

Ragnhild's expression was suddenly much more thoughtful, and Abigail smiled again, a bit more broadly.

"I suppose that analysis could be the result of the fact that I'm a Grayson, not a Manticoran. I've noticed—no offense, Midshipwoman—that you Manties think of the current government of the Republic, whoever it happens to be at the moment, as the font of all evil in the known universe. Not surprising, I suppose, given your experiences with them over the last, oh, sixty or seventy T-years.

"We Graysons, on the other hand, spent as long as your entire Star Kingdom's existed thinking that way about Masada. We're less fixated on governments and more fixated on ideologies, you might say—religious ones in our own case, of course. And we've seen more than enough evidence of displaced Masadans turning to freelance thuggery and atrocities and popping up in the most peculiar places after being run out of Endicott by the Occupation, like those so-called 'Defiant' fanatics who attacked Princess Ruth and Helen's sister in Erewhon last year. So, with all due respect, even if the Captain does think these are probably official Havenite naval units under officially sanctioned orders, I'm not so sure. And if they aren't," her smile disappeared, and her gray-blue eyes were suddenly very, very cold, "then the Deneb Accords don't come into it at all, do they?"

"No, Ma'am," Ragnhild said, slowly. "I don't suppose they do."

"In which case, and speaking as someone with more personal experience with pirates than I ever wanted to have," Abigail continued from behind those frozen eyes, "I would be extremely surprised if quite a few of the people aboard that freighter haven't thoroughly qualified themselves for the death penalty. In which case, that's precisely what they're going to receive, isn't it?"

"Yes, Ma'am," Ragnhild agreed soberly, and Abigail nodded in response and returned her attention to her instruments.

"May I ask another question, Ma'am?" Ragnhild said after a moment, and Abigail's chuckle dispelled some of her eyes' lingering chill.

"Ragnhild, you're on your middy cruise. You're *expected* to ask questions."

"Well, in that case, Ma'am, do you think Bogey Three got off a signal to Bogey One?"

"I don't know," Abigail admitted, "but the only reason I can think of for their *not* getting one off would be that we did enough collateral damage to take out their main communications array. That's distinctly possible, of course. Merchies don't have the communications redundancy of a warship, and all their command and control systems, including communications, are bunched a lot more tightly. I don't think we should go around counting on Divine Providence to have arranged that for us, though. The Tester probably wouldn't like it."

This time, her smile was actually a grin, although neither of them really found the probability that the freighter had sent a warning to her armed consorts especially amusing.

"No, Ma'am, I imagine not," Ragnhild replied, after

a moment, with a smile of her own. She'd been a bit surprised, initially, by the fact that Lieutenant Hearns showed absolutely no inclination to proselytize for the Church of Humanity Unchained. But if the Lieutenant made no attempt to recruit active converts, she also made no effort to disguise her own religious beliefs—which appeared, truth to tell, to be far less rigid than Ragnhild had always assumed most Graysons' convictions must be—even surrounded by a secular lot of Manticorans.

"In any case," Abigail said, indicating the time display which showed just over sixteen minutes had passed since they began their deceleration, "we should be finding out just who these people *really* are for ourselves in another hundred and four minutes or so."

Chapter Twenty-Four

"Update the tactical log, if you please, Ms. Zilwicki," Commander FitzGerald said.

"Aye, aye, Sir," Helen acknowledged crisply.

Her hands flicked across her panel, entering the proper commands, even though she and the Exec both knew the AuxCon computers had already updated the tac log backups automatically, just as they did every five minutes whenever the ship was at General Quarters. Despite that, The Book called for a manual doublecheck every half-hour. The tactical logs were the detailed record of every sensor datum, every helm change, every order or computer input which affected *Hexapuma*'s tactical stance in any way. On ships like *Hexapuma*, which boasted an Auxilliary Control position, they were maintained by AuxCon personnel in order to free the primary bridge personnel from that distraction. On ships without an AuxCon, their maintenance was overseen by the tactical officer's senior petty officer. Their purposes were manifold, but especially included analysis by BuWeaps and Operational Research, the Navy commands charged with evaluating and updating tactical doctrine. And, in the event that any court of inquiry was ever called, the logs would form the crucial body of evidence for all concerned.

Which was why The Book was just a tad paranoid about making certain those logs were properly backed up.

And, in this case, she suspected FitzGerald also saw it as a way to keep at least one of his snotties' minds occupied doing something besides fretting. Which wasn't necessarily a bad idea.

In a way, Helen found her present assignment immensely satisfying. It wasn't often a mere midshipwoman was allowed to assume the position of a heavy cruiser's tactical officer, even if only as backup. For the next few heady minutes or hours, Auxiliary Control's entire tac section was hers—all hers. Well, hers and the Exec's. And, she conceded with just a hint of sourness, Paulo d'Arezzo's, too, if she counted the electronic warfare subsection. The keypads and computer links at *her* fingertips controlled all the sleek, deadly firepower of an *Edward Saganami*-class cruiser, and for the first time it was as if she could actually *feel* all that power, all that potential for maneuver and combat, as if it were an extension of her own muscles and nerves.

It was odd, really, she reflected. She'd participated in—and performed well in—training simulations in which she'd been the tactical officer of everything from a *Shrike*- or *Ferret*-class LAC to a *Medusa*-class pod superdreadnought. Others in which she'd been not the tactical officer, but the "Captain" herself. Many of those scenarios had been intensely, even terrifyingly, lifelike, and some had been conducted right here, aboard *Hexapuma*, using AuxCon as a simulator. And yet not one of them had given her the same sense of fusion with a warship's power as the one she found herself experiencing now, in the hushed, cool quiet of *Hexapuma*'s fully manned Auxiliary Control.

Probably, because this time I know it really is *real.*

Which, she admitted to herself, was also why her satisfaction wasn't unalloyed. Because it was real . . . exactly as her responsibilities would be if anything happened to the bridge. And that was more than enough, however unlikely it might be, to send icy butterflies cavorting through the stomach of even the hardiest midshipwoman.

Unless, of course, the snotty in question is a complete and utter idiot. Which I hope *I'm not . . . Daddy's occasional observations to the contrary notwithstanding.*

"Ms. Zilwicki, I have something," Sensor Tech 1/c Marshall said quietly, and Helen turned towards the tracking rating responsible for monitoring the outermost shell of *Hexapuma*'s remote sensor arrays. All of them were reporting only via relayed, light-speed channels to prevent the bogeys from realizing they were out there, so whatever was coming in was at least thirty minutes out of date, but naval personnel got used to skewed information loop timing.

Now a data code strobed brightly on Marshall's display. It hadn't been there a moment before, and even as the sensor tech tapped it with her fingertip, the single code turned into a spilling stream of data.

Helen leaned closer, and her eyes widened.

"Good work, Marshall," she said, and turned her chair to face FitzGerald. "Commander, we've just received confirmation that Lieutenant Hearns and Captain Einarsson have executed their attack on Bogey Three. The outer shell picked up their impeller signatures right on the projected time chop and detected at least two heavy bursts of laser fire approximately thirty seconds later. According to the emissions data Marshall is pulling in from the array, the pinnaces and the Nuncian LACs all went to maximum decel approximately thirty seconds before the attack . . . and Bogey Three was still sitting exactly where she was after it."

"Very good, Ms. Zilwicki," Ansten FitzGerald replied. And it *was* very good, he reflected, watching the com display which tied him to the bridge. Marshall and Zilwicki had spotted, evaluated, and passed on the data a good ten seconds faster than CIC's highly trained and experienced personnel had managed to get the same information to Naomi Kaplan. And, almost equally as good, Zilwicki had seen to it both that he knew Marshall had brought the information to her attention and that Marshall knew Zilwicki had made certain he did.

Of course, one reason they'd been quicker off the mark than CIC was that they hadn't wasted any time double-checking their information before reporting it to him. But it was still excellent work, and he was about to say something more to them when Captain Terekhov spoke over the AuxCon-to-Bridge com link.

"CIC reports that Lieutenant Hearns has executed her attack, Ansten."

"Yes, Sir." FitzGerald nodded to the visual pickup. "Ms. Zilwicki just brought that information to my attention."

"She did, eh?" Terekhov smiled. "It sounds as if you have a fairly competent team over there, XO."

"Oh, not too shabby, I suppose, Skipper," he said, glancing up to give Helen and Marshall a quick wink. Then he returned his full attention to Terekhov. "I don't suppose we have direct confirmation from Lieutenant Hearns, Sir?"

"No, but that's not surprising," Terekhov replied, and FitzGerald nodded. The question had been worth asking, but neither Abigail's pinnaces nor Einarsson's LAC could possibly have hit *Hexapuma* direct with a communications laser at that range—certainly not without Bogey One knowing they had. Still, she might have tried relaying through one of the other arrays.

"The sensor data was picked up by one of the epsilon arrays and relayed around the periphery to one of the delta arrays via grav-pulse," Terekhov continued, as if he'd read at least part of his XO's thoughts. "The delta array was far enough out on the flank to have a com laser transmission path to us that cleared the bogeys by a safe margin. All of which, by the way, means it took just over forty minutes for the information to reach us."

He looked expectantly at the exec, and FitzGerald nodded again.

"Which happens to be five minutes longer than it would've taken for a transmission direct from Bogey Three to Bogey One," he said.

"Indeed it is. And Bogey One hasn't so much as

blinked. So there's at least a chance Hearns managed to knock out Three's communications."

"Or just to do enough damage to knock them back *temporarily*, Skipper," FitzGerald pointed out. Terekhov grimaced, but he didn't disagree. Nor was his grimace aimed at FitzGerald; it was one of an executive officer's responsibilities to present every reasonable possible alternative analysis to his CO.

"At any rate," Terekhov continued, "they're continuing on, and if they keep it up for another forty minutes or so, they're ours."

"Yes, Sir." FitzGerald nodded again. Actually, the bogeys were already "theirs." Their overtake velocity was down to under sixteen thousand KPS, and the range was down to less than fifty-two light-seconds. Given that *Hexapuma*'s maximum powered missile range from rest was over twenty-nine million kilometers and that the range was less than *sixteen* million, both those ships were already within her reach . . . and probably doomed, if Aivars Terekhov had been prepared to settle for simple outright destruction. Which, of course, he wasn't.

"I have to admit, Skipper," the exec said after a few seconds, "when you first came up with this idea, I had my doubts. Mind you, *I* couldn't think of anything better, given all the balls you had in the air. I was still afraid this one was tailor-made for Murphy, but it looks like you've outsmarted him this time."

"That remains to be seen," Terekhov cautioned, although an eager light flickered deep in his blue eyes. Then his expression sobered. "And whatever happens here, there's still a damned good chance we've already killed some of the good guys, if there were any left aboard Bogey Three."

"We probably have," FitzGerald agreed unflinchingly. "And if so, I'm sorry. But if I were a merchant spacer aboard that ship, Skipper, I'd *damned* sure want us to at least try to retake her, even if there was a chance I'd be killed!"

"I know, Ansten. I know. And I agree with you. None

of which will make me feel a lot better if I have just killed some of them."

There wasn't much FitzGerald could offer in the way of comforting responses to that. Especially not when he knew he would have felt exactly the same way in the Captain's place. That he *did* feel exactly the same way, for that matter.

"Well, Skipper," he said instead with a grim smile, "in that case, I guess the best thing for us to do is to concentrate on taking out our frustrations on Mr. *Mars* and Friend."

"Sir, we're being hailed by the bogeys."

Terekhov turned his chair to face Lieutenant Commander Nagchaudhuri and cocked one eyebrow.

"It's voice-only," the com officer added.

"Voice-only? That's interesting." Terekhov stroked the underside of his chin with a thumb. Actually, he'd expected to hear from the bogeys long before. Almost twenty minutes had passed since they'd received confirmation of Lieutenant Hearns' initial attack. The range was down to less than four and a half million kilometers, well inside even the Peeps' powered missile envelope, and the bogeys' overtake velocity was down to only seventy-six hundred kilometers per second. Had *Hexapuma*'s pursuers deliberately waited, letting the "freighter's" crew sweat under the knowledge that they were in missile range, as a psychological measure? Then he shrugged. "Put it on speaker, please."

"Aye, aye, Sir."

"Freighter *Nijmegen*, this is Captain Daumier of the heavy cruiser *Anhur*. Cut your accel immediately and stand by for rendezvous!"

The voice was harsh, hard-edged, with the flat accent of the slums of Nouveau Paris. There was a chill menace to it, despite the absence of any overt threats, and it was female.

"Odd, wouldn't you say, Ansten?" Terekhov murmured, and the executive officer nodded.

"In a lot of ways, Skipper. That's a Peep talking, all right. But why voice-only? And why not identify *Anhur* as a Havenite vessel?"

"Maybe she's pretending to be a 'regular' pirate, Skipper," Ginger Lewis offered from her own quadrant of Terekhov's com screen, and he made a small gesture, inviting her to amplify her thought.

"On my first deployment to Silesia, the Peeps had organized a complicated commerce-raiding operation designed, at least in part, to look as much as possible like regular pirate attacks on our merchant traffic," she said. "Could this be more of the same?"

"Why bother?" Naomi Kaplan's question wasn't a challenge. The tac officer was simply thinking aloud, and Ginger shrugged.

"One of their objects then was to keep ONI guessing about whether what we faced were Peeps or simply the normal scum, taking advantage of how the war was distracting us from Silesia. But another one—and more important in their thinking—was to keep the Andies from realizing they were operating in the Empire's backyard. They didn't want to drive the Andy Navy into our arms by looking as if they were threatening Imperial territory. Could they be thinking the same way about the Sollies now?"

"Trying to avoid provoking the League by stepping on OFS' toes in an area it's always considered its private turf, you mean?" Terekhov said.

"Yes, Sir." *Hexapuma*'s Engineer shrugged again. "Mind you, Skipper, I can't see any reason why they should be worried about it. We're the ones trying to expand into the area, not them, and the Sollies must know that. So I'm not saying it makes a lot of sense, just that it's the only explanation for their behavior that springs to my mind."

"Well, they're not likely to make anyone believe they're 'regular pirates' with a woman in command," Kaplan observed sourly. "Too many real pirates are neobarbs from backwaters even less enlightened than Nuncio. Some of them remind me of those hard-line bastards on Masada, actually." She grimaced. "The idiots are convinced no one can run a hard-assed lot like *them* unless he shaves and has testicles!"

"Now, Naomi," Nagchaudhuri said soothingly. "There are *some* female pirate skippers. Just not very many."

"And by and large, the women who've commanded pirates have been one hell of a lot nastier than the men," FitzGerald agreed.

"True." Terekhov nodded. "Still, there's something about this—"

"Excuse me, Sir," Nagchaudhuri interrupted. "*Anhur*'s repeating her message."

"Missile launch!" one of Kaplan's ratings announced suddenly. "I have a single missile launch from Bogey One!"

Kaplan's eyes flashed back to her plot. A single inbound missile showed on it as a red triangle, apex pointed directly at *Hexapuma* while it moved steadily across the display. The tac officer scanned the data sidebars, then relaxed and looked back up at her captain.

"Classify this as a warning shot, Skipper," she said. "It's coming in under max acceleration. From their current base velocity, that gives them a maximum range of less than three-point-two million klicks before burnout. Considering the geometry, the actual effective envelope against us is only a tad over two million at launch . . . and the range is four-point-four-point-eight million."

Terekhov nodded. If *Anhur* had actually intended to hit an impeller-drive target—even a clumsy, lumbering, half-lamed one like "*Nijmegen*"—at this range, they would have fired at a much lower acceleration to extend the missile drive's endurance so that it could track the evading ship. This bird would be inert and harmless as it coasted ballistically past *Hexapuma*, which meant it was simply a pointed reminder that Captain Daumier's ship had the range to kill the freighter at any moment, if that was what she decided to do.

"Same message?" he asked Nagchaudhuri.

"Yes, Sir. Almost word for word, in fact."

"Well," Terekhov made himself smile as he watched the missile icon continuing to speed in *Hexapuma*'s general direction, "given that there's no one aboard ship who could produce a believable Rembrandter accent, I think we'll just decline to answer Captain Daumier for the moment."

One or two people chuckled, and he looked at Kaplan.

"Keep an eye on them, Guns. They may get frustrated by our silence and decide to fire something with a bit more lethal intent."

"Aye, aye, Skipper."

Terekhov leaned comfortably back in his command chair and crossed his legs, his expression serene, with the confident assurance expected of the commander of one of Her Majesty's starships. And if there was a hidden, fiery core of anticipation behind those blue eyes, that was no one's business but his.

Helen tried very hard to look as calm as everyone about her in AuxCon It wasn't easy, and she wondered how difficult it was for the others. Especially, she thought with mixed resentment and reluctant admiration, for Paulo d'Arezzo. The overly handsome midshipman seemed impervious to the taut anticipation winding tightet and tighter at Helen's own center. The only possible indication that he shared any of her own tension was a very slight narrowing of his gray eyes as he sat with the three EW ratings Lieutenant Bagwell had assigned to assist him, watching his displays with quiet, efficient competence.

Twelve minutes had passed since *Anhur*'s first transmission. Despite the Captain's high reputation as a tactician, Helen had never really believed he would succeed in drawing his enemies into pursuing him so unwaveringly for so long. The range was down to 586,000 kilometers—less than two light-seconds, and barely eighty thousand kilometers outside theoretical energy weapon range—and *Anhur*'s overtake velocity was barely two thousand KPS.

Brilliant, she thought admiringly, yet her mouth was undeniably dry. *But there's a downside to all this. Sure, we've sucked the bad guys in exactly where we wanted them. Which means we're about to enter the energy weapon envelope of two opponents simultaneously.*

The possible consequences of that made for some unhappy thoughts which, although she had no way of knowing it, were very similar to some which had crossed Ansten FitzGerald's mind. But while she was unaware of the XO's reservations, she suspected Captain Daumier was even less happy than she was, if not for exactly the same reasons. The Peep officer's voice had become steadily harsher, harder, and more impatient over the last ten minutes or so. There'd also been two more missiles, and the second one had been a hot bird—a laser head that detonated barely sixty thousand kilometers clear of the ship.

The Captain hadn't turned a hair as the missile came rumbling down on his command. Helen's fingers had itched, almost quivering with the urge to bring up *Hexapuma*'s missile defenses, but the Captain simply sat there, watching the missile bore in, and smiled thinly.

"Not this one," he'd said calmly to Lieutenant Commander Kaplan. "She's not quite pissed off enough yet to kill a golden goose, and a ship like the real *Nijmegen* would be worth several times any cargo she could be carrying out here in the Verge. She won't just blow that away when she figures she can have us in energy range—or close enough for pinnaces and boarding shuttles, for God's sake!—in another twenty minutes, and take us intact."

He'd been right, but Helen had decided she never wanted to play cards against the Captain. He was too—

"All right, Guns," the Captain said in an even, conversational tone that sliced the silence on both bridges like a scalpel. "Execute Abattoir in thirty seconds."

"Aye, aye, Sir," Kaplan said crisply. "Execute Abattoir in three-zero seconds." She pressed a stud on her console, and her voice sounded over every earbug aboard

Hexapuma. "All hands, this is the Tac Officer. Stand by to execute Abattoir on my command."

Helen found her eyes suddenly glued to the time display, watching the seconds slide away.

"Abattoir," she thought. *An ugly name, but fitting, if the Captain's plan works out. . . .*

Stress did strange things to her time sense, she discovered. On the one hand, she was focused, intense, feeling each second flash past and go speeding off into eternity like a pulser dart. On the other, the time display's numerals seemed to drag unbearably. It was as if each of them glowed slowly to life, then flowed into the next so gradually she could actually *see* the change. Her pulse rate seemed to have tripled, yet each breath was its own distinct inhalation and exhalation. And then, suddenly, the hyper-intensive cocoon which had enveloped her burst, expelling her into a world of frantic activity, as Naomi Kaplan pressed a red button at the center of her number one keypad.

Only a single command sped outward from the button, but that command was the first pebble in a landslide. It activated a cascade of carefully organized secondary commands, and each of those commands, in turn, activated its own cascade, and things began to happen.

HMS *Hexapuma*'s impeller wedge snapped abruptly to full power. Senior Chief Clary's joystick went hard over, and the heavy cruiser snarled around to starboard in a six-hundred-gravity, hundred-and-eighty-degree turn. Her sidewalls snapped into existence; tethered EW drones popped out to port and starboard; her energy weapons ran out, locking their gravity lenses to the edges of the sidewalls' "gun ports"; and radar and lidar lashed the two Havenite ships like savage whips.

It was the worst nightmare of any pirate—a fat, defenseless merchie, transformed with brutal suddenness from terrified prey into one of the most dangerous warships in space at a range where evasion was impossible . . . and survival almost equally unlikely.

It took *Hexapuma* fourteen seconds to go from standby

to full combat readiness. The EW drones' systems were still coming on-line, but Kaplan's fire control computers had been running continuously updated tracks on both targets for hours. The missiles in her tubes' firing queues had been programmed for three broadsides in advance, and the firing solutions had been updated every fifteen seconds from the instant Bogey One and Bogey Two entered her maximum missile range. Now, even as she turned, a double broadside roared from her tubes, oriented itself, and drove headlong for Bogey Two.

At such a short range, they were maximum-power shots, and current-generation Manticoran missile drives at that power setting produced an acceleration of over 900 KPS^2. Worse, from the enemy's viewpoint, the bogeys were rushing to meet them at over two thousand KPS. Flight time was under thirty-four seconds, and it took the bogeys' tactical crews precious seconds to realize what had happened. Bogey Two's anti-missile crews got off a single counter-missile. Just one . . . that missed. The Haven-built destroyer's laser clusters managed to intercept three of the incoming laser heads. The others—*all* the others—ripped through the desperate, inner-boundary defenses and detonated in a single, cataclysmic instant that trapped the doomed vessel at the heart of a hell-born spider's lightning web.

The destroyer's sidewalls didn't even flicker. She simply vanished in the flash of a fusion plant which had taken at least a dozen direct hits.

But Kaplan wasn't even watching the destroyer. She'd known what was going to happen to it, and she'd assigned a single one of her petty officer assistants to the tin can. If, by some miracle, the destroyer somehow managed to survive, the noncom was authorized to continue the missile engagement on his own. Kaplan could do that, because she hadn't assigned a single one of her missile tubes to Bogey One . . . also known as *Anhur*.

Helen knew she was witnessing a brilliantly planned, ruthlessly executed assassination, not a battle. But she was a tactical specialist herself, however junior a practitioner she might still be. She recognized a work of art when she saw one, even if its sheer, brutal efficiency did send an icy chill of horror straight through her.

Aivars Terekhov felt no horror. He felt only exultation and vengeful satisfaction. The *Desforge*-class destroyer had been no more than an irritant. A distraction. A foe which was too unimportant to worry about taking intact. The cruiser was the target *he* wanted—the flagship, where the senior officers and relevant data the cold-blooded professional in him needed to capture would be found. And he was glad it was so, for it was also the cruiser—the *Mars*-class cruiser—the avenger within him needed to crush. There must be nothing to distract him from *Anhur*, and so he and Kaplan had planned the destroyer's total destruction to clear the path to her.

Hexapuma settled on her new heading, her bow directly towards *Anhur*. Not so many years ago it would have been a suicidal position, exposing the wide-open throat of her wedge to any weapon her enemy might fire. But *Hexapuma* possessed a bow wall even tougher than the conventional sidewalls covering her flanks, and *Anhur* didn't.

There were ports in *Hexapuma*'s bow wall for the two massive grasers and three lasers she mounted as chase weapons. Like her broadside energy mounts, they were heavier than most battlecruisers had carried at the beginning of the Havenite Wars. In fact, they'd been scaled up even more than her broadside weapons, because they were no longer required to share space with missile tubes now that the RMN's broadside tubes had acquired the ability to fire radically off-bore, and the Manticoran cruiser's fire control had *Anhur* in a lock of iron. It took *Hexapuma* another twenty-seven seconds to reverse her heading—twenty-seven seconds in which the missiles which doomed Bogey Two were sent hurtling through space and the bogeys' overtake velocity closed the range between them by 54,362 kilometers.

Then Terekhov's ship settled on her new heading at maximum military power. She decelerated towards *Anhur* at seven hundred and twenty gravities even as Bogey One continued to decelerate towards her at 531g, and that, too, was something *Hexapuma* wasn't supposed to be able to do. The single enormous tactical drawback to the new bow wall technology was that an impeller wedge had to be open at both ends to function. When the RMN had introduced the new system, it had accepted that ships with raised bow walls would be unable to accelerate and had been happy to do it, given the fact that, for the first time in history, an impeller-drive ship would be protected against the deadly "down the throat" rake which was every tactician's dream.

But BuShips had felt it could do better, and it had in the *Saganami-C*s. *Hexapuma*'s bow wall could be brought up in two stages. The second stage was the original wall that completely sealed the front of her wedge, protected against fire from any angle or weapon, and reduced her acceleration to zero. The *first* stage wasn't a complete wall, however. It was a much smaller, circular shield, its diameter less than twice the ship's extreme beam. It offered no protection against beams coming in from acute angles, and a laserhead could actually slip right past it before detonating. But against the energy weapons of a single target, *Hexapuma* could place that defense directly between her hull and the enemy . . . and continue to accelerate at full efficiency.

The sheer stupefaction of the savagely reversed trap paralyzed Anhur's bridge crew, just as Terekhov had intended. Most of their brains gibbered that this could not be happening, and even the parts that worked had no idea what to do about it. A heavy cruiser could not reverse course that quickly. A ship of so much tonnage could not accelerate at that rate. And though they knew RMN heavy cruisers had bow walls, they didn't know a thing about the new technology. Which meant, so far as they could know, that Hexapuma couldn't have hers up. But without it, engaging bow-to-stern, chaser-to-chaser, was suicide for both ships! And yet, that was precisely what the Manticoran maniac roaring down on them was doing.

It took another thirty-one seconds—thirty-one seconds in which the range dropped by another 108,684 kilometers and their closing velocity fell to just over fifteen hundred KPS—for the *Mars*-class cruiser's captain to reimpose her will on her own ship's maneuvers.

It was obvious when she did. Anhur's bow rose, relative to Hexapuma, which simultaneously dipped her stern, since she was decelerating directly towards the Manticoran ship. Obviously, Daumier—if that was really the other captain's name, Terekhov thought viciously—had elected to stand her ship on her tail, presenting only the roof of her impeller wedge to Hexapuma's bow chasers as they closed. She probably hoped she could get far enough around to present her own broadside, then roll back up to hit Hexapuma from astern with a raking broadside as they crossed over one another.

Unfortunately for her, the range was down to 423,522 kilometers . . . 50,000 kilometers inside the range at which *Hexapuma*'s chasers could have burned through the bow or stern wall *Anhur* didn't have.

"Open fire," Aivars Terekhov said in a calm, almost conversational tone, and Naomi Kaplan stabbed the firing key just as *Anhur* began her maneuver.

In their arrogant confidence that *they* were the hunters, *Anhur*'s crew hadn't even completely cleared for action. Only her missile crews and half a dozen energy mounts were fully closed up, with the crews in skinsuits, and the outer spaces normally evacuated of atmosphere for combat were wide open and fully pressurized. Almost three-quarters of her crew had been in normal working dress, not skinsuits, when *Hexapuma* turned ferociously upon them, and not one of them had the time to do anything about it. They just had time to realize how hideously vulnerable they were, and then the tsunami struck.

Both grasers and two of the three lasers scored direct hits. Even worse for Bogey One, it took the light-speed weapons 1.4 seconds to reach her . . . and her attitude change had begun just in time to open the angle far enough for one of the graser hits to snake past her heavily armored hammerhead and smash directly into the unarmored roof of the main section of her spindle-shaped hull.

At that range, unopposed by any sidewall, *Hexapuma*'s energy weapons could have disemboweled a superdreadnought. What they did to a mere heavy cruiser was unspeakable.

Anhur's after hammerhead shattered. Heavy armor, battle steel structural members, impeller nodes, power runs, chase weapons, sensor arrays—all of them blew apart, ripped and torn like tissue paper. The energy weapons' superconductor rings erupted in volcanic secondary explosions as they arced across. The forward impeller rooms were brutally opened to space, more superconductors gave up their stored energy, and still *Hexapuma*'s rage tore deeper and deeper. Through internal armored bulkheads. Through weapons compartments. Through magazines. Through berthing compartments, mess compartments, damage control points, life-support rooms, and boat bays. Her fire ripped a third of the way up the full length of the central spindle before its fury was finally spent. Broadside weapons were taken from the side, unprotected by the ship's heavy side armor as the energy fire came from the one angle the ship's designers had assumed it simply could not. Still more uncontrolled power surges and secondary explosions lashed out, erupting along the flanks of the central vortex of destruction, and her after fusion plant managed to go into emergency shutdown a fraction of an instant before the Goshawk-Three reactor's unstable bottle would have failed.

The stricken cruiser reeled aside, after impeller ring completely down, wedge flickering, sidewalls stripped away from the after half of her hull. In that single firing pass, in the space of less than six seconds, HMS *Hexapuma* and Captain Aivars Aleksovitch Terekhov killed over thirty-five percent of her ship's company outright and wounded another nineteen percent. Thirty-one percent of *Anhur*'s shipboard weapons had been destroyed. Her maximum possible acceleration had been reduced by over fifty percent. She'd lost forty-seven percent of her sidewalls, all of her after alpha and beta nodes, and her Warshawski sails. Fifty percent of her power generation was gone, her after fire control and sensor arrays had been gutted, and almost two-thirds of her tactical computers had been thrown into uncontrolled shutdown by power spikes and secondary explosions.

No ship in the galaxy could survive that punishment and remain in action, no matter what incentive her crew might have to avoid surrender.

"*Enemy cruiser!*" The voice screaming in Terekhov's earbug was no longer hard and harsh—it was raw and ugly with sheer, naked terror. "Enemy cruiser, we surrender! *We surrender!* Cease fire! *For God's sake, cease fire!*"

For just an instant, an ugly light blazed in arctic-blue eyes that glowed now with furnace heat. The order to continue firing hovered on the tip of Terekhov's tongue, with the salt-sweet taste of blood and the copper bitterness of his own dead, crying out for vengeance. But then those eyes closed. His jaw clenched, and silence hovered on *Hexapuma*'s command deck while the voice of *Anhur*'s captain screamed for mercy.

And then Aivars Terekhov opened his eyes and jabbed a finger at Nagchaudhuri. The com officer pressed a button and swallowed.

"Live mike, Sir," he said hoarsely, and Terekhov nodded once, hard and choppy.

"*Anhur*," he said in a voice colder than the space beyond *Hexapuma*'s hull, "this is Captain Aivars Terekhov, commanding Her Majesty's Starship *Hexapuma*. You will cut your wedge now. You will shut down all active sensors. You will stand by to receive my boarders. You will not resist them in any way, before or after they enter your vessel. And you will *not* purge your computers. If you deviate from these instructions in any detail whatsoever, I will destroy you. Is that clearly understood?"

More than one person on his own bridge swallowed hard

as they recognized the icy, total sincerity of his promise. *Anhur's* captain couldn't see his expression, but she didn't need to. She'd already seen what he could do.

"Understood! Understood, Captain Terekhov!" she said instantly, gabbling the words so quickly in her terror that they were almost incomprehensible. Almost. "We understand!"

"Good," Terekhov said very, very softly.

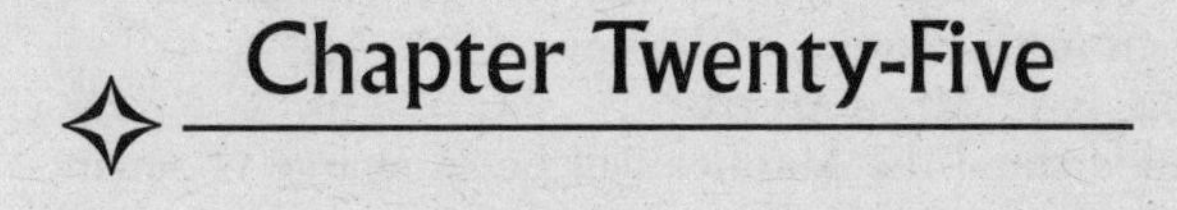

Chapter Twenty-Five

Helen Zilwicki swallowed hard. She was glad her skinsuit's helmet at least partially concealed her expression from the pinnace's other passengers, although she couldn't help wondering how many of them felt the same way.

She turned her head, glancing at the midshipman seated to her left. She would have preferred being paired with Leo Stottmeister, since neither Aikawa nor Ragnhild were available, but she hadn't been consulted. Commander FitzGerald had simply looked at the three middies still aboard *Hexapuma*, then jabbed with a forefinger, assigning Leo to his pinnace and Helen and Paulo d'Arezzo to the one with Commander Lewis and Lieutenant Commander Frank Henshaw, *Hexapuma*'s second engineer. Then he'd looked at all three midshipmen, and his expression had been grim.

"It's going to be bad over there," he'd told them flatly. "Whatever you can imagine, it's going to be worse. You three are being assigned primarily to assist me, Commander Lewis, and Commander Henshaw. Despite that, you may find yourselves in positions where *you* have to make on-the-spot decisions. If so, use your own judgment and keep me or Commander Lewis informed at all times. Major Kaczmarczyk and Lieutenant Kelso will be responsible for securing enemy personnel. You'll leave that to them and their Marines. Our job is to secure the ship herself, and in doing so, we will be guided by three primary considerations. First, the security and safety of our own people. Second, the need to secure the ship's systems and deal with damage which might threaten further destruction of the ship. Third, the need to prevent any acts of sabotage or data erasure. Are there any questions?"

"Yes, Sir." It had been d'Arezzo, and Helen had glanced at him from the corner of her eye.

"What is it, Mr. d'Arezzo?"

"I understand the Marines will be in charge of securing the prisoners, Sir. But what about their wounded? I'm sure we're going to be running into trapped injured personnel—and, for that matter, probably unhurt crewmembers—once we start clearing wreckage and opening damaged compartments."

"That's why you have sidearms, Mr. d'Arezzo. All of you," the Exec's eyes had bored into theirs, "remember what you're dealing with here. Commander Orban's sickbay attendants will have primary responsibility for stabilizing any wounded personnel and returning them to *Hexapuma* for treatment. No matter who these people are, or what they've done, we'll see to it that they receive proper medical attention. But don't make the mistake of lowering your guards simply because this ship has surrendered. At the moment, her people are probably too terrified and shocked—and grateful to be alive—to pose any threat, but don't *rely* on that. It only takes one lunatic holdout with a grenade or a pulse rifle to kill you or an entire work party. And it won't make you, or your parents, feel one bit better to know whoever killed you was shot himself five seconds later. Do you read me on this one, People?"

"Yes, Sir!" they'd replied in unison, and he'd nodded.

"All right." He'd jerked his head at the waiting pinnace boarding tubes. "Get aboard, then."

Now Helen looked out the port beside her as Commander Lewis' pinnace held station to port of and just below *Anhur*'s broken hull. It was the closest Helen had ever come to a Havenite-designed vessel, and her blood ran cold as the damage the ship had suffered truly become clear. There was a difference, she discovered, between floating here beside the wreck, looking at it with her own eyes, and even the best visual image on a display. The shattered cruiser was just to sunward of the pinnace, and drifting wreckage—some in chunks as large as the pinnace itself—drifted hard-edged and black across Nuncio-B's brilliance. Her mind replayed Commander FitzGerald's warning, and she knew he was right. It *was* going to be worse than she could possibly imagine inside that murdered ship.

She listened to the rattle of orders as Lieutenant Angelique Kelso's First Platoon's shuttles docked. Only *Anhur*'s forward boat bay would hold atmosphere, and Captain Kaczmarczyk was obviously disinclined to take any avoidable chances. Kelso had her first squad in full battle armor, and he sent them in first to secure the bay galleries before the remainder of the skinsuited Marines boarded.

Aivars Terekhov stared at the main bridge display. Its imagery was relayed from Angelique Kelso's helmet pickup as she and her Marines took control of *Anhur*'s single functional boat bay. There were no signs of damage in the immaculate boat bay. Or, at least, not of physical damage to the ship. The white-faced, shocked officer waiting to greet Kelso as she came aboard was another matter. His left arm hung in a blood-spotted sling, his crimson uniform tunic was torn and covered with dust, where it wasn't dotted with dried fire-suppressive foam, his left cheek was badly blistered; and the hair on the left side of his head was singed. At least half the personnel with him showed greater or lesser signs of the carnage which had been wreaked upon their ship, but that wasn't what made Terekhov stare at the display in disbelief. Only two of the crewmen in the boat bay were in skinsuits; the others still wore the uniforms in which they'd been surprised by his crushing attack, and those uniforms didn't belong to the Republic of Haven.

Or, rather, they *no longer* belonged to the Republic of Haven.

"Well," he said after a moment, as the first, sharp astonishment eased, "I have to admit this is . . . an unexpected development."

Someone snorted, and he glanced up. Naomi Kaplan stood beside his command chair, watching—along with the rest of *Hexapuma*'s skeleton bridge watch—as Kelso finished securing the boat bay gallery and the rest of her Marines followed First Squad aboard.

"State Security?" The tac officer shook her head, her expression an odd combination of surprise as deep as Terekhov's own and profound distaste. "Skipper, 'unexpected' is putting it pretty damned mildly, if you'll pardon my saying so!"

"Maybe."

Terekhov felt himself coming back on balance, although the sight of the uniforms which had filled any citizen of the *People's* Republic of Haven with terror had brought something much stronger than distaste back to him. For four months after the Battle of Hyacinth, he and his surviving personnel had been in StateSec custody. Only four months, but it had been more than long enough, and a fresh, hot flicker of hatred pushed the last wisps of surprise out of his mind.

The State Security thugs who'd run the POW camp which had engulfed his pitiful handful of survivors had treated them with the viciousness of despair as Eighth Fleet smashed unstoppably into the People's Republic. They'd taken out their fear and hatred on their prisoners with a casual brutality not even the foreknowledge of inevitable defeat had been able to fully deter. Beatings had been common. Several of his people had been raped. Some had been tortured. At least three who other survivors swore had been captured alive and uninjured simply disappeared. And then, in rapid fire, came word of the cease-fire High Ridge was stupid enough to accept . . . followed eight local days later by news of the Theisman coup against Oscar Saint-Just.

Those eight days had been bad. For those days, StateSec had believed in miracles again—had once again believed its personnel would never be called to account—and some among them had indulged in an even more savage orgy of vengeance upon the hated Manties. Terekhov himself had been protected, at least, by his critical wounds, because the People's Navy had run the local hospital, and the hospital commandant had been a woman of moral courage who refused to allow even StateSec access to her patients. But his people hadn't been, and all the evidence suggested that the two men and one woman who'd vanished had been murdered during that interval . . . probably only after undergoing the sort of vicious torture certain elements of the SS had made their chosen speciality.

The Peeps had conducted their own investigation afterward, in an effort to determine exactly what had happened, and despite himself, he'd been forced to believe it was a serious attempt. Unfortunately, few StateSec witnesses had been available. Most had been killed when Marines from the local naval picket stormed the SS planetary HQ and POW camps and the howling mobs of local citizens lynched every StateSec trooper, informant, and hanger-on they could catch. The local SS offices had been looted and burned, and most of their records had gone with them. Some of those records had probably been destroyed by StateSec personnel themselves, but the result was the same. Even the most painstaking investigation was unable to establish what had happened. In the end, the military tribunal impaneled on Thomas Theisman's direct authority for the investigation had concluded that all evidence suggested Terekhov's people had been murdered in cold blood by unknown StateSec personnel while in Havenite custody. The captain who'd headed the tribunal had personally apologized to Terekhov, acknowledging the People's Republic's guilt, and he had no doubt that, had the cease-fire ever been transformed into a formal treaty, the new Havenite government would have echoed that acknowledgment and made whatever restitution it could. But the people actually responsible were almost certainly either already dead or had somehow evaded custody.

And now this.

He closed his eyes for a moment, face-to-face with a dark and ugly side of himself. The hunger which filled him when Kaplan told him Bogey One was a *Mars*-class heavy cruiser, for all its strength, couldn't match the hot, personal hatred that uniform kicked to roaring life. And the man wearing it, like everyone else aboard *Anhur*, was Aivars Terekhov's prisoner. A prisoner who was almost certainly a pirate, not a prisoner of war whose actions had enjoyed the sanction of any government or the protection of the Deneb Accords.

And the penalty for piracy was death.

"'Maybe'?" Kaplan turned to look at him. "Skipper, are you saying *you* expected something like this? Or that anyone should have?"

"No." Terekhov opened his eyes, and his expression was calm, his tone almost normal, as he turned his chair to face the diminutive tac officer. "I didn't expect anything of the sort, Guns. Although, if you'll recall, I did caution at the time that we couldn't afford to automatically assume we were dealing with Peep naval units."

Despite herself, one of Kaplan's eyebrows tried to creep upward, and he surprised himself with a genuine chuckle.

"Oh, I admit I was mostly throwing out a sheet anchor just to be on the safe side and protect the Captain's reputation for infallibility. I *expected* either regular Navy units, or else that these ships had been disposed of through a black-market operation—either by the Havenite government or by some Peep admiral looking to build himself a nest egg before disappearing into retirement. But we've known for a long time now that some of the worst elements of the People's Navy and StateSec simply ran for it when Theisman pulled Saint-Just down. At least two of their destroyers and a light cruiser eventually turned up in Silesia, and there have been unconfirmed reports of other ex-Peep units hiring out as mercenaries. I suppose what surprises *me* most about this is that anyone would take the risk of continuing to wear StateSec uniform."

"Pirates are pirates, Skip," Kaplan said grimly. "What they choose to wear doesn't make any difference."

"No, I don't suppose it does," Terekhov said quietly. But it did. He knew it did.

"*Wolverine*, this is Hawk-Papa-Two. I have a message for Captain Einarsson."

One hundred and two seconds passed. Then—

"Yes, Lieutenant Hearns? This is Einarsson."

"Captain," Abigail said, watching Bogey Three grow steadily larger ahead of her two pinnaces, "we've just received word from *Hexapuma*. Bogey Two's been destroyed with all hands. Bogey One, confirmed as a Havenite heavy cruiser, has been heavily damaged and forced to surrender. Captain Terekhov has Marines aboard her, and Navy rescue and salvage parties are boarding now. He says she's suffered severe personnel casualties, and his present estimate is that damage to the ship itself is too heavy to make repair practical."

"That's wonderful news, Lieutenant!" Einarsson replied, a minute and a half later. "Unless something changes drastically in the next fifteen minutes or so, it looks like a clean sweep."

"Yes, Sir," Abigail agreed. *And the fact that they were Peep ships after all justifies the Captain's decision to attack without challenging them first*, she added to herself. She was surprised by how relieved that made her feel . . . and also to realize that in the Captain's place, she'd probably have done exactly the same thing, Peeps or no Peeps.

"I suppose you should go ahead and talk to them, Lieutenant," the Nuncian officer continued from the far end of the communications line without awaiting for Abigail's response. "She's your bird, after all."

"Why, thank you, Sir! We'll see to it. Hawk-Papa-Two, clear."

Abigail hoped the surprise she felt hadn't shown in her reply. Einarsson *was* the senior officer present, even if he was currently well over thirty million kilometers away. The pinnaces, with their higher acceleration, had overshot Bogey Three by less than twenty-seven million kilometers, 5.2 million less than *Wolverine*'s overshoot. And that same higher acceleration had brought them back to within 1.3 million kilometers while the Nuncian LACs had begun the return journey only two minutes ago. Assuming Bogey Three stayed as motionless as she'd been ever since Abigail's fly-by attack, she'd decelerate to a zero/zero intercept in another eleven minutes. There'd never been much question that her pinnaces were going to do the actual intercepting, but she had to admit Einarsson had surprised her by formally—and spontaneously—admitting that a mere female lieutenant deserved full credit. It was true, perhaps, but Abigail had enjoyed too much firsthand experience of how difficult it was for an old-school, dyed-in-the-wool patriarch to voluntarily admit any such thing.

She switched to the merchant guard frequency and spoke into her com again.

"Unknown freighter," she said, and her soft Grayson accent was cold as space and ribbed with battle steel, "this is Lieutenant Abigail Hearns, of Her Majesty's Starship *Hexapuma*, aboard the pinnace approaching from your zero-zero-five zero-seven-two. Your consorts have been destroyed or captured in the inner system. You will stand by to be boarded by my Marines. Any resistance will be met with lethal force. Is that clear, unknown freighter?"

Only silence answered, and she frowned.

"Unknown freighter," she said again, "respond to my previous message immediately!"

Still, only silence, and her frown deepened. She thought for a few moments, then switched frequencies again, this time to Lieutenant Mann aboard the second pinnace.

"Lieutenant Mann, this is Hearns. Have you been monitoring my communications?"

"Affirmative, Lieutenant,"

"I suppose the most likely reason for their communications silence is that we did somehow manage take out their com section. That would certainly explain why they apparently never said a word to Bogey One about our attack. I just can't quite believe we did that kind of damage. Even if we managed to take out their laser array, they ought to be able to respond via omnidirectional radio at this piddling range!"

"Agreed." Mann was silent for three or four seconds, obviously thinking hard. Then he came back over the link. "What about the possibility that you did enough damage to take out their receivers? Or enough that the people who'd normally be mounting com watch are off dealing with more pressing damage?"

"Of the two, the second one makes more sense. But I don't like the feel of this. Something isn't right. I can't explain exactly why I'm so sure, but I am."

"Well," Mann said after a heartbeat or two, "I'm just a Marine. I'm not prepared to question a Navy officer's judgment in a case like this—especially not after Captain Terekhov and Major Kaczmarczyk made it abundantly clear the Navy officer in question is in command. How do you want to handle it?"

He had not, Abigail noted, made any remarks about religion or superstition.

"I think we have no choice but to go ahead and board," she said, after a moment. "But until we know more about what's going on aboard her, I'd prefer to limit our exposure. We'll take one of your squads, two of my Engineering ratings, and both midshipmen across without docking, and both pinnaces will withdraw to five hundred kilometers before we crack a hatch."

"Aye, aye, Ma'am," Mann agreed. Abigail was more than a little surprised by the total lack of argument, but she only nodded.

"Very well, Lieutenant. Get your squad saddled up. We should be ready to go EVA in about seven minutes."

"Aye, aye, Ma'am," Lieutenant Mann said again. The tall, black-haired lieutenant rubbed his neatly trimmed goatee and looked over his shoulder in the troop compartment of pinnace Hawk-Papa-Three. "You heard, Sergeant?"

"Aye, Skipper." Platoon Sergeant David Crites, Third Platoon's senior NCO, had blue eyes, salt-and-pepper hair, despite his prolong, and a no-nonsense manner. Usually. This time he rubbed his own beard, a considerably bushier and generally more majestic proposition than his lieutenant's, and grinned. "Probably be simplest to just go ahead and take McCollom's squad, seeing's how he's right here, conveniently located next to the hatch, and all."

"Well, if he's the best we have available, I suppose he'll have to do," Mann agreed with a sigh, and the skin around his hazel eyes crinkled in a smile as he looked at Lance Corporal Wendell McCollom.

McCollum, who ran Second Squad for him, stood a hundred and ninety-three centimeters tall, with dark hair and a prominent nose. He was also just a tad on the plump side for a proper recruiting poster, and he and Crites, who'd known one another for almost twenty T-years, were known for punning contests that could go on literally for hours.

What mattered most at this moment, however, was that Second Squad and its plump lance corporal happened to have the highest training marks for the assault role in *Hexapuma*'s entire Marine detachment. Which was why McCollum's people were the only ones—aside from Mann and Crites—in full battle armor.

"Try not to open any exploding paint lockers this time, Corporal McCollom," the lieutenant said sternly.

"One little mistake, and they never let you forget about it," McCollom said sadly, then regarded his youthful platoon commander with a mournful, accusatory eye. "I still think that was an underhanded trick, even for an officer . . . Sir."

"Underhanded?" Mann returned the corporal's regard innocently. "I thought it made a nice change from the usual audio alarms. And, as the Sergeant pointed out to me at the time he—I mean *I*—thought of it," he admonished with a twinkle in his eye, "you really should pay more attention to possible booby traps in training scenarios."

"I do now, Sir."

All three smiled, and Aikawa Kagiyama, who sat watching them, wished he felt remotely as calm as they appeared. At least some of it had to be an act, he thought. The way warriors throughout the ages had put on relaxed faces to demonstrate their confidence before facing the unknown. Yet there was a tough, resilient professionalism underneath the act. Mann was the youngest of the three, but there was no question of his authority, however light the hand with which he exercised it, and Aikawa thought that was probably what he envied most.

The lieutenant scratched his chin for a moment, thoughtfully, then looked at Aikawa, whose anxiety level ratcheted abruptly upward.

"It seems you're going on a little excursion with us, Mr. Kagiyama. I don't know what we're likely to be walking into over there, but my people will look after you. Just remember two things. One, you're a midshipman on your first deployment, not Preston of the Spaceways. Stay out of trouble, keep an eye on the people around you who've done this sort of thing before, and leave your sidearm holstered unless somebody tells you differently. Second, your skinsuit's a hell of a lot better at stopping pulser darts and other nasty things than bare skin, but it's not battle armor. So do all of us a favor and try to keep the battle armor between you and any unpleasantness we run into."

It was, Aikawa reflected, like being told to keep his hands in his pockets. Which, under the circumstances, he found almost comforting.

"Do you think Lieutenant Hearns is right to be concerned, Sir?" he asked after a moment.

"I don't know." If Mann thought Aikawa's question

was out of line, no sign of it showed. "But I do know she's not the kind to jump at shadows. I suppose we'll find out in a few minutes." He looked back at Crites and McCollum. "Let's get our people helmeted up."

"Aye, aye, Sir."

The battle-armored Marines locked their heavily armored helmets into place while Aikawa sealed his own clear, globular helmet. Never a large person, he felt like a midget in his standard Navy skinsuit beside the towering, armored Marines. The soot-black battle armor's limbs swelled with exoskeletal "muscles," and the pulse rifles most of them carried looked little larger than toys in their gauntleted hands. The two plasma gunners had exchanged their energy weapons for tribarrels, and he knew the grenadiers carried only standard HE and frag rounds without any plasma grenades. He still felt dwarfed and insignificant armed with nothing more than the pulser holstered at his right hip.

As he waited to leave the pinnace, he thought about what Mann had just said. It was interesting. All of *Hexapuma*'s Marines seemed to accord Lieutenant Hearns' judgment a degree of respect Aikawa was fairly sure was rare for someone of her rank. Especially a *naval* officer of her rank. She seemed completely unaware of it, too. He wondered how much of it went back to what had happened in Tiberian and how much of it was the effect of Lieutenant Gutierrez's presence.

"Two minutes, Lieutenant Mann," he heard the pinnace's pilot announce over his skinsuit com.

"Understood," Mann replied, and made a "wind it up" circular gesture with his right hand at Crites and McCollum. Both noncoms nodded, and Aikawa—obedient to Mann's admonition—stayed carefully out of the way while the hulking, armored Marines moved towards the airlock.

Helen followed SCPO Wanderman down the passageway towards Environmental Three. Paulo d'Arezzo had been split off to accompany Commander Lewis to *Anhur*'s single remaining fusion plant, and Lieutenant Commander Henshaw had sent her with Wanderman while he picked his way through the wreckage to what was left of the after impeller rooms. She was astonished by how much she missed d'Arezzo. His standoffishness was a pain in the ass, but his apparent calmness had been more comforting than she cared to admit. He was the only person in the entire boarding party who approached her own youthful lack of experience, and she'd taken an unexpected sort of strength from that sense of shared identity.

"Just a minute, Ma'am," Wanderman said suddenly, and she came to a halt behind him. The petty officer and the other two ratings with him blocked her view, and she wondered what the problem was.

"What d'you think, Senior Chief?" one of the ratings asked.

"I don't think it was a direct hit. Looks more like a secondary explosion. But whatever it was, it made a hell of a mess."

"Wonder how they got pressure back in here?" the rating said.

"One of the reasons I think it was a secondary," Wanderman replied. "Anything that got this deep from the outside and did that kind of damage would've left a breach all the way in that would've been hell to seal. But if something like a superconductor ring blew this deep in, it could have shredded the passage this way and opened a small breach clear to the skin without opening up the entire side of the ship."

"Kinda makes you wish they'd lost the grav plates, doesn't it?" the other rating put in.

"Freefall would help," Wanderman agreed. "But I think if we stay to port we'll be all right. Just watch your footing."

Helen's curiosity was almost more than she could stand—especially since, technically, she was the senior (as in *only*) officer present. Under the circumstances, however, she wasn't about to attempt to assert authority over a noncom with Wanderman's years of experience.

And if she'd been tempted to, the thought of Commander Lewis' reaction to her temerity would have depressed the temptation immediately. But she still—

Wanderman and the others moved aside, and Helen abruptly wished they hadn't.

The entire right-hand side of the passage ahead had been ripped as if by a huge, angry talon. It was splintered and broken, half-melted and recongealed in places, for a distance of nine or ten meters. The damage crossed one of the ship's emergency blast doors, and the door's starboard panel had obviously never had a chance to move before whatever titanic blow had torn the passage apart froze it.

And neither had the crewmen who'd been in the passage when that blow hit.

She couldn't even tell how many of them there'd been. The port bulkhead was pitted where fragments of the starboard bulkhead had ricocheted from it, but the marks were hard to see because of the blood patterns splashed across it. It looked as if some lunatic with a spray gun of gore had been interrupted halfway through repainting the passage, using bits of human tissue and scraps of human bone to provide texture to her work. Severed limbs, blasted torsos, fingers, bits of uniform, an intact boot with its owner's foot still in it, a human head canted up against the lower edge of the frozen blast door like a discarded basketball. . . . And, worst of all, the contorted body of a man who'd obviously been badly hit by the explosion but miraculously not killed outright when it shattered both his legs. A man whose rupturing lungs had vomited blood from mouth and nose while his fingers clawed at the deck as the passage depressurized about him.

Wanderman's right, a small, still voice said beneath her horror. *It couldn't have been a direct hit. This big a breach would've depressurized the passage almost instantly if it went all the way through. And he must have taken several minutes to die, lying here, unable to get away. . . .*

She felt the senior chief watching her from the corner of one eye, and she made herself stand there for a moment, looking out over that scene of unspeakable carnage. Then she drew a deep breath.

"I believe you suggested keeping to port, Senior Chief?" she said, gazing at the badly damaged decksole along the starboard side. Her voice sounded strange to her, without the quivers of shock she felt running through her body.

"Yes, Ma'am."

"Well," she said, "since I'm the lightest person here, I suppose I should go first to check the footing."

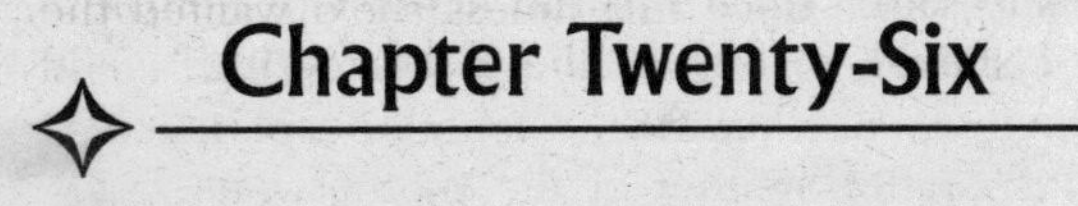

Chapter Twenty-Six

Ragnhild Pavletic and Aikawa Kagiyama floated across the crystal vacuum towards Bogey Three. This far from Nuncio-B, they might as well have been in the depths of interstellar space. The system primary was no help at all when it came to making out details of the freighter's damage, and Aikawa wished at least one of the pinnaces had remained close enough to lend the assistance of its powerful lights. But Lieutenant Hearns had been adamant about withdrawing both of them to a safe distance.

Probably another reason I wish they were close enough, he thought wryly. *I don't like the notion of their* needing *a safety perimeter.*

Lieutenant Hearns hadn't specified what she was leaving a safe distance against, but it didn't take a hyperphysicist to figure it out. The *Dromedary* was unarmed, and it sure as hell couldn't hope to ram something as small and agile as a pinnace, even if it had possessed a functioning impeller wedge. But it did have a fusion plant, and that plant was still active, according to the ship's emissions signature. And if someone put his mind to it, he'd had time to get around the safety interlocks if he'd really wanted to.

Not a comforting thought, he reflected, and looked at Ragnhild.

Her face was visible in the backwash of her helmet's heads-up display just as his must be, and she seemed to feel his glance. She turned her head and looked back at him, and her tight smile looked as anxious as he felt. Both of them knew they'd been included in the boarding party solely as part of their training. Lieutenant Hearns had even had to leave Hawk-Papa-Two in the hands of the flight engineer in order to bring Ragnhild along, and she'd never have done that unless she'd wanted the midshipwoman here for a specific purpose. Which could *not* have anything to do with the lengthy experience in this sort of operation neither of the snotties had.

Aikawa wanted to say something to Ragnhild—whether to encourage her or seek encouragement he couldn't have said. But he kept his mouth shut and only flipped his head in the skinsuited equivalent of a shrug. She nodded back, and they returned their attention to the task at hand, trailing along behind Lieutenant Hearns, Lieutenant Gutierrez, Lieutenant Mann, and the battle-armored Marines.

It took another fifteen minutes to complete the crossing. Most of Bogey Three's running lights were out, but it was unlikely that was because of battle damage. Far more probably, the prize crew had never bothered to turn them on. Why should they, way out here, hiding? But Aikawa wished they had. The freighter's enormous, unlit bulk was an ill-defined mass, like a fog-shrouded mountain, "visible" only by extrapolation from the starscape its looming bulk blocked. The lack of lights deprived him of any reference points and left him feeling uncomfortably like an ant cowering under a descending boot heel.

Judging from the crisp comments and commands flowing back and forth between Lieutenant Mann and his Marines, they, at least, were unaffected by Aikawa's forebodings. They moved briskly, the brilliant circles of illumination from their battle armor's powerful lamps carving slices of solidity out of stygian blackness as they danced across hull plating. They didn't really need lights, given their armor's powerful built-in imaging systems and sensors, Aikawa knew. Were they using the lamps to help out the hapless Navy types less liberally equipped to see in total blackness? Or were they possibly a bit more oppressed by the darkness than their crisp, matter-of-fact voices suggested?

He rather hoped it was the latter, he discovered.

It took another half-hour to locate a maintenance lock. The lock's outer hatch opened readily enough to the standard emergency code on the keypad, and it was large enough to admit their entire party with only a little crowding. Aikawa was delighted to cram into it, since he had a pretty shrewd notion of which two members' junior status would have had them bringing up the rear if it had been necessary to lock through in two waves.

The inner hatch opened into a cavernous equipment bay. The egglike shapes of four one-man heavy maintenance hardsuits were neatly racked along one bulkhead, and bright overhead lights shone on workbenches, racked tools, and bins of electronic components and repair parts. It wasn't as spotless as the same machine shop would have been aboard *Hexapuma*, but the equipment was obviously well maintained and organized.

The Marines moved out, armor sensors and old-fashioned eyeballs probing carefully. Aikawa had never really appreciated just how many potential human-sized hiding places there were aboard a starship. It wasn't exactly an environment which encouraged designers to leave lots of wasted space, but there were still plenty of nooks and crannies big enough to conceal a person. Or even two or three of them at once. Not that anyone but an idiot would suddenly fling himself from ambush to attack an entire squad of battle-armored Marines.

Of course, the fact he was an idiot wouldn't be very much comfort to those of us who aren't *in battle armor. I'm sure Mann would see to it whoever it was came down with a serious case of dead, of course . . . not that*

that would be all that much comfort either, now I think about it.

Lieutenant Hearns had downloaded an inboard schematic of the standard *Dromedary* design to her memo board, and she consulted it as the point Marines led the way from the machine shop/equipment bay. Gutierrez loomed at her right shoulder, carrying a flechette gun to supplement his usual sidearm, and Mann followed at her left, where he could see the memo pad display. They turned to starboard—up-ship—and Lance Corporal McCollom detailed two Marines to bring up the rear and watch their backs. Aikawa thought that was an excellent idea.

They'd traveled about fifty meters and passed through one open set of blast doors when they found the first bodies.

"What do you think, Lieutenant?"

Aikawa was struck by how calm Lieutenant Hearns sounded as she stood looking down at the mangled bodies in the enormous puddle of congealing blood. He was glad he had his helmet on, and he tried to not even imagine the stink of blood and ruptured internal organs which must fill the passageway.

"More than one weapon, Ma'am." The Marine went down on one armored knee, his tone almost clinical, and examined one of the bodies closely while McCollum's squad spread out, pulse rifles and tribarrels ready. "What do you think, Sarge? Flechette guns from up-passage?"

"From the spray patterns, I'd say so, yeah, Skipper," Sergeant Crites replied. He turned, looking down a side passage to the right. "Somebody with a pulse rifle down that way, looks like."

"And it wasn't all one-sided, either," Mann said.

"No, Sir. Whoever had the flechettes took out these two," Crites indicated the two worst mangled bodies, wearing what looked like standard coveralls, although it was hard to be certain after the knife-edged flechettes finished. "Looks like they'd probably just come out of the side passage when they got hit. But the boy with the pulse rifle was behind them, and he's the one who got this fellow."

The sergeant prodded the third body with a toe. It wore a gray uniform blouse and black trousers, and Aikawa frowned. There was something about . . .

"State Security." Mann made the two words sound like an obscenity.

"Are you sure?" Lieutenant Hearns asked. "I don't think I've ever seen a picture of an SS officer without a tunic."

"I'm sure," Mann said. "I recognize the collar insignia. And the belt buckle." He straightened. "I'd hoped we were at least through with *these* motherless bastards. Pardon, Ma'am."

"Don't worry about it," the Lieutenant said dryly. "I've been out of the nest for a while now, Lieutenant. And the terminology's certainly appropriate in this instance." Then she sighed. "This doesn't look good."

"No, it doesn't," Mann agreed.

Gutierrez looked as if he wanted to say something a bit stronger than that, but he kept his mouth shut. No doubt his armsman's responsibility to keep the Lieutenant out of harm's way was clashing with his recognition that running risks was part of a naval officer's job description. His own Marine background probably helped him keep it in perspective. Well, that and the fact that he knew the Lieutenant would rip his head off if he tried to stop her.

"Kinda have to wonder whether these two," Sergeant Crites indicated the coveralled bodies, "were from the original crew, or if there was a falling out amongst the prize crew the Peeps put aboard?"

"I don't know," Lieutenant Hearns said grimly. "But I suppose there's only one way to find out."

It took the better part of three more hours to sweep the ship. Even then, they'd actually examined only a tiny portion of the freighter's interior. A battalion of Marines could have been hidden in the enormous cargo holds, but it became steadily more apparent as they went along that there couldn't be very many—if any—live enemies left aboard. At least one of the freighter's cargo shuttles was missing, and it was possible the survivors of the on-board massacre had escaped in it while the pinnaces were too far away to see them. They could have gotten away with that if they'd launched on thrusters rather than bring up their wedge, and even at a low initial acceleration, they could be anywhere in an enormous volume of space by now. But if any survivors had bailed out that way, there couldn't have been many of them.

The bodies were scattered about, some singly, some—like the first ones they'd discovered—in small clumps and groups. Most of the dead had been killed with flechette guns, but about a quarter had been killed by the higher-powered darts of military-grade pulse rifles. At least one appeared to have been strangled to death, and three had either been stabbed or had their throats cut, and Abigail Hearns found it difficult to imagine what it must have been like. What had possessed these people? What sort of insanity had led them to spend the last two hours of their lives hunting one another down and killing each other? Her orders from Captain Terekhov had prohibited her from identifying herself to them, at least until Bogey One and Bogey Two had been dealt with, as part of the effort to prevent them from warning their armed consorts there was a Manticoran warship in the system. But they had to have had enough sensor capability to realize what had happened and that the pinnaces and LACs which had inflicted the damage would be back to take them into custody. So why hadn't they simply waited?

The answer was waiting when they finally got to the ship's engineering spaces.

"Hold it up, Sir," Coporal McCollom said. "Alverson's outside the power room, and he says the hatch is locked. From the inside, it looks like, but he hasn't tried to force it yet."

"Everybody, hold where you are," Mann ordered. Then

he looked at Abigail. "How do you want to handle this, Lieutenant?"

"Well," Abigail said, her thoughts racing ahead of the words, "if whoever is inside was inclined to suicide, she's already had plenty of time to blow herself up. Unless, of course," she smiled without humor, "whoever it is is deliberately waiting until she's positive at least some of our people are on board."

"Sounds unlikely," Mann said. "On the other hand, people do unlikely things. And anyone far enough gone to still be wearing a StateSec uniform's probably a little less stable than most to begin with."

"'Less stable.'" Abigail surprised herself with a harsh chuckle. "Lieutenant, anybody that far gone is so far around the bend she can't even see it in her rear view mirror!"

"We Marines are just naturally gifted with a talent for concise summations," Mann said modestly. "Besides, I've been taking law school courses by e-mail. Still, I'd say it's more likely whoever locked himself inside was trying to keep someone *else* from blowing the ship."

Abigail nodded and glanced at the two midshipmen standing beside her and trying to look as if they weren't eavesdropping. Not that there was any reason they shouldn't be. They were both doing their best to look calm, and they were doing a pretty fair job, actually. Aside from a certain tightness in Ragnhild's shoulders and the fact that the fingers of Aikawa's right hand were drumming lightly on his holstered pulser, there was very little to give away their tension. She supposed she could have left both of them aboard the pinnaces; it wasn't exactly as if she'd had a pressing need for junior officers. But leaving future officers wrapped up in tissue paper didn't do anyone any favors.

"Recommendations, Ms. Pavletic? Mr. Kagiyama?" Both middies twitched as if she'd poked them, then they looked once—quickly—at each other before they turned to face her.

"I think Lieutenant Mann's probably right, Ma'am,"

Ragnhild said. "Like you say, if somebody wanted to kill herself and blow the ship, she's had plenty of time. But if somebody else wanted to blow it, and I objected, I'd probably try to keep them out of the main reactor compartment, too."

"I agree, Ma'am," Aikawa said. "And if that's the case, whoever's in there's probably nervous as a 'cat with a hexapuma at the base of his tree. I'd recommend approaching him a little carefully."

"That seems like sound advice," Abigail said gravely, watching Mateo's face as he towered over the midshipmen from behind and tried not to smile. No doubt, she thought, he was remembering someone else's snotty cruise.

She gazed back at him for a second, then squared her shoulders, walked briskly across to the bulkhead communications panel just beside the fusion room hatch, and pressed the call key.

Nothing happened for several seconds, and she pressed again. Two or three more seconds oozed past. Then—

"What?"

The single word was harsh, hard-edged and grating with hostility and yet washed out with exhaustion.

"I am Lieutenant Abigail Hearns, of Her Majesty's Starship *Hexapuma*." This wasn't the moment to complicate things by trying to explain what a Grayson was doing so far from home. "We've taken possession of the ship. I think it's probably time you came out of there."

The intercom was totally silent for perhaps three heartbeats. Then it rattled back to life.

"*What* did you say? Who did you say you were?!"

"Lieutenant Hearns, of the *Hexapuma*," she repeated. "Our ship's captured the heavy cruiser—the *Anhur*, I believe—and destroyed the destroyer, and so far, my boarding party hasn't found anyone alive out here. I think it's time you came out," she said again, firmly.

"Wait."

The voice was still harsh, but there was life in it now, incredulity and a desperate need to hope confronted by the fear of yet another trap. Abigail tried—and failed—to imagine what that voice's owner must have been through, and her failure gave her patience.

"Activate your visual pickup," the voice said after a moment.

The bulkhead com was a simple, bare-bones unit. It could be set for voice-only or for voice with two-way visual, but not for visual only one way. Apparently the delay had been to give the man inside the fusion room time to cover his pickup, because Abigail's end showed only a featureless blur. She stood calmly, facing her own pickup, then stepped back far enough to be sure that it could see her Navy skinsuit.

"Take off your helmet, please," the voice said, and she complied. There was silence, and then the voice said, "We're coming out."

Mann made a quick hand gesture, and three of McCollum's Marines stepped to one side, covering the hatch with pulse rifles. Mateo Gutierrez had followed Abigail to the com. Now he simply brought his flechette gun to a muzzle-down readiness position, ready to snap it up and fire with snakelike quickness if it was needed. Scarcely had he and the Marines settled into position when the hatch moved smoothly aside.

A dark-haired man, perhaps a hundred and eighty centimeters tall, stood in the opening. His eyes widened, and his empty hands moved farther away from his sides, as he saw the three Marines behind the pulse rifles trained upon him.

"Lieutenant Josh Baranyai," he said quickly. "Third officer of the *Emerald Dawn*."

"Lieutenant Hearns," Abigail said, and he turned his eyes away from the pulse rifles almost convulsively. She smiled as reassuringly as she could. "Are you alone, Lieutenant Baranyai?"

"No." He paused and cleared his throat. "No, Lieutenant. There are eleven of us."

"Can you tell us what happened out here?" she asked, waving one hand to indicate the rest of the corpse-littered vessel.

"Not for certain." Baranyai looked back at the Marines, then at Abigail again.

"Step forward out of the hatch, please," Abigail said. "I don't wish to appear discourteous, but until we know exactly what happened and sort out exactly who's who, we're going to have to proceed cautiously. Which, I'm afraid, means all of you will have to be searched for weapons. I hope you'll forgive any necessary discourtesy."

Baranyai laughed. The sound was just a little on the hysterical side, but it carried a surprising amount of genuine amusement, as well.

"Lieutenant Hearns, after the last couple of months, I can't think of anything we wouldn't be prepared to forgive if we get out of this alive!"

He stepped fully out into the passageway, still holding his arms well out to either side, and stood patiently as one of McCollum's skinsuited Marines quickly searched him.

"Clear, Ma'am," she said to Abigail when she was finished, and Abigail beckoned for Baranyai to join her (and the silently hovering Gutierrez) as the next person—this one female—emerged hesitantly from the fusion room.

"Now, Lieutenant Baranyai. What can you tell me?"

"They took us about two, two and a half months back," he said, scrubbing his mouth with the back of his hand and blinking rapidly. Then he shook himself and drew a deep breath.

"They took us two and a half months back," he repeated more calmly. "Jumped us just short of the hyper limit leaving New Tuscany. We were a half-hour shy of translation when they matched vectors with us. Came out of nowhere, as far as we could tell." He shrugged. "I figure they probably came in under stealth, but the Company never has spent a credit more on sensors than it had to. They could have come thundering up firing flares, and *we* wouldn't've seen them!

"The first thing Captain Bacon knew, they were right there, and they told him that if he tried to use the com, they'd blow us out of space." Baranyai shrugged again.

"With a heavy cruiser's broadside aimed right at him, he didn't have much choice. So they came aboard."

The Solarian merchant officer crossed his arms in front of him, rubbing his palms up and down his forearms as if he were cold.

"They were lunatics," he said flatly. "Most of them, we found out later, were 'security troops' for the previous regime out in the People's Republic of Haven. Apparently they actually crewed entire starships with 'security' personnel to keep an eye on their regular navy units!"

He looked at Abigail as if, even now, he found that difficult to believe, and she nodded.

"Yes, they did. We've had . . . quite a bit of experience with them ourselves. The previous Havenite regime wasn't noted for moderation."

"I'll take your word for it," Baranyai said. "I might not have, once, but I will now, for damned sure. Somehow the 'faxes don't seem to've reported the full story on the People's Republic. Nothing I ever saw said anything about homicidal maniacs being put in charge of the asylum!"

"Not all Havenites are maniacs. We aren't too fond of them, of course, but honesty compels me to admit that the present regime genuinely seems to have done everything it can to expose and eradicate the excesses of its predecessors." It came out sounding more stilted than Abigail had intended, but it was nothing less than the truth.

"I can believe that, too, from the way these people carried on," Baranyai said. "Their commander—'Citizen Commodore Clignet,' he called himself—could rant and rave for a half-hour at a time, and at the drop of the hat, about the 'recidivists' and 'class traitors' and 'enemies of the Revolution' and 'betrayers of the People' who'd conspired to overthrow the legitimate government of the People's Republic and murder somebody called Saint-Just."

Abigail nodded again, and Baranyai looked at her helplessly.

"I thought the Havenite head of state was named Pierre," he protested.

"He was. Saint-Just replaced him after he died in a coup attempt."

"If you say so."

Baranyai shook his head, and Abigail found herself smothering a smile at the way the Solly's confusion put the all-consuming importance of the war against Haven and the reasons for it into brutal perspective from a Solarian viewpoint.

"Anyway," the merchant spacer continued, "Clignet apparently sees himself as point man for the counterattack to 'save the Revolution.' He isn't just a common, garden variety, scum of the universe pirate, in his own eyes, at least. And he's real big on maintaining 'revolutionary discipline.'" Baranyai shivered again. "As nearly as I can tell, that's just an excuse to indulge in torture. Anybody—and I mean *anybody*—who steps out of line, discharges his duties inadequately, or just pisses Clignet and his toadies off is lucky if he gets off alive. Most of them're lucky if they manage to kill themselves before Clignet's enforcers get their hands on them. And our people caught it just as badly as his did. Apparently, the way he sees it, you're either entirely on his side or entirely on the other side, in which case you deserve anything he can think up to do to you.

"Captain Bacon lasted about two weeks," the lieutenant said bleakly, "and it took him about three days to die. Sophia Abercrombie, our second engineer, went a week later. But we weren't the only ones. Actually, I think some of his people were delighted to see us because it gave them the chance to divert him to another target. As nearly as I ever managed to figure it out, Clignet and Daumier and a half dozen other senior officers have been holding things together through a combination of loot, the opportunity for their people to amuse themselves with any prisoners, and an organized reign of terror of their own. We were the bottom rung of the ladder, but anybody who even looked like getting out of step was fair game.

"I'm still not clear on what happened today," he went

on. "They had us scattered out in working parties, as usual, when someone blew the hell out of Engineering. Was that you people?"

"I'm afraid so," Abigail admitted soberly. "I'm sorry if we killed any of your people, Lieutenant. But with only one hyper-capable ship and targets over a half light-hour apart—" She shrugged.

"I understand." Baranyai closed his eyes for a moment, his face wrung with pain, but when he opened them again, they met Abigail's levelly. "I wish it hadn't happened, but I understand. And," he managed a crooked, infinitely bitter smile, "if you hadn't done it, we'd probably all've been dead in a few months, anyway. Or wishing we were."

He inhaled deeply.

"Anyway. You blew the crap out of the ship. Citizen Lieutenant Eisenhower, the prize master Clignet had assigned to *Emerald Dawn*, was one of his inner circle. He started screaming at us to put the hyper generator and the after impellers back on-line. But there was no point trying—they're dockyard jobs, both of them. His own engineering officer told him the same thing. At which point apparently he ordered his people to blow up the ship and themselves with it.

"After, of course, killing off the rest of our people so we couldn't interfere."

He fell silent again, staring off at something only he could see. Then he gave himself a shake and his eyes refocused on Abigail.

"I guess at least a few of his people decided they didn't want to be martyrs to the Revolution, after all. *We* sure as hell didn't have any weapons, but *somebody* started shooting. I think Steve Demosthenes—he was our second officer—was in After Impeller when you hit us. I don't know. But I grabbed every one of my people I could get my hands on and dragged them down here. I figured they'd play hell trying to blow up the ship with anything short of the fusion plant, whoever won the shooting match, and there was at least a fair chance whoever had shot us up would follow up with a boarding party sooner or later. Either way, this was the only place I could think of to go, and, at least, as a bridge officer, I knew the security override codes so they couldn't just unlock the hatch from the bridge. And . . . here we are."

He waved both hands in a vague, yet all-inclusive gesture at the ship about them, and Abigail nodded.

"Yes, you are," she said quietly. "Lieutenant Baranyai, I wish you and your people hadn't had to endure everything you've been through, and I deeply regret the deaths of your fellow officers and crew. I wish we hadn't been forced to add to them. But, on behalf of *Hexapuma* and the Star Kingdom of Manticore, I give you my word all of you will be repatriated to the Solarian League at the earliest possible moment."

"At the moment, Lieutenant Hearns," Baranyai said with simple, heartfelt sincerity, "I can't think of anything we could want more than that."

"Then let's get my pinnaces in here and lift you people off."

Chapter Twenty-Seven

"What do you think will happen to them?" Ragnhild asked quietly.

"To the Peeps? Or Baranyai's people?" Helen asked in reply.

All of *Hexapuma*'s midshipmen sat around the commons table in Snotty Row. Two local days had passed since the destruction of Commodore Henri Clignet's "People's First Liberation Squadron" and the recapture of *Emerald Dawn*.

There'd been enough left of *Anhur*'s impellers to get her under way under a mere fifty gravities' acceleration, and the savagely battered wreck now lay in a parking orbit around Pontifex. *Emerald Dawn*'s helpless hulk had been towed in by a half a dozen LACs and occupied an orbit not far from her erstwhile captor. Baranyai had been able to confirm that one of the freighter's heavy shuttles was missing, but no one had found any trace of it, so far. Eventually, Helen felt sure, it would turn up somewhere. Probably someplace on the surface of Pontifex, abandoned by whoever had used it to get there. Exactly how the Peep escapees thought that they were going to blend into such an isolated local population was more than she could say, but she supposed they figured that making the attempt beat the alternatives.

"All of them, I guess," Ragnhild said. "But I was thinking mostly about the Peeps."

"Fuck the Peeps," Aikawa said, so harshly Helen glanced at him in some surprise. "You talked to Baranyai, just like me, Ragnhild. Do you think for a minute they don't deserve whatever they get?"

"I didn't say I felt *sorry* for them, Aikawa," Ragnhild responded. "I just said I wondered what would happen to them in the end."

"Whatever it is, it'll be better than they have coming," Aikawa muttered, staring down at the hands clenched before him on the tabletop.

"I heard the Exec talking to Commander Nagchaudhuri this afternoon," Leo Stottmeister said. "He said the Captain's going to ask President Adolfsson to hold them here, at least temporarily."

"Makes sense to me," Helen said. "We sure don't have the space aboard ship for them!"

"No, we don't," Leo agreed. "But I don't think that's all the Captain has in mind." He looked around the table and saw all of them looking back at him. "The Exec told the Commander that the Captain's going to recommend to Admiral Khumalo that Clignet and Daumier and all of their people be handed over to the Peeps, along with all the evidence we've been able to collect about their activities."

"Oh, my!" Helen sat back in her chair, her lips half-parted in a sudden smile. "That's . . . evil," she said admiringly.

Clignet, as part of the megalomania which had driven him to dream—apparently sincerely—of someday restoring the People's Republic in all its malevolent glory, had kept a detailed personal log of his "squadron's" activities. He'd lovingly detailed each prize they'd taken, by name, registry, and cargo. Listed the profits they'd earned by disposing of them, the star systems where they'd been sold, even the names of the brokers through whose hands they'd passed. He'd recorded the other rogue Peep units he'd been in contact with, and the "Liberation Force in Exile" organization which had grown up among them. He'd also meticulously listed the names of those he'd ordered executed for "treason against the People" . . . including at least forty people who'd never been citizens of the People's Republic in the first place. And he'd kept an equally thorough list of his personnel who had most distinguished themselves "for their zeal in the People's service."

That information alone would have been enough to get most of them hanged in the Star Kingdom. But there was a cool, deliciously vicious elegance in the thought of handing them back to the restored Republic of Haven. Not even the most virulent Manticoran patriot could doubt for a moment what sort of welcome President Eloise Pritchart's government and Admiral Thomas Theisman's Navy would extend to Henri Clignet and his homicidal band.

And they'll just hate the thought of being executed by the counterrevolutionaries as garden variety rapists, thugs, and murderers. And—oh, my—when Pritchart *and* Theisman *have to admit these people are out there and that they came originally from the Republic—! I wonder just how many birds we* would *hit with that stone? Daddy and Web would love it!*

"I agree that it's appropriate," Paulo d'Arezzo said quietly. "And don't get me wrong, I don't feel a gram of sympathy for them on that score. But I've got to tell you, Aikawa, after what I saw in *Anhur*, it's hard not to feel at least a little . . . I don't know. Not *sorry*, but—"

He shrugged uncomfortably, and the others all looked at him. He looked back, not exactly defiantly, but . . . stubbornly. As if he expected them to jump down his throat for daring to say anything smacking of even the tiniest sympathy for the StateSec survivors.

But they didn't. Not at once, at any rate, and Helen realized she felt an odd sort of respect for him for having dared to say what he just had. And, as her mind went back over the horrors she'd seen aboard *Anhur*, she also realized she felt at least a trace of agreement with him.

"I know what you mean." She hadn't realized she was going to say anything until the words were already out, and d'Arezzo seemed even more surprised than the others to hear them. "It was . . . pretty bad," she told Aikawa and Ragnhild, and Leo nodded in sober agreement. "I know you guys must've seen plenty of bodies and blood aboard *Emerald Dawn*, but there was this one stretch of passageway in *Anhur*. Couldn't have been more than fifteen, twenty meters—twenty-five, max. We counted seventeen dead in that one space. Took one of Commander Orban's forensic sniffer units to do it, too. The . . . parts were so mixed up together, and so . . . chopped up and burned we couldn't even tell for sure which bits went with which, so we DNAed the whole heap of scraps to see how many people were in it. And that was just one stretch, Aikawa. So far, we've confirmed over two hundred dead."

"So?" Aikawa looked at her almost angrily—not so much at her personally, as at the suggestion that anything should make him feel the slightest trace of sympathy for the people who'd done what had happened to *Emerald Dawn*'s crew.

"She and Paulo have a point, Aikawa," Leo said somberly. "I don't know about anyone else, but I'll admit it—I puked my guts up when we finally got into their after impeller rooms. Jesus. If I *never* see that kind of mess again, it'll be twenty years too soon. And the Skipper did it all with one salvo from our bow chasers. Can you *imagine* what would have happened with a full broadside?"

"Okay, okay," the smaller midshipman said. "I admit it was pretty horrible. I could tell that much from the visual imagery. But a lot of people who never murdered anyone, or raped anyone, or tortured anyone just for the hell of it, have had equally terrible things happen to them in naval combat. You guys're trying to tell me that makes up for everything they did to helpless prisoners in cold blood?"

He sounded almost incredulous, and Helen shook her head.

"No, of course not. It's just, well—"

"It's just that *we* feel guilty, too," d'Arezzo said softly. Helen turned her head, staring at him in surprise as he put his finger unerringly on the concept she'd been fumbling towards.

"Yes," she said slowly, looking into those gray eyes as if, in some way, she were seeing their owner for the first time. "Yes, that's exactly what I meant." She turned to look at the others, especially Aikawa. "It's not that I don't think they deserve whatever horrible thing happens to them, Aikawa. I just don't want *us* to turn into *them* giving it to them. What we did to that ship ought to constitute sufficient punishment for anything anyone could ever do. I don't say it does, I said it *ought* to. And if I'm going to like myself, I don't want to turn into someone who *wants* to personally punish even someone like Clignet even more terribly. I'll pull the lever myself, if they sentence the bastard to hang. Don't get me wrong. But if we can hand them over to someone else—someone who has every bit as much justification and legal jurisdiction as we do, who will proceed after due legal process to punish them further—then I say let's do it."

"Why?" Aikawa demanded. Much of the belligerence had gone out of his tone, but he wasn't quite prepared to give up the fight yet. "Just so we can keep our hands clean?"

"Not our hands, Aikawa," d'Arezzo said. "They're already dirty, and I think Helen and I are both equally willing to get them even dirtier, if that's what our duty requires." He shook his head. "It's not our hands we're worried about; it's our souls."

Aikawa had opened his mouth. Now he shut it again very slowly. He looked back and forth between Helen and d'Arezzo, then at Leo.

"He's got a point," Leo repeated, and Helen nodded in slow, emphatic agreement. Aikawa frowned, but then he shrugged.

"Okay," he said. "Maybe you all do, Leo. And maybe I'll feel differently in a few weeks, or a few months. If I do, I guess it'd be better not to've done a lot of things I'll start wishing I could undo. Besides," he managed an expression far closer to his normal grin, "what really matters is that the bastards get the chop, not that *we* give it to them. So I guess if the Captain wants to be generous and give Pritchart and Theisman a present, I can go along with that, too."

"Geez, Aikawa, your saintly compassion and kindliness leave me breathless," Helen said dryly, and joined the general chuckle that ran around the table after her sentence. Yet even as she chuckled, she was thinking about the unsuspected depths Paulo d'Arezzo had just revealed. And the even more disturbing thought that perhaps those depths had been unsuspected only by her. . . .

"It feels good to get back to a routine, Skipper," Ansten FitzGerald said frankly as he and Terekhov sat in the captain's quarters drinking Chief Steward Agnelli's delicious coffee. The desk between them was littered with paperwork and record chips as they caught up on all of the routine details of *Hexapuma*'s day-to-day existence.

"Yes. Yes, it does." Terekhov heard the profound satisfaction in his own voice. He didn't know if the vicious pounding he'd given *Anhur* had finally laid to rest the demons of Hyacinth. Frankly, he doubted it. But he knew he'd at least made some progress against them, and the demonstration that he hadn't lost his touch after all had been, in his humble opinion, pretty damned convincing. Best of all, he hadn't given in to the almost overwhelming compulsion to hang or space Clignet and his surviving oficers—that cold-blooded, murdering, sadistic bitch Daumier, at the very least—himself. He would never have doubted for a moment that they'd had it coming; but the question of whether he'd done it for justice's sake or simply to slake the fires of his own vengeance in blood was one he never wanted to have to answer. And not just for himself. It would have been one he had to answer for Sinead, as well, even if she never, ever asked him.

"Still," he said, thinking aloud, "we were lucky."

"Some people make their own luck, Skip," FitzGerald said, regarding him through a tiny wisp of steam across his own coffee cup.

"Don't give me that, Ansten." Terekhov smiled crookedly. "Tell me you didn't think I'd gone off my nut when I opted to suck them in *that* close—if you can!"

"Well . . . " FitzGerald began, startled that the Captain had brought that particular point up between them.

"Of course you did. For God's sake, Ansten! We've got Mark 16s in the tubes. I could've pounded either one of them—or both—into scrap, with no option but to surrender, without ever letting them into energy range at all. Couldn't I?"

"Yes, Sir, you could have," FitzGerald said quietly. "And I suppose, if I'm going to be honest, I did wonder if not doing that was the best tactical choice."

Even now, the exec was more than a little surprised they could have this conversation. He remembered all his earlier doubts about Aivars Terekhov and the scars Hyacinth must have left behind. And, truth to tell, he wasn't convinced yet that he'd been wrong to harbor them. But the action against *Anhur* and Clignet's psychopaths had gone a long way toward resolving them. And, more importantly, in many ways, it seemed to have resolved a lingering constraint in his relationship with his Captain.

"I won't lie to you, Ansten," Terekhov said, after a moment, looking down into his cup. "When we found out they were Peeps—and especially that one of them was a *Mars* class—it *did* affect my judgment. It made me even more determined not just to defeat them, but to *smash* them. Ansten," he looked up from the coffee's brown depths, and his blue eyes were dark, without the distancing reserve FitzGerald had become accustomed to, "I wanted to do every single thing we did to them. I *know* what that ship looked like inside when we finished with her, and I wanted to see it. I wanted to *smell* it."

FitzGerald gazed at him, his own eyes gray, calm mirrors. Perhaps they wouldn't have been so calm if he hadn't heard Terekhov's tone. If he hadn't recognized his Captain's own realization of the demons he carried around with him.

"But," Terekhov continued, "whatever I wanted, I'd already decided on exactly the sort of engagement I planned to fight if I could get whoever it was that close. I'd made that decision before I knew they were Peeps. Not because I wanted to punish the same people who massacred *my* people at Hyacinth, but because I wanted—needed—to take them out, whoever they were, so fast and so hard, from such a close range and at such a low relative velocity, that they wouldn't even dream of dumping their computer cores when I told them not to."

"Well, Skip," FitzGerald said with a slow smile, "you certainly did that."

"Yes, I did," Terekhov agreed with a slight smile of his own. "But now that it's over, I realize I need you to help me watch myself." His smile disappeared, and he looked at FitzGerald very levelly. "There's only one person aboard any warship with whom its captain can truly let down his guard, and that's his exec. You're the one person aboard the *Kitty* I can discuss this with—and the one person in a position to tell me if you think I'm stepping over the line without damaging discipline or undermining the chain of command. That's why I'm telling you this. Because I need you to know I *want* your input in a case like this."

"I—" FitzGerald paused and sipped coffee, deeply touched by his Captain's admission. The relationship he'd just described was the one which ought to exist between every successful captain and his executive officer, yet the degree and level of frankness he'd asked for—and offered—was attained only too rarely. And FitzGerald wondered if *he* would have had the moral strength and courage to admit to another officer, especially one of his *subordinate* officers, that he'd ever doubted his own judgment. Not because he was stupid enough to believe they wouldn't realize he had, but because admitting it simply wasn't the way the game was played.

"I'll bear that in mind, Skipper," he said quietly, after a moment.

"Good." Terekhov leaned back with a more comfortable smile, holding his coffee cup and its saucer in his lap. He gazed around the cabin for a moment, as if composing his thoughts, then grimaced.

"I'm starting work on my post-battle reports, and I'm looking forward to seeing yours and the rest of our officers. I'm especially curious as to whether or not the rest of you are going to identify the one weakness I've discovered about the new ship types."

"Like the lack of manpower?" FitzGerald asked dryly, and Terekhov chuckled.

"Exactly like the lack of manpower," he agreed. "We were swamped trying to deal with *Anhur*'s casualties and damages. Even with the Nuncians to take up so much of the slack, we didn't begin to have the warm bodies we would've needed if we'd had to board a couple of intact ships. And as for doing that *and* making critical repairs, especially if we'd already had to detach some of the Marines—!"

"I never thought I'd say reducing the Marine detachments was a mistake, Skipper," FitzGerald said, shaking his head, "but it really is going to be a problem for us on detached operations like this."

"I know. I know." Terekhov sighed. Then he shrugged. "On the other hand, what we need right now more than anything else is a warfighting navy, not a peacekeeping one, and so far, these designs are one hell of a lot more efficient as pure fighting machines. We'll just have to learn to cope with the problems in other operational regimes. And let's be honest—if we'd been conducting regular anti-pirate operations instead of taking on semi-modern heavy cruisers, we wouldn't've felt the strain quite so badly."

"Probably not," FitzGerald conceded. "But for the people who get stuck pulling this sort of assignment, it's going to be an ongoing pain in the ass, and no mistake about it."

"Agreed. But speaking about the difference between our little soiree here and 'regular anti-pirate operations,' what do you think about our discoveries in *Anhur*'s computers?"

"I think it's past time we settled accounts with Manpower once and for all," FitzGerald said grimly, his expression hard. "And probably with all the rest of those bloodsucking Mesan bastards."

"My, my! You *are* upset," Terekhov observed with a lightness which fooled neither of them.

"Skipper, Clignet's logs virtually admit Manpower's recruited every damned refugee StateSec ship they can get their hands on!"

"Unsavory of them, I admit," Terekhov acknowledged, picking up his saucer and crossing his legs as he leaned back to sip coffee. "Not, on the other hand, really a surprise, I think. Now is it?"

"Hiring StateSec scum? Damned right *that's* a surprise, Skipper! Or it sure as hell is one where *I'm* concerned!"

"Actually, 'hiring' isn't exactly the right verb. It's more like placing independent contractors on retainer. And the contractors are working on commission, not direct payment. All Manpower's doing, really, is providing some initial maintenance and resupply *gratis*, then pointing their new . . . associates at profitable hunting grounds. And, of course, helping dispose of their plunder. Let's face it, Ansten; some of the biggest Solly merchant lines have always been in bed with the more successful pirates. They use them against competitors, and supplying them with information and weapons buys them immunity for ships traveling under their own house transponder codes. Hell, *Edward Saganami* was killed in action against 'pirates' subsidized by Mesa and the contemporary Silesian government! Not a lot of change there."

"All right," FitzGerald muttered, just a bit rebelliously. "I'll admit it—Mesa and its multistellars have always been outlaws, and they've always been perfectly comfortable working with the most murderous scum out there. But I still think recruiting StateSec units and rogue People's Navy ships is a new departure for them. And, give the Devil his due, Skip—I always thought the Peeps were as serious as we were about enforcing the Cherwell Convention, at least."

"I suppose it is a new departure for Manpower, in some ways," Terekhov conceded. "If nothing else, they're recruiting ships whose weapons, electronics, and crew quality come a hell of a lot closer to matching that of contemporary navies. It's not up to our weight, maybe. Or the Andies'. But it comes a lot closer, and these units probably *are* a match for the older ones we're using for routine commerce protection away from the front-line systems. And it also guarantees deniability. After all, these ships are already outlaws against their own star nation—or hard-core patriots, fighting to restore the legitimate government *of* their star nation, depending on your perspective. They've got their own reasons for doing anything they do, and Manpower can stand back and fling its hands piously into the air in horror right along with the best of them if any of their rogues get themselves caught.

"By the same token, though, these people are all orphans. They're not even privateers working with a viable—or semi-viable—planetary or system liberation organization, like some of the folks we've dealt with in Silesia for so long. As you just pointed out, opposition to the genetic slave trade's always been a core policy of Haven, whether it was the People's Republic or just the Republic. The fact that these people are willing to sign on with slavers cuts the last real link with where they came from or who they used to claim to be.

"So they don't have anywhere else to go, whatever lies

they may tell themselves, and there's no countervailing loyalty to draw them away from their new associates. The best kind of mercenaries, Ansten—people no one can hire away from you, because they aren't officially your employees, and even if they were, they don't have anywhere to go! And, as pirates, they pay their own way with the loot they're taking from the people you want hurt in the first place. Talk about making war pay for itself!"

"Skipper," FitzGerald said in pained tones, "*please* don't sound like you actually admire these bastards!"

"Admiration doesn't come into it. Understanding what they're trying to do, now—that's another matter. And I don't. Understand, I mean."

"Excuse me?" FitzGerald looked at him quizzically. "Weren't you the one who was just explaining about how all of this is such a great advantage for them?"

"That was all in the tactical sense—or, at most, the operational sense. I'm talking about figuring out the *strategic* sense in what they're doing. Aside from taking a certain vengeful pleasure in blacking our eyes after all we've done to them over the centuries, and maybe using people who used to be Peeps to do it with, I don't see what they're trying to accomplish. *Anhur* and 'Citizen Commodore Clignet' would obviously have added to the pressure on us here in the Cluster, if they hadn't gotten their chops busted so quickly. But his log entries pretty clearly imply that Manpower has acquired an entire little fleet of ex-Peep rogue units. And, apparently, even more ship commanders they can help acquire vessels and suitable crews from other sources. So where are they? Are they planning to try to swamp us out here in the Cluster? If they are, where's the rest of them? And are they really stupid enough to think discovering hordes of ex-Peeps flailing about in the Cluster wouldn't make Queen Elizabeth even more determined to drive the annexation through? Ansten, by now the entire *galaxy* knows the Queen wants to occupy the Haven System, depopulate Nouveau Paris, plow the entire planet with salt, and then nuke it into a billiard ball to make sure she didn't miss any microbes. Show her a batch of 'Citizen Commodore Clignets,' and she'll find the reinforcements she needs to hold the Cluster even if she has to buy them from the Sollies out of the Privy Purse!"

"That might be . . . just a . . . bit of an overstatement, Skipper." FitzGerald's voice quivered, and his lips twitched. He paused and inhaled deeply. "On the other hand, I will concede Her Majesty is just a *little* irked with Peeps in general, and the old regime in particular. Something about that assassination attempt in Grayson, I think."

"Exactly. Oh, she's going to be pissed off wherever and whenever they turn up. And I don't expect Manpower to hold off using them just because they don't want to hurt Her Majesty's feelings. But I don't think they're clumsy enough to make heavy use of them here, if their object in the long run is to encourage us to stay out of the Cluster. I could be wrong about that. And it's possible any of their tame Peeps they chose to use here would be just one of several strings to their bow. But they started recruiting these people, according to Clignet, long before we ever discovered the Lynx Terminus. So they obviously had something in mind to do with them before the Cluster became an issue. And I'd very much like to know what that 'something' was."

"Put that way, I have to agree," FitzGerald said thoughtfully.

"Well, I'm sure we'll both keep turning it over in the backs of our brains for the foreseeable future. In the meantime, I think we can give ourselves at least a modest pat on the back for dealing with Clignet and his butchers. And then get back to the boring, day-to-day duties we expected when we first arrived in Nuncio."

"Yes, Sir," FitzGerald sighed. "I've already got Tobias running preliminary updates on our charts, and I promised him he can have the snotties when he needs them. I guess we can settle down for the real survey activity tomorrow, or the next day."

"Time estimate to completion?"

"With all of the remote arrays we deployed against Clignet, we've already got a pretty damned good 'eye in the sky.' We're going to have to use the pinnaces to pick some of them up if we want to recover them—which," he added dryly, "I'm assuming, given their price tags, we do?"

"You assume correctly," Terekhov said even more dryly.

"Well, about a quarter of them've exhausted their endurance, so we're going to have to go out and get them. That's the bad news. The good news is that they've given us enough reach that we can probably complete the survey within another nine to ten T-days."

"That *is* good news. At that rate, we'll be able to pull out for Celebrant almost exactly on schedule, despite playing around with Clignet. Outstanding, Mr. Exec!"

"We strive to please, Skip. Of course," the XO smiled nastily, "doing it's going to require certain snotties to work their butts off. Which may not be such a bad thing, given some of the experiences they have to work their way past," he added more seriously.

"No, not a bad thing at all," Terekhov said. "Of course, I don't see any reason to explain to our long-suffering snotties that we're doing this for their own good. Think of all the generations of oppressed midshipmen who'd feel cheated if this one figured out their heartless, hard-driving, taskmaster superiors actually *care* what happens to them!"

Chapter Twenty-Eight

Helen opened the hatch and started to step through it, then stopped abruptly.

She'd discovered the small observation dome early in her second week aboard *Hexapuma*. It was never used. The optical heads spotted along the cruiser's hull, and especially here between the boat bays, gave multiply overlapping coverage. They allowed the boat bay flight control officer far better visibility from the displays in his command station than any human eye could have provided, even from this marvelously placed perch. But the dome was still here, and, in some emergency, with the normal command station knocked out, someone stationed here might actually do some good. Personally, Helen doubted it, but she didn't really care, either. Whatever the logic of its construction, it gave her a place to sit alone with God's handiwork and think.

It was very quiet in the dome. The hand-thick armorplast blister on the bottom of *Hexapuma*'s central spindle was tougher than thirty or forty centimeters of the best prespace armor imaginable, and the dome boasted its own armored hatch. There were only two comfortable chairs, a communications panel, and the controls required to configure and maneuver the small grav-lens telescope. The quiet whisper of air through the ventilating ducts was the only sound, and the silent presence of the stars was her only companionship whenever she came here to be alone. To think. To work her way through things . . . like the carnage and butchery she'd seen aboard *Anhur*.

And that made it a very precious treasure aboard a warship, where privacy was always all but impossible.

Which was why she felt a sudden, burning sense of resentment when she discovered that someone else had discovered *her* refuge. And not just any someone.

Paulo d'Arezzo looked up as the hatch opened, then popped upright as he saw Helen. An odd expression flashed over his too-handsome face—a flicker of emotions too fast and complex for her to read. Surprise, obviously. And disappointment—probably the mirror image of her own resentment, if he'd believed, as she had, that no one else had discovered this refuge. But something else, too. Something darker, colder. Black and clinging and bitter as poison, that danced just beyond grasp or recognition.

Whatever it was, it vanished as quickly as it had come, replaced by the familiar, masklike expression she detested so thoroughly.

"I'm sorry if I startled you," she said stiffly. "I hadn't realized the compartment was occupied."

"That's all right." He, too, sounded stiff, a bit stilted. "I was just about finished here today, anyway." He turned half-away from her to pick something up. His movements seemed hurried, a bit too quick, and, almost despite herself, Helen stepped farther into the small, compartment and looked over his shoulder.

It was a sketch pad. Not an electronic pad: an old-fashioned paper pad, with a rough-toothed surface for equally old-fashioned pencils or pastels or charcoal sticks. Cathy Montaigne sometimes used a similar pad, although she'd always insisted she was nothing but a dabbler. Helen wasn't so sure about that. Cathy was certainly untrained, and her work wasn't up to professional standards, perhaps, but there was something to it. A feel. A sense of . . . interpretation. *Something*. Helen didn't have the training to describe what that "something" was, but she recognized it when she saw it.

Just as she recognized it when she saw Paulo's pad. Except that Paulo obviously had both the raw talent and training Cathy lacked.

She inhaled sharply as she recognized the sketch. Saw the shattered, broken hammerhead looming against Nuncio-B, surrounded by wreckage and splintered ruin. It was a stark composition, graphite on paper, blackest shadow and pitiless, blazing light, jagged edges, and the cruel beauty of sunlight on sheared battle steel. And somehow the images conveyed not just broken plating and pieces of hull. They conveyed the violence which had created them, the artist's awareness of the pain, death, and blood waiting within that truncated hull. And the promise that the loss of some precious innocence, almost like virginity, waited with those horrors.

Paulo looked back over his shoulder at the sound of her indrawn breath, and his face blanked. He reached out, his hand moving faster, and slapped the cover over the pad, almost as if he was ashamed she'd seen it. He looked away from her again, his head partly bent, and jammed the pad up into the satchel she'd often seen him carrying without wondering what might be inside it.

"'Scuse me," he muttered, and started to brush past her towards the hatch.

"Wait." Her hand closed on his elbow before she even realized she was going to speak. He stopped instantly, looking down at her hand for perhaps a second, then looked up at her face.

"Why?" he asked.

"Because—" Helen paused, suddenly aware she didn't know the answer to that question. She started to release her grip, ready to apologize and let him go. But then she looked into those gray, aloof eyes, and they weren't aloof. There was a darkness in them, the same darkness, Helen knew, which had brought *her* here to think and be alone. But there was an edge of something else, as well.

Loneliness, she thought wonderingly. Perhaps even . . . fear?

"Because I'd like to talk to you," she said, and was astonished by the fact that it was the truth.

"About what?" His deep, resonant voice carried the familiar standoffishness. Not rude, or dismissive, but with that unmistakable sense of distance. She felt an equally familiar flicker of irritation, but this time she'd seen his eyes, and his sketch. There was more to Paulo d'Arezzo, she realized, than she'd ever bothered to notice before, and that sent a dull throb of shame through her.

"About the reason you're here." She waved her free hand at the quiet, dimly illuminated dome. "About the reason *I'm* here."

For an instant, he looked as if he meant to pull free and continue on his way. Then he shrugged.

"I come here to think."

"So do I." She smiled crookedly. "It's hard to find someplace to do that, isn't it?"

"If you want to be left alone to do it," he agreed. It could have been a pointed comment on her intrusion into his solitude, but it wasn't. He looked back out at the pinprick stars, and his expression softened. "I think this has to be the most peaceful spot in the entire ship," he said quietly.

"It's the most peaceful one I've been able to find, anyway," she agreed. She pointed at the chair he'd been sitting in when she arrived. He looked at it, then shrugged and sat back down. She settled herself into the other chair, and pivoted it to face him.

"It bothers you, doesn't it?" She twitched one hand at the closed sketch pad in his satchel. "What we saw aboard *Anhur*—that bothers you as much as it bothers me, doesn't it?"

"Yes." He looked away, out into the peaceful blackness. "Yes, it does."

"Want to talk about it?"

He looked back at her quickly, his expression surprised, and she wondered if he, too, was remembering their conversation with Aikawa in Snotty Row.

"I don't know," he said, after a moment. "I haven't really been able to put it into words for myself, much less anyone else."

"Me, either," she admitted, and it was her turn to look off into the stars. "It was . . . awful. Horrible. And yet . . ." Her voice trailed off, and she shook her head slowly.

"And yet, there was that awful sense of triumph, wasn't there?" His soft question pulled her eyes back to him as if he were a magnet. "That sense of *winning*. Of having proven we were faster, tougher—smarter. Of being better than they were."

"Yes." She nodded slowly. "I guess there was. And maybe there *should* have been. We *were* faster and tougher—this time, at least. And they were exactly what we joined the Navy to stop. Shouldn't there be some sense of triumph, of victory, when we stop murderers and rapists and torturers from hurting anyone else, ever again?"

"Maybe." His nostrils flared as he drew a deep breath, then shook his head. "No, not 'maybe.' You're right. And it's not as if you or I gave the orders, or fired the weapons. Not this time. But the truth is, when you come right down to it, however evil they might've been—and I grant you, they *were* evil, any way you want to define the term—they were still human beings. I saw what happened to them, and my imagination's good enough to picture at least some of what it must've been like *when* it happened. And no one should feel triumphant over having done that to someone else, however much they may have deserved to have it done to them. Nobody should . . . and I do. So what does that say about me?"

"Feeling qualms about wearing the uniform?" she asked almost gently.

"No." He shook his head again, firmly. "Like I said when we were talking with the others. This *is* why I joined, and I don't have any qualms about doing the job. About stopping people like this. Not even about firing on—killing—people in other navies who're just like you and me, just doing what duty requires of them. I don't think it's the actual killing. I think it's the fact that I can see how horrible it was and feel responsible for it without feeling guilty. Shouldn't there be some guilt? I hate the fact that I helped do that to other humans, and I regret that it had to happen to anyone, but I don't feel *guilty*, Helen. Sick at heart. Revolted. Horrified. All those things. But not guilty. What does that say about me? That I can kill people and not feel guilty?"

He looked at her, the gray eyes bottomless, and she folded her arms across her breasts.

"It says you're human. And don't be too sure you don't feel guilty. Or that you won't, in time. My father says most people do, that it's a societal survival mechanism. But some people don't. And he says that doesn't necessarily make them evil, or sociopathic monsters. Sometimes it just means they see more clearly. That they don't lie to themselves. There are choices we have to make. Sometimes they're easy, and sometimes they're hard. And sometimes our responsibility to the people we care about, or the things we believe in, or people who can't defend themselves, doesn't leave us any choice at all."

"I don't know." He shook his head. "That seems too . . . simplistic. It's like giving myself some kind of moral get out of jail free card."

"No, it isn't," she said quietly. "Believe me. Guilt and horror can be independent of each other. You can feel one whether you feel the other or not."

"What are you talking about?" He sat back, his forearms on the chair armrests, and looked at her intently, as if he'd heard something she hadn't quite said. "You're not talking about *Anhur* at all, are you?"

Once again, his perceptiveness surprised her. She considered him for a few seconds, then shook her head.

"No. I'm talking about something that happened years ago, back on Old Earth."

"When the Scrags kidnapped you?"

"You knew about that?" She blinked, and he actually chuckled.

"The story got pretty good coverage in the 'faxes," he pointed out. "Especially with the Manpower connection. And I had reasons of my own for following the stories." Again something flickered deep in his eyes. Then he smiled. "And neither your father nor Lady Montaigne have been particularly . . . inconspicuous since you came home." His expression sobered. "I've always figured the newsies didn't get the whole story, but the part they did get was bloody enough. It must've been pretty bad for a kid—what, fourteen T-years old?"

"Yeah, but that wasn't what I meant." He raised both eyebrows, and she twitched her shoulders uncomfortably, unable to believe she was about to tell Paulo d'Arezzo, of all people, something she'd never even told Aikawa or Ragnhild. She drew a deep breath. "Before Daddy and . . . the others found me, and Berry and Lars, there were three men. They'd grabbed Berry and Lars before I came along. They'd raped Berry and beaten her—badly. They were going to kill her, probably pretty soon, I think. But I didn't know that when they came after *me*."

He was staring at her now, his eyes wide, and she drew another breath.

"I was already pretty good at the *Neue-Stil*," she said flatly. "I was scared—I'd just gotten away from the Scrags, and I'd known they were going to kill me if I didn't make a break. I had all the adrenaline in the galaxy pumping through me, and *nobody* was going to make me go back. So when these three came at me in the dark, I killed them."

"You killed them," he repeated.

"Yes." She met his eyes steadily. "All three of them. Broke their necks. I can still feel the bones snapping. And I felt nauseated, and sick, and wondered what kind of monster I was. The nausea comes back to me, sometimes. But I remember I'm still here, still alive. And that Berry and Lars are still alive. And I tell you this completely honestly, Paulo—I may feel nauseated, and I may wish it had never happened, but I don't feel guilty and I do feel . . . triumphant. I can look myself in the eye and tell myself I did what had to be done, without waffling, and that I'd do it again. And I think that's the question you have to ask yourself about *Anhur*. You've already said you'd do the same thing again if you had to. Doesn't that mean it's what has to be done? What you have to do to be *you*? And if that's true, why should you feel guilty?"

He looked at her silently for several seconds, then nodded slowly.

"I'm not sure there isn't a gaping hole in your logic, but that doesn't make you wrong. I'll have to think about it."

"Oh, yeah," she agreed with a wry smile. "You have to think about it, Paulo. A lot. *I* sure as hell did! And don't think for a minute I'm not having a few bad moments over what happened to *Anhur*. You'd have to be psycho not to. Just don't get all bent out of shape trying to take the blood guilt of the universe onto your shoulders."

"That's, ah, a . . . profound bit of advice."

"I know," she said cheerfully. "I'm paraphrasing what Master Tye told *me* after Old Chicago. He's a lot more profound than I am. 'Course *most* people are more profound than me, when you come down to it."

"Don't sell yourself too short."

"Sure, sure." She waved one hand in a dismissive gesture, and he shook his head with what might have been the first completely open smile she'd ever seen from him. It transformed his usual, detached expression into something totally different, and she cocked her head.

"Look," she said, feeling a returning edge of awkwardness but refusing to let it deter her, "this may not be any of my business. But why is it that you, well . . . keep to yourself so much?"

"I don't," he said, instantly, smile disappearing, and it was her turn to shake her head.

"Oh, yes, you do. And I'm beginning to realize I was

even slower than usual not to realize it isn't for the reasons I thought it was."

"I don't know what you're talking about," he said stiffly.

"I'm talking about the fact that it isn't because you think you're so much better than everyone else, after all."

"Because I think *what?*" He stared at her in such obvious consternation she had to chuckle.

"Well, that was my first thought. And I can be kind of mentally lazy sometimes. Somehow I never managed to get beyond thought number one to number two or number three." She shrugged. "I see somebody who's obviously spent that much money on biosculpt, and I automatically assume they have to have a pretty high opinion of themselves."

"Biosculpt?" He was still staring at her, and, abruptly, he laughed. It was not a cheerful sound, and he grimaced as he touched his face. "*Biosculpt?* You think that's what this is?"

"Well, yeah," she said, a bit defensively. "You're going to try to tell me it's not?"

"No," he said. "It's not biosculpt. It's genetics."

"You're kidding me!" She eyed him skeptically. "People don't come down the chute looking *that* good without a little help, Mr. d'Arezzo!"

"I didn't say it was *natural* genetics," he said, his deep, musical voice suddenly so harsh that she sat bolt upright. His eyes met hers, and the cool gray was no longer cool. It was hot, like molten quartz. And then, suddenly, shockingly, he stuck out his tongue at her.

It was a gesture she'd seen before—seen from "terrorists" like Jeremy X and scholars like Web Du Havel. But she'd never seen the genetic bar code of a genetically engineered slave on the tongue of a fellow Naval officer. He showed it to her for perhaps five seconds, then closed his mouth, gray eyes still blazing.

"If you think I'm good-looking," Paulo said bitterly, "you should have seen my mother. I never did—or not that I remember, anyway. She died when I was less than a year old. But my father's described her to me often enough. He had to describe her because he couldn't *show* me—Manpower doesn't let its slaves have pictures of each other."

Helen stared at him, and he stared back defiantly, almost hostilely.

"I didn't know," she said finally, softly.

"No reason you should've." He drew a deep breath and looked away, taut shoulders relaxing ever so slightly. "It's . . . not something I like to talk about. And," he looked back at her, "it's not as if *I* remember ever being a slave. Dad does, and sometimes it eats at him. And the fact that he and I—and my mother—were specifically *designed* to be attractive because that's what 'pleasure slaves' are supposed to be, *that* does eat at me sometimes. But he's never forgotten it was the Navy that intercepted the slaver we were on. My mother was killed in the process, but he never blamed the Navy, and neither did I. At least she died *free*, by God! That's why he took Captain d'Arezzo's name for our surname when he filed for citizenship. And why *I* joined the Navy."

"I can see that," she said, and deep inside she was kicking herself for not having recognized the signs. Surely someone who'd spent as much time with ex-slaves and the Anti-Slavery League as she had should have seen them. But why had he never dropped so much as a hint about it in her presence? He must have known Cathy Montaigne's adopted daughter would come as close to understanding as anyone who'd never been a slave could!

"Yeah," he said, almost as if he'd been reading her mind. "Yeah, I imagine you can see it, if anybody aboard the *Kitty* can. But it's not something I talk about. Not because I'm ashamed, really. But because . . . because talking about it takes away from *me*. It focuses on where I came from, the cold, sick 'businessmen' who built me and never even considered my parents or me human."

He looked out the dome, his mouth twisted.

"I guess you can also understand why I'm not quite so impressed with my 'good looks' as other people are," he said in a low, harsh voice. "Sometimes it goes a lot further than that. When you know a bunch of twisted bastards designed you to look good—to be a nice, attractive piece of meat when they put you on the block or rented you out—having people chase after you just because you look so goddamned *good* turns your stomach. It's not you they want. Not the you that lives inside you, the one that does things like this." He slapped the sketchpad's satchel. "It's *this*." He touched his face again. "This . . . *packaging*."

"I've known quite a few ex-slaves by now, Paulo," she said, keeping her voice normal, "and most of them have demons. Couldn't really be any other way, I guess. But whatever happened to them, whatever was *done* to them, and whatever those motherless bastards in Mesa may think about them, they're people, and the fact that someone else thought they were property doesn't make it true. It just means people who think they're fucking gods decided they were toys. And some toys, Paulo d'Arezzo, are very, very dangerous. In the end, that's what's going to finish Manpower off, you know. People like Jeremy X. And Web Du Havel. And you."

He looked at her suspiciously, as if he suspected she was shooting him a line, and she chuckled again, nastily.

"Paulo, for all intents and purposes, Cathy Montaigne's my mom, and you know all about Daddy. Do you think they don't have a pretty damned shrewd idea how many ex-slaves, and children of ex-slaves, have gone into the Star Kingdom's military? We get good marks for enforcing the Cherwell Convention. That attracts a lot of people—people like you—and the way we attract people like you is one reason we enforce the Cherwell Convention as well as we do. It's a reinforcing feedback loop. And then, of course, there's Torch."

"I know." He looked down, watching his right index finger draw circles on his kneecap. "That was something I really wanted to talk to you about—Torch, and your sister, I mean. But I— That is, it's been so long, and—"

"Paulo," she said, almost gently, "I've known a *lot* of ex-slaves, all right? Some of them are like Jeremy or

Web. They wear where they came from right out on their sleeves and throw it into the galaxy's teeth. It *defines* who they are, and they're ready to rip Manpower's throat out with their bare teeth. Others just want to pretend it never happened. And then there's a whole bunch who don't want to pretend it didn't happen but who do want to get on with who they are. They don't want to talk about it. They don't want people to cut them extra slack, make exceptions for them out of some sort of misplaced, third-party guilt. And they don't want pity, or to be defined by those around them in terms of their victimhood. Obviously I haven't bothered to get to know you as well as I should've, or this wouldn't be coming as such a surprise to me. But I do know you well enough to know, especially now, that you're part of that hard-headed, stiff-necked, stubborn bunch that's determined to succeed without whining, without excuses, or special allowances. The kind who're too damned stubborn for their own good and too damned stupid to know it. Sort of like Gryphon Highlanders."

She grinned at him, and to his own obvious surprise, he smiled back.

"I guess maybe we are sort of alike," he said finally. "In a way."

"And who'd've thunk it?" she replied with that same toothy grin.

"It probably wouldn't have hurt to've had this discussion earlier," he added.

"Nope, not a bit," she agreed.

"Still, I suppose it's not too late to start over," he observed.

"Not as long as you don't expect me to stop being my usual stubborn, insufferable, basically shallow self," she said.

"I don't know if all of that self-putdown is entirely fair," he said thoughtfully. "I never really thought of you as stubborn."

"As soon as I get over my unaccustomed feeling of contrition for having misjudged the motivation for that nose-in-the-air, superior attitude of yours, you'll pay for that," she assured him.

"I look forward to it with fear and trembling."

"Smartest thing you've said all day," she told him ominously, and then they both laughed.

Chapter Twenty-Nine

"And I suppose Aleksandra's going to say *this* isn't significant, either," Henri Krietzmann said sourly.

"Of course she is," Joachim Alquezar snorted.

The two of them sat on the seaside villa's terrace, gazing out across the ocean into the ashes of sunset. Stars had just begun to prick the cobalt vault above them, the remnants of a light supper lay on the table between them, a driftwood fire burned in a stone and brick outdoor fireplace with a copper hood, and Alquezar leaned back in a chaise lounge. An old-fashioned wooden match flared in the twilight, and smoke wreathed upward as he lit a cigar. Krietzmann sniffed appreciatively at the aromatic tendrils, then reached for his beer.

"I'm beginning to really, really dislike that woman," he said almost whimsically, and Alquezar chuckled.

"Even Bernardus dislikes her, whether he's willing to admit it or not," the San Miguelian said. "After all, what's not to dislike?"

It was Krietzmann's turn to snort in bitter amusement, but there was an unpalatable amount of truth in Alquezar's quip.

"I just don't understand the way her mind works," the

Dresdener admitted after a moment. "Bad enough Nordbrandt and those 'Freedom Alliance' maniacs are blowing people up and shooting them almost at random on Kornati, but at least everyone realizes they're lunatics. Westman, though." He shook his head, scowling at the memory of the reports from Montana which had arrived only that morning. "Westman is Old Establishment. He's not a marginalized hyper-nationalist politician—he's a wealthy, propertied *aristocrat*, or what passes for one on Montana. And he's smarter than Nordbrandt. She started off with a massacre; *he* started with a joke. She followed up with assassinations and scattered bombings; he followed up by blowing up the headquarters of one of the most hated off-world organizations on his homeworld . . . and still did it without killing a single soul. He's like, like—"

"Like that ante-diaspora fictional character Bernardus was talking about?"

"Yes, exactly!" Krietzmann nodded vigorously. "What was his name . . . the Crimson—No! The Scarlet Pimpernel, that was it!"

"Maybe so," Alquezar said. "But I hope you won't think me shallow for pointing out that I, and the other RTU shareholders and directors, aren't exactly amused by his choice of targets. However much debonair style and elegance he may display as he goes about his nefarious business."

"Of course not. But," Krietzmann gazed at him levelly in the light of the oil lamps burning on the table as darkness settled fully in, "I hope you don't expect me to shed a lot of tears over your losses, either."

Alquezar looked at him sharply, eyebrows lowered for just a moment, then snorted and shook his head.

"No," he said softly, and paused to draw upon his cigar. The tip glowed like a small, red planet, and he launched an almost perfect smoke ring onto the evening breeze. "No, Henri. I don't. And I shouldn't. But the fact that I feel that way, and that other people on San Miguel and Rembrandt—like Ineka Vaandrager—are going to have even stronger feelings about it, is only another proof of

Westman's shrewdness. He found a target guaranteed to polarize feelings on *both* sides of his particular political divide, and that takes brains. You say you have trouble understanding Aleksandra's take on this? Well, *I* just wish I understood how someone who's obviously as bright as Westman is could have bought into something like this in the first place. He ought to be getting behind us and pushing, not blowing us up!"

"Bright isn't the same thing as well-informed or open-minded," Krietzmann pointed out. "And everything I've been able to piece together suggests that Westman takes the Montanan fetish for stubborn individuality to previously uncharted heights—especially where Rembrandt and the RTU is concerned. Not to put too fine a point on it, he hates your guts. He doesn't really care *why* you people were so busy sewing up the Cluster's shipping. All he knows—or wants to know—is that you were doing it, that you were about as ruthless about it as you could possibly have been, and that his world's one of several which feels it was royally screwed by your so-called 'negotiating technique.'"

The Convention President shrugged.

"I don't really blame him for that. If you people had enmeshed Dresden in your cozy little empire against our will, I'd probably resent you just as much as he does. The only real difference between Westman and me is that, first, I believe Bernardus when he tells me how he first conceived of the Trade Union, and why. And, second, whatever his real motives—and yours—might have been, annexation by Manticore represents the greatest single opportunity, and not just in economic terms, which has ever fallen the entire Cluster's way. I'm willing to forgive an awful lot to capitalize on that opportunity. But Westman's too focused on the old equation to realize how completely it's been changed."

"That's basically what Bernardus said," Alquezar said. "I suppose I follow the analysis intellectually. It's just that the mindset which can ignore all of that is so far away from the universe *I* live in that I can't get my understanding wrapped around the possibility it can even exist. Not on any emotional level."

"You'd better," Krietzmann said bleakly. "In the end, I think he's more likely to succeed in killing the Constitution than Nordbrandt is."

"Really?" Alquezar cocked his head. "I don't think I disagree with you, but I'd like to hear your reasoning."

"How much reasoning's involved?" Krietzmann grunted. "Oh, all right."

He leaned back in his own chaise lounge, cradling his beer mug.

"At the moment, O my esteemed fellow conspirator, you have about sixty-two percent of the delegates in your vest pocket. And Nordbrandt's extremism's actually pushed about ten percent of that total into your corner, I'd estimate. But Tonkovic and Andre Yvernau—and Lababibi—have an iron lock on the other thirty-eight percent. They've got most of the Cluster's oligarchs, aside from the delegates you and Bernardus can deliver from the RTU planets, and Nordbrandt pushed about ten percent of *them* away from your side and into Tonkovic's pocket when she punched the economic warfare button. Most of them could care less what happens on Kornati . . . as long as it doesn't splash onto their own comfortable little preserves. But with her blowing up banks and shooting bankers, not to mention the local oligarchs, her particular version of destabilization threatens to spill over into other systems, and they're not about to sign on to anything that would, as they see it, hamper their existing political and law-enforcement machinery for dealing with neo-bolsheviks and anarchists on their own worlds. And, since it takes a two-thirds majority to vote out a draft Constitution, as long as she can hold on to the five or six percent of the delegates you still need, she can stonewall the entire process and try to extort concessions out of you. Out of *us*."

"We agree so far," Alquezar said as Krietzmann paused to sip beer. "But that still doesn't explain why you should think Westman's more dangerous than Nordbrandt."

"Oh, don't be Socratic, Joachim!" Krietzmann said a bit impatiently. "You know as well as I do that Aleksandra Tonkovic and Samiha Lababibi have absolutely no intention of actually blocking the annexation. If they do kill the Constitution, it'll be by accident, because they genuinely believe that line Aleksandra was spouting right after Nordbrandt's first attack—that Manticore won't *let* the process fail. I think they're both—especially Aleksandra—too prone to view the Star Kingdom through the distortion of their domestic political experience, but that's how they see things. At the moment, at least. But if anything ever happens to crack that sublime confidence of theirs, they'll probably stop holding out for impossible demands and settle for the best fast, down-and-dirty compromise they can get.

"But if Westman pisses off enough of *your* oligarchs—the ones you and Bernardus roped up and convinced to support the annexation in the first place—we're screwed. If he ever convinces enough of them that he and people who think like him can inflict serious damage on everything the Trade Union's managed to build up, a significant percentage of them—possibly an outright majority—would switch over to Tonkovic's side in a heartbeat, and you know it. And if they do, they'll shift the balance drastically. Not just here at the Convention, either. If Rembrandt and San Miguel and the rest of the RTU planets start opposing annexation, instead of supporting it, it's going to fail."

"You're right," Alquezar sighed after a moment. "That's another reason Bernardus went home to Rembrandt. He wanted Vaandrager out of the chairmanship before she could build a support bloc strong enough to challenge his control or get herself too deeply burrowed into the system government. Because she's exactly the sort to do what you're afraid of, especially if Westman can convince anyone outside his home system to throw in with his Montana Independence Movement."

"So," Krietzmann said, "what do we do about it?"

"If I had the answer to that one," Alquezar replied sourly, "I wouldn't need to worry about Aleksandra and Samiha. I could just wave my magic wand and fix everything!"

"Well, we're going to have to come up with *something.*"

"I know. I know." Alquezar drew on his cigar again. "I sent a memo to Baroness Medusa this afternoon, right after the dispatch boat from Montana got here. I expressed very much the same concerns you just have, and I suggested to her that it might be time for Her Majesty's official representative here to take a more . . . direct approach."

Krietzmann looked at him with a hint of uneasiness, and the San Miguelian shrugged irritably.

"It's not an ideal solution, even if she does step in, and I know it. The problem is, I think we're fresh out of ideal solutions, Henri."

" . . . not an ideal solution, Milady," Gregor O'Shaughnessy said, "but I'm afraid of the way the situation's escalating."

"Madam Governor," Rear Admiral Khumalo said heavily, "I must reiterate my concerns about becoming overly involved on the local level in the Cluster's politics."

"With all due respect, Admiral," O'Shaughnessy shot back a bit sharply, "you were the one who wanted to intervene against Nordbrandt after the first Kornati bombing in Karlovac."

"Yes, I was, Mr. O'Shaughnessy," Khumalo rumbled. "But that was rather a different situation from this, as I hope you'll admit. Nordbrandt is a killer, a murderess on a mass scale. Dropping Marines onto Kornati, assuming the local planetary government invited us to do so, to hunt down a cold-blooded, calculating killer would be one thing. Dropping Marines onto Montana to go after one of its most prominent citizens, who's apparently well on his way to becoming some sort of folk hero—or antihero—and hasn't killed a a stray dog yet, much less members of the local parliament, would be another thing entirely."

"But we're already engaged there on a day-to-day

basis," O'Shaughnessy said. "We've had a presence in the system—and, arguably—a responsibility to support President Suttles' government ever since he gave us permission to station your support ships there. For that matter, we could provide the support direct from those ships."

"Those ships are neither designed for nor capable of providing that sort of support," Khumalo said frostily. "*Ericsson* is essentially nothing more than a freighter hull wrapped around machine shops and storage for spare parts. Her entire complement's under two hundred—technicians, not combat personnel. And *Volcano*'s only an ammunition ship, with an even smaller crew. They've got military-grade impellers, compensators, and particle shielding and minimal sidewalls, but they aren't warships and they *are* totally unsuited to this sort of task. Even assuming that asking any of our ships to perform that task was a good idea. Which it isn't."

"I think—" O'Shaughnessy began, but Dame Estelle raised her hand. He closed his mouth, looking at her, and she smiled crookedly.

"In this instance, Gregor, Admiral Khumalo has a point," she said. "A very good point, in fact. There'd be substantial local popular support if we intervened in Split. So far, Nordbrandt's still at the stage of evoking far more horror, revulsion, and repugnance than widespread support. She's done a lot more damage to her own planet than Westman has, and she's made it perfectly clear she's escalated her strategy of pure terror to go after anyone who 'collaborates' with us or the elected Kornatian government on *any* issue, not just the annexation.

"She's using a sledgehammer, a brute force approach. Westman's using a rapier. So far, at least, his target selection's had exactly the opposite effect from Nordbrandt's. As far as I can see, there's no immediate danger of his turning around Montana's support for the annexation, but he's more likely to have that effect in the long run than she is. More to the point, from the perspective of the Convention, he's more likely to generate a significant shift in the balance of power between Alquezar's Constitutional

Unionists and Tonkovic's Constitutional Liberals. But from our *tactical* perspective, the most significant difference between him and Nordbrandt is that we're the air cav, rushing to the rescue, if we go after her, whereas we become the sinister foreign conquerors on Montana if we intervene in their local affairs to go after *him* and make even the tiniest mistake."

"But, Milady," O'Shaughnessy protested respectfully, "I'm afraid we'll be making a mistake anyway, and not a tiny one, if we *don't* take action in regard to Montana."

"Personally," Khumalo said, "I'm still in favor of dropping a battalion or so of Marines on Nordbrandt's head. Let's go in fast and hard, yank her up, and hand her worthless, murderous ass to the Kornatian courts. Let them execute her after a scrupulously fair trial before a jury of her fellow citizens—God knows they've already got enough evidence to hang her two or three times! All we'd do would be to apprehend her, then stand aside and let the local legal establishment do its job. As you say, she's hardly a poster girl for the orderly political process on Kornati, and this steady expansion of her 'manifesto' shows a degree of creeping extremism that comes pretty damned close to classic megalomania. She's starting to remind me of Cordelia Ransom!"

He snorted, and several of his listeners, including Dame Estelle Matsuko, winced at the all too apt comparison.

"Dispose of her, first, and we free ourselves to go after Westman in the most effective manner and without distractions. And as a bonus, when we do, we'll already have buffed up our halo by helping take out someone who's obviously a stone-cold terrorist and assassin."

"It's tempting, Admiral," the Provisional Governor replied. "Believe me, it's *very* tempting. But I'm still leery of sending in our own troops, especially in that kind of strength. The domestic political situation is . . . complex, and as far as we can tell from here, very much in a state of flux. The only thing I can think of that could begin to legitimize Nordbrandt's efforts in the eyes of a significant percentage of the Kornatian public would be for us to go after her in a way that validates her charges about her own government's corruption and our imperial pretensions. If we appear to be supporting a suppressive regime simply because its opposition doesn't want to be 'taken over' by the Star Kingdom, we could lose any moral high ground in a hurry."

"With all due respect, Madam Governor," Khumalo said, deliberately using the same formula O'Shaughnessy had, "if we can't act on Kornati, where *can* we act? This is a clear-cut, unambiguous example of terrorism against the legally elected government of a sovereign planet. Mr. Westman, so far, has only stolen a few hundred thousand dollars' worth of Manticoran property, embarrassed a dozen or so of our nationals, and destroyed several hundred million dollars worth of private property, none of which was owned by his own government or any citizen of his planet. And, I repeat, so far he's been extraordinarily careful not to kill or even injure *anyone*."

"You're right." Medusa really wished she could disagree. She had an uncomfortable suspicion that she wanted to do that because her private estimate of Khumalo was so low. Which, she admitted as she considered his analysis, might have been just a bit unfair of her.

"I think," she said, looking around the conference table at O'Shaughnessy, Khumalo, Captain Shoupe, Commander Chandler, and Colonel Oliver Gray, the commander of her own Marine contingent, "we're all at least in agreement that, at the moment, the two star systems which present actual threats to the annexation and to the security of the Constitutional Convention are Montana and Split?"

"I'm sure we all agree on that much, Milady," O'Shaughnessy said. "I'd like to point out one additional difference between Westman and Nordbrandt, however."

"Go ahead," she invited.

"All reports from Split," her intelligence chief said, letting his eyes travel around the conference table, "indicate that, despite all the damage she's done, Nordbrandt's still operating effectively on a logistical shoestring. She's using civilian small arms and explosives, not military-grade weapons, and so far there's no indication she possesses sophisticated communications or antisurveillance gear. And, frankly, I think one reason she's launched this campaign of assassination against local landowners and industrialists is that she doesn't have the military wherewithal to take on really hard targets. She got away with her initial attack because of lengthy, meticulous preplanning and because no one saw it coming, and most of her successful bombing attacks since have been possible only because the local authorities are still gearing up to go after her and because she's chosen targets on the basis of their vulnerability, not their importance. She's going after the ones she *can* hit, not necessarily the ones she'd *like* to hit.

"Westman's a whole different breed of 'cat. He's obviously much better funded, and the Montanan government's managed to trace at least one purchase of Solarian coms and encryption software he made before going underground. They think he's acquired at least some off-world military supplies, as well. He's definitely used military-grade explosives in at least one strike, and according to our local Manticoran surveyors, the guerrillas he deployed for his first attack were armed with what appear to have been fairly modern Solly military small arms. In addition, his two operations to date have displayed an impressive degree of intelligence-gathering capacity and planning capability, and he's demonstrated he most certainly *can* hit hard targets.

"Nordbrandt and the FAK probably took weeks to plan that first bombing attack. Westman and his Montana Independence Movement mounted their first operation within twelve hours of the time our surveyors went into the field. Not even *our* people knew where they were going until they actually started out, so there's no way he could have known in advance, either. Which means he put the entire thing together on the fly, and carried it off faultlessly, with a maximum of twelve hours of planning time. And when he went after the RTU's facilities, he slid right through the kind of security Nordbrandt's been very careful to stay well clear of to hit a pinpoint target with devastating effectiveness. Not only is he using a scalpel instead of a chainsaw, but he's using it much, much more effectively than she is."

"So you're arguing," Dame Estelle said, "that even if Nordbrandt's killing more people and wreaking more general destruction, Westman's the more dangerous, harder to suppress of the two threats?"

"More or less. But what I was really trying to say, Milady, is that while I'm willing to concede Nordbrandt is the more appropriate target *at the moment*, in the long run, we're going to have to deal with both of them, and the sooner the better in either case. I'd really prefer not to see us get bogged down or locked into a focus or concentration on the FAK that distracts us from acting against the MIM at the earliest possible moment. And I think it's essential to come up with strategies against both threats."

"I see." Baroness Medusa leaned back, steepling her fingers across her midsection, and let her chair rock gently while she pondered. Both Khumalo and O'Shaughnessy had valid points. But given her severely limited resources, how could she deal with either of them, far less both?

Silence stretched out for several minutes while her subordinates watched her think. Then her eyes narrowed. She considered possibilities and options for a few more moments, then let her chair come back upright with an air of finality.

"Very well," she said crisply. "Admiral, your point about Kornati is well taken. I'm not sure we have the resources to actually swoop in and scoop Nordbrandt out of the woodwork for the local authorities, but Split's definitely the place for us to make our presence known and offer direct cooperation to the local government and its law-enforcement agencies. At the same time, I feel a definite lack of firsthand, reliable analysis on the situation there. Not just where the terrorist threat's concerned, but on several fronts. That being the case, I want a trustworthy set of eyes on the ground. Someone who can give us a clear, accurate idea of exactly what's going on and how best to deal with it. And I want a presence in the system to back him up—an impressive one."

"Milady?" Khumalo said cautiously, when she paused.

"I want *Hexapuma*."

"Madam Governor," the rear admiral began in instant, automatic protest, "*Hexapuma*'s the most powerful, most modern unit I have. I can't in good conscience recommend diverting her from her current duties to act as a local policeman in Split."

"I don't recall asking you to recommend anything, Admiral," the baroness observed, and Khumalo's dark face flushed.

"No, Ma'am," he said stiffly. "But I am the station commander. The deployment of my assets is *my* responsibility."

He stopped short of pointing out that his use of the verb "recommend" had been an act of courtesy on his part. Along with the responsibility for the deployment of his units came the legal right to decide what those deployments ought to be, regardless of anyone else's ideas. But courteous or not, he obviously intended to be stubborn about it, and Medusa locked eyes with him for a moment, then nodded in grudging respect for his moral courage . . . if that was what it was.

"Very well, Admiral," she said, dropping back from openly confronting her military commander, "what would you recommend?"

"We don't need *Hexapuma* for this particular operation, Madam Governor," he said, still very formally. "Any of our older units could perform the same function. If we feel a cruiser's necessary for reasons of prestige, Captain Anders' *Warlock* could handle the assignment equally well. And using an older unit would allow me to retain *Hexapuma* where she'll be most effective against pirates or other external threats. Moreover, *Warlock* has a larger Marine detachment than *Hexapuma*, and Captain Anders has been in the Cluster for almost seven months, substantially longer than Captain Terekhov. As such, he's had much more opportunity to develop a feel for local political nuances."

O'Shaughnessy stirred in his seat, but a quick glance from the Provisional Governor kept his mouth shut on whatever he'd been about to say. Then she looked back at Khumalo.

"I see your logic, Admiral. But, forgive me, wouldn't it be fair to say that, barring a direct attack by the Solarian League or some incredibly long-range invasion by the Republic of Haven, even your older units ought to be markedly superior to anything they're likely to meet? Specifically, exactly what sort of pirate do you anticipate meeting out here that's so dangerous only a ship as powerful as *Hexapuma* could reasonably expect to defeat it?"

"Well," Khumalo said slowly, his expression manifestly unhappy, "if you put it that way, Milady, it does sound unlikely. Although," he added, rallying gamely, "it's a naval officer's responsibility to plan for the unlikely, as well as the likely."

"Of course," she agreed. "But, to continue, you also mentioned the fact that Captain Anders has been in the Cluster longer than Captain Terekhov has. That's certainly true, and the point clearly has merit. However, meaning no disrespect whatever to Captain Anders, my impression of Captain Terekhov is that he has considerably more facility when it comes to 'thinking outside the box.' In this sort of situation, I rather think mental flexibility and the willingness to consider . . . unconventional realities, shall we say?—outweigh simple time on station. And while I certainly respect Captain Anders, I think we might also agree that Captain Terekhov's Foreign Office experience could be rather useful to us in the present circumstances."

Khumalo's eyes flickered. He seemed about to say something, but then visibly restrained himself, and she hid a thin, unamused smile. She'd wondered how much it bothered him to have a senior subordinate whose diplomatic experience vastly exceeded his own. The answer, apparently, was that it bothered him quite a lot.

Which is just too bad for him, she thought coldly. *I need Terekhov, and I mean to have him.*

"As to the fact that *Warlock* has a larger Marine detachment," she continued aloud, "I'm not at all convinced this is a situation in which simple numbers can provide a solution. It isn't the total number of troops which can be deployed, not given the difference between our technical capabilities and those of the locals. It's the *effectiveness* with which our Marines can be deployed that's going to matter, and, again, with no disrespect to Captain Anders, I have a higher degree of confidence in Captain Terekhov's ability to employ his forces effectively."

She paused and smiled pleasantly at the rear admiral. He looked back at her, his expression set, and she cocked her head to one side.

"Finally," she continued, "it's my understanding that after Captain Saunders, Terekhov is your senior ranking officer. Since I scarcely believe it would be appropriate to transfer *Hercules* to Split, that means he's the most senior officer you could send, doesn't it?"

"Yes, Ma'am," Khumalo admitted in a rather tight voice.

"Well, under the circumstances, I believe it would be most appropriate to assign this responsibility to the most senior officer we have available. Whoever we send is going to be dealing with the highest levels of the Kornatian and Montanan governments. Both from the perspective of courtesy and proving to them that we take this situation seriously, we ought to send them an officer senior enough to command their respect while demonstrating our own."

Khumalo said nothing for a second or two. Legally, Baroness Medusa couldn't directly order him to send *Hexapuma* to Split or Montana. He was the Talbott Station commander. The Provisional Governor might request or suggest. She could assign specific tasks, require him to perform specific duties. But the actual management of the military resources under his command when it came to accomplishing those tasks or duties was his affair. He was the one with the legal authority to employ those units as *he* felt best.

But any station commander who blithely ignored the desires of his civilian superior was almost as big an idiot as one who acquiesced in those desires against his better judgment. And while Khumalo continued to feel this particular mission would scarcely represent the most effective employment for HMS *Hexapuma*, the Provisional Governor had made several telling points. Points which would loom large if he chose to ignore them and his superiors in the current Admiralty decided to question his own judgment.

"Very well, Madam Governor," he said, unable to totally keep an edge of harshness out of his tone. "I'm not certain I'm fully convinced, but you've made several valid arguments. More to the point, perhaps, you're Her Majesty's direct political and administrative representative here in the Cluster. As such, it's clearly the responsibility and duty of Her Majesty's Navy to aid and assist you in any way possible, including the provision of the military support you feel would be most appropriate in support of your overriding mission. I'll recall *Hexapuma* and place her at your disposal for this operation."

"Thank you, Admiral," Dame Estelle said, with a gracious smile warm enough that Khumalo actually found himself smiling back.

"Where, precisely, is *Hexapuma* at the moment?" she asked.

"Nuncio, Milady," Captain Shoupe said promptly, like the excellent staff officer she was. She glanced at Khumalo from the corner of one eye but kept her attention focused on the Provisional Governor. "Assuming Captain Terekhov adheres to his projected schedule, he'll be there for another day or so. Of course, something could've come up to delay his departure. If nothing has, however, he should be departing for Celebrant within the next twenty-four to forty-eight standard-hours. His voyage time from Nuncio to Celebrant should be about ten and a half T-days. We'd have to dispatch couriers to both systems to ensure that he got the recall order."

"But he'd most probably be in Celebrant when he received it?"

"Yes, Milady. He would."

"Good!" Dame Estelle said, with an enthusiasm which brought a puzzled expression to Rear Admiral Khumalo's face. She smiled broadly at him. "If he starts from Celebrant," she said, "it would scarcely be out of his way at all to drop by Rembrandt on the way to Split, now would it?"

Chapter Thirty

"Pontifex Traffic Control, this is *Hexapuma*, requesting clearance to depart planetary parking orbit."

"*Hexapuma*, this is Commodore Karlberg," an unexpected voice replied to Lieutenant Commander Nagchaudhuri's routine hail instead of the duty traffic controller. "You are clear to depart Pontifex orbit, with our profound thanks. We won't forget what you people did for us. Good luck, and good hunting."

Nagchaudhuri glanced at Captain Terekhov, seated in his command chair at the center of *Hexapuma*'s bridge. Terekhov looked back at him, then pressed a stud on the arm of his chair.

"I'm glad we could help, Commodore," he told the Nuncian Navy's commanding officer. "I hope you won't have any other unpleasant visitors, but if anything untoward does turn up, you ought to be seeing another Queen's ship in the next few weeks. In the meantime, thank you for the good wishes."

"You earned them, Captain. Oh, and we'll keep a real close eye on your prisoners until the Provisional Governor decides exactly what she wants to do with them."

"Thank you, Sir. I never doubted you would. Terekhov, clear."

"Least we can do for you, Captain. Karlberg, clear."

Terekhov nodded to Nagchaudhuri, who closed down the circuit, then turned his command chair to face Lieutenant Commander Wright.

"All right, Commander. We've got clearance, so why don't we just step along smartly now?"

"Aye, aye, Sir." The Astrogator grinned and looked at Senior Chief Clary. "Helm, execute planned orbital departure maneuver."

"Aye, aye, Sir. Breaking orbit now," Clary acknowledged, and *Hexapuma* raised her nose and moved ahead at a steady one hundred gravities' acceleration.

"Maintain present accel until Point Able," Wright directed. "Then come to zero-zero-three by two-seven-niner at five hundred gravities."

"Maintain current acceleration to Point Able, then alter to zero-zero-three by two-seven-niner at five-zero-zero gravities, aye, Sir," Clary replied, and Terekhov tipped his command chair back in profound satisfaction as his ship accelerated slowly clear of Pontifex near-space traffic. Seventy-five light-years to Celebrant, he thought. Ten and half days for the rest of the universe, or a little over seven by *Hexapuma*'s internal clocks. The downtime the voyage offered would be welcomed by everyone on board.

Hexapuma's twelve days in Nuncio had been as productive as they had been hectically busy. Two ex-Peep pirate vessels destroyed or captured, *Emerald Dawn* retaken (even if she was going to require the lengthy services of a well equipped repair ship before she ever left Nuncio again), and the meticulous updating of the Navy's astrography on the Nuncio System. President Adolfsson's government and citizens had made their enthusiastic approval of *Hexapuma*'s efforts on their behalf clear, and he and his crew could depart secure in the knowledge that this star system, at least, harbored no reservations about the desirability of inclusion in the Star Kingdom.

And the prize money for retaking Emerald Dawn—*not*

to mention the head money for the "pirates" we killed or captured—doesn't particularly depress our people, either.

But most importantly of all, in Terekhov's view of the universe, *Hexapuma*'s crew was no longer an unknown quantity. And it was clear that same crew no longer harbored any reservations, if it ever had, about the competency of its captain. That was worth quite a lot, he told himself. Quite a lot, indeed.

"Approaching Point Able," Senior Chief Clary announced.

"Very well, Helm," he acknowledged, and he smiled.

"Over there!"

Captain Barto Jezic, Kornatian National Police, looked up in irritation as the harshly whispered warning came over the com.

"This is Team Leader!" he snapped into his own boom mike. "Who the hell said that, and where the hell are you? Over."

There was a moment of intense silence. Every one of Jezic's people recognized that tone of voice. It was rather famous throughout the entire KNP, in fact. Someone was about to sprout a brand new anal orifice, unless he was very, very lucky.

"Uh, sorry, Team Leader," the hapless focus of his wrath said after a moment. "This is Blue Three. Second story of Main Admin, eastern side. I have movement on the south side of Macek Avenue. Five—no, correction, *seven*—human heat sources. Over."

"That's better, Blue Three," Jezic growled, more than a little mollified by Blue Three's prompt clarification. Well, that, and the fact that it looked as if their information had been accurate, after all.

"All units," the captain continued, "Team Leader. Stand by to execute. Remember, damn it, we need *prisoners*, this time, not just bodies! Team Leader, clear."

He eased forward from his own position, fifty meters from his official command post, and flipped his own visor down over his eyes. He would cheerfully have traded two fingers from his left hand for really modern gear, but what he had would have to do. At least it had decent light-gathering capabilities and infrared, which meant he didn't have to go to active sensors to sweep Macek Avenue himself.

There they were! He felt the adrenaline spike and forced himself to inhale deeply. He was astonished to find his hands trembling on his rifle—not in fear, but in anticipation . . . and raw fury. He didn't like that. The KNP's senior SWAT officer was supposed to be a professional. But the last thirty days of Agnes Nordbrandt's murderous campaign had eroded that professionalism more than he cared to admit.

He waited a few heartbeats, until he felt confident he could keep his voice crisp, unshadowed by his sudden, blazing hatred, then keyed his com again.

"Blue One, Team Leader."

"Blue One, go," Lieutenant Aranka Budak's voice came back over his headset.

"Blue One, they're heading towards your position in the parking garage. You're authorized to take them as soon as all seven identified hostiles cross the perimeter of your engagement zone. ROE Bravo apply. Acknowledge."

"Team Leader, Blue One is authorized to take seven—repeat, *seven*—hostiles into custody as soon as all have crossed my zone perimeter. Rules of Engagement Bravo are in effect. Blue One, over."

Jezic grunted in satisfaction. He didn't know how Intelligence had broken FAK's security on this one. He had his suspicions, which included the probable serious violation of someone's guarantee against self-incrimination. No doubt the courts would eventually have something severe to say about that, and Jezic wouldn't object when they did. He wasn't particularly delighted by the notion that his own organization might be resorting to that sort of interrogation technique. There were times when you simply *had* to have the information—sometimes when innocent lives were on the line—and he wouldn't shed any tears for the tender sensibilities of terrorist murderers. But once any police force started cutting that kind of corner, it was only a matter of time before people who *weren't* terrorists found themselves subject to the same abuses. Worse, each time it happened, it got easier to justify doing it again, for progressively less vital reasons. And enough of that could make Nordbrandt's accusations into ugly truths.

But however the information had been developed, he was delighted to have it, and he'd studied it as intensively as time had permitted. If only their . . . informant was also right about who was *leading* this attack!

He pushed that thought down—again—and watched the developing situation in silence. He'd hoped the bastards would come in along Macek. That was why he'd put Aranka on that flank. Lieutenant Budak and her special weapons squad were the best he had—in his opinion, the best the entire National Police had. If he couldn't be out on the flank himself, there was no one else on Kornati that he would have preferred to see in his place.

Juras Divkovic slipped through the rainy shadows as quietly as the night breeze.

Unlike some of Agnes Nordbrandt's original recruits, Divkovic had never doubted there would be blood in the streets before it was all over. The whole system was so rotten, so riddled with corruption, grafters, self-seeking, dishonest politicians, all controlled by the filthy money of people like that traitor Tonkovic, that it couldn't be any other way. Some of Nordbrandt's initial supporters hadn't shared that hard awareness. They'd talked boldly enough about the "people in arms" and the "armed struggle," but they hadn't really *meant* it. They were theorists, effete dilettantes—silly upperclass poseurs afraid, when it came right down to it, of getting a little blood on their hands. Or risking their own precious hides.

It was a good thing Nordbrandt had insisted on a cellular organization from the outset. Without it, he was certain, the whiners and fairweather "activists" would have sold the entire FAK leadership to the collaborationists running Kornati just to save their own asses. But they couldn't betray people they didn't know, and Nordbrandt had been smart enough to create two totally separate organizations. One composed of the big talkers with the testicles of timid gnats who could be counted on for financial contributions, political activism, agitation and demonstrations, but not for the Movement's *real* work. And a second, composed of people like Divkovic, who'd known from the outset what would have to be done and demonstrated their willingness to do it. The people who had begun building the infrastructure the FAK required years before the time had come for open conflict.

Most of the first organization had either gone to ground, hiding from both sides, or, worse, turned themselves into eager informants in a desperate attempt to disassociate themselves from the FAK's armed campaign. Some had even succeeded, but none of them were any great loss. In fact, their disappearance pleased Divkovic. None of them had actually known anything useful about *his* side of the FAK, so the self-serving informants could do no real damage to operations. And their defection got them out of his way, reduced the threat of future security breaches . . . and left the direction of the Movement firmly in the hands of people like Divkovic himself. Now that there was no longer any need for Nordbrandt to jolly the weak sisters along, the Movement had rolled up its sleeves and gotten down to the serious business of kicking the accursed Manties out of Split and restructuring Kornati.

He held up his left hand, halting his strike group, and went down on one knee behind a trash barrel. He leveled his binoculars across it, gazing out over the wide boulevard at the Treasury Department compound, fifteen blocks from the Nemanja Building. This was the deepest they'd struck into Karlovac itself since the attack on the Parliament Building, and Divkovic was determined to make it a success. The darkness and misty rain were on his side, as was the lateness of the hour, but none of it helped visibility, and he spared a moment to wish his people had equipment as good as the gear Tonkovic and her flunkies were able to provide to their so-called "Police."

They didn't, unfortunately, although they'd at least gotten their hands on a few modern weapons. Divkovic himself carried a pulse rifle, 'liberated' from the Rendulic police arsenal in one of the Movement's early attacks. Such weapons were too expensive for most civilians—only someone with the resources of the government could afford them—which was why most of his people were still armed with chemical-powered weapons. Just like most of their equipment, they had to make do with what they could get their hands on, and despite their revolutionary ardor, that put them at a severe disadvantage. Still, his old-fashioned, pure optic binoculars were enough to bring the lighted window on the fifth floor of the main administration building into sharp focus. He couldn't see much in the way of details, but the conference room blazed with light, despite the hour.

That was the Movement's handiwork, he thought with vengeful satisfaction. The tremors their strikes were sending through Kornati's corrupt economy and political structure had panicked the pigs rooting around in the public trough. Now Treasury Secretary Grabovac had summoned her flunkies to an emergency meeting in her frantic efforts to shore up the Establishment's sagging house of cards. It was fitting that they should meet in the dark of night, like maggots crawling through the belly of a rotting carcass . . . and that Grabovac and her bootlicking stooges had decided to trust in the secrecy of their meeting time rather than bolstering their normal night security forces.

Thoughts of security forces brought his glasses around in another long, slow scan of the grounds. This Treasury compound was usually a secondary, or even tertiary, management node. Its three buildings and central parking garage were an isolated government enclave in one of the poorer sections of the capital that thrust in towards its center, and it was used mainly for routine record storage and clerical functions. That was one reason it had been chosen for tonight's meeting—because no one had believed the Movement would suspect that anything important would take place in such a low-security, low-level facility.

According to their intelligence, the only on-site security was internal. Little more than watchmen, although they'd been issued weapons and ammunition since the FAK began operations. Most of them were overaged, out-of-shape people who should already have been drawing pensions—the sort who'd be like sheep before the wolves of his own well-trained, motivated people. The fact that, look though he might, he couldn't see a single one of them walking the outside perimeter of the compound, rain or no rain, said volumes about their preparedness, he thought with grim amusement.

Grabovac's personal security team would be a more serious proposition. But according to their information, it consisted of only three men, and they'd be in or directly outside the conference room itself.

He returned his attention to the conference room window one last time and saw a blur, a shifting shadow against the window, as someone moved inside the room as if to demonstrate that it was occupied, just as it was supposed to be. He inhaled in satisfaction, lowered the binoculars, and cased them with deliberate movements. Then he turned to his second in command, whom he knew only as "Tyrannicide."

"All right," he breathed in a throaty whisper, scarcely louder than the rainy wind. "They're in the conference room, just like they're supposed to be. Let's go."

Tyrannicide nodded. He rose, cradling his pulse rifle—liberated in the same raid as Divkovic's—in his arms, and beckoned to the other two men of his section. All three started directly across the avenue towards the fire escape Divkovic had selected as the secondary point of entry, floating through the night's misty ambiguity like vague spirits. Karlovac City's street lighting had never been more than barely adequate; on nights like this, it was little more than a gesture towards providing any kind of visibility.

Which was good, Divkovic thought, watching them go for a moment. Then he turned and led his own four-person section towards the parking garage. The conference room was less than ten meters down the hall from the garage's fifth-floor access door, and his smile was ugly as he visualized the expressions of the doomed administrative underlings summoned to their emergency meeting.

"Shit!"

Jezic was glad he hadn't keyed his mike as the heartfelt expletive escaped. So much for comprehensive intelligence!

He watched what was supposed to have been a single, unified FAK strike team split into two sections and thought furiously. They might not be proceeding exactly as Intelligence had predicted, but they *were* here. Which meant news of the Treasury Department's emergency, secret meeting had leaked to them, exactly as the KNP had feared. That was fairly ugly confirmation that their own internal security procedures had been compromised, although the fact that the attack hadn't been canceled when the meeting was moved elsewhere and the trap was set in its place probably indicated the leak was somewhere on the Treasury side. And from one of the less senior day-workers, at that. Someone who hadn't been in the loop when the last-minute cancellation had been decided upon.

But that could be left for later. His problem was that two separate forces were going to run into different parts of his own teams, and do so at different times. The three people headed for the far end of the Admin Building were almost certainly planning to use one of the exterior fire escapes to gain access to the fifth floor as one prong of a pincer attack on the conference room. That was going to take them directly into his Red Team. And given how much farther they'd have to go, they were probably going to run into Red Team at least four or five minutes before the parking garage team crossed Aranka Budak's third-floor perimeter. As soon as anyone challenged them or demanded their surrender, the alarm would be raised, at which point the *other* group of terrorists would turn around and try to vanish. Given the damnable efficiency with which they'd been using storm drains, sewers, service conduits, and all the other various underground connections of Karlovac to escape after launching their attacks, it was possible—although not, in his opinion, bloody likely—that they'd succeed in disappearing, too.

That would be bad enough under any circumstances, but if Nordbrandt really was present tonight herself . . .

"Red One, Team Leader," he rasped over the com. "Hold off as long as you can! I want the garage team as far into Blue One's zone as possible. Team Leader, over."

"Team Leader, Red One copies," Sergeant Slavko Maksimovac said. "I'll hold as long as I can, Barto, but they're coming right down my throat. Red One, over."

Jezic was about to reply when everything began happening at once.

Divkovic didn't know what warned him. Maybe it was simply the instincts of a predator. Or perhaps it was something else—an injudicious movement by one of Lieutenant Budak's people, or a dull gleam of reflected light off something that shouldn't have been there. It could even have been nothing at all, nothing but an overactive imagination that, just this once, was right.

Whatever it was, it brought the muzzle of his pulse rifle snapping up to the ready position, and he froze where he was, at the foot of the parking garage ramp. The dark-haired woman behind him almost ran into him, and he hissed at her to move to his left. The next member of the team fanned out to the right, and Divkovic stood motionless, nostrils flared, eyes probing the poorly illuminated garage.

He hesitated for less than three seconds, then made his decision and signaled for his section of the strike team to withdraw. He hated to abort the mission, especially when he had no means of communication with Tyrannicide's people. But both parts of the operation had been planned to succeed on their own, if necessary. So if he was wrong, all it meant was that Tyrannicide's team would carry through the attack without him, while if his suddenly jangling suspicions were justified, continuing could lead his entire cell straight into disaster.

"Oh, *crap*!" Barto Jezic snarled in bitter frustration as the terrorists' parking garage prong stopped where it was, fanned out briefly, and then began withdrawing. He'd really wanted prisoners, especially if— But there was no time to think about that now, and it was still possible . . .

"All units, Team Leader!" he barked. "Able Zulu. *Able Zulu!*"

Juras Divkovic cursed vilely as the multimillion-candlepower searchlights on top of the main administration building snapped to blinding, brilliant life. Their dazzling beams lanced out through the misty rain, slamming into his people's retinas like fists. The sudden shock effect was literally stunning, and his entire team froze.

"This is Captain Barto Jezic, National Police!" a hugely amplified voice crashed out. "You are under our guns! Surrender or die!"

Someone behind Divkovic whimpered, and the terrorist cell leader bared his teeth in a vicious snarl. His brain raced, trying to consider too many things at once. The bastards had *known* they were coming. That was the only way those lights could have been waiting in position. But he hadn't seen a sign of anyone on the way in. Did that mean his planned escape route was still clear? Or did it mean he simply hadn't seen whoever was prepared to block it? Or—

"You're running out of time!" the grayback's amplified voice roared. "Drop your weapons and surrender—*now!*"

Divkovic hesitated, wavering. It was, he suddenly discovered, far easier to be totally committed when it was a matter of killing someone *else*. The abrupt discovery that he was afraid to die filled him with a sudden, towering rage—a fury directed as much at his own previously unsuspected weakness as at the establishment thugs who'd ambushed him.

"What do we—?" the woman behind him began, and Divkovic's anger peaked. He whipped around towards her, lips parted to snarl his rage at her.

The sudden movement of the lead terrorist, the rise of his weapon, had inspired—or terrified—two of his followers. They flung themselves to the sides, going prone. And then Jezic saw the muzzle flashes of chemical-powered rifles as they opened fire on the searchlights.

There was no one on the building's roof. The lights were remotely controlled, although the terrorists had no way of knowing that. But opening fire at all was a fatal mistake. Under Able Zulu, the Rules of Engagement changed.

"Blue Team, Blue One!" Aranka Budak snapped over the com. *"Take them!"*

Juras Divkovic had one fleeting moment to realize what was happening. An instant to recognize that his unsuspected cowardice, if that was what it was, didn't matter. Wasn't going to have the chance to seduce him into surrender—and survival—after all.

He was fleetingly aware of more fire, from Tyrannicide's direction. Had Tyrannicide's people opened fire when his idiots did? Or had it been more grays? Or—?

"Cease fi—" he began to bellow, out of some pointless instinct.

Barto Jezic saw it happening, and there was nothing he could do to stop it. For that matter, he wasn't even certain he would have tried to stop it if he'd been able to. Budak's command was in policy and in accordance with the Rules of Engagement currently in force.

It was exactly the correct response, however final it might have been.

A tornado of pulser fire slammed back at Divkovic and his companions. The pulse rifles were bad enough, but there were two old-fashioned, multibarreled bulky miniguns, as well. Slower-firing and less destructive than a tribarrel they might have been, but a thousand rounds per minute, even from an obsolete nitrocellulose weapon, were quite sufficient to turn a human body into a finely suspended red mist.

The shattering explosion when something hit the detonator of the commercial explosives tucked away inside one of the terrorist's backpacks was almost anticlimactic.

Jezic swore in mingled frustration and satisfaction. He really had wanted those people alive. But he was too honest with himself to pretend he didn't feel a deep, vicious sense of triumph as his people took the terrorists down.

The mingled snarl of pulser fire, civilian-made rifles, and minigun thunder from the direction of Sergeant Maksimovac's Red Team ended as abruptly as Aranka's fire had, and Jezic swore again, then relaxed and shrugged his shoulders.

He'd accomplished his primary goal by stopping the attack dead in its tracks, he reminded himself. And if there was enough left down there for the forensic specialists, he might find out he'd done quite a bit better than that. . . .

"You're joking!" Vulk Rajkovic looked at Colonel Brigita Basaricek's face on his com screen. The National Police's commanding officer was a tall, hawk-faced woman with dark hair and eyes in the KNP's pearl-gray tunic. At the moment, her eyes gleamed, although her expression remained guarded, as though she were unwilling to believe her own news.

"The attack itself was stopped dead, Mr. Vice President," she said. "There's no question that every one of the terrorists was killed. As to the other, well, the forensic people don't have a lot to work with. Apparently she was personally carrying one of the explosive charges they'd planned to use to level the garage on their way out."

"But you think it was actually her?" Rajkovic pressed.

"Mr. Vice President, I think there's a good chance of it," Basaricek replied after a momentary hesitation. "Again, I have to stress that forensics doesn't have much. But the information we had before the attack was that it was under the operational control of the man they called Icepick, but that Nordbrandt herself was in overall command. The fact that Secretary Grabovac was supposed to be there in person apparently made the meeting important enough for her to decide it justified her own presence. You know how she's insisted on that 'lead from the front' image from the beginning."

She paused until Rajkovic nodded. Much as he'd come to hate and loathe Agnes Nordbrandt, no one had ever called her a coward. And, much as he hated to admit it, her habit of personally accompanying certain especially high profile attacks had earned her a grudging respect—though certainly not admiration—from some segments of the planetary press. He wasn't certain if she insisted on doing that for exactly that reason, or if it was because of her own fanaticism, and it didn't matter. Particularly not if Basaricek's information was correct.

"At any rate, we've positively identified 'Icepick' among the dead," the KNP's commander continued. "We'd already known he was one of her most senior action cell leaders. Now that we've managed to run his fingerprints, we can ID him as one Juras Divkovic. His father was killed—apparently by some of my own people, I'm sorry to say, though it might have been some of the militia we were forced to call out—when the Odak factory riots got out of hand eight years ago. From everything I've seen on him and his family, it's hard to blame him for being bitter as hell, and he's got two brothers. Both of them disappeared right after the attack on the Nemanja Building, just like 'Icepick,' so I'm afraid we may be running into them sometime soon, as well.

"In addition to him, however, we also recovered the bodies—or partial remains, at least—of six other people. One of them was female and, from the low-light surveillance footage Lieutenant Budak's people got just before it all fell into the crapper, looked an awful lot like Nordbrandt. As I say, she was carrying a heavy explosive charge which detonated during the firefight, so the biggest pieces of her body we've been able to recover aren't much. What we have is being transported to our central forensics lab for examination, but it's not like we have the sort of technology someone like the Star Kingdom or the Sollies has, and it was a powerful explosion. It's going to take us days or even weeks just to sort out which body parts go together. We may never be able to say for certain that it was or wasn't her."

"But if it was . . ." Rajkovic's voice trailed off as he contemplated the devastating impact Nordbrandt's death would have on the FAK. It was unlikely to stop the lunatics she'd set in motion in their tracks, but it would certainly be a body blow.

"All right," he said, shaking himself back to the present. "Do the best you can to confirm that one way or the other, Colonel. And in the meantime, we need to make sure this doesn't hit the press. The last thing we need is for it to look as if we've made unfounded claims that she's dead if it turns out later that she actually isn't!"

"Ah, Sir, that may be a problem."

"Problem?" Rajkovic's tone sharpened, and the colonel's mouth twitched unhappily.

"Mr. Vice President, the gunfire didn't last long, but it was quite . . . noticeable," she said. "And the explosion was even more so. All the commotion attracted a lot of attention, including the press. At least three news teams got there even before the forensics vans. Our people were under orders to keep their mouths shut and refer all inquiries to the official public information officers, of course. Unfortunately, one of the questions our PIO was asked by a reporter was whether or not he could *confirm* Nordbrandt was among the dead. So it looks to me like someone leaked the possibility to them when they first hit the scene."

She grimaced again, more strongly, and shook her head.

"I'm sorry, Sir. I know how sensitive this information is, and how important it was to keep it under wraps until we did have confirmation. But it appears it's already gotten out. The only people who could've leaked it are all KNP personnel, and if I can find out who it was, I assure you they'll be hearing directly from me about it, but the damage is already done, I'm afraid."

"I see." Rajkovic frowned, then shrugged. "Done is done, Colonel. If you can find out who did it, give him—or her—a few extra kicks from me, but you're right. We can't shove the cat back into the bag. We'll just have to be as forthcoming as we can while making it clear we don't *have* any confirmation for them. Not that they'll pay the least attention to us," he predicted with a sigh.

Chapter Thirty-One

Captain Damien Harahap, Solarian Gendarmerie, known as "Firebrand," was not a happy man.

He sat at a small table in the Karlovac bar, nursing one of the capital city breweries' justly famed beers, and his gaze dropped for a moment to the old-fashioned printed newspaper on the table. He'd never much cared for such primitive versions of a proper 'fax, and he particularly resented the inability to go straight to a decent infonet to follow up the articles. He sometimes wondered how intelligence agents had done their jobs properly in preelectronic days. They must have spent literally hours every day just rummaging around through reams and reams of ink-smeary, finger-staining paper!

But this particular newspaper was especially infuriating because it suggested so much while confirming absolutely nothing. Oh, if he decided to take all the reporters' speculation and editorial commentary at face value, the news was disastrous. But he would almost have preferred to know that was true than to be reduced to *guessing* about things this way.

"NORDBRANDT DEAD?" "FAK TERRORIST FOUNDER KILLED!" "DEATH OF A MURDERER!"

The headlines, with the possible exception of the first, didn't seem to have much doubt. It wasn't until he got into the articles themselves that the questions became evident. The *Karlovac Tribune-Herald*, which had bannered its afternoon's edition with the first headline, had been the most resistant to the general euphoria. As its lead writer had noted, "Government spokesmen continue to stress that no positive identification of Nordbrandt's remains has been made. Forensics specialists caution that it may never be possible to absolutely confirm that the remains in the National Police's hands are indeed those of the infamous terrorist. Nonetheless, there appears to be significant reason to believe she has, indeed, been killed."

Which would be just my luck, he thought bitterly. *Two days ago. Just two days ago! If I'd gotten here* two days *earlier, she would've been too busy meeting with me to get her lunatic ass blown away like this!*

It took all his formidable self-control to keep his expression tranquil and sip his beer as if he had no cares at all. Especially when he thought about all the spadework he'd done, all the preparation. Wasted. Just thrown away because the bloodthirsty bitch just *had* to go out into the field playing soldier!

He drew a deep breath and commanded himself to break the feedback loop of his temper. He was only making himself angrier by brooding on all his wasted time and effort, and there was no point in it. Besides, it was bad tradecraft.

He snorted in wry amusement at the thought. But it was true, and he took a deeper pull at his beer and sat back to think.

He'd underestimated her. He'd sensed a certain capacity for violence in her, recognized her as a potentially lethal tool, but he'd never imagined she might prove *this* violent. Her first attack on the planetary parliament had been more than sufficiently spectacular—in fact, he'd been astounded, upon his arrival here, to learn she'd managed to carry out such an operation successfully. But the ensuing pattern of assassinations, bombing attacks on exposed portions of the Kornatian infrastructure, and general mayhem were even more surprising, in a way. Either he'd significantly underestimated the size of her organization, or else Kornati's security forces were even more inept than he'd believed possible.

Calm down, Damien. She probably had *managed to put together a bigger organization than you thought. But she might not have, too. You haven't really had enough chance to analyze the operations she pulled off successfully to make a meaningful estimate of the organization she needed to do it. You're still reacting to these damned "newspaper" articles, and you* know *there's more than a little hysteria in the way they've been reporting things. This planet doesn't have much tradition of violence in politics. The emergence of* any *violent terrorist organization's obviously taken them by surprise. That's probably enough right there to explain how she managed the Nemanja bombing! And of course the newsies are figuring it took some kind of massive organization to pull it off. Just like the government is inevitably going to insist there are only a handful of the lunatic fringe out there throwing bombs.*

The truth was that what looked to the local media like a carefully planned and orchestrated program of attacks might well be nothing of the sort. More than half the bombings appeared to have targeted things like public transportation stations and power transmission lines. Those sorts of targets were both highly visible and extremely difficult for even the best trained, most experienced security forces to protect. Most of those attacks could very well have represented nothing more than opportunity targets. The massive fire touched off by the bombing attack on the petrochemical storage tanks at Kornati's fifth-largest refinery would have required more planning and faced more significant opposition from both public and private security forces, but most of the other industry-oriented attacks had been on smaller factories or branch offices of banking and investment firms. Again, widespread strikes on relatively lightly defended targets which had helped generate a public *perception* of some sort of terrorist tsunami.

No, she hasn't really gone after all that many "hard" targets after all, has she? It just looks that way. Then again, that's what terrorist campaigns are all about. There's no way she and her true believers could ever have hoped to defeat the planetary government in an open, standup fight. But if she'd been able to convince enough of the public that the government couldn't crush her, *either. Couldn't prevent her from hitting any target she chose. . . .*

Except that it was beginning to look as if the government had done just that.

He sighed, finished his beer, tossed a couple of local coins onto the tabletop, and stood. He tucked the folded newspaper under his arm—not because he was particularly interested in keeping it, but because leaving it behind might prick someone's curiosity if they'd noticed how intently he'd been scanning it earlier. It probably didn't much matter either way, but that sort of professional consideration was programmed into him on an almost instinctual level.

He stepped out onto the sidewalk and turned towards the local subway station.

It was a warm, sunnily pleasant day, as if deliberately designed to mock his gloomy thoughts, and he ambled along. He was halfway to the stairs leading down to the subway when someone stepped up close behind him. Instincts jangled, but before he could do more than inhale once, something hard pressed against the base of his spine.

"Keep walking . . . Firebrand," a voice said very quietly somewhere behind his left ear.

In all the bad holo dramas Harahap had ever seen, the steely-eyed, strong-jawed intelligence agent would have swept backwards with his elbow, catching his invisible assailant unerringly in the solar plexus, simultaneously disarming and disabling him. Then he would have paused to straighten his jacket before turning to his whooping, gasping foe, collecting his dropped weapon, and delivering some clever witticism for the defeated underling to relay to his superiors.

Life being life, and considering how difficult it was to survive when one's spine was blown in two, Damien Harahap kept walking.

His mind raced as they continued past the subway entrance. His first thought was that in the wake of Nordbrandt's death, her organization had come sufficiently unraveled for his cover to have been blown to the Kornatian National Police. But as he pondered it, he decided that didn't make a lot of sense. If the graybacks knew who he really was, they'd probably have approached this in a totally different manner. There were certain rules planets in the Verge knew better than to break, and one of them was that they never arrested and tried—far less thought about imprisoning—Gendarmerie intelligence agents. No Verge government could afford the retribution Frontier Security would visit upon anyone who dared embarrass OFS that way. Besides, if the police meant to arrest him, why not simply do so? The fellow behind him had certainly gotten the drop on him with embarrassing ease. There was no reason to believe a larger arrest team couldn't have done the same thing. For that matter, the fellow behind him had had plenty of opportunities to inform him he was being taken into custody.

That left, so far as Harahap could see, only two real possibilities. The first, and more frightening, was that the KNP had decided not to take him into custody at all. They might know exactly who he was and believe he'd had even more to do with organizing and equipping the FAK *before* the Nemanja bombing than he had. If that were so, they might have decided to send a message to his superiors—or to *him,* at least—by simply making him disappear. In which case this relaxing little stroll was going to end in an alley somewhere with a pulser dart in his brain. Or, more likely, with his throat slit and his wallet stolen—an unfortunate victim of a violent robbery whose demise owed absolutely *nothing* to the Kornatian government whose parliamentary representatives he'd helped to murder. And if he did end up there, OFS would probably let it go. After all, one couldn't make an omelet without cracking the occasional egg. There were plenty more where he'd come from, and at least Kornati would have played by the rules and refrained from embarrassing Frontier Security in the Solly press.

The thought made him breathe harder and faster, but he didn't really think that was what was happening. How much of that was because he so desperately *wanted* it not to be was more than he was prepared to say, even to himself.

The second and, he sincerely hoped, more likely possibility was that Nordbrandt's organization hadn't been completely rolled up and that some remnant of it had recognized him when he turned up at the appointed contact point. In that case, whoever it was might be prepared to assume Nordbrandt's mantle and continue her struggle, in which case he—or she—undoubtedly wanted "Firebrand's" support more badly than ever. Or, he might have been recognized by one of Nordbrandt's survivors who only wanted a way off-planet and figured "Firebrand" was his best chance of arranging or extorting a ticket.

Of the various possibilities for his abduction, only the hope that it was one of Nordbrandt's people, regardless of his captor's precise demands, offered much chance for Harahap's continued breathing, so he decided to operate on that assumption.

They'd walked another eight or nine blocks before the man behind him spoke again.

"In the middle of the next block. Number 721. On your right. Up the steps, in the front door, and continue to the end of the hall."

Harahap allowed himself a small nod and started looking for street numbers.

The next block consisted of tall, narrow tenement buildings. Back on prespace Old Earth, they might have been called "brownstones." Here on Kornati they were called "one-suns" because they were packed so closely together that only one wall had windows to admit sunlight. These particular one-suns were a bit more rundown than some, but not as badly as many others. It was an industrial district, and the blue-collar workers who lived here earned enough money to aspire to a somewhat higher standard of living.

They came to Number 721, and Harahap turned to his right and up the steps as if this had been his destination all along. The front door had been repainted fairly recently, in a deep, dark green that seemed out of place in this grimy, urban setting. It wasn't locked—doors seldom were in this part of town, where renters could rely on their neighbors to break the kneecaps of anyone stupid enough to try to rob or burglarize any of their fellow residents—and it opened at his touch.

He walked down the hallway, smelling a combination of cooking, faint mildew, and people living too close together. The door at the end of the hall swung open at his approach, and he stepped through it to find himself face-to-face with a dark-haired, dark-eyed, dark-complexioned woman of medium height.

"I suspected the rumors of your unfortunate demise were exaggerated, Ms. Nordbrandt," he said calmly.

"So I decided to let them think they'd gotten me, at least for a week or two," Agnes Nordbrandt said thirty-odd minutes later.

She and Harahap faced one another across a small table in the one-sun apartment's tiny kitchen. A pot of some sort of soup or stew simmered on the old-fashioned stovetop behind him, and he sat with his hands on the table, a mug of surprisingly good tea clasped loosely between them, while he watched her face. It seemed thinner than at their last meeting, harder. And there was a brighter, fiercer glitter in her dark eyes. The nascent fanaticism he'd sensed from the outset was stronger. He'd seen that before, in his line of work.

There were some who harbored a natural predatory streak, sometimes without ever suspecting it themselves. People who turned out to have a taste for blood, who actually enjoyed doing what still went by the euphemism of "wet work." Agnes Nordbrandt, it appeared, fell into that category.

"They *did* get some good people," she continued more harshly, then stopped and made herself relax. "And, while I suppose the reports of my death may be disheartening to some of our cells, I expect the blow to the government's credibility when it turns out I'm *not* dead to more than offset any interim damage."

"I see." He sipped tea, then returned the mug to the table and smiled ever so slightly. "On the other hand, I don't believe any of the newspaper articles I've read said that the government ever claimed you were. It's all been pure media speculation, with government spokesmen persistently cautioning people that there's no proof you're not alive."

"I know." Her grin was positively vicious. "That's one reason the entire idea appeals to me so much. The government can argue all it wants that it never tried to claim I was dead. But no one'll remember that, especially when I begin all my communiques announcing my continued existence with 'Despite the corrupt governing elite's terrified efforts to claim they had silenced my voice of opposition . . .'"

"I see," he repeated. She was right, and she was also demonstrating a rather more sophisticated grasp of effective propaganda and psych war than he'd really expected out of her. Which, he chided himself, had been foolish. She had, after all, been a successful Kornatian politician before the annexation vote destroyed her constituency. Of course, she remained fundamentally a lunatic, but she was clearly a lunatic with good tactical instincts, however poor her grasp of the strategic realities might prove in the end.

"How long are you planning to pull back on your operations?"

"You noticed that, did you?" Nordbrandt seemed pleased by his perceptiveness. "I figure another couple of weeks, maybe three, with nothing more than a few, widely isolated operations—the sorts of thing action cells might come up with on their own if they were completely cut off from central guidance—should pretty much convince all the press pundits I'm safely dead. And it should also encourage Rajkovic and Basaricek to believe the same thing, whether they admit it to anyone else—or even themselves—or not. Or, at least, for the grays and General Suka's people to relax and lower their guards just a little. Which ought to make the wave of attacks I'm planning to punctuate my statement of continued health even more effective."

"Can you afford to take the pressure off for that long?"

"For two weeks, certainly. Three?" She shrugged. "That may be a bit more problematical. Not so much here on Kornati, but on Flax. I don't want the Constitutional Convention too comfortable with the notion that they don't face any opposition."

"I see your point," he said. "On the other hand, I've just come from Montana. You've heard about Westman and his Independence Alliance's attack on Rembrandt's facilities there?"

"No. Last I heard, he was still playing around stealing people's clothes."

Her disdain for Westman's opening operation was obvious . . . and, Harahap thought, proved that whatever her own strengths might be, her understanding of the full possibilities of psychological warfare were, in fact, almost as limited as he'd first thought they were. Or perhaps it would be more fair to her to say she suffered from tunnel vision. She was too enamored of the raw violence of her own chosen tactics to consider the possibilities inherent in any other approach.

"Well, that might have been a bit silly," Harahap conceded, catering to her prejudices. "If it was, though, he's decided to take a rather . . . firmer approach since."

He proceeded to tell her all about Westman's attack on the RTU's Montana headquarters. By the time he was done, she was chuckling in open admiration. Of course, Harahap had chosen not to stress the careful precautions Westman had taken to avoid casualties.

"I love it!" she announced. "And, to be honest, I never thought Westman would have it in him. I always figured him for just one more useless cretin of a Montanan aristocrat—like Tonkovic and her cronies here on Kornati."

It occurred to Harahap, not for the first time, that the citizens of the Talbott Cluster, including an amazing number of those who should have known better, were sadly ignorant about the societies of their sister worlds. True, Westman was what passed for an "aristocrat" on Montana, but the mind boggled at the thought of him as, say, a New Tuscany oligarch. Whatever their other faults, the Montanans would have laughed themselves silly at the very prospect.

"He did seem to be taking things lightly, just at first," he said. "But he's gotten more serious since. And he's decided to sign on with our Central Liberation Committee. That's what we finally decided to call ourselves. Has a nice ring to it, doesn't it?" he added with a smile.

"He has?" Nordbrandt demanded, eyes narrowing as she ignored his humorous question.

"He has," Harahap said more seriously. "Which is one reason I suspect that even if you decided to take the full three weeks before announcing you're still alive, someone else'll help keep the pressure on. And we'll be providing him with modern weapons and support to do it with. As I told you we might the last time I was here, we seem to've come into a bit of an unexpected stock dividend from Van Dort's RTU, and our contacts have come through with modern weapons, night vision optics, communications hardware, and military-grade explosives. May I assume you'd like a few of those goodies yourself?"

"You certainly may," she said with the fervency of someone who, since their last conversation, had experienced the realities of operating from the wrong side of a capability imbalance. "How soon can we expect to see them?"

"They're in transit," he told her, and watched her eyes glitter. "Unfortunately, it's still going to take them about sixty T-days to get here. Freighters aren't exactly speed demons, and we need our delivery boys to be so ordinary-looking they slide in under the authorities' radar." She looked disappointed at the thought of taking that long to get her hands on her previously unanticipated new toys, and he smiled crookedly. "Besides," he continued, "I imagine you'll be able to make good use of all that time. After all, we're going to have to figure out how to land—and hide, here on the planet—something on the order of a thousand tons of weapons, ammunition, and explosives."

"A thousand?" Her eyes glowed, and he nodded.

"At least," he said gently. "And it could be twice that. That was the minimum quantity I was assured of when I set out. They were still assembling the shipment, though, and the numbers may well have gone up since. Can you handle and hide that big a consignment?"

"Oh, yes," she told him quietly. "I think you can rely on that!"

"Celebrant Traffic Control, this is HMS *Hexapuma* requesting clearance to an assigned parking orbit."

Lieutenant Commander Nagchaudhuri sat patiently at his communications panel after transmitting Captain Terekhov's request. Like all the other systems out here, Celebrant certainly didn't possess any FTL com capability, and *Hexapuma* had just crossed the G4 star's 20.24-light-minute hyper limit. The star system's habitable planet, which also rejoiced in the name Celebrant, was directly between the ship and its primary, with an orbital radius of just under eleven light-minutes, so it would be at least eighteen minutes before any response could be received by *Hexapuma*.

That was perfectly all right with Terekhov. At this range, even the sorts of sensors available in the Cluster should have gotten a clear fix on *Hexapuma*'s hyper footprint and impeller wedge, so they knew someone was coming. And it was only courteous to let them know as soon as possible who that someone was.

He gazed into his maneuvering plot, watching his ship's green bead move steadily closer to the planet of its destination, and, somewhat to his own surprise, discovered that he felt . . . content. They'd done good work in Nuncio. It might not be as dramatic and glorious as charging into combat against the Republic of Haven's massed fleet, but it was good, *useful* work. Work that was going to have profound, positive consequences for the future of the entire Star Kingdom in the fullness of time.

And let's be honest. Even if we were serving with Eighth Fleet, we'd probably spend most of our time sitting around in parking orbit, waiting for an enemy attack or preparing for one of our own. That's what duty with the Fleet is—ninety-nine percent boredom and one percent sheer, howling terror. I suppose the same is true enough out here, but at least we can spend some of that ninety-nine percent of the time doing useful things, like survey work to update our charts. Besides, these people need *us an awful lot worse than the Star Kingdom needs one more heavy cruiser serving with Eighth Fleet or Home Fleet. And every single thing we do lays one more brick in the notion that the Star Kingdom is* worth *something. That its protection and freedoms actually* mean *something.*

How odd. He'd known he'd taken a savage satisfaction in destroying *Anhur* and her consort. But exactly when had he slipped over from being here because someone *had* to be here to being content that he was the one who actually *was* here?

He didn't know, but as he gazed at the blue and white icon indicating an inhabited world named Celebrant, he actually found himself looking forward to discovering what new routine, boring, absolutely vital and essential tasks awaited them here.

Chapter Thirty-Two

"You know, Boss, we can't keep this up forever," Luis Palacios remarked as he slid the final charge into its hole.

"You think Suttles and his yahoos can actually find their ass with both hands?" Stephen Westman shot back with a chuckle.

"Matter of fact, they can, Boss. Well, maybe not *Suttles*, but Trevor Bannister's no fool, and you know it. Reckon that's why we're taking all these precautions you insist on."

Chief Marshal Trevor Bannister commanded the Montana Marshals Service, the police force with jurisdiction over the entire star system. Like their fellow Montanans, the marshals made something of a fetish out of appearing as calm and unhurried as was physically possible. Unfortunately, appearances could be deceiving, and the marshals had an enviable record for cracking even the most difficult of cases. Prior to the recent unpleasantness, Bannister and Westman had also been close friends. Which, Westman knew, wouldn't for a moment deter Bannister from hunting him, and all his men, down. The Chief Marshal had a well-earned reputation for integrity and stubbornness that was monumental even for a Montanan.

"All right." Westman nodded. "I'll grant you old Trevor's bright enough. And he's a pretty good dog to set on any trail. But if we keep on being careful, sticking to the rules for security, he's going to play hell catching up with us."

"Reckon you're right." Palacios tamped the charge, and his nimble fingers began fitting the detonator. "That wasn't the point I was aiming to make, though."

He fell silent, working carefully at his task and obviously concentrating hard, and Westman stood behind him, watching him with affectionate exasperation. Luis Palacios had been Westman's father's foreman before the old man's death. He'd been respectfully warning his new, younger boss against mistakes for as long as Westman could remember. And he preferred to do it by throwing out cryptic utterances until sheer frustration compelled Westman to ask him what he meant.

Like now.

"All right, Luis," he sighed. "What point *were* you aiming to make?"

"The point that we can't keep hitting them hard enough to convince the Manties and Rembrandters to mosey on home and not start hurting people," Palacios said, turning to look up at him, and his voice was very, very serious.

Westman looked back down at him in the lantern light. The artificial light did strange things to Palacios' expression. The foreman's scarred face looked older, thinner. The shadows seemed to add still more gravity to the already grave set of his mouth and eyes, and Westman wondered if they did the same thing to his face. Silence lingered for several seconds, and then Westman shrugged.

"You're right," he agreed quietly. "I mean to postpone the moment as long as possible, but I've always said it was bound to happen if they wouldn't listen to reason. You know that."

"Yep." Palacios gave the charge and its detonator one last, careful examination, then stood. He slapped his palms together, dusting them off, then reached into his shirt pocket for a twist of the dried native plant the colonists had named backy. It didn't really look like Old Earth tobacco, but it was pleasant-tasting, mildly stimulating, and easily grown and cured. Palacios cut himself a short length, popped it into his mouth, and began to chew.

"Thing is, Boss," he said, after a moment, "you've warned all of us about that. And we've believed you. Problem is, I'm not so sure you've believed yourself."

"What do you mean?"

If any other man alive had said that to Stephen Westman, he'd have been furious. At least angry at the implication that he'd lied to himself. But Luis Palacios wasn't "any other man." He was the person who probably knew Westman better than Westman knew himself.

"Boss, I'm not saying you haven't considered the possibility of actually hurting, even killing, the people who get in our way pretty damned seriously. And I'm not saying you're not willing to get your hands dirty, even bloody, if you have to. And I'm not even saying I think you'll hesitate if the time comes to do any of those things. But the truth is, Boss—and you know it as well as I do, if you're honest with yourself—you don't *want* to do it. Matter of fact, I don't expect there's a single thing in the world you want less. Except maybe—maybe—to see the Manties take us over."

"I never said I *did* want to." Westman's voice was harsh, not with anger, but with resolution. "But I will. If I have to."

"Never doubted it," Palacios said simply. "But you've been moving heaven and earth to avoid it. And, truth to tell, I don't much like what I reckon it's going to do to you if it comes down to it. Don't expect I'll much care for how the other folks on this planet'll think about all of us, for that matter. Not that I'm about to pack it in on you at this point. I just want you to be thinking about the fact that we've probably come pretty close to playing this string all the way out. Reckon we'll get away with it today without hurting anybody. It won't be that way much longer, though. And sooner or later, we're gonna come up against some of Trevor's boys and girls, and we're all gonna have guns in our hands. The boys and me, we'll back you all the way. You know that. And I don't reckon most of us are gonna have anywhere near the problem *you* are when it comes to squeezing those triggers, 'cause we're all perfectly willing to let you do the thinking. But you're the one's gonna have to live with those decisions."

He paused again, looking very levelly into Westman's eyes.

"I've known you a lot of years, Boss. Grown pretty fond of you, too. But it's not gonna be so very much longer before you have to make those decisions, and I don't want you making one that's gonna eat you up alive from the inside. So you'd best be thinking *real* hard about how much blood—and whose—you're really ready to shed."

Stephen Westman looked back into his foreman's eyes for several seconds, then nodded.

"I'll think about it," he promised. "But I've already done a lot of that. I don't think I'm going to change my mind, Luis."

"If you don't, you don't," Palacios said philosophically. "Either way, the boys and I'll back your play."

"I know you will," Westman said softly. "I know you will."

"He said they're going to *what*?"

Warren Suttles sat back behind his desk in the spacious, sun-drenched office of the System President and looked at Chief Marshal Bannister in shock. Bannister was a man of only medium height—a bit on the short side, actually, for Montana—with a head of thick, grizzled red hair and dark eyes. He was deeply tanned and, despite a job which kept him behind a desk far too much of the time, he was fighting a mainly successful battle against the thickening of his middle. He was also a taciturn, soft-spoken man with a reputation for never using two words when he could do the job with one—or with a grunt.

Which was the main reason he didn't reply to what he recognized as a rhetorical question. It wasn't the only reason. As a matter of simple fact, Trevor Bannister found Warren Suttles the silliest excuse for a chief executive of any of the three system presidents he'd served as Chief Marshal. Suttles wasn't a bad man; he just wasn't a very strong one, and the spinmasters and political handlers who'd gotten him elected weren't any better. For all practical purposes, the so-called "Suttles Administration" was little better than a committee whose nominal head would've had trouble deciding what color to paint his bedroom without first commissioning multiple popular opinion polls. It was unfortunate, in many ways, that Warren Suttles was President instead of Stephen Westman. Although, when it came right down to it, little though Bannister *respected* Suttles, the President's policies—especially where the annexation issue was concerned—were far better for Montana's future than Westman's were. He didn't like admitting that. If there was anyone on Montana who liked Bernardus Van Dort less than Stephen Westman did, it was almost certainly Trevor Bannister, and the thought of supporting anything Van Dort thought was a good idea stuck in his craw sideways. But he'd managed to choke it down, because however much he loathed Van Dort, Suttles was right about the future, and his administration's policy of embracing the annexation was the only one that made sense.

And even if it didn't, this son of a bitch's the duly elected President of my star system, his policies represent the freely expressed will of damned near three quarters of the electorate, and I'm bound—both by law and my personal oath—to enforce the law and to protect and preserve the Constitution of Montana against all *enemies, foreign or domestic. Including enemies who happen to be close personal friends.*

"Can he really *do* that?" Suttles asked, finally moving on from useless questions to some which might actually be worth answering.

"Mr. President," Bannister pointed out, "the man's done every other single thing he said he would."

Warren Suttles clenched his jaw and managed—somehow—to keep himself from glowering at the man seated across his desk from him. If he'd thought for a minute that he could politically survive firing Bannister, he would've done it in a heartbeat. Or he liked to think he would have. The fact was, that he wasn't sure he would've had the nerve to do it even if it had been politically feasible. Which, of course, it wasn't. Trevor Bannister was an institution, the most successful, most hard driving, most dedicated, most decorated, most everything-in-the-damned-world Chief Marshal in the history of Montana. And he wasn't even impolite. It was just that he managed to make Warren Suttles feel like an idiot—or feel pretty confident Bannister *thought* he was an idiot—with apparent effortlessness.

"I'm aware of that, Chief Marshal," the System President said after a moment. "Just as I'm aware that, so far, we don't seem to've come a single centimeter closer to apprehending him than we were after that first escapade of his."

That was about as close to a direct criticism of Bannister's campaign against the Montana Independence Movement as Suttles was prepared to come, and the verbal shot bounced off Bannister's armor without so much as a scuff mark. He simply sat there, gazing attentively and respectfully at the System President, and waited.

"What I meant, Chief Marshal," Suttles continued a bit stiffly, "was that it seems incredible to me that even Mr. Westman and his henchmen could pull this one off. I'm not saying they can't; I'm just saying I don't understand how they *can*, and I'd appreciate any insight into their capabilities you could offer me."

"Well, Mr. President, I can't say positively, of course. What it looks like is that he got to the old service tunnels under the bank. They're supposed to be sealed off, and the ceramacrete plugs the Treasury put in sixty, seventy T-years ago are ten meters thick. They're also supposed to be alarmed, and the alarms are supposed to be monitored twenty-seven hours a day. On the face of it, it shouldn't be possible for him to get through them, but it seems pretty clear that he did. Say what you will about the man, he's got a way of doing what he sets his mind to."

"You don't think this time he might be bluffing?"

"Mr. President, I've played a lot of poker with Steve Westman. One thing about him; he don't bluff worth a damn, and he never has. He's not bluffing this time."

"So you think he's actually planted explosives under the System Bank of Montana?"

"Yes, Sir. I do."

"And he'll actually set them off?"

"Don't see any other reason to've put them there."

"My God, Chief Marshal! If he sets those things off, blows up the *national* bank, it'll be a devastating blow to the entire economy! He could trigger a full-scale recession!"

"I expect he's thought of that, Mr. President."

"But he's gone to such pains to avoid angering the public. What makes you think he's ready to change that pattern here?"

"Mr. President, he's told us all along he's prepared to go to the mat over this. That he's prepared to risk being killed himself, and to kill other people, if that's what it takes. And everything he's done so far's been a direct, logical escalation from the last thing he did. Sure, he's going to piss off a lot of people if he blows the economy into a recession. However, pissing people off is what he's been after all along. And however pissed they're going to be at him, he's figuring they're going to be just as pissed at you, me, and the rest of the Administration, for *letting* him do it. The man's willing to get himself killed over this—you really think he's going to lose sleep over people thinking unkind thoughts about him?"

Suttles felt his teeth trying to grind together, but this time, he knew, at least two-thirds of his frustration was directed at the absent Westman, not at Bannister. Well, maybe a bit less than two-thirds.

"All right, Chief Marshal. If you're convinced he's serious about it, and if you're also convinced he's somehow planted explosive charges in the bank service tunnels, why don't we send someone down to disarm them?"

"Mostly because Steve obviously thought of that, too. He warned us not to, and I'm pretty sure if we try something like that anyway, we'll just set them off early."

"Don't we have experts who specialize in disarming bombs and disposing of explosives?"

"We do. So does the Navy. I've talked to them. They say there's at least a dozen ways he could have rigged his charges to go off the instant anyone steps into those tunnels, assuming that's where the bombs are."

"They're not even willing to *try*?"

"Of course they are. Question is, are we willing to send them in?"

"Of course we are! How can you even think of *not* sending them?"

"First, because I'd just as soon not get them killed," Bannister said calmly. "And, second, because if we do get them killed, sending them in after Westman's taken such pains to warn us not to—to specifically tell us the charges'll detonate if we do—it'll be a mite difficult to convince the public *he's* the one responsible for their deaths."

"Of course he'd be responsible for their deaths! He's the one who put the damned bombs there in the first place!"

"Not saying he didn't. All I'm saying is the public perception's going to be that *your* Administration sent those bomb disposal experts in *knowing* the bombs would go off—and kill them—if you did. They'll blame Westman, all right. But they'll blame you for ignoring his warning almost as much as they'll blame him. And do you really want the voters thinking we're just as clumsy, stupid, and ineffectual as Westman's been claiming we are right along?"

Suttles opened his mouth to snap a reply, then paused. A part of him couldn't help wondering if just possibly

Trevor Bannister secretly agreed with Westman. Was it possible the Chief Marshal, for all his famed devotion to duty, actually wanted Westman to win? Possibly enough to see to it that Westman's attacks succeeded?

But that thought wasn't what froze him in mid-snap. Partly because, even at his most irritated, he knew the very idea was ludicrous. Not that it was impossible Bannister agreed with Westman, but that he would have permitted that agreement to deflect him a single millimeter from his duty. But mostly he froze because he'd suddenly realized that the Chief Marshal had a point.

"Have you talked to the Treasury Secretary about this, Chief Marshal?" he asked instead of saying what he'd started to say.

"I have."

"What was his estimate of the consequences if the bombs go off?"

"I understand he's prepared to give you his formal estimate at the emergency Cabinet meeting, Mr. President."

"I'm sure he is. And I'm sure you expect me to make my decision only after every member of the Cabinet's had a chance to express his or her own views on exactly what I ought to be doing."

There was an ever so slightly biting edge to the President's voice, and Suttles was rather pleased to see a faint spark of surprise in Bannister's dark eyes.

"However," he continued, "let's not waste time pretending anything any of them say is going to weigh as heavily as what *you* recommend, Chief Marshal. So just go ahead and tell me what Secretary Stiles had to say."

"He estimates, worst-case scenario, that we'll lose about two weeks worth of electronic records. Everything's backed up immediately on the Bank's secondary computer net, and twice a month a complete new backup's generated for the remote storage location in the New Swans. Unfortunately, Westman timed this to hit just before the bi-monthly backup, and the secondary computer net is in the Bank building's subcellars . . . which means they're even closer to the bombs—assuming they're really there—than the *primary* computers. 'Pears he's managed to cut the land line to the New Swans site to prevent any emergency dumps, too, and the Bank's security staff's already evacuated the building—my orders, Mr. President—so even if there was time, there's no access for physical downloads.

"Course, losing the records is only part of it. When those bombs go, they're gonna take the Bank's mainframes—all three of 'em—with them. According to the Secretary, we can probably reconstitute about eighty percent of the electronic records from hardcopy records and electronic records at secondary locations, but it'll take weeks—at best—to get the job done. I 'spect he's being overoptimistic in that estimate, Mr. President, 'cause just finding replacements for the Bank's central net's gonna be a real bear. But that's what he's going to tell you."

"And did he happen to mention what effect he expects that to have on the economy?"

"I don't think he has the least idea, Mr. President. I don't think anyone does. It's never happened before. I don't expect it to be good, and neither does he, but his feeling is that unless it sparks an outright panic—which, *I* think is unlikely—the effect should stop well short of the sort of panic-induced recession you referred to earlier."

"Which isn't the same thing as saying that it won't cost us millions, possibly even billions."

"No, Mr. President. It isn't."

"And your recommendation is still that we accept the damage rather than sending in bomb disposal units to try to prevent it?"

"Mr. President, if I thought there was a chance in hell of disarming those bombs without setting them off, I'd personally lead our BDUs into those tunnels. I don't think there is. So I'm recommending we not get people killed in addition to the damage we're already going to take. The bombs are going off, Sir. Do we really want to get our own people killed, and assume the political consequences stemming from the electorate's view that we did it because we were too stupid to take Westman's word for what would happen?"

Suttles looked at him for several moments in silence. Then the System President inhaled deeply, planted his hands on his desktop, and shoved himself erect.

"All right, Chief Marshal," he sighed. "Let's get on into the Cabinet meeting. And, if you don't mind," he actually managed a smile, "let me at least pretend to listen to everyone else before I decide we're going to do things your way."

"Of course, Mr. President," Trevor Bannister said, and rose with considerably more genuine respect for his President than usual.

Be damned, he thought, following Suttles out of the office, *might just be the man's got a spine, after all. Be nice if he had a brain to go with it, but who knows? It may turn out he's even got one of those if he ever decides to stand up on his hind legs and* use *it*.

Chapter Thirty-Three

"Well, what do you make of it, Andrieaux?" Samiha Lababibi asked.

"What do you mean, what do I make of it?"

The Spindle System President and New Tuscany's senior delegate sat in a private dining room at one of the most exclusive restaurants in Thimble. It was a *very* private dining room—one whose security against any known listening device was guaranteed, as was the discretion of the wait staff which served diners in it.

"Andrieaux, let's not play games, please," Lababibi said with a winsome smile. She picked up the wine bottle and poured fresh glasses for both of them. "The probability that Nordbrandt's dead is bound to affect everyone's calculations. What I'm asking for is your estimate of how it's going to affect Alquezar's, Aleksandra's . . . and ours."

"Surely it's much too early to be formulating new policies on the basis of something which hasn't even been confirmed yet," Andrieaux Yvernau protested gracefully, and Lababibi's smile took on a slightly set air. He sipped his wine appreciatively, then set down the glass with a sigh. "Personally, I find the entire matter extraordinarily tiresome," he said. "I'd like to think that if she really is dead—and I do devoutly hope she is—we might be allowed at least a few days, or weeks, of peace before we have to return to the fray with Alquezar's hooligans."

"It's extremely unlikely Joachim is going to give us that sort of vacation, Andrieaux," Lababibi pointed out. *And*, she didn't add aloud, *if you want a little rest, you smug, self-satisfied ass, you might think about the fact that my own life was ever so much more restful before that crazed bitch drove me into your waiting arms—yours and Aleksandra's.*

"Really, Samiha, what does it matter what Joachim's willing to give us? As long as we hold firm, he and that disgusting Krietzmann have no choice but to await *our* response." He smiled thinly. "According to reports I've received from certain people officially on the other side, our *dear* friend Bernardus is having steadily mounting problems holding the RTU-backed delegates for Alquezar. And if *they* come over to our side—"

He shrugged, his smile turning into something remarkably like a smirk.

"They haven't shown any signs of breaking with him yet," Lababibi pointed out.

"Not openly, no. But you know there have to be fissures under the surface, Samiha. They can't possibly be comfortable siding with lower-class cretins like Krietzmann, whatever Van Dort and Alquezar are demanding. It's only a matter of time before they start coming over, and when they do, Alquezar will have no choice but to accept the 'compromise' between Aleksandra's demands and my own, far more moderate position."

"And you don't see Nordbrandt's death affecting that equation in any way?"

"I didn't say that," Yvernau said with a patient sigh. "What I *said* is that it's too early to be formulating new policies when all we can do is speculate upon the effect her demise is likely to have. Although, if I had to guess, I'd be tempted to wager it will strengthen my position more than anyone else's. To some extent, of course, Aleksandra's contention that Nordbrandt never represented any serious threat will be validated. Insofar as that view is accepted, it will also tend to validate her stand in holding out for the most liberal possible protection of our existing legal codes and societies. However, it will also take some of the pressure off certain of her . . . less enthusiastic supporters, shall we say?"

He darted a look across the table at Lababibi, who returned it with an expression of complete tranquility. An expression, she knew, which fooled neither of them. She had, indeed, been driven into Tonkovic's camp by the wave of panic Nordbrandt's extremism had sent surging through the Spindle System oligarchs. If Nordbrandt truly was gone, and if her organization truly was crippled, some of that panic might begin to subside. In which case, the pressure being exerted on Lababibi to maintain a united front with Tonkovic might also ebb. It might even be possible to move back towards a position based on *principle* instead of other peoples' panic.

Not that Yvernau would be particularly happy if she managed that.

"If," he continued, "Aleksandra's bloc of votes begins to show signs of crumbling, Alquezar will scent blood. He and Krietzmann—and Bernardus, if he ever deigns to return from Rembrandt—will begin to press their demands that we accept the Star Kingdom's legal code lock, stock, and barrel with even greater fervency. Which, of course, will only stiffen Aleksandra's opposition. I suspect we'll see a period of gradual erosion of her support base, unless, of course, some replacement for Nordbrandt appears. But it will be a *gradual* process, one which will take weeks, even months, to show any significant effect on the balance of power in the Convention. Eventually, of course, the balance will tip against her. But she already knows that as well as you and I do, whether she chooses to admit it or not. Which means that somewhere deep inside she's already accepted that she'll never get everything she's holding out for. So if I choose my moment properly, when I step forward to present my compromise platform—one which gives Alquezar perhaps half of what he wants—she'll endorse it. And if both of us unite in a sudden surge of goodwill and the spirit of compromise, Alquezar will find it extremely difficult not to meet us halfway."

"And if he refuses to, anyway?"

"Then he loses his own oligarchs," Yvernau said simply. "Not even Van Dort will be able to hold them if Alquezar first throws away a chance for a compromise solution and, second, makes it clear the draft Constitution *he* favors will strip them of every single legal protection they've spent centuries acquiring. Which means, in the end, that I and those who think like me will get everything we've wanted all along. Effectively total local autonomy in return for a unified interstellar fiscal, trade, diplomatic, and military policy emanating from Manticore."

"And you believe this will take weeks. Even months."

"I think it's extremely likely to," Yvernau acknowledged.

"You're not concerned about Baroness Medusa's warnings that our time isn't unlimited? Nor worried that if things stretch out that long the Star Kingdom may simply decide to walk away? To take the position that if we can't put our own house into order well enough to report out a draft Constitution after all this time, then obviously we're not really serious about joining the Star Kingdom at all?"

"I think there will probably be some internal, domestic pressure for the Star Kingdom to do that," Yvernau said calmly. "In this instance, however, I think Aleksandra is correct. The Queen of Manticore herself has committed her crown and prestige to the annexation. If she's actually told Medusa there's a time limit—if our beloved Provisional Governor hasn't simply manufactured the threat to push us along—I suspect her 'time limit' actually contains a large measure of bluff. She might want a Constitution hastened, and she might not be prepared to use force to suppress opposition to the annexation, but neither is she going to simply walk away and present to the galaxy at large the impression that she's abandoned us to Frontier Security."

"I see."

Lababibi nodded slowly, as if in agreement with her dinner companion, but underneath her calm surface she wondered just how overconfident Yvernau—and Tonkovic—were actually being.

"Do you think she's actually dead?" Baroness Medusa asked as she gazed around a dinner table of her own. This one sat in the luxurious—by Spindle standards—mansion allocated as the official residence of Her Majesty's Provisional Governor. And this dining room was guarded by far more effective antisnooping systems than protected the one in which Samiha Lababibi and Andrieaux Yvernau were dining at that very moment.

"I don't know, Milady," Gregor O'Shaughnessy admitted. "I wish we'd had some of our own forensics people on-site, although I'm not really sure even that would have helped a lot.

"From Colonel Basaricek's report, it certainly sounds as if she could be gone, but Basaricek herself points out that her evidence is extremely problematical. I've requested a copy of the KNP's low-light imagery. Once we have it, we may be able to enhance the quality sufficiently to make a more positive estimation of whether or not it really was Nordbrandt. Of course, even for a dispatch boat, the transit time between here and Split is over seven days one-way, so it'll be at least another week before it could possibly get here."

"Excuse me, Gregor," Commander Chandler said, "but if we're requesting copies of the imagery, why don't we simply offer our own forensic services to determine whether or not the remains are hers?"

"I considered that, Ambrose," O'Shaughnessy told Rear Admiral Khumalo's intelligence officer. "But then I read the full appendices Basaricek had appended to her basic report."

"I skimmed them myself," Chandler said. He grimaced. "I can't say I understood everything in them. Or even most of what was in them, for that matter."

Rear Admiral Khumalo frowned from his seat at the foot of the table as Chandler made that admission. Dame Estelle saw it and wondered whether Khumalo's problem was that he felt Chandler *should* have understood the technical material, or if he was just irritated with the ONI officer for admitting ignorance in the presence of civilians.

"I didn't understand them either." O'Shaughnessy didn't even glance at Khumalo, but the Provisional Governor suspected him of deliberately drawing a little fire away from his uniformed colleague. "But, *because* I didn't understand them, I went and asked Major Cateaux for her analysis."

Several people sat a bit straighter, listening more intently, at the mention of Major Cateaux. Sandra Cateaux was the senior Marine physician assigned to the understrength battalion stationed in Spindle.

"She reviewed the material," O'Shaughnessy told them. "And when she finished, she told me what I'd been afraid she was going to." He shrugged. "The short version is that if the remains the KNP recovered had been those of a Manticoran citizen, the Major could easily have identified the victim. But because they're the remains of a Kornatian citizen, she doesn't have the base information she requires for a genetic determination. Apparently Nordbrandt never had a genetic scan—they're rarely performed by the current Kornatian medical establishment—and, so far as the KNP's been able to determine, no samples of her blood or tissue were retained by her physicians. Or else, as I suspect was the case, she and her organization saw to it that any samples which had been retained were properly disappeared when she decided to go underground.

"As for more mundane, not to say primitive, forensic techniques, apparently Ms. Nordbrandt hadn't previously suffered any physical injuries which would have left identifying markers in the rather, um . . . finely divided remains. The Kornatians do have her dental records; unfortunately, they didn't recover enough teeth for a positive ID.

"In short, according to Major Cateaux, the available material and records simply aren't enough to conclusively determine from the physical evidence whether or not the remains belong to Nordbrandt."

"What about genetic comparisons to family members?" Captain Shoupe asked. Khumalo's chief of staff was frowning intently as she leaned forward to look down the length of the table at O'Shaughnessy.

"That might be a possibility," Dame Estelle's intelligence chief acknowledged. "Except, unfortunately, for the fact that Ms. Nordbrandt was adopted." Shoupe winced, and O'Shaughnessy nodded. "That's right. She was a foundling. Colonel Basaricek's looking into it, but she's not optimistic about her investigators turning up anything that would guide us at this late date to Nordbrandt's biological family."

"So all we can really say is that it *may* be Nordbrandt," Khumalo rumbled with an expression of profound disapproval.

"I'm afraid so, Admiral," O'Shaughnessy said regretfully, and a gloomy silence fell briefly over the table.

"There may be some indirect, inferential evidence," Chandler said after a moment. All eyes turned in his direction, and he shrugged.

"While Gregor was consulting with Major Cateaux, I spent some time analyzing the news reportage from Kornati and cross-indexing it with Colonel Basaricek's report on FAK activity. The two salient points which struck me, once I'd stripped away all of the newsies' verbiage and wild speculation, were that, first, Nordbrandt hasn't stepped forward to announce she's still alive. And, second, the tempo of FAK attacks has dropped radically. Obviously, as Gregor's just pointed out, all our information is over a T-week out of date simply because of the time it spends in transit. Nonetheless, the pattern I'm referring to had been established over a period of almost eight days before Vice President Rajkovic sent Basaricek's report to the Convention."

"Those are both excellent points, Ambrose," O'Shaughnessy said. "It does seem peculiar for a terrorist leader who's been reported killed by government forces not to announce she's still alive . . . if she *is* still alive. The uncertainty among her followers would have to have a pronounced negative effect on their ability and willingness to continue the struggle. For that matter, it's a bit odd that no one's come forward claiming to be her spokesperson even if she's actually dead, just to try to hold her movement together."

"That might depend on just how disordered they are in the wake of her death," Captain Shoupe suggested. "Maybe there's nobody left in a sufficiently clear position of command to organize that sort of hoax."

"More likely, they just don't think it would work," Chandler said. Shoupe looked at him, and he shrugged again. "Nordbrandt was FAK's sole spokeswoman. She was the terrorists' public face, the voice which openly—proudly—accepted responsibility for their atrocities in their collective name. If she were still alive and not seriously incapacitated, she'd never rely on a spokesperson to inform her homeworld of that. So either she *isn't* still alive, or else she *is* seriously incapacitated. Or, for some reason, she's chosen not to announce her survival, despite her decision's probable negative impact on her own organization."

"Can anybody suggest a reason why she might make a choice like that?" Dame Estelle asked.

"*I* can't, Milady," Chandler said. "On the other hand, I wasn't privy to her plans before this attack went sour. I'm certainly not privy to whatever's going through the FAK's collective mind at this point. It's entirely possible there might be some tactical or strategic advantage in allowing the Kornatian authorities to believe she's dead. I simply can't imagine what it might be from the limited information we possess."

"I have to agree with Ambrose, Milady," O'Shaughnessy

said. "I can't think of any advantage it might gain for them, either. As he says, none of us have any sort of inside line to what these people might be thinking or planning, but his second point—that the FAK's been almost somnolent since her reported death—may also be significant. It may well be she was just as charismatic and central to her organization's operations and existence as her role as its sole spokeswoman, as Ambrose puts it, might suggest. If she was, and if she's dead, then the FAK may very well be disintegrating even as we speak."

"Now *that's* a pleasant thought, Mr. O'Shaughnessy," Rear Admiral Khumalo observed.

"Yes, it is," the Provisional Governor agreed. "And, to be honest, I think it's what President Tonkovic thinks is happening. She's still talking in terms of our providing 'technical' assistance—reconnaissance and intelligence support and modern weapons for her own law enforcement and military personnel—rather than the actual insertion of our own troops. I, personally, don't plan on investing too much confidence in the notion that Nordbrandt's gone and the FAK is going—certainly not without additional evidence. But the possibility obviously exists. And if it happens to be true, it would free us to turn our primary attention to Mr. Westman and his Montana Independence Movement."

"Which," Khumalo sighed gloomily, "is a problem less likely to yield to simple solutions than Ms. Nordbrandt appears to have been."

"Excuse me, Skipper."

"Yes, Amal?" Aivars Terekhov looked up from his discussion with Ansten FitzGerald and Ginger Lewis as Lieutenant Commander Nagchaudhuri poked his head into the bridge briefing room.

"Sorry to disturb you, but a dispatch boat's just arrived from Spindle, Sir," *Hexapuma*'s communications officer said. "She's already uploaded her dispatches to us."

"Really?" Terekhov tipped his chair back, turning it

away from the table to face the hatch. "May I assume we have new orders?"

"Yes, Sir, we do. I've copied them for you," Nagchaudhuri said, extending a message board. But Terekhov shook his head.

"Just give me the gist of them."

"Yes, Sir. We're to return to Spindle via Rembrandt, picking up Mr. Bernardus Van Dort from Vermeer *en route*."

"Van Dort? Was there any explanation of why we're to collect him?"

"No, Sir. Of course, all I've done so far is to decrypt our orders. There was a lot more in the download, including news reports from Spindle and a hefty amount of private correspondence for you from Admiral Khumalo and the Provisional Governor. I'd say there's a fair chance something in there may give us a clue or two, Skipper."

"You have a point," Terekhov agreed, and turned to look at FitzGerald and Lewis again.

"Well, the good news is that at least the Celebrants don't seem to be experiencing the problems that Nuncio was. We can pull out in good conscience without worrying about abandoning them to some outside threat. Or, at least, any *known* outside threat." He smiled thinly.

"True enough, Skipper," FitzGerald agreed. "I wish we'd had more than eight days in-system, though. Our astrogation database updates are just getting started, and I hate to stop now."

"It's a pain, but it's not the end of the universe," Terekhov said. "We had to take the first couple of days to introduce ourselves to the Celebrants. Frankly, I think that was time well spent—probably better than if we'd launched straight into the survey, when all's said, Ansten. The relationship between the people who live here and the Star Kingdom's more important than the coordinates of some minor system body."

"You've got me there, Skip," FitzGerald said.

"Very well. Amal."

"Yes, Sir?"

"First, a message to President Shaw's office. Inform them that we're under orders to depart as soon as possible for Spindle. This is only a heads-up for general information. I'll want to send him a personal message before we actually depart."

"Aye, Sir."

"Second, a message for the dispatch boat's skipper. Unless he has specific orders to continue on to some other system, I'll want him to return directly to Spindle. We'll upload our logs, including our reports on events in Nuncio, as well as any mail our people want to send ahead. The dispatch boat can shave three days, absolute, off our own arrival time, even assuming we don't have to lay over in Rembrandt while we wait for Mr. Van Dort."

"Aye, Sir," Nagchaudhuri repeated.

"Third, general broadcast to all our small craft and away duty and leave parties. All hands to repair onboard immediately."

"Aye, Sir."

"I think that's it for now. Get back to me as soon as you can on the dispatch boat's availability, please."

"Yes, Sir. I'll see to it."

Nagchaudhuri stepped back through the hatch on to the bridge, and Terekhov glanced at his two senior subordinates.

"What do you think they're up to, Skip?" FitzGerald asked after a moment.

"Not a clue in the universe," Terekhov told him with a grin.

"Me neither," Ginger Lewis said. "But, in the words of an old prespace book I read once, 'Curiouser and curiouser.'"

"Jesus Christ."

Stephen Westman couldn't have said whether he meant it as a prayer or a curse. He sat in his underground headquarters with Luis Palacios, staring at the news footage which had finally arrived from the Split System. That footage was over forty days old; the Talbott Cluster wasn't served by the fast commercial dispatch boats the interstellar news services used to tie more important bits of the galaxy together, and the news had crossed the hundred and twenty light-years between Split and Montana aboard a regular freighter. Which meant it had crossed slowly. Not that the delay in transit had made it any better.

"My God, Boss," Palacios said. "She's got to be a frigging maniac!"

"I wish I could disagree," Westman replied.

He looked down at his hands and was astounded to see they weren't shaking like leaves. They ought to have been. And he was vaguely surprised he wasn't actively nauseated by the gory imagery of the atrocity Agnes Nordbrandt had committed.

"They attacked their own parliament building while Parliament was in session!" Palacios muttered. "What were they *thinking*?"

"What do you think they were thinking?" Westman snorted bitterly. "Look at this 'manifesto' of theirs! They're not trying to convince people to support them—they're declaring war against their entire government, not just the annexation effort. Hell, Luis—they've gone to war against their entire society! And it looks like they don't give a good goddamn who they kill in the course of it. Look at this body count. And it's from their very first damned operation. Operation! It was a goddamned *massacre*! They *wanted* the highest possible casualty totals—that's why they had two damned waves of fucking bombs!"

He sat back, shaking his head, thinking about how hard he and his people had worked to avoid killing *anyone*, much less innocent bystanders. The spectacular destruction of the System Bank of Montana had antagonized a sizable percentage of Montana's electorate, exactly as Westman had anticipated. He hadn't really liked pissing off that many people, but it was inevitable that the majority of Montanans were going to oppose his objectives, at least initially. After all, almost three-quarters of them had voted in favor of annexation. So there wasn't a lot of point pussyfooting around and trying to avoid hurt feelings. He'd made his point that he was prepared to attack economic targets other than the hated Rembrandter presence on Montana. And he'd made his secondary point, that he was prepared to disrupt the entire star system's economy, if that was what it took to get all the assorted and accursed off-worlders off Montana once and for all. But he'd also managed to do it without killing, or even injuring anyone.

Frankly, he'd been surprised no bomb disposal experts had been sent into the bank's cellars in an effort to defuse his bombs. Delighted, but surprised. He'd expected that they would be, despite the airy confidence to the contrary he'd adopted for his followers' benefit. And he'd known that if the Marshals Service or the military had sent bomb disposal units into the tunnels, some or all of those men and women would have been killed by his antitampering arrangements. He'd anticipated that Trevor Bannister would know he wasn't bluffing, but he'd been very much afraid that halfwitted jackass Suttles and the rest of his Cabinet would reject Trevor's advice.

Yet they hadn't, and because they hadn't, he still wasn't a murderer.

It wouldn't last, of course. As Luis had pointed out, sooner or later people were going to be killed. But one thing he was grimly determined upon was that he would never resort to general and indiscriminate slaughter. His government had no right to subvert the Montana Constitution, and *no* off-worlders had the right to exploit and economically enslave his planet. He would fight those people, and those who served them, in any way he must. Yet he'd also do his best to minimize casualties even among their ranks. And before he embarked on the deliberate massacre of innocent men, women, and children, he would turn himself in, and all his men with him.

Still, he thought, drawing a deep breath and getting a grip on his shock, he was still a long way away from that kind of decision. And he had no intention of finding himself forced to make it.

But I do have another *decision to make. "Firebrand" and his Central Liberation Committee are supporting both me and Nordbrandt. Do I really want to be associated, even indirectly, with someone who could do something like this? Nobody outside the Central Liberation Committee would ever know I was, but* I'd *know. And Firebrand was so enthusiastic about Nordbrandt and her plans. My God,* his eyes narrowed, momentarily harder than blue flint, in fresh realization, *the whole time he was standing here telling me how he admired my "restraint," he was already in bed with a murderous bitch like this!*

I should tell him to bugger off and stay the hell away from me, if he's so fond of bloodthirsty lunatics. The last thing I need is to be associated with someone like Nordbrandt!

But he was right. I do need the weapons and other support he's offered to provide. And so far, at least, there's been no pressure to change my operational methods. If there is any pressure, I can always just say goodbye and don't screen us, we'll screen you.

He gazed off into nothingness, at things only he could see, and wrestled with his own demons even as he shied away from a demoness named Nordbrandt.

Chapter Thirty-Four

"Welcome to Rembrandt, Captain Terekhov!"

The big, burly captain in the uniform of the Rembrandt System Navy held out his hand and shook Terekhov's firmly. More than firmly, really; whether he meant to be or not, he was clearly a knuckle crusher.

"I'm Captain Groenhuijen, Admiral Van Der Wildt's chief of staff. On her behalf, and that of the entire Navy, I officially welcome you to the Rembrandt System."

"Thank you, Sir," Aivars Terekhov replied, hoping he would get his hand back without permanent damage. Arjan Groenhuijen was a good eight centimeters shorter than he was, but the Rembrandter was thick chested and broad shouldered, with long, powerful arms and sinewy hands. Terekhov suspected that he was one of those physical fitness types who spent most of his free hours in the weight room.

The dark-haired Rembrandter finally released his hand, and beamed at him.

"It's a genuine pleasure to see you here, Captain Terekhov. You aren't the first RMN vessel we've seen, of course. But you are the most modern and most powerful. I'm impressed, Captain. Most impressed."

"Time permitting, Sir," Terekhov said, resisting a temptation to wiggle his fingers to make sure all of them were still in working order, "I'd be honored to give you a tour. I'm afraid, however, if I've read the urgency attached to my instructions properly, that this will be a very brief visit."

"True, I'm afraid." Groenhuijen's expression sobered. "President Tinkhof has stressed the importance of assisting any Manticoran vessel, especially any Queen's ship, visiting our space. According to the correspondence which has passed back and forth between her office, Admiral Van Der Wildt's office, and Mr. Van Dort, in this instance the greatest assistance we can provide will be to get you turned around and on your way quickly. Do you have any pressing logistics requirements?"

"No, Sir. Thank you. We're still in remarkably good shape on the logistics side." Terekhov didn't mention the missiles he'd expended in Nuncio. Those expenditures couldn't have been made good out of Rembrandt stocks. Besides, his next stop was Spindle itself, where the station's service squadron would be able to supply any of his needs.

"Excellent!" Groenhuijen rubbed his hands together, once again beaming. "In that case, I'm to inform you that Mr. Van Dort will, with your permission, come aboard at zero-seven-thirty hours local. Admiral Van Der Wildt's arranged his transportation to your vessel."

"That will be quite convenient, Sir. One point, however. My orders are to transport Mr. Van Dort to Spindle as expeditiously as possible. No mention was made of any staff or assistants. We are, of course, prepared to carry any such staff, but my XO and Logistics Officer would like to know if we're expecting any additional passengers, so that they can make arrangements for their accommodations and comfort."

"That's very kind of you, Captain. However, Mr. Van Dort will be traveling by himself. As is his customary practice."

Something about the Rembrandter's tone piqued

Terekhov's curiosity, and he looked more closely at the other man.

"I see. May I ask if you're aware of any special needs Mr. Van Dort might have?"

For a moment, it seemed Groenhuijen wasn't going to answer. Then the RSN captain gave a smile which contained very little humor.

"Mr. Van Dort routinely travels by himself, Captain. It is his way, you understand." He waited until Terekhov had nodded. "Nonetheless, there are those here in Rembrandt who . . . worry about him. He is not, perhaps, universally beloved throughout the Cluster, or even here on Rembrandt these days. And he's driving himself hard—very hard—to make the annexation a success. It isn't really my place to say this, but there are those of us who regard him as a national treasure, a man upon whom a great many things depend, and for whom we have enormous respect. It would please me—and Admiral Van Der Wildt—to think he had someone specifically . . . looking after his needs. Whether he's prepared to take someone along for that purpose or not."

Terekhov looked into Groenhuijen's eyes and was startled by what he saw there. The bluff, hand-crushing naval officer's admiration and concern for Bernardus Van Dort were obvious. And despite his rank, the Rembrandter also looked like a young boy, running around behind the back of a beloved uncle to be sure he was properly looked after.

"I see, Sir," Terekhov said. "We'll be expecting him. And I promise we'll take good care of him."

"Midshipwoman Pavletic reports to the Executive Officer as directed, Sir!" Ragnhild Pavletic said, bracing to attention before Ansten FitzGerald's desk.

"Midshipwoman Zilwicki reports to the Executive Officer as directed, Sir!" Helen Zilwicki echoed, coming to attention beside her.

"Stand easy," FitzGerald said gravely, and hid a smile as both snotties obeyed. Their expressions were those of two young women whose consciences were spic and span, without trace of sin. But something about their body language, a slight tightness to the shoulders, perhaps, suggested both of them were earnestly searching their memories for some infraction sufficiently serious to have landed them in front of the XO himself.

"First," he continued, in that same grave tone, "neither of you is in trouble." Without moving a muscle, they managed to radiate enormous relief. "Second, I have an additional duty looking for someone to be assigned to it. At the moment, it looks like one of you is going to be the lucky recipient. However, I wanted to discuss it with both of you in order to determine which is best suited to it."

The middies glanced at one another from the corners of their eyes, then looked attentively at their superior.

"In about two hours," FitzGerald said, "Mr. Bernardus Van Dort will be coming aboard the *Nasty Kitty*. Excuse me," he grinned wickedly at their expressions, especially Ragnhild's, "I mean, of course, aboard *Hexapuma*," he corrected himself. Then his tone sobered. "I presume both of you know who he is?"

"Ah, we saw him on Flax, at the banquet, Sir," Helen said. "I believe we were told he was an important commercial representative from Rembrandt, but no one explained anything more than that to us."

"I did hear, Sir," Ragnhild added, "that he was—or had been—a very senior board member of the Rembrandt Trade Union." FitzGerald quirked an eyebrow at her, and she smiled slightly. "My family's deeply involved in the Star Kingdom's merchant marine, Sir. I guess some of the family instincts rubbed off on me. I tend to pick up odd bits and pieces of information—the kind a merchant spacer might find useful."

"I see. As a matter of fact, Ms. Pavletic, I was aware of your family background. It's one of the reasons I'm considering you for this assignment."

FitzGerald let both of them digest that for a few seconds, then brought his chair upright behind his desk.

"What both of you just said about Mr. Van Dort is perfectly accurate, as far as it goes. However, it would be more accurate to say he *is* the RTU. He was its founder, and he's still its largest stockholder. For most of the last sixty T-years, he's been Chairman of the Board of a four-system 'trade association' which is effectively a star nation in its own right. Mr. Van Dort resigned his position as Chairman specifically to organize the annexation vote. That, too, could be said to be his personal brainchild, although he isn't and never has been a politician as we would understand the term in the Star Kingdom. In short, although he's technically only one more private citizen here in the Cluster, he's an *extremely* influential and important private citizen."

He paused to let them think over what he'd said, then continued.

"The reason I'm telling you all this is that we've been instructed by Admiral Khumalo, at Baroness Medusa's request, to transport Mr. Van Dort to Spindle. I'm not prepared at this time to go into the exact reasons the Provisional Governor made that request. It's probable, however, that we'll be moving on from Spindle, and that Mr. Van Dort will accompany us. I'm sure both of you are intelligent enough to deduce that in such a circumstance we would be functioning in a support capacity for any mission Mr. Van Dort might undertake at the Baroness' request. We've just been informed, however, that it's Mr. Van Dort's practice to travel by himself, without staff. Apparently, to be blunt about it, this is a personal foible of his, almost an affectation. I suppose he must have a staff here in Rembrandt, and possibly one already in place in Spindle, but he'll have no such staff support aboard *Hexapuma*, unless he drafts some of the people we assume he has in Spindle for that purpose after our arrival.

"In the meantime, however, Captain Terekhov has decided it would be wise to assign him a personal aide. It's entirely possible such an assignment would never amount to being more than a personal go-for. It's also possible, however, that the individual assigned to him would find him or herself involved in significantly more important duties and responsibilities. Since this insistence of his on traveling without an entire stable of assistants seems to be an important part of his self-image, the Captain doesn't wish to make it obvious that he's trying to circumvent it. Accordingly, he's decided to assign a midshipman to the task. Someone junior enough to avoid triggering any automatic rejection of an official aide, but with sufficient personal background knowledge and experience to serve that function, anyway. Which is what brings me to the two of you."

He paused again, this time obviously waiting for them to say something. Helen glanced at Ragnhild, then looked back at the Exec.

"May I ask why it does, Sir?" she asked.

"You may. Ms. Pavletic and Mr. Sottmeister are the only two of our midshipmen with connections to our own merchant marine. Of the two, Ms. Pavletic's family's been more deeply involved for a longer time. Specifically, Pavletic, Tilliotson, and Ellett is one of the Star Kingdom's oldest shipping lines. This, I believe, would probably put her in the best position of any of our middies to 'talk shop' with Mr. Van Dort. Although I'm sure the Captain would prefer not to have to find a replacement pilot for Hawk-Papa-One, I'm afraid Mr. Van Dort takes precedence even over that.

"You, on the other hand, Ms. Zilwicki, are effectively the adopted daughter of Catherine Montaigne. You have personal, first-hand experience of how someone operating at the highest level of the Star Kingdom's politics goes about her business. Then there's your relationship to Queen Berry. And the fact that your father is one of the Star Kingdom's most effective, ah . . . intelligence operatives. Whereas Ms. Pavletic would be in a position to address the business side of Mr. Van Dort's responsibilities and achievements, you'd be in a better position to appreciate any political requirements he might have."

"Sir, PT and E may be one of the older lines, but

we're not exactly crowding the Hauptman Cartel. We're not that big an outfit," Ragnhild protested.

"And, Sir, with all due respect, while I may have seen Cathy—I mean, Ms. Montaigne—in action, I've never been especially interested in politics. Certainly not on the level Mr. Van Dort seems to be."

"Noted, and noted. Nonetheless, however inadequate you may feel your qualifications are, they are superior in this regard to those of your fellow snotties. So, one of you is going to draw the assignment. What we're here to determine is which one it will be."

FitzGerald smiled at their expressions, then pointed at the chairs behind them.

"Sit," he said, and they sat.

"Good." He smiled again. "The interview process will now begin."

"Welcome aboard *Hexapuma*, Mr. Van Dort," Captain Terekhov said, standing just inside the boarding tube as his guest came aboard from the Rembrandt Navy shuttle.

"Thank you." The tall, fair-haired Rembrandter reached out to shake the captain's hand. Unlike Captain Groenhuijen, he showed no particular inclination to mangle the digits in his grasp.

"I've been instructed by Baroness Medusa to personally thank you for your willingness to return to Spindle with us," Terekhov continued.

"That's very kind of her, but no thanks are necessary. I'm not certain I can provide the assistance she needs, but anything I can do, I certainly will."

"No one could possibly ask more than that. May I introduce Commander FitzGerald, my Executive Officer?"

"Commander," Van Dort acknowledged, shaking the XO's hand.

"And this is Commander Lewis, my Engineer."

"Commander Lewis." Van Dort smiled as the engineering officer stepped forward. "I well recall my own days as a merchant spacer. Which means I know who really keeps any ship running."

"I see you're as perceptive as everyone said you were, Sir," Ginger Lewis said with a smile of her own, and he chuckled.

"And this," the captain continued, "is Midshipwoman Zilwicki."

Van Dort turned towards Helen with a smile, then paused. It was a tiny thing, no more than a momentary hesitation, but she saw something flicker in his eyes.

"Midshipwoman," he murmured after a moment, and offered her his hand in turn.

"Mr. Van Dort. This is an honor, Sir."

The Rembrandter made a tiny, graceful brushing-away gesture with his free hand, his eyes still on her face, and Terekhov smiled.

"With your permission, Sir, I've taken the liberty of assigning Ms. Zilwicki to get you settled in aboard *Hexapuma* and to serve as my personal liaison with you. I believe you'll find she has considerably more experience with the sorts of responsibilities facing you than you might expect from someone of her age and lack of seniority."

Van Dort had opened his mouth, as if to politely reject the offer, but he closed it again at Terekhov's final sentence. Instead of speaking, he simply gazed at Helen for another second or two, and she felt uncomfortably as if he'd just put her on some sort of invisible scale that weighed her abilities with meticulous precision. Or as if he knew something about her she didn't know herself. Which was ridiculous.

"That's very considerate of you, Captain," he said finally. "I trust Ms. Zilwicki won't find my requirements too onerous."

"Oh, I wouldn't worry too much about that, Sir," Terekhov murmured with a wicked little smile. "After all, Ms. Zilwicki's on her snotty cruise. She's *supposed* to find her duties onerous."

"So what's he like?" Leo Stottmeister demanded.

"Van Dort?" Helen looked up from the maintenance

manual on her reader. She, Leo, Aikawa, and Paulo d'Arezzo were off duty, and she'd been boning up on maintenance procedures for the broadside graser mounts. Abigail Hearns intended to conduct a verbal exam on the subject the next day, and Helen believed in being prepared.

"No, the Andermani Emperor," Leo said, rolling his eyes in exasperation. "Of course Van Dort!"

"He's a nice enough guy. For an old geezer." Helen shrugged.

"Scuttlebutt says he's a real hard-ass political type. Some kind of hired gun the Provisional Governor is calling in."

"Then scuttlebutt has its head up its ass," Helen replied tartly.

"Hey! I'm just saying what I've heard," Leo said a touch defensively. "If I'm wrong, straighten me out, don't bite my head off!"

Helen ran her hands through her hair with a grimace.

"I really do have to study this maintenance manual."

"Bull," Leo shot back. "You know that stuff forward and backward—you've aced every proficiency exam we've had!"

"He's got a point, Helen," Aikawa said with a grin. "If you don't want to talk about it, that's one thing. But you really need to come up with a better excuse than that."

"All right. All right!" She grinned back, acknowledging defeat. "But you guys have to understand, I've spent probably less than two hours with him so far. It isn't like I can tell you what he's thinking or anything like that. Or, for that matter, like I would if I could."

She accompanied the last sentence with a stern gaze, and her audience nodded in acknowledgment.

"Having said that, I think he really is a nice guy. He's worried, I can tell you that much, although I don't know how much *he* knows about what the Baroness has in mind. He seems to be as smart as they come, too. And he spends most of his time buried in briefing papers and personal correspondence from what looks like people all over the Cluster. I guess the reason I kind of snapped at you, Leo, is that the one thing he isn't is a 'hired gun.' This is a very serious player—maybe even more serious, in some ways, than Cathy Montaigne—and this entire annexation idea was pretty much his brainstorm. I don't know what Baroness Medusa's thinking, but she's just latched onto the man who probably has the most political horsepower of anybody in the entire Cluster. When you combine that with the fact that she had *Hexapuma* divert to Rembrandt specifically to pick him up instead of just sending a dispatch boat for him, I'd say she's probably got him—and us—earmarked for something pretty damned significant, wouldn't you?"

"I wonder if Terekhov's picked up Van Dort yet?" Rear Admiral Khumalo murmured.

"I beg your pardon, Sir? Were you speaking to me?"

"What?" Khumalo shook himself and straightened in his chair. "Sorry, Loretta. I suppose I was actually just thinking out loud. I was wondering if *Hexapuma*'s reached Rembrandt yet."

"She probably has," Captain Shoupe said after a quick, reflexive glance at the date/time display on the briefing room bulkhead. The rear admiral's daily staff conference had just broken up, and abandoned coffee and teacups stood forlornly beside mostly empty carafes.

"I certainly hope so," Khumalo said, and the chief of staff looked quickly back at him. His broad face looked weary, far more worried than he'd permitted it to look during the staff meeting.

"If she hasn't already, I'm sure she will in the next day or so, Sir," she said encouragingly.

"The sooner the better," Khumalo said. "I'm not sure I'm prepared to admit it to Mr. O'Shaughnessy, but the situation on Montana's threatening to get badly out of hand. I'm still more than a little uneasy about the entire notion of meddling in their internal political quarrels, but given this latest news . . ." He shook his head. "If Van Dort—and Terekhov, I suppose—really can do anything about it, then the sooner we get them there, the better."

Shoupe kept her expression carefully neutral, but she was a little taken aback by Khumalo's attitude. Her superior must be even more concerned about the Montana Independence Movement than she'd thought to have changed his position that radically.

"May I ask if the Provisional Governor's firmly decided Montana has priority over Split, Sir?" she asked respectfully.

"You may, and I don't know," Khumalo replied with a half-smile, half-grimace. "All I can say is that with it looking more and more as if the Kornatians really did nail Nordbrandt, Montana's relative priority's risen pretty steeply. Especially after Westman's last little trick!"

Shoupe nodded. News of the MIM's destruction of the Montana System Bank's headquarters had reached Spindle the day before.

Why, oh why, she wondered, *couldn't our problem-child star systems be closer to each other. Or to us, for that matter*.

Split lay just over 60.6 LY from Spindle. Montana was 82.5 LY from Spindle, and over a hundred and twenty from Split. Even a warship like *Hexapuma* would require more than eight days to make the trip from Spindle to Split. Montana was the next best thing to twelve days away, and the trip from Montana *to* Split would require better than seventeen days. All of which made coordination between Spindle and what looked like being the Cluster's two true flashpoints a genuine, unmitigated pain in the ass. Just getting information back and forth, even using the speedy dispatch boats which routinely traveled in the riskier Theta Bands of hyper-space, took literally weeks. No matter what Rear Admiral Khumalo or Baroness Medusa decided to do, they could absolutely count on the fact that the information on which their decision was based was out of date.

"I suppose we should concentrate on being glad Nordbrandt and the FAK seem to be out of business, Sir," she suggested after a moment. "That doesn't make dealing with Mr. Westman any more attractive, but at least it's an improvement over having to deal with both at once!"

"A point, Loretta," Khumalo agreed with a tired smile. "Definitely a point."

Chapter Thirty-Five

"The Captain's compliments, Sir, and the pinnace will depart from Boat Bay Three in thirty minutes."

"Thank you, Helen." Bernardus Van Dort smiled and shook his head. "You didn't really have to come and deliver that message in person, you know. The com would have worked just fine."

"First of all, I didn't mind delivering it in person, Sir. Second, when the Captain 'suggests' that a snotty personally deliver a message to an important guest aboard his ship, the snotty in question gets on her little feet, trots right down the passage, and delivers said message."

Van Dort laughed out loud, and Helen Zilwicki grinned at him. Their relationship had come a long way in the seven days—six by *Hexapuma*'s internal clocks—since he'd come on board. At first, Helen thought, he'd started out regretting having accepted her as his aide. He seemed, for all his accomplishments and personal wealth, a very private man. And, she thought, a lonely one. He'd certainly been politely distant from her, with a sort of cool courtesy that discouraged any familiarity. Indeed, in some ways he'd seemed even more distant from her than from anyone else in the entire ship, as if he were deliberately keeping her at arm's length. He'd gotten a bit more comfortable, but he still maintained that sense of distance, of watchfulness.

Yet she'd come to realize there was a warm and caring person under that isolated, detached shell of his, and she wondered why a man like that lived such a solitary life. No doubt he did have large, capable staffs to serve him at home on Rembrandt. And, equally no doubt, he could call on the RTU staffers on any planet in the Cluster to provide him with secretaries and assistants at need. But he should have had a permanent, personal staff. At least one private aide to travel with him whenever travel was necessary. Someone who was as much a confidant as an administrative assistant.

Someone to keep him company.

There had to be a reason he didn't, and she wished she dared to ask him what it was.

"Will you be free to accompany me to the meeting, Helen?" he asked, and she looked at him in surprise.

"I . . . don't know, Sir. As far as I know, the possibility hasn't been discussed. I'm sure that if you'd like me to, the Captain would authorize it."

"Well, it's occurred to me that if I'm going to be continuing aboard the *Kitty*," he shared another grin with her, "it would be just as well for my 'aide' to be up to speed on what we're trying to accomplish. And I've come to realize you're actually quite a bright young woman, despite occasional attempts to pretend otherwise." His expression grew more serious. "I think you could be of even greater assistance if you were fully informed on the parameters of my mission. And there are a few other reasons I think it might be a good idea to have you along."

"Sir," she said, "I'm deeply flattered. But I'm only a middy. I'm not at all sure the Provisional Governor would approve of someone that junior being fully briefed on a mission that was important enough to haul you all the way back to Spindle from Rembrandt."

"If I tell her I've come to rely on your assistance and that I'd like you informed—and that you'll keep your mouth shut about any sensitive information—I feel sure I could overcome any objections she might have. And you *would* keep your mouth shut, wouldn't you?"

"Yes, Sir! Of course I would!"

"I rather thought so," he said with a slight smile. "Then again, I'd hardly expect less from the daughter of Anton Zilwicki."

Helen couldn't help herself. This time she didn't just look at him in surprise, she gawked at him, and he chuckled.

"Helen, Helen!" He shook his head. "I've made it a priority to remain as closely informed as possible on events in the Star Kingdom ever since *Harvest Joy* came sailing out of the Lynx Terminus. I know all about that affair in Erewhon. In fact, I probably know more about it than most native-born Manticorans. That feature story Yael Underwood did on your father just before the Stein funeral caught my eye, especially in light of what happened in Erewhon and, later, in Congo. I'm sure he got parts of it wrong, but he obviously got a lot right, too. It took me all of an hour and a half to put you and your surname together with his, especially after I remembered that the newsies said he had a daughter at the Manticoran Naval Academy."

"Sir, I'm not a spook. Daddy may be some sort of superspy, although given the fact that everybody in the entire galaxy seems to know now what he does for a living, his active spying days must be pretty much over. But I never even *wanted* to be a spook."

"I never assumed you did. But, as I say, you're intelligent, you've demonstrated tact and initiative in the time we've been together, and whether you want to be a 'spook' or not, your father's example when it comes to maintaining operational security has to've rubbed off on you at least a little. Besides," he looked away, "you remind me of someone."

She started to ask who, then stopped herself.

"Well, Sir," she said, instead, with a crooked smile, "I'm sure you could have your pick of people far better qualified than I am. But if you want me, and if the Captain doesn't have any objections, I'd be honored to help out anyway I can."

"Excellent!" He looked back down at her with a broad smile. "I'll speak to him immediately."

"Bernardus!" Dame Estelle Matsuko swept across the room to greet her visitor. "Thank you for coming!"

"Madam Governor, anything I can do to be of service is, of course, yours for the asking," he said graciously, and actually bent over her hand to bestow a kiss upon it.

The old boy's got the chivalrous courtesy bit down cold, Helen Zilwicki thought admiringly, trailing along behind the rest of the party as befitted her astronomically junior status.

"That's very good of you," the Provisional Governor said much more seriously. "Especially since I know how badly you wanted to get away from Spindle."

"That was a tactical decision, Madam Governor, not a reflection of any desire to quit the fray before the annexation's completed."

"Good," she said, "because 'the fray's' gotten progressively uglier since you left, and I need you." She waved her hand at another door, through which Helen could just make out an enormous conference table and at least half a dozen more people, including Rear Admiral Khumalo. "Please, come join us. We have a lot to talk about."

" . . . so unless we can get a handle on the situation in Montana, I'm afraid we'll be looking at an even greater problem than the ones we faced on Kornati," Gregor O'Shaughnessy completed his general background briefing somberly. "The steady escalation of the MIM's operations is heading Westman and his people towards an inevitable direct confrontation with the Montanan security forces. Despite all his efforts to avoid inflicting casualties, he's going to find himself in a shooting war with his own government, and the fact is, he's much more dangerous than Nordbrandt ever was. If it does come to a direct military confrontation between him and the Montanan System's police and military, he's going to do a lot more damage than Nordbrandt did because he doesn't believe in terror as a weapon. Put most simply, he's a guerilla, not a terrorist at all. He's not going to divert from his attacks on what we might call legitimate targets to waste his time taking out vulnerable civilian targets for the terror effect or just because he can rack up impressive kill numbers."

Bernardus Van Dort nodded slowly and thoughtfully, and Dame Estelle cocked her head at him.

"From your expression, I take it you find yourself basically in agreement with Gregor's assessment, Bernardus?"

"Yes, I do," he admitted. Then he shook his head, his expression rueful. "This is mostly my fault, you know. Where Montana's concerned, I mean. I let Ineka Vaandrager—"

He broke off and frowned.

"No," he continued after a moment, "let's be honest. I *used* Ineka to win the most favorable possible concessions from Montana. I never did like her tactics, but I had rather different priorities at the time, so I gave her her head. Which is one reason Westman hates my guts."

"Have you actually met, Sir?" O'Shaughnessy asked. "Do you know one another personally?"

"Oh, yes, Mr. O'Shaughnessy," Van Dort said softly. "We've met."

"Would he agree to meet with you again now if you asked him to?" Dame Estelle asked, and his eyebrows rose in surprise.

"Madam Governor—Dame Estelle, I doubt there's anyone in the entire Cluster he'd be *less* likely to meet with. For a lot of reasons. But especially not when his operations on Montana seem to be going so well. I'm sure that if I asked him to meet me, he'd see it as further evidence that he's in a position of strength. And, to be perfectly honest, in his boots, I'd hate my guts, too. Lord knows our 'negotiators' gave his entire planet sufficient reason to be . . . unfond of us, shall I say?"

"What I have in mind," the Provisional Governor said, "is to send you to speak to him not in your own right, not as a representative of the Trade Union, or even of the Constitutional Convention, but as my direct representative. As, if you will, the direct representative of the Star Kingdom of Manticore. And I would prefer for the invitation to be issued very openly, very publicly, so that he knows everyone else on the planet knows I've sent you as my personal envoy."

"Ah! You believe he's an astute enough psychologist to recognize that refusing to so much as meet with me under those circumstances would undermine the image of the gentleman guerrilla he's been at such pains to create?"

"That's one way to put it. I prefer to think of it as his recognizing he has to appear as reasonable and as rational as any outlaw can if he doesn't want to lose the struggle for public opinion the way Nordbrandt was in the process of losing it in Split. But the way you described it also works. Especially given that he's just about reached the limit of how far he can go without major bloodshed. He's got to recognize that. So if he is inclined towards any sort of negotiated settlement, he's got to be feeling pressure, the awareness that there's a line he can't cross without pretty much ruling out any negotiated resolution. I think he'd probably be willing to talk to almost anyone, under those circumstances, before stepping across that line."

"So you've definitely concluded Nordbrandt is dead?" Van Dort asked.

"I wouldn't go that far. I'll admit that the continued lower tempo of FAK operations and the fact that no one's heard the slightest claim that she *isn't* dead is inclining me strongly in that direction. But that's not the same thing as feeling confident she's gone. On the other hand, I have to prioritize threats somehow, and as long as Kornati stays more or less quiet, Montana has to become my first priority."

"I can understand that," he said, nodding again in agreement.

"Then I hope you can understand this, too, Bernardus," Medusa said very seriously. "I've discussed the situation on Kornati, on Montana, and here on Flax with all the Convention's major political leaders and reported the results of those conversations to the Foreign and Home Secretaries. I've also reported my own observations of the balance of power in the Convention and the apparent—as opposed, in some cases, to the claimed—objectives of the various groupings. In return, I've received instructions from Her Majesty's Government, and, on the basis of those instructions, I'm very much afraid the Government's patience isn't without limit."

Van Dort sat very still, watching her face intently.

"Aleksandra Tonkovic and her allies," the baroness continued levelly, "are playing with fire, and they either don't realize it or else won't admit it to themselves. Despite the situation in her own home system and in Montana, Tonkovic continues to hold out for a virtual guarantee of total local autonomy for all the systems in the Cluster. Not just in the sense of home rule, but in the sense of picking and choosing—and mostly rejecting, so far as I can tell—the provisions of the Star Kingdom's Constitution which they'll accept as binding upon them.

"My analysts—" she flashed a smile at O'Shaughnessy "—continue to assure me that much of her apparently total intransigence is a negotiating ploy. They may be right. But what I don't seem to be able to get her to believe is that Her Majesty has certain standards of her own, which any draft Constitution must meet to be acceptable. Tonkovic's proposals don't even come close. And the fact that she may intend at some unspecified future time to relax her demands in the hope of achieving a favorable compromise resolution is, unfortunately, largely lost on the Manticoran public and on the members of Parliament. She isn't merely polarizing the debate here in the Cluster; she's also polarizing it at home, in Manticore. And that, Bernardus, is something

Queen Elizabeth does *not* need when she's in the middle of a war.

"The bottom line is this. I've been informed by Her Majesty's Government that if an *acceptable* draft Constitution isn't voted out of the Convention within the next five standard months, the Star Kingdom of Manticore will withdraw its decision to accept the Talbott Cluster's request to be admitted to the Star Kingdom. If the delegates to the Convention are unwilling or unable to produce a Constitution which will meet the test of acceptability by the Manticoran Parliament *and* provide the legal mechanisms for the swift, effective suppression of murderous criminals like Nordbrandt, the Star Kingdom will settle for Lynx and leave the rest of the Cluster to its own devices."

Van Dort's face had gone white, and there was a long moment of silence when Dame Estelle finished. Then he cleared his throat.

"I can't blame your Government for feeling that way," he said quietly. "As a citizen of Rembrandt, as someone who lives here in the Cluster and who knows what Frontier Security will do to us if we don't obtain the Star Kingdom's protection, however, the very thought of what you're describing terrifies me. Have you had this same conversation with Aleksandra, Madam Governor?"

"I haven't discussed it quite as openly and frankly as I have with you," she said. "I've never been on the same terms of intimacy and confidence with her that I have with you and Henri Krietzmann and Joachim Alquezar. Not surprisingly, I suppose, given her basic political platform. But I've informed her that an outside time limit exists."

"And her reaction?"

"Ostensibly, she accepts the warning and assures me she's working diligently to resolve all existing problems as quickly as possible. Actually, I think, she believes I'm lying."

Van Dort looked shocked, and Dame Estelle waved one hand.

"What I mean, Bernardus, is that I believe she's convinced herself any hard time limit is my own invention, a ploy I came up with to pressure her into accepting Joachim's draft. I may be wrong, and I hope I am. But even if I'm not, she seems to be missing the point that the time limit I'm talking about is the last one the *Government* is prepared to accept. If the polarization she's creating here, and that's spilling over into domestic debate on this issue in the Star Kingdom, continues to grow stronger, official time limits will cease to matter. It will become politically impossible for the Crown to carry through the annexation, whatever the Queen's personal desires, in the face of powerfully opposed domestic opinion. That's one reason I believe it's essential for us to make the strongest possible effort to bring about at least a cease-fire on Montana and Kornati. If we can just stop the fighting and prevent further bloodshed, we ought to be able to put the brakes on at least some of the steadily growing domestic opposition to the annexation. And that, Bernardus, is why I need you. Badly."

"I understand, Madam Governor. And I assure you, I'll do everything in my power to get you those cease-fires."

HMS *Hexapuma* accelerated steadily away from the planet of Flax once again. Her magazines had been topped up—in fact, they were at 110 percent of nominal wartime levels—and her crew was supremely confident of its ability, and its Captain's, to deal with any threat she might encounter.

Not all the people aboard her were quite so optimistic. Her Captain and senior officers—and one lowly midshipwoman—knew too much about the ticking political clock. Some threats couldn't be blown out of space with a salvo of Mark 16 missiles. Nor could they be solved by a quick sortie by a company of Marines. And somehow aiming a single anxious man, be he ever so smart, determined, and politically savvy, at problems like that seemed a frail hope.

Unfortunately, he appeared to be the only weapon they had.

Admiral Gregoire Bourmont and Admiral Isidor Hegedusic, Monican System Navy, stood side-by-side in the space station gallery and watched reaction thrusters flare as the first of the long, lean ships slid gracefully to a stop relative to the station. Tractor beams reached out for her, nudging her bow hammerhead into the station's waiting space dock, and Hegedusic shook his head with a bemused expression.

"When you told me about it, I didn't really believe you. It just didn't seem possible."

"I know what you mean," Bourmont agreed. "I had much the same reaction when Roberto—I mean, President Tyler—told me about it."

Hegedusic glanced sideways at the Republic of Monica's chief of naval operations. That "slip of the tongue" was typical of him. Bourmont was part of the unfortunately sizable percentage of the MSN's officer corps who owed his successful career more to connections than to ability. Hegedusic had always suspected that somewhere inside the man knew it, too. Despite his exalted naval rank, Bourmont's ego simply wouldn't permit him to let anyone forget he was on a first-name basis with the President. And the CNO didn't seem to have a clue how petty and insecure it made him look.

Of course, Hegedusic thought, turning back to the armorplast as a second, identical shape approached the station, *sometimes even the most petty of people hit a goddamned jackpot*.

"It's going to take at least a week or so for all of them to get here," Bourmont continued. "We should be able to get the first of them into yard hands within the next ten to twelve days. After that, we'll have to see exactly how long the necessary alterations actually take. Between you and me, I think this Levakonic is grossly optimistic, Technodyne bigshot or not. This isn't a Solly yard. Even with the assistance of his 'tech reps,' it's going to take longer than he keeps assuring everyone it will. Bardasano and Anismovna apparently came to the same conclusion, because I've been informed that an additional draft of a hundred and twenty Jessyk Combine technicians will arrive shortly aboard one of the Combine's 'special ops' ships. Apparently, she's passing through on business of her own, so Bardasano decided to reinforce Levakonic's Technodyne people on her own. They're primarily civilian techs, but they should still be of considerable assistance."

"I'm sure they will, Sir. And we'll certainly do everything we can to expedite."

"I know, Isidor. That's one reason I picked you for the command." Bourmont slapped the junior admiral on the shoulder. "And I imagine the thought of actually getting to command them in action has to be what they call an efficiency motivator, doesn't it? I know it certainly would be for *me*, if I were twenty T-years younger!"

"Yes, Sir. It certainly does," Hegedusic agreed, despite the fact that Bourmont had never commanded anything in action. The closest he'd ever come was escorting transports full of Monican mercenaries from their home system to wherever OFS needed to employ them.

"Good man!" Bourmont slapped his shoulder again. "You and I also need to go over the manning requirements again," he said. "We're going to be short of trained personnel however we go about it, and I think it's important to begin cycling our people through as soon as we can get the first two or three of the new ships back into service. We'll use them as schools and, hopefully, we'll have basically competent cadres to place aboard each successive ship as she leaves the yard."

"Yes, Sir," Hegedusic said, exactly as if he hadn't already written a memo to Bourmont's office proposing exactly the same thing. He watched the docking battlecruiser for a moment longer, then turned his head to look at his superior.

"One question, Sir. Even if we get cadres trained the way you're talking about, we're going to be in an awkward position during the actual transition. We'll have lots of battlecruisers waiting for crews, and lots of personnel training to crew them, but most of our existing ships are going to be undermanned and in the process of being laid up as their people transition to the battlecruisers."

"And your point is?" Bourmont asked when he paused.

"I'm just a little worried about our home security while we're in that position, Sir. It would be embarrassing if an emergency came up and the Navy wasn't able to respond."

"Um." Bourmont frowned, tugging at his lower lip, then shrugged. "Unfortunately, I don't see any way around it, Isidor. Oh, we'll schedule things to keep our more powerful and modern units manned longest, but there's no way to avoid the draw-down you're talking about."

"No, Sir. But I was wondering if we might ask Mr. Levakonic if it would be possible to deploy some of his 'missile pods' to cover our more important installations. As I understand it, they're pretty much suited to indefinite deployment, as long as they can be serviced regularly, so it wouldn't be as if we were actually expending them. And I'd feel a lot better with some additional firepower to back us up."

"Um," Bourmont said again, frowning. "I think you're probably being overly concerned, Isidor," he said finally, "but that doesn't mean you're wrong. And it *would* be embarrassing to be caught out that way, however unlikely I might think it would be. The missile pods won't be arriving for a couple of months, but I'll discuss the idea with Levakonic. And if it won't throw us behind schedule, I think it's a good one."

"Thank you, Sir. It would make me feel a lot better."

"Me, too, now that you've brought it up," Bourmont conceded, and grimaced. "It's going to be a real strain to pull this one off," he went on. "And I'll be honest, the thought of actually mounting the operation's enough to make me nervous. But I think the planning's fundamentally sound, and the President's convinced the potential gains far outweigh the risks. On the whole, I'm strongly inclined to agree. But it's going to be up to you to actually make all the parts fit together and work, Isidor. Are you ready for the challenge?"

"Yes, Sir," Hegedusic replied, his eyes clinging to the second battlecruiser as she nuzzled into her own space dock. "Yes sir, I am."

Agnes Nordbrandt sat in the safe-house's kitchen, sipping hot tea, and waited.

She liked kitchens, she reflected. Even small, cramped ones like this. It was something about the soothing, sustaining ritual of preparing food. The smells and tastes and textures that wrapped a comforting cocoon around the cook. She got up and crossed to the lower of the two stacked ovens, bending over to peer in through the glass window in its door, and smiled. The Kornatian "turkey" really did rather resemble the Terran species which had given it its name, and the one in the roasting bag had turned a rich, golden brown. It would be ready for the celebratory dinner soon.

She turned away and walked out of the kitchen. The one-sun's narrow hall was dark, even though it was only midafternoon, because her apartment was located at the very back of the building. The lack of sunlight bothered her sometimes, but there were advantages to her apartment's location. Among other things, it had permitted her to cut an emergency escape hatch from her bedroom to an old sewer tunnel which connected with the Karlovac storm drains she and the Movement had used so often and to such good effect. Sooner or later, they were going to lose that mobility advantage—or, at least, have it significantly reduced. But for the moment, they still knew their way around the capital city's underbelly far better than the KNP did.

She climbed the steep, narrow stair at the back of the one-sun. It was supposed to serve as an emergency stair to be used only if the elevators were out. Given that the elevators hadn't worked once in the entire time she'd been in the building, the stairs saw a lot more use than they were supposed to. She grimaced wryly at the thought as she made her steady way upward.

I wonder how Rajkovic and Basaricek are going to feel when they find out I'm alive after all? I'd love to see their faces. Then again, I'd love to see their reaction to the knowledge that I've been hiding right under their noses from the very beginning. They just don't seem to get it. Maybe they figure I have to have some big, elaborate command post to be effective? But that would be stupid. I can handle everything I need to handle with nothing more than one personal com and a couple of trustworthy runners. And that lets me disappear tracelessly into the capital's population—just one more poor, anonymous young widow, struggling to keep a roof over her head on the miserable social support payments the government makes available. And I actually collect the credit drafts, too. She grinned at the thought. *Setting* that *up before I went underground wasn't easy, but it's paid off big time.*

She shook her head, still bemused by the opposition's myopia. Maybe it was the fact that the people looking for her knew she'd always been relatively affluent. Her adoptive parents had been well enough off to send her to private schools and pay most of her tuition when she went off to college. Her parliamentary career had paid pretty well, too, not to mention the noneconomic perks that had gone with it. So maybe it simply never occurred to the people looking for her that she would quite cheerfully hide in plain sight simply by becoming poor.

It had been one of her better ideas, she decided yet again as she crossed the one-sun's flat roof to the clothesline. Drawing a regular social support stipend turned her into the purloined letter so far as government agencies were concerned. She was right there, in plain sight, yet hidden and anonymous behind an absolutely legitimate social support account number and case file. They *knew* exactly who she was, and that she was harmless, so they ignored her completely.

And the same principle applied to her choice of safe-houses. When a woman was poor enough, she became effectively invisible, and the densely populated tenements of the Karlovac slums became an infinitely better hiding place than some camouflaged bunker tucked away in the mountains.

Not to mention the fact that the tenements are much more convenient to my work.

She walked along the clothesline, blinking against the bright sunlight, her short hair—auburn now, not black—blowing on the brisk breeze that flapped the sheets and towels pinned to the line. The vanes of the mushroom-headed ventilators whirred, and she enjoyed the warmth on her skin. She tested each sheet, each towel, for dampness with her hand, thus explaining to anyone who happened to glance in her direction what routine, harmless task had brought her to the roof at this particular moment.

She glanced at her chrono. That was one of her few concessions to her role of terrorist commander. It was a very good chrono, worth more than a full year of her one-sun apartment's rent. But she'd had that expensive timepiece remounted in a cheap, battered case suited to the sort of chrono a poverty-stricken widow might reasonably possess. She didn't care what it looked like; only that it kept perfect time.

Which it did.

The first explosion thundered across the capital precisely on schedule. A thick cloud of debris, flame, and smoke shot up near the city's center, and Nordbrandt ran to the front edge of the one-sun's roof. There was no risk of giving herself away now—everyone who could was moving, craning her neck, trying to see what was happening. Indeed, she'd have aroused suspicion if she *hadn't* rushed to stare off towards the plume of smoke rising out of the swelling mushroom of dust.

Then the second explosion bellowed.

The first had been a delivery truck, parked—in the same parking space in which it had been parked every day for the last three weeks—outside the main city post office. Had anybody examined that truck on any day except today, they would have found it loaded with legitimate parcels and packages being delivered to the post office by the courier service whose name was painted on its sides. But last night the courier service employee, who belonged to one of Nordbrandt's cells, had loaded his vehicle with something else before he parked it, set the timer, locked it, and walked away. And the truck had simply sat there, waiting until mid-afternoon, when the post office would be most crowded.

She shaded her eyes with her hand, staring towards the post office. Or, rather, towards the flaming, tumbled heap of rubble which had *been* the post office. She could see one or two people staggering around, clutching broken limbs or bleeding wounds. More lay writhing—or motionless—on the sidewalks, and half a dozen ground vehicles added their own smoke and flame to the hellish scene. Kornati's tech base was sufficiently primitive that most vehicles still used petrochemical fuels, and tendrils of liquid fire flowed across the pavement, seeking the storm drains, as bleeding fuel tanks gushed flame. And she could see other people already beginning to rip and tear at the wreckage in frantic efforts to rescue anyone who might be trapped under it.

Gutsy of them, a cold, thoughtful corner of her brain acknowledged. *Especially after the way we set up the Nemanja bombing. Maybe it's time we started setting follow-up charges again.*

She turned her attention towards the second explosion, but it was farther away. She could see the smoke, hear sirens, but she couldn't actually *see* anything. Not that she needed to. Another truck, from the same courier service, had been parked in a basement garage under the city's largest department store. Judging from the smoke and dust cloud, the bomb must have been even more successful than she'd hoped.

Then the third bomb detonated—the one in the stolen ambulance parked under the marquee of the Sadik

Kozarcanic Army Hospital. She'd had her doubts about that one. There'd been a far higher chance that the team charged with placing the ambulance would be detected and intercepted, which would have alerted the authorities to the fact that an operation was underway. And even if they weren't, security remained too tight, despite the growing certainty she and the Movement had both been killed, for them to get the ambulance close enough to do the kind of structural damage they'd managed at the post office and department store. But she'd decided it was still worth the risk as a psychological blow. They hadn't attacked hospitals before. And, in fact, she had no intention of adding hospitals to the list. Not *civilian* hospitals, anyway. But there was no way for the government or the general public to *know* that, now was there?

The fourth bomb went off, but it was clear across the city, too far away for her to see it from here. Not that she needed to. The neat operational planning file in her head checked it off as sharp, harsh thunder rattled the one-sun's windows.

First Planetary Bank, she thought cheerfully. Again, they hadn't been able to get the bomb actually inside the building perimeter, and the Bank building itself was built more like a bunker than a commercial establishment. But, knowing they wouldn't be able to place the bomb as close as they wanted, she and Drazen Divkovic, Juras' brother, had put the bomb under a tanker truck. In theory, it contained fuel oil; in fact, Drazen had sealed the tank and filled it with natural gas, creating what was in effect a primitive fuel-air bomb.

Then Drazen himself had driven the truck into position, stopped it, gotten out, and opened the hood to bend over the turbine, obviously checking for malfunction. He'd tinkered with it until he heard the first explosion. Then he'd smashed the fuel line with a single, carefully placed blow from a wrench, to make sure no one else could drive it away, and vanished into a subway station. By the time anyone realized the "driver" had abandoned his truck, Drazen had been kilometers away. And by then it was much too late for anyone to move the deadly vehicle before it exploded like a tactical nuclear warhead.

The vaults may survive. I don't think any of the rest of the building will, though.

She looked out at the plumes of smoke one more time, then, shaking her head in obvious disbelief and horror, turned and headed back towards the stairwell. She wanted to get back to her apartment and its cheap, tiny HD in time to see if the news channels played her prerecorded message claiming responsibility for the bombing attack in the name of the FAK. And, just incidentally, informing the Kornatian public that she wasn't dead, after all.

She was halfway down the stairs when the fifth and final bomb of this attack exploded in yet a third delivery truck. That one was parked outside the Karlovac Metropolitan Museum, and she spared a moment to hope the museum's fire suppression systems would save most of its artworks. It was probably a little schizophrenic to hope one of her own attacks would be less than totally successful, but she couldn't help it.

She shook her head at her own perversity as she reached the bottom of the stairs and checked her chrono again. Assuming her delivery arrangements worked, the news outlets wouldn't have her recorded message for another few minutes. It would be interesting to see how long it took the first news service to get it on the air.

And while she waited, she just had time to check the turkey again and put the bread into the other oven.

Chapter Thirty-Six

"So much for the demise of the Freedom Alliance," Baroness Medusa said bitterly.

Gregor O'Shaughnessy simply nodded. There wasn't much else to do as he and the Provisional Governor watched the news clips which Colonel Basaricek had appended to her official report.

It was bad, he thought. Worse even than the Nemanja bombing. The casualty count was higher, the damage was spread across a wider area of the city and—especially in the area of that tank truck bomb—far more severe, and the sheer psychological shock effect after the extended false calm was equally severe. The commentary on the news clips Basaricek had included carried a new, harsher flavor than the reportage before Nordbrandt's assumed death had. Much of that anger was directed at the FAK, but a disturbing amount of it was aimed squarely at the Kornatian government this time.

"I don't like how critical they're being of Rajkovic and Basaricek," Dame Estelle said, as if she'd been reading his mind, and he nodded again.

"Hard to blame them, really, Milady. Oh, the newsies ought to know better. Probably do, really. But after the sense of euphoria, the belief the storm was over, this had to have a major psychological effect."

"Well, now we know why she didn't bother to disabuse us of the fond assumption that we'd actually managed to kill her. And while you're being so understanding about their reporters, Gregor, you might bear in mind that one reason those same reporters are hammering the government right now is to keep from admitting *they* were the ones—not Vice President Rajkovic or Colonel Basaricek—who announced that the lack of activity meant she had to be dead. Rajkovic was always careful to keep cautioning people that there was no proof of that."

"Granted, Milady. But it would be unrealistic to expect anything else out of them, really. And at least it proves Kornati really does have a free press, doesn't it?"

The baroness gave a sharp crack of laughter and shook her head.

"You're not usually the one looking for the silver lining, Gregor. Do I really sound like I need cheering up that badly?"

"I wouldn't put it quite that way, Milady." He smiled crookedly at her. "In fact, I think I may be the one who needs the cheering up this time."

They turned their attention back to the grim sights and sounds from the wounded city. It didn't take much longer to get to the end, and Dame Estelle turned off the HD with an almost vicious jab at the remote. She sat for a moment longer, still glowering at the blank unit, and then shook herself and turned back to O'Shaughnessy.

"The timing on this could have been better," she said with massive understatement. Twelve days had passed since *Hexapuma* had departed for Montana. Probably the cruiser was already in-system and decelerating towards the planet in the continued blissful belief that the situation in Split was under control.

"Yes, Milady," he agreed, "the timing could indeed be better. But however inconvenient it may be, my immediate impression is that this—" he gestured vaguely in the direction of the silent HD "—fundamentally changes our analysis of which flashpoint is the more dangerous. And the more deserving of our most effective intervention."

"No argument," Dame Estelle said. "Although there is the interesting question of exactly how well inclined towards Aleksandra Tonkovic I am at this particular moment. And, assuming we do put Split at the head of our list, there's also the question of whether or not we can afford to spend the time to hand it to Terekhov and Bernardus. It may be time for us to stop worrying about our 'storm trooper' image or whether or not we'll be seen as supporting suppression and just drop Colonel Gray's Marines in on Nordbrandt's head. Crush her as quickly as possible and then hope we can repair any damage once the shooting's stopped. And if we do that, we can send someone else—like Captain Anders and *Warlock*—like Khumalo wanted in the first place."

"Part of me's inclined to think it *is* time to reach for a hammer, Milady," O'Shaughnessy agreed. "But remember what Colonel Basaricek had to say about how well hidden Nordbrandt's cells are. We can't use a hammer unless we know where the nail is, and we don't. Without proper intelligence backup to tell him where to find the enemy, Colonel Gray can't really accomplish much more than the KNP. It's not a case of the Kornatians not having enough manpower or firepower; it's a case of their not being able to aim it properly."

"I know." Dame Estelle scrubbed her face with the palms of her hands, and grimaced. "It's probably as much sheer frustration as anything else," she admitted. "But I want these people, Gregor. I want them badly."

"We all do, Milady."

O'Shaughnessy thought for a moment, scratching one eyebrow as he pondered. Then he shrugged.

"The bottom line, I think, Milady, is still that the Kornatians do need the technical support Tonkovic has been requesting. I think it's probable they also need advice and a small, fast response strike force they can use as a precision instrument against identified targets. I know Ms. Tonkovic hasn't asked for those, but I think her planet needs both of them far more than they need us to simply dump modern weapons on their own security forces. And if we decide to intervene in support of the local government at all, the political equation still calls for us to make the strongest possible statement about the *quality* of the assistance we're prepared to offer our friends in the area. And for that, *Hexapuma*, especially with Mr. Van Dort on board, is still our biggest counter. Besides, *Warlock* isn't in Spindle any longer."

The Provisional Governor nodded. *Warlock* was on her way to Tillerman, at the far end of Rear Admiral Khumalo's southern patrol line. It would take almost three weeks just to get word to Captain Anders to take his ship to Split, and another twenty-six days for him to actually do it.

Too many fires and not enough ships to put them out with, she thought.

"Who *is* still available here in Spindle?" she asked after a moment.

"I'd have to screen Captain Shoupe to be certain, but I believe that aside from *Hercules*, there's only a destroyer or two and the service squadron ships."

"And a destroyer's too small to make the kind of statement we want to make, while a superdreadnought's too big, however ancient and decrepit she might be," Dame Estelle said gloomily.

"Probably, yes. The fact is, Milady, that if we immediately send orders to *Hexapuma*, she can be in Split in roughly twenty-eight days. And that's probably about as quickly as we could get anything else bigger than a destroyer there. Not to mention the fact that they'd have Mr. Van Dort along, as well."

"I know." Dame Estelle laid her palms on her desk and frowned thoughtfully down at the backs of her hands. "Whatever we're going to do, we ought to do it quickly. I have a meeting with Tonkovic scheduled for this afternoon. She requested it as soon as the reports arrived, but I didn't want to see her until I'd had a chance to view them myself. I believe it's time I spoke clearly to her, without ambiguity. I don't expect her to enjoy the conversation, and I think I'll just see what she has to say before I make any hard and fast decisions. But go ahead and prepare a full download for Terekhov and Van Dort. Whether or not we actually decide to send them to Split, they'll need to know what's going on there."

"So that's Montana," Lieutenant Commander Kaplan said.

She sat at the bridge briefing room's conference table with Terekhov's other department heads, Bernardus Van Dort, and one midshipwoman who was acutely aware of her own insignificant rank. The blue and white image of the planet about which *Hexapuma* had just settled into orbit floated before them in the conference table's holo display. The service ships Khumalo had stationed there to support his "Southern Patrol"—Captain Lewis Sedgewick's HMS *Ericsson* and Commander Mira Badmachin's HMS *Volcano*—were bright dots of reflected sunlight in their somewhat higher permanent parking orbits, hanging above the image of the planet like tiny stars.

"Pretty planet," Lieutenant Commander Nagchaudhuri said. "The mountains remind me a little of Gryphon. Although—" he showed Helen a half-grin, "—I understand the climate's a lot better."

"*Most* climates are a lot better than Gryphon's," Commander FitzGerald said, smiling openly at the midshipwoman, and a general chuckle ran around the table.

"Montana is a nice planet," Terekhov said, his tone announcing that it was time to get down to business. "And, from all the background information available to me, the Montanans seem to be nice people."

"They are, Aivars," Van Dort said. "Very nice people—in their own, deliberately rough-hewn way. They're generous, gracious to guests, and incredibly stubborn."

There was something about his tone, some tiny shadow in his expression, that came and went so quickly Helen wasn't certain she'd actually seen it. If she had, no one else seemed to have noticed it, and he went on briskly.

"I've already contacted President Suttles and Chief Marshal Bannister. I can't say Bannister seemed delighted to see me on his com, but we have a bit of a personal history that probably explains his initial reaction. Once I explained to him why we were here, he got rather more enthusiastic. Not hopeful, but willing, at least, to give it a try. And, as I'd hoped, Westman's been to some pains to establish a communications link to the system government. If Westman will agree to meet with me at all, Suttles and Bannister think they can probably arrange the details within the next two or three days."

"I hate to have to ask this, Mr. Van Dort," Terekhov said after a moment, "but my intel files say Trevor Bannister and Westman have been friends literally since boyhood. Is it your impression after speaking to Bannister that we can rely on his loyalty to the government?"

"Captain," Van Dort began in a surprisingly sharp voice, "that question is simply—"

He chopped himself off and closed his mouth for a moment. Then he shook his head.

"Personal integrity is the single most important ingredient in the Montana honor code, Aivars." His voice was very level, as if he were making a special effort to keep it that way. "Nothing's more central to their notion of honorable conduct, and both Westman and Bannister are honorable men. If Bannister sympathized with the MIM deeply enough to aid Westman's operations, he would've resigned his office and joined Westman openly." He smiled crookedly. "Not the most effective possible approach, I suppose, but Machiavelli wouldn't have been able to *give* his book away on Montana." His smile vanished. "I think that's one reason they resented Ineka Vaandrager's negotiating techniques so deeply."

"It sounds like we could have worse honor codes to deal with," Terekhov said. He looked as if he were about to add something more, but instead, he shrugged and turned to Captain Kaczmarczyk.

"Given what Mr. Van Dort's just said, Tadislaw, I

think we need to reconsider our security arrangements for any meeting."

"Sir," the Marine began, "with all due respect for Mr. Van Dort, and accepting that everything he's just said about the Montanans is completely accurate, it's still my responsibility to see to it that—"

"I know what you're going to say, Major." Terekhov's voice was just a bit crisper. "But we're here to help negotiate a peaceful settlement, or at least a cease-fire. And we're not going to manage that if we offend local leaders or suggest we believe they'll act dishonorably. More to the point, perhaps, everything we've seen from Mr. Westman suggests that he does take his personal integrity seriously. Under the circumstances, if he promises a safe conduct, I'm not going to a meeting with him surrounded by battle-armored Marines bristling with plasma rifles and tribarrels. Nor am I going to insist that he come here."

He and the Marine locked eyes for a moment, and then Kaczmarczyk nodded.

"Aye, aye, Sir," he said levelly. "For the record, I'm not at all happy about exposing you or Mr. Van Dort to any unavoidable risk. But that's your decision, not mine. I hope you won't object, however, if I provide the tightest security I can within whatever guidelines you're willing to agree to? Navy captains and Crown envoys aren't exactly considered expendable assets, you know."

He did not, Helen noted, comment on the expendability or lack thereof of midshipwomen attached to the said Crown envoy as an assistant.

"I find this latest news from home disturbing," Aleksandra Tonkovic said in a low voice. "Very disturbing. The destruction, the deaths, the degree of panic . . ." She shook her head slowly. "To think that a handful of murderous lunatics could to this much damage to an entire planet. It just doesn't seem possible."

"It doesn't take a huge army to create panic when the people in it are willing to murder civilians in job lots. And the focused attention of the news media can make even a relatively small terrorist organization seem far larger than it is . . . Madam President," Baroness Medusa said.

Tonkovic's eyes flicked to the Provisional Governor's face as Dame Estelle addressed her not as a delegate to the Constitutional Convention but rather as the Kornati head of state. Dame Estelle looked back steadily for a heartbeat or two, then continued in the same measured tones.

"Nonetheless, it seems evident from this latest series of attacks, and from Colonel Basaricek's reports, that the FAK's membership is, in fact, larger and more widespread than previously believed. Admittedly, they had weeks to plan and implement this most recent operation, but it took more manpower—and better preattack intelligence—to set it up than earlier reports indicated they should have."

Silence hovered between them until, after several moments, Tonkovic shrugged slightly.

"Yes," she acknowledged. "There are more of them than we'd thought. There must be. We already knew they had a tight cellular organization. Now we're beginning to suspect Nordbrandt must have done at least some of the preliminary organizational work before the annexation plebiscite ever came along. We always knew she was a nationalist extremist. We just never suspected she might have been building up an organization like this all along. No doubt she initially intended it as a defense against Frontier Security."

"No doubt," Dame Estelle agreed, noting once again that Nordbrandt had obviously hit a deeper nerve with the economic side of her terrorist platform than any of the Cluster's oligarchs really wanted to admit. Even now, Tonkovic seemed constitutionally incapable of admitting that the discontent which had fueled Nordbrandt's original recruiting drive clearly stemmed from a much broader spectrum of issues than the annexation plebiscite alone.

"The fact that they're more deeply entrenched and apparently more numerous than we'd suspected, however," the Kornatian continued, "gives added weight to our request for reconnaissance support and modern weapons for our security forces. I know we've discussed the pros and cons of direct Manticoran military intervention, but I continue to believe there's much point in the arguments coming from Vice President Rajkovic and the Cabinet against launching a full-scale military effort. We can deal with Nordbrandt's butchers ourselves, if we only have the tools to find her and the weapons to defeat her once we do. But we *do* need that support, and I believe also that some evidence that the Star Kingdom stands with us at this moment would be psychologically very beneficial to the vast majority of Kornatians who continue to support the annexation."

"I don't disagree," Dame Estelle replied. "However, to be brutally frank, Madam President, there seems to me to be a slight discrepancy between your request, as Kornati's head of state, for assistance from the Star Kingdom and your position, as Kornati's chief delegate to the Convention. On the one hand, you're requesting that we send assistance to your planet, making our support for your government clear, while on the other hand, you are insisting in debate here that the preservation of full local autonomy necessarily means full integration of your star system into the Star Kingdom isn't possible."

Tonkovic's lips compressed, and despite her years of experience as a politician, anger flickered in her green eyes. The Provisional Governor simply sat, hands folded loosely on the desk before her, and waited.

"Madam Governor," the Kornatian said after a moment, "I'd hoped we might deal with what all of us recognize as mass murder by a common criminal without engaging in acrimonious political debate."

"I'm not engaging in 'acrimonious political debate,' Madam President. I'm pointing out a fundamental inconsistency in your position. One which, I hope you'll forgive my mentioning, I've pointed out to you several times before. I don't for a moment believe you intend to deliberately sabotage the annexation effort. And I'm quite certain you believe your reading of the politics of the Convention here and of the annexation campaign, both here and in the Star Kingdom, is accurate. However, as Her Majesty's personal representative in the Cluster, I would be remiss in my duties if I didn't suggest to you that it is somewhat unreasonable to insist on one hand that we demonstrate our support for you against domestic terrorists while insisting on the other that we must grant you an extraordinarily broad special status and admit you to the Star Kingdom, as full citizens, without requiring you to abide by the same laws under which we require all the rest of our citizens to live."

"I'm not accustomed to having guns held to my head, Madam Governor," Tonkovic said harshly.

"Then I would suggest to you, Madam President, that you shouldn't try to hold guns to other people's heads," Dame Estelle said unflinchingly. Their eyes locked, and silence hovered for a few, fragile seconds before she continued levelly.

"I haven't attempted, nor does the Star Kingdom have any desire to attempt, to arbitrarily dictate to your world or to your personal conscience. *You* sought annexation by the Star Kingdom; no one in the Star Kingdom enticed you into doing so in any way. If, in the end, you decide requesting annexation was a mistake, you have every right to change your mind. You also have every right to explain to the Star Kingdom the terms under which you would like to become a member of it. But, Madam President, the *Star Kingdom* retains the right to tell you your terms aren't acceptable. And if they aren't, the Star Kingdom is under no obligation to assist you in suppressing local criminal elements opposed not simply to the idea of annexation, but apparently to what they perceive as other long-standing grievances within your society. You cannot expect us to intervene as outside policemen in a conflict of this nature and magnitude while simultaneously insisting that you must receive special, privileged status, effectively placing you above the law, within the Star Kingdom as your price for joining it."

Tonkovic's face was pale and set. Baroness Medusa

found her sympathy for the other woman was severely limited. She'd tried repeatedly, while observing all the tactful, diplomatic niceties, to warn Tonkovic she was, indeed, playing with fire. Perhaps she'd finally found a big enough club to get through to her.

"Obviously," Tonkovic said in a taut voice, "there is a greater gap between my position and objectives and your perception of them than I had believed, Madam Governor. With all due respect, I would point out to you that there's a distinct difference between political debates and strategies, whose objective is simply to obtain the most equitable balance between long-held, hard-won local freedoms and a new central government, and the cold-blooded murder of innocent civilians by a collection of homicidal criminals. Should I assume from what you've just said that my only options are to acquiesce to every single demand of Joachim Alquezar's clique, or else to see my homeworld left entirely on its own to continue this struggle alone against butchers and murderers? Murderers who *began* their campaign of slaughter because they objected to our seeking closer relations with the Star Kingdom?"

"I haven't said anything about mutually exclusive options, Madam President. However, it may be that the crux of our problem is found in your use of the term 'seeking closer relations with the Star Kingdom.' What Mr. Alquezar and his supporters are seeking is membership *in* the Star Kingdom, not merely an alliance *with* the Star Kingdom. There's a distinct difference between the two."

"We have now reached the point of straining over fine linguistic points of implication and inference," Tonkovic said harshly. "I repeat, am I to understand that my official request for the Star Kingdom's assistance in dealing with the so-called Freedom Alliance of Kornati is conditional upon my immediate acceptance in the name of the Split System of the Alquezar draft proposal for the Constitution?"

Baroness Medusa allowed the hard, brittle silence

to linger between them for several seconds. Then she smiled, ever so slightly.

"No, Madam President. We aren't quite at that point yet. However, if you request the Star Kingdom's assistance, we will render that assistance in whatever we believe to be the most effective manner. Our representatives will deal directly with the representatives of your planetary government actually present on Kornati, on a face-to-face basis. And you had best understand that just as you retain the right to change your mind about seeking annexation, we retain the right to inform the Constitutional Convention that we will not extend membership in the Star Kingdom to any or all of the star systems represented here, collectively *or as individuals*."

She looked directly into Tonkovic's eyes.

"My Queen and her Government would very much prefer to avoid taking that drastic step. It is for that reason we've waited so patiently for so long for an internal resolution of the long delay in the reporting out of a draft Constitution. Yet our patience, as I've attempted to impress upon you before, isn't unlimited. We will not allow this delay to stretch out indefinitely. I am now officially informing you, and will be sending a formal note to the same effect to all other delegations here on Flax within the next two hours, that we require the acceptance of a draft Constitution by this Convention within a period of no more than one hundred and fifty standard days. If I, as the Queen's representative in Talbott, haven't received a draft Constitution within that time, the Star Kingdom of Manticore will either withdraw the offer of membership to *all* systems in the Talbott Cluster or else present to the Constitutional Convention a list of specific star systems whose inclusion in the Star Kingdom will no longer be acceptable in Her Majesty's eyes. I would suggest to you that it wouldn't be wise of you to find your own system on that list."

The silence that followed was harder—and colder—than ever. Hatred burned in Aleksandra Tonkovic's eyes. Hatred,

Dame Estelle thought, all the stronger because Tonkovic was so unaccustomed to finding herself in the weaker position in any political confrontation. She was used to the political warfare of a single star system, to holding the whip—either as head of state itself or at the very least as one of the movers and shakers of the controlling political establishment. She wasn't accustomed to dealing with other star systems and their leaders as equals. And she was even less accustomed to the sour-tasting realization that she and her entire star system might be regarded as an insignificant, bothersome, backward, easily dispensed with distraction by someone like the Star Kingdom of Manticore.

Whatever the outcome of the annexation debate, Dame Estelle Matsuko knew she personally had just made an implacable, lifelong enemy. Which was fine with her. She believed firmly that the best measure of anyone's character was the enemies they made.

She allowed the silence to linger once more, then gave Tonkovic a small, cool, polite smile.

"Do you wish me to send orders to Captain Terekhov and the *Hexapuma* to proceed to Split and render assistance to your government, Madam President?" she asked pleasantly.

"Which dispatch boat has the current duty, Loretta?" Rear Admiral Khumalo asked.

"The *Destiny*, I believe, Sir. Lieutenant Quayle. May I ask why you wanted to know?"

"Because we're about to send him off to Montana," Khumalo said. He and Captain Shoupe exchanged eloquent glances, and then the rear admiral shrugged. "There's no one to blame for it except Nordbrandt. And it's hardly the first time some poor Navy ship's been harried back and forth between pillar and post. Can't even blame the political leadership this time."

"No, Sir." Shoupe sat for a moment, making mental calculations, then cocked her head at her boss. "Do you think Terekhov and Van Dort are going to get much done in the next eleven days, Sir?"

"I gave up believing in miracles about the same time I gave up believing in the tooth fairy, Loretta," Khumalo rumbled like an irritated boar. Then he snorted and shook his head. "I suppose it's possible they might make a little progress, and at the moment, I'm prepared to settle for whatever we can get. But I don't see any way they're going to manage anything significant in that much time. And if they are making progress, we're likely to undo most of it by snatching them out of the star system with absolutely no warning."

"I imagine you're right, Sir," Shoupe sighed. "I assume Baroness Medusa will send dispatches and directions along with the recall?"

"You assume correctly." Khumalo managed a tart smile. "In this case, to a large extent, ours truly isn't to wonder why. Go ahead and draft a dispatch to Terekhov directing him to transport Mr. Van Dort to Split in the most expeditious manner and to render such assistance to Mr. Van Dort in his efforts there as may be directed in the Provisional Governor's dispatches."

"Yes, Sir," she said. "I'll get right on it."

Chapter Thirty-Seven

The unarmed air car approached the agreed upon meeting site at exactly the agreed upon time.

Stephen Westman stood leaning against a tree, arms folded across his chest, and watched it come. It had taken two full days of cautious contacts and secret negotiation to arrange this meeting, and there was a certain fitting irony, though he'd be unable to share it with his "guests," to the location he'd chosen. The last off-worlder he'd met here had been the man called "Firebrand," whose objectives had been somewhat different from these off-worlders'. He wondered if Van Dort and the Manties in the air car would find the scenery as spectacular as Firebrand had.

The air car circled the site once, then settled to a neat landing the better part of seventy meters from Westman. The turbines whined as they spooled down, and Westman straightened, letting his arms fall to his side. Luis Palacios had wanted to be here, but Westman had turned him down. Although the MIM leader had complete faith in Chief Marshal Bannister's integrity, he had somewhat less confidence in Bernardus Van Dort's. And he'd never met any Manticoran—aside, he corrected himself with a snort of amusement, from those Manty surveyors he'd encountered on the banks of the Schuyler River. For all he knew, Manties might be almost as treacherous as Sollies.

The passenger side hatch opened, and Trevor Bannister climbed out. The strength of the pang Westman felt as he saw his old friend for the first time in months surprised him. He wondered if Trevor felt the same way, but no expression crossed the Chief Marshal's face as he made a quick but thorough survey of the surroundings, then turned and walked slowly to his waiting "host."

"Afternoon, Trevor," Westman said.

"Steve." Bannister nodded, then shoved his Stetson well back on his head and gazed out over the New Missouri Gorge. "Nice scenery."

"Seemed appropriate."

The two men looked at one another for a moment, then Westman smiled.

"Don't see any desperate ambushers?"

"Didn't expect to." Bannister took off his hat and ran his fingers through his grizzled red hair. "You might want to think about the fact that the people in this air car also took your word that they had safe conduct," he said. Westman looked surprised, and the Chief Marshal snorted. "These aren't Montanans, Steve. Matter of fact, they're senior representatives of those antichrists you've been campaigning against. But they still took your word. You might want to consider what that says about whether or not you can trust what they say."

"Point taken." Westman nodded. "All the same, a dishonest man can trust an honest man to stay honest. Doesn't necessarily work the other way 'round."

"Reckon there's something in that," Bannister conceded. Then put his hat back on, turned, and waved to the passengers still in the air car.

Westman watched them disembark. Van Dort was easy to recognize, even at this distance, thanks to his height. Besides, Westman had met the Rembrandter personally. The thought was like an under-ripe persimmon, and his mouth twisted briefly before his eyes moved on to the other new arrivals.

The bearded man beside Van Dort also had blond hair and blue eyes. In fact, Westman thought with a certain inner amusement, the meeting site seemed to be crowded with tallish, blond-haired men. But the amusement faded as the off-worlders got closer and he looked into Aivars Terekhov's blue eyes. This wasn't a man to take lightly, he realized.

His concentration on the two men had held his attention until they were almost up to him. He looked past them then, at the final person to climb out of the air car, and the last flicker of amusement disappeared. He'd been told Van Dort and Captain Terekhov would be accompanied by a single aide, a Manticoran midshipwoman. Some sort of very junior lieutenant, Bannister's messenger had told him. But no one had warned him what she looked like, and despite all his own formidable self-control, his eyes darted to Trevor Bannister's face.

The Chief Marshal looked back at him, once again expressionless as a sphinx, and Westman winced mentally. It must have been like a punch in the belly when he saw that dark-haired, dark-eyed, solidly muscled young woman. Especially when he saw her standing with Bernardus Van Dort.

"Steve," Bannister said in a professionally detached tone, "I don't have to introduce you to Mr. Van Dort, I know, but this," he gestured at the Manticoran captain, "is Captain Aivars Terekhov, commanding officer of HMS *Hexapuma*. And this," he gestured at the young woman standing respectfully behind Van Dort and Terekhov, and his voice never even wavered, "is Midshipwoman Helen Zilwicki."

"Welcome," Westman said, shaking aside his own reaction to the young woman. "Wish I could say it's a pleasure to see you gentlemen, but I never was much good at polite lies. Nothing personal, but seeing you two on Montanan soil under any circumstances doesn't exactly make me want to do handsprings of delight."

"Chief Marshal Bannister reminded me that you're a blunt-spoken man," Van Dort said with a smile of what looked like genuine amusement. "I can work with that. In fact, I've been accused of being just a little too blunt-spoken myself, upon occasion."

"Hope you won't take this wrongly," Westman said, "but that's not the only thing you've been accused of. Especially not here on Montana."

"I'm sure it isn't," the Rembrandter conceded. "As a matter of fact, if I were a Montanan, I'd probably harbor quite a bit of—ill-will, shall we say?—where Rembrandt and the Trade Union were concerned."

One of Westman's eyebrows quirked at the admission. Of course, he reminded himself, words cost nothing. And even if Van Dort's statement was completely accurate, it didn't mean a thing about the Rembrandter's ultimate objectives.

"As I'm sure you've noticed," he said, "I've had my people put up a tent over there, under the trees. It's quite a nice tent, actually—used to belong to some Manticoran surveyors, I believe—and it's air-conditioned. I thought we might all like to get out of the sun and sit down someplace cool for this little talk you gentlemen wanted."

Helen was confused. There was something going on between Westman, Van Dort, and—of all people—Chief Marshal Bannister. She didn't have a clue what it was, but somehow she felt certain *she* was mixed up in it somehow. Which was preposterous, of course, except for the fact that she knew it was the truth.

She followed the four men to the waiting tent. Its side still carried the rampant manticore of the Star Kingdom's coat of arms, and she felt a flicker of amused respect for Westman's audacity. He was making a none-too-subtle point by flaunting his trophy, but it also provided a comfortable place for the representatives of the various sides to sit down and talk.

All four men found seats around the camp table inside

the tent. There was a fifth chair, but Helen chose to stand, hands clasped loosely behind her, at Van Dort's shoulder. She felt Westman's eyes flicker over her again, once more with that odd expression of almost-recognition. He looked as if he were about to insist that she sit down, which would have been in keeping with the elaborate Montanan social code. But he glanced at Van Dort and Bannister, then visibly changed his mind.

"All right," he said after a moment. "This meeting was your idea, I understand, Mr. Van Dort. That being the case, I reckon it's only fair to give you the floor first."

"Thank you," Van Dort said, but he didn't seem in any great hurry. He sat for a moment, his hands lightly folded on the camp table while he gazed out through the window-configured tent wall across the magnificent sweep of the New Missouri River Gorge. He sat that way for several seconds before he brought his gaze back inside and focused on Westman.

"I'm here," he said, "not as a representative of Rembrandt, but as the personal representative of Baroness Medusa, Queen Elizabeth's Provisional Governor for the Talbott Cluster. I don't expect you to forget I'm a Rembrandter. Nor do I expect you to forget all the reasons you have for disliking me personally, or for distrusting and detesting Rembrandt and the Trade Union. If you wish to discuss our past policies and how we went about implementing them, I'm quite prepared to do so. However, I'd like to request that you allow me to speak as Baroness Medusa's envoy first. I suspect," he allowed himself a crooked smile, "that if we get into debating Montana-Rembrandt relations, we'll be here for the next several days. At least."

Westman's mouth twitched. It looked, Helen thought, as if the Montanan had felt a sudden urge to smile back at Van Dort. If he had, he managed to suppress it quite handily, though.

"Speaking as Baroness Medusa's representative, then," Van Dort continued, "I've been instructed to ask you to set forth your exact objections to the annexation of the Montana System, at the freely voted upon request of its citizens, by the Star Kingdom of Manticore. I realize you've published your manifesto, and knowing Montanans, I have no doubt that it honestly represents your convictions. What Baroness Medusa would like to do is to give you the opportunity to expand upon your manifesto's statements. She hopes, frankly, to open a direct dialogue. To give you a channel through which both of you may straightforwardly set forth your views and opinions. Whether or not this ultimately achieves anything is, of course, impossible to predict. But Baroness Medusa feels, and I believe with reason, that without such a dialogue, there's no hope at all of arriving at a negotiated resolution of the current situation."

"I see," Westman said after frowning for several seconds. Then he shook his head—not in rejection, but to indicate a certain dubiousness, Helen thought.

"That all sounds very reasonable," the guerrilla leader went on. "But I'm just a mite skeptical. And, truth be told, it's a mite difficult for me to forget who you are. You just mentioned freely voted upon requests, but everybody in the Cluster knows the entire annexation plebiscite came out of Rembrandt. And that you personally were the driving force behind it, at least at first. I hope you won't take this wrongly, but that tends to taint the whole notion in my eyes."

"I don't blame you," Van Dort said calmly. "As I said, I'd prefer not to debate all of the past strains and tensions between Montana and the RTU. I will acknowledge freely, however, that the RTU's policies were part of a carefully planned strategy to build the economic power of the RTU's member systems as rapidly as possible. In pursuit of those policies, we did some things which, quite frankly, were one-sided and unfair to other systems. Montana was such a system, and, as such, you have every right to resent and dislike us.

"I regret the fact that all of that's true, but I'd be lying if I said I wouldn't do exactly the same again under the same circumstances. This entire Cluster's been looking down the barrel of Frontier Security's pulser for a long time now. I saw that coming even before OFS started looking our way, and I came up with the RTU as the best strategy to protect my own homeworld. I didn't think there was any way I could hope to protect anyone else, so I didn't try to. But the discovery of the Lynx Terminus changed all that.

"My point is simply this: the policies which made Rembrandt an economic aggressor were intended to defend Rembrandt. When I saw an opportunity for an even better defensive strategy—annexation by the Star Kingdom—I leapt at it. And, in the process, I finally did find a way I could hope to protect the rest of the Cluster. You may not believe that was my motivation, but it was. And whether it was or not, and all personal considerations aside, you should consider the advantages and disadvantages of the proposal not on the basis of where it originated, but on the basis of what it can mean for your own world and your own objectives. That's what Baroness Medusa's asking you to do—and the reason she hopes to open a dialogue with you."

"I see." Westman sat back, rubbing his chin thoughtfully.

"I see," he repeated. "Unfortunately, at the moment, it seems to me that my objectives and Baroness Medusa's are mutually exclusive. I don't want Montana to join the Star Kingdom; she wants to annex it for her Queen." He shook his head again. "Not a whole lot of room for compromise there, I think."

"I don't believe I said anything about compromises, Mr. Westman." Westman's eyebrows rose, and Van Dort smiled again, thinly, this time. "Assuming your own government remains committed to seeking annexation, and assuming the Constitutional Convention drafts a Constitution which is mutually acceptable to our citizens and Manticore, Montana *will* become a member of the Star Kingdom."

Westman's eyes flashed, but Van Dort met his fiery gaze steadily.

"That isn't meant to sound gratuitously confrontational," the Rembrandter said. "However, the fact is that, like any guerrilla movement, yours can only succeed if a significant percentage of the Montanan population decides to support it. Without that, your movement is ultimately doomed, and the question simply becomes how much damage you do to your own star system and, indirectly, to the Star Kingdom at large before it's ultimately suppressed."

"I expect you might find the amount of damage we can do more than you'd care for," Westman half-snapped.

"Baroness Medusa finds the damage you've already done more than she cares for. But that doesn't mean the Star Kingdom isn't prepared to absorb even more damage if it must. And, I repeat, the Star Kingdom will only be involved in attempting to forcibly suppress your actions if the majority of your fellow Montanans continue to desire to become citizens *of* the Star Kingdom. Should that be true, however, and should an acceptable Constitution be drafted and approved by the Manticoran Parliament and the legislatures of the Cluster's member star systems, the Star Kingdom will commit whatever resources are necessary to bring an end to violence here on Montana."

"Better listen to him, Steve," Chief Marshal Bannister said shortly. "So far, you're up against me, and I'm basically a cop. If the annexation goes through and you're still blowing things up, or, even worse, having shootouts with me and my people, the Manticorans will send in Marines. And those Marines'll have battle armor, orbital surveillance systems, armored vehicles, and all the things I *don't* have. You're good. I'll admit that. In fact, I think you may be better than I am. But you're not good enough to stand up to that kind of an opponent. Especially not if everyone else is rooting for the other side."

Westman's face tightened. It looked to Helen as if he would have liked to reject what both Van Dort and Bannister had said. But the man was obviously too realistic to fool himself. Yet there was something in his eyes. Something that seemed to suggest at least a kernel of doubt.

I wonder, she thought. *Does he have access—or think he has access—to some sort of off-world support? Something that might give him an edge, or at least some kind of equalizer, against modern military hardware? But if he does, where the hell is it coming from? And where the hell is Daddy when I* need *a super-spook?*

"Whether or not I can win in the end is one thing," Westman said after a few, tense seconds. "Whether or not what I believe in requires me to try is something else. And whether or not this planet will be worth annexing after we're done is still another something else."

"Forgive me, Mr. Westman," Captain Terekhov said, "but I believe you're missing part of Mr. Van Dort's point."

"Which is?" Westman asked.

"What Baroness Medusa is trying to tell you, Sir," the Captain said calmly, "is that the amount of damage is immaterial. The Star Kingdom isn't interested in annexing Montana because of the wealth you don't have. Obviously, in the long term, we believe Montana, like all the Cluster's star systems, will become more prosperous and represent a net economic gain for the Star Kingdom as a whole. But, to be perfectly honest, the Lynx Terminus represents the only powerful selfish reason for us to be involved in this region, and there are many countervailing reasons why we *shouldn't* be here. At the possible expense of belaboring a point, the entire question of annexation only arose after the citizens of the Cluster requested it. The Star Kingdom's commitment to the annexation of Montana is a moral one, not an economic one. Damage can be repaired. Destroyed facilities can be rebuilt. The legal and moral obligations of a government to protect its citizens—both in their persons and property and in their right to live under the government of their choice—aren't negotiable."

Westman sat back, regarding the Captain through narrow eyes. There was a speculative light in them, Helen thought. It was as if what the Captain had just said puzzled him. Or surprised him, at least.

"It's those legal and moral obligations I'm fighting

for," the Montanan said, his voice quiet. "I don't believe the government has the legal right to discard our own Constitution. This star system was settled by a bunch of fools who'd fallen in love with an over-romanticized fantasy about a time and place, Captain. They didn't have a clue about how accurate or inaccurate their fantasy was, and it didn't matter. They set up a government and a Constitution predicated on principles of independence, orneriness, the freedom of the individual, and the individual's responsibility to look after himself and stand up for what he believes in. I don't say they built the perfect government. Hell, I don't even say the system we had before this annexation plebiscite came along was what they actually had in mind in the first place! But it was *my* government. It was a government of my friends and my neighbors, and of people I didn't much care for, but it didn't involve any foreign queens, or any baronesses, or any kingdoms and parliaments. I won't stand by and see my planet sold out to someone else, no matter how good a price some of the folks who live here think they're getting. I won't give up the laws and customs my ancestors built, brick by brick, on *this* planet, not on Rembrandt, and not on Manticore."

"So to protect our government and way of life you're willing to blow up buildings and eventually kill people—and you and I both know that's coming, Steve—to prevent your fellow citizens from doing what three-quarters of them voted to do?" Chief Marshal Bannister shook his head. "Steve, I've always respected your guts and integrity, and God knows I've come to respect your ability. But that's just plain loco. You can't *preserve* something by blowing it up and shooting it."

Westman looked stubborn, and Van Dort pushed back from the table.

"Mr. Westman, we're not going to magically resolve issues like this in a single meeting, even with the best of intentions. Probably not in half a dozen meetings. I think we've made at least a start on explaining our position to you. As I say, Baroness Medusa invites you to send a detailed explanation of your own views and desires to her. She doesn't want to browbeat you into some sort of abject surrender. Mind you," he let a flicker of a smile show, "I don't think she'd object if you suddenly decided you *wanted* to turn in your guns! But she's not foolish enough to expect that. What she hopes, I think, is that she may be able to convince you that what you fear isn't going to happen. That, unlike the Trade Union, the Star Kingdom isn't interested in squeezing every drop of profit it can out of the Cluster. That you won't give up your individual liberties, or your right to local self-government. But she can't do that, and you can't explain your concerns and your reservations to her, if there's no communication between you except bombs and pulser darts."

He paused, looking into Westman's eyes.

"We'll be here in Montana for at least the next few weeks. Rather than continue the discussion at this time and risk turning a debate into a quarrel that backs people into positions they can't get out of later, I think we'd be wise to consider this a good beginning and call it a day. Before we do that, though, I'd like to address one other point, if I may."

Westman looked back at him for several seconds, then made a small inviting gesture for him to continue.

"Up to this point," Van Dort said quietly, "all your operations have been directed against property, not people. Don't think for a moment that Baroness Medusa is unaware of the extraordinary effort you've made to keep it that way. She recognizes—as I'm sure Captain Terekhov could confirm—that you've deliberately handicapped your operational flexibility and, in fact, accepted a greater degree of risk to your organization, in order to avoid killing. But as Chief Marshal Bannister just pointed out, you must be aware that you won't be able to do that much longer. At the moment, there's a huge distinction between you, your actions, and your apparent objectives, on the one hand, and those of butchers like Agnes Nordbrandt, on the other."

Something flashed in Westman's eyes at Nordbrandt's

name, Helen realized. She didn't know what, but that moment of intense emotion was impossible to hide.

"Right now," Van Dort continued, "you're technically a criminal. You've broken the law and conspired with others to break the law, and God only knows how many millions of stellars worth of damage you've done. But you're not a murderer like Nordbrandt. I think you might want to consider keeping it that way. I'm not trying to convince you to surrender your weapons or turn yourself in. Not yet, anyway. But I do think you should very carefully consider the possibility of declaring at least a temporary cease-fire."

"And give you time to finish voting out your draft Constitution without opposition?" Westman demanded.

"Possibly. Maybe even probably. But I submit that whatever you do here on Montana, you won't stop the other systems represented at the Convention from voting out a Constitution if they decide to do it. If a Constitution is voted out, and *if* the Montanan legislature votes to ratify it, and *if* the Star Kingdom's Parliament votes to accept it, then—if your principles leave you no other choice—you can always start shooting again. But do you really have to push things to the point that people get killed, and no one in your organization—not just you, but *no one*—can ever step back from the brink, before you even know a viable Constitution's going to be put into place?"

"Listen to the man, Steve," Bannister said quietly. "He makes sense. Don't make my boys and girls and your people kill each other when there may never even be any need for it."

"I won't say yes or no to the possibility of a cease-fire," Westman said bluntly. "Not here, not without a chance to think about it and talk it over with my people. But," he hesitated, looking back and forth between Van Dort and Bannister, then gave a short, jerky nod. "But I *will* think about it, and I will discuss it with my people." He smiled tightly at the Rembrandter. "You got at least that much of what you wanted, Mr. Van Dort."

✧ ✧ ✧

Helen followed Captain Terekhov and Van Dort back towards the air car. Bannister and Westman walked a little apart from the other two, talking quietly. From their expressions, Helen suspected they were discussing personal matters, and she wondered what it must feel like to find close friends suddenly enemies over something like this.

The Captain and Van Dort reached the air car and climbed aboard. Helen waited politely for Bannister to do the same, and the Chief Marshal shook Westman's hand and did. She started to step past the guerrilla leader to follow the others, but Westman raised a hand.

"Just a minute, please, Ms. . . . Zilwicki, was it?"

"Helen Zilwicki," she said a bit stiffly, glancing towards the air car and wishing fervently that at least one of her superiors was in earshot.

"I won't keep you," he said courteously, "but there's something I'd like to ask you, if I may."

"Of course, Sir," she agreed, although it was the last thing in the world she wanted to do.

"You remind me of someone," he said quietly, his eyes on her face. "You remind me of her a lot. Did Mr. Van Dort ever mention Suzanne Bannister to you?"

"Suzanne Bannister?" Helen repeated, trying to keep her eyes from widening at the surname. She shook her head. "No, he hasn't."

"Ah." Westman seemed to consider that for a moment, then nodded. "I wondered," he said, and inhaled deeply. "Economic warfare isn't the only thing that lies between Rembrandt and Montana, Ms. Zilwicki," he said softly, then he nodded to her again, politely, and walked briskly away.

She gazed after him for several seconds, wondering what he meant. Then she shook herself and turned back towards the air car.

Bernardus Van Dort and Trevor Bannister sat side by side, watching her, and she suddenly wondered how she'd managed to miss the pain on both their faces whenever they looked at her.

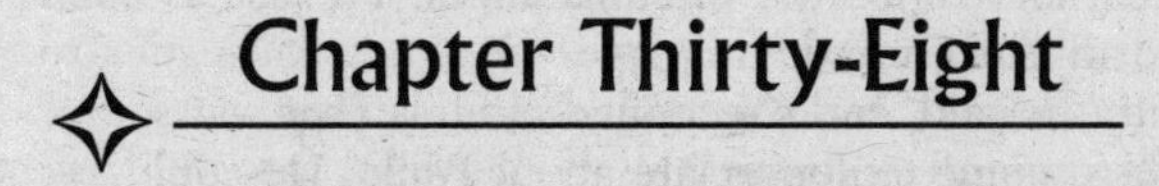

Chapter Thirty-Eight

The stars outside the armorplast dome were dominated by the huge cloud-swirled blue marble of the planet called Montana. There were fewer ships and orbital constructs circling it than there would have been back home, but Helen had grown accustomed to the sparser traffic here in the Verge. Now she lay sprawled across one comfortable chair, staring at the huge storm system dominating the planet's eastern hemisphere. One of the things spacers missed was the feel and smell of weather, and for someone from Gryphon, where it was always lively (to say the very least), the sense of deprivation sometimes hit hard.

But it wasn't really weather that was bothering her, and she knew it.

The hatch opened with its familiar silent speed, and she looked up quickly, then relaxed.

"How'd it go?" Paulo d'Arezzo asked.

Helen gazed at him thoughtfully, reflecting on how much their relationship had changed over the past month. It was sometimes hard to remember how standoffish she'd thought he was . . . until she saw him with the other middies. It wasn't the nose-in-the-air sense of superiority she'd once thought it was, but Paulo was an intensely private person. She wondered, sometimes, if anyone else aboard *Hexapuma* had the least idea about his background and the demons he carried quietly around with him. Even now, she wasn't prepared to ask him, but she thought she knew the answer.

"Better than I expected, in some ways," she said after a moment in response to his question.

"Can you talk about it?"

"They didn't tell me not to, but they didn't tell me I could, either. Under the circumstances, I'd just as soon not, if you don't mind."

"Fine," he said, and she smiled at him. That was something she'd come to appreciate about Paulo. He could ask a question like that without giving the impression he was trying to entice her into telling him something she shouldn't. He was simply asking if she could talk about it, and he was perfectly prepared to talk about something else entirely if she told him she couldn't. Even Aikawa would have looked disappointed if she'd told him no; Paulo didn't.

He dropped into the other chair, propped his heels on the edge of the com console, and dug out his sketch pad. He began to work, and she watched him from her comfortable drape across her own chair.

"Is this the only place on board where you sketch?" she asked several minutes later, into the quiet, companionable sound of soft pencil lead kissing sharp-toothed paper.

"Pretty much," he said, eyes on the pad and his gracefully moving pencil. He paused and glanced up at her with an off-center smile. "It's kind of a private thing for me. I started doing it as much for a sort of therapy as anything else. Now—" He shrugged. "I guess it's kind of like Leo's poetry."

"Leo writes *poetry*?" Helen felt both eyebrows rise, and he shook his head with a chuckle.

"You didn't know?"

"No, I certainly didn't!" She looked at him suspiciously. "You're not just pulling my leg to see if it'll come off in your hand, are you?"

"Me? Never!" He chuckled again. "Besides, I understand you're a very dangerous person. Wouldn't be very safe to try pulling *your* leg, now would it?"

"So how come you know about his poetry and I don't?"

"Far be it from me to suggest that you can sometimes be a bit unobservant," he said, his pencil moving across the paper again. "On the other hand, I sometimes have to wonder where all of your father's sneaky, all-seeing, spymaster genes went, because you sure didn't get any of them!"

"Ha ha, very funny," she said with a grimace. "You aren't going to tell me how you found out, are you?"

"Nope."

He looked up with another smile, then returned his attention to his artwork, and she glowered at the top of his head. For somebody who didn't mingle worth a damn, he seemed to do an extraordinarily good job of picking up information. In fact, he seemed to do quite a number of things extraordinarily well in his quiet loner's kind of way.

"Paulo?"

"Yes?" he looked back up, his expression intent, as if some odd note in her voice had alerted him.

"I need some advice."

"I'm not exactly the best person to ask, if it's a social question," he cautioned, with something almost like panic in his eyes.

"You're going to have to get over that rabbit-in-the-headlights reaction to mingling with other people, you know. A successful naval officer doesn't have to be a howling extrovert, I suppose. But a hermit's going to experience a certain difficulty in building sound professional relationships."

"Sure, sure!" He raised his hand, waving his pencil at her admonishingly. "Stop criticizing and ask your question."

"I said I'd prefer not to talk about the meeting, but there was one really weird thing, and I'm not sure what to do about it."

"What do you mean, 'weird'?"

"As we were leaving, Westman asked me if Mr. Van Dort had ever mentioned someone named Suzanne Bannister."

"He did what?" Paulo frowned with the expression of someone who knew he didn't have all the information required to understand something. "Why would he do that?"

"I don't know." She turned her eyes away, gazing back out the armorplast at the storm system. "He said I reminded him of someone, then asked me if Mr. Van Dort had ever mentioned her. And I don't think the last name's exactly a coincidence," she added.

"Bannister? I guess not!"

He sat there for several seconds, frowning at her profile.

"You're worried that he had some kind of ulterior motive for telling you, aren't you?" he asked finally, and she gave an irritated little shrug.

"No, not really . . . most of the time. But I can't be sure. And even if he doesn't, I've got a strong feeling it might be painful to Mr. Van Dort if I brought it up.

"Well," Paulo said, "it seems to me you've got three options. First, you can keep your mouth shut and never bring the question up. Second, you can ask Van Dort who this Suzanne Bannister was. Or, third, if you really think Westman might've had some sort of ulterior motive, you could report it to the Skipper and see what *he* thinks you should do about it."

"I'd already pretty much come up with those same options on my own. If you were me, which one would you choose?"

"Without being there and actually hearing what he said to you, I'm not prepared to say," he said thoughtfully. "If you're reasonably certain this isn't simply a case of Westman looking for some way to upset Van Dort or create some kind of suspicion between him and the Skipper—or between him and you, for that matter—then maybe you should just go ahead and ask him. If you're seriously afraid it *is* a way to make trouble, you should probably tell the Skipper without letting Van Dort know anything about it. Let the Skipper decide the best way to handle it." He shrugged. "Bottom line, Helen, I don't think anyone else can make that decision for you."

"No," she agreed, yet even as she did, she realized just talking to Paulo about it had helped her decide what to do.

"Yes, Helen? What can I do for you?

Bernardus Van Dort laid aside the old-fashioned stylus with which he'd been scribbling longhand notes when the cabin hatch chime sound. He tipped back his chair, smiled, and indicated the small couch on the other side of the cabin he'd been assigned.

Helen settled down and looked at him, wondering one last time if she was doing the right thing. But she'd made her mind up, and she inhaled unobtrusively.

"I hope I'm not out of line, Sir," she said. "But someone suggested that I reminded him of someone called Suzanne Bannister."

For just an instant, Van Dort's face froze. All expression vanished, and for that moment, Helen felt as if she were looking at an old-fashioned marble statue. Then he smiled again, but this time the smile was crooked and contained no humor at all.

"Was it Westman? Or Trevor?" His voice was as calm and courteous as ever, yet wrapped around a tension, almost a wariness, she'd never heard from him before.

"It was Mr. Westman," she said steadily, meeting his gaze without flinching, and he nodded.

"I thought it probably was. Trevor and I haven't mentioned Suzanne to one another in over twenty years."

"Sir, if it's none of my business, just tell me so. But when Mr. Westman mentioned her—I don't know. It was as if he really, really wanted me to know and, I think, to ask you about her. And as if his reasons didn't have anything at all to do with the annexation or why we're here."

"You're wrong about that, Helen," Van Dort looked away at last. He gazed intently at a perfectly bare patch of bulkhead. "It has quite a lot to do with why we're here—why *I'm* here, at any rate—even if only indirectly."

He was silent for a long time, still gazing at the bulkhead. The blindness in his eyes made Helen regret that she'd begun the entire conversation, but he hadn't bitten her head off or told her to go away. He simply sat there, and she couldn't just leave him wherever he'd wandered to.

"Who was she, Sir?" she asked quietly.

"My wife," he said, very, very softly.

Helen stiffened, her eyes opening wide. She'd never heard that Van Dort had been married. Then again, she thought, she hadn't actually heard *anything* about his personal life.

Van Dort's eyes finally released the bulkhead and returned to her face. He studied her features, then nodded slowly.

"I see why he told you to ask. You look so much like her. You could be *her* again, or at least her daughter. That's why I almost refused Captain Terekhov's offer to assign you as my aide. It was too much like how I met her, in many ways."

"Would . . . would you care to talk about it, Sir?"

"No." He smiled again, wryly. "But that doesn't mean I shouldn't explain it to you, anyway. I probably should've explained it to Baroness Medusa before she asked me to come here, for that matter. I suppose it comes under the heading of 'potential conflicts of interest.'"

She said nothing, only looked at him, and he faced her fully.

"How old do you think I am, Helen?"

"I'm not sure, Sir," she said slowly. "You're obviously first-gen prolong, if you'll pardon my saying so. I guess . . . sixty T-years?"

"I'm well past eighty," he said. Her eyebrows arched, and he chuckled humorlessly. "I may well have been the first person in the Talbott Cluster to receive prolong. My father was merchant-owner of two freighters when I was born. My mother and I lived aboard, with him, until I was almost sixteen and he sent me off to Old Earth to college. He had a freight concession from one of the Solly shipping lines, and he made regular runs deeper into the League. Prolong wasn't available here, but he took me along on those trips into the Old League and had the therapies started when I was about fourteen.

"You're what—third-generation, I suppose?" He looked the question at her, and she nodded. "Your father?"

"Second-generation."

"Well, I imagine there are enough first-gen recipients in the Star Kingdom for you to realize that first-generation prolong's effects aren't very evident until you're well into your biological thirties." She nodded again, and he grimaced. "Given the fact that prolong wasn't generally available here, the handful of us who'd gotten it the way I did tended not to mention it. It creates a certain resentment when your contemporaries discover you're going to live three or even four times as long as they are. So the fact that I'd received the prolong therapies wasn't general knowledge, and most people simply assumed I naturally looked younger than my age.

"Then I met Suzanne."

He fell silent again, gazing into the past, and this time there was a deep, bittersweet joy in his smile. A joy compounded equally of happiness and pain, Helen thought without knowing why she was so certain.

"I was the skipper of one of my father's ships at the time. I was probably, oh, thirty-three or thirty-four, and Dad had almost a dozen ships by then. By Verge standards, we were indecently wealthy, but Dad already had his eye on Frontier Security. He knew they were coming, and he was afraid of what it would mean for all of us, but especially for Mom and me. He died of a heart attack—he was only fifty-six—the same year I met Suzanne, before he could think of any way to protect us. But it was his concern that started me in the direction of the Trade Union and led directly to where we all are now.

"But that was all in the future the day I brought *Geertruida's Pride* to Montana. Suzanne was Trevor's older sister. He was only a baby, probably less than five T-years old, when I met her. She was a lieutenant in the customs service, and she commanded the inspection party they sent aboard to clear our cargo for landing. She really did look amazingly like you, Helen. Oh, the uniform was different, and she looked a few bio-years older than you do, but when I first saw you standing there, just inside the boarding tube, I thought—"

He shook his head, his eyes bright.

"Anyway, I fell for her. Dear *God*, did I fall! In my entire life, I have never met and don't believe I ever will meet another woman with that much sheer zest for life. With as much intelligence and strength of will. As much courage. And she, God forgive me, fell in love with me.

"I should have realized she looked young for her age. I should've trusted her enough to tell her I'd received prolong. But I'd kept quiet about it for so long it was a reflex to keep on saying nothing. So I did keep quiet. I was here long enough for both of us to realize how deeply we were attracted to one another. And I came back, for a long visit, three months later. I was here almost five T-months that time, and when I left, we were married."

He closed his eyes, his face wrung with pain.

"That was when I told her I was a prolong recipient and that, as a surprise honeymoon gift, I'd arranged a trip to Beowulf itself for her to receive the same therapies. And that was when I found out she was too old. That she was her father's daughter by his *first* wife, and that she was over twenty years older than Trevor."

He was silent again for what seemed like minutes. Then he inhaled deeply and opened his eyes.

"There are myths from Old Earth, from almost every culture and civilization there ever was, of immortal beings—elves, gods and goddesses, nymphs, demigods—who fall in love with mortals. They all end badly, one way or another. Mine was no exception. She forgave me for not telling her, of course. That made it almost worse. I'm not saying we didn't love each other very much, and that we didn't take a tremendous joy in one another, but the entire time, we knew I was going to lose her. I think she felt worst about the thought that she'd be 'deserting' me. Leaving me behind. We had two daughters, Phillipia and Mechelina. They'd received prolong at the earliest possible age, of course, and I think it made Suzanne feel better when she reflected on the fact that we'd have each other when she was gone.

"I also think the fact she hadn't received prolong made her more aware of her mortality, gave her the sense that she had less time in which to do all the things she wanted to do. When I came up with the idea for the Trade Union, she was one of my most enthusiastic backers. And she threw herself into the project the same way she did everything, with every gram of her energy, every scrap of ability.

"Her brother, Trevor, was old enough by then that he'd already begun his career in the Marshals Service, and he didn't think much of the idea. He never really understood, I think, that Suzanne and I were trying to build some sort of bastion here in the Cluster that might be able to resist Frontier Security. He'd never forgiven me, anyway, for marrying his sister without warning her I was going to outlive her by a century or two, and now I'd seduced her into helping me loot the economies of other planets, other star systems. He and his best friend, Stephen Westman—young, intemperate hotheads, the pair of them, even for Montanans—were both convinced I was a ruthless, self-centered bastard who didn't give much of a rat's ass—to use Westman's charming turn of phrase—for anyone else as long as I got what I wanted. Suzanne was . . . irritated with them for their attitude, and she *did* have a temper. Words were exchanged, and feelings were badly hurt on both sides. But Suzanne and I were certain that, eventually, they'd come to understand what we were doing, and why."

He picked up the stylus again, turning it in his fingers.

"By that time, Suzanne and I were both in our fifties, and she was beginning to look noticeably older than I did. Still an amazingly attractive woman, and not just in my opinion, but definitely the older of the two. It hurt her, I think. No, I *know* it did, but she found it useful, too. She was one of the RTU's best negotiators. She could make people who loathed and distrusted the entire concept decide it was a good idea, and she used that attractive-but-mature, decisive personality and appearance like some sort of lethal weapon. I, on the other hand, looked too young, too wet behind the ears, to make some people happy, so I often let her handle the negotiations. Sometimes we double-teamed the other side, with her hitting them high and me hitting them low, and we usually traveled together. She was my wife, my friend, my lover, my partner—she and the girls were everything in the universe to me, and just like my mother and father, we spent most of our time living aboard one or another of the Van Dort Line ships.

"I'd originally been scheduled to go open a round of negotiations with New Tuscany, but she decided to go, instead. She said she could handle the assignment at least as well as I could've, and by going, she could free me up to stay home and deal with some other problems which had arisen. So I took the shuttle up with her and the girls, kissed them, watched them board the *Anneloes* and set out for New Tuscany.

"I never saw any of them again."

Helen's jaw tightened—in pain, not really in surprise.

"We never found out what happened," Van Dort said softly. "The ship simply . . . vanished. It could've been almost anything. The most logical explanation was pirates, although she was armed, and there hadn't been much pirate activity in the Cluster for two or three years. But we never found out, never knew. They were just . . . gone.

"I didn't take it well. I'd spent so long worrying about her shorter life expectancy, thinking about how I was going to lose her, about how I should have told her before I ever married her, of how incredibly lucky I'd been that she loved me anyway. But it never occurred to me in my worst nightmares that the last thing I'd ever see of her was her and our daughters smiling, waving goodbye. That they'd just be . . . erased out of my life, like some deleted computer file.

"I refused to deal with it, refused to come to grips with it, because if I'd done that, I would have had to admit it'd happened. Instead, I buried myself in my work. I dedicated myself to making the Trade Union the success Suzanne and I had dreamed it could be. And anything that got in the way of that success was my enemy.

"Trevor blamed me for her death for years. I don't think he does anymore, but he was younger then. He seemed to feel I'd *sent* her to New Tuscany, because it wasn't important enough for me to waste my own time on. It was my fault, as he saw it, that she was ever on that ship in the first place. And the way I refused to face my own loss, to admit it or let the rest of the universe see my wounds, convinced him I was just as cold, callous, and scheming as he'd ever suspected.

"And as if I were determined to confirm the validity of his opinions, I brought Ineka Vaandrager on board. I justified it then on the grounds that time was getting short, that Frontier Security was beginning to look more hungrily in our direction, and it was. That's the worst of it; I can still justify everything I did on that basis and know it was true. But I can never run away from the suspicion that I would've turned to Ineka anyway. That I just didn't care. I'm sure Westman's bone-deep resentment and distrust of the RTU stems from that period, the five or ten T-years after Suzanne's death. And that's why I understand why Montanans might not be particularly fond of me.

"It's also the reason I turned so eagerly to the possibility of building support for a Cluster-wide annexation plebiscite when *Harvest Joy* came out of the Lynx Terminus. It was like my last chance for salvation. To prove—to

Suzanne, I think, more than anyone else—that the RTU wasn't just a money machine for Rembrandt and for me personally. That it really was intended to stop Frontier Security, and that I was willing to abandon it entirely, even after all these years, if the possibility of protecting *all* of the Cluster offered itself."

He stopped and looked up from the stylus in his hands. He met Helen's gaze, and he smiled sadly.

"I've never explained all of that to anyone before. Joachim Alquezar knows, I think. And a few others probably suspect. But that's the true story of how the plebiscite came to be, and why. And also the reason Montana is special to me in so many ways. And why Steve Westman's doing what he's doing."

He shook his head, his smile sadder than ever.

"Ridiculous, isn't it? All of this springing from the mistakes of one man who was too stupid to tell the woman he loved the truth before he asked her to marry him?"

"Mr. Van Dort," Helen said, after a moment, "it may not be my place to say this, but I think you're being too hard on yourself. Yes, you should've told her about the prolong. But not telling her wasn't an act of betrayal—*she* certainly didn't see it that way, or she wouldn't have stayed. And it sounds to me like the two of you had a marriage which was a genuine partnership. My father and mother had that sort of marriage, I think. I never knew Mom well enough to really know, but I do know Daddy and Cathy Montaigne are like that, and I like to think that someday I may find someone I can have that kind of relationship—that kind of life—with. And whatever might've happened someday because you had prolong and she didn't, that wasn't why you lost her and your daughters. You lost them because of circumstances beyond your control. Beyond *anyone's* control. It could've happened to anyone. It happened to happen to you and to them. I lost my mother because of circumstances beyond anyone's control, and even with all the love my father's given me, there were times I wanted to strike out at the universe. Wanted to take it by the throat and strangle it for stealing my mother from me. And unlike you, I knew precisely how she died, knew it was her choice, as well as her duty.

"So don't blame yourself for their deaths. And don't blame yourself for being bitter because they died. That's called being a human being.

"As for Westman and Chief Marshal Bannister and their attitudes towards the Trade Union and even the annexation, all you can do is all you can do. Maybe you weren't exactly the nicest person in the world while you were trying to build up the RTU, but that doesn't mean it's tainted or poisoned somehow. And if the annexation goes through, I can't think of a better possible memorial for your wife and daughters."

"I've tried to tell myself that," he half-whispered.

"Good," Helen said more briskly. "Because it's true. And now that I know about Suzanne, and your daughters, and all the rest of your deep, dark secrets, be warned! The next time I see you sinking into a slough of despond or starting to feel overly sorry for yourself, I'm going to kick you—with infinite respect, of course!—right in the ass."

He blinked, both eyebrows flying up. And then, to her relief, he began to laugh. He laughed for quite a long time, with a deep, full-throated amusement she'd never really expected to see from him. But finally, the laughter eased into chuckles, and he shook his head at her.

"You're even more like Suzanne than I thought. That's exactly what she would've told me under the same circumstances."

"I thought she sounded like a smart lady," Helen said in a satisfied tone.

"Oh, yes. *Very* like Suzanne . . . and that," he added in a softer voice, "is probably the greatest compliment I could ever pay anyone."

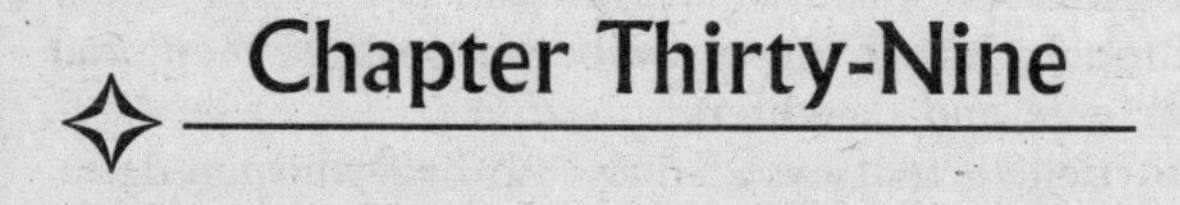

Chapter Thirty-Nine

The dispatch boat from Spindle began uploading its message queue well before it reached Montana planetary orbit. Lieutenant Hansen McGraw, the com officer of the watch, watched the message headers scroll up on his display. Most were protected by multilevel encryption, and he waited patiently while the computers sorted through the traffic. Half a dozen of the larger message files, he noted, were personal-only for Captain Terekhov and Bernardus Van Dort. One of them, however, carried a lower security classification and a higher priority rating. He downloaded that one to a message board, and handed it to Senior Chief Harris.

"Deliver this to the Exec, please, Senior Chief."

"Aye, aye, Sir," Harris said, and tucked the message board under his arm. He carried it across the bridge to the lift, down one deck, and along a passage to the wardroom, where he stepped through the open hatch and cleared his throat politely.

"Yes, Senior Chief?" Lieutenant Frances Olivetti, *Hexapuma*'s third astrogator, happened to be sitting closest to the hatch.

"Message for the XO, Ma'am."

"Bring it on over, please, Senior Chief," Ansten FitzGerald said from where he sat in the midst of a pinochle game with Ginger Lewis, Lieutenant Commander Nagchaudhuri, and Lieutenant Jefferson Kobe.

"Yes, Sir." Harris crossed to the executive officer. He handed over the message board, then stood waiting, hands clasped behind him, while FitzGerald opened the message file and scanned it. His eyes narrowed and he frowned slightly, obviously thinking hard. Then he looked back up at Harris.

"Who has the standby pinnace?"

"Ms. Pavletic, Sir," the senior chief replied.

"In that case, please inform her that I anticipate she'll be leaving the ship to collect the Captain and his party within the next few minutes, Senior Chief."

"Aye, aye, Sir." Harris came briefly to attention, then headed back out through the hatch while FitzGerald plugged his personal com into the shipboard system and punched in a combination.

"Bridge, Officer of the Watch speaking," Tobias Wright's voice replied.

"Toby, it's the Exec. I need to speak to Hansen, please."

"Yes, Sir. Wait one, please."

There was a very brief pause; then Lieutenant McGraw answered.

"You wanted me, Sir?"

"Yes, I did, Hansen. Please make a general signal to all work and shore parties to return on board."

"Yes, Sir. Should I indicate immediate priority?"

"No," FitzGerald said after a brief consideration. "Instruct them to return directly, but to expedite any extended tasks."

"Aye, aye, Sir."

"Thank you. FitzGerald, clear," the executive officer said.

He switched off his com and returned his attention to his cards. Several people looked as if they'd have liked to ask him questions, but none of them did. Aikawa

Kagiyama, who was in the process of suffering abject annihilation across a chessboard at Abigail Hearns's hands, found it even more difficult to concentrate on his game. There was only one logical reason for the instructions the XO had issued: *Hexapuma* had just received new orders which required her to go someplace else.

He frowned, part of his mind trying to decide whether to sacrifice a knight or his single remaining bishop in an effort to briefly stave off the lieutenant's merciless attack, while the rest of his mind considered the implications of new orders. *Hexapuma* had been in Montana for just under eleven T-days, and it had been nine days since the Captain and Van Dort's first meeting with Westman. Aikawa didn't know how well that effort had been going. He knew Van Dort had met with Westman a second time, but he couldn't pick up a single hint about what they might have discussed. It was deeply frustrating for someone who prided himself on always knowing what was going on. And the fact that Helen really *did* know but refused to tell him was even more frustrating. He respected her refusal to gossip about the details to which she might be privy, but all the respect in the galaxy wasn't going to make him feel any less curious.

"Are you planning to move sometime soon?" Lieutenant Hearns asked pleasantly, and he gave himself a shake.

"Sorry, Ma'am. I guess I was woolgathering."

He looked back down at the board and interposed his king's knight. Lieutenant Hearns' castle swooped down and took it instantly.

"Mate in four moves," she informed him with a smile.

Aikawa grunted in exasperation as he realized she was right. He started to tip over his king, then stopped himself. It might just be possible, he thought, studying the board carefully, that he could at least make her take an additional two or three moves to finish him off. Which was about the best any of the midshipmen, with the sole exception of Ragnhild Pavletic, had so far managed.

He shelved consideration of what their new orders

might be and gave himself over to the intense examination of the board.

"Flight Ops, this is Hawk-Papa-One, requesting clearance for a direct transit to *Hexapuma* Alpha's current location," Ragnhild Pavletic said into her boom mike.

"Hawk-Papa-One, Flight Ops," Lieutenant Sheets' voice replied in her earbug. "Hold while we clear your flight plan."

"Flight Ops, Hawk-Papa-One copies."

Ragnhild sat back in the pilot's seat and considered her projected trip. As always, the exact location of Captain Terekhov—"*Hexapuma* Alpha"—was monitored whenever he was off the ship. As such, she knew that he, Bernardus Van Dort, and Helen Zilwicki were currently in a restaurant rejoicing in the name of The Rare Sirloin. It was supposed to be one of the better restaurants in Brewster, the Montana capital. Ragnhild didn't know about that personally, of course. Unlike *some* midshipwomen, she thought, she hadn't been invited to eat there no less than three times in the last week.

On the other hand, I haven't been expected to pull my full watch assignment on board ship as well as going haring off dirt-side every time Van Dort does, either.

She was surprised Helen didn't show more signs of exhaustion. She was spending most of her putative free time assisting Van Dort aboard ship, whenever she wasn't somewhere on the planet with him. She was still finding time—somehow—for regular exercise and sparring sessions, but that was about it, and her bunk time was suffering. Still, there did seem to be the odd half-hour here and there Ragnhild couldn't quite account for. And, interestingly enough, there seemed to be matching holes in Paulo d'Arezzo's known whereabouts.

The thought of Helen spending time with the too-pretty midshipman was fairly preposterous. But not as preposterous as it would once have been, she reminded herself. Something had happened to alter their relationship, and no one else in Snotty Row seemed to have any idea what it might have been. Whatever it was, it didn't seem to have any romantic overtones—thank God—but it was all very odd. And if she and Paulo were sneaking off somewhere, where was it? As big as *Hexapuma* was, there weren't that many places aboard her where two people could evade observation.

No, she told herself once again, it had to be a simple coincidence.

"Hawk-Papa-One, Flight Ops," Lieutenant Sheets said suddenly.

"Flight Ops, Hawk-Papa-One," Ragnhild acknowledged.

"Hawk-Papa-One, you are cleared to *Hexapuma* Alpha's current location. Flight path Tango Foxtrot to Brewster Interplanetary, Pad Seven-Two. Contact Brewster Flight Control on Navy Channel Niner-Three at the two hundred klick line for final approach instructions."

"Flight Ops, Hawk-Papa-One copies flight path Tango Foxtrot to Brewster Interplanetary, Pad Seven-Two, contacting Brewster Flight Control on November Charlie Niner-Three at the two-zero-zero klick line for final approach instructions."

"Hawk-Papa-One, Flight Ops. Confirm. You are cleared to separate at your discretion."

"Flight Ops, Hawk-Papa-One separating now." She looked over her shoulder at the pinnace's flight engineer. "Chief, disengage the umbilicals."

"Disengage umbilicals, aye, Ma'am." The flight engineer tapped commands into his console and watched telltales flicker from green, through red, to amber as the pinnace's service connections to the ship were severed.

"Confirm all umbilicals disengaged, Ms. Pavletic."

"Thank you, Chief." Ragnhild glanced over her own displays, doublechecking the umbilicals' status, and nodded in satisfaction. She keyed her mike again. "Flight Ops, Hawk-Papa-One confirms clean separation at zero-niner-thirty-five."

"Hawk-Papa-One, Flight Ops. Confirm. You are cleared to apply thrust."

"Flight Ops, Hawk-Papa-One. Applying thrust now."

The pinnace's bow thrusters flared as Ragnhild backed the sleek craft out of its docking arms. She watched the boat bay bulkhead's smart-painted range marks and numbers glide past as the pinnace moved slowly astern. She came up on the departure mark exactly on the tick and at exactly the correct velocity, she noted with pleasure, and the reaction thrusters gimbaled upward, pushing the pinnace down and out of the bay. Once she had sufficient separation, she dropped the nose, closed the bow thruster ports, and engaged the main thrusters. This flight would be too short to bother with the impeller wedge—they'd already be configuring for atmosphere by the time they were sufficiently clear of the ship to activate the wedge—and she settled back to enjoy a good old-fashioned airfoil flight.

"Well, this is a fine kettle of fish," Aivars Terekhov commented sourly as he finished reading the last of his personal dispatches from Rear Admiral Khumalo and Baroness Medusa.

"That's certainly one way to put it," Van Dort agreed. His personal dispatches were even more voluminous than Terekhov's, and he was still reading. He looked up from the current message and grimaced.

"Joachim Alquezar commented to me once that Aleksandra Tonkovic, just after the Nemanja bombing, said something to the effect that we wouldn't need a silver bullet to kill N1ordbrandt. I'm beginning to wonder about that."

"It does seem she has some sort of evil fairy looking out for her, doesn't it?" Terekhov said sourly.

"So far, at any rate. But what's impressed me even more than her unpleasant propensity for surviving is her sheer malevolence. You do realize that by now she's killed something over thirty-six hundred people, most of them civilians, in her bombing attacks alone?"

"Which doesn't even count the wounded. Or the cops—or the frigging firemen!" Terekhov snarled, and Van Dort looked up quickly.

Even that mild an obscenity was unusual from Terekhov. Van Dort and the Manticoran captain had become quite close over the thirty-five days he'd spent aboard *Hexapuma*. He liked and admired Terekhov, and he'd come to know the Manticoran well enough to realize that that language indicated far more anger from him than it would have from someone else.

"She's certainly a very different proposition from Westman," the Rembrandter said after a moment. "And the people she's recruited obviously have much more deep-seated grievances than Westman does."

"To put it mildly." Terekhov tipped his chair back behind his desk and cocked his head at Van Dort. "I'm not really familiar with Split," he said, "and the standard briefing on the system was fairly superficial, I'm afraid. My impression, though, is that the system's economy and government is set up quite differently from Montana's."

"They are," Van Dort said. "Economically, Montana's beef and leatherwork command decent prices even in other systems here in the Cluster, and they also ship it Shell-ward. They have some extractive industries in their asteroid belt, also for export, and they don't *import* all that much. By and large their industry's domestically self-sufficient for the consumer market, although their heavy industry's more limited. They import heavy machine tools, and all their spacecraft are built out-system, for example. And their self-sufficiency stems in part from the fact that they're willing to settle for technology that's adequate to their needs but hardly cutting edge.

"Montana isn't a wealthy planet by any stretch, but it maintains a marginally favorable trade balance and there isn't actually any widespread poverty. That's an unusual accomplishment in the Verge, and whether Westman and his people want to admit it or not, the RTU's shipping strength is one reason they're able to pull it off.

"The other way Montana differs from Kornati is that it's much easier, relatively speaking, for someone who works his posterior off and enjoys at least a little luck to move from the lowest income brackets to a position of comparative affluence. These people make an absolute fetish out of rugged individualism, and there's still a lot of unclaimed land and free range. Their entire legal code and society are set up to encourage individual enterprise to *use* those opportunities, and their wealthier citizens look aggressively for investment opportunities.

"Kornati's a much more typical Verge planet. They don't have an attractive export commodity, like Montana's beef. There's not enough wealth in the system to attract imports from outside the Cluster, and although their domestic industry's growing steadily, the *rate* of increase is low. Since they have nothing to export, but still have to import critical commodities—like off-world computers, trained engineers, and machine tools—if they want to build up their local infrastructure, their balance of trade's . . . unfavorable, to say the very least. That exacerbates the biggest economic problem Kornati faces: lack of investment capital. Since they can't attract it from outside, what they really need is to find some way to pry loose enough domestic investment to at least prime the pump the way other systems have managed.

"The Dresden System, for example, was even poorer than Split thirty T-years ago. By now, Dresden's on the brink of catching up with Split, and even without the possibility of the annexation, Dresden's gross system product would probably pass Split's within the next ten T-years. It's not that Dresden's wealthier than Split—in fact, the system's actually quite a bit poorer. It's just that the Dresdeners've managed to begin a self-sustaining domestic expansion by encouraging entrepreneurship and taking advantage of every opportunity—including energetic cooperation with the RTU—that falls their way. The oligarchs on Kornati, by and large, are more interested in sitting on what they have than in risking their wealth in the sorts of enterprises which might bolster the economy as a whole. They aren't quite a kleptocracy, and that's about the best I can say for them."

The Rembrandter's expression mirrored his contempt for the ruling families of Split, and he shook his head.

"The truth is that while the situation on Kornati isn't actually anywhere near so bad as Nordbrandt's agit-prop paints it, it isn't good. In fact, it's pretty damned bad. You saw the slum areas in Thimble while you were in Spindle?" Terekhov nodded, and Van Dort waved a hand. "Well, the housing in Thimble's slums is two or three notches above the quality of housing available in Karlovac's. And the social support payments on Kornati have only about sixty percent of the buying power of equivalent safety net stipends on Flax. Starvation isn't much of a problem, because the government does heavily subsidize food for those receiving social support, but it's no damned picnic to be poor there."

"I gathered that from the briefing papers," Terekhov said, indicating the chip folio-littered desk, "and I didn't understand it. According to other parts of the package, the Kornatians are fiercely devoted to individual civil rights. How does a nation with that sort of attitude justify not providing an adequate safety net for its people? I realize there's a difference between having the right to have the government leave you alone and depending on the government to take care of you, but it still strikes me as reflecting contradictory attitudes."

"Because it does, in a way," Van Dort agreed. "As you say, their civil rights tradition is that the citizen has the right to be free of undue government interference, not to be taken care of *by* the government. When that tradition first evolved, about a hundred and fifty T-years ago, the economy was far less stratified than it is now, the middle class was much larger, relatively speaking, and the electorate in general was far more involved in politics.

"But over the last seventy or eighty T-years, that's changed. The economy's stagnated, compared to other systems in the area, even as the population's increased steeply. The poor and the very poor—the underclass, if you will—has grown enormously relative to the total population, and the middle class has been severely pinched. And there's a growing attitude on the part of some Kornatian political leaders that the civil rights of *voting* citizens are important, but that those of citizens who don't vote are more . . . negotiable. Especially when the citizens involved pose a threat to public safety and stability."

"This is the local 'autonomy' and 'freedoms' Tonkovic wants to preserve?" Terekhov asked bitingly, and Van Dort shrugged.

"Aleksandra's looking out for her own interests and those of her fellow oligarchs. And, to be blunt, most of them are a pretty sorry lot. There are exceptions. The Rajkovic family, for example. And the Kovacics. Did your briefings give you much detail on the Kornatian political set up?"

"Not a lot," Terekhov admitted. "Or, rather, I have a whole kettle of alphabet soup full of political party acronyms, but without any local perspective, they don't mean a whole lot to me."

"I see." Van Dort pursed his lips, thinking for several seconds, then shrugged.

"All right," he said, "here's the 'Fast and Dirty Rembrandt Guide to Kornatian Politics,' by B. Van Dort. I've already given it, in somewhat greater detail, to Dame Estelle and Mr. O'Shaughnessy, which I suspect has something to do with the nature of our instructions from the Baroness. Do bear in mind, though, that what I'm about to tell you is from the perspective of someone on the outside looking in."

He raised both eyebrows at Terekhov until the Manticoran nodded, then began.

"Aleksandra Tonkovic's the leader of the Democratic Centralist Party. Despite its rather liberal-sounding name, the DCP is, in my humble opinion, anything but 'centralist,' and it certainly doesn't believe in anything a Rembrandter or a Montanan would call 'democracy.' Essentially, its platform is dedicated to maintaining the current social and political order on Kornati. It's an oligarchical party, dominated by the Tonkovic family and perhaps a dozen of its closest allies, who tend to regard the planet as their personal property.

"The Social Moderate Party is the DCP's closest political ally. For all intents and purposes, their platforms are identical these days, although when the SMP was first formed, it actually was considerably to the 'left' of the Centralists. The generation of DCP leadership before Tonkovic successfully co-opted the SMP, but the appearance of a compromise platform, evolved after annual conferences between their 'independent' party leaderships, was too valuable to give up through an official merger.

"Vuk Rajkovic, on the other hand, is the leader of the Reconciliation Party. In a lot of ways, the RP is more of an umbrella organization than a properly organized political party. Several minor parties merged under Rajkovic's leadership, and they, in turn, reached out to other splinter groups. One of them, by the way, was Nordbrandt's National Redemption Party. Which, I imagine, didn't do Rajkovic's political base a bit of good when she decided to begin blowing people up.

"The biggest difference between the Reconciliation Party and Tonkovic and her allies is that Rajkovic genuinely believes the Kornatian upper classes—of which he is most decidedly a prominent member—must voluntarily share political power with the middle and lower classes and work aggressively to open the door to economic opportunity for those same groups. I'm not prepared to say how much of this position's based on altruism and how much is based on a coldly rational analysis of the current state of the Split System. There've certainly been occasions on which he's couched his arguments in the most cold-blooded, self-interested terms possible. But when he's done that, he's usually been talking to his fellow oligarchs, and speaking as someone who's occasionally attempted to locate a few drops of altruism in *Rembrandter* oligarchs, I suspect he's discovered that self interest is the only argument that particular audience understands.

"The most significant thing about the last presidential election was that the Reconciliation Party launched an aggressive voter registration campaign among the working class districts of Kornati's major cities. I don't think

Tonkovic and her allies believed that effort could have any practical effect on the outcome of the campaign, but they found out differently. Tonkovic only won because two other candidates withdrew and threw their support to her. Even so, she managed to outpoll Rajkovic by a majority of barely six percent on Election Day, and that was with *eleven percent* of the total vote split between eight additional candidates."

Van Dort paused, smiling nastily, and chuckled.

"That must've come pretty close to scaring Aleksandra right out of her knickers," he said with relish. "Especially because, under the Kornatian Constitution, the vice presidency goes to the *presidential* candidate who pulled the second-highest total of votes. Which means—"

"Which means the fellow she had to leave in charge on Kornati when she went scampering off to Spindle is her worst political enemy," Terekhov finished for him, and it was his turn to chuckle. Then he shook his head. "Lord! What idiot thought up *that* system? I can't conceive of anything better designed to cripple the executive branch!"

"I expect that's exactly what the drafters of the original Constitution had in mind. Not that it's meant a lot over the past several decades, since, until the Reconciliation Party came along, there wasn't really any significant difference between the platforms of any of the presidential candidates who stood much chance of winning either office.

"But, after the last presidential election, Rajkovic and his allies—which, at that time, still included Agnes Nordbrandt—controlled the vice presidency and about forty-five percent of the seats in the Kornatian Parliament. Tonkovic's Democratic Centralists and the Social Moderates between them controlled the presidency and about fifty-two percent of Parliament, and the remaining three percent or so of the vote was scattered among more than a dozen marginal so-called parties, many of which managed to elect only a single deputy. I haven't seen the most recent figures, but when Nordbrandt's NRP disintegrated during the plebiscite campaign, Rajkovic lost enough deputies to drop his representation in Parliament to around forty-three percent, and Tonkovic picked up about half of what Rajkovic lost. I have no idea, at this point, how Nordbrandt's terrorist campaign has affected the balance in Parliament. I'd expect that from Rajkovic's perspective, the effect hasn't been good.

"On the other hand, Aleksandra has the problem that her strongest, most serious political rival is the acting head of state back home. Because he's only the *acting* head of state, he's pretty much stuck with the Cabinet Tonkovic selected and Parliament approved before annexation ever came up. She probably figures that the combination of passive resistance within the Cabinet, plus the fact that he doesn't control a majority in Parliament, will prevent Rajkovic from doing anything especially dangerous while she deals with the Constitutional Convention in Spindle. On the other hand, he is at home, at the center of the government and the entire political system, which gives him the home court advantage to set against all of her efforts to hobble him."

"That," Terekhov said, after a moment, "sounds like a remarkably good recipe for political and economic disaster."

"It isn't a good situation, but it isn't quite as bad as a bare recitation of the political alliances and maneuverings involved might suggest. For instance, a surprisingly high percentage of their civil service is both honest and reasonably efficient, despite the oligrachic political system. As far as I can tell, the Kornatian National Police are also reasonably honest and efficient, and Colonel Basaricek does her level best to keep her people out of politics and out of the hip pockets of the local elite. In fact, she's apparently been working on reinforcing a more traditional view of the entire citizenry's civil rights among her personnel over the last five or ten T-years. Enough so that she's drawn some noticeable political flak from people who value domestic tranquility over the rights of troublemakers.

"The biggest political problem's the way the electorate's grown increasingly apathetic over the past several decades. There's always been a strong tradition of patronage on Kornati, and these days that translates into clients who vote in accordance with their patrons' desires in return for a degree of security and protection in an economy that isn't doing well. Coupled with the extremely low level of voter registration, that's how a very small percentage of the total population's managed to take control of the legislative process. Which is another huge difference between Split and Dresden . . . and one reason Dresden is overtaking Split economically so rapidly."

"We've seen that system before," Terekhov said grimly. "It was called the People's Republic of Haven."

"Split isn't anywhere near that bad yet, but I'd have to say it has the potential to end up that way. Unless, of course, Rajkovic's accomplishment in the last presidential election reverses the trend. My impression is that, at least until Nordbrandt started killing people, Aleksandra and her colleagues believed Rajkovic's campaign represented an anomaly. I think they hoped—probably with reason—that if they managed to stymie his efforts to make genuine, large-scale progress in opening up the system, as his party platform called for, the first-time voters who came out in his support would decide the system doesn't work, after all. If they go home again, and decline to vote in future elections, it'll be business as usual for the oligarchs."

"And that's why Tonkovic doesn't want anybody upsetting her own little playhouse, is that it?"

"I'd say so, yes." Van Dort looked troubled. "I wondered what Aleksandra had in mind when she supported the original plebiscite so enthusiastically. In my opinion, she was driven far more by fear of being ingested by Frontier Security than by the advantages membership in the Star Kingdom might bring to her planet and its economy. Where the majority of the Convention's delegates, including a majority of the oligarchs, see annexation as an opportunity to improve the lives, health, and life expectancy of their worlds' citizens, Aleksandra doesn't, really.

"I'm not saying the other oligarchs are saints, because they're not. They figure that if the economy improves for everyone, those already at the top of the heap will improve *their* situations even more. But I do think most of them're able to look at least a short distance past the limits of their own greedy self-interest. I don't really think Aleksandra is. Worse, I don't think she realizes she *isn't*. She and the people she associates with on Kornati—the people she thinks of as the 'real' Kornatians—are quite well off as things are. The people who aren't 'real' to her don't matter. Don't even exist, except as threats to the ones who *are* 'real.' So what they want the Star Kingdom to do is to protect them from the League's bureaucratic nightmare and otherwise leave them alone. And I'm afraid Aleksandra, despite having quite a good mind, actually, has been extrapolating from her own experience in Split when she visualizes the Star Kingdom. I'm convinced that when she and her closest associates decided to support the plebiscite, they believed the Star Kingdom's version of representative government was essentially a façade. That they'd be able to continue business as usual even after the annexation went through."

"Well, they're in for a disappointment," Terekhov said with a harsh chuckle. "Just wait until a few sharp Manticoran business types start lining up local partners! Investment capital won't be a problem much longer, and once the Kornatians have hard money in their pockets, and something to spend it on, the economic climate's going to undergo a major change. And when that happens, their comfortable little closed political shop is going to find its windows smashed in, too. If they didn't like what happened in the last presidential election, they *really* won't like what a Manticoran election looks like!"

"I think they believe that since the Star Kingdom requires its citizens to pay taxes before they're allowed to vote, they'll be able to control the situation. That the Manticoran system's set up to give the Star Kingdom's upper class control of the electorate while maintaining the fiction that the lower classes have any real political power," Van Dort said, and Terekhov barked a sharp laugh.

"That's because they don't understand how high a percentage of our people do pay taxes. Or maybe they think our tax codes are as complicated and buggered up as theirs are as a way to chisel people out of the franchise."

"Not all of our tax codes are that bad," Van Dort protested.

"Oh, *please*, Bernardus!" Terekhov shook his head in disgust. "Oh, I'll grant you Rembrandt isn't quite as bad as the others, but I've taken a look at the rat's nest of tax provisions some of you people have out here. I've seen hyper-space astrogation problems that were simpler! No wonder nobody knows what the hell is going on. But the Star Kingdom's personal tax provisions are a lot simpler—I filled out my entire tax return in less than ten minutes, on a single-page e-form, last year, even with the emergency war taxes. And all the Star Kingdom requires to vote is that a citizen pay at least one cent more in taxes than he receives in government transfer payments and subsidies. Once the infusion of investment capital hits your local economies, there're going to be an awful lot of franchised voters. And somehow I don't think they're going to be very fond of Ms. Tonkovic and her friends. In fact, I think they'll probably line solidly up behind Mr. Rajkovic."

"Which is precisely what's driving her delaying tactics now," Van Dort said. "I doubt she's truly realized just how wrong her original analysis of the Star Kingdom's political structure really was even now, but she *has* begun to realize that it *was* wrong. Unfortunately, from her perspective, she's now committed to supporting the annexation. Worse, she's probably realized that even if she could opt out on behalf of the Split System, despite the plebiscite vote—which would be political suicide for her personally, at a bare minimum—Split would simply find itself encysted within the Star Kingdom once the rest of the Cluster joined it. The odds of her being able to maintain her neat little closed system under those circumstances would be minute. So instead, she's fighting for a Constitution which will not simply leave the existing economic structures and control mechanisms in place in Split, but actually give them the imprimatur of an official constitutional guarantee backed by the Crown. That's the 'local autonomy' she keeps harping on—the right of individual star systems to determine who holds the franchise within their own political structures."

"It's not going to happen," Terekhov said flatly. "Her Majesty will never stand for it. It's too close to the old PRH, and no Manticoran monarch or government would even consider letting it stand."

"It's a pity you can't just announce that to the Kornatians," Van Dort mused. "It might even separate some of the FAK's rank and file from Nordbrandt."

"Assuming they were prepared to believe *anybody* where political promises are concerned."

"There is that," Van Dort conceded. Then he smiled. The expression was so unexpected Terekhov blinked in surprise.

"What?" the Manticoran asked.

"I was just reading between the lines of Baroness Medusa's instructions. She must have twisted Aleksandra's arm right to the brink of dislocation."

Terekhov cocked an eyebrow, and Van Dort chuckled.

"Given everything I just told you about the relationship between Aleksandra and Rajkovic, do you think she really wants us rummaging around in Split, outside her ability to control what we do? If she's requested Manticoran support on the basis outlined in my instructions, with *Rajkovic* approving or disapproving our actions on the spot, then Dame Estelle must have figured out a way to screw a pulser muzzle straight into her ear canal. This could actually be fairly interesting."

"But it does take us away from Montana," Terekhov pointed out.

"Yes, it does. I'm not sure that that's a bad thing, though."

"Why not?"

"I've been spending a fair amount of time with Trevor Bannister." A shadow flickered briefly through Van Dort's eyes and vanished. "We've covered a lot of ground, including dealing, more or less, at least, with some personal matters that could have gotten in the way. In addition, though, I've been through Trevor's intelligence summaries and compared them to what I personally know about Stephen Westman. I'm inclined to think that what Nordbrandt's been doing on Kornati's something of a bucket of cold water for Westman. A horrible example, if you will, of where his own operations could go if he and his followers find themselves increasingly isolated from the Montanan mainstream. And I also think meeting you and talking with you, as well as listening to Baroness Medusa's message to him, may actually have started getting the notion that Manticore isn't a clone of Frontier Security through his skull. Leaving him alone to think about it for a while might not be a bad idea."

"I hope that's not just whistling in the dark," Terekhov said. "Either way, though, we have our movement orders."

"Yes, we do." Van Dort frowned with the expression of a man trying to remember something that was at the tip of his mental tongue. Then he snapped his fingers.

"What?" Terekhov asked.

"I almost forgot. When I was down at Trevor's office this morning, he gave me a new piece of information. I'm not sure where he got it—he's protecting his sources carefully—but it seems Westman's been in contact with at least one off-worlder who appears to be very . . . supportive of his position."

"He has?" Terekhov frowned. "I don't like the sound of that."

"Neither do I. The last thing we need is some sort of interstellar coordinating committee operating Cluster-wide."

"Absolutely. Do we know anything about this mysterious stranger?"

"Not much," Van Dort admitted. "All we really know is that he met with Westman about two T-months ago and that he was identified only by the codename 'Firebrand.' What he and Westman discussed, where 'Firebrand' came from, and where he went when he left, are all unanswered questions, but the name itself has some unpleasant connotations from our perspective."

"It does, indeed."

Terekhov frowned some more, then shrugged.

"Well, there's nothing we can do about it for now," he said, and reached out to punch an address combination into his desktop com.

"Bridge, Officer of the Watch speaking," Lieutenant Commander Kaplan said.

"Are all our people back aboard, Naomi?"

"Yes, Sir. They are."

"Very well. In that case, request permission from Montana Traffic Control for us to leave orbit and depart the system for Split.

"Well, 'Firebrand,'" Aldona Anisimovna said as Damien Harahap walked into the conference room attached to her Estelle Arms Hotel suite on Monica. "Welcome back. How was your trip?"

"Long, Ms. Anisimovna," he replied. In fact, he'd left Monica better than three T-months ago. He'd spent most of that time traveling between star systems, penned up in the confines of a dispatch boat, and he wanted a long, soaking bath, a thick, rare steak with baked potato and sour cream, and several hours of convivial female companionship—in that order.

Anisimovna and Bardasano sat on the other side of the crystal-topped conference table. Izrok Levakonic was supposed to be there, but there was no sign of him. Harahap nodded his head in the direction of Levakonic's empty chair in silent question, and Anisimovna smiled.

"Izrok's out at Eroica Station," she said. "He's helping out with a minor technical problem the Monican Navy's experiencing, and he'll probably be stuck out there for the next few days. Go ahead with your report. Isabel and I will see to it that he's brought up to date."

"Of course, Ma'am."

'Technical problem,' is it? Harahap snorted mentally behind his expressionless eyes. *And just how much would that have to do with all those battlecruisers which have miraculously appeared here in Monica?*

The Gendarmerie captain was beginning to suspect that the scale of Anisimovna's plans was considerably more audacious than he'd believed possible. It all seemed extraordinarily risky, assuming he was starting to get it figured out correctly. But somehow he doubted even Manpower would have been prepared to make the investment that many hundreds of thousands of tons of battlecruiser represented unless it was pretty damned sure of success.

In any case, that part of the operation wasn't his responsibility.

"While I was gone," he began, "I contacted Westman in Montana, Nordbrandt in Split, and Jeffers in Tillerman. The quick overview is that, of the three, Nordbrandt's definitely the best suited to our needs. Jeffers talks a good fight, but my impression is that he's actually too shy to come out of the woodwork without a great deal of additional encouragement. Westman's the big question mark. I suspect that in terms of capability, he leaves both the other two in the dust. And my impression is that he's deeply committed to his beliefs. But he's also much more opposed to inflicting casualties. In terms of representing a serious threat to his own government, or to OFS, he's probably the most dangerous. But in terms of our need for a threat which is spectacular, however genuine it may or may not be, his disinclination to kill people is definitely a strike against him."

He looked back and forth between the two women. Both of them were listening intently, and Bardasano had a memo pad in front of her. They weren't going to interrupt him with questions until he'd finished his basic presentation, he realized. That was nice. Too many of his uniformed superiors were too in love with demonstrating their own insightful intelligence to keep their mouths shut until people who knew what was really happening could finish explaining it to them in short sentences of single-syllable words.

"I'd like to discuss each of these three possibilities in increasing order of value, if that's acceptable?" he asked. Anisimovna nodded, and he smiled.

"Thank you. In that case, let's get Jeffers out of the way. First of all, Jeffers doesn't have a very good grasp of operational security," Harahap began. "In fact, I wouldn't be surprised if he's already been pretty thoroughly penetrated by local counterintelligence types. When I spoke to him, he said he . . ."

Chapter Forty

"Damn, I *hate* this kind of shit," Captain Duan Binyan muttered as the Jessyk Combine's armed freighter *Marianne* decelerated towards Kornati orbit.

"Why they pay us the big money," Annette De Chabrol, *Marianne*'s first officer said philosophically. The tension around her brown eyes gave the lie to her calm tone, though, and Duan snorted.

He kept his eyes on the maneuvering plot as the freighter's velocity dropped steadily. So far, so good, he thought. And at least they'd been able to grease a few useful palms at this stop. *Marianne*'s false registry and collection of bogus transponder codes could get them in and out of most star systems, especially out here in the Verge. In fact, she spent at least half her career pretending to be another ship entirely, especially when she had "special consignments" on board. But in many ways, Duan would have felt better transporting a cargo of slaves than running this particular load in through Kornatian customs.

Unfortunately, when you commanded one of Jessyk's "special units" and Ms. Isabel Bardasano personally explained that your mission was Priority One, you nodded, saluted, and went off and did whatever it was she'd requested. Quickly and well.

He'd made his rendezvous with the local Jessyk cargo agent a full light-year short of the Split System and precisely on time, despite having been diverted to drop off that load of technicians in Monica. No one had told him what that was all about, but he was used to that. He had his suspicions, anyway, and he'd been rather amused by the technicians' uneasy expressions when they discovered what their accommodations aboard *Marianne* usually housed.

Still, only *Marianne*'s superior speed had let him make the rendezvous on schedule, and he was glad it had. That far out in interstellar space, he and the agent's dispatch boat could be confident of remaining unobserved while last-minute instructions were passed. The good news was that it meant that this time, at least, he was coming in with a complete local background brief and knew the arrangements to receive his cargo at least appeared to be in place and secure. The bad news was that the agent had also brought them up to date on the local political situation, and Duan didn't much care for what he'd heard about one Agnes Nordbrandt.

No one had told him specifically that he was delivering weapons to the FAK, but it didn't take a hyper-physicist to figure it out. He didn't have a clue *why* he was, other than the fact that Isabel Bardasano thought it was a Good Idea. Given Bardasano's reputation, that was more than enough for Duan Binyan.

But there was obviously only one group on Kornati who could possibly require the better part of four thousand tons of small arms, unpowered body armor, encrypted communicators, stealthed counter-grav surveillance sats and drones, and military-grade explosives. And given the local authorities' ugly attitude, Duan Binyan didn't even want to think about what would happen to anyone caught running modern weapons into the hands of the "Freedom Alliance of Kornati."

Of course, he thought glumly, *they can't kill us any*

deader than the frigging Manties would if they caught us with a special consignment. They've made that *clear enough.*

"Are there any Manty transponders out there?" he asked, prompted by unpleasant thoughts of the Royal Manticoran Navy.

Zeno Egervary, *Marianne*'s communications officer—and also her chief security officer—glanced at his own display for a moment, then shook his head.

"Nothing. Not even a merchie."

"Good," Duan muttered, and slouched a bit more comfortably in his command chair.

Even without a special consignment aboard, *Marianne* had obviously been designed as a slaver, and she carried all of the necessary equipment. Which meant, under the Manticorans' "equipment clause" interpretation of the Cherwell Convention, she *was* a slaver, and her crew was guilty of slaving, even if there were no slaves physically present. And since the Manties seemed determined to move into the area, their nasty habit of executing slavers gave Duan Binyan a rather burning desire to be certain there were none about.

Fortunately, *Marianne*'s sensor suite was good enough for Egervary to be sure there weren't. In fact, her sensors were far more capable than any legitimate merchantship—especially one that looked as decrepit as she did—ever carried. Nor was that the only unusual thing about her. The four-million-ton freighter might look like a tramp whose owners routinely skimped on maintenance, but she had a military-grade hyper generator and particle screening. Her acceleration was no greater than that of other merchantmen her size, but she could reach the Epsilon Bands and sustain a velocity of .7 *c* once she got there, which gave her a maximum apparent velocity of over 1,442 *c*, thirty-two percent faster than a "typical" merchie. He would have liked to have military-grade impellers and a military-grade compensator, as well, but those would have been almost impossible to disguise and would have cut massively into her cargo capacity. And if he couldn't have those, at least her designers had provided her with eyes and ears as good as most military vessels boasted, which was at least equally important to a ship which had to operate covertly.

She was also armed, although no one in his right mind—and certainly not Duan Binyan—would ever confuse her with a warship. She didn't make any effort to pretend she *wasn't* armed, although her official papers significantly understated the power of the two lasers she mounted in each broadside and her engineering log always showed that at least one of them was down for lack of spare parts. The Verge could be a dangerous place, and probably ten or fifteen percent of the merchies which plied it were armed, after a fashion, at least. The "inoperable" broadside mount was simply part of *Marianne*'s down-at-the-heels masquerade, and half her point defense clusters and counter-missiles tubes were concealed behind jettisonable plating, again in keeping with her pretense of parsimonious owners.

All in all, *Marianne* was capable of holding her own against any pirate she was likely to meet. She could even encounter a light warship—a destroyer, say—from one of the podunk navies out here with a more than even chance of success. And on at least two occasions, *Marianne* herself had turned "pirate" for specific operations. On the other hand, any modern warship would turn her into so much drifting debris in short order. Which was the reason Duan and his crew vastly preferred to depend upon stealth and guile.

"We're coming up on the outer orbital beacon," De Chabrol announced, and Duan nodded in acknowledgment.

"Go ahead and insert us."

"Okay," De Chabrol acknowledged, and Duan chuckled. His ship might be armed, but no one would ever mistake her bridge routine for something a man-of-war would have tolerated for an instant!

Agnes Nordbrandt sat in the passenger seat of the battered freight copter as it whirred noisily through the night. Counter-grav air lorries would have been more efficient, and they were common enough on Kornati these days that she probably could have rented one or two without arousing suspicion. But helicopters were cheaper, and so ubiquitous no one could possibly stop all of them for random searches.

This particular helicopter was operating under a perfectly legitimate transponder, although the freight company which owned it wasn't aware of tonight's trip. The pilot, whose mother had been hospitalized for the last eight T-years, was one of the freight company's senior pilots . . . and also a member of Drazen Divkovic's FAK cell. He'd been with the company for twelve T-years, and part of his arrangement with his employer was that he could use company vehicles to moonlight to supplement the regular salary which somehow had to pay for his mother's hospitalization as well as feed his own wife and children.

Knowing all of that, unfortunately, didn't make Nordbrandt noticeably happier.

The problem was the helicopter's maximum cargo capacity of only twenty-five tons. She had five more, similar helicopters, although two of them couldn't be used long, since they'd been stolen for this operation. Still, even with all six of them, she could transport only a hundred and fifty tons in a single flight. Which meant it would require twenty-six round trips by all six to move her arriving bounty of destruction.

In some ways, that wasn't entirely bad. She'd made arrangements to spread the weapons between several dispersed locations, and that would've required her to break the entire consignment down into smaller increments, anyway. But it was going to take at least a couple of days to move everything, and that much exposure was dangerous.

She didn't like coming out into the open this way herself, either. Not out of any sense of cowardice, although she was honest enough to admit she *was* afraid on a personal level, but because if the graybacks managed to capture or kill her, the effect on the FAK would be devastating. Indeed, the fact that she'd supposedly been killed once would probably make the psychological effect even worse if she actually was arrested or killed. Yet she didn't have much choice, at least for this first stage of the delivery operation. She had to be on hand, had to be confident her arrangements were working, and had to be available to resolve any last-minute complications which reared their ugly heads.

She'd chosen the delivery site with care, because landing the shuttle was the most hazardous single element of the operation. "Firebrand" had assured her his agents would be well versed in clandestine deliveries, and that they'd be capable of flying a nape-of-the-earth course. She'd taken him at his word and selected a site in the rugged Komazec Hills. It was only three hundred kilometers from Karlovac, but the rough terrain provided plenty of concealed spots. And the hills were close enough to the capital that a cargo shuttle making dispersed deliveries to legitimate customers could duck into their valleys and ridgelines for cover against standard air traffic and police radars without arousing undue suspicion.

There was still a major degree of risk, and most of it was the fault of her own operations. What she thought of as her "I'm Back" strike in the capital lay almost seven T-weeks in the past, but the entire planet was still reeling from its effects. The thought gave her a great deal of satisfaction, but the wildly successful attacks had bloodied the graybacks' nose badly enough to ensure a high degree of alertness. The biggest danger was that some spaceport security officer would doublecheck the cargo shuttle's delivery manifests and discover that the legitimate businesses to which the shuttle was supposedly making direct deliveries weren't expecting anything of the sort. But Firebrand's contacts had managed to find a customs agent willing to look the other way for a price. He was the one who'd certify the shuttle's cargo as whatever innocuous civilian machine tools or spare parts its manifest showed, and he was also the one responsible for confirming the delivery orders. So as long as he stayed bought, the shuttle should be able to lift out from the port without challenge, disappear into the hills, and meet with Nordbrandt's helicopters.

She really wished she could take delivery directly from the spaceport. She and Firebrand had considered the possibility, and it had been attractive in many ways. But the decisive point had been her inability to transport that much cargo in a single flight. She couldn't risk moving her own people in and out through the spaceport security perimeter that often. If anyone saw them meeting out here in the middle of the night, it would sound every security alarm on the planet, of course. But she had a far better chance of not being seen *here* at all than she would have had of entering and leaving a public spaceport that many times.

Her own helicopter flew along openly enough, trusting in its legitimate transponder code, until it reached the Black River. The Black flowed out of the Komazec Hills to join the larger Liku River which flowed through the heart of Karlovac. The Black was far smaller than the Liku, but it was big enough to have chewed a deep gorge through the Komazecs, and Nordbrandt's pilot abruptly cut his transponder, dipped down into the gorge, and throttled back to a forward speed of no more than fifty kilometers per hour. Twenty-three minutes later, he lifted up over the edge of the gorge, crossed a ridgeline, slid down the further side to an altitude of thirty meters, traveled another twelve kilometers, and then set neatly down in an overgrown, bone-dry wheat field. The farm to which the wheat field belonged had been abandoned when its owner had the misfortune to be walking across the Mall on the day of the Nemanja bombing.

Nordbrandt wasn't immune to the harsh irony which made this particular landing site available. She hadn't had anything in particular against the farm's owner. He'd simply been in the wrong place at the wrong time and become a martyr to Kornatian independence. And now his death was making a second contribution, she thought, as she swung down through the passenger door into the tall wheat.

Two of the other helicopters were already present, and as she walked across the field, two more came clattering in to land. Unless the police had redeployed their ground surveillance satellites since she went underground, she had a window of almost five hours before the next overhead pass. If she'd been in charge of the graybacks, those satellites *would* have been redeployed. According to the sources she still had inside the government, however, they hadn't. Apparently no one realized she'd managed to obtain full information on the recon network while she was still a member of Parliament.

Of course, it's always possible that they've turned my sources. In which case, they probably have *redeployed the birds. In which case the KNP and SDF will come screaming in on us sometime in the next, oh, half-hour or so. Another of those little uncertainties that make life so . . . interesting.*

She checked her disguised, expensive chrono. The cargo shuttle was late, but that was fair enough, because so was the sixth and final freight copter. Timing on something like this never worked out exactly to schedule, and she'd allowed for slippage when she and Drazen devised the plan.

She sat on an abandoned piece of farm equipment, gazing up at the stars. A heavy overcast was coming up from the south, gradually devouring the stars in that direction, and her thoughts silently urged the cloud pack on. If it moved in, covered their operation, it would be that much less likely that any chance overflight—or even one of the grays' recon satellites—would notice this peculiar congregation of freight vehicles.

She was still sending encouraging thoughts in the clouds' direction when the cargo shuttle swept almost silently up and over the tree-covered ridge north of the farm. Its air-breathing turbines were much quieter than Nordbrandt's clattering helicopters had been, and it moved with the peculiar grace of a counter-grav vehicle which had slipped the trammeling bounds first formally described by Sir Isaac Newton, so many weary centuries before.

The shuttle had full rough-field capability, and its pilot obviously knew his business. It swept once around the field, perhaps ten meters up, then ghosted in to land. A personnel hatch opened, and a single man in civilian clothing climbed out of the cockpit. Nordbrandt pushed up from her improvised seat and walked across the field to meet him.

"You have something for me," she said calmly.

"Yes, I do," he confirmed, equally casually. "As you requested, we've made the load up in twenty-ton lots, loaded on standard helo freight pallets. And just as a bonus, we used counter-grav pallets."

"That's good." It was hard to keep a combination of thankfulness and irritation out of her matter-of-fact voice. Thankfulness, because the counter-grav units would let them move the cargo so much more rapidly and easily. Irritation, because she and Drazen should have thought to ask for them at the outset.

"Yeah," the pilot agreed. "You told us you wanted twelve pallets—that's two hundred and forty tons, total—but I only see five choppers."

His tone made the statement a question, and Nordbrandt nodded. It wasn't really any of his business, but there was no point in rudeness. The Central Liberation Committee had just demonstrated how valuable it could be, so she supposed she'd better cut its representatives some slack rather than risk irritating them.

"Our sixth copter's on its way in now. It ought to be here in the next fifteen minutes. It'll take them about an hour, on average, to reach their destinations. Say another hour and a half on the ground to unload—and we can probably cut that even further, with the counter-grav, because we won't need the forklifts after all—and another hour to get back here. That's four hours, which leaves us another hour to load the second group of pallets and clear out before any of the graybacks'—the police's, I mean—surveillance satellites get a good look at this field."

The pilot looked at her just a bit dubiously, then shrugged.

"Once I kick it out the hatch, it's your responsibility. The schedule sounds a little tight to me, but I'm out of here in forty minutes, whatever happens."

With that, he walked back to the shuttle and opened the exterior cargo controls' access door. The dim light of the instrument panel gilded his face in a wash of red and green, and he began entering commands.

The shuttle's computers obediently opened the huge after hatch. The two hundred-plus tons of military equipment occupied only a fraction of the cargo hold, and more commands fired up the pallets' built-in counter-grav units. An overhead tractor grab picked up the first pallet, moved it smoothly down the cargo ramp, and held it motionless, hovering a meter above the ground, until half a dozen eager hands grabbed the handholds and towed it out of the way.

The trio of FAK members guided the floating munitions across to one of the waiting helicopters while the tractor grab went back for a second load. Three more Kornatians were waiting, and quickly turned it towards a second copter. The third pallet was on its way out of the hold almost before they had number two clear, and Nordbrandt nodded in profound satisfaction.

She stood to one side, staying out of the way, while her people guided the pallets into the helicopters' cargo compartments. They loaded the copter which had farthest to go first, and it lifted away into the night, its movements slower and more ponderous than when it arrived, even before the second was fully loaded.

She stood quietly, watching as five of the freight copters headed out. By then, the cargo shuttle was completely empty. The additional pallets were moved into the concealment of a convenient barn, and the shuttle closed its hatches, fired up its turbines, and disappeared the way it had come. Nordbrandt gave the landing site one more look, noting the trampled tracks in the wheat field, then climbed up into the sixth and final helicopter. It would drop her off where other secure transportation was waiting to return her to her tenement safe-house before it returned for its second load.

"Make sure you set the timers before you lift out with your final load," she told the pilot, raising her voice over the clatter of the rotors.

He nodded hard, his expression serious, and she sat back in satisfaction. She'd anticipated that using the wheat field as the transfer point would leave the dry, ripe wheat trampled and beaten down. Most probably, no one would have noticed anything this far out in the boonies, but she intended to take no chances. Sometime early the next morning, well before sunrise, a fire would break out in one of the derelict farm's abandoned buildings. It would spread to the wheat field, and probably to the orchards beyond. By the time the local rural fire department responded, all signs that anyone had visited the farm would be erased.

All very sad, she thought. The abandoned farm, its owner dead at terrorist hands, totally destroyed by fire. Tragic. But at least there wouldn't be anyone still living there to be threatened by the flames, and it wasn't as if the farm still represented a livelihood for anyone. That was about all anyone would think about it. It certainly wouldn't occur to them that the FAK would waste its time burning down a single, isolated, abandoned farm in the middle of nowhere.

She sat back in her seat, thinking of all the expanded potential the helicopter's cargo represented, and smiled thinly.

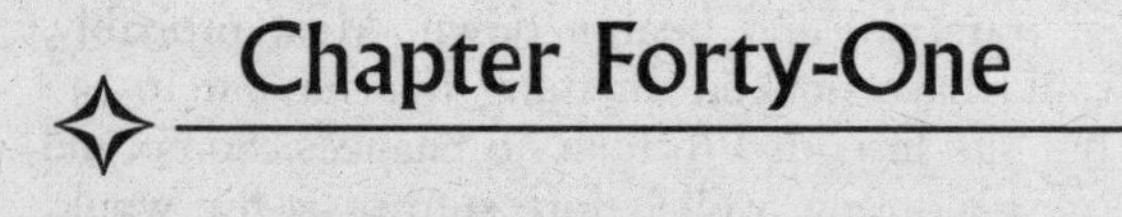

Chapter Forty-One

HMS *Hexapuma* slid into orbit around Kornati with the polished professionalism to be expected from one of the galaxy's premier navies. Aivars Terekhov observed the maneuver from the center of his smoothly humming bridge with profound satisfaction. *Hexapuma* was seventeen days out of Montana—a rapid passage by anyone's standards—and between them, he and Ansten FitzGerald had turned the ship into a precision instrument.

But however satisfied he felt about that, Terekhov cherished no illusions that his responsibilities in Split would be easily discharged. Amal Nagchaudhuri's department had been monitoring the Kornatian news channels ever since *Hexapuma* translated back into normal-space. There'd been no more major incidents in the last several weeks, but there had been a handful of minor attacks—little more than pinpricks, really. It seemed apparent they were intended more to keep the public reminded the rumors of Nordbrandt's demise had been wildly exaggerated than to do any significant damage. And they clearly were succeeding. Even if the newsies' commentary hadn't made that point, the fervency with which Kornati Traffic Control welcomed *Hexapuma* would have made it abundantly clear the locals had pinned an enormous amount of hope on the capabilities of his ship and crew.

The problem with heightened expectations, he reminded himself, *is that they lead to heightened dejection if they're disappointed. And as good as my people are, the chances of our finding Van Dort's silver bullet aren't exactly overwhelming.*

The ship settled precisely into her assigned position, and Senior Chief Clary rang off main thrusters and reconfigured for automatic station keeping. Terekhov nodded in satisfaction, then turned towards Communications as a chime sounded.

Lieutenant Commander Nagchaudhuri listened for a few moments, then looked up.

"Skipper, I have a Ms. Darinka Djerdja on the line. She's Vice President Rajkovic's personal assistant, and she asks if it would be convenient for you to speak to the Vice President."

Despite himself, Terekhov felt an eyebrow rise. Evidently, the locals were even more eager to talk to him than he'd anticipated.

"Do we have visual?"

"Yes, Sir," Nagchaudhuri replied.

"Then please inform Ms. Djerdja that I would be honored to speak to the Vice President. When he comes on the line, put it on my display here, please."

"Aye, aye, Sir."

It took less than four minutes. Then a stocky, dark-haired man of medium height appeared on Terekhov's display. Vice President Vuk Rajkovic had steady gray eyes, a strong chin, and ears that could have been used for airfoils. They stuck out sharply on either side of his head, and they would have made him look ridiculous if not for the concentrated purpose in those piercing eyes.

"Captain Terekhov, I'm Vuk Rajkovic," the big-eared man said in a deep, whiskey-smooth baritone.

"Mr. Vice President, this is an honor," Terekhov replied, and Rajkovic snorted.

"This, Captain, is a case of the cavalry riding to the

rescue. Or, I certainly hope it is—and that we haven't waited too long to call for help."

"Mr. Vice President, I assure you we'll do anything and everything we can," Terekhov said, conscious of both Van Dort's briefing on the local political situation and his own instructions from Baroness Medusa. "However, I hope no one in Split has unrealistic expectations about just what we *can* do."

"I don't expect miracles, Captain," Rajkovic reassured him. "I'm afraid some members of my Cabinet and Parliament probably do. And I *know* those idiots who report the news do. But I recognize that you have a single ship, with limited manpower, and no more idea where to find these lunatics than we have. I suppose what I'm really hoping for is two things. First, I'd be absolutely delighted if you were able to break the FAK wide open in a single brilliantly conceived and executed operation, after all. Second, failing that—which, frankly, seems likely to me—I'd be extremely gratified by even one or two relatively minor successes. If it's possible for us to score a few victories, even small ones, with your assistance, then the notion that the entire resources of the Star Kingdom stand ready to assist us further should be a major morale enhancer for all of our people."

"I see." Terekhov gazed at the face on his com. Obviously Rajkovic wanted him to know he was only too well aware that *Hexapuma* was unlikely to slay the FAK dragon with a single stroke of the sword. And, the captain conceded, the expectations attached to the Vice President's second hope were both pragmatic and realistic.

"We'll certainly give it our very best effort, Mr. Vice President," he assured Rajkovic.

"No one could ask for more, Captain. Would it be possible for you—and for Mr. Van Dort—to meet with me in the President's Mansion this afternoon?"

"It'll take at least a little while to get *Hexapuma* snugged down, Sir. However, I'd estimate that Mr. Van Dort and I could be available to you within ninety minutes or so. Two hours would be better, frankly."

"Two hours would be more than satisfactory, Captain. My calendar's been cleared for the afternoon. Please com Ms. Djerdja when you're ready to join us here. I'd like to have Mavro Kanjer, my Secretary of Justice, and Colonel Basaricek and General Suka present, as well. I should be able to get them here between the time you leave your ship and the time you reach the spaceport and we can find transportation to the President's Mansion for you."

"Of course, Mr. Vice President."

"Until then, Captain," Rajkovic said with a warm smile, and disappeared from Terekhov's display.

The captain looked up. Helen Zilwicki was at Tactical with Naomi Kaplan while Ragnhild Pavletic was at Communications with Nagchaudhuri, and Terekhov pointed a finger in Helen's direction.

"Ms. Zilwicki, you're relieved. Please go inform Mr. Van Dort that we'll be leaving the ship within two hours to meet with Vice President Rajkovic and his senior military and police officers. Then prepare yourself to accompany us."

"Yes, Sir." Helen stood and faced Kaplan. "Ma'am, I request relief."

"Ms. Zilwicki, you stand relieved," Kaplan replied gravely, and Helen braced briefly to attention, then headed for the lift.

Terekhov was already pointing the same finger at Ragnhild.

"Ms. Pavletic, you also are relieved. Report to Boat Bay One and assemble Pinnace One's crew. You'll transport Mr. Van Dort and me to the Karlovac spaceport and remain there to return us to the ship after our meeting with Vice President Rajkovic. See to it that you're fully cognizant with local flight control procedures and that our flight's fully cleared. In addition, contact the senior KNP officer at the spaceport—I'm sure Karlovac Flight Control can put you in touch with him—and ask him to com Major Kaczmarczyk to coordinate security overwatch for the pinnace."

"Yes, Sir!" Ragnhild said. She stood and turned towards Nagchaudhuri to request relief, but Terekhov was already punching a combination into his own com.

"Major Kaczmarczyk," a voice said a moment later, and the bristle-cut Marine appeared on his display.

"Tadislaw, Mr. Van Dort and I are going down to meet with the Kornatian Vice President and his senior cops. I want you present for the meeting. In addition, I think it's time for a proper show of force. Nordbrandt's demonstrated that she's ambitious, if nothing else. If she sees an opportunity to take out the Manticoran big shots sent to help hunt her down, I expect her to take it. Even if she doesn't, a demonstration of our own capabilities won't hurt a thing."

"Yes, Sir. I understand," Kaczmarczyk said when Terekhov paused.

"Ms. Pavletic will have Pinnace One. I've instructed her to contact Karlovac Flight Control for clearance and a flight plan, and also to request that the senior police officer at the spaceport contact you. I expect you'll be hearing from him sometime in the next ten to fifteen minutes. When you discuss arrangements with him, make it clear you intend to provide security for our party between the spaceport and the President's Mansion, as well. If he needs to clear that with his own superiors, he should have time before we actually head down."

"Aye, aye, Sir. I'll get right on it."

"Good. Terekhov, clear."

The captain cut the com link and looked up. Ragnhild had already disappeared in Helen's wake, and he gazed at the tactical plot. There were more orbital installations and traffic than he'd anticipated from Bernardus' description of the Split economy and tech base, although the plot still looked incredibly sparse compared to what it would have shown around Manticore, Sphinx, or Gryphon.

"Guns."

"Yes, Sir?" Naomi Kaplan said.

"I want to know just what orbital assets the Kornatians have. I expect they'll be perfectly willing to brief us on their capabilities, but sometimes there's a discrepancy between what people tell you they can do and the capabilities of the hardware they actually have in place. Put out some arrays to give us a look at the far side of the planet. Then run a detailed analysis of every ship and satellite out there. I'd like you and Lieutenant Hearns to be prepared to give me a full-dress brief on your findings right after breakfast tomorrow."

"Aye, aye, Sir. We'll be there," Kaplan assured him, and began giving instructions of her own to her ratings.

Terekhov gave the plot one more brief examination, glanced at the main visual display and the huge blue and white globe of Kornati, then stood. If he was going to go call upon the local head of state, acting or no, it behooved him to make the best impression that he could, and Chief Steward Agnelli would never forgive him if he didn't give her enough time to make him what *she* considered presentable.

"They're here."

The voice didn't identify itself. On the other hand, it didn't have to. First, because Nordbrandt recognized it. And, second, because it was speaking over one of the secure military coms which had been landed the evening before. Only four people, including Nordbrandt, had so far received those.

"You're positive?" she asked.

"They've contacted the graybacks to clear their small craft into the spaceport," Drazen Divkovic replied. "I'm not sure of their arrival time, but Rajkovic'll want to see them as soon as possible."

"Agreed."

Nordbrandt frowned at the drably painted wall of her one-sun's kitchen. She knew why Drazen had contacted her directly this way, and a part of her agreed with him. But it was too soon. The Manties' guard would be up, and the essentially civilian weapons her action groups had used against Kornatian opposition would be grossly inadequate against Manticoran hardware. Her people needed the time to become reasonably proficient with their new weapons before they crossed swords with the Manties.

"Take no action at this time," she said.

She could visualize the expression of frustration her words sent flickering across Divkovic's face. He'd been fiery and impatient enough even before his brother was killed. But he was also disciplined.

"Acknowledged. Clear," was all he said, and the link went dead.

Nordbrandt put the fist-sized com back into its hiding place in the flour canister, stopped by the oven to check the bread whose rich aroma filled the kitchen, then sat back down to consider the implications.

They'd known the Manties were coming. Tonkovic was unaware one of her own aides at her precious Constitutional Convention was a FAK sympathizer and information source, and that source had informed Nordbrandt almost as quickly as Tonkovic had informed Rajkovic. But the man hadn't been able to tell Nordbrandt when *Hexapuma* would arrive, and the actual timing was . . . inconvenient.

She'd arranged for the second load of weapons to be landed that very night. Things had gone so well the first time that she'd decided to go ahead and run in a full shuttle load—over a thousand tons—in a single flight. Since she had enough from the first load tucked away in her twelve separate caches to meet her immediate operational needs in and around the capital, she'd decided to risk landing that large a chunk of the total consignment at Charlie One, the carefully hidden base training camp also known as "Camp Freedom."

Charlie One had been located with security in mind, which meant it was incredibly inconveniently placed to support operations in or around Karlovac. Or any of Kornati's other major cities. Or even moderately large towns, for that matter. But its very isolation should mean it would be reasonably safe to hold the majority of the new weapons and equipment there for at least a short time—long enough, certainly, to carefully disperse it all to secondary hidden locations.

But all of that had been predicated on relative freedom of movement, and certainly hadn't included the intrusion of a Manticoran warship. She rather suspected that Firebrand's delivery crew would be less than delighted by *that* turn of events.

"You're shitting me."

"I wish!" Annette De Chabrol shot back.

"A goddamned Manty *cruiser*?" Duan Binyan stared at her, still trying to scrub the last rags of sleep out of his brain.

"A *Saganami*-class, no less!" De Chabrol snarled. "The son of a bitch is sitting in a parking orbit less than a thousand kilometers from us right this instant!"

"All right. All right! Calm down," Duan urged. She looked at him out of his cabin com as if she thought he were an idiot, and he shrugged.

"So there's a Manty cruiser in orbit with us," he said, just a bit more calmly than he actually felt. "So what? We're a legitimate merchantship, certified by the locals' own customs inspectors, and we're here to pick up and drop off a half-dozen small consignments and a dozen passengers. It's all logged with Traffic Control—*and* with Customs and the KNP—and it was set up months ago. There's absolutely no reason for these Manties to be any more suspicious of us than the Kornatians are."

De Chabrol stared at him for three seconds, then shook herself.

"That's all well and good, Binyan," she said in a marginally calmer voice. "But it overlooks one little point. The Kornatians' sensors suck; Manty sensors most empathically do *not*. This cruiser's a helluva lot more likely to spot anything out of the ordinary we might do . . . like landing, oh, I don't know—say, another thousand tons or so of prohibited military-grade weapons for a bunch of murdering terrorists."

Her tone was withering, and Duan was forced to admit she had a point.

"I don't have any more desire to stick my reproductive equipment into a power outlet than you do," he said. "Unfortunately, we may not have a lot of choice. Nordbrandt's people have already set up tonight's delivery, and we don't have any way to tell them we're not coming. We can always simply scrub the delivery *without* telling them, of course. But there's no telling how they'll react if we don't show up."

"What? You expect them to call the authorities and say, 'Hi, this is your friendly local terrorist organization speaking. Those nasty people in the *Marianne* were supposed to deliver a thousand tons of weapons and explosives to us so we could kill more of you, and they didn't. So we're ratting them out to you. Go arrest them'?"

"No," he said with considerable restraint. "What I'm afraid of is that if we don't make the delivery, someone in their part of the pipeline is going to ask one question too many, stay in the wrong place just too long, or panic and start trying to contact their own leaders—*something* that ends up drawing the local cops' attention. And if that happens, and they get busted, and the locals roll up the delivery chain and find us at the end of it, I don't doubt for a minute that Mr. *Saganami*-class cruiser will very cheerfully board us or blow us out of space at their request."

"So why don't we just *leave*? Let them go ahead and roll up the locals! It's no skin off our ass if they do."

"Oh, yes, it is. Nordbrandt's contact for this shipment's the Jessyk agent here on Kornati. If we pull out, and Nordbrandt's people get nailed, there's no way they won't tell the authorities exactly who was supposed to deliver their weapons . . . and didn't. And if it's escaped your attention, our agent doesn't have diplomatic immunity. The locals will bust him in a heartbeat, and when they do, they'll hand him over to the Manties. And the one thing we can't afford is for the Manties to start wondering why the Jessyk Combine—a *Mesan* transstellar corporation—is shipping weapons to terrorists in the Talbott Cluster. Believe me," he looked into her eyes, "there's more going on here than just a weapons drop to a bunch of lunatics. If you and I do *anything* that compromises the rest of Bardasano's operation, we'll be lucky if we manage to kill ourselves before her wet work teams catch up with us."

De Chabrol had opened her mouth in fresh protest. She closed it again.

"Yeah," Duan said dryly. "What I thought myself."

"So we go ahead with the drop as planned?"

"Only the next scheduled phase. Between what we already have down and the next load, they'll have almost a third of the entire consignment. That's a hell of a lot more than they had before, and we'll explain that the arrival of this Manty cruiser means we have to haul ass. I'm pretty sure Nordbrandt will understand. And even if she doesn't, even if we wind up ratted out, Bardasano won't blame *us* for it. Or, she *probably* won't, at least. She came up through covert ops herself, and they say she's got enough experience to recognize what field ops realistically can and can't do when Murphy turns up. If we manage to make that much of our drop and get away clean, I think she'll agree it was the best we could do under the circumstances."

"I hope you're right. And I hope we do get away with it."

"So do I. But the bottom line is that Bardasano's more likely to order us popped if we screw up this operation than the Manties are, even if they grab us under the equipment clause."

"What a charming incentive," De Chabrol muttered, and Duan chuckled in sardonic agreement.

Chapter Forty-Two

"Thank you for coming, Captain Terekhov. And you, Mr. Van Dort."

In person, Helen thought as Darinka Djerdja led them into the Vice President's presence, Vuk Rajkovic projected even more sheer presence than he had over the com. He was scarcely a handsome man, but, then, neither was Helen's father, and no one had ever accused Anton Zilwicki of weakness.

The Vice President stood at the head of the long, wooden table in the palatial conference room one floor down from the Executive Office in the Presidential Mansion of Kornati. The paneled wall behind him bore the great seal of Kornati above the crossed staffs of the planetary flag and the presidential standard. The chairs around the table were old-fashioned, unpowered swivel armchairs which, despite their obsolete design, looked almost sinfully comfortable. The carpet was a deep, cobalt blue, with the planetary seal in white and gold, and old-fashioned HD screens lined one entire wall.

There were no windows. This room was located near the center of the Presidential Mansion, deep enough inside to defeat most external listening devices.

"We wish no one'd had to come, Mr. Vice President," Captain Terekhov said gravely. "But we'll be delighted to do anything we can to assist you."

"Thank you," Rajkovic repeated, and quickly introduced the other two men and one woman already present.

Secretary of Justice Mavro Kanjer, of average height, average build, and medium complexion, stood before the chair immediately to the Vice President's right. Of all the Kornatians, physically he was by far the least prepossessing. Colonel Brigita Basaricek, tall and fair-haired in the gray tunic and dark blue trousers of the Kornatian National Police, rose from the chair to Kanjer's right as their off-world guests were ushered into the conference room. General Vlacic Suka, in the dark green tunic and cherry-red trousers of the Kornatian Defense Forces, stood to the Vice President's left. Suka was almost as dark as Rajkovic, but taller, with grizzled gray hair, thinning on top, and a VanDyke beard considerably more aggressive and bushy than the Captain's. His face was lined with age, fatigue, and worry.

"Captain Terekhov," the Vice President continued, "I've met over the com, and Mr. Van Dort's familiar to all of us, of course. However—"

He looked past Van Dort and arched his eyebrows politely.

"Mr. Vice President," the Captain said, "this is Captain Kaczmarczyk, commanding officer of *Hexapuma*'s Marine detachment. And Midshipwoman Zilwicki, who's acting as Mr. Van Dort's aide."

"I see." Rajkovic nodded to Kaczmarczyk and Helen, then waved a hand at the waiting chairs. "Please, be seated."

His visitors obeyed, and he and his subordinates settled back down in their own chairs. The Vice President looked around the faces at the table, then back at the Captain.

"I can understand why you'd want Captain Kaczmarczyk present, Captain. I'm sure he, Colonel Basaricek, and General Suka have a great deal to discuss. I understand," he smiled thinly, "that the Captain's Marines have already made quite an impression on our citizens."

"I hope not a bad impression, Sir."

"Oh, I suspect it made a *very* bad impression on a certain segment of our population, Captain," Colonel Basaricek said with what Helen thought was an evil smile. "I can't begin to tell you how bad an impression I hope you made on them."

"That was one of the objects of the exercise, Colonel," the Captain acknowledged, and smiled back at her.

Ragnhild Pavletic and her pinnace were parked prominently on one of the central pads of the Karlovac spaceport. The dorsal turret's heavy pulse cannon were manned, and the entire pad was ringed by two full squads of battle-armored Marines, complete with heavy weapons. And as an additional touch, two full-spectrum battlefield sensor drones floated overhead on their counter-grav. One was high enough to be immune to virtually any man-portable weapon Kornati might possess; the second was much lower, deliberately exposed to possible hostile fire in order to make sure everyone could see it and know it was there.

A third squad of armored Marines had added themselves to the security perimeter of the Presidential Mansion, and a third sensor drone was deployed above the mansion's grounds.

"The other object, Colonel," Captain Kaczmarczyk said, "was to land a sufficient reaction force on the off-chance that we might be able to entice Nordbrandt's people into going after Captain Terekhov and Mr. Van Dort. Unfortunately, they seem to've declined the bait."

"They may not decline it indefinitely, Captain," Secretary Kanjer said sourly in what would otherwise have been a pleasant tenor. "Although they *have* shown a pronounced distaste for taking on targets that can shoot back."

"I'm not sure that's fair, Mavro." General Suka's voice was deeper than Kanjer's, though less deep—and considerably rougher—than Rajkovic's, and he shook his head at the Justice Secretary. "Oh, I'll admit they've shown more discipline than I'd like when it comes to avoiding attacks on targets that are prepared to shoot back. And I'll also admit it's tempting to call them a pack of murdering cowards. But I'm afraid it's not so much that they're *afraid*, as that they recognize that going directly up against the armed forces or Colonel Basaricek's special weapons teams would be a losing proposition."

"With all due respect, General," Van Dort said, "while they may not be cowards in the physical sense, they certainly are cowards in a moral sense. They've adopted the coward's strategy of striking at the helpless and the vulnerable, using them as pawns against an opponent—their own legally elected government—they can't challenge directly."

He seemed to be watching the Vice President carefully out of the corner of one eye as he addressed the general. Secretary Kanjer looked as if he were in full agreement, but Rajkovic's mouth tightened.

"I don't disagree with your basic analysis, Mr. Van Dort," he said after a moment. "But, just between the people in this room, Nordbrandt couldn't have assembled the cadre of killers she has if we hadn't helped. I'm not saying her claims that we've created a veritable hell on earth on Kornati aren't wildly exaggerated. But there are abuses here, and poverty, and those create embittered people."

So Bernardus—Mr. Van Dort—got him to admit it right up front, Helen thought. *Clever*.

"Abuses are no justification for mass murder, Mr. Vice President," Kanjer said sharply.

Van Dort had briefed Helen on the Kornatian political system, and she knew Kanjer was one of the Cabinet officers who'd been appointed by Tonkovic before she left for Spindle. Cabinet meetings around here must be . . . interesting.

"Justification for murder, no," Rajkovic said in a frosty tone. "Reason, possibly yes."

He locked eyes with Kanjer, and Suka shifted uneasily at the apparent tension between the Vice President and the Justice Secretary. Basaricek, on the other hand, nodded.

"With all due respect, Mr. Secretary, the Vice President has a point," she told her own civilian superior. "The fact that so many people feel disenfranchised is another factor, of course, but the perception that the system's fundamentally unfair, in some ways, is a huge part of what made it possible for Nordbrandt to get this far."

Kanjer looked as if he wanted to say something sharp to her, but he glanced at the Vice President's expression and thought better of it.

"Would you care to expand on that, Colonel?" Van Dort inquired in a tone, Helen noticed, which gave very little indication of whether he found Rajkovic or Kanjer more persuasive.

"I think a lot of people have failed to realize," Basaricek said, turning to face Van Dort directly, "that long before the plebiscite, the core of Nordbrandt's Nationalist Redemption Party was composed of extraordinarily angry people. People who, rightly or wrongly, believed they had legitimate grievances against the system. Most of those people, in my opinion, would've done better to look a little closer to home for the causes of their failures and their problems. But if that was true for a lot of them, some of them had definite justification for feeling the government, or the courts, or the Social Support Administration had failed them. I know, because my people tend to find themselves in the middle when someone who's just plain desperate tries to take matters into her own hands."

She glanced at Kanjer, and her expression held a definite edge of challenge. Not defiance, but as though she dared the Justice Secretary to deny what she'd just said. Kanjer looked like he would have preferred to do just that, but he didn't. Helen wondered if that was because he didn't want to disagree openly with Rajkovic, or because he knew he honestly couldn't.

"Even before the NRP's more moderate members started falling away because of her opposition to the annexation," Basaricek continued, "she'd been recruiting an inner cadre from that bitter, alienated hard core of her most fervent supporters. As the moderates bailed out on her, she came to effectively rely exclusively on the hardliners. There never were very many of them as a percentage of the total population, but even a tiny percentage of a planetary population is a large absolute number. Probably only a minority of even her closest supporters were prepared to cross the line into illegal actions, but that was still enough to let her organize FAK cells in most of our major urban areas."

"May I ask how the population as a whole views her and her organization at this point?" Van Dort asked.

Basaricek glanced at Rajkovic, who nodded for her to go ahead and take the question.

"They're afraid," the KNP colonel said bluntly. "So far, we've had only scattered, isolated successes against them. They hold the advantage in terms of choosing where and when they're going to strike, and what the public primarily sees is that the terrorists consistently manage to attack vulnerable targets, while the police and military have been largely unable to stop them."

"We've managed to stop them every time we got timely intelligence, Colonel," Kanjer pointed out stiffly. "We *have* had our successes."

"Yes, Sir, we have. But I stand by my categorization: they've been scattered and isolated." She went on speaking to her superior, but it seemed to Helen her remarks were actually directed to Van Dort and the Captain. "You know we've managed to break no more than half a dozen cells, including the two we pretty much wiped out the night we thought we might've gotten Nordbrandt herself. We managed to identify all but one of the other cells we've managed to take down by keeping tabs on people we already knew were particularly embittered members of the NRP. I'm afraid we've pretty much exhausted the possibilities there, however. We're looking for a couple of dozen of the party faithful who disappeared at the same time Nordbrandt did, and we're keeping our eye on as many of the NRP's one-time core members as we can, but there are limits on our manpower. And the truth probably is that most of them would never dream of murdering anyone."

She turned her head, looking directly at Van Dort.

"It's hard to explain to frightened people that this is primarily a war of intelligence," she said. "That until we can identify and locate the FAK leadership, all we can do is adopt a reactive stance. Which means the terrorists are free to choose the point of attack, and they certainly aren't going to attack where we're strongest."

"I understand," Van Dort said. He leaned back in his chair and looked at Rajkovic.

"Mr. Vice President, Baroness Medusa and I have discussed the general situation in the Cluster and, specifically, here in Split. Captain Terekhov and I have further discussed it, in light of the dispatches we received from the Provisional Governor when she ordered us here from Montana. It seems to us that historical experience demonstrates that the successful suppression of this sort of movement must always include a two-pronged approach.

"On the one hand, obviously, the military threat must be contained and neutralized. That's usually fairly straightforward, if not necessarily simple. Colonel Basaricek's just finished explaining a large part of the reason why it's not simple. Nonetheless, it isn't impossible, either, and Baroness Medusa's prepared to offer assistance in the effort. She's dispatching the chartered transport *Joanna* from Spindle, with two full-strength companies of Royal Manticoran Marines on board. One company is drawn from the battalion assigned to her personal command on Flax. The other is drawn from rear Admiral Khumalo's flagship, the *Hercules*. They'll be accompanied by their integral heavy weapons platoons, two assault shuttles, and three Fleet pinnaces, and they'll take over in the purely military support role when they arrive. That, unfortunately, will probably not be for another week or two, at the soonest. They will, however, remain on assignment to you until such time as the military situation is under control."

Helen watched all four of the Kornatians sit up straighter, their eyes brighter, and Van Dort smiled. But then his smile faded just a bit.

"But in addition to neutralizing the military threat, remedial action must be taken to repair the abuses which helped create the threat in the first place. You can't eliminate resistance by simply shooting resisters, not unless you're prepared to embrace a policy of outright terror yourselves. Your tradition of vigilance where civil rights are concerned suggests to me that you probably aren't prepared to do that. Besides, it would be ultimately futile, unless you're willing to accept a *permanent* police state. Any time you arrest or kill someone who's perceived as striking out against genuine injustice, you simply create another martyr, which only provides recruits to the other side. It doesn't necessarily mean the terrorists are *right*; it simply means you're generating a supply of people who *think* the terrorists are right. So to cut off their support at its base, you must make it evident you're prepared to address the issues which spawned the resistance movement in the first place. Do it from a position of strength, by all means, and don't allow yourselves to be driven into making huge, unjustified concessions. But those issues *must* be addressed, and some sort of consensus about them must be reached, if you're to have any hope of finally and completely eliminating the threat."

The Kornatians looked at one another. Basaricek had no expression at all. Kanjer looked frankly mutinous, and General Suka looked as if he'd just bitten into something spoiled. Vice President Rajkovic looked thoughtful, and he leaned back, resting his right forearm on the conference table, and gazed at Van Dort speculatively.

"I hope you'll pardon me for saying this, Mr. Van Dort, but given the Trade Union's reputation, this talk of reform sounds just a bit odd from you."

"I'm sure it does, Mr. Vice President," Van Dort said

wryly. "As a matter of fact, however, that's precisely the process I'm in the middle of right now, myself. In a sense, the entire annexation plebiscite was an effort to make right all the regrettable things the RTU—and I—did in our efforts to protect ourselves from Frontier Security. I don't know if you've heard that Ms. Vaandrager is no longer the RTU's chairwoman?"

Rajkovic's eyes seemed to narrow, Helen thought, and Suka actually blinked. Van Dort smiled humorlessly.

"Ms. Vaandrager was my mistake. I've acted, not completely too late, I hope, to correct it. I'm also attempting to convince certain stubborn, pigheaded Montanans that the Trade Union has turned over a new leaf and, more importantly, that the Star Kingdom isn't interested in brutally exploiting their economy. And in addition, I've been working closely with Joachim Alquezar and Henri Krietzmann at the Constitutional Convention, and now with Baroness Medusa, in an effort to finalize a draft Constitution which will let the annexation move forward. Not, I'm sorry to say, without significant resistance."

Rajkovic's expression went as blank as Basaricek's at the obvious reference to Aleksandra Tonkovic. Suka's face, on the other hand, darkened, and his jaw clenched, while Kanjer stiffened angrily.

"My point is this, Mr. Vice President," Van Dort said levelly. "If the annexation goes through, and if the Split System's political and economic systems undergo the changes the annexation will inevitably bring in its wake, the abuses and poverty which, as Colonel Basaricek has pointed out, helped to fuel the FAK, will be enormously alleviated."

"Excuse me, Mr. Vice President," Kanjer rumbled, his facial muscles tight, "but I seem to be hearing an indictment of our entire government and economy. While I certainly appreciate the offer of assistance from the Star Kingdom—and from Mr. Van Dort—I must say I don't believe we represent a brutally repressive regime."

"Nor do I," Suka said, eyeing his Vice President almost defiantly.

"Gentlemen," Rajkovic replied gently, "I don't believe that either. I'm not certain it's fair to say Mr. Van Dort does, for that matter. However, I think honesty compels us to admit we don't exactly represent a perfectly equitable regime, either."

Kanjer clamped his jaw, and Suka looked rebellious. The Vice President shook his head and smiled at the general.

"Vlacic, Vlacic! How many years have we known each other now? How many times have we sat down over an excellent dinner and shaken our heads over the problems we both see in our society and economy?"

"I may have seen problems," Suka said stiffly, "but we're certainly no worse than many other star systems. And we're far better than many, for that matter!"

"Of course you are, General," Van Dort said. "There are systems I could think of right here in the Cluster who, I believe, have problems more severe than any you face here. And God knows there're systems *outside* the Cluster which are just plain nightmares. For that matter, I can think of star systems in the Shell, and even in the Old League itself, whose political structures are far more inequitable than anything here in Split. But that doesn't mean there aren't areas in which you can improve upon what you already have. And all I'm saying is that if the annexation goes through, those areas *will be* improved."

"And just why are you telling us this?" Kanjer demanded suspiciously.

"For two reasons, Mr. Secretary," Van Dort said. "First, it's necessary to launch a propaganda counteroffensive. Yes, a huge majority of the franchised population voted in favor of annexation. But the franchise is so limited here, because of the nonregistration of eligible voters, that the vote in favor was actually a minority of the total pool of potential voters. Nordbrandt knows that. She's played upon it in her propaganda. And it's not enough for the government to respond by simply reciting the vote totals over and over again. You have to come out swinging, in a way which convinces the majority of those who didn't vote that annexation is a good thing. That it will have positive consequences for them in their own lives. At the moment, Nordbrandt's arguing that it will benefit only the 'moneyed interests' and 'oligarchs,' and only at the expense of everyone else. You need to not only dispute her claims, but effectively debunk them."

Rajkovic and Basaricek were both nodding, and even Kanjer and Suka looked a bit more relaxed, Helen thought. But she also knew Van Dort hadn't dropped the other shoe yet.

Then he did.

"And second," he said quietly, "to be completely honest, President Tonkovic's position at the Constitutional Convention isn't helpful."

Suka's already dark complexion turned an alarming shade of red. He quivered with visible outrage, and Kanjer sat bolt upright in his chair, his expression furious, but Van Dort faced him calmly.

"Mr. Secretary, before you say anything, has President Tonkovic informed your government that she's been informed by Baroness Medusa that a hard time limit for the approval of a Constitution exists? That if a draft Constitution hasn't been approved within the next one hundred and twenty-two standard days, the Star Kingdom of Manticore will either withdraw the offer of annexation completely, or else provide a list of specific individual star systems whose admission to the Star Kingdom will be rejected?"

Kanjer had started to open his mouth. Now he froze, eyes widening, and darted a look at Rajkovic. But the Vice President seemed as startled as the Justice Secretary himself.

"Excuse me," Rajkovic said after moment. "I have to be absolutely clear on this point. Are you telling us, as Baroness Medusa's personal representative, that she's informed President Tonkovic of this?"

"She has," Van Dort said levelly.

"She informed President Tonkovic before she ordered you from Montana to Split?" the Vice President pressed.

"According to her dispatches to me, yes."

The Kornatians looked at one another, and Helen could see them doing the math. Recognizing that a message from Tonkovic containing that same information could have reached Kornati almost three weeks earlier. That their head of state hadn't informed them, neither in her capacity as their delegate to the Convention, nor as their head of state, who was constitutionally required to keep their Parliament informed in diplomatic matters, about an official message from the Provisional Governor.

"It's not my intention, or the Provisional Governor's, to present Kornati with a constitutional crisis," Van Dort said gently. "But this is something you're going to have to deal with. How you do it is up to you. But it's my responsibility to inform you that the problem, and the deadline, exist. And, to be perfectly honest, I believe it's a point which is going to have to be addressed in your campaign—should you decide to wage one—to convince the nonvoters of the Split System that annexation is a good thing for them."

"This . . . is going to create additional problems," Rajkovic said slowly. Colonel Basaricek nodded in emphatic agreement; Secretary Kanjer and General Suka looked as if they were in a state of shock. "In the short term, however," the Vice President continued, "may we assume you and Captain Terekhov *are* prepared to assist us actively in the military efforts to suppress the threat represented by the FAK?"

"Of course we are, Mr. Vice President," the Captain said. "The nonmilitary response Mr. Van Dort's described has to be part of a long-term solution, but it also has to be very carefully thought through. And as he says, constitutional crises aren't what we came to provoke. In the immediate short term, we'll cooperate with you fully against Nordbrandt and her killers. And I really do believe, Sir," he added, his blue eyes colder than ice, "that she won't enjoy what happens."

✧ ✧ ✧

"Well, thank God for that," Annette De Chabrol murmured fervently as the *Marianne* accelerated steadily away from Kornati.

Duan Binyan and Franz Anhier, the ship's engineer, were careful to hold her acceleration down to an ambling pace appropriate to her decrepit appearance. But that was fine with De Chabrol. She was less concerned with acceleration rates than she was with headings, and at the moment *Marianne* was headed directly away from HMS *Hexapuma*.

"I have to admit, I'm a little surprised Nordbrandt took it that well," Zeno Egervary said, and Duan laughed sharply.

"I don't know how 'well' she took it," he said. "We never spoke directly to her, after all. But there wasn't much else she could do. I was never that worried about *her* reaction—or, rather, I was *less* worried about her reaction than I was about the possibility of somebody spotting us actually unloading her goddamned weapons."

"You seemed confident enough we could pull it off when you were explaining everything to *me*," De Chabrol said in a sour tone, but she smiled as she said it.

"I was just more confident we'd be in deeper shit if we didn't try than I was that we'd get away with it!"

"Well, either way, I'm with Annette," Egervary said. "Just get me away from that fucking Manty cruiser, and I'll be a happy man."

"I'm always in favor of promoting happiness among my officers and crew," Duan told him with a smile. "So we'll just leave Mr. Manty sitting here in Split while we get on with business elsewhere."

He turned to De Chabrol, and his smile grew broader.

"Plot us a course to Montana, Annette."

Chapter Forty-Three

"I understand that we need to train our people with the new weapons before we start using them, Sister Alpha."

Drazen Divkovic's tone and manner were both as respectful as always, but he had a certain air of stubbornness, Nordbrandt thought. He always did, for that matter. Stubbornness, determination, sheer bloody-mindedness—call it what you would, it was one of the qualities which made him so effective.

"And I understand you want to begin making *effective* use of them as soon as possible, Brother Dagger," she replied. "I know all our brothers and sisters do. My only concern is that our eagerness to take the fight to the oppressors may betray us into striking before we're truly prepared."

"Yet we're already making use of the new equipment, Sister Alpha," Drazen pointed out, and Nordbrandt nodded, even though neither he nor anyone else could see her.

Although Drazen was always careful to address her, even in their face-to-face meetings, as "Sister Alpha," she normally referred to him by his actual name in those meetings, rather than his FAK name. It wasn't that she was any less security-conscious than he, but she never met with more than a single cell leader at a time, and she knew the given names of more of them than she really ought to. There was no point pretending she didn't, as long as not doing so didn't threaten their security, and it was good for their morale, helped nourish their sense of unity. She told herself that, and it was true, but it was also true that the human within the revolutionary leader, the extrovert who'd become a successful politician, hungered for the occasional pretense of normality. The ability to call an old companion by name. To pretend to forget for that fleeting moment that she—and they—must be forever vigilant, forever on guard.

But neither of them would risk that informality now, because she was meeting simultaneously with the leaders of no less than eleven cells.

She would never have dared to do that in person, but the encrypted military coms from the Central Liberation Committee enormously enhanced her communications flexibility. She had to admit that the belief she'd taken away from her first meeting with Firebrand—that what had eventually become the CLC would probably never amount to more than words—had done him a gross disservice. She could scarcely believe the cornucopia of weapons and explosives, man-portable surface-to-air missiles, night vision equipment, and body armor even the abbreviated CLC consignment had delivered to them. And the military coms were almost better than the guns and explosives.

She reminded herself yet again that she mustn't extend some sort of magical faith to the new tech advantages she'd received. Good as the coms might be, the damned Manties could undoubtedly match them. But not until they knew to look for them. And not even the Manties could direction find on the coms when they weren't broadcasting.

One advantage of Kornati's relatively primitive technology level was that an enormous percentage of their telecommunications still passed over old-fashioned optic cable. In some cases, over actual *copper*. In this particular instance, she and her cell leaders had simply plugged their coms into the existing hardwired communications net, then placed a conference call. The coms' built-in encryption was more secure than anything the local authorities might possess, and the wire connection meant there was no broadcast signal for listening stations to pick up. And they'd been designed to be used in exactly this way, as well as in the normal, wireless mode. Their software continually monitored any landline connection to detect any tap, all of which meant it was now possible for her to teleconference with her top leadership.

As long as we're still careful, and don't start taking the ability for granted, she reminded herself sternly.

"Yes, Brother Dagger," she acknowledged. "We are already using some of the new equipment. But we're phasing it in gradually. And we're still not using it—or relying on it—in the field."

"Excuse me, Sister Alpha," another leader said, "but that may be a false distinction. No, we're not in the field. But if we screw up during this discussion, if we give ourselves away and the grays pounce, it's going to cost the Movement a hell of a lot more than losing one action cell in the field."

"Point taken, Brother Scimitar," she admitted ungrudgingly. One mistake she was determined not to make was to create some sort of personality cult in which her senior subordinates were unwilling to challenge what they saw as possible errors of judgment on her part.

"I think what Brother Dagger's suggesting, Sister Alpha," a third cell leader said, "is that we should consider the possibility of using some of the new weapons in smaller, secondary operations that would let us gain experience with them."

"Not exactly, Sister Rapier," Drazen said. "I agree that we should use them at first in small operations, that expose us to only limited damage if we lose the strike team. But what I'm really suggesting is that we should begin stepping up our training schedule."

"In what way, Brother Dagger?" Nordbrandt asked.

"We had a big part of the shipment delivered to . . . a secure location," Drazen said, and Nordbrandt smiled in approval. Drazen had been in charge of the delivery of the bulk of the equipment to Camp Freedom, but he wasn't about to share that information with *anyone* who didn't need to know it. Not even people he knew were the leaders of Nordbrandt's most trusted central cadre.

"And?" she invited, when he paused.

"I think we could safely transport a couple of action groups to that location. I've had my own team studying manuals and learning to field strip and maintain the new equipment. Most of it's actually fairly simple—what they call 'soldier-proof,' I think. But, anyway, my team is far enough along to need someplace to actually fire the weapons and do some serious hands-on practice. And I think we need to set up a permanent training cadre, probably at the same secure location, though I guess we might want to set up another one, separated from any of the rest of our operational locations. Let us spend some time—at least a few days—working with the new weapons. Not the missiles, or the plasma rifles, or the crew-served weapons. Let's get our toes wet with the small arms and the grenade launchers—they're not so very different from the civilian weapons we've already been using, except that they've got higher rates of fire and longer ranges. Well, and they inflict a lot more damage if you hit something.

"Anyway. Let us check ourselves out on them, then see about a few small-scale operations, somewhere away from the capital. We're going to have to do that sooner or later, Sister Alpha. Let's go ahead and get started."

No one else said anything, but she could almost physically feel their agreement with Drazen. And as she considered the proposal, she found herself sharing that agreement.

"All right, Brother Dagger. I think your suggestion has merit. I'll approve it. And since your team's that far along, and since you already know where the secure location is,

I believe your cell should be the first to cycle through the training program. Is there any other business we *all* need to discuss?"

No one replied, and she nodded to herself in satisfaction.

"Very well then, Brothers and Sisters. I'll continue this in private with Brother Dagger. The rest of you should disconnect now. You know our communications schedule, and I'll expect to speak to each of you at the scheduled time. Go now."

There were no verbal responses; just a series of musical tones and the blinking of extinguished telltale lights as the other cell leaders disconnected, leaving only Drazen.

"This is a good idea, I think," she complimented him. "Do you have secure transportation, or do we need to work something out?"

"I've already got it arranged," he said, and she could almost hear him smiling. "I figured you'd probably approve it. And if you didn't, I could always just cancel the arrangements."

"Initiative's a good thing," she said with a chuckle. "How soon can you move your team to Camp Freedom?"

"This evening, if that's all right with you."

"That quickly? I *am* impressed." She considered for several seconds, then shrugged to herself. "All right, it's authorized. Go ahead and alert your team."

"That's odd," Sensor Tech 1/c Liam Johnson murmured.

Abigail Hearns looked up from her own console in CIC at the rating's quiet comment. She and Aikawa Kagiyama had just been reexamining—playing with, really—the sensor data on Kornati's orbital space activity Captain Terekhov had asked Naomi Kaplan to run down when *Hexapuma* first arrived in Split. It wasn't exactly exciting, but it was good practice, and there hadn't been a lot else for Aikawa to do during the current watch.

Johnson was studying his own display, and Abigail frowned. The sensor tech was responsible for monitoring the orbital sensor arrays *Hexapuma* had deployed around

Kornati. Even a planet as poor and technically backward as Kornati had an enormous amount of aerial traffic, and trying to monitor it was a stiff challenge, even with *Hexapuma*'s sophisticated ability to collect and analyze the data. For the Kornatians themselves, it was more of a matter of brute manpower and making do, given their limited and relatively primitive computer capability. Air traffic control worked fairly well, but it really relied upon the fact that most of the pilots involved *wanted* to obey the traffic controllers, and the Kornatian ground radar stations weren't all that terribly difficult to evade.

But what was impossible for the Kornatians, was simply difficult for *Hexapuma*'s CIC. Sensors and computer programs designed to handle hundreds, even thousands, of individual targets moving on every conceivable vector in spherical volumes measured in light-hours, were quite capable of searching for patterns that shouldn't be there—and flaws in patterns that *should* be there—in something as small and confined as a single planet's airspace.

Abigail rose from her own chair and crossed to Johnson's station.

"What have you got, Liam?"

"I don't know, Ma'am. It may not be anything, actually."

"Tell me about it."

"It might be better if I showed you, Ma'am."

"All right, show me," she said, leaning one forearm lightly on the sensor tech's shoulder as she leaned over his display.

"I was doing a standard analysis run of yesterday's data," Johnson explained, tapping keys rapidly.

"Which data set?"

"Northern hemisphere air traffic, Ma'am. Quadrant Charlie-Golf."

"I didn't know there *was* any air traffic up there," Abigail said with a smile.

"Well, there isn't much, Ma'am, and that's a fact. Most of it's south of the Charlie line, but there's actually more local traffic than you might expect, given the population level, and about five or six regularly scheduled air transport routes that come up from the smaller continent—Dalmatia—and cross the pole on their way down to Karlovac and Kutina or going the other way on the return leg. They come straight through Charlie-Golf, but it really is what you might call a quiet chunk of airspace as far as through traffic is concerned.

"The local air traffic's so high because *ground* traffic's pretty nearly nonexistent in the area. The airspace's an awful lot less crowded than someplace like Karlovac, of course, but with no decent local roads, everybody who does move around, does it by air."

"Okay," she said. "I've got the location, now. And this was yesterday's data?"

"Yes, Ma'am. The time chop would be from about seventeen-thirty to midnight, local."

"Okay," she repeated, nodding to herself more than to him as she mentally settled the references into place.

"All right, Ma'am." Johnson tapped a last command sequence and sat back with his arms folded. "Watch this."

The data take from the array watching that portion of Kornati's airspace played itself out on Johnson's display at a considerable time compression rate. The little icons of aircraft went streaking across the plot, trailing glow-worms of light behind them. The regularly scheduled transport aircraft were easy to identify. Not only were they bigger, and normally at a higher altitude, but they were also faster, moving on straight-line courses, and their transponder codes were crisp and clear.

The local traffic was much more erratic. No doubt a lot of it was nothing more than local delivery aircraft, dropping off overnight parcels to the isolated homesteads in the area. Others were probably joy-riding teenagers, buzzing around in old jalopies. And at least one larger, slower aircraft was identified by its transponder as a tour bus of high school students on a nature field trip. None of that traffic seemed ever to have heard of the notion of straight lines. They wove and twisted, plaiting their scattered flight paths across Johnson's display, and if there was any pattern to them, Abigail couldn't see it.

Johnson looked up at her, one eyebrow raised, and she shrugged.

"Looks like so much spaghetti to me," she admitted, and he chuckled.

"Trust me, Ma'am—I didn't spot it by eyeball, either. Assuming there's really anything to it, that is. I was running standard analysis packages, and the computer spotted this."

He tapped one of the macros he'd set up, and the same timespread replayed itself. But this time the computers were obviously filtering out the bulk of the traffic. In fact, there were less than a dozen contacts, and Abigail felt *both* eyebrows rising.

"Run that again."

"Yes, Ma'am," he said, and she straightened up, folding her own arms and cocking her head as she watched. There was no time association she could see between the contacts Johnson's data manipulation had pulled out. The first appeared at 17:43 hours local. The others were scattered out at apparently random intervals between then and 24:05 local. But what they *did* have in common was that regardless of when they crossed into the quadrant, they each terminated at exactly the same spot.

And they stayed there.

"That *is* odd," she said.

"I thought so, Ma'am," he agreed. "I'd set the system filters to show me any location where more than five flight paths terminated, and this was the only one that turned up, aside from a couple of small towns scattered around the area." He shrugged. "I've been trying to think of some reason for them to do that. So far, I haven't been able to come up with one. I mean, I guess they could all be going on a fishing trip together, and it just happened to take them six and a half hours to get together. But if it was me, I think I'd try to schedule my arrivals a little closer together than that. Besides, this is *yesterday's* take, and I've already done a search of today's. We still don't have a single departure from that location, so whoever they are, they're still there, right?"

"That's certainly the conclusion which would leap to the front of my own powerful brain," Abigail said, and Johnson grinned at her. But then his grin faded into a much more sober expression.

"The problem is, Ma'am, that according to passive scans of the area, there's nothing down there but a river and some trees. Not a helicopter, not an air car, not even a log cabin or an old pup tent."

"To quote Commander Lewis, 'Curiouser and curiouser,'" Abigail said. She gazed at the plot for several more seconds, then shook her head. "Sensor Tech Johnson, I think it's time we consulted with older and wiser heads."

"Johnson and Abigail are right, Skipper," Naomi Kaplan said flatly. "We've got ten aerial vehicles of some sort—analysis suggests at least six of them were private air cars—all landing at exactly the same spot, and then just disappearing. And a standard passive scan of the landing area shows absolutely nothing there now. Except, of course, that they *have* to be there, because they never took off again."

"I see." Terekhov leaned back, gazing at the holo map projected by the unit in the center of the briefing room table. "I suppose we could do an active scan," he said slowly. "But if there is anyone down there, and they pick it up, they'll know they've been spotted."

"Well, before we do that, Skipper, you might want to look at this." Kaplan gave him the smile of a successful sideshow conjurer, and the holo map disappeared. In its place was a detailed computer schematic of a single small portion of the total map, showing contour lines, streams, rocks, even individual trees, and Kaplan looked at it fondly.

"That, Skipper, is from one of Tadislaw's stealthed battlefield recon drones. They don't begin to have the raw computational power we do, and they sure as hell don't have our range, but they're specifically designed for taking close, unobtrusive looks. So when I decided I wanted more detail on the area, I got hold of Lieutenant Mann, and he and Sergeant Crites went out to the main airport in Karlovac to inspect the aircraft there. And somehow one of their drones accidentally got itself tractored to the skin of one of the regularly scheduled transports that cross through the area. And it fell off again right about . . . *here*."

A bright, irregular line appeared on the map, which obediently zoomed in still closer on the roughly wedge-shaped area it contained, and Terekhov's eyes narrowed.

"This, Skipper," Kaplan said, her tone and manner now completely serious as she leaned forward, using a stylus as a pointer, "is the thermal signature of a carefully hidden access—one big enough for an air car or even one of the Kornatians' big freight helicopters, if you fold the rotors—to a large underground structure of some sort. And this," the stylus moved to the side, "is a ventilation system designed to disguise the waste heat. And this over here," the stylus moved again, "is what looks like a pretty well camouflaged observation post, placed high enough on this hill to command most of this entire end of the river valley all of this is tucked away in. And this right here," her voice sharpened and her eyes narrowed, "is a pattern of earth and leaves that were turned over fairly recently—probably within the last seventy to eighty hours—that happens to be big enough to cover the marks the landing skids of a good sized shuttle or a really big counter-grav air lorry might have left. If that's what it is, it can't have been there for more than seventy-seven hours, unless whatever left them had better stealth capacity than anything of ours does, because that's how long ago we put Johnson's array up and tasked it to watch this area."

"And we couldn't pick any of this up with our own array?"

"Whoever put this in, did an excellent job," Kaplan said. "My best estimate is that the Defense Force's recon satellites wouldn't have seen this at all using their optical or heat sensors. There are power sources down there, but they're also extremely well shielded—so well that even Tadislaw's drone can't isolate point sources reliably. You can do that with enough dirt or ceramacrete. I don't think anything the KDF has could spot this without going active with radar mapping. *We* couldn't spot it from up here, using purely passive systems, partly because of the sheer depth of atmosphere, partly because of the dense tree cover and how good a job they did of hiding it when they put it in, and partly because for all the computational power we've got, our arrays simply aren't designed for detailed tactical work in this type of environment. The Marines' equipment is, and that's why Tadislaw's drone could spot what we couldn't."

"All right, that makes sense." Terekhov sat gazing at the holo for several more seconds, thinking hard, then nodded.

"This is on the planet, so it's clearly in Suka and Basaricek's jurisdiction. Both of them would be more than mildly irritated if we crashed the party without even mentioning it to them. On the other hand, none of their units have the same ability we do for getting in hard and fast. So it's time I brought them up to speed, but I think I need to talk to someone else first."

He punched a combination into the conference table com.

"Ground One, Kaczmarczyk speaking," a voice said.

"Tadislaw, it's the Captain."

"Good afternoon, Sir," Captain Kaczmarczyk said from his command post at the spaceport. "How can I help you this afternoon?"

"Commander Kaplan and I have just been discussing some equipment you lost earlier today."

"Ah! *That* equipment."

"Yes. I think we're going to want to go collect it this evening. Has Commander Kaplan shared her analysis of the data with you?"

"Yes, Sir. She uploaded it to me about a half-hour ago."

"Good. Who have you got down there who could go get your toy back?"

"Lieutenant Kelso's platoon has the duty this evening, Sir. She's got enough battle armor for two of her squads."

"I'll leave that to your judgment, Tadislaw. It's not my area of expertise. Just bear in mind that we don't have any idea what might be waiting underneath. I'd recommend against assuming there won't be any modern weapons down there, though."

"I think that's wise, Sir. Should I plan on local participation?"

"I think so. I'll speak to Colonel Basaricek. If she feels we should get the Defense Force involved, we'll be bringing General Suka on board, as well. I'd really prefer to keep it as closely held as possible, but I think good manners require that we have at least some of the locals along in the follow up wave. Unless I tell you differently, plan on going in first with our people. And work out the details for a covert insertion. I'd really like your people to be on the ground and kicking in the doors before whoever's down there has a clue you're coming."

"Yes, Sir. Gunny Urizar's down here with me. She and I'll sit down with Kelso and put together an ops plan for your approval. I should have something in an hour or two."

"I'll try to get back to you sooner than that with Basaricek's reaction to the news," Terekhov promised.

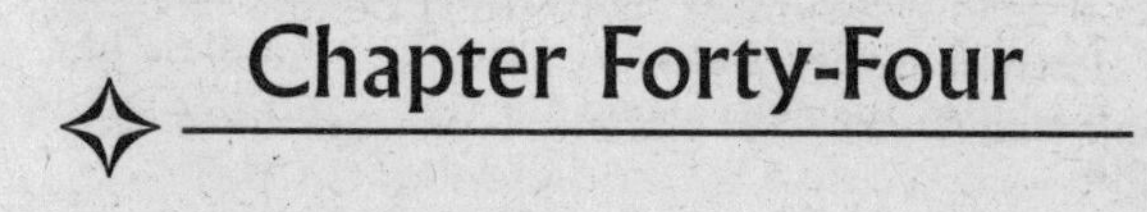

Chapter Forty-Four

Barto Jezic looked around, just a bit uncomfortably, as he stepped into the spaceport hangar and saw the Manticoran Marines strapping into their equipment. It was a clear, breezy evening, a far cry from the rainy night when the police captain's SWAT teams had foiled the terrorist attack on the Macek Avenue Treasury compound, and he felt more than a little out of his depth.

"Excuse me, Captain," a voice said behind him in an oddly musical foreign accent.

He turned and saw a tall, female noncom. He wasn't familiar with Manticoran rank insignia, but she seemed to have an awful lot of chevrons stenciled on the upper arm of her coal-black powered armor. There was something particularly sleek and deadly looking about that armor, he thought, unable to suppress a pang of envy as he considered what his people could have done with it when Nordbrandt and her murderers began their attacks.

"Yes, Sergeant—?"

"Urizar, Sir. Sergeant Major Hermelinda Urizar. If you happen to hear someone talking about 'the Gunny,' that's me."

She smiled, white teeth flashing in a naturally dark complexion which was even more darkly tanned, and he smiled back.

"Captain Barto Jezic, Kornatian National Police." He started to hold out his hand, then paused, glancing at her armor's powered gauntlets, and her smile grew broader.

"'S okay, Captain," she said, extending her own hand. "I've got the governors kicked in. They limit the armor's force levels to what my muscles could do unassisted."

Jezic decided to take her word for it, but it was still hard not to flinch as his hand disappeared into the Sergeant Major's hugely armored paw. To his relief, her grip was no more than firm, and he recovered his hand unmashed.

"I'm supposed to be looking for Captain Kaczmarczyk, Sergeant Major," he said, and she nodded.

"I know, Sir. The Captain asked me to keep an eye out for you. He's over there with Lieutenant Kelso." She waved in the direction of three more Marines—two armored like the sergeant major—standing around a portable holo table in one corner of the hangar. "If you'll come with me, Sir, I'll get you hooked up with him."

"Thank you," he said, but he hesitated a moment, and Urizar cocked an eyebrow at him. "I've got two unmarked vans full of SWAT people parked out on the apron. Your perimeter teams cleared us through, but I didn't know if I could go ahead and bring them inside the hangar. Colonel Basaricek told me she wants a low profile on this entire op, though. I'd like to get them inside, under cover, if I can."

"Not a problem, Sir." The sergeant major reached up and touched a small stud on the side of the boom mike headset she wore. "Central, Hawk-Mike-One-Three." She waited a heartbeat, then said, "Cassidy, Urizar. We've got a couple of unmarked vans on the apron full of KNP SWAT troopers and their equipment." She looked a question at Jezic with the last phrase, and he nodded vigorously. "We need to get them inside and out of sight. Take care of it."

She stood for a moment, obviously listening to a response, then nodded in satisfaction.

"Central, Hawk-Mike-Alpha," she said then. "Skipper? Captain Jezic and his people are here."

One of the armored Marines by the holo table straightened and looked in their direction, then waved for them to join him, and Urizar grinned at Jezic.

"Right this way, Captain."

The Kornatian followed her across the hangar which formed the central core of the Manticorans' "Ground One" dirt-side base. It seemed quite crowded with Manticorans. Of course, a lot of that could be because of the amount of space the two pinnaces—each about the size of a Kornatian heavy air transport—took up. About twenty or thirty of the Marines, in addition to Urizar and the trio by the holo table, were in the sleek, black powered armor.

Most of the Manticorans Jezic had seen—which wasn't all that many, really, he admitted—were taller than average Kornatians. That probably had something to do with the fact that they got better diets and medical care from childhood, he reflected. But the battle armor added at least another fifteen centimeters to their height, and the armor's arms and legs swelled smoothly with artificial "muscles." Most of the armored Marines were liberally festooned with weaponry and other equipment, but another twenty-odd Marines in armored skinsuits were still checking out their personal gear. That much, at least, was reassuringly familiar, even though the weapons and equipment were far more advanced than anything with which he'd ever trained.

Despite the crowding and bustle, people stepped aside to clear the way for Urizar to escort him to Captain Kaczmarczyk. He saw curiosity in many of the Marines' eyes, but none of the disdain or tolerant contempt he'd been half afraid he might. Watching them prep themselves and their high-tech equipment made him painfully aware of how primitively his own people were equipped in comparison. But if *they* were aware of it, they let no sign of it show.

"Captain Jezic." The speaker was an exception to the apparent rule that only giants were accepted for service in the Manticoran Marines. He was probably at least a centimeter shorter than Jezic himself—or would have been, if he hadn't been in battle armor—and his brown hair was clipped so short his scalp was clearly visible.

This time Jezic didn't hesitate when the Marine offered his gauntleted hand, and the Manticoran's odd amber-green eyes smiled as they shook.

"I'm Captain Kaczmarczyk. It's good to meet you. I'm assuming they grabbed you with no notice at all and told you to get over here yesterday, so you haven't been briefed in on exactly what's going on?"

"More or less," Jezic agreed, and smiled. He was beginning to feel much more at home. These people might have better equipment than his did, but he recognized the same sort of professionalism when he saw it. "Colonel Basaricek gave me a very cursory briefing on the terrain, showed me some still shots of it I gather you transmitted to her, and explained how your ship came to spot the target. But aside from the fact that we're along primarily to provide a local police presence and to observe while you people do the heavy lifting, I don't know a thing about the operational plan."

"Typical," Kaczmarczyk chuckled. "The guy at the sharp end's usually the last one to get the word in our shop, too." He waved a hand at the other armored Marine by the holo table. "This is Lieutenant Angelique Kelso, Captain Jezic. She's First Platoon's CO, and it's her people who are throwing our little party tonight."

Kelso was as tall as Urizar, at least ten or twelve centimeters taller than Kaczmarczyk, with chestnut hair and blue eyes. She shook Jezic's hand with a welcoming smile, and nodded welcomingly to him.

"And this is Lieutenant William Hedges," Kaczmarczyk continued, indicating the dark-haired young man standing beside Kelso, not in battle armor, but in an armored skinsuit. Jezic had to remind himself that all of the people around him were at least second-generation prolong recipients. He himself had received only the first-generation therapies, and even Kaczmarczyk looked as if he could have been the same age as one of Jezic's nephews. Despite his load of weapons and gear, Hedges looked as if he should still be shooting marbles in a schoolyard somewhere.

"Lieutenant Hedges runs Third Platoon, Captain Jezic," Kaczmarczyk told him. "Lieutenant Kelso's borrowing one of his squads for the op; he and his other two squads are taking over base security while we're away. That," he pointed at the battle-armored Marines under the pinnaces' sharply swept wings, "is First Platoon's First and Second Squads. Each of our platoons has two squads worth of battle armor, and Lieutenant Kelso," he grinned at the platoon commander, "is a bit on the greedy side, so she kept the best toys for herself."

"That's not fair, Skipper," Kelso protested with an absolutely straight face. "You know I didn't have any choice. Michael here can't be trusted with sharp objects."

"Sure, sure," Kaczmarczyk agreed, rolling his eyes at Jezic. Then his expression grew more serious.

"If you'll take a look here, Captain, this is what the terrain actually looks like."

Jezic tried not to look like a little boy with his nose firmly against the candy store window as he studied the exquisitely detailed holo map hovering above the table. The information they had on the footprint of the installation hidden under that seemingly innocuous terrain had been highlighted in red, and he oriented himself quickly.

"What we're planning to do, in simplest terms, Captain," Kaczmarczyk said, "is to drop Lieutenant Kelso and her armored people on individual counter-grav. We'll toss them out in a high-altitude/low-opening drop from several kilometers out. They'll freefall towards the installation, using skydiving techniques and their armor's thrusters, and pop their counter-grav at the minimum safe altitude. That ought to put them on the ground, right on top of the the bad guys before they have any idea we're coming.

"Her first objective will be to secure or destroy this structure here." He indicated the stubby, camouflaged tower on top of the hill. "We can't tell whether this tower—it looks like more of a tall bunker, really—is just an observation post, or if it mounts heavy weapons. Since we can't tell for certain, we'll go ahead and be sure it's neutralized, just to be on the safe side.

"While one of First Squad's fire teams takes care of that, her second squad will set up over here, covering the one apparent vehicle ramp we've identified. They'll be dropping in heavy-assault configuration, with maximum firepower and minimum endurance. Hopefully, the entire operation will be over very quickly, but we're bringing in backup power units for their armor and weapons in the event that it turns into some kind of siege operation and they have to stay on site for more than a couple of hours. With the plasma cannon, heavy tribarrels, and grenade launchers they'll be bringing in, I don't think anything's likely to get out of the ramp and away from us.

"First Squad's second fire team will set up right here." Kaczmarczyk indicated the ventilation system which had been identified. "Its primary mission will be to serve as Lieutenant Kelso's tactical reserve until the rest of us get onto the ground. However, it will also be equipped with Suppressant Three." Jezic looked at him, and he shook his head as if mildly irritated with himself. "Sorry, Captain. That's our current sleepy gas. If the fire team can get onto its objective before the bad guys realize what's going on and switch off their ventilators, it may be able to put the majority of the opposition to sleep, which would *really* make the rest of the job a lot easier."

"I can certainly see that," Jezic said feelingly. "And I wish *we* had an effective—'sleepy gas,' did you call it?" Kaczmarczyk nodded, and Jezic shrugged. "The best incapacitants we've got are irritants and nausea-inducing agents. I understand the Defense Forces have some fairly effective lethal agents, but something that actually put people to sleep would be very useful to the KNP."

"Gunny," Kaczmarczyk said, looking past Jezic to Urizar.

"Make a note to remind me to see how much Suppressant Three we've got in stores. We should have enough to let the Captain here have at least a few canisters. And remind me to inventory our stun guns, too, now I'm thinking about it. Police forces are going to have a lot more need for something like that than we do."

"Aye, Sir," the sergeant major replied.

"Now," Kaczmarczyk said, turning back to Jezic and continuing before the Kornatian could thank him for the implied generosity, "once Lieutenant Kelso's on the ground and has the site basically secured, we'll bring in the rest of First Platoon and Lieutenant Hedge's Second Squad. They'll be in regular Marine skinnies, which're probably as good as any of your local body armor, but not anywhere near as tough as battle armor. They'll spread out to take over the perimeter, and Second Squad, as soon as it's been relieved from that duty, will execute the break-in into the underground installations. The pinnaces will lift back off as soon as everyone's on the ground. They'll provide air cover and ground support, if needed, and, along with the recon drones we'll be deploying, they'll keep an eye out for escapees. We haven't been able to spot them so far, but the people who managed to put in something this well concealed are damned sure going to have bolt holes to let them scurry out the back door if someone kicks in the front door."

"That's been our experience," Jezic agreed. "I hate these bastards, you understand, but they usually plan pretty well. At first, a lot of it was obviously the work of amateurs, but even then, they usually managed to cover all the bases. Since then, they've gotten less elaborate and more practical. In fact, I hate to admit it, but they've demonstrated a pretty steep learning curve."

"Nobody ever promised the bad guys'll be stupid and incompetent just because they're bad guys," Kaczmarczyk said philosophically.

"No, but somebody should have!" Jezic shot back, and all of the Marines standing around him chuckled.

"I do have one question, Captain," Kaczmarczyk said

after a moment, his expression much more serious. "The one thing I know I don't have a good feel for is exactly how fanatical these people are. Or maybe what I mean is how *suicidal* they might be."

"That's a hard one, Captain. We know they're fanatical enough to blow up department stores full of civilians. And which," Jezic added grimly, "they knew contained two child day-care centers. But, to be perfectly honest, we haven't managed to corner enough of them to know how likely they are to blow *themselves* up for the glory of the Movement." His mouth twisted bitterly. "If this place is as important as its isolation and concealment indicate, I'd think that they'd be more likely to do something like that here than if we'd only cornered a strike team out in the open somewhere. I'd have to say the possibility exists, but I can't begin to tell you how likely it actually is."

"I was afraid that was what you're going to say," Kaczmarczyk said unhappily. "That's one reason I'm really hoping we can get the Suppressant Three in there before they shut down their air system. Not even battle armor will protect someone from a big enough explosion."

"I don't imagine it will," Jezic said. "On the other hand, they obviously are depending on concealment, and this isn't something they put in yesterday, or even last week. I know our recon satellites didn't pick any of this up, and they're not as good as yours are, by a long chalk. But this—" he indicated the holo map "—was a major project. I'm willing to bet Nordbrandt's people built this damned thing even before the annexation plebiscite came up. I can't prove that—yet—but I did have Colonel Basaricek pull the file recon footage for this area. The stuff we've gotten since we reinforced and redeployed our recon assets after the Nemanja bombing. None of it shows what your drones managed to pick up, but it doesn't show any evidence of construction, either. So this has been in and underground, with time for the vegetation and foliage around it to recover, for at least that long."

Kaczmarczyk nodded, though, from his expression,

he wasn't too sure where Jezic was headed, and the Kornatian smiled.

"Setting up an effective self-destruct you can be sure will work in an emergency but *won't* go off unless you tell it to isn't as easy as entertainment writers would like us to think it is, Captain. Especially the second bit."

He smiled again, more nastily, and this time Kaczmarczyk smiled back.

"True," the Manticoran agreed. "Accidents can be so . . . permanent if something like that screws up."

"Exactly. My point, though, is that while they've almost certainly had the time to put something like that in, I'm not at all certain they've felt any urgency to do so. After all, we've never given any sign that we suspected something like this might be up there, and they're probably feeling about as confident about their security as any terrorist bunch is likely to let itself feel. That being the case, I doubt they'll be able to improvise an effective self-destruct system in the time available to them if we get in hard and fast enough."

"I'd say there's a good chance you're right," Kaczmarczyk agreed. "On the other hand, I've never been real enthusiastic about including 'there's a good chance' in my mission planning."

"Neither am I. But when it's all you have, it's all you have."

Jezic paused, hesitating for a moment as he recalled another part of his truncated briefing from Colonel Basaricek, then shrugged and plunged on in.

"There is one other point, Captain," he said, his tone more formal than it had been, and Kaczmarczyk gave him a sharp glance.

"Yes, Captain?" His tone was also more formal, Jezic noted.

"We don't *know* anyone in this installation is violating the law," the police officer said. "I realize the circumstances are extraordinary. And as Colonel Basaricek pointed out to me, martial law's been declared and Parliament's voted to authorize the use of the regular military—which would also cover your people, in this case—for duties which would otherwise fall squarely to the National Police. However, that doesn't absolve the government, or the police, from our responsibilities under the Constitution."

He paused again, and Kaczmarczyk nodded.

"You're a Marine, Captain Kaczmarczyk. So are all your personnel, and military training's necessarily different from police training. You said you intend to 'neutralize' the tower, or bunker, or whatever it is, as quickly as possible. I have to ask you if that means you plan to employ deadly force without first calling upon any suspects to surrender without resistance?"

He thought he saw a flicker of respect in those amber-green eyes. He *knew* he saw a grimace of what was probably irritation on Lieutenant Hedges' face, and Lieutenant Kelso gave him a tight, teeth-baring smile that was totally devoid of humor.

"Let me put it to you this way, Captain Jezic," Kaczmarczyk said, after a moment. "The question you've just raised was addressed by Captain Terekhov when he alerted me for this mission. He emphasized to me that the observance of Kornatian law was of paramount importance. However, although I realize this is essentially a police operation, the nature of this particular installation makes it *effectively* a military operation. I've attempted to strike the best compromise I can between those two differing sets of requirements and priorities.

"The instant the first of my Marines hits the objective, he'll deploy remote speaker systems which will begin broadcasting a demand for the occupants of the installation to surrender and come out of their hidey holes without weapons, and warning that we're prepared to employ deadly force if they don't immediately comply. If that demand's obeyed, we won't fire a shot. If, however, it is *not* obeyed, or the instant a shot is fired at one of my people or we discover we're looking at heavy weapons sited for immediate use, it will cease to be a police operation and become a military strike. Under those conditions, my people will be instructed to accept surrenders *so long as it doesn't endanger them or any other of my personnel.*"

His strange eyes met Jezic's levelly, unflinchingly, and the police captain understood he was hearing a nonnegotiable position. Still—

"And the neutralization of the tower, Captain?"

"Anybody in it will've heard the surrender demand, Captain. Sergeant Cassidy's team will be under orders to take out any heavy weapons without inflicting casualties, if possible. I will not, however, expose my people to fire from that position. If it's impossible to neutralize its weapons without destroying it outright, then I *will* order it destroyed unless anyone inside it comes out and surrenders instantly. I hope it'll be possible to shut it down without killing anyone. But if it contains heavy weapons, I'm going to accept that as proof the people in this installation are engaged in illegal activities, and as criminals, the preservation of their lives takes second place to the preservation of the lives of my personnel."

Jezic hovered on the brink of protesting, but he didn't. He didn't because he recognized the logic of the Manticoran's position. And because it was vital for his star nation to retain not simply the cooperation of the Manticorans, but their *active* cooperation. And he didn't because he was a SWAT officer—because all too often in his career, he'd been called into situations where the parameters and options were very much like the ones Kaczmarczyk faced here.

"All right, Captain Kaczmarczyk," he said finally. "I understand your position, and I respect it. I suppose we'll all just have to hope for the best, won't we?

Ragnhild Pavletic sat in her flight couch, on Hawk-Papa-Two's flight deck tonight, with her right hand lightly on her stick, and watched the clean, crisp twinkle of the stars. Major Kaczmarczyk had specifically requested her for this mission, and she felt flattered. She also felt nervous.

People were going to be killed tonight. Whatever the

Major wanted, however much everyone would prefer to take them all prisoner, it wasn't going to happen—she knew that with absolute assurance. And if anyone tried to bug out by air, Ragnhild Pavletic or Coxswain 1/c Tussey, flying Hawk-Papa-Three, were supposed to nail them.

"Nail them," she thought, lips twisting in a humorless smile. *I suppose it sounds better than "kill them" or "blow them into tiny bleeding pieces." But it means the same thing. And this time it won't be the computers taking a preprogrammed shot. It'll be* my *hand on the trigger.*

She didn't much care for that but, to her surprise, it didn't frighten her, either. She knew what the FAK had done here on Kornati.

Yet she wasn't looking forward to it, and so she watched the brilliant, uncaring stars as Hawk-Papa-Two knifed along on the very edge of space, and wished human beings could settle their affairs with the same clean, cool detachment.

Platoon Sergeant George Antrim, First Platoon's senior noncom, stood and moved to the center of the pinnace. Unlike Lieutenant Kelso, Antrim was in a standard armored skinsuit, and he crossed to stand beside the pinnace's flight engineer at the jump master's station.

"Approaching drop," he announced, over his skinsuit com to the battle-armored Marines. "Prepare to drop."

The armored Marines stood and moved to the port side of the pinnace. The standard airlock was on the starboard side of the hull. The port side of the fuselage was configured for just this situation, and Antrim nodded to the flight engineer.

"Open her up."

"Opening now," the Navy puke replied, and a hatch four meters across slid open in the side of the pinnace. Everyone in the passenger compartment, including the flight engineer, was skinsuited or armored, with helmet sealed, for reasons which were obvious as the compartment instantly depressurized. Baffles forward of the hatch broke the slipstream, providing a pocket of protected airspace outside it, and Captain Kaczmarczyk and Sergeant Major Urizar stepped up to the opening.

"Confirm drop acquisition," Antrim said, and twenty-six armored thumbs rose on twenty-six armored right hands as every one of the queued Marines confirmed that his armor's internal computer had pinpointed the coordinates of the drop zone and projected it onto his visor's heads-up display. The sergeant nodded in approval, and checked the jump display projected into his own helmet's HUD again.

"Drop point in . . . forty-five seconds," he announced.

The appointed seconds raced away, and Antrim spoke one last time.

"Go!"

Captain Tadislaw Kaczmarczyk thrust himself out and away from Hawk-Papa-Two. His external sound pickup was adjusted to its lowest sensitivity, but the ear-piercing wail of the pinnace's turbines was still deafening. For just an instant, the air around him seemed almost calm; then his plummeting body crossed the boundary between the baffles' protective bubble and the air beyond.

Despite his protective armor, he grunted in shock as Kornati's atmosphere punched savagely at him. It was a sensation he'd felt before, although he hated to think what it would have been like for someone without armor.

He flung out his armored arms and legs, simultaneously triggering his suit's built-in thrusters, stabilizing himself in midair. This section of Kornati was virtually unpopulated, an endless forest of virgin, indigenous hardwoods and evergreens, which undoubtedly explained why the bad guys had chosen it for their installation. It also meant there were no artificial light sources below him. He gazed down into a vast, black void—the bottom of the greedy well of gravity into which he'd cast himself—and he could see nothing.

Until he brought his low-light systems on-line, that was.

Instantly, the forested terrain below him—*very* far

below him—snapped into visibility. He was still far too high to make out details, and from his altitude, he seemed scarcely to be moving at all, despite a forward velocity of more than six hundred kilometers per hour. His rigidly extended limbs meant his angle of descent was shallow, and the glowing green crosshair of his objective floated above the horizon line projected across his HUD. The armor's exoskeletal "muscles" meant he could hold his posture forever, despite the clawing pressure of the steadily thickening atmosphere, and he adjusted his position carefully, dropping the crosshair directly onto the horizon line. A soft audio tone confirmed that he was back on trajectory, and he settled down.

Minutes ticked past as he continued to slice through the air, First Platoon's first two squads stretched behind him like some formation of stooping hawks. The ground beneath drew steadily closer, and his speed across it became increasingly apparent. He checked his altitude. It was down to little more than a thousand meters, and the crosshair began to blink—slowly, at first, then more and more rapidly. Another audio tone sounded—this one sharp and insistent, not soft—and he popped his counter-grav.

It wasn't like a standard counter-grav belt or harness. There wasn't room for one of those, or not for one with the power he needed tonight, at any rate. Instead, the backpack harness strapped between his armored shoulder blades popped open. A tether deployed from it, and an instant later, the extraordinarily powerful counter-grav generator at the tether's far end snapped to full power, with no gradual windup.

Kaczmarczyk grunted again, this time explosively, as his airspeed checked abruptly. He swung on the end of the tether, outside the actual field of the generator, and the treetops flashing past below him slowed. They reached up for his boots, but he was coming down far more gradually now, and he checked his HUD one more time.

Right on the money. Good to know I haven't lost my touch.

✧ ✧ ✧

First Platoon hit the ground almost precisely on its objective.

Almost precisely.

Even with the best computer support available, there was bound to be at least some scatter in a HALO drop from that far out. For the most part, the error was less than twenty meters, but Private 1/c Franz Taluqdar, of First Squad, was just a bit farther off than that. In fact, Private Taluqdar found himself coming down almost directly in front of the ridgeline tower which was his objective.

Taluqdar didn't know what, if anything, that bunker was armed with. If it was armed and the weaponry was of local manufacture, the odds were pretty good that his armor would protect him from it. But "pretty good" were two words Taluqdar didn't much care for, especially not in reference to sharp pointy things and his own personal hide. He therefore decided that landing in the potential field of fire of the possible bunker's hypothetical weapons was contraindicated and proceeded to do something which would certainly have cost him his PFC stripe in a training exercise.

He jettisoned his counter-grav while he was still ten meters off the ground and hit his suit thrusters.

Battle armor thrusters, unlike the jump gear which allowed an armored Marine to cover ground at an amazing rate in long, low leaps, had a strictly limited endurance. They were intended for extra-atmospheric maneuvers, not for the bottom of a gravity well, and it was expected that their users would avoid full-power emergency burns even there.

Private Taluqdar had other ideas, which, taken all together, violated about fifteen safety regulations.

His trajectory altered abruptly, first dropping in the instant he cut his tether, and then angling sharply upward as his thrusters flared. He reached the apogee of his flight path, swept his body—and his thrusters—through a neat arc, and shifted abruptly to an equally sharp angle of descent. It was all instinct, training, and eyeball estimates, but it worked. Instead of landing in front of the tower, he touched neatly down atop it.

And promptly crashed straight through its camouflaged canopy as inertia and the mass of his armor had their way.

Captain Kaczmarczyk hit the release button to deploy his own speaker unit just before he smashed through the tree canopy and hit the ground. The self-contained unit arced away from him, ping-ponging off branches and spinning sideways before stabilizing into a hover fifteen meters in the air. He hit the ground hard, his armor—freshly smeared with the Kornatian ecosystem's version of chlorophyl—absorbing most of the shock, and tucked and rolled. He came back upright, pulse rifle ready, and heard his own thunderous, recorded voice bellowing from his speaker unit.

"Attention! Attention! This is Captain Kaczmarczyk, Royal Manticoran Marines! Surrender and come out without weapons and with your hands on top of your heads! Repeat, surrender and come out without weapons and with your hands on your heads immediately! You are under arrest for suspected illegal terrorist activities, and resistance or noncompliance will be met with deadly force! Repeat, you are under arrest! Surrender immediately, or face the consequences!"

The backup speakers were silent. They were scarcely needed to cover the area of the installation—even with his external audio cranked down, the sound of his amplified voice was almost deafening—and his own unit had sent out a signal to shut the others down. Had his speaker malfunctioned, Kelso's would have taken over. And if hers had malfunctioned in turn, Sergeant Cassidy's would have taken over.

Satisfied that the warning had been issued, and leaving the speaker set to repeat it over and over again—both so there wouldn't be any question that the bad guys had been given the opportunity to surrender, and also for the morale effect it was bound to have—he turned towards the ridgeline position.

Just in time to see one of his Marines land directly on top of it and disappear.

Private Taluqdar caught a scrap of the captain's surrender demand as his armor smashed through the camouflage-patterned thermal canopy covering the open top of the tower.

The single Kornatian who had been standing there, half-asleep in the middle of his long, boring watch, had just started to jerk fully upright in reaction to the thundering voice, when two meters of night-black armor came crashing down on the log platform behind him. His surprise was as complete as surprise could possibly be, and he whipped around, instinctively clawing for the weapon holstered at his hip.

It was exactly the wrong reaction.

Taluqdar knew he was supposed to call upon any "suspects" to surrender before blowing them away. But Franz Taluqdar was also a combat veteran, and there was something about the weapon behind the sentry. Something his experience recognized even if his brain didn't have time to put it altogether. Something that changed the entire threat parameter of the operation.

Something that activated his combat reflexes, instead of the demand to surrender.

Kaczmarczyk's head whipped up as the hissing, supersonic "*Crack-crack-crack!*" of a firing pulser came from the direction of the ridgeline. His armor's sensors instantly identified it as the product of a M32a5 pulse rifle on full auto, and he swallowed a mental curse. So much for giving the other side a chance to surrender first!

"Hawk-Mike-Alpha!" a voice his armor's HUD tagged as one of First Squad's riflemen came up on his com. "Hawk-Mike-One, Pandora. *Pandora!*"

Kaczmarczyk's concern about timing and surrender demands disappeared abruptly.

"All Hawks, Hawk-Mike-Alpha!" he snapped. "Pandora! I say again, Pandora! *Case Zulu!* I say again, Case Zulu is now in force!"

Taluqdar heard the Skipper, but as far as he was concerned, Case Zulu had applied from the instant his conscious thoughts caught up with his reflexes and recognized the weapon mounted on the platform railing as a plasma rifle.

It shouldn't have been there. There shouldn't have been *any* plasma rifles on Kornati, aside from a very small number held by the System Defense Force, all of which had been positively accounted for. But there it was, and even before the warning had gone out to the rest of the platoon, Taluqdar was placing the breaching charge on the floor of the log platform, which was also the roof of the bunker beneath.

He slapped the shaped ring charge into place, thumbed the detonator, and stepped back as far as the platform would allow. Five seconds later the charge detonated with a loud "*Whumpf!*" which blew a gaping opening through the heavy logs. Taluqdar tossed a frag grenade through for good measure, waited for it to detonate, and then dropped through feet-first in pursuit.

Aboard the second pinnace, circling around as it prepared to land the rest of the Marines and his own SWAT personnel, Captain Barto Jezic, monitoring the Marines' communications net over a borrowed headset, also heard Captain Kaczmarczyk, and his jaw clenched.

He knew the Marines hadn't really expected to face modern, off-world weapons any more than he had. But Kaczmarczyk and his people were professionals. They'd allowed for it in their planning, and the Pandora warning had moved them abruptly to an entirely different set of rules of engagement.

They were no longer there to apprehend; they were there to "neutralize."

To destroy.

Jezic closed his eyes briefly, praying that at least some of the people down there—people who had to be terrorists, if they had off-world weapons, however they'd gotten them—would be fast enough to surrender while they were still alive."

Drazen Divkovic, "Brother Dagger," rolled out of his bunk, clawing his way frantically up out of the depths of sleep. The incredible volume of the surrender demand had penetrated into the warren of underground bunkers and passages which had been built long before the National Reformation Party had been transformed into the Freedom Alliance of Kornati. But he'd only begun to rouse when the first explosions began.

How? *How?!* If Camp Freedom had been spotted when the off-world weapons were actually landed, it would have been hit *then*, not three nights later! And how could they have—

"Drazen! *Drazen!*" It was Jelena Krleza, his second-in-command, screaming through the open door. "We're under attack!" she announced unnecessarily. *"It's the fucking Manties!"*

Drazen's heart seemed to stop. Manties? *Manticorans?*

It couldn't be. It simply *could* not be! But it was, and he cursed himself for not having set up some sort of self-destruct. But this site had been here so long, been so secure. He hadn't been able to believe it had been compromised, not after they'd landed the weapons and no one had even blinked! Only now—

"Get your weapons!" he bellowed. "Get your weapons! Man your positions!"

He snatched up the belt-fed grenade launcher he'd chosen as his own personal weapon and dashed for the door, wishing with all his heart that he'd had the opportunity to actually practice with it.

Second Squad was in assault configuration. Its regular plasma rifles had been replaced with heavier weapons, which were normally crew-served. Its riflemen had traded in their usual pulse rifles for heavy tribarrels fed from five thousand-round, backpack tanks of alternating HE and armor-piercing ammunition.

Now Second Squad went to Case Zulu, and the plasma rifles fired. The camouflaged door to the underground vehicle ramp was only earth-covered logs, less than a half-meter thick. It simply vanished, and a tornado of tribarrel fire ripped through the opening. Grenades followed, and the squad's first section went in behind them, charging into the inferno of exploding fuel tanks and blazing vehicles, tribarrels ready.

First Squad's second fire team looked for a way to dump the sleeping gas into the ventilation system, but there were no intakes. All they had was the exhaust from the system, and they moved swiftly to their alternate assigned role under Case Zulu, deploying rapidly outward to take over the perimeter while Second Squad broke in through the vehicle entrance. Even as they did, Sergeant Cassidy's team went up the ridge in the long, flying leaps of their jump gear, and more breaching charges thundered as they blew their way in through the sides of the tower/bunker and followed Private Taluqdar down into the bowels of the installation beneath.

Chapter Forty-Five

"My God, Aivars." Bernardus Van Dort's face was ashen as he looked up from the report. "A *thousand tons* of modern weapons?"

"That's Kaczmarczyk's best estimate." Terekhov sat behind his desk in his day cabin, and his expression was as grim as his voice. "He may be off in either direction, but I doubt he's very far off."

"But, dear God, where did they *come* from?"

"We don't know. And we may not find out. We only have five prisoners, and three of them are critically wounded. Doctor Orban's doing what he can, but he's pretty sure we're going to lose at least one of them."

"And your own losses?" Van Dort asked, his voice softer.

"Two dead, one wounded," Terekhov said harshly. "Either some of these people were suicidal, or else they didn't know what the hell they were doing! Using plasma grenades in an underground tunnel?" He shook his head viciously. "Sure, they killed two of my Marines, but the same grenades killed at least fifteen of their people—possibly more!"

Van Dort shook his head, not in disbelief, but like a man who wished he could disbelieve.

"What do we know about their casualties?" he asked after a moment.

"So far Tadislaw's confirmed at least seventy bodies. That number may very well go up. At the moment, only his Marines are equipped for search and rescue operations in there. Without armor, or at least skinsuits, nobody can get through the fires and the heat."

Van Dort closed his eyes, trying—and, he knew, failing—to imagine what it must have been like in those narrow, underground passages when modern weapons turned them into a roaring inferno.

"I don't know what I feel," he admitted after several moments, opening his eyes again. "It was a massacre," he said, and raised one hand before Terekhov could open his mouth to protest his choice of nouns. "I said a massacre, Aivars, not an *atrocity*. At least we tried to give these people a chance to surrender, which is more than they've done. And if we've killed seventy or eighty of them, that's a drop in a bucket compared to the thousands of civilians—including *children*—they and their . . . colleagues have slaughtered. But it's still—what? ninety-plus percent of everyone in their base when we arrived?" He shook his head again. "Even knowing who they were, what they've done, that kind of death rate . . ."

His voice trailed off, and he shook his head again, but Terekhov barked a hard, sharp-edged laugh.

"If you want someone to spend your pity on, Bernardus, I can find you some much more deserving candidates!"

"It isn't pity, Aivars, it's—"

"I'm a naval officer, Bernardus," Terekhov interrupted. "Oh, sure I spent twenty-eight T-years as a Foreign Office weenie, but I was a Naval officer for eleven T-years first, and I've been a Naval officer for *fifteen* T-years since. I've spent too many years cleaning up after people who do things like this, and that affects your perspective. We call them 'pirates,' or sometimes 'slavers,' but they're no different, when you come right down to it, from Nordbrandt and her butchers. The only difference is the justification they use for their butchery, and I, for one, am not going to shed one single tear for *these* butchers!"

Van Dort gazed at his friend's bleak expression. Maybe Terekhov was a harder man than he was—hardened by his profession, and experience. Yet, even if he was, Van Dort knew he was right. FAK's actions had put its members beyond the pale. Whatever twisted justification they gave themselves for their actions, they'd reduced human beings—men, women, and children—to tools. To readily expended pawns. To *things* to be destroyed in a coldblooded, calculated ploy to terrify and demoralize their opponents.

And yet . . . and yet . . .

There was a part of Bernardus Van Dort which couldn't help being horrified. Couldn't accept that any human beings, whatever their crimes, could be wiped away in such transcendent horror without some corner of his soul crying out in protest. And even if he could have shed that soul-deep repugnance, he didn't want to. Because the day he could do that, he would become someone else.

"Well, whatever else it's done," he said at length, "it has to be a body blow to the FAK. It's more than three times their *total* casualties to date, and all inflicted in less than two hours. That kind of damage has to knock even fanatics like Nordbrandt back on their heels."

"And losing a thousand tons of modern weapons has to make a hole in their offensive capabilities," Terekhov pointed out. But there was something odd about his voice, and Van Dort looked up quickly.

The Manticoran's eyes were distant, almost unfocused, as he gazed across the cabin at the bulkhead portrait of his wife. He sat that way for over a full minute, rubbing the thumb and first two fingers of his right hand together in a slow, circular movement.

"What is it, Aivars?" Van Dort finally asked.

"Hmph?" Terekhov shook himself, and his eyes refocused on Van Dort's face. "What?"

"I asked what you were thinking about."

"Oh." The Manticoran tossed his right hand in a

throwing-away gesture. "I was just thinking about their weapons."

"What about them?"

"Tadislaw already has First Platoon's armorers examining their find. So far, everything's been Solarian manufacture. Some of the small arms are at least twenty T-years old, but all of them are in excellent shape. Replacement parts, some a lot newer than the weapons themselves, indicate they were all refurbished and reconditioned before they were delivered to Nordbrandt. The crew-served weapons they've looked at so far seem to be newer than that, though, and they've turned up modern com gear, reconnaissance systems, night vision equipment, body armor, military-grade explosives and detonators . . ." The captain shook his head. "Bernardus, they had everything they needed to equip a battalion of light infantry—*modern* light infantry—complete with heavy weapons support, buried in that hole in the ground."

"I realize that," Van Dort said.

"You're missing my point. They had it *buried* in a *hole in the ground*. Why? If they had this kind of equipment, why weren't they *using* it? They could've blasted their way right through anything the Kornatian police could put in their way. Hell, for that matter, they could've blasted their way through anything Suka's *System Defense Force* could have thrown at them, unless the SDF was prepared to resort to saturation airstrikes! Nordbrandt could have invaded the Nemanja Building and taken the entire Parliament hostage on the very first day of her offensive, instead of just bombing it with *civilian* explosives. So why didn't she?"

Van Dort blinked, then frowned.

"I don't know," he admitted slowly. "Unless they *didn't* have them then." He inhaled deeply, still thinking. "Maybe you said it yourself. You said they were either suicidal or didn't know what they were doing. Maybe they just hadn't had the weapons long enough."

"That's exactly what I was thinking. But if they didn't have them stockpiled to begin with, where did they come from? How did they get here? I can't believe Nordbrandt had a big enough war chest socked away to *pay* for them, but the kind of rogue arms dealer who'd deal with someone like her would demand cash in advance, and he wouldn't sell them cheap. So who did pay for them? And when did they deliver them? And while we're asking questions like that, how do we know this is the only stockpile she had?"

"I don't know," Van Dort admitted again. "But I think we'd better find out."

Agnes Nordbrandt's hands trembled as she switched off the com and returned it to its hiding place in the canister of flour. She put the canister back into the cabinet, closed the door, and switched on the HD. But there was only regularly scheduled programming, none of the screaming news bulletins which would go streaming out when the government announced its stunning victory.

How? How had they *done* it? How had they even spotted Camp Freedom in the first place?

Was it *her* fault? That second load of weapons and equipment—had they spotted the delivery shuttle after all? Tracked it to Camp Freedom?

No. No, it couldn't have been the delivery. If they'd spotted that, they would have attacked before this. They would never have risked waiting until we might have dispersed the weapons to other locations.

But if not that, then what?

Drazen. It must have been Drazen's people. Yet how could it have been? They'd made dozens—scores—of careful, stealthy trips in and out of Camp Freedom since the Nemanja bombing without anyone ever noticing a thing. And Drazen had been even more cautious than usual. Less than a dozen individual flights—nondescript personal air cars and copters—buried in the background of an entire hemisphere's routine, civilian traffic. Their flight paths had been almost random. Even their arrival times had been staggered over a window more than six *hours* wide! There was no way they could have been spotted. No way their courses and arrivals could have been connected with one another.

The Manties, she thought. *The goddamned, murdering* Manties. *They did it. Them and their sensors and their jackbooted Marines!*

It was the only answer. Only the Manties had the technical capability to pluck a handful of innocent-looking flights out of the clutter of everyone else's air traffic. Only the same greedy, avaricious, grasping imperialists out to devour her planet. They were the only ones who could have spotted Drazen, and their mercenary so-called "Marines" were the only troops in the star system who could have butchered everyone in Camp Freedom like so many helpless sheep hurled into a furnace.

Hot tears burned the backs of her eyes, but she refused to shed them. She wouldn't weep. She would *not* weep! Not even though the hired thugs of the interstellar appetite waiting to rape her world and the corrupt regime of local despots waiting to help them do it had murdered Drazen and his entire cell. Had burned them like so many logs in a fire and butchered over ninety other people—friends, colleagues, brothers and sisters of the armed struggle, some of whom she'd known for literally two-thirds of her entire life—with them.

She would not weep.

They may have destroyed Camp Freedom, she told herself fiercely, *but they don't know about the other arms caches. They don't know the Movement still has modern weapons, still has dozens of times the firepower and capability we had at the beginning!*

She told herself that, and resolutely refused to consider the fact that whatever the FAK might have, the government had the Star Kingdom of Manticore.

"So now what do we do?"

Vice President Vuk Rajkovic looked around the table at the members of "his" Cabinet, although less than a quarter of them had been chosen by him.

"What do you mean, Mr. Vice President?" Mavro Kanjer asked.

"You know perfectly well what I mean, Mavro," Rajkovic told the Secretary of Justice flatly. "You were there when Van Dort told us what Aleksandra *didn't* tell us." Several people shifted uneasily, and Rajkovic stabbed them with an angry glare. "*All* of you know, by now. Don't pretend for one moment you don't! And if any of you want to try to, I'm officially informing you now that I have formal confirmation of Van Dort's statements from Baroness Medusa herself. President Tonkovic was informed *six weeks ago* that a hard deadline existed, and she *still* hasn't informed her own government of that fact."

People looked away from him. Some looked down at the table, some at the walls, and some at each other. Then, finally, Vesna Grabovac looked up and met his gaze squarely.

"What do *you* think we should do, Mr. Vice President?" the Treasury Secretary asked.

"I think we should consider the fact that President Tonkovic was required by our Constitution to inform the rest of her government—and, especially, Parliament—of that communication from the Provisional Governor 'without delay.' I submit to you that six weeks—over a quarter of the total time remaining to the Constitutional Convention—constitutes a very significant delay."

"Are you suggesting she be recalled to face Parliamentary questioning?" Alenka Mestrovic, the Education Secretary demanded.

"I think the possibility should be considered very strongly, yes," Rajkovic said unflinchingly.

"We can hardly sustain a constitutional crisis at a moment when we've just learned Nordbrandt and her lunatics are in possession of modern, off-world weapons!" Kanjer protested.

"My God, Mavro!" It was Goran Majoli, Secretary of Commerce and one of Rajkovic's strongest allies in the Cabinet. "We—or, rather, the Manticorans—just seized over a *thousand tons* of those 'modern weapons' and killed over a hundred of her murderers in the process! If we can't face the possibility of an open political debate about our own President's compliance with the Constitution now, then when do you suggest we *will* be able to?"

Kanjer glared at Majoli. Obviously, Rajkovic thought, Kanjer felt that "never" would be a very good time to consider Aleksandra's conduct.

Voices started up all around the table, with a contentiousness not even the most broad-minded could have dignified with a term as civilized as "debate." Rajkovic let the wrangling stretch out for several minutes, then hammered on the wooden block with his gavel. The crisp, sharp sound brought the raised voices to an abrupt, slithering stop, and he glared at all of them.

"This is a meeting of the Cabinet, not a sandbox full of fighting children!" Even some of Tonkovic's most avid supporters had the grace to look embarrassed at that, and he swept his eyes over all of them.

"Obviously, we aren't going to reach consensus on this this afternoon," he said flatly. "It is, however, a matter we're going to have to settle, and soon. Whatever President Tonkovic may think, I cannot justify not passing that information on directly to Parliament now that it's been officially communicated to me by the Provisional Governor."

The silence became deathly still as Tonkovic's partisans realized what he was saying, and he met their gazes levelly.

"I called this meeting, and asked the question that I did, primarily as a matter of courtesy. In my judgment, the destruction of so much of Nordbrandt's organization, and the capture and destruction of so many off-world weapons, should have a calming effect on public opinion. I believe there won't be a better time for me to grasp the nettle and bring this information to Parliament's attention without provoking widespread public outrage and protests. I'll do so in as noninflammatory a fashion as I possibly can, but all of you know as well as I do that, however public opinion reacts, Parliament won't take it well. And Parliament may, at its own discretion, summon any elected official—including the President—to answer before its members for the proper discharge of his or her duties."

"And you'll just *happen* to suggest that they ought to do so in this case, eh?" Kanjer demanded with an ugly expression.

"I'll suggest nothing of the sort," Rajkovic replied coldly. "If that were what I wanted to suggest, however, it would be unnecessary, and you know it as well as I do."

"I know you're planning on staging what amounts to a *coup d'etat*!" Kanjer retorted angrily.

"Oh, bullshit, Mavro!" Majoli snapped. "You can't accuse Vuk of staging a coup when all he's doing is what the Constitution flatly *requires* him to do! Or do you suggest he should violate the Constitution in order to protect someone else who's already doing the same thing?"

Kanjer snarled at the Commerce Secretary, and Rajkovic hammered the gavel again. Kanjer and Majoli sat back from the table almost simultaneously, still glaring at one another, and the Vice President shook his head.

"I'll be dispatching an official report of the raid and its results to Spindle by tomorrow or the next day. Anyone who wishes to communicate with President Tonkovic is welcome to send his or her messages via the same courier. Frankly, I invite you to do so. Whether you believe this or not, Mavro, I'd far rather resolve this *without* a constitutional crisis. And I've been acting head of state long enough to have a very good idea of just how unpleasant it would be to have the job permanently, thank you!

"I have also, however, been summoned to appear before Parliament tomorrow afternoon. The exact reason Parliament wishes to see me hasn't been vouchsafed, but I suspect we can all deduce what it is they want to talk about. And when they ask me questions, Ladies and Gentlemen, I *will* answer them—fully, frankly, and as completely as I can. What will come of that, I don't know, but I suggest that it behooves all of President Tonkovic's friends to convince her that there are matters here on Kornati which require her urgent attention."

✧ ✧ ✧

"Sir? Do you have a minute?"

"What is it, Lajos?" Aivars Terekhov replied, glancing up from the paperwork on his computer display to find Surgeon Commander Orban looking in through the open hatch of his bridge briefing room.

"Sir, I don't know if this is important, but I thought I should mention it to you."

"Mention what to me?" Terekhov raised one eyebrow and half-turned towards the hatch with his elbow on the briefing room table.

"Well, Sir," Orban said slowly, "normally, under the Beowulf Code, what a patient says under heavy medication is privileged doctor-patient information."

Terekhov felt his muscles freeze. The Star Kingdom subscribed firmly to the bioethics of the Beowulf Code. Most physicians would have been prepared to face prison themselves rather than violate it.

"I believe, Doctor," he said slowly, "that your responsibilities as a Queen's officer supersede that particular privilege under certain circumstances."

"Yes, Sir, they do," Orban said, his eyes even darker than usual. "I don't like it, but they do. For that matter, under the circumstances, I suspect the old Hippocratic Oath would, even though it was hardly written for a case like this."

"Like what?" Terekhov made his voice remain calm and patient.

"One of my patients, one of the terrorists, is under some fairly heavy pain medication, Sir," the surgeon commander said slowly. "I'd say he's got no more than a seventy percent chance, even with quick heal." He frowned, then waved one hand impatiently. "Whatever. The important thing is that he's fairly delusional at the moment. He thinks the SBAs and I are someone called 'Drazen' or 'Brother Dagger,' and he keeps trying to make some kind of report to us."

"What sort of report, Doctor?" Terekhov asked very intently.

"I don't know, Sir. We're recording it, but his voice

is pretty much gone and it's all fairly garbled. In fact, most of it seems to be so much gibberish. But there's one name he keeps saying over and over again. It seems to have something to do with all the weapons they had down there. I think this fellow's been thrown back to before the attack, because he keeps telling this 'Drazen' fellow that 'the shipment has been delivered.'"

"'The shipment'?" Terekhov repeated sharply, and Orban nodded. "And you said he keeps repeating a name?"

"Yes, Sir." The physician shrugged. "I guess it must be a code name of some sort. I mean, 'Firebrand' could hardly be someone's real name, could it?"

"'*Firebrand*'? Is Dr. Orban sure about that, Aivars?" Van Dort demanded.

"Whether *he* is or not, the recorder is," Terekhov said harshly. "I played it back myself. And then I had Guthrie Bagwell digitally enhance it. That's the name he keeps saying. And he's telling this 'Drazen' that he—our wounded terrorist—personally took delivery of 'Firebrand's guns.' I don't think there can be any reasonable doubt. This 'Firebrand' character is how Nordbrandt got her hands on at least—*at least*, Bernardus—a thousand tons of modern weapons. Do you think it's just a coincidence that your friend Westman's been having some sort of contact with someone using the same name?"

"No. No, of course it isn't." Van Dort rubbed his face with his palms, then drew a deep breath and laid his hands flat on the tabletop in front of him and stared at their backs.

"Then maybe Mr. Westman has just been stringing us along," Terekhov suggested, his tone even harsher.

"Maybe," Van Dort said. Then he shook his head. "Of course it's possible. Anything's possible—especially in a situation like this! But why? The one thing about Westman, from the very beginning, was how determined he's been to minimize casualties. *Minimize* them. There couldn't be a bigger difference between his attitude and

Nordbrandt's! Why would he be dealing with someone who's connected with *her*?"

"I can think of only two reasons." If Terekhov's voice was less harsh, it was much colder. "First, we've been wrong about Westman from the start. Maybe he's just smarter than Nordbrandt, not less bloodthirsty. He could simply've decided to start out more slowly, so he'd be able to make a stronger case to the Montanan public for having been forced to it by the reactionary forces of a corrupt regime when he unleashes his *own* bloodbath.

"Second—and, to be honest, the one I would infinitely prefer—this 'Firebrand' is simply that rogue arms dealer I mentioned to you once before. Somebody peddling arms wherever he can find a buyer, who's managed to contact both Westman and Nordbrandt. In that case, Westman really may be as different from Nordbrandt as we always thought he was."

"But how could a single arms dealer make contact in such a relatively short period with two such totally different people? Neither of whom were on some directory of would-be freedom fighters or terrorists before they went underground, and that wasn't all that long ago. So how did he find both of them so promptly?" Van Dort objected. "Especially when the two people in question live on planets over a light-century apart?"

"That, Bernardus, may be the one ray of sunlight in this entire thing," Terekhov said grimly. "I've been worried—for that matter, the Office of Naval Intelligence and Gregor O'Shaughnessy have been worried—that certain . . . outside interests might be interested in destabilizing the Cluster to prevent the annexation from succeeding. It might just be that this 'Firebrand' is the front man for somebody trying to do just that."

"By feeding weapons to local terrorists, or possible terrorists," Van Dort said.

"Absolutely. And, if that's the case, and if your estimate of Mr. Westman is accurate, we may finally have caught a break."

Van Dort looked up at him, trying to understand

how the probable confirmation that the Solarian League was actively working against the annexation effort could possibly be construed as "a break," and Terekhov smiled slowly. It wasn't an excessively pleasant smile.

"We're going back to Montana, Bernardus. I'll leave one platoon of Marines, with battle armor, one pinnace, and orbital sensor arrays, to support the Kornatians until Baroness Medusa's reinforcements get here. But you and I, and the *Kitty*, are returning immediately to Montana. Where we're going to confront Mr. Westman with the media coverage, and the government reports, and our *own* records, of what Agnes Nordbrandt's been doing here in Split. We're going to ask him if he really wants to be associated with a murderous bitch like her, and then, when he denies he ever could be, we're going to hit him squarely between the eyes with the fact that he's been buying guns from the same supplier she has and see how he likes that."

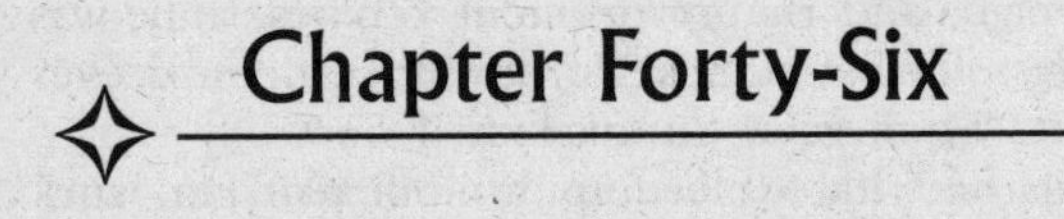

Chapter Forty-Six

Aleksandra Tonkovic sat in the golden sunlight spilling through the windows of her office on the planet Flax and glared at the neat, formal words before her. The entire Constitutional Convention had received precisely the same report on the FAK raid, and at least that bastard Rajkovic had been careful to keep any of his poisonous, scarcely veiled anticipation out of a document he knew so many other star system's political representatives were going to see.

Her personal correspondence had been another matter, of course.

No doubt he would insist he was merely doing his duty as Planetary Vice President. As the dutiful servant of Parliament. But she knew Vuk Rajkovic. Knew he'd never shared her vision of Kornati's future. No wonder he and that rabble rouser Nordbrandt had been such bosom buddies for so long! His Reconciliation Party might as well have publicly acknowledged that Nordbrandt's National Reformation Party was no more than an auxiliary adjunct of its own!

She gritted her teeth, inhaled deeply, and forced herself to step back—a little, at least—from her rage.

Fair was fair, she told herself sternly. Whatever his other faults, Rajkovic had never hidden his core beliefs. That was one of the things which made him dangerous. He had a carefully built reputation as an honest politician, one who not only couldn't be bought, but one who also meant exactly what he said. Tonkovic had enjoyed such a reputation with the electorate, but there'd been a difference; Rajkovic enjoyed the same reputation among his fellow politicians.

No, none of the idiots who followed Rajkovic's lead could ever claim they hadn't known exactly where he was going. Unless, of course, they willfully kept their eyes screwed shut throughout the journey.

Tonkovic had hated leaving him behind to work behind her back, but there was no one besides herself she could trust to represent the Split System properly, and the Reconciliation bloc in Parliament had been large enough to virtually guarantee Rajkovic would have been sent, if *she* hadn't come. In which case, the Split System would have found itself firmly aligned with those idiots Van Dort and Alquezar and their junkyard dog, Krietzmann.

And now this.

She'd hoped his onetime association with Nordbrandt might cripple him politically when the FAK began its atrocities. Not that she'd ever wanted the attacks themselves, of course. But it would have been so fitting to see his career ended by the bloodthirsty terrorism of the very elements he'd argued for so long needed to be given greater access to power. Surely the unprovoked mayhem wreaked by the ignorant, childish, brutishly vicious rabble of that "dispossessed" and "unfairly excluded" underclass he was so fond of championing, should have destroyed his credibility.

Instead, he'd emerged from the carnage as a decisive national leader, a figure of reassuring calm and inflexible determination, dealing with the crisis while Tonkovic was in an entirely different star system. Someone who was enough the Mob's own to have credibility with it and simultaneously "respectable" enough to be seen by the oligarchical party leaders as their only real conduit to the underclass which had suddenly assumed such a frightening, bogeyman presence.

Although she'd consistently played down the FAK's threat, privately, Tonkovic had been as frightened as anyone else by its initial, spectacular successes. She'd wanted to blame Rajkovic for not having seen it coming, but she'd known that would have been absurd. Another part of her had blamed him for not acting more decisively after it began, but her contacts back on Kornati made it clear he—and, of course, *her* Cabinet appointees—had been doing everything possible. And another part of her had hoped that if Nordbrandt wasn't going to be crushed—which, of course, Tonkovic wanted her to be—at least Rajkovic's image of decisiveness would erode under the fear and hatred generated by the FAK's bombing campaigns.

It had even looked as if that much was happening . . . until that even more unmitigated bastard Van Dort and the fucking Royal Manticoran Navy moved in and smashed Nordbrandt's hidden weapons cache. Only fifteen days ago. Was it really only *fifteen days* since that devastating blow had staggered not simply Nordbrandt's murderous organization but the entire political calculus of Kornati?

The sheer, stunning scope of the defeat inflicted upon the FAK and, even more importantly, its future capabilities, had enormously strengthened Rajkovic's hand. Especially after Nordbrandt's resurrection and the terrorists' resurgence. Even people who might otherwise have remained calm and collected enough to recognize that the Reformation Party's platform was just as dangerous, in the long run, as any terrorist bomb, thought he could walk on water! The idiots ought to have realized Nordbrandt was only the tip of an iceberg, no more than the first outrider of the barbarian invasion Rajkovic's entire political philosophy was busy opening doors for.

Even after Nordbrandt was defeated—as Tonkovic had

never doubted she inevitably would be—she'd serve as an incendiary example to all of those useless, lazy, underproductive parasites who wanted to overturn the established bastions of society and loot the economy in some sort of crazed redistribution campaign. And the "*rights*" Rajkovic kept telling those same parasites they had would be the justification the Mob used to sanctify its demolition work! Unless the sane elements of Kornatian society were very, very lucky, they'd find themselves facing an entire succession of Nordbrandt clones. Tonkovic doubted any of them would possess the venomous capability of the original, but that wouldn't prevent them from doing enormous damage.

Which was why it was more important than ever to ensure that Kornati retained the law enforcement and economic mechanisms to guarantee another Nordbrandt couldn't succeed where the FAK failed. That was why she'd decided against passing on that insufferable prig Medusa's arrogant and humiliating demand that she surrender the principles she'd come to Spindle to fight for.

Even now, she couldn't believe Medusa was so foolish as to believe she could convince anyone who knew how the game was played that the Alexander Government's warnings about a set deadline were anything but a ploy. A bluff. One more attempt to browbeat her into surrendering Kornati's essential sovereignty. The Star Kingdom of Manticore had invested too much prestige in this annexation. Allowing the annexation to fail and Frontier Security to snap up the Cluster after all would be a devastating blow to its interstellar credibility. If she only stood her ground—if those cowards back on Kornati only let her call Manticore's bluff—Prime Minister Alexander would find some perfectly logical "reason of state" to extend the deadline.

And even if he didn't, how much worse off could they be? If they surrendered their full sovereignty, then everything that mattered about Kornati would be destroyed, possibly within months, certainly within years. Far better to hold their position on the basis of principle. And if the Manticorans carried out their cowardly threat and specifically excluded the Split System from their precious Star Kingdom because Split refused to cave in, she and her government could face the people of Kornati with their heads high. The fault would lie elsewhere, and Kornati would be free to pursue its own destiny. Best of all, the Star Kingdom which had refused to grant them membership as if they were some sort of moral pariahs would protect them from State Security after all by its simple presence.

So of course she hadn't told anyone back home about Medusa's insulting, intolerable demands. If she had, some of the weaklings in Parliament might have been panicked into insisting that they throw away the last shreds of self-determination. And if she never told anyone, the government would at least have plausible deniability. They could blame their homeworld's exclusion from the Star Kingdom on her. On a single, courageous woman who'd taken it upon herself to save her planet's ancient liberties. It might be hard on her, initially. But ultimately, her actions would prove justified, and she would return once more to her rightful place in the world of the Kornatian politics.

But did Rajkovic understand that? Of course he didn't! Or, even worse, he didn't care. It well might be that his own vengeful political ambitions drove him to seize this opportunity to destroy her, regardless of the ultimate cost to Kornati.

She looked at the letter—the official letter, on official parchment, not a simple electronic message—once more, and her jaw clenched. It was very short and to the point.

Presidential Mansion
Karlovac
December 13, 1920 PD

Madam President,

At the command of Parliament, I must request you to return to Kornati by the first available transportation. Your presence before the Special Committee on Annexation and the Standing Committee on Constitutional Law is required.

By command of the Parliament and people of Kornati,

Vuk Ljudevit Rajkovic
Planetary Vice President

The sentences, the phrasing, were purely formal, defined by centuries of custom and law, yet she heard Rajkovic's gloating triumph in every syllable. He hadn't been able to defeat her at the polls, and so he'd embraced this sordid maneuver to steal the office he'd been unable to win.

She inhaled another deep breath and gave herself a fierce mental shake.

This wasn't the end. Yes, she'd been recalled to appear before Parliament, and the phrasing made it clear it would be an adversarial proceeding. And, yes, Parliament had the authority to remove her from office if it determined she'd violated the constitutional limits upon her powers as Planetary President and Special Envoy, or failed to discharge her responsibilities to either office. But her Democratic Centralists and their allies still commanded a majority in Parliament, and it would require a two-thirds vote to sustain an impeachment. Rajkovic and his cronies would never be able to muster that many votes for what was so obviously a partisan effort to steal the presidency.

She looked at the letter one last time, then stood and tossed it contemptuously onto her desk.

She had people to see before she returned home to confront that pygmy Rajkovic and his contemptible allies.

Forty-five days after leaving the Montana System for Split, and twenty-two days since the destruction of the FAK base, HMS *Hexapuma* came back over the Montana alpha wall 19.8 light-minutes from the system primary.

The spectacular blue radiance of a hyper-transit radiated from her sails like sheet lightning, and she folded them back into an impeller wedge and began accelerating in-system from a base velocity of just under fifteen thousand kilometers per second.

Aivars Terekhov sat on his bridge, watching the G1 star grow before his ship, and then looked at Amal Nagchaudhuri.

"Record a message to Chief Marshal Bannister, please," he said, and Nagchaudhuri touched a control stud.

"Live mike, Skipper."

"Chief Marshal," Terekhov began. "Mr. Van Dort and I have returned to Montana after uncovering information on Kornati which, we believe, should have a significant bearing on Mr. Westman's opposition to the annexation. We would greatly appreciate it if you could contact him and inform him that we would like to speak to him again. We should enter Montana orbit in approximately two hours and twenty-five minutes, and Mr. Van Dort and I are both looking forward, on a personal level, to seeing you again. If it would be convenient, we'd very much enjoy having dinner with you at, say, the Rare Sirloin. If that would be possible, would you care to make reservations for our regular table, or should I?"

He stopped and watched while Nagchaudhuri played back the recording through his own earbug. Then the com officer nodded.

"Clear copy, Skipper."

"Go ahead and send it," Terekhov said.

"Aye, aye, Sir."

"What are you going to do, Boss?" Luis Palacios asked.

"I don't rightly know," Stephen Westman replied. It wasn't an admission he would—or could—have made to anyone else.

The two of them sat under the aspens outside the hidden mouth of the MIM's cave headquarters, gazing across the small mountain valley. The air was cooler than it had been, and the brisk, elusive smell of autumn was approaching. Palacios' jaw worked steadily, rhythmically, on a chew of backy while they listened to the wind, whispering in the leaves, and silence fell between them once more.

It was a comfortable silence. The silence of a leader and his follower. Of two old friends. And of a patron and the old and faithful retainer who'd long since earned the right to speak his own mind. And who knew now, at this moment, that there was no need for him to do so.

Westman sat in that silence, and the brain behind his blue eyes was busy.

How had it come to this? He could look back and see every step, every decision, and, truth to tell, he had no regrets even now. In fact—his lips twitched as he remembered barefooted off-worlders in their underwear limping off down a mountain trail—some of it had been just plain *fun*.

But then the temptation to smile faded. It wasn't that he was no longer prepared to fight, to die—even to kill—for what he believed was right. It wasn't even that he was no longer prepared to take Luis and his other followers with him. It was that he was no longer confident that what he had believed in *was* right.

There. He'd admitted it. He had doubts. Not about whether or not the RTU had cheated and abused Montana. Not about whether or not that arrogant bastard Van Dort should've told Suzanne the truth about his prolong before he trapped her into marriage. And certainly not about how far he was prepared to go to prevent the organized rape of his planet by greedy, corrupt off-worlders. But . . .

But what if they *weren't* greedy, corrupt off-worlders, out to clearcut his world and turn all its citizens into debt-enslaved peons on the planet their ancestors had made their home? What if he *had* permitted his hatred for Rembrandt to automatically extend itself to anyone Rembrandt—and Van Dort—thought good? And what if—most disturbing thought of all, in oh, so *many* ways—he had been wrong about Bernardus Van Dort himself?

Surely not! Surely he couldn't have been wrong about *all* of that! But, the same stubborn integrity which had turned him into a guerrilla demanded insistently, what if he had? And, that dogged integrity insisted, it *was* possible. After all, what did he actually know about the Star Kingdom of Manticore? Nothing, when it came down to it. Only that its vast wealth was based on its shipping and astrographic advantages, and that had only resonated in his own mind with Rembrandt's position in the Cluster. He knew it was a kingdom, with a hereditary queen and an aristocracy, and that was enough to raise any good Montanan's hackles. Yet if Van Dort and the Manticoran captain, Terekhov, were to be believed, it was the selfish resistance of oligarchs like Aleksandra Tonkovic which was stalling the annexation. And if the Star Kingdom was what Westman feared, why should someone like Tonkovic resist the Constitution proposed by Joachim Alquezar and Henri Krietzmann? And, for that matter, what could a Dresdener possibly have in common with one of the wealthiest oligarchs San Miguel—charter partner in the RTU—had ever produced?

Face it, Stevie, he told himself, *this mess is a whole bunch more complicated than you thought it was when you decided to jump right in like the hard-assed, stubborn, always-sure-you-know-all-the-answers country boy jackass you've always been.*

Even as he thought it, he knew he was being unfair to himself.

But not very, his stubborn doubt insisted. *Sure, a man has to take a stand for what he knows is right, and it's too late to take a stand after the fight's already lost. But a man ought to be certain he knows what he's fighting* against—*not just what he's fighting* for—*before he gets ready to kill people, or asks people who trust him to kill people. And what if you don't like Van Dort? Nobody says you have to.* He *doesn't even say you have to. Hell,* Trevor *says I should listen to him, and he was Suzanne's brother!*

He frowned, remembering, once again seeing his best

friend's glamorous older sister through the adoring eyes of a small boy. What had he been? Ten? No, he doubted he'd been even that old. But he remembered the day Suzanne left with her wealthy off-world husband. He remembered the day Trevor told him Suzanne's husband would live a thousand years, while she grew old and died. And he remembered the day—no little boy, now, but a man grown, a man of the Founding Families—when Suzanne came back to Montana to explain why her precious, treacherous husband was trying to make all the rest of the Cluster the economic slaves of Rembrandt.

His jaw clenched as he relived that moment of betrayal. The instant he realized that somehow Suzanne had been changed. That the strong, magnificent person he remembered had been brainwashed into spouting the Rembrandt line. And then the even worse betrayal, when she died. Died before she had time to come to her senses and realize how she'd been used.

He remembered it all, so clearly. Was it truly possible he'd perceived it all wrongly?

No. Van Dort himself admitted Rembrandt had been committed to building its economy at everyone else's expense. But the reason for it . . . Was it possible he was also telling the truth about his reasons for it? And about the reasons he'd abandoned fifty T-years of consistent policy when another opportunity offered?

And did it really matter *why* Van Dort had done what he'd done?

"I expect I'll meet with them again, after all, Luis," he said, finally.

"Figured you might, Boss," Palacios said, as if fifteen seconds and not fifteen minutes had passed between question and answer.

He spat backy juice, and then the two of them sat silently once more, gazing out over the valley.

"He says he'll meet with you," Trevor Bannister said.

"Under the same conditions?" Terekhov asked.

"Well, it seems to've worked last time," Bannister said with a shrug. Then his expression changed, ever so slightly. "One thing, though. He seems pretty insistent that your midshipwoman—Ms. Zilwicki, was it?—come along again."

"Ms. Zilwicki?" Almost unconsciously, Terekhov looked up from his com to where Helen sat side-by-side with Ragnhild Pavletic, watching Abigail Hearns demonstrate something at Tactical. Then he looked back at Bannister. "Did he say why?"

"No, he didn't. Might be I could guess, but I expect you'd do better asking Van Dort." Bannister paused, then continued grudgingly. "One thing I can tell you, though. If he's asking you to bring Ms. Zilwicki along, it damned sure means he's not planning anything . . . untoward."

Terekhov started to ask what he meant, then changed his mind, remembering Van Dort's cryptic comments about his personal history with Bannister. There was something going on here, and if it meant one of his officers—especially one of his midshipmen—might be being placed in danger, it was his responsibility to find out what that something was. But if Helen would have been endangered by it, Bernardus would have told him. Of that much, he was certain.

"Tell Mr. Westman his word is sufficient bond for me. Mr. Van Dort and I will meet him at any time or place of his choosing. And if he wishes Ms. Zilwicki to be present, I'm sure that can be arranged, also."

Something flickered in Bannister's eyes. Surprise, Terekhov thought. Or possibly approval. Maybe even a combination of the two.

"I'll tell him," the Chief Marshal said. "I imagine I can get the message to him sometime this evening. Would tomorrow afternoon be too early for you?"

"The sooner the better, Chief Marshal."

"Flight Ops, this is Hawk-Papa-One. Request departure clearance for Brewster Spaceport."

"Hawk-Papa-One, Flight Ops. Wait one."

Helen sat in the pinnace's comfortable seat, listening

through the open flight deck hatch, as Ragnhild talked to Flight Ops. She'd decided it would be an ignoble emotion, unworthy of one such as herself, to feel base envy for all the extra time her friend was getting on the flight deck. She suspected from some of Ragnhild's comments and one or two of Lieutenant Hearns' remarks that Ragnhild might be seriously considering putting in for duty with the LAC squadrons after their snotty cruise. It would certainly be an appropriate choice for someone with her knack for tactics and amply demonstrated flying ability.

The conversation between Ragnhild and Flight Ops was cut off as the hatch slid shut, and Helen looked back out her viewport, watching the brightly lit boat bay begin to move as Ragnhild lifted the pinnace clear of the docking arms and applied thrust.

She didn't know everything the Captain and Mr. Van Dort wanted to tell Westman, but she had a pretty shrewd suspicion of the main thrust of their message.

It would be interesting to see how he responded.

Stephen Westman watched the air car settle once again beside the tent he'd . . . appropriated from the Manticoran survey party. They were certainly prompt. And from the sound of Trevor's message, they genuinely believed they had some sort of new information for him. Although he was unable to imagine what they might have discovered in Split that would have any bearing on the situation here in Montana.

Face it, boy, he thought. *A part of you damned well hopes they* did *find something. This resistance movement thing is no job for a man who's started to have more questions than answers.*

Stephen Westman, Helen thought, really was a remarkably handsome man. She'd been concentrating more on what he had to say than what he looked like during their first meeting, but his sheer physical charisma had been evident even then. Today, in what was probably his best Stetson, and wearing one of the peculiar neck ornaments the Montanans called "bolos" with a jeweled slide in the form of a rearing black stallion that glittered in the sunlight, the tall, broad-shouldered man presented a truly imposing appearance.

Yet even as she acknowledged that, she sensed something different about him. Not any absence of assurance, but . . . something almost like that.

No, she thought slowly. *That's not quite right. He looks like . . . like someone who's self-confident enough to admit to himself that he's no longer positive about something he thought he knew all about.*

The instant the thought crossed her mind, she scolded herself for it. Wishful thinking wasn't what anyone needed just now, even from a lowly midshipwoman/"aide." She hoped the Captain and Mr. Van Dort were more resistant than she was to the temptation to read what she knew all of them wanted to see into the MIM founder's attitude.

"Captain Terekhov," the Montanan said, extending his hand in greeting. "Mr. Van Dort."

That really *was* different, Helen realized. He didn't seem particularly happy to see the Rembrandter, and there was still unconcealed dislike in his eyes, even if he did manage to keep it out of his expression. But the crackling undertone of hostility which had been so noticeable at their first meeting was far less pronounced this time.

"Mr. Westman," the Captain greeted him, then stood aside as Trevor Bannister climbed out of the air car and extended his hand to Westman.

"Trevor."

"Steve."

The two men nodded to one another, and Westman waved at the familiar tent.

"If y'all would care to step into my office?" he invited with just a trace of a mischievous smile.

"So," Westman said, laying his Stetson on a corner of the camp table and looking across it at his guests.

"Trevor tells me you gentlemen believe you've discovered something I ought to know?" He smiled thinly. "I trust you'll both bear in mind that I'm going to be inclined to be just a mite suspicious about the altruism that brings you here."

"I'd be disappointed if you weren't," Aivars Terekhov said with an answering smile.

"Then I'd suggest you just fire away."

"Very well," Terekhov said without so much as a glance at Van Dort. It was Terekhov's Marines who'd turned up the evidence, after all. And there was no point in adding the additional barrier of Westman's personal antipathy for the Rembrandter to the equation.

"We know you've said—and, so far, at least, demonstrated by your actions—that you don't see yourself as the sort of outright terrorist Agnes Nordbrandt's decided to become."

Westman's lips tightened ever so slightly at the words "so far, at least," but he simply sat, waiting courteously, for Terekhov to continue.

"While we were in Split," the captain continued, watching the Montanan's face carefully, "we located one of Nordbrandt's base camps. One platoon of my Marines raided it. The FAK suffered very close to one hundred percent casualties, over a hundred of them fatal, in an operation which lasted about twenty minutes."

Westman's eyes narrowed, as if he realized Terekhov had deliberately underscored the speed and totality with which a single platoon of Captain Kaczmarczyk's Marines had demolished the Freedom Alliance base.

"Afterward, we discovered just over a thousand tons of modern, off-world weapons." Terekhov watched Westman's expression even more closely than before. "All of them were of Solarian manufacture, and in first-rate condition. Information from one of the captured terrorists indicated that they'd been supplied—very recently—to Nordbrandt through the offices of someone called 'Firebrand.' "

Trevor Bannister had told his off-world allies Westman was famous among his friends for his inability to bluff across a poker table. Now Terekhov saw a quick, brief flare of recognition in the Montanan's blue eyes. It vanished as quickly as it had come, but not quickly enough to hide itself.

"When we were in Montana previously, Mr. Westman," Terekhov said quietly, "the name 'Firebrand' also came up here." Westman's eyes flickered again, although his expression itself might have been carved out of pleasantly attentive stone. "That suggests to me, Sir, that there's a closer association between you and your organization, on the one hand, and Agnes Nordbrandt and her organization, on the other, than you've previously implied."

Oh, he didn't like that *one!* Helen thought.

The expression which had given away so little turned obsidian-hard, but even that was less flinty than his eyes. His nostrils flared as he inhaled a sharp, angry breath, but then he made himself stop, clearly reaching for self-control before he opened his mouth.

"There is *no* association between the Independence Movement and the FAK," he said then, icily, his casual Montanan manner of speaking far less noticeable than usual. "I've never personally met, corresponded with, or communicated in any way with Agnes Nordbrandt, and I despise her methods."

That's an interesting statement, Helen thought as her father's training kicked in. *Mad as he is, he picked his words pretty carefully, I think. Especially that word "personally."*

"One need not approve of someone's methods or tactics to work with them," the Captain pointed out. "In the end, though, the methods of those one is prepared to associate with, even if only indirectly, are likely to color one's own achievements." He held the Montanan's eyes levelly across the table. "And it might be well for you to consider who else might see an advantage in supporting the . . . aspirations of two people as different from one another as you and Agnes Nordbrandt."

"I could say the same of you, Captain," Westman

replied, letting his eyes shift to Mr. Van Dort's face. "The fact that your Star Kingdom's seen fit to associate its policies with someone like the Trade Union strikes me as sufficient reason to question its ultimate objectives."

"I understand that." The Captain actually chuckled with what seemed genuine humor. "You made that clear enough the *first* time we met, Mr. Westman. I've done my best, as has Mr. Van Dort, for that matter, to answer your concerns on that head. But I strongly suggest you consider the scale of our find. We captured or destroyed a *thousand tons* of weapons, Mr. Westman—in one base. Whether we got all of them or not, I honestly can't say at this point, although I suspect it was probably the majority of those landed for her *so far*. But we know you invested in at least some weapons yourself before you went underground, so obviously, you've had to make your own contacts and come up with the cash to pay for them. Based on that experience, how likely do you think it is that the FAK managed to pay for that much modern hardware out of its own resources? And if it didn't, if someone's prepared to subsidize someone like Nordbrandt on the scale those weapons represent, what might *his* objectives be?"

Westman felt his shoulders tighten as the Manticoran's level-voiced questions recalled his own doubts about "Firebrand's" honesty.

You were never stupid enough to believe all he was spouting about how much of what he and his "Central Liberation Committee" were doing was based on "altruism," Stevie, he reminded himself. *And it's not like you were signing up to follow him wherever he led. But still . . .*

He made himself sit back in his chair, looking across the table at Terekhov, and inhaled deeply.

"And just who do *you* think might be prepared to subsidize . . . someone like Nordbrandt?" he asked.

Not a muscle in Terekhov's face so much as twitched, but a fierce bolt of exultation ripped through him as Westman asked the question he'd prayed for.

"I'd start," he said calmly, "by considering who—aside from patriots such as yourself, of course—might think the Star Kingdom's presence in the Cluster was a bad thing. And I'd also ask myself who they might prefer to see here *instead* of the Star Kingdom. If whoever supplied Nordbrandt is also prepared to supply weapons to . . . someone else, on a similar scale, then the supplier must have both extensive resources and extensive contacts with those weapons' source."

He gazed into Westman's eyes, pausing, waiting with the same precision he would have used to time a missile salvo. Then—

"And I'd reflect on the fact that every one of those weapons, every round of ammunition, every bit of equipment, came from somewhere in the Solarian League."

I really, really *never want to play cards against the Captain,* Helen reflected as Hawk-Papa-One sliced across the boundary between Montana's indigo atmosphere and the still blackness of space.

She didn't know where or how it was all going to end, but the Captain had obviously gotten to Westman. Whether the Montanan would be able to step far enough back from his own commitment to Montanan independence to really consider what the Captain had suggested remained to be seen, but she suspected the odds were good.

Whether or not Westman would be prepared to give up his vendetta against the annexation—and the Rembrandt Trade Union—no matter who he might unknowingly have allied with was, of course, another question entirely.

Chapter Forty-Seven

"I do*n't* believe this shit."

"What?" Duan Binyan looked up, startled by the sheer venom in Zeno Egervary's voice. The *Marianne* was thirty days out of Split, decelerating towards the last planet on her delivery schedule, and Egervary sat glaring at his tactical display.

"That bastard Manticoran," Egervary snarled, and Duan frowned, wondering why Egervary sounded so upset.

"What about them?" he asked. "We knew they had a couple of support ships stationed here."

"Not them," Egervary grated. "That frigging cruiser from Split!"

"What about her?" Duan demanded. He was getting past surprise at the security officer's obviously frightened fury to alarm, and his tone was considerably sharper.

"She's here, too," Egervary spat. "Right here in Montana orbit!"

"*What?*"

Duan bounced out of his command chair and across to Egervary's station almost before he realized he was moving. Not for the first time, he made a mental note to insist that if *Marianne* was going to be sent out on this sort of mission he really wanted a proper tactical repeater where he could get at it without leaving his own chair. It was only an absentminded flicker at the bottom of his brain, however. His attention was too firmly fixed on Egervary's plot to spare it any more than that.

"Are you sure?" he demanded as he gazed down at the icons of the ships in orbit around the planet. There weren't many. The icon representing the warship floated in a parking orbit all its own, and there were only two merchantmen—one a Rembrandter, and the other a Solarian, from their transponder codes, the two service ships they'd known about, and half a dozen Montanan LACs to keep it company.

"Unless you know some reason for two Manty cruisers to both be squawking the same transponder code, then, yeah, I'm pretty goddamned positive."

Egervary's tone was scarcely what anyone would have called respectfully disciplined, but Duan paid that little attention. If Egervary's identification was accurate, he had every reason to be worried as hell.

"I don't like this, Binyan." Annette De Chabrol's voice was sharper than usual, if not quite as taut as Egervary's.

"I'm not particularly crazy about it myself, Annette," he replied acidly, still staring down at the plot while his mind whirred.

"They must've spotted the goddamned drop after all," Egervary said. "The bastards nailed the fucking terrorists, then ran on ahead to grab our asses when we showed up here! We're *fucked*, people!"

Duan glanced sideways at him. Zeno Egervary's language wasn't exactly what you'd care for your sweet old grandmother to hear at the best of times, but he was obviously under more stress than usual. Which could be bad. Egervary was good at his job—both his jobs—but he was also the least stable of *Marianne*'s officers.

"Calm down, Zeno," the captain said as soothingly as he could. Egervary gave him an incredulous look, and Duan shrugged.

"They did *not* spot the drop, Zeno. If they'd spotted that, they would have nailed *us* at the same time. We didn't break orbit for over four hours after we made the delivery and recovered the shuttle. You think they would've let us just sit there that long, then actually leave the system, if they'd known what we'd been doing?"

He held Egervary's eyes with his own, and the security head seemed to settle down a bit.

A very *tiny* bit.

"Then they must've picked up one of the locals with some of the new guns right after we left," he said. "They busted him, and he sang like a bird. *That's* how they knew to come on ahead and wait for us."

"And just how do you figure that? *I* didn't tell anybody where we were going next—did you?"

Egervary was still glaring at him, but he gave his head a choppy shake, and Duan shrugged.

"Well, if you didn't, and if I didn't, I'm damned sure Annette didn't. So how do you think *they* could have figured it out."

"What about the port agent?" Egervary demanded. "*He* knew what we were doing. If they picked someone up and whoever it was turned him in, he could've told them."

"He couldn't tell them what he didn't know," Duan riposted. "This operation was tightly compartmentalized, Zeno. Our Kornati agent knew we were coming and made the arrangements for us, including assembling our cover cargo, and he could have spilled that part of it. But he didn't know where we were going next. The flight plan we filed with him had us heading for Tillerman as our next port of call, and that's also the destination for the cargo we took on there. We didn't say a word about stopping off at Montana. So the only place he could have sent them is straight ahead to Tillerman."

Egervary frowned, obviously trying to find a hole in Duan's logic. The captain folded his arms, leaning one hip against the tactical console and waited.

One advantage of *Marianne*'s military-grade hyper

generator and particle screening was that her speed would let her stop off at Montana long enough to contact the locals waiting for their special cargo and still make it to Tillerman on time. A regular merchantman would have been too slow for that, and not even the Jessyk agent on Kornati had known about *Marianne*'s superior speed.

"Then what do *you* think she's doing here?" Egervary challenged.

"I don't have the least idea. The only thing I'm pretty damned confident of is that there's no way they could have predicted that *we'd* be coming here."

"Whether they could predict it or not, they're here now," De Chabrol pointed out tartly, and Duan nodded.

"Yes, they are. "

"So what do we do?" his executive officer demanded, and he frowned.

If Egervary had spotted the Manty sooner, his options might have been a lot better. Unfortunately, even *Marianne*'s sensor suite had a strictly limited range, especially against targets not obliging enough to have an impeller wedge up. From the look of Egervary's plot, the Manty's parking orbit must have brought her around from the far side of the planet within the last six or seven minutes. Unfortunately, by the time the cruiser was on the right side of the planet and the range was down to something which let Egervary spot her and check her transponder code, *Marianne* had already made turnover and begun decelerating towards the planet. Now she was twelve minutes past turnover, down to a velocity of 14,769 KPS and about 56.8 million kilometers from the planet, still decelerating at her dignified, tramp freighter's rate of two hundred gravities.

Part of the Jessyk Combine officer wanted to avoid the planet altogether. Despite his soothing words to Egervary, he, too, felt his hackles rising as he looked at that silent icon. What *had* brought the Manty here? Duan had seen enough bizarre coincidences to know they happened, but this one was more bizarre than most . . . assuming it was, in fact, a coincidence at all. Under the circumstances, and especially given the nature of the ship under his command and his cargo, he felt no burning desire to find out if it was.

Unfortunately he didn't have much choice. His ship was two hours and three minutes out of Montana orbit. If she suddenly changed course away from the planet, she'd make System Flight Control mildly curious, to say the least. Nor could she magically stop where she was and escape back across the hyper limit. Unless she altered acceleration radically, it was still going to take her two hours to decelerate to rest relative to the system primary, whatever she did. That meant she was committed to at least a flyby of the planet, and not stopping as she went by was certain to arouse the Manty skipper's suspicions.

And if the Manty got suspicious, there was no way *Marianne* could hope to stay away from her long enough to escape into hyper.

"We'll have to continue on profile," he said finally. Egervary looked as if he wanted to protest, and De Chabrol and Iakovos Sandkaran, the communications officer, didn't look much happier. "We're already committed to making planetfall," he pointed out. "If we try anything else, they're bound to figure we're up to something shady."

"But we're not supposed to be here," De Chabrol pointed out.

"And nobody in the system knows we're not," Duan countered. "Unless you want to suggest the Manty pulled our flight plan from the Split traffic control people?" He snorted. "That wouldn't make any more sense than the notion that they'd somehow run on ahead of us to lurk in ambush, now would it?"

"Maybe not, but what if they recognize us?" Egervary asked.

He looked more than a little pinched around the nostrils, and Duan remembered that Egervary—only his name hadn't been "Egervary" then—had been a "guest" of the Royal Manticoran Navy once before. Fortunately, he'd been acting as the tactical officer aboard a pirate cruiser in Silesia at the time, rather than serving aboard a slaver. Since he hadn't been in the database of the battlecruiser which had taken his ship and he'd been "only" a pirate, he'd been turned over to the local Silesian system governor rather than simply executed by the Manties. Getting him back from a Silly system governor had been trivially easy for Jessyk, but it seemed to have permanently affected Egervary's nerve where Manticoran warships were concerned.

Probably because he figures he is *in their database now*, Duan thought sarcastically. But his sarcastic amusement faded quickly. Finding yourself in the Manty Navy's database under the heading of previously arrested pirate or slaver was a virtual guarantee of the death sentence the *second* time they apprehended you.

"There's not any reason they should recognize us," he said, looking Egervary in the eye. "If they didn't spot us doing anything we shouldn't have been doing in Split, there's no reason for them to have done anything except check our transponder code. Why waste time taking a close look at one more rusty tramp—especially one that heads out of the system within less than nine hours of your own arrival? Right?"

Egervary looked at him for a moment, then gave a jerky nod.

"All right, then." Duan turned to Sandkaran. "Have we contacted Flight Control yet, Iakovos?"

"No," Sandkaran said, shaking his head.

"And we haven't started squawking our transponder code yet, right?" Another headshake. "Good. Let's crank up a new transponder—the *Golden Butterfly*, I think. Get it ready, then contact Flight Control and request a parking orbit as *Butterfly*. Don't put the transponder on-line until they call you back up and whack you on the wrist for not having it up. Be a little crabby when they do, like a typical lazy merchant spacer. Then put the *Butterfly* code up. By the time we actually make orbit, the Manty should already have been informed by Flight Control that we're coming under our new name."

"What should I give them for purpose of visit?"

"Good question." Duan thought for a moment, then snorted. "Whatever this guy's doing here, I don't propose to do anything that could make him suspicious of us. The customers waiting on this planet don't know exactly when we're supposed to arrive, anyway. They won't think anything one way or the other if we don't contact them with the right ID code. So I think this time our hatches will just stay sealed nice and tight. If the Combine had a shipping agent on the planet, I'd try telling them we were just dropping off a company message on our way through. Unfortunately, we don't have an agent here. So I think our best bet is to haul out that busted oxygen tank."

Understanding showed in Sandkaran's eyes. Annette actually chuckled, and even Egervary cracked a slight smile. *Marianne* carried a severely damaged liquid oxygen tank everywhere she went. It was her excuse for stopping at planets where she couldn't produce a legitimate cargo or other reason for being there. The tank was identical to the ones in her life-support plant, and stopping to replace something like that at the earliest possible moment would make sense for any merchantship. Especially for a freighter as dilapidated as *Marianne* appeared to be, since such a ship would undoubtedly be operating on a thinner safety margin than better maintained vessels.

"Be sure you declare an emergency and explain its nature when you call up Flight Control, Iakovos," Duan directed.

"Do you think Westman's going to call it quits?" Aikawa Kagiyama asked quietly.

He and Helen were sitting at the tactical station. Officially, they had the tac watch, since The Book required Tactical to be manned at all times aboard Manticoran warships. Since absolutely nothing was likely to happen at the moment, it made sense to give both Lieutenant

Commander Kaplan and Lieutenant Hearns some down-time. It was also an opportunity for a couple of snotties to get a little more "independent" tac time on their logs. So, officially, Helen was Tac Officer of the Watch with Aikawa as her assistant.

Now she glanced at him quizzically, and he shrugged.

"I'm not asking you to betray any confidences, Helen. On the other hand, do you really think there's anyone in the ship who hasn't figured out roughly why we hurried our buns back here so quickly? Or that the Skipper and Van Dort must've had *some* reason to go dirt-side and see him again?"

"Well, put that way, I guess not," she admitted.

Now that she thought about it, Aikawa and Ragnhild had put remarkably little energy into bugging her for details. The other two denizens of Snotty Row didn't count. Paulo, of course, never tried to weasel information out of her, and Leo Sottmeister had been left behind on Kornati, along with *Hexapuma*'s third pinnace and Lieutenant Kelso's platoon.

But apparently Aikawa's curiosity had finally gotten the better of his—limited—ability to control it. She looked back at the main plot without really seeing it and considered what she'd seen and heard.

"I don't know what he's going to decide, Aikawa," she said finally, slowly. "I'll tell you this, though. He isn't a bit like Nordbrandt must be. I figure he could be as stubborn and as dangerous as they come over something he really believes in. And I think he really believed in keeping us out of Montana when he started all this. But I'm not so sure he does, anymore. Or, at least, I think he's figured out it's not as black-and-white as he thought it was. I guess the real question's whether or not he's flexible enough to admit we're not the original font of all evil and be sensible about this."

"And do you think he is?"

"I don't know," she repeated honestly. "I hope so, but I wouldn't even venture a guess at this point."

"What I was afraid of," Aikawa sighed. "I guess it would have been too easy for—"

He broke off as a soft chime sounded and an icon on the tactical plot changed. He and Helen both looked at it.

"'*Golden Butterfly*,'" Aikawa repeated, reading the name which had appeared as the incoming merchantship brought its transponder on-line and CIC updated the plot. "They think up some pretty screwy names for merchies, don't they?"

"See?" Duan smiled as Montana System Flight Control accepted their ID and the ostensible reason for their visit. The pleasant young woman who'd taken their call hadn't even fussed very hard over the previous absence of any transponder code, and Sandkaran had been suitably apologetic. Now he was turning the microphone over to Azadeh Shirafkin, *Marianne*'s—or, for the moment, *Golden Butterfly*'s—purser.

"I told you," Duan went on to De Chabrol and Egervary as the young woman made sympathetic noises over Shirafkin's explanation of their supposed emergency. "We'll just slide in under their radar horizon by not calling any attention to ourselves, pick up our new oxygen tank, and then—very quietly—get the hell out of here again."

"It works for me," Egervary said fervently.

Aikawa Kagiyama felt bored. Standing a tactical watch was all very well, but it would have been nice if there'd been something a bit more energetic than Montana's anemic traffic to keep an eye on. Even the arrival of a typical tramp for a routine repair call was a welcome diversion . . . which said something significant about just how boring things had been *before* the weirdly named *Golden Butterfly* arrived.

For want of anything else to do, he decided to run a tracking exercise on the freighter, which was now less than fifteen minutes from entering orbit. She was moving at barely 1,703 KPS, and only 736,096 kilometers out, and he had an almost perfect sensor angle, right up the kilt of her wedge.

He studied the information on his display. Aside from the fact that her active sensor emissions seemed just a bit more energetic than he would have expected out of a ship like her, the data was thoroughly uninteresting. He almost pulled the sensors off of her, then shrugged. If he was bored, the ratings manning CIC probably were, as well. He might as well give them something to do, too, so he punched in the command for a routine evaluation of the ship.

He wasn't at all prepared for what came back a moment later.

Helen was no longer sitting at Tactical. Lieutenant Commander Kaplan was, and Helen actually found it a bit difficult to see the plot from where she stood. Perhaps that was because Abigail Hearns, Guthrie Bagwell, Ansten FitzGerald, and Captain Terekhov were all crowded in, peering over Kaplan's shoulder as a noticeably nervous Aikawa took the lot of them back through his impromptu tracking exercise.

". . . so, then, Ma'am, I asked CIC to do an evaluation. Just as a drill. I never expected to get *this* back from them."

He looked up at the circle of astronomically senior faces looming over him, and Captain Terekhov's hand gripped his shoulder.

"Good work, Aikawa," he said quietly. "*Very* good work."

"Skipper," Aikawa's face flushed with obvious pleasure, "I wish I deserved the credit. But it was just one of those things. I can't even say I had 'a feeling,' because I sure as heck didn't!"

"That doesn't matter," FitzGerald told him. "What matters is that you *did* it."

"Even that wouldn't have mattered if you hadn't had Abigail and me pull in everything we could while we were in Kornati orbit, Skipper," Kaplan pointed out.

Terekhov nodded almost absently, his mind busy.

Whoever that was over there, he doubted very much that the ship's real name was *Golden Butterfly*. And he was quite certain the other vessel's commander had no idea *Hexapuma* had gotten a complete emissions map off of her before she left Split. If he'd even suspected that, he would never have been stupid enough to try using a false transponder code.

"Whoever that is, he's gutsy," FitzGerald remarked. Aikawa looked up at him, and the XO snorted. "Coming right up on us this way takes about a kiloton of nerve. We've been squawking our transponder ever since we went into orbit, so he has to know who we are."

"Might be nerve," Kaplan said. "But it could be desperation, too. I'm betting there's either something here on Montana he absolutely has to do, or else he didn't realize we were here until it was too late to do anything but come on in and ask for a parking orbit of his own."

"I'm inclined to think you're right, Guns," Terekhov said. "Or even that it's both—something he has to do *and* a late pickup on our presence. The question is what we do about it."

"Well, Sir," Abigail said, "we know one of the two transponder codes they've used must be false. For all we know both of them may, but at least one has to be bogus. That's sufficient reason to board and examine her under interstellar law, isn't it?"

"Yes, it is," Terekhov agreed. "And I think that's what we'll do." He turned to FitzGerald. "Get hold of Tadislaw, Ansten. Tell him I'll want a boarding party ready to go within the next fifteen minutes."

"Skipper, you know she's armed," FitzGerald said. "We picked up that much in Split, and look how quickly she got here. Whatever else she is, she *isn't* a standard merchie. We don't know what else they may have hidden away over there."

"Can't be helped," Terekhov replied. "According to this," he tapped the detailed readout from the Split data, "she's got two lasers in each broadside plus some point defense. It'll take her at least five or ten minutes to clear away the broadside weapons, and there's no way she can do that at this range without our seeing it coming. Same for anything she has hidden, except that she'll have to take the time to clear away the false plating or whatever over it first, as well. Her point defense could come up faster, but it's not going to hurt us if we clear for action ourselves before we tell her we're coming to visit. Unless they've got some sort of death wish, they're not going to argue with a heavy cruiser that's obviously ready to turn them into drifting wreckage."

"Flight Ops, Hawk-Papa-One is ready to depart."

Ragnhild Pavletic heard the edge of excitement sharpening her tone and forced herself to step back from it just a bit.

"Hawk-Papa-One, Flight Ops. You are cleared to depart. No traffic, repeat, no traffic."

"Flight Ops, Hawk-Papa-One copies no traffic on flight path and cleared to depart. Departing now."

The sharpness had smoothed back down into properly crisp professionalism, she was pleased to note as she fed power to the thrusters. They goosed the pinnace sharply, pushing the small craft clear of *Hexapuma*'s radar shadow, and she watched her proximity radar. Hawk-Papa-One cleared the pinnace's impeller wedge safety perimeter quickly, and the pressure of acceleration vanished as she brought the wedge up and went to four hundred gravities.

She'd left the flight deck hatch open, and she glanced over her shoulder through it, past the small cubbyhole of the flight engineer. Lieutenant Hedges and a full squad of his platoon occupied about a third of the passenger compartment.

"Attention freighter *Golden Butterfly*!" She heard the Skipper's voice come up on the com as she settled down on course for the freighter. "*Golden Butterfly*, this is Captain Terekhov of Her Majesty's Starship *Hexapuma*. You are ordered to stand by for boarding and examination. My boarding party is *en route* now. You will open your hatches immediately."

"—will open your hatches immediately."

"*Jesus Christ!*" Egervary gasped, and Duan Binyan snapped upright in his chair. He heard Annette De Chabrol inhale sharply, but it scarcely registered. He was staring at his plot, where the Manticoran heavy cruiser's impeller wedge had just snapped up. Even as he watched, her sidewalls were coming up, as well, and her broadside energy mounts were training out as she went to battle stations.

"So much for they'll never suspect anything!" Egervary half-shouted, wheeling towards Duan. "They knew all along, goddamn it, just like I said! They were fucking *waiting* for us and we fucking well sailed right up to them!"

"Shut up!" Duan snapped.

"Why? What the fuck does it matter now? We're dead—we are fucking *dead*! When they come aboard, find out what we are, they'll—"

"He said to shut up, Zeno," Annette said viciously, turning on the security officer with a snarl, "so goddamn *shut your face*!"

Egervary managed to clamp his jaws together, but his facial muscles twitched and jumped and a thick sheen of sweat oozed down his forehead. His hands trembled visibly, and he turned back to his console with something almost like a whimper.

Duan Binyan wanted to whimper himself.

The money was always good for someone willing to serve on one of the Jessyk Combine's "special ships," and the risks weren't really all *that* great. Despite the best efforts of people like the Star Kingdom of Manticore and the Republic of Haven, no more than five percent of slave ships were ever apprehended. Most were stopped by people like the Solarian League, where, by and large, the worst a crewman had to worry about was a brief incarceration before the Combine or Manpower bribed him out of jail. No more than a handful were stopped by the Star Kingdom or the Republic in any given year. But the crews on that handful were seldom ever heard of again. Manticore and Haven, for all they hated one another, both took genetic slaving seriously, and the penalty under the law of either star nation was death.

But the odds against being one of those handful of ships were so high, and the money was so good, Jessyk could always find someone to take the chance. Someone like Duan Binyan, who suddenly realized all the money in the galaxy was no use at all to a dead man.

"What are we going to do, Binyan?" De Chabrol asked urgently, her voice lowered so only he could hear.

"I don't—" Duan broke off and wiped perspiration from his own face. "I don't think there's anything we *can* do, Annette," he admitted hoarsely. "That's a *heavy cruiser*. She can turn us into vapor anytime she feels like it. If we don't open the hatches, she may just decide to do it. Or, just as bad, she'll blow her way in, and her Marines will come in shooting. Do you want Marines in battle armor burning down that hatch?" he demanded, jerking a thumb at the bridge lift hatch.

"But they're *Manties*," she protested, her eyes desperate. It was all she had to say, and Duan's mouth tightened.

"What do you want me to say, Annette? If we let them in and they find out what we are, they may kill us—all right," he said quickly as she opened her mouth, "they probably *will* kill us! But if we try to stop them, there's no question what'll happen. At least if we open up, we'll live a little longer!"

"I say blow the fucking ship and take the motherless bastards with us!" Egervary said. Duan wheeled towards him, and the security officer bared his teeth in a rictuslike grin. His dark eyes were huge, and his nostrils flared. "Those holier-than-thou motherfuckers are all so hot to kill anyone who does anything *they* don't approve of! Who the hell died and made them God? I say we take as many to hell with us as we can!"

"That's the stupidest thing you've said yet!" Duan snapped. "You may want to die, but I sure don't!"

"Like what you want's going to make a difference!" Egervary jeered. "We're *dead*, Binyan. That's what happens when the Manties come on board. Well, if I've got to die, so do they!"

The security officer hovered on the brink of outright madness in his terror, Duan realized. And that terror, as all too often happened, was feeding his rage, fanning it like a furnace.

"No," the captain said flatly, forcing his voice to project a calm he was far from feeling. "We're going to do exactly what they tell us to, Zeno. *Exactly*."

"You think so?" Egervary's grin was wider and more maniacal than ever, and he whipped back around to his panel.

Duan Binyan had an instant to realize what that grin had meant, and he lunged towards the security officer screaming in protest.

"Stand by, Lieutenant Hedges," Ragnhild said. "We'll be coming up on her main personnel hatch in another five minutes."

"Right, Ragnhild," Michael Hedges acknowledged with a smile.

He was one of the very few people serving in *Hexapuma* who looked almost as young as Ragnhild did. It was unfortunate that he'd had the bad judgment to become a Marine rather than a *Navy* officer, but he was awfully cute anyway. Of course, he was considerably senior to her, but Regs only prohibited relationships between officers in the same chain of command. Technically, that included Marines aboard a ship, but it was a technicality that was winked at most of the time. So maybe it wasn't such a bad thing he was a Marine after all. . . .

She smiled back at him and returned her attention to her HUD, and one eyebrow rose as she saw half a dozen patches of plating blowing away from the freighter's hull. One of the sudden openings was almost directly in front of the pinnace, and she saw something in it. It was an indistinct, barely visible shape, but there was something naggingly familiar about that half-glimpsed form, and it seemed to be turning to point in her direction.

God, it's a—!

Ragnhild Pavletic never completed the thought.

The universe punched Helen Zilwicki in the belly. Nothing else could have explained the sudden, hoarse exhalation. The way her heart stopped and her lungs froze as Hawk-Papa-One exploded.

Point defense cluster, an icy voice said in the back of her brain, clear and precise—a stranger's voice, surely not her own.

Shock at the sheer, suicidal stupidity of what they'd just seen gripped every officer on *Hexapuma*'s bridge. Every officer but one.

"Laser clusters only—force neutralization!" Captain Aivars Aleksandrovich Terekhov snapped. "*Fire!*"

"*You fucking idiot!*" Duan howled.

His hands closed on Egervary's neck from behind. His shoulders and arms heaved ferociously, and the security officer flew up out of his seat. All Duan had really been thinking about was getting the maniac away from the tactical panel before he did something even stupider—as if there'd been anything stupider he *could* do! He succeeded in that, but the savage, panic-driven strength with which he tore Egervary away from the console also snapped the man's neck like a stick.

The corpse was still in midair when *Hexapuma* fired.

The range was less than four thousand kilometers.

At that range, point defense lasers capable of taking out incoming, wildly evading missiles at ranges of sixty or seventy thousand kilometers were more than enough to deal with any unarmored target not protected by a sidewall or an impeller wedge. It wasn't often that a warship had the opportunity to use its point defense against even hostile small craft, far less another starship, because nobody was insane enough not to surrender when a naval vessel got that close.

Usually, at any rate.

The good news for *Marianne* was that *Hexapuma*'s laser clusters were far less powerful than her broadside energy mounts. One of the heavy cruiser's grasers would have blown entirely through the freighter's civilian hull, and probably broken her back in the process. The laser clusters wouldn't do that, but dozens of them studded each of *Hexapuma*'s flanks, and the Royal Manticoran Navy believed in being prepared. Rare though the opportunity to use the normally defensive weapons offensively might have been, BuWeaps had considered how best to do so when the chance offered itself, and Naomi Kaplan's vengeful finger punched up a stored fire plan. The tactical computer considered the data coming back to it from the active sensors briefly—*very* briefly—then established its targets, assigned each of them a threat value, assigned them to specific point defense stations, and opened fire.

Stilettos of coherent light stabbed out from *Hexapuma*. Each of a cluster's eight lasers was capable of cycling at one shot every sixteen seconds. That was one shot every two seconds from every cluster in *Hexapuma*'s starboard broadside and *Marianne*'s hull plating seemed to erupt outward. The strobing laser clusters tracked across her, precisely, carefully, almost literally unable to miss at such an absurdly short range, as *Hexapuma* savaged the ship which had killed her pinnace. They scourged her with whips of barbed energy, shattering and smashing, wiping away weapons, sensors, impeller nodes.

It took precisely twenty-three seconds from the instant Terekhov gave the command to fire to reduce the ship which had just murdered eighteen of his people to a shattered, broken wreck that would never move under its own power again.

Alarms screamed. The bridge quivered and jerked like a small boat in a gale as *Marianne*'s four-million-ton hull shuddered in agony. Transfer energy hammered her as *Hexapuma*'s fury flayed alloy flesh from her bones.

There were other screams, here and there throughout her hull. Human screams, not electronic ones, and—for the most part—very brief. Low-powered laser clusters might be, compared to regular broadside weapons, but atmosphere belched out of the holes smashed into her. Some of it came from cargo holds, but most came from the ship's compartments. From impeller rooms which were torn open by laser talons, spilling men and women in coveralls and shirt sleeves into the merciless vacuum. From passageways inboard from targeted laser clusters. From berthing quarters directly inboard from her broadside lasers. From messing compartments inboard from her main broadside sensor array.

There were fifty-seven men and women aboard *Marianne* before *Hexapuma* fired. That was an extraordinarily large crew for a merchantship, but then most merchantships never had to worry about cargoes of desperate slaves.

By the time Zeno Egervary's body hit the deck and stopped sliding, there were fourteen still-living men and women aboard the freighter's shredded wreck.

"*Cease fire!*" the terror-distorted voice screamed over the com. "*For God's sake, cease fire!* We surrender! *We surrender!*"

Aivars Terekhov's face was like hammered iron. His visual display showed the rapidly dispersing wreckage of Ragnhild Pavletic's pinnace. The pieces were very, very small.

"Who's speaking?" Frozen helium was warmer than that voice.

"This is . . . this is Duan Binyan," the other voice gasped, jagged and shrill with panic. "I'm . . . I was the captain, but I swear to God I never ordered that! *I swear it!*"

"Whether you ordered it or not, it was your responsibility, *Captain*," Terekhov said with a flat, terrible emphasis. "I will be sending a second pinnace. This one will contain a full platoon of battle-armored Marines. At the first sign of resistance, they will employ lethal force. Is that understood, *Captain*?"

"Yes. *Yes!*"

"Then understand this, as well. You've just murdered men and women of the armed forces of the Star Kingdom of Manticore. As such you are guilty, at the very least, of piracy, for which the sentence is death. I suggest, *Captain*, that you spend the next few minutes trying to think of some reason I might consider letting you continue to live."

Aivars Terekhov smiled. It was a terrifying expression.

"Think hard, *Captain*," he advised almost gently. "Think *very* hard."

Chapter Forty-Eight

Helen knelt on the decksole and slowly, carefully dialed the locker's combination. Aikawa was on duty—the Captain was keeping him there, she knew, because he blamed himself. If he hadn't identified the freighter, none of this would have happened. It was foolish to condemn himself for it, but he did, and the Skipper was too wise to let him sit and brood.

But someone had to do this, and it was Helen's job.

Her hands shook as she gently lifted the lid, and she blinked hard, trying to clear her eyes of the sudden tears. She couldn't. They came too hard, too fast, and she covered her mouth with her hands, rocking on her knees as she wept silently. She couldn't do this. She couldn't. But she had to. It was the last thing she would ever be able to do for her friend . . . and she couldn't.

She didn't hear the hatch open behind her. She was too lost in her grief. But she felt the hand on her shoulder, and she looked up quickly.

Paulo d'Arezzo looked down at her, his handsome face tight with grief of its own. She stared up into his gray eyes through tear-spangled vision, and he went down into a crouch beside her.

"I can't," she whispered almost inaudibly. "I can't *do* this, Paulo."

"I'm sorry," he said softly, and her sobs broke free at last. He went fully to his knees, and before she knew what was happening, his arms were around her, holding her. She started to pull away—not from the embrace, but from the humiliation of her weakness. But she couldn't do that, either. The arms around her tightened, holding her with gently implacable strength, and a hand touched the back of her head.

"She was your friend," Paulo said softly into her ear. "You loved her. Go ahead. Cry for her . . . and then I'll help you do this."

It was too much. It broke her control, and with it her resistance, and she pressed her face into his shoulder and wept for her dead.

Aivars Terekhov walked into the bridge briefing room with a face of battle steel. His blue eyes were hard and cold, and grief-fired rage slept only uneasily behind that azure ice.

Captain Tadislaw Kaczmarczyk followed him into the compartment. The Marine peeled off to take a seat beside Guthrie Bagwell, but Terekhov crossed to the head of the table and took his place, then let his eyes range over the officers gathered around it.

Abigail Hearns looked as if she'd wept, yet there was a calmness, almost a serenity, about her at odds with everyone else in the compartment. There was steel under the serenity, the unyielding and inflexible steel of Grayson, but there was acceptance, too. Not forgiveness for the people who'd murdered her midshipwoman, but the acceptance that to care—to love—was to surrender one's self to the pain of loss . . . and that to refuse to love was to refuse to live.

Naomi Kaplan showed no acceptance. Not yet. The fury still smoked in her dark brown eyes, hot from hatred's forge. There wasn't enough vengeance in the universe to slake Kaplan's ferocious rage, but enough time hadn't yet passed for her to realize that.

Ansten FitzGerald, Guthrie Bagwell, Ginger Lewis, Tadislaw Kaczmarczyk, and Amal Nagchaudhuri were all, to greater or lesser extent, mirrors of Kaplan.

It was the suddenness of it, Terekhov thought. The stupidity. These people—all of them, even, or especially, Abigail—had seen combat. Had seen people killed. Lost friends. But the incredible, casual speed with which a young midshipwoman, the crew of Hawk-Papa-One, and fifteen Marines had been wiped away before their eyes . . . That was something else. And all of it had been for absolutely nothing. The man who'd apparently killed them out of panic and terror-induced vengefulness was dead. So were the vast majority of his crew mates.

All for nothing, he thought, remembering Ragnhild's face, all the times she'd piloted his pinnace. Remembering how she'd tried to hide her frustration at the youthfulness of her appearance, her joy when the pinnace gave her wings. Remembering all the incredible promise of the life which had been wiped away as if it had never existed.

No, he told himself, angry with his own thoughts. *No, not as if she'd never existed. She* did *exist. That's why this* hurts *so much.*

"Before I say anything else," he said quietly, "there will be no self-recrimination. If anyone in this ship is to blame for what happened to our people on that pinnace, that person is me. I sent them across, knowing that ship was armed."

People stirred around the table. Most of them looked away. But Abigail Hearns looked straight into his eyes, and shook her head. She said nothing, yet she didn't need to, and somehow Terekhov found himself looking back into her eyes. And then, to his own surprise, he nodded once, accepting her gentle correction.

"Skipper," FitzGerald began, "you couldn't have—"

"I didn't say I made the wrong decision, based on the information we had, Ansten," Terekhov interrupted.

"We're Queen's officers. Queen's officers die in the line of duty. And Queen's officers send other people places where *they* die. Someone had to take that pinnace across, and as I said at the time, only a lunatic would've tried to stop it. One did." He inhaled deeply. "But it was still their job to go, and my job to send them. I did. No one else in this ship did. I will not have any officer—or midshipman—under my command blaming himself for not possessing the godlike power of clairvoyance to predict what was going to happen."

He let his eyes circle the table one more time, and this time all of them looked back at him. He nodded in satisfaction, then flipped his right hand and turned his attention to Kaczmarczyk.

"Tadislaw, suppose you brief everyone on what we've learned so far."

"Yes, Sir." Kaczmarczyk drew his memo pad from the case at his belt and keyed the display alive.

"This vessel belonged to the Jessyk Combine," he began. "Given its construction and outfitting, it clearly falls under the equipment clause of the Cherwell Convention. As such, all members of its crew are legally liable to the death sentence, even without reference to what happened to Hawk-Papa-One. They realize this, and the surviving personnel are falling all over themselves trying to provide sufficient information to buy their lives.

"What we've learned so far—"

Stephen Westman watched the air car settle beside the tent once again.

Maybe I should just leave it permanently set up here, he thought wryly. *It'd be a lot less work than constantly putting it up and taking it down again.*

The hatches opened and the familiar "guests" climbed out once more. But this time, the midshipwoman wasn't present, and he felt a flicker of surprise.

Greetings were exchanged, and then he, Terekhov, Van Dort, and Trevor Bannister were once again seated around the camp table.

"I have to say this is a surprise," he said. "I sort of figured you'd leave me to stew a mite longer."

"We planned to," Van Dort said. "But something's come up. Something you should know about before you make any decisions."

"Like what?" Westman recognized the hardness that crept into his voice whenever he addressed Bernardus Van Dort. He did his best to restrain it, but a lifetime of hostility couldn't be that readily overcome even by someone who was positive he wanted to overcome it. And Westman remained far from certain he did.

"You may have noticed Ms. Zilwicki isn't with us," Terekhov said, pulling the Montanan's eyes to him. "I've relieved her of all other duties to allow her to deal with the effects of Midshipwoman Pavletic."

Westman stiffened in his chair. He remembered the other midshipwoman. He hadn't met her, the way he had Zilwicki, but some of his . . . friends in Brewster had managed to get pictures of her when they photographed Terekhov's planeted pinnace, and he remembered the way they'd joked about how young she looked.

"Effects?" he repeated.

"Yes. Ms. Pavletic, the flight crew of her pinnace, and fifteen of my Marines were killed five hours before the Chief Marshal contacted you. Their pinnace was destroyed by an armed merchantship in orbit around Montana."

The Manticoran's voice was crisper than ever, Westman noticed. The words came quickly and sharply, with the honed steel edges of a bowie knife. And then he saw the same steel in the blue eyes regarding him across the table.

"That vessel, Mr. Westman, was here to deliver weapons to you." Westman felt his heart miss a beat, and a sudden, icy chill went through him. "She was squawking the transponder code of a vessel registered as the *Golden Butterfly*, but her actual name, inasmuch as she had one, was apparently *Marianne*. She sailed directly from Split, where she'd delivered a sizable consignment of weapons to Ms. Nordbrandt, as arranged by a gentleman going by the name of 'Firebrand' for something called the Central Liberation Committee. Does any of this ring a bell, Mr. Westman?"

"Parts of it," he acknowledged, returning Terekhov's gaze steadily. "If you want me to say I'm sorry to hear about the loss of your people, I am," he continued, hoping the Manticoran heard the sincerity in his voice. "But while I personally had nothing to do with their deaths, I'd point out that it was the threat of open warfare here on Montana that brought you to this star system. I regret the losses you've suffered. I don't apologize for seeking the weapons and equipment I require from someone who willingly offered them to me."

"Ah, yes. The generous and altruistic Mr. Firebrand," Van Dort said. Westman realized that the two off-worlders were double-teaming him. Unfortunately, the recognition didn't make the tactic any less effective.

"*Marianne*'s surviving crew members—there weren't many—were most eager to tell us anything we wanted to know," the Rembrandter continued. "I think *you* should know what they told us, as well. But before I share that with you, I'd like Trevor to comment on what I'm about to tell you."

Westman looked at Van Dort's brother-in-law. The Chief Marshal looked as if he would have preferred being somewhere else, but his eyes were as steady as ever as he returned Westman's gaze.

"My people sat in on the interrogations, Steve," he said flatly. "I've viewed recordings of the pertinent portions of them. And Captain Terekhov's people got the *Marianne*'s computers pretty much intact. One of the prisoners, an Annette De Chabrol, took down the security protocols so they could access them. The output I've seen so far confirms what the surviving crew members have told us."

Westman looked at him for a few more moments, then nodded slowly. He understood why Van Dort—or Terekhov—had ensured that Bannister would be able to verify the truthfulness, or at least accuracy, of whatever they were about to tell him.

"*Marianne*," Van Dort's flat voice reclaimed Westman's attention, "wasn't working for anything called the Central Liberation Committee. To the best of her crew's knowledge, there *is* no Central Liberation Committee. *Marianne* was owned and operated by the Jessyk Combine."

Westman felt the sudden shock congealing his features, but there was nothing he could do about it. *Jessyk Combine?* Impossible!

"The weapons were being delivered to 'resistance groups' in the Cluster on the direct orders of Isabel Bardasano, a cadet member of the Jessyk Board of Directors who specializes in covert operations, 'wet work,' and the transportation of genetic slaves," Van Dort continued implacably. "*Marianne* was equipped and outfitted as a slaver. She *was* a slaver, and the survivors of her crew include her commanding officer, who's carried out quite a few 'special operations' for Jessyk over the years. As far as he's aware, this was simply one more."

He stopped. Just like that. He simply stopped talking, sat back in his chair, and looked at Westman across the table.

Westman looked back—*stared* back—in stunned disbelief. It couldn't be. It couldn't! Why should the Jessyk Combine, one of the worst of the Mesan transstellars, provide weapons to a resistance movement determined to keep *all* off-worlders off of Montanan soil? It didn't make sense!

And yet. . . .

And yet it did. His jaw clenched as he realized his worst suspicions about Firebrand had fallen far, far short of the truth. Whatever he'd thought he was accomplishing, "Firebrand" and his masters had been *using* him,

The realization was sickening. But even worse was the question of *why* they'd done it. He tried desperately to avoid the inevitable conclusion, but his own accursed integrity wouldn't let him. It forced him to look the truth squarely in the eye.

The only reason any Mesan corporation would have helped him keep the Star Kingdom out of Montana was to hold the door open for Frontier Security. If he succeeded in driving Manticore out, it would only be to let Frontier Security—and Mesa—in instead.

"I—" he began finally, only to stop. He cleared his throat. "I didn't know Mesa was involved," he said. "The fact that it was doesn't necessarily mean Manticore wears a white hat—" his eyes flicked to Terekhov's white beret almost against his will, and he snatched them back under control as he continued "—but that's no excuse for dealing with someone like Mesa."

"Mesa may not be the only one you were dealing with, Steve," Bannister said heavily. "According to the bastards aboard that ship, their next port of call wasn't Mesa—it was Monica."

"*Monica?*" Westman didn't even tried to hide his confusion this time.

"Yep." Bannister nodded. "Monica. Their entire supply mission was staged through 'President' Tyler's little playground. And, as I expect you'll recall, the biggest single customer for Monica's mercenaries is the Office of Frontier Security. So what does that say about the people who were lining up to help you so eagerly?"

"It says," Westman said slowly, "that there's fools and then there's damned fools. And I reckon that this time around, I've been one of the *damned* fools. And whatever I may think of the Star Kingdom of Manticore, *or* of Rembrandt, I expect that this time I owe you gentlemen my thanks. If I'd accepted the 'assistance' of scum like that, I'd have slit my own throat when I found out afterward."

"The question, Steve," Bannister said, "is what you're going to do now you *have* found out. You're a stubborn man, even for a Montanan. Hell, you hold *my* grudges longer than I do! But it's time you faced the truth, boy. I know you're pissed at Rembrandt for what it's done to Montana. All right, you've got a right to be. I know you're pissed at Bernardus, and I know why. Personally, I reckon we've nursed that particular pet hate long enough Suzanne would be kicking us both in the ass if she were here now. But that's up to you. I'm not going to tell you how to feel about Bernardus as a man. But as Baroness Medusa's representative, I think you'd damned well better listen to what he's saying, because it's the truth, Steve. The *truth*. The Star Kingdom of Manticore may not be perfect, but it's one *damned* sight better than anything we're ever going to get out of Frontier Security and somebody like Mesa. Smell the coffee, Steve."

Stephen Westman looked at his oldest friend, and knew—however fiercely he might fight against admitting it—that Trevor was right. He struggled with himself, and with his stubborn, Montanan pride, for endless seconds. Then he inhaled deeply.

"All right, Trevor," he said wearily. "Expect you're right. It just plain goes against the grain to admit I've been *that* stupid. I don't say I like it. And don't you go expecting me to ever love Manticore or—especially!—Rembrandt. But I'll allow as how neither one of them can hold a candle to what Frontier Security'd do to us. And I will be *damned* if I'll let myself or my people be used by something like Mesa. Of course, I'll have to talk it over with the boys before we make any hard and fast decisions, you realize."

"You do that. And I expect you might find it a mite easier to talk them around if you mention what Bernardus here negotiated with President Suttles before we came out for this little visit."

Westman looked a question at him, and the Chief Marshal chuckled.

"Old Bernardus may not be up to Ineka Vaandrager's weight as a pure, dyed-in-the-wool bitch, but he's a pretty persuasive negotiator in his own right. He started by saying Rembrandt'll refuse to press charges for the destruction of its enclave here on Montana. He followed that up by telling the President he already had Baroness Medusa's approval of an amnesty offer for all of you on the part of the Star Kingdom if you'd surrender your weapons and give up all this nonsense. And he suggested to the President that if Rembrandt was prepared to forgive you, and Manticore was prepared to forgive you, it might just be he ought to consider exercising his pardoning power to promise you boys amnesty under Montanan law if you lay down your guns."

"Are you serious?" Westman looked at Bannister, then back and forth between him and Van Dort and Terekhov. Bannister only chuckled, and Westman felt his jaw set. "I never asked for any favors, Trevor! I went into this with my eyes open. I'm willing to face the music for what I did!"

"No doubt you are, Mr. Westman," Terekhov said. "I can respect that, even if it does seem just a little stiff-necked even for a Montanan. But however willing *you* may be to face the music, don't you think you owe it to your men to accept the offer for them? Or, at least, to give them the option?"

Westman glared at him for a few seconds. Then his shoulders slumped and he shook his head wearily.

"Reckon you're right," he sighed. "I reckon you're right."

"So you think he'll come in, Captain Terekhov?" Warren Suttles asked.

"I think he will, Mr. President. On the other hand, I'm not the best judge of the way Mr. Westman's, or any other Montanan's, mind works. No offense, Sir."

"None taken," Suttles said with a smile, and looked at Bannister. "Your opinion, Chief Marshal?"

"Oh, he'll come in, Mr. President," Bannister said confidently. "He'll kick, and he'll whine, and he'll bellyache. And come a few more T-years down the road, he'll point at every little thing that goes wrong and tell me how much better it would've been if he'd only kept Manticore out of our system. But that's Steve. He'll always be crossgrained and ornery as a pseudorattler with a broken tooth. But if he gives you his word, he'll keep it. And when he starts bellyaching down the road, he'll know he's just making a fool out of himself, and it won't bother him a bit."

Suttles' smile turned into a chuckle, and he shook his head.

"If he'll just stop blowing up the planet, I can live with all of that," the President said. "I can even live with how pissed off the rest of the Cabinet's going to be when I announce the amnesty!"

Chapter Forty-Nine

"Thank you for joining us, Madam President," Andrija Gazi said, smiling as Aleksandra Tonkovic walked regally into the hearing room and settled herself behind the long, polished witness' table.

"The Planetary President is the servant of Parliament, Mr. Chairman," Tonkovic replied, with a smile as gracious as Gazi's own. "It's my pleasure to appear before the committee and to provide any information it may require."

"We appreciate that, Madam President. It makes a refreshing change from some chief executives with whom Parliament's been forced to deal."

Gazi's smile was thinner this time, and Tonkovic was careful not to return it at all. Gazi was a member of her own Democratic Centralist Party, as well as Chairman of the Special Committee on Annexation. She'd taken pains to be certain Andrija wound up in that position, and she was glad now that she had. But she couldn't appear publicly to support his barbed comments about the acting chief executive Parliament had been forced to deal with while she was in Spindle.

Twelve days had passed since she'd received the

summons to return home. It felt both much longer and far shorter as she sat in the sunlight spilling through the conference room's tall windows. From where she sat, she could see the Nemanja Building, surrounded by the scaffolding of repair work. She'd been surprised by how much that firsthand sight of the damage Nordbrandt had wreaked had shaken her, but she had no time to think about that right now. She'd spent three days of frenetic activity on Flax, doing her best to ensure the Constitutional Liberal Party's effectiveness in her absence. Then she'd made the eight-and-a-half-day voyage home, studying her notes, thinking about her committee appearances, and—much though she hated to admit it—worrying. She'd arrived late the previous afternoon, and there simply hadn't been time for her to touch bases with many of her allies. The DCP's general secretary had given her the best briefing he could in the time available, and she'd had dinner with a dozen party leaders, but she was only too well aware of how long she'd been off-world. It was a good thing she was starting with Gazi's committee. Under his management, she'd have a little more time to get her feet back under her before the more adversarial proceedings to come.

"For the most part," Gazi continued, "this will be an informal examination. Unless the situation seems to require it, we'll relax the full rigor of standard parliamentary procedure. We'll invite you, Madam President, to make a brief report on the progress of the Constitutional Convention and its deliberations. Thereafter, each member of the Special Committee will be allocated fifteen minutes in which to inquire more fully into points of particular interest.

"I understand you'll also be appearing before Deputy Krizanic's committee this afternoon." Gazi allowed the merest flicker of distaste to dance across his well-trained features, but his urbane voice went smoothly on. "We thought our own day's business should be concluded by the noon hour, and that we would then break for lunch. In light of your appointment with Deputy Krizanic and her committee, we're planning to adjourn for the day at that time in order to give you some time to refresh yourself and rest between committee appearances. We would, therefore, also request that you make time available to appear before us on Thursday, as well. At that time, the Special Committee's members will each be allotted an additional thirty minutes in order to pursue more fully the points which particularly interest them. Would that be acceptable to you, Madam President?"

"Chairman Gazi, my time is Parliament's. My only concern would be to prevent conflicts between the committees' schedules. I feel confident I can rely on you and Chairwoman Krizanic to avoid that."

"As always, Madam President, you are as gracious as you are diligent in our planet's service," Gazi said, beaming upon her in his best statesman's fashion. She inclined her head with proper modesty, and he cleared his throat and rapped his gavel once, sharply, on the wooden block beside his microphone.

"In that case, the Committee will come to order." The eight men and women behind the raised, horseshoe-shaped table at the head of the hearing room sat a bit straighter, and Gazi nodded to Tonkovic.

"If you'd care to begin, Madam President."

"Thank you, Mr. Chairman."

She took a sip of water and made a minor production out of arranging her old-fashioned notecards before her on the table. Then she looked up with a smile that was both confident and sober.

"Mr. Chairman, Ms. Vice Chairman, Honorable Members of the Committee. As you all know, following the plebiscite vote, it was decided by Parliament that the delegation to the Constitutional Convention on Flax should be headed by our own head of state. Accordingly, as Parliament had directed, I made arrangements to transfer authority to my Vice President and departed for the Spindle System. Once there—"

Gazi and the other members of the committee listened attentively, nodding occasionally, as she launched into her account of her stewardship of Kornati's interests at the convention.

"Thank you, Madam President," Gazi said the better part of an hour later. "You've been speaking for some time now. Would you like to take a short recess before we proceed?"

"No, thank you, Mr. Chairman." She smiled again, a bit more impishly this time. "I've spent sufficient time in Parliament myself to develop my endurance as a speaker," she added demurely.

A general chuckle ran around the hearing room, and several committee members actually allowed themselves to laugh. Gazi rationed himself to a decorous, appreciative chuckle and shook his head at her with an answering smile.

"Very well then, Madam President. In that case, we'll proceed to the members' allocated time. Deputy Ranjina?"

"Thank you, Mr. Chairman," Tamara Ranjina said. "And thank you, Madam President, for that thorough presentation."

Tonkovic inclined her head in a gracious nod. Anything more would have been too effusive, given that Ranjina was the ranking Reconciliation Party member of the Special Committee. Under Parliament's rules, that made her Gazi's Vice Chairwoman, although it was extremely unlikely Andrija had maintained anything closer than a politely frosty relationship with her. Personally, Tonkovic considered Ranjina a nonentity. It had always puzzled her why someone who'd once enjoyed a secure niche within the Social Moderate Party should have shifted her allegiance to the Reconciliationists.

"Madam President," Ranjina continued now, her tone pleasant, "I listened with considerable interest to your account of your representation of Kornati at the Constitutional Convention. There are, however, one or two points upon which I still remain just a little bit confused. Perhaps you could illuminate my confusion for me?"

"I'll certainly be happy to attempt to, Madam Vice Chairwoman."

"Thank you. There was one minor element about your otherwise comprehensive report which struck me as a little odd, Madam President. I refer to the fact that Baroness Medusa, Queen Elizabeth's Provisional Governor, repeatedly and specifically informed you that your delaying tactics at the Convention were threatening to derail not simply the Convention but the entire annexation effort and that you didn't see fit to report that information to this committee. Could you possibly explain why that was?"

Ranjina's pleasant voice never changed. The smile never left her face. Yet her question hit the hearing room like a hand grenade. Gazi's face turned an alarming shade of puce. Two of the other committee members appeared as dumbfounded—and enraged—as their chairman, and a single heartbeat of silence hovered in the question's wake. Then the stunned silence vanished into a rising turmoil of whispered agitation among the staffers sitting behind the committee members and those sitting behind Tonkovic herself.

For her own part, Tonkovic felt herself staring in sheer, incredulous shock at the woman on the other side of the horseshoe. She couldn't believe Ranjina had possessed the unadulterated gall to make such an outrageous statement in an open committee hearing. It simply wasn't done. One didn't seek to ambush and humiliate the Planetary President! It was obvious from Gazi's reaction that Ranjina had given him no hint of what she intended to say. Clearly the treacherous bitch had realized the chairman would have muzzled her—or, at the very least, warned Tonkovic—if he'd dreamed she was about to launch such a crude, bare-knuckled assault on the dignity of Tonkovic's office.

It took the President several seconds to be certain she had control of her own temper. She bitterly begrudged the delay, the way it made her look unprepared and caught off guard, but she knew the one thing she couldn't afford to do in front of the news services' cameras was to give the impertinent bitch the tongue-lashing she so abundantly deserved.

"Madam Vice Chairwoman," she said then, coldly, "Spindle is seven and a half days away from Split, even by dispatch boat. Given that communications delay—fifteen days, I would remind you, for two-way message transmission—it was my responsibility as Kornati's representative to the Convention, *and* as Planetary President, to determine how best to proceed in negotiations with the other delegates and with Baroness Medusa. It wasn't possible for me to confer with this committee or with Parliament as a whole before deciding upon my responses to specific situations as they arose. That, if you will recall, was one of the primary reasons it was decided to send the Planetary President herself to head our delegation."

"Forgive me, Madam President," Ranjina said calmly, apparently totally unaffected by the icy precision and coldly focused fury of Tonkovic's reply, "but I didn't ask you about responses to specific situations *at the Convention*. I inquired as to why you hadn't seen fit to inform us of Baroness Medusa's communications to you."

"As I have just explained," Tonkovic said, aware that she was biting off the edges of her words but unable to completely stop herself, "it requires fifteen days for a message to travel from Split to Spindle and back again. It wasn't practical to, nor, I submit, would anyone have expected me to attempt to, communicate to Parliament every exchange between myself and members of other delegations or the Provisional Governor herself."

"Madam President, I'm afraid you're either missing my point or deliberately seeking to evade it." This time Ranjina's own voice had become the blade of a frozen knife. "You were informed over four T-months ago by Baroness Medusa that the continued deadlock in the Constitutional Convention—which all reports available to me suggest stemmed primarily from the deliberate efforts of the Constitutional Liberal Party, which you organized in Spindle—was threatening the annexation effort. You were informed by Baroness Medusa three T-months ago that the Star Kingdom of Manticore would no longer consider itself bound to honor its agreement to annex the Talbott Cluster if a draft constitution wasn't voted out of the Convention within a reasonable time. And you were informed two T-months ago that a hard and fast time limit of one hundred fifty standard days existed, after which, in the absence of a draft Constitution, Queen Elizabeth's Government would either withdraw the offer of annexation in its entirety or else submit a list of star systems which the Star Kingdom would exclude from any future annexation, and that the Split System would appear on that list."

The whispered exchanges which had been provoked by Ranjina's initial assault had vanished into a rising tide of consternation as the Vice Chairwoman's ice-cold voice rolled on. Tonkovic's expression was mottled with the ivory-white of shock and the deep crimson of rage. She couldn't believe it. She could *not* believe that even a Reconciliation Party hack like Ranjina would *do* something like this! It violated every aspect of the code against washing political dirty laundry in public. Even the most bitter partisan conflicts between the established parties had *some* rules, some limits. The reaction of the reporters behind her made it all too clear the substance of Ranjina's coldly enumerated accusations had never been made public, and the Planetary President ground her teeth together in mingled humiliation and fury.

She glared at Gazi, her blazing green eyes demanding that he call Ranjina to heel, but the committee chairman appeared as stunned as Tonkovic herself. He was dazed, trying to think of a way to derail Ranjina, but obviously without success. He didn't know how to deal with it, because this sort of brutal frontal attack simply wasn't done by a member of the Kornatian political establishment. He reached for his gavel, yet he hesitated, trying to find an acceptable pretext for shutting her up. But there wasn't one. However crude, however vicious, her attack, she'd remained totally within her right to use her allocated time in any fashion she chose. And she wasn't finished yet

"It's all very well to talk about delegated authority and communications delays, Madam President. But by your own admission, the maximum delay for an exchange of views was only fifteen days. Not one hundred forty days, not ninety-two days, not even sixty-one days—*fifteen* days. I submit to you that it's one thing to speak of the need to deal with immediate crises as they arise, but that it's quite another to knowingly commit your entire government to a policy of your own creation without so much as warning a single soul on this planet that you were doing so. A policy you've been specifically warned may very well end in the exclusion of our star system from the annexation which over seventy percent of our registered voters approved. That isn't simply arrogance, Madam President. It verges upon the assumption on your part of dictatorial powers and the patent abuse of your office."

Tonkovic's jaw dropped in sheer disbelief. That wasn't a question, wasn't even a disguised policy position statement on Ranjina's part. It was an indictment. One delivered in an ambush such as no Planetary President of Kornati had walked into in well over two hundred T-years.

The hubbub behind her rose to a confused roar, and Gazi's gavel was finally hammering, pounding thunderously. But it was too late. The damage was done, and Aleksandra Tonkovic watched the solemn hearing disintegrate into a shouting match between her allies and her enemies within the Special Committee while the cameras watched every detail of the fiasco.

"Captain Terekhov, Mr. Van Dort, the Montana System owes the two of you a debt which I doubt we'll ever be able to repay," President Warren Suttles said. The President was a politician, but just this once, at least, there was nothing but sincerity in his face and voice. "Stephen Westman and the entire rank and file of the Montana Independence Movement have agreed to surrender to the Marshals Service and to turn in all their heavy weapons. The threat of guerrilla warfare and insurrection on this planet, with all of the damage and deaths that might have entailed, has just been removed thanks to your efforts."

Terekhov, Van Dort, and a still-subdued Helen Zilwicki sat in the President's office along with Chief Marshal Bannister. The captain waved one deprecating hand, but the President shook his head.

"No. You can't just wave it off, Captain. We do owe you an enormous debt. I wish there were something we could do to at least begin paying down some of the interest!"

"Actually, Mr. President," Terekhov said diffidently, "there *is* one little thing you could do for us."

"Anything!" Suttles said expansively, and Bannister closed his eyes in momentary pain. He'd helped craft this particular ambush himself, but it still hurt to see its intended prey walk into it with such utter innocence.

"Well, Mr. President," Terekhov said, "there's a Solarian-registry freighter, the *Copenhagen*, in Montana orbit, and . . ."

"My God, Aivars! What we just did to that poor man!" Van Dort shook his head, trying hard—and unsuccessfully—not to laugh as their pinnace returned to *Hexapuma*.

"What?" Terekhov replied innocently. "He *did* owe us a favor, Bernardus, you know."

Chapter Fifty

"You do realize, Skipper, that you're shooting craps with your career?"

"Nonsense, Ansten." Terekhov shook his head with a half-smile, but FitzGerald wasn't buying it.

"You told me, once, that you might need me to warn you that what you had in mind was a little risky," the XO reminded him. "Well, the Sollies're going to go apeshit . . . and that may be the *good* news!"

The captain and his exec sat in *Hexapuma*'s number two pinnace, and FitzGerald pointed out the viewport at the mountainous bulk of the Kalokainos Shipping-owned freighter *Copenhagen*.

"I think the admiralty courts call this 'piracy,'" he said.

"Nonsense," Terekhov replied airily. "This is a simple and obvious case of salvage of an abandoned vessel."

"Which you arranged to have 'abandoned' in the first place!"

Terekhov was gazing out the viewport, watching *Copenhagen* draw steadily closer. Privately, he was prepared to admit FitzGerald had a point. Several of them, in fact. But what he was prepared to admit to himself was quite different from what he was prepared to admit to anyone else.

"Another thing you might want to think about, Skipper," FitzGerald said, in the tone of the man looking for a telling argument, "is the amount of grief you may be buying for Montana when the Sollies find out the part Suttles agreed to play in this little charade."

"President Suttles is showing a perfectly reasonable and prudent concern, under the circumstances, Ansten." Terekhov's expression was that of someone widows and orphans could safely trust with their final penny. FitzGerald's expression, however, only got more skeptical, and Terekhov smiled again, a bit more broadly than before.

"Given the fact that a Solarian-registry vessel was apprehended in the very act of supplying illegal weapons to terrorists on his planet, President Suttles has every right to be concerned. Since there was a second Solarian-registry vessel in orbit at exactly the same time, and since Kalokainos Shipping and the Jessyk Combine are known to have coordinated their interests in several areas of the Verge, the discovery that *Marianne* belonged to Jessyk amply justifies his decision that *Copenhagen* merits investigation, as well. And since the entire Montanan navy consists of LACs, without a single hyper-capable unit, he obviously couldn't count on preventing *Copenhagen* from fleeing the system to avoid investigation if, indeed, her ship's company had been involved in this nefarious plot. So he clearly had no choice but to remove *Copenhagen*'s crew for interrogation."

"And you think that . . . fairy tale is going to convince the League Suttles didn't have a thing to do with the rest of this?" FitzGerald gestured at *Copenhagen* again, as the pinnace decelerated to rest relative to the big freighter.

"I think that, either way, it isn't going to matter," Terekhov said much more seriously. FitzGerald looked at him, and he shrugged. "If the annexation goes through, the League won't be looking at a single, unsupported Verge system; it'll be looking at a member system of the Star Kingdom of Manticore. At which point, it will become *our* responsibility to protect Suttles from Frontier Security. And," his tone turned more serious still, almost grim, "if you people find what I'm very much afraid you're going to, Suttles and everyone else who ever favored the annexation are going to find themselves in much worse trouble than anything *this* could produce unless we do something about it."

The pinnace pilot was playing his maneuvering thrusters with a skill which reminded Terekhov of Ragnhild Pavletic. The memory sent a fresh stab of pain through him, but he allowed no trace of it to shadow his expression as he gazed back out through the port again. He watched as the pilot carefully aligned the pinnace's airlock with the freighter's emergency personnel hatch. A single skinsuited crewman stepped through the airlock's open outer hatch and drifted gracefully across to *Copenhagen*'s hull, where he opened a small access cover and tapped a command sequence into the keypad behind it. The personnel hatch considered the command ("unofficially" acquired from Trevor Bannister after *Copenhagen*'s crew accepted his invitation as involuntary guests of Montana) and obediently extruded its boarding tube to mate with the pinnace's lock.

FitzGerald sat studying the captain's profile and trying to think of a fresh argument which might bring Terekhov to his senses. It wasn't that he didn't understand what the other man had in mind, or even that he disagreed with Terekhov's suspicions or the captain's conviction that something had to be done to prove or disprove what he feared. It was the method Terekhov had selected . . . and, perhaps even more, what FitzGerald suspected the captain had in mind if his investigation confirmed his worst fears.

The green light came on above the airlock's inner hatch, indicating a good seal and pressure in the tube, and Terekhov nodded.

"Time to get your people on board."

"Skipper, at least send one of the other ships straight

to Spindle," FitzGerald half-blurted, but Terekhov shook his head.

He was gazing back along the center aisle, watching Aikawa Kagiyama. The midshipman looked better, but his shoulders still hunched, as if they were bearing up under a burden of guilt, and Terekhov was worried about him. That was one reason he'd assigned Aikawa to FitzGerald's party.

Lieutenant MacIntyre would be along as FitzGerald's engineer, with Lieutenant Olivetti as his astrogator and Lieutenant Kobe to handle his communications. That was as many officers as Terekhov could spare, but it was still going to leave FitzGerald shorthanded, since only Olivetti was watch-qualified. MacIntyre and Kobe were both junior-grade lieutenants, capable enough in their specialties, but with limited experience. In fact, MacIntyre had something of a reputation for being sharp-tongued and waspish with enlisted personnel and noncoms. Terekhov suspected that it sprang from her own lack of self-confidence, and he hoped this assignment might help to turn that around. But he'd also decided FitzGerald needed at least a little more support, so he'd attached Aikawa. The midshipman wasn't watch-certified, yet, but he was a levelheaded sort who was actually better at managing enlisted personnel than MacIntyre was. He could take on at least some of the load . . . and getting him out of *Hexapuma* would also get him out of an environment where every single sight and sound and smell reminded him of Ragnhild's death.

"Admiral Khumalo's going to think you should've sent word directly to him, Sir," FitzGerald said flatly, in his strongest statement of disagreement yet.

Terekhov looked back at him, touched by the concern in his executive officer's expression.

"Thank you for worrying, Ansten," he said quietly, "but the decision's made. I only have three hyper-capable units, aside from *Hexapuma* herself—and, of course, *Copenhagen*. I can't spare any of them for a direct flight to Spindle, but *Ericsson* will continue on to Spindle from Dresden.

She'll deliver my complete report to the Admiral and the Provisional Governor."

"But—"

"I think we should move on to something else," Terekhov said firmly, and FitzGerald closed his mouth. He looked for a moment at the CO about whose resolution he'd nursed such reservations when they first met, six months before, and knew there was no point in arguing.

"Yes, Sir," he said finally, and Terekhov smiled gently and patted him on the forearm.

"Good. And now, let's get your people aboard your new command. You've got a lot to do before you break orbit."

Aleksandra Tonkovic stood with a welcoming smile as her butler ushered Tomaz Zovan into the library of her Karlovac townhouse.

"Tomaz," she greeted, holding out her hand.

"Madam President," he replied as he took it, and her smile turned into a slight frown at the unexpected formality. Zovan was a Democratic Centralist and a forty-T-year veteran of Parliament. She'd known him literally since childhood, and if he'd never been one of the most brilliant intellects Parliament had ever known, he'd always been a loyal, dependable wheel-horse for the Party and her own administration. As such, he was accustomed to addressing her by her given name, at least in private.

"Why so formal, Tomaz?" she asked, after a moment. "I understood this was to be a social visit."

"I wasn't fully confident of the security of my com when I had my secretary make the appointment, Madam President," he replied, and grimaced. "Rajkovic and Basaricek swear they aren't using Manty technology to monitor all calls from the Nemanja Building, but—"

He broke off with a shrug, and Tonkovic's face tightened.

"Surely not even he would go that far!"

"Madam President," Zovan said, deliberately emphasizing

the title, "how can we be sure of that? He hasn't returned the seal of office to you, has he? Doesn't it seem likely at least part of the reason he hasn't is to keep you from finding out exactly what he's been up to? What he's *still* up to?"

Tonkovic started to protest that Zovan was being unnecessarily paranoid. To be sure, Rajkovic *ought* to have returned the seal of office to her, and with it her formal authority as head of state, as soon as she set foot back on Kornatian soil. He hadn't, and she'd been back for over nine days now. It was infuriating and insulting, but it wasn't—quite—illegal. Technically, a confirming vote of Parliament was required to transfer that authority back and forth, even if he'd handed the seal directly to her. And given the current tone of Parliament, and her continuing appearances before the Special Committee on Annexation and even more acrimonious appearances before Cuijeta Krizanic's Standing Committee on Constitutional Law, she'd decided not to press the matter. Some of the exchanges between her supporters and opponents—not all of them Reconciliationalists, either—were becoming decidedly ugly. However little she'd cared to admit it to herself, she hadn't been certain Parliament would back her if she demanded Rajkovic hand the seal over, and she couldn't afford the loss of political capital if it had declined to do so.

Besides, she hadn't needed the official return of her authority to monitor what was happening inside "his" Cabinet. Mavro Kanjer and Alenka Mestrovic kept her fully informed on anything Rajkovic said at Cabinet meetings, and Kanjer, as Justice Secretary, would certainly have known about any communications taps the Manticoran detachment from Spindle was maintaining.

She decided against explaining any of that. If someone wanted to get sticky, Mavro and Alenka were technically violating the law to keep her informed when someone else was acting head of state. Zovan certainly wouldn't pass on anything she told him in confidence, but under the circumstances, the fewer people who knew, the better.

"I think you're unduly concerned, Tomaz," she said instead. "But, now that you're here, please, sit down. Have a drink, and then tell me what this is all about."

"I appreciate the offer, Madam President. And I may take you up on the drink later. But I think I'd better explain why I needed to see you first, not last."

"As you wish. But at least please sit down."

She pointed at one of the comfortable chairs which sat facing her own, and Zovan settled obediently into it. But he didn't relax. He sat forward, on the edge of the seat, his hands resting on his knees, and actually leaned slightly towards her.

"Now, Tomaz," she said. "What *is* this all about?"

"Madam President, officially, I'm not supposed to know this. Or, at least, I'm not supposed to admit I do. Under the circumstances, however, I thought it my duty to come to you about it immediately."

His voice was somber, his expression grim, and Tonkovic felt a formless chill run through her.

"This afternoon," he continued, "Krizanic spoke to the other members of the Standing Committee behind closed doors. Afterward, Judita Debevic came to my office."

He paused, and Tonkovic nodded slightly. Debevic was the leader of the Social Moderates and vice chairwoman of the committee.

"Madam President," Zovan said heavily, "she'd come to ask me unofficially if I'd be prepared to serve as your advocate in a formal impeachment debate."

Despite decades of political experience and discipline, Tonkovic flinched physically. She sat staring at her visitor for at least ten seconds, conscious only of a vast, singing emptiness, before she could shake her brain back into operation.

No sitting president had ever been successfully impeached! Only one bill of impeachment had ever been voted out in Kornatian history, and it had failed. By a narrow margin, perhaps, but failed. Surely not even Rajkovic was stupid enough to think an impeachment could be sustained against *her* on such flimsy grounds!

Yet even as she told herself that, she felt an undeniable tingle of fear. Rajkovic's Reconciliationists had gotten the chairmanship of the Standing Committee on Constitutional Law for Krizanic as part of the share out of committee chairmanships after the last presidential election. That had seemed reasonable, with Tonkovic's party and its allies' control of the presidency and a working majority in Parliament. But although Cuijeta Krizanic might be the committee's chairwoman, five of its eight members were either Democratic Centralists or Social Moderates. That ought to have guaranteed the failure of any motion before the committee for an impeachment.

But Debevic would never have asked Zovan if he would act as Tonkovic's advocate if she weren't deeply concerned that articles of impeachment might—probably would—be voted out. She'd spoken to Zovan unofficially, but she'd known Tomaz would inform Tonkovic as quickly as possible. It was a way for her to warn the Planetary President without violating her constitutional duty to maintain confidentiality on any deliberations before the committee.

That meant Debevic was afraid of losing at least two "safe" votes, and Tonkovic's eyes narrowed as she ran back over the committee's membership mentally, trying to decide who the traitors might be.

"Did Judita happen to mention how soon she needed an answer from you?"

"She wanted an immediate reply, Madam President." Zovan's tone was even heavier. "Needless to say, I assured her I would be honored to represent you, should such an unthinkable event come to pass."

"Thank you, Tomaz. Thank you very much," she said, smiling, as warmly as she could around the freezing void which seemed to fill her as she realized the event in question was far more thinkable than she'd ever imagined it could be.

"Mr. Levakonic is here, Admiral."

"Show him in immediately," Isidor Hegedusic said.

The Monican admiral stood as his wiry visitor was ushered in. He didn't walk around his desk to greet Levakonic, however. He'd requested this meeting almost a week ago.

"Mr. Levakonic," he said, holding out his hand. "Thank you for coming." Despite himself, his tone added an unspoken "finally."

"Admiral Hegedusic," Levakonic replied, taking the hand and shaking it with a bright smile. "I'm sorry I couldn't get out here sooner. I was so tied up in meetings with President Tyler, Ms. Anisimovna, and Ms. Bardasano that I've hardly had time to catch my breath. Every time I thought I could schedule the flight out to Eroica Station, something else came up. Please forgive me."

"Of course," Hegedusic said, far more graciously than he felt. At the moment, Eroica Station, the Monican Navy's primary shipyard, was well on its way towards opposition from Monica. Flight time from the planet to Eroica Station, traveling with the rest of the Eroica belt, was almost eight hours, so he supposed it was even possible Levakonic was telling the truth rather than that he'd delayed until it suited him as a way to remind his neobarb allies of their place.

Possible. Which wasn't to be confused with "likely."

"But now that I'm here, Admiral," Levakonic continued briskly, "I'm obviously excited about seeing how well the work is proceeding. And, of course, to learn what else it is I can do for you?"

"The first of the battlecruisers went in for refit almost two standard months ago, as I'm sure you know," Hegedusic said. "I'm afraid progress has been slower than anticipated, however. It'll be at least another month and a half before the first of them recommissions."

"That long?" Levakonic frowned, as if this were the first he'd heard of any delays. Which, Hegedusic was forced to admit, was at least possible. His own reports to Admiral Bourmont had been drawing attention to the slippage for weeks now, but it would have been very like the Chief of Naval Operations to . . . refrain from passing that unhappy news along.

"I'd hoped our technical representatives would have been able to hasten that process for you, Admiral. Indeed, it was my understanding they'd done just that."

"Your people have been extraordinarily helpful," Hegedusic told him, which was nothing less than the truth. "I think the problem's that the capacity of our facilities was overestimated when the original schedule was projected. I've been reporting our difficulties to my superiors—" which meant, as Levakonic no doubt understood, Bourmont "—for some time now. I'd hoped you'd been informed."

"Unfortunately, I wasn't." Levakonic shook his head with another frown. "I could have arranged another additional draft of our own yard workers and some additional equipment if I'd known. Now, by the time I could get word back to Yildun, it would be too late to get additional help out here in time to make much of a difference."

"I'm sorry the word didn't get back to you in time. An oversight on someone's part, I'm sure."

"No doubt," Levakonic agreed, and Hegedusic thought he might detect the beginning of genuine respect—or, at least, sympathy for a competent officer trying to get a job done despite his superiors. "Well," the Solly went on briskly, "I'll still look forward to inspecting the work. And, obviously, if I can think of anything to speed the process up, I'll definitely bring it to your attention."

"Thank you. I'd appreciate that," Hegedusic said sincerely. "However, the real reason I wanted to speak to you has to do with the missile pods."

"Don't tell me they've been delayed, too!" Levakonic said with a levity Hegedusic suspected was just a bit forced.

"No, they arrived on schedule early last week," the admiral reassured him. "What I wanted to inquire into was the possibility of deploying some of them here, in Monica, to bolster Eroica Station's security when we began drawing down our existing naval strength to find personnel to man the new vessels. We're recruiting additional men, but we're still going to have to lay up every existing ship. I don't like being that vulnerable."

"I don't blame you"

Levakonic thought for a moment, then nodded and looked back at Hegedusic.

"I don't see why that should be a problem," he said so readily Hegedusic was hard pressed to hide his surprise. "We'll need at least a couple of weeks—a month would be better—to overhaul them before they'll be ready for deployment in Lynx. But you ought to have enough of the new battlecruisers in commission to let me began picking the pods back up with time to spare. Even if that doesn't happen, we probably wouldn't have to deploy more than thirty or forty pods—a hundred or so, at most. If it's no more than that, we could almost certainly overhaul them aboard ship on our way to Lynx."

"To be honest, I'd prefer to deploy as many of them here as we can," Hegedusic said. "On the other hand, I realize I'm probably oversensitive where Eroica's security is concerned. But I'll deeply appreciate the ability to deploy any of them."

"I understand completely, Admiral," Levakonic assured him. "I'll talk to my project officers about it while I'm out here. We'll want to discuss exact numbers with you, but I'll authorize the deployment before I return to Monica."

"Thank you," Hegedusic said, even more sincerely.

"Admiral," Levakonic told him with a desert-dry smile, "Technodyne has a lot of money tied up in this operation. And, to be honest, we're extremely hopeful of having the opportunity to look at some of the Manties' new technology first-hand. We're deeply committed to making the project a success, and this sounds to me like a perfectly reasonable request."

"I'd hoped you might see it that way," Hegedusic said. "And I'm relieved you do. So," he stood again, and this time he did walk around his desk, "let's go arrange that tour of the yard for you."

✧ ✧ ✧

"So," Bernardus Van Dort said quietly, standing beside Terekhov's command chair on *Hexapuma*'s bridge, watching the main plot as the *Copenhagen* headed out of Montana orbit under new management, "when do you start trying to throw me off your ship?"

"I beg your pardon?" Terekhov turned his head to look at him.

"The way I have it figured," Van Dort said thoughtfully, "you're going to say something about how instrumental I was in convincing Westman to call it quits. And then you're going to argue that I really ought to stay here on Montana to make sure nothing else goes wrong. And, of course, you'll promise to pick me up here on the way back from the rendezvous to return me to Spindle."

"That's what you think, is it?" Terekhov had the definite look of a man sparring for time, and Van Dort smiled cheerfully at him.

"Well, you certainly tried hard enough to manufacture some 'reasonable' reason to ship me off aboard *Ericsson*. Which, as my keen intelligence noted at the time, was the only one of your three messengers which won't be coming back here to Montana before you go haring off to your rendezvous with *Copenhagen*."

"I think," Terekhov said after a moment, "that we should take this conversation to my briefing room." He looked past Van Dort to Naomi Kaplan. "Guns, you have the bridge."

"Aye, aye, Sir. I have the bridge," she replied, and Terekhov climbed out of his chair and beckoned for Van Dort to follow him.

The briefing room hatch closed behind them, and the Manticoran turned to face the civilian.

"Now," he said, "suppose you tell me just what sort of nefarious scheming you've imputed to me."

"Oh, really, Aivars!" Van Dort rolled his eyes. "I've known more or less what you had in mind ever since you got me and Trevor Bannister to help you figure out how to steal *Copenhagen*."

"Borrow," Terekhov corrected almost absently, and Van Dort snorted magnificently.

"Oh, forgive me!" he begged earnestly. "Of course I meant 'borrow'! And stop trying to divert me."

"I'm not trying to divert anyone," Terekhov protested. Van Dort gave him a fulminating look, and he shrugged. "Anyway, go on with your exposition of my Machiavellian motives."

"Aivars," Van Dort said much more seriously, "there's only one reason for you to 'borrow' a Solly freighter, load one of your remote sensor drones into its hold, and send it off to Monica. Especially when you follow that up by sending orders to any units at Dresden, Talbott, and Tillerman to join you here before you go off to rendezvous with *Copenhagen* on her return. And, extra especially, when the rendezvous you've set is a hundred light-years from Montana . . . and only thirty-eight from Monica."

"It's just a routine precaution."

"Which, undoubtedly, is the reason you never told the Montanans about *Marianne*'s last trip to Monica. You know, the one when Duan and his cutthroats dropped off the Technodyne technicians?"

"Well, maybe not *totally* routine."

"Oh, stop it! You even commandeered Suttles' only dispatch boat to carry your message to Tillerman. And ordered it to return straight here and accompany you to the rendezvous."

"All right, Bernardus," Terekhov said flatly. "I already knew you're a clever man. Now tell me why I shouldn't leave you behind?"

"Because I won't stay," Van Dort said, equally flatly.

"Don't be stupid. Of course you'll stay."

"Not unless you're prepared to use Marines to put me forcibly dirt-side," Van Dort told him unflinchingly.

"Bernardus, be reasonable!"

"I don't think so. You've got this set up so that by the time *Ericsson* gets to Spindle, it'll be too late for Khumalo or Baroness Medusa to get dispatches to you forbidding you to leave Montana. You and whatever units you can round up from Khumalo's 'Southern Patrol' to go with you. And if *Copenhagen* reports what you and I both suspect she will, you'll be moving directly from your rendezvous to Monica. Oh, don't bother trying to look innocent at me, damn it! What the *hell* do you think you're doing?"

"Using the initiative expected of a senior officer of the Queen," Terekhov told him, without a flicker of humor.

"And making damned certain no one can stop you. *And* that the Star Kingdom will have 'plausible deniability' if it all hits the fan. The Queen will be able to disavow your actions with the absolutely truthful statement that not one of your superiors knew what you were planning to do and that your actions, in their entirety, were unauthorized."

"Possibly."

"Well, you're not doing it without me."

"Why not?" For the first time there was more than a little exasperation in Terekhov's voice, and Van Dort smiled thinly.

"Partly because I refuse to pretend you pulled the wool over my eyes, as well. I don't intend to look *that* stupid to the rest of the galaxy. And partly because if both of us go along on this idiot's errand of yours, the Queen will have two loose warheads to blame it on. But mostly?" He held Terekhov's gaze with a fiery, unflinching eye. "Mostly because I started this entire mess when I came up with the brilliant notion of organizing the plebiscite. If you want to come right down to it, Aivars, everything that's happened, including Nordbrandt and Westman *and* Monica is my fault. So if someone's going to get his idiot self killed, and possibly quite a few other people along with him, I'm going along for the ride."

"Bernardus, that has to be the most arrogant thing I've ever heard anyone say in my entire life. One man, no matter who he is, can't possibly take the entire credit—or blame—for the actions of everyone in an entire cluster the size of Talbott!"

"Maybe not." Van Dort's voice dropped, and he looked

away at last. "Maybe not. But I've spent my entire adult life trying to keep Frontier Security's claws off of my planet, and I've supped with the Devil to do it. I've connived, and I've pressured people, and I've extorted concessions to squeeze the last stellar out of entire planets. Whether I meant to or not, I've given my obsession my wife and my daughters. Fifteen days ago I gave it Ragnhild Pavletic and your Marines. I fed all of them into the furnace, and the absolute hell of it is that I'd do it all again. So if those Frontier Security bastards—or anyone else—think they're going to come charging in at this point and take over everything I care about, everything I've mortgaged my soul and poured out my life and the lives of the people I love to keep out of the Sollies' clutches, I'm *damned* well going to be there when they find out they're wrong!"

There was a moment of silence. Then Terekhov cleared his throat.

"All right," he said finally. "You're a bigger idiot than you seem to think I am, but if you're going to be this whiny about it, I suppose you can come along."

"Thanks," Van Dort said. He inhaled deeply, then turned back to face his friend again, and Terekhov gave him an off-center smile.

"Even if my suspicions are confirmed," he said quietly, "it's not such a sure thing Frontier Security's wrong, you know."

"I've come to know you and your people better than that, Aivars," Van Dort said, equally quietly. "You may not survive, but they *will* be wrong."

Chapter Fifty-One

"No, Samiha, the news from Split *doesn't* sound very good, does it?" Andrieaux Yvernau agreed. His tone was grave, but he couldn't quite hide the gleam in his eye . . . assuming he'd made the effort in the first place. He seemed poised on a needlepoint of strange excitement and defiance, midway between exhilaration and bitterness.

"I'm worried about what this may mean for the CLP, Andrieaux," Lababibi said with a concern that was only partly feigned. "Aleksandra's been the heart and soul of the Liberals from the very beginning. Now that she's been recalled, even her own delegation is beginning to slip away. And I don't think the example has been lost on a couple of the other delegation heads."

"The more fools they for not having secured the full, informed approval of their own governments," Yvernau said scornfully. "Did they think the respectable classes wouldn't understand? *Ptahhhh!*" He actually spat on the expensive carpet, his features twisted with disdain. "Now look what they've done to themselves! Every one of them, sitting in his expensive office every night, wondering when the hounds baying at *his* heels will drag him down. And it'll happen to more than a few of them, Samiha. You mark my words! When the implications of Medusa's insolent time limit sink home, the fact that the idiots didn't get clear, unequivocal approval for their positions will give their opponents—and possibly their 'friends,' as well—back home the excuse to make the entire delay *their* fault. They'll find themselves sacrificed by the gutless wonders who can't wait to scramble onto Alquezar's wagon and fawn all over Medusa, whining 'It wasn't *our* fault! *We* didn't know what they were *doing*!'"

Lababibi frowned ever so slightly. Even that was more expression than she'd intended to show, but the scalding venom of Yvernau's angry contempt surprised her. The New Tuscan had always prided himself on his self-control, his detached amusement at the inept maneuvers of the lesser mortals around him. He'd known he was far superior to any of them, that it was only a matter of biding his time until destiny inevitably handed him the opportunity for which he waited.

Unfortunately, the idiot never counted on Elizabeth losing her patience with all the irritating pygmies—like him—buzzing around the Convention like so many gnats. And my own Cabinet wants me to go on cooperating *with this fool?* She shook her head mentally. *Talk about riding the ship down in flames!*

Lababibi's problem was, in many ways, the opposite of Aleksandra Tonkovic's. Since the Convention was being held on her own homeworld, every single member of the Spindle System government—not to mention every semi-literate in the street—knew every detail of what was happening. Well, every *public* detail, at any rate. There were still some things which were thankfully confidential. God bless smoke-filled rooms and their spiritual descendants!

But more than enough was known to prevent Lababibi from exercising anything remotely resembling the freedom Tonkovic had enjoyed . . . until she was yanked back to Split. Which had its upside, of course. At least no one could drag her home and accuse her of concealing critical information or formulating her own policies. The bad news was that she had no choice but to execute the policies dictated to her, whether she thought they were insane or not.

"If you think so many of the Liberal delegates are going to be recalled, what do you propose we do about it?" she asked Yvernau.

"I propose that we see how many of the stupid sheep are still willing to stand up like men—at least until they get dragged home by the scruff of their fleece."

"That sounds very poetic," she said tartly. "Now, would you care to be just a bit more specific?"

"The basic situation is very simple, Samiha." Yvernau's voice took on the lecturing note Lababibi most detested. "In essence, Medusa's informed all of us that we're under the gun. That we face a time limit, imposed by Manticore, within which we *must* yield to the Star Kingdom's demand for a complete surrender of our sovereignty. If we decline to lick Queen Elizabeth's hand like proper little lap dogs, then she'll kick us aside and leave us to languish in the outer dark. Where, as the final element of her threat runs, we'll undoubtedly be devoured by Frontier Security."

He paused, and while Lababibi would have disputed the tone and purpose of the Manticorans' statement, he'd certainly summed up the consequences accurately enough in his own, viciously angry way.

"However," he continued, "the truth isn't quite that cut and dried, because Aleksandra had a point. If they carry their threat through, and if Frontier Security does scoop us up, Manticore's prestige and diplomatic reliability will suffer severe damage. Possibly even irreparable damage, given how much dispute there is over the Manties' and Haven's versions of their prewar diplomatic exchanges. They're in a worse position to afford damage to their credibility than anyone else I can possibly think of."

"So you still think, despite the formal communique from Prime Minister Alexander in the Queen's name, that it's really a bluff?" Lababibi managed to keep the incredulity out of her voice somehow.

"More than a bluff, but far short of an irrevocable policy statement. They may be threatening to do it, but it's the last thing they really want to do."

You flaming idiot. *Just what*, Lababibi thought scathingly, *makes you think this Cluster is important enough to Manticore for them to waste time trying to* bluff *us? About the only thing I can say for you, Andrieaux Yvernau, is that you're not a* whole *lot stupider than my own political lords and masters.*

"If that's the case, what do we do about it?" she asked, rounding her eyes and giving him her best "troubled-but-trusting" expression.

"We treat it as a bluff," he said decisively.

"I beg your pardon? Didn't you just say it was more than that?"

"Of course. But if we stand fast, tell them we're prepared to reject their demands even at the risk of their abandoning the entire process, we'll be able to use Medusa's own policy against Alquezar and his so-called 'moderate' cronies. They're already terrified we're going to pull the house down around their ears. I say we convince them that's *exactly* what we'll do unless they meet us at least half way. And once they're convinced of that, we offer them the compromise platform I've been working on all along. They'll be so scared, so desperate to do anything to save the annexation, that they'll accept the compromise rather than call *our* bluff and risk losing everything."

"And if they do decide to 'call our bluff' and count on the portion of the Alexander statement that says Manticore will pick and choose which of the Cluster's systems it will annex and which it will exclude?"

"There are two possibilities, assuming—which I, for one, don't—that these frightened little minds have the fortitude to go eyeball-to-eyeball with us. One is that Manticore's genuinely willing to exclude and abandon our star systems, despite the diplomatic fallout of such an action. The second is that our governments back home will disavow our positions and cave in, making the best deals they can with Alquezar after removing us from our delegations.

"Personally, I don't think the Manticorans have the balls to go through with the exclusion. And, even if they do, I don't see them allowing Frontier Security to snap us up. The Manties couldn't afford to see their new systems here in the Cluster invaded by cysts of the League. So whether it's what they want to do or not, they'll have to include us under the same security umbrella as their possessions here. That's why I'll recommend to my government that even if everyone else signs up like good little peasants, we refuse."

"And if they don't?"

"If they don't, then they disavow my actions," Yvernau said unflinchingly.

Lababibi rather doubted he could really visualize a situation in which his government might actually do that. His personality was too fundamentally arrogant for him to believe on any emotional level that even the universe itself could ultimately fail to do his bidding. And there was probably an element of desperation in his disbelief, as well. His final refuge was to deny the reality of the threat bearing down upon him. Yet whether or not he could fully accept the possibility of his political demise, he was at least intellectually aware of the possibility. And so, in his own way, he was showing considerable political courage. Of a nasty, contemptuous sort, perhaps, but still courage.

Which was quite possibly the single virtue he possessed.

"Have you discussed this with the other CLP delegates?"

"With the majority of them."

"And they said—?"

"I got a generally positive response."

Meaning at least a quarter of them told you to take a hike, she thought. The problem was, her fellow Spindalian oligarchs were unlikely to agree with that sane quarter. They'd undoubtedly be willing to take Yvernau's second option when his bluff failed, but Lababibi felt no particular desire to obey their instructions to refuse to surrender only to have them disavow her when it didn't work.

My God. He may actually be able to produce the votes he needs to try this insanity simply because people are too frightened to face their home political establishments without trying it!

"So when do you plan on laying this . . . strategy before the Convention?"

"Tomorrow or the next day. I still have one or two people I need to talk to, first."

"I see."

"And do you think the Spindle System will stand with us?"

"I'll certainly discuss it with my Cabinet and the legislature's leadership this afternoon," she assured him. "Frankly, at this point, I wouldn't venture to predict what they're likely to say. All I can tell you at the moment is that so far they've been very firm about supporting the CLP position ever since Nordbrandt started killing people."

"Then I'll take that as a good sign," Yvernau told her. "And now, if you'll forgive me, I have to go. I have an appointment with the Rembrandt delegation." He smiled thinly. "I don't think Van Dort's control is quite as firm as he believes. And since he's off running errands for Medusa like a good little brown-noser, he's not exactly around to keep them in line anyway, is he?"

"So what do we do about Yvernau's latest brainstorm?" Henri Krietzmann asked.

"Nothing," Joachim Alquezar replied with a nonchalance which had to be at least partly assumed, Krietzmann thought.

"He might actually get those stupid dinosaurs to stand up in front of the glacier with him, you know," the Dresdener pointed out.

"In which case they'll be found a thousand years later with buttercups frozen in their stomachs," Alquezar said scornfully. "That's the best they'll be able to hope for—to stay frozen exactly where they are while the rest of us sign up with Star Kingdom and leave them in our dust. But that's not what's going to happen."

"No?"

"No. I give it ten T-years, twenty-five at the outside, before they get themselves tossed out of office by a new crop of political leaders who'll come begging, hats in hand, to be allowed to join the Star Kingdom on our terms. I don't think any other result's possible, in the long term. Not when they see what membership in the Star Kingdom's going to do for our economies and our citizens."

"I think you may be being overly optimistic," Krietzmann said, his eyes troubled. He raised his left hand, the one with the missing fingers, in an exasperated sort of wave. "Unless we're willing to embargo their economies, they'll still share in any general economic improvement in the Cluster. Not to the same extent, maybe, but I'm afraid they may see enough domestic improvement to keep a lid on things a lot longer than you're predicting."

"Perhaps they will," Alquezar conceded. "And if they do, I'll be very sorry for the rest of their population. But all *we* can do is the best we can. And, to be brutally frank, Henri, our fundamental responsibility's to our *own* star systems. We can't justify endangering our own people's future out of concern for the consequences of the actions of a handful of self-interested, self-absorbed, self-serving political parasites in other systems."

It was a beautiful late morning. She looked up at a blue sky, swept by orderly lines of blindingly white clouds and polished by a brisk easterly wind, and felt the sheer, vibrant energy of the day. It danced on her skin like some sort of elemental life force, and she leaned back in the chaise lounge on the townhouse roof, closed her eyes, and tilted her face up to the sun.

With her eyes closed, she could forget—temporarily, at least—the political crisis. Just as she could forget the extra guards, armed now with the latest in off-world weapons, either directly from Manticoran stores or from weapons captured from the FAK base camp, who stood watchfully at the corners of the rooftop terrace.

Nordbrandt was still out there, she thought. Rajkovic and his vulture allies were circling, ready to try their luck at a judicial *coup d'état*, and the terrorists' "great leader" was still uncaught, unpunished. She was undoubtedly planning yet another attack, but could Kornati's so-called political leadership be bothered to do anything about it? Not until they'd finished the gladiatorial circus of the impeachment attempt.

A part of Aleksandra Tonkovic's brain was aware she was being unfair—where finishing off the FAK was concerned, at least. Rajkovic and his cronies knew Nordbrandt was still alive, still active. That was the reason the detachment of Manty Marines was still camped at the spaceport, providing surveillance and security. It was going to take more than simple planning and good luck for Nordbrandt to get through that security umbrella, and Tonkovic knew it. No wonder the terrorists were lying low, licking their wounds. Yet another part of her couldn't help wishing the FAK *would* get through . . . or at least make the attempt and fail. That sort of proof that the base camp raid hadn't magically finished off the terrorist threat might at least help show Rajkovic up for the fraud he was.

"Excuse me, Madam President." It was her butler, and she pried one eye open and looked up at him.

"Yes, Luka?"

"Secretary Kanjer is here, Madam President. He asks if it would be convenient for you to receive him?"

Both of Tonkovic's eyes popped open. Kanjer, here? Without a prior appointment? Her mouth felt unaccountably dry, but she swallowed to moisten it and sat upright on the lounge.

"Of course it will," she said calmly, reaching for a

robe and shrugging into it. She belted the sash around her waist, and nodded. "Show him up, Luka."

"At once, Madam President."

The butler disappeared with the soundless, magical efficiency of his kind. He reappeared minutes later, with Mavro Kanjer in tow.

"Secretary Kanjer, Madam President," he murmured, and vanished again.

"Have a seat, Mavro," Tonkovic invited, pointing at the chairs around an umbrella-shaded table. The normally vocal Justice Secretary nodded jerkily and sat without a word. That was a bad sign, she thought, but she said nothing, only smiled and settled into a chair on the other side of the table.

"To what do I owe the pleasure?" she asked lightly, once she was seated.

"Mrsic is going to move for a formal impeachment tomorrow morning," Kanjer said bluntly.

Despite Zovan's warning, it hit her like a fist.

"That seems unlikely," she heard her own voice say, and Kanjer grimaced.

"Aleksandra, it's been coming for weeks," he said. "I admit, I didn't see it either—not until Parliament voted to call you home. And even then, I didn't think *this* would happen. But I was wrong. They have the votes on the Standing Committee to report out a bill of impeachment, and they're going to."

"That *bastard*!" she hissed as the cold hammer of reality began to shatter the armor of her detachment. "That miserable, traitorous *son of a bitch*! He won't get away with it—he *won't*, I tell you!"

"Who won't?" Kanjer's expression was more than a little confused.

"That bastard Rajkovic, of course! He may think he can steal the presidency this way, but he's got another thought or two coming!"

"*Rajkovic?*" Kanjer stared at her. "Didn't you hear what I said? The motion's coming from Mrsic—*Eldijana* Mrsic."

"Mrsic?" Tonkovic blinked as the name finally registered. Eldijana Mrsic wasn't a Reconciliationist. She wasn't even a Social Moderate. She was the senior Democratic Centralist on Cuijeta Krizanic's Standing Committee.

"That's what I'm trying to tell you," Kanjer said. "It's coming from inside the Party, Aleksandra."

"But . . . but how did Rajkovic get to Mrsic?" Tonkovic asked in bewilderment.

"He didn't, Aleksandra," Kanjer said almost gently. "Alenka and I have been telling you all along that Rajkovic hasn't been in secret communication with Parliament. Hasn't been tapping your communications. Hasn't been using the KNP against you and your supporters. You just haven't been listening."

"But . . ." She stared at him, confused, and he shook his head.

"Vuk Rajkovic's no saint, Aleksandra. He's an experienced politician, and he can be just as sneaky and devious as any of the rest of us. But he didn't have to be this time. He didn't pressure Parliament into recalling you. All he did was pass on the information Medusa put into his possession through Van Dort. Parliament did the rest. And now Parliament is pushing the impeachment movement."

"But why? What about our majority?" she asked.

"We don't have one on this issue. Nordbrandt scared too many people, and the Manties got too much credit from those terrified people when they took out her base camp and all those weapons. And, to be perfectly blunt, Aleksandra, the threat that your policies in Spindle could get us blacklisted by the Star Kingdom frightened them even worse than Nordbrandt. That's why the Party's fracturing over the impeachment vote. Some of our deputies actually *want* you removed from office, because they're scared of exactly the same things and they blame you for it. But more of them are frightened of the consequences at the polls if you remain as Party leader. They want you out, Aleksandra. They believe you've become a dangerous political liability, and they won't support you. At best, they'll abstain when it comes down to the vote. And if they do, you'll lose."

"What are you saying? Are you saying the impeachment would *succeed*?"

"Yes," he said, and there was a certain kindness in the brutally brief reply. She shook her head, dazed, almost bemused, and he reached across the table and took her lax right hand between both of his own.

"I know what you tried to do," he said. "And I believe the majority of the Party does. But it's not a big enough majority. Not with the Reconciliationist bloc in Parliament. If you're impeached, the impeachment will be sustained. Comfortably."

Tonkovic swallowed. This was a nightmare. It couldn't be happening—not to *her*.

"What should I—? I mean, how—?"

"You have to resign," Kanjer told her gently. Her eyes flashed in instant rejection, and he tightened his clasp on her hand. "Listen to me, Aleksandra! You *have* to resign. If you don't, they'll hound you out of office, anyway. It's going to happen. The only choice you have is how you leave."

"And why should I make it easy for the traitorous bastards?" she snapped with a return of spirit. "If they want to be rats scurrying over the side before the ship sinks, why should I give a single solitary *damn* about what they want?"

"Because if you don't, it's the end of your political career."

"And how much 'political career' does a President who resigns in disgrace have? No Planetary President's *ever* resigned, and you know it!"

"This is a panic reaction," Kanjer said. "The people who ought to recognize what you're trying to do are too frightened to defend you at the moment. But that doesn't mean they won't eventually realize you were right. That by stampeding into the Manties' arms under Alquezar's terms they've thrown away their best—possibly their only—hope of preserving our way of life and, not to put too fine a point on it, their own positions.

"But when that day comes, they'll still be a political force. Not as strong a force as before they threw away all their advantages, but still a force. And the only force dedicated to protecting what's left of our society. When they finally wake up and recognize what they've done, how bad the situation is, they'll need a leader. One who didn't stampede right along with them.

"You, Aleksandra. They'll need *you*."

"What is this?" she demanded bitterly. "Some kind of cheerleader speech? Did they pick you to hand me my walking papers because they figured you could sugarcoat the pill, Mavro?"

"I don't blame you for feeling that way," he said, meeting her gaze unflinchingly. "But I'm not sugarcoating anything. It's going to be ugly, and it's going to be humiliating. For a while—possibly even for two or three T-years—you're going to be, at best, a voice crying in the wilderness. But I'm dead serious. Eventually, what's left of the Centralists and Moderates are going to realize they need a leader of stature. And you, as the woman who became a political martyr trying to protect them from their own panic, will be the only logical choice. That's why you have to resign *now*, before the impeachment bill's voted out. While it's still *your* choice, and you can tell the people who've abandoned you that you're walking away, with your head high, until the day they realize what a dreadful mistake they've made."

He paused, then shook his head.

"I can't promise you it'll work out the way I'm predicting," he admitted. "But you always said I was one of the best political strategists you knew. Maybe I am, and maybe I'm not. But, in all honesty, what other choice to you have?"

She stared at him, listening to the sunny morning's wind popping the umbrella fringe like jubilantly clapping little hands, and tried to think of an answer to his question.

Chapter Fifty-Two

It was lonely in Snotty Row.

Aikawa was away in *Copenhagen*. Leo was still on Kornati. And Ragnhild was . . . gone. Only Helen and Paulo remained.

Helen sat in the observation dome, her heels on the edge of the seat cushion, her knees tucked up under her chin and her arms wrapped around her shins, and gazed out at the growing number of vessels in Montana orbit while she thought. It was very peaceful under the dome, and she let her eyes rest on *Hexapuma*'s nearest orbital neighbor.

The heavy cruiser *Warlock* had been at Dresden when *Ericsson* arrived with Captain Terekhov's orders for any Navy ships in the system to join him in Montana. Captain Anders was junior to Captain Terekhov. As such, he'd had no choice but to obey, whatever he might think about his orders, and he and the destroyer *Javelin* had arrived in Montana two days before. Helen didn't know exactly what the Skipper had told Anders and Lieutenant Commander Jeffers, *Javelin*'s CO, he had in mind. He might not have told them anything yet, she thought. But everybody aboard the *Nasty Kitty* had a pretty good idea by now, and she suspected the inter-ship grapevine must have carried at least a few hints to Anders and Jeffers.

Then, this morning, more ships had come in, this time from Talbott. *Volcano* had returned with Commander Eleanor Hope's *Vigilant*, another *Star Knight*-class cruiser, and the light cruiser *Gallant*, a sister of the Skipper's old *Defiant*, in tow, accompanied by two more destroyers—*Rondeau* and *Aria*, both old *Chanson*-class ships.

It was turning into a fairly respectable little squadron, she reflected. True, most of its ships verged on obsolescent, by Manticoran standards, but those standards were a bit high by anyone else's measure.

Of course, it was also, in many ways, a *stolen* squadron. All those ships were part of Rear Admiral Khumalo's "Southern Patrol," one of the mainstays of his anti-piracy strategy. Technically, the Skipper was within his rights to call them in, and communications delays over interstellar distances required that officers exercise their initiative. The more senior an officer became, the more initiative she was expected to demonstrate, but countermanding a superior officer's orders, and especially those of a station commander, wasn't something to undertake lightly. An officer who did so had damned well better be able to demonstrate that her actions had been justified.

Still, if she got herself killed in the process, she'd at least neatly avoid the all but inevitable court of inquiry her actions would provoke.

The thought made Helen smile with sour amusement. She wished she could share it with Paulo, but he was on duty. Which was one reason she'd come here now, when she could sit with her thoughts and the dim quiet *without* having to share them with him.

Her smile faded as she reflected on the fact that she was actually glad to be able to avoid him, at least for the moment. Not happy, just glad. Or, perhaps, the word she really needed was *relieved*. Although that, too, carried connotations that weren't quite right.

In some ways, she and Paulo rattled around like two lonely peas in Snotty Row. The midshipmen's quarters had been designed to house up to eight people. Just the two of them found themselves with almost too much space, although that was a concept they would have found difficult to visualize when they first joined *Hexapuma*'s company.

In other ways, though, the space was entirely too confined. With no one to hide behind, there was no room for Paulo to be his old, standoffish self, even if he'd wanted to. Which posed complications of its own, especially in light of the Articles of War's ban on physical intimacy with other military personnel in the same chain of command.

The fact was that, now that she understood where Paulo's good looks had really come from, and even more since she'd gotten over her own silly prejudices and begun to know the person behind those features, she found him . . . attractive. *Very* attractive, if she was going to be honest, which she very much wished she could avoid. The comfort he'd given her after Ragnhild's death, she'd come to realize, was completely typical of him, despite his aversion to letting people get too close. Of course, Ragnhild had become his friend, as well as Helen's, but not in the same way. He'd known her for less than six T-months; Helen had known her for four T-years. He and Ragnhild had gotten just close enough for him to realize how much her death had hurt Helen, and for it to hurt him enough that he, too, had needed to draw comfort from another.

That sharing, when she'd wept on his shoulder and his own tears had kissed her hair, had changed the relationship between them. What had been growing into a friendship as close, in its own way, as her friendship with Aikawa and Ragnhild, had become something else. Something far more intense, and more than a little frightening.

Helen had been what she'd thought of as "romantically involved" before. Several times, in fact. Sometimes it had been fun; other times, sheer frustration had made her want to kill the idiot. Like most Manticoran adolescents, she'd been reasonably well instructed in the basics of human sexuality, and she'd found those lessons valuable in those romantic involvements. That, too, had been fun. On occasion, *lots* of fun, she admitted cheerfully.

But none of those relationships had begun as whatever was growing between her and Paulo had. She hadn't started out disliking the other person intensely, for one thing. And the other person had never carried Paulo's history and background around with him. Never possessed near godlike handsomeness . . . and despised its source. There was an ingrained, intense suspicion in Paulo. A defensive reaction against the attractiveness designed into his genes to make him a more sellable commercial commodity. He didn't want people to desire him for his appearance, and that jagged, wounded part of him was always only too ready to assume anyone who *did* desire him was, in fact, drawn to his physical attractiveness.

Had Helen decided to pursue him aggressively, it would have been like trying to embrace an Old Earth porcupine. And, in the end, almost certainly as futile as it would have been painful. So it was possibly a good thing she wasn't certain she wanted to "pursue" him at all. Yet she suspected that he, like her, felt the changes in whatever was growing between them. It was already too intense for Helen to call it mere friendship, but hadn't—quite—toppled over into anything else yet.

Yet.

She grimaced, looking out through the armorplast, and felt a reverberation of loss as she saw a pinnace separate from *Vigilant* and head for *Hexapuma*. It reminded her of so much, and along with the loss, she felt a stab of guilt. Ragnhild had been gone for barely three weeks, and it seemed grotesque that the death of one of Helen's two closest friends could have had such a powerful effect on drawing her and Paulo closer. It felt almost like a betrayal of her friend's memory. And yet there was a sense of rightness to it, as well. As if it were an affirmation that life went on.

She sighed, then shook her head as her chrono chimed softly.

It was time to report for duty herself, and she shoved herself up out of the comfortable chair as *Vigilant*'s pinnace began its final approach to *Hexapuma*.

No doubt Commander Hope was coming aboard to find out what all of this was about, Helen thought, and smiled again, crookedly, wishing she could be a fly on the Skipper's cabin bulkhead.

"Well, I thought that went fairly well," Terekhov said as the cabin hatch closed behind Eleanor Hope and Lieutenant Commander Osborne Diamond, her executive officer.

"You did, did you . . . Sir?" Ginger Lewis responded, and he turned to look at her. She sat in one of his comfortable armchairs, just to one side of Sinead's portrait. Terekhov was certain the juxtapositioning was a coincidence, but he was struck again by how much Commander Lewis looked like a younger, slightly taller version of his wife.

Which isn't precisely what you need to be thinking about your acting XO, Aivars, he told himself wryly.

"Yes, I did," he replied. He poured himself a fresh cup of coffee from the carafe Joanna Agnelli had provided, leaned back, and crossed his legs. "Why? Didn't you?" he asked innocently.

"Skipper, far be it from me to suggest you're talking through your beret, but Hope doesn't care much for this little brainstorm of yours. And she still doesn't know the half of it, whatever she may suspect."

"Nonsense. Just a little perfectly understandable . . . apprehension at having her previous orders overruled on such short notice, I'm sure."

"Sure it was," Ginger said, shaking her head with a smile. Then her expression sobered. "Skipper, I don't much care for Hope. She looks to me like an ass-coverer who abhors the very thought of sticking her neck out. When she figures out what you're really planning, she's going to have three kinds of hissy fit."

"What I'm really planning?" Terekhov arched his eyebrows, and she snorted.

"I'm an engineer, not a tactical officer, Sir. I check the gizmos and widgets, oil the parts, wind the ship up, and make her go wherever you lordly tactical types decide. And I do my best to patch up the holes you same tactical types eventually get blown in my perfectly good ship. Still, I'm not exactly brain dead, and I've had six months now to watch you in action. Do you really think I haven't figured it out?"

Terekhov considered her thoughtfully. He'd found himself missing Ansten FitzGerald more and more badly since sending him off to Monica seventeen days ago. Indeed, he'd been more than a little surprised by just how badly. The executive officer wasn't brilliant, but he was far, far from stupid, and he was also competent and experienced and possessed the courage of his convictions. He'd become exactly the sort of sounding board a good XO was supposed to be, even when Terekhov never said a word to him. Simply visualizing FitzGerald's probable response was often all he needed to do.

Ginger Lewis was different. Although, as she'd just pointed out, she was an engineering specialist, not a tac officer, she had a first-class brain—a better one than FitzGerald's, as a matter of fact. Possibly even a better one than Terekhov himself had, he often thought. And the fact that she'd come up as a mustang, without ever attending Saganami Island, gave her a different perspective. It was as if thinking outside the box came naturally for her, and she possessed a degree of irreverence which was both rare in a regular officer and refreshing. In many ways, he realized, she was almost more valuable to him in the present circumstances than FitzGerald himself might have been.

"I imagine you've deduced most of it, Ginger," he conceded after a moment. "And you're probably right that Hope isn't going to be delighted when *she* finds out. Assuming, of course, that worse comes to worst and we do end up provoking a major interstellar incident."

"You remember, back in 281, when Duchess Harrington blew that Peep Q-ship out of space in Basilisk,

Skipper? You know, the one that got her convicted as a mass murderer in absentia by the Peeps?" Ginger asked, and he nodded.

"Well, *that* was 'a major interstellar incident,'" she said. "What you've got in mind is going to be something else entirely. Something I'm not sure they've actually invented a word for yet. Although, now that I think about it, 'act of war' might come pretty close."

He considered disagreeing with her, but he didn't.

She was right, after all.

"I knew Yvernau was an idiot," Dame Estelle Matsuko said over the appetizer. "I never realized he was directly descended from a lemming, though."

"'Lemming,' Milady?" Gregor O'Shaughnessy repeated, and she wrinkled her nose and reached for her wineglass. She sipped, then set the glass back down and brushed her lips with a napkin.

"It's a species they have on Medusa," she told him. "Actually, the name goes back to an Old Earth species. The Medusan version was named because it has some similar habits. Specifically, at irregular intervals, enormous masses of them get together and either charge off the edge of a high cliff or swim straight out to sea until they drown."

"Why in the world do they do that?"

"Usually because they breed like Old Earth rabbits, only more so. Their numbers grow to a level which threatens to destroy their environment, and that seems to be their genetically programmed mechanism for reducing the population pressure."

"It seems a bit excessive," the analyst observed.

"Mother Nature can afford to be excessive," Medusa pointed out. "There are always plenty more where they came from, after all."

"True," O'Shaughnessy conceded, then cocked his head. "Actually, that's not a bad metaphor for Yvernau, now that I think about it. He and his fellow oligarchs really are threatening their own environment, and like those . . . lemmings of yours, there are, unfortunately, plenty more where he came from. Although, to be fair, I was also rather taken with Alquezar's metaphor during the debate."

"'Dinosaurs with stomachs full of frozen buttercups,'" Medusa quoted with a certain relish. "Something wrong with it, though. I don't think it was dinosaurs with buttercup-stuffed tummies. I think it was . . . elephants? Hippopotami? Something warm-blooded, anyway. But it *was* a nice turn of phrase, I'll grant you that."

"And Yvernau didn't like it very much, either," O'Shaughnessy said with poorly suppressed glee.

"No. No, he didn't," the baroness agreed judiciously.

She and her guest fell silent as uniformed Navy stewards, assigned to her support staff along with Colonel Gray's Marines, removed the appetizers and replaced them with the soup course. It was a delicious local concoction of chicken, rice and a local grain which closely resembled pearl barley, and the Provisional Governor sampled it appreciatively.

"So how do you think the New Tuscan government's going to react to his little fiasco, Milady?" O'Shaughnessy asked. He was officially *her* analyst and intelligence chief, but he'd long since discovered that in political matters, she was often better at his job than he was.

"Hard to say," she replied thoughtfully. "What they ought to do is get behind him and help him over the cliff, of course. I just wish I were confident they'll see it that way."

"About a third of his own delegation would cheerfully shoot him on the Convention floor," O'Shaughnessy observed, and she nodded.

"They certainly would. And they could make a nice profit selling tickets. Did you see Lababibi's expression when she realized his motion was going to fail?"

"Yes, Milady." O'Shaughnessy smirked. Undeniably, he smirked. "I'll almost guarantee you her instructions were to support him. She must've been delighted that Spindle's position as host meant she had to vote last."

Medusa nodded. She'd been watching Yvernau's expression almost as closely as Lababibi's when the Spindle System President rose to cast her vote. The New Tuscan had obviously counted hers as being in the bag, and his furious consternation when she voted against his motion had been almost as obvious as her own delight.

"It's been obvious for weeks—months—Lababibi despises Yvernau," she said. "He's probably the only person in the entire Convention who didn't know it. And you're right about her instructions. But the motion had already failed before the vote got to her, so she's not even going to have to pay the price of disobeying orders. She's the woman who put them firmly on the winners' side instead of death-locking them to the losers, the way she'd been told do to. And she got to kick Yvernau publicly in a particularly sensitive spot in the process. Talk about having your cake and eating it, too!"

She and her analyst smiled nastily at one another. Then she shook her head.

"It should be evident to anyone with a measurable IQ that Yvernau's policy's been proven a disastrous failure, Gregor. Sheer, cynical pragmatism, as well as principle, ought to turn his supporters back home against him. But the members of the New Tuscan political elite—I use the term loosely, you understand—have more than a little lemming in their own genotypes. Why else would they have set up the rules for their delegation the way they did?"

"It probably seemed like a good idea at the time."

"So did the first Peep attack on Grayson," the baroness said dryly, and the analyst chuckled. But his humor was fleeting, and he frowned.

"You may be right, Milady," he said slowly. "Everything I've managed to put together about Yvernau suggests that even now, he's not going to relinquish control of the delegation without direct, nondiscretionary orders from home. And as long as he wants to stay obstinate, there's nothing the rest of the New Tuscan delegates here on Flax can do about it. I'd like to think the system government's bright enough to send instructions from home to override him, though."

"You'd like to think that, but *do* you?"

The analyst sighed after considering it for several seconds. "Not really."

"I'm not overly optimistic myself. I thought Tonkovic was bad, but at least the Kornatians called her home and hammered her hard enough for her to resign." The dispatch boat from Split had brought the news the day before. "But I'm afraid the New Tuscan oligarchs are even more stubborn and a lot more monolithic than the Kornatians."

"Yes, Milady, they are. My best prediction at the moment is that there's about an eighty percent chance they'll leave Yvernau here, still heading their delegation. I figure there's a seventy percent chance they won't send him any new instructions, either. They'll let him continue standing in front of the air lorry until it runs him down, hoping for the best. After that, though, I don't know what they'll do. That's why I was asking you. It looks to *me* as if it's too close to call at this point. There's almost an even chance they'll buy into this notion of his that they can do just fine without us, thank you."

"That's my reading of the situation, too," Medusa said. "And he's probably right that we'll find ourselves obliged to prevent anyone else from moving in on them. But for the rest of it—" She shook her head. "Either New Tuscany's going to turn into some sort of police state, or else the current management's going to get bounced out on its collective posterior when the New Tuscan electorate sees what's happening to the rest of the Cluster without their participation."

"Which could be even messier than Nordbrandt's efforts on Kornati," O'Shaughnessy said grimly.

"That's what happens to closed, exploitative ruling classes which insist on trying to tie the cork down more tightly instead of reforming themselves or at least venting the pressure in some controlled fashion," Medusa agreed sadly. Then she shook herself.

"There's not much we can do if they're going to insist on some sort of mutual suicide pact," she said. "On the other hand, it looks like the rest of the Cluster's falling into line behind Alquezar and Krietzmann quite nicely."

"Yes, it does." O'Shaughnessy made no particular effort to hide his satisfaction, and the Provisional Governor returned his broad smile with interest. "Given what Terekhov and Van Dort did to Nordbrandt and the FAK, and now the approval of the Alquezar draft Constitution virtually in its entirety, I'd have to say the annexation logjam seems to be breaking up. The one thing I was most worried about—once the Government finally decided to go ahead and impose a hard and fast deadline—was the effect all of the death and destruction on Kornati was going to have on domestic political opinion back home. Tonkovic and Yvernau's delaying tactics never had a hope of standing up to the threat of exclusion, but I had my doubts about whether or not Parliament would approve the annexation, even with the Queen getting behind and pushing hard, if it thought we were going to be looking at a constant, running sore in Split."

"I think you might've been underestimating both Her Majesty's grip on the present Parliament and the electorate's intestinal fortitude," Medusa said. "On the other hand, you might not have been. Either way, I'm glad there's not going to be any more spectacular bloodshed and explosions coming out of the Cluster."

"Very well, Amal," Terekhov said. "General signal to the Squadron. All units prepare to depart Montana orbit and proceed in company to Point Midway."

"Aye, aye, Sir," Lieutenant Commander Nagchaudhuri acknowledged, and Terekhov glanced around his bridge.

Hexapuma was understrength, what with the Marines she'd left on Kornati, the casualties she'd suffered when Hawk-Papa-One was destroyed, and the detachment of Ansten FitzGerald's party to *Copenhagen*. The same number of casualties and detached personnel would have made a relatively minor hole in the company of an older ship, like *Warlock* or *Vigilant*. Aboard *Hexapuma*, it represented a significant reduction in manpower. He'd been tempted to "borrow" a few people from the other ships, but not very strongly. He knew the temper of his weapon. He preferred to see it slightly understrength rather than risk introducing flaws into it at this critical moment.

He turned his attention to the main plot. The green icons of twelve ships gleamed upon it now. In addition to *Hexapuma*'s own, there were two other heavy cruisers—*Warlock* and *Vigilant*—and three light cruisers—*Gallant* and *Audacious*, both sisters of his dead *Defiant*, and *Aegis*, one of the new *Avalon*-class ships, almost as modern as *Hexapuma*. That was the core of "his" squadron's combat power, but they were supported by four destroyers—*Javelin* and *Janissary*, both relatively modern, and the ancient (though neither of them was really any older than *Warlock*) *Rondeau* and *Aria*. The ten warships were accompanied by the dispatch boat he'd impressed from its assignment to the Montanan government and by HMS *Volcano*.

He let his attention linger on *Volcano*'s light code for a moment, then laid his forearms precisely along the armrests of his command chair and rotated it to face Lieutenant Commander Wright.

"All right, Tobias," he said, his voice calm, unshadowed by any trace of uncertainty. "Take us out of here."

Chapter Fifty-Three

HMS *Ericsson* erupted over the hyper wall into the Spindle system in a starburst of blue transit energy twenty-seven days after leaving Dresden.

She sent her identity and notice that she carried dispatches to HMS *Hercules* via grav-pulse as soon as she made translation, and a trickle of consternation flowed uphill as the news of her arrival wended its way towards the superdreadnought's flag deck. *Ericsson* was a depot ship. She wasn't a dispatch boat, and she *was* supposed to be permanently stationed in Montana, supporting the Southern Patrol.

No one knew what she was doing here, but no one expected it to be good.

"Dispatches?" Captain Loretta Shoupe frowned at *Hercules*' com officer. "From Montana?"

"That's what I'm assuming at the moment, Ma'am," the lieutenant commander said. "But assume is all I can do. Unless you want me to send a query back?"

Shoupe considered. According to the time chop on the arrival message, it had been receipted nineteen minutes before it was actually delivered to her. Allowing for decryption time and the fact that the communications officer had hand-delivered it to her, which had required him to walk it up six decks and down the next best thing to a quarter-kilometer of passages, that wasn't too bad. But the total transit time for *Ericsson* from the hyper limit to Flax orbit would be approximately two and a half hours, which meant it would be another two hours and fifteen minutes before she reached *Hercules*.

She scanned the brief message again. Whatever dispatch *Ericsson* was carrying, it was obviously important, since she'd listed it as Priority Alpha-Three. That called for it to be delivered via secure recording medium rather than transmitted.

"Yes," she said. "Ask them to confirm the originator and the addressee of their dispatches."

"From Terekhov, you say?" It was Rear Admiral Augustus Khumalo's turn to frown. "Aboard *Ericsson*?"

"Yes, Sir." Shoupe stood just inside the hatch of his day cabin, and he beckoned for her to come further in and take a seat. "It's from Terekhov," she continued as she obeyed the silent order, "but she didn't come direct from Montana. According to her arrival message, she's inbound from Dresden."

"*Dresden?*" Khumalo sat straighter behind his desk, and his frown deepened. "What the hell was she doing in Dresden?"

"I don't know yet, Sir. I'm guessing Terekhov sent her there for some reason before she came on to Spindle."

"But she's carrying Alpha-Three priority dispatches from *Terekhov*, not from anyone in Dresden?"

"That's correct, Sir. Lieutenant Commander Spears requested and received confirmation of that."

"That's ridiculous," Khumalo fumed. "If his message is so damned important, why send it so roundabout? Going by way of Dresden added almost three weeks to the direct transit time! Besides," his frown became an active scowl, "there's a dispatch boat assigned to the Montanan government, and *she* could have made the trip direct from Montana in ten days, a fifth of the time he he took sending it this way!"

"I know, Sir. But I'm afraid I don't have enough information even to speculate on what's going on. Except to say we'll know one way or another in about—" she checked her chrono "—another hour and fifty-eight minutes."

"He's done *what*?"

Baroness Medusa wasn't doing any frowning. She was staring at Rear Admiral Khumalo in stark disbelief.

"It's all in his dispatch, Milady," Khumalo said in the voice of a man still dealing with his own disbelief. "He's come up with some wild suspicion that the Republic of Monica—*Monica*, of all damned places!—is preparing some lunatic military operation here in the Cluster."

"So he stole a merchantship—a *Solarian* merchantship—put a Navy crew on board her, and sent her off to violate Monica's territorial space?" the Provisional Governor demanded.

"Ah, actually, Milady," Shoupe said a bit nervously, "that part of it makes a certain amount of sense."

"*None* of this makes any sense, Loretta!" Khumalo snarled. "The man's chasing phantoms!"

"That's obviously one possibility, Sir," Shoupe acknowledged. "But it's not the only one," she added stubbornly. Admiral and Provisional Governor alike turned to stare at her, and she shrugged. "I'm not saying he's right, Sir. There's no way for any of us to know that at this point. But if he *is* right, the sooner we confirm it, the better. And if we can possibly keep the Monicans from realizing we have confirmed it, the advantage could be enormous. And—"

"And going to call on Monica to investigate with a Queen's ship would make that impossible," Baroness Medusa finished for her.

"Exactly. A freighter, on the other hand, especially a *Solly* freighter, probably has a pretty good chance of getting in and out without arousing any suspicion."

"But if it *does* arouse any suspicion, and it's stopped

and searched, the discovery that it has a Navy crew—a Navy crew that *stole* the ship in the first place—will make the situation ten times as bad as if he'd sailed straight through Monica in *Hexapuma*!" Khumalo threw in.

"Excuse me," Gregor O'Shaughnessy said, "but I came in on this late. What makes Captain Terekhov think the Monicans are up to something in the first place?"

"That's . . . a little involved," Commander Chandler said. Khumalo's intelligence officer glanced at the rear admiral considerably more nervously than Shoupe had. "He's included a summary of all the evidence which forms the basis of his analysis, and he's copied his intelligence files for you and the Provisional Governor, so you can check both the evidence and his conclusions for yourself. The short version's that he and Van Dort have an informant who claims the Jessyk Combine delivered a large number of shipyard technicians, well versed in naval applications, to Monica. Apparently, according to this same source, Jessyk's sending in a flock of freighters configured as minelayers, as well. At *Jessyk's* cost, not Monica's. And the same ship that delivered the technicians saw what looked like two very large repair or depot ships in Monica, at Eroica Station, its main naval yard, when it dropped off the techs. And it was *also* the ship used to run arms to Nordbrandt and Westman."

"Westman!" the baroness said suddenly. "That's another thing. What's happening with Westman in the middle of all this?"

"That's actually one of the bright points, Milady," Chandler replied. "Apparently, Westman's laid down his weapons and accepted an amnesty offer from President Suttles."

"Well, thank God there's *some* good news!" Khumalo grated.

"Forgive me, Admiral," O'Shaughnessy said, "but assuming this merchantship—*Copenhagen*, you said it was called?" Khumalo nodded, and the civilian intelligence specialist continued. "Well, assuming *Copenhagen* gets into and out of Monica without being intercepted or boarded, where's the problem?"

"Where's the problem?" Khumalo repeated. "Where's the *problem*?" He glared at O'Shaughnessy. "I'll tell you where the *problem* is, Mr. O'Shaughnessy. Not content to steal a Solarian-registry freighter—a fact which is *going* to come out, eventually, you may be sure—and use it to violate a sovereign star nation's territoriality, Captain Terekhov's also seen fit to order every unit of the Southern Patrol in Tillerman, Talbott, and Dresden to join him in Montana. He's assembled himself an entire squadron—somewhere between eight and fifteen Queen's ships, depending on who was in-system and who was in transit between—and, assuming he kept to the schedule which he so *kindly* provided to us, he left Montana with that squadron ten days ago."

"Going where?" O'Shaughnessy was noticeably paler than he'd been a moment before, and Khumalo seemed to take a certain gloomy satisfaction in the change.

"His immediate objective is a point approximately one hundred light-years from Montana—thirty-eight light-years from Monica—where he expects to rendezvous with *Copenhagen* sometime in the next ten days to two weeks."

"Jesus Christ," O'Shaughnessy said prayerfully, "please tell me he's *not* going to—?"

"It's the only explanation for why he chose this peculiar way to get his dispatches to the Admiral in the first place, Gregor," Shoupe said heavily. "He's made it physically impossible for us to stop him."

"He's a frigging lunatic!" O'Shaughnessy snapped in a horrified voice. "What kind of loose warhead is the Navy *giving* ships to, goddamn it?"

Shoupe glared at him, anger sparkling in her dark brown eyes, and even Khumalo gave him a dirty look. The rear admiral opened his mouth, but Dame Estelle's raised hand stopped him. The Provisional Governor gave O'Shaughnessy a stern look, and pointed one index finger at him like a pistol.

"Don't let your prejudices run away with your mouth before you engage your brain, Gregor." She didn't even raise her voice, but it stung like the flick of a whip. O'Shaughnessy flinched visibly, and she gave him a cold, level stare. "Captain Terekhov's intentionally arranged matters so that he becomes the obvious sacrificial lamb if one becomes necessary. I once knew another Navy captain who would've done precisely the same thing *if* she'd believed what he apparently does. He may be wrong, but he is *not* a lunatic, and he's deliberately placed his career on the chopping block. Not simply to back up what he believes in, but so that the Queen will be free to court-martial him if she needs to prove to the galaxy at large that her Government had nothing to do with his totally unauthorized foray."

"I—" O'Shaughnessy paused and cleared his throat. "Forgive me, Admiral. Loretta. Ambrose." He bowed to each uniformed officer in turn. "The Provisional Governor's right. I spoke before I thought."

"Believe me, Mr. O'Shaughnessy," Khumalo said heavily, "I doubt very much that you could possibly think of anything unflattering to say about Captain Terekhov's mental processes which hasn't already passed through my own mind. Which isn't to say the Provisional Governor's wrong in any way. It's just that the entire notion seems so preposterous, so bizarre, I simply can't believe it's possible."

"I think . . . I think *I* can, actually," O'Shaughnessy said after a moment.

"Excuse me?" Khumalo blinked at him.

"If—and I say *if*—someone in the League's been deliberately stirring up and arming people like Nordbrandt and Westman to destabilize the Cluster, and if that same someone's prepared to upgrade the Monicans' naval capabilities, then it could actually make sense," the civilian said slowly.

"If they expect Monica to take *us* on, it had better be one damned massive upgrade of their capabilities!" Khumalo snorted.

"Granted. But maybe not quite as massive as you're assuming, Admiral."

Khumalo started to say something quickly, but O'Shaughnessy shook his head.

"I'm not questioning your naval judgment. But if Terekhov and Van Dort have put this together the way it sounds to me they have, then this is essentially a *political* operation which simply happens to have a military component. Oh," he waved both hands, "it's far too complicated, and it requires a degree of confidence verging on blind arrogance, but God knows the Sollies have demonstrated plenty of arrogance in the past. I think it's literally impossible for the sort of people who'd try something like this to conceive of a situation they can't control—or at least spin the way they want it—because they're so confident they have the power of the entire League behind them."

"Maybe so, but it's still ridiculous," Khumalo said. "Let's say they've tripled the Monican Navy's combat power." He barked a harsh laugh. "Hell, let's say they've increased it by a factor of *ten*! So what? We could still wipe them out in an afternoon with a single division of SD(P)s or a squadron of CLACs!"

"Possibly. All right, *probably*," O'Shaughnessy amended at the rear admiral's exasperated look. "But it's entirely possible that whoever put this thing together doesn't really care what happens to the Monicans. All they may care about is creating a pretext—an armed clash in the Cluster—that gives the Monicans an initial victory or two. Are you going to argue that an upgraded Monican Navy couldn't defeat your presently deployed forces? Especially if it caught them dispersed, by surprise, and engaged them in separate, isolated actions with its own forces concentrated for each attack?"

Khumalo glared again, but this time he was forced, grudgingly, to shake his head.

"Well suppose the Monicans did just that, and then called in Frontier Security, claiming *we'd* started it and asking for Solarian peacekeeping forces. What do you think would happen then?"

Khumalo's jaw clamped hard, and O'Shaughnessy nodded.

"It sounds to me as if Terekhov's already neutralized the terrorist movements which were supposed to destabilize things from the civilian, political side," he said. "If the Monicans or their Solly partners are looking for something they can use to spin the Solly media, they may already have everything they need, but at least it's not going to get any worse. And if he can neutralize the Monican Navy—assuming the Monicans really are part of a coordinated operation—he may just manage to stall the entire operation."

"Then you think he's right?" Shoupe asked.

"I don't have the least idea whether he's right or not," O'Shaughnessy said flatly. "In fact, I'm busy praying he's dead wrong. But I think it's *possible* he isn't, and if there really is something to his suspicions, then I hope to God he manages to pull this off."

"I don't know *what* I think," Khumalo said after a few heartbeats of silence. "But if he *is* right, we're going to need more firepower than I have right now. Loretta," he turned to his chief of staff, "draft a message to the Admiralty, highest priority. Attach copies of Terekhov's dispatches—*all* his dispatches—and request immediate reinforcement of the Lynx Terminus. Further inform them that I'll be ordering the remainder of my present forces to concentrate to cover the southern edge of the Cluster and that I'm moving on Monica personally with every ship available here in Spindle as soon as possible. Inform them," he looked across at the Provisional Governor, meeting her eyes levelly, "that although I remain uncertain of Captain Terekhov's conclusions, I endorse his actions and intend to support him to the best of my ability. I want that off by dispatch boat to Lynx and Manticore as quickly as humanly possible."

"Aye, aye, Sir," Shoupe said crisply, eyes gleaming with approval.

"It's going to be too late to make very much difference to Terekhov, either way, Loretta," the rear admiral said quietly.

"Maybe so, Admiral," she replied. "But maybe not, too."

"I sure hope this is going to work, Sir," Aikawa Kagiyama said quietly.

He and Ansten FitzGerald sat on *Copenhagen*'s flight deck as the freighter accelerated steadily inward from the system's hyper limit. The merchantship's bridge was actually smaller than *Hexapuma*'s, but it seemed incredibly vast because it was uncluttered by the elaborate plots, data displays, weapons consoles, and multiple command stations of a warship. It had been rather nice, in many ways, to have the space during the thirty-three-day voyage from Montana. At the moment, however, it simply served to remind Aikawa that he was aboard an unarmed, unarmored, absolutely defenseless, *slow* merchant vessel about to enter a potentially hostile star system under false pretenses.

It was not a pleasant thought.

"Well," FitzGerald said thoughtfully, glancing across at the midshipman manning the freighter's sensors, such as they were and what there were of them, "it's got a better chance of working than a visit from the *Nasty Kitty* would have, Mr. Kagiyama."

Despite the tension, Aikawa actually chuckled, and FitzGerald was glad to see it. The young man's humor still lacked the spontaneity and edge of mischievous wickedness which normally typified it, but at least he was no longer troubled by obvious bouts of depression. The Captain had been right. Assigning him to *Copenhagen* and working his posterior off had done wonders. And FitzGerald was also grateful for the time it had given him to get to know the youngster better. With only five officers, including Aikawa, in the entire ship, he'd learned more about each of them in the last T-month than in the previous six.

Not that learning more about some of them had been as pleasant as learning about others.

The freighter's acting captain glanced at the small com

screen which showed the view from the optical pickup mounted on Lieutenant MacIntyre's skinsuit helmet. The engineering officer's personnel management skills impressed FitzGerald even less here in *Copenhagen* than in *Hexapuma*. The smaller ship's company only magnified her ability to irritate and annoy the experienced ratings and noncoms under her command, and FitzGerald was beginning to question whether or not his and the Captain's original theory about the reason for that was accurate. Lack of self-confidence was one thing, but some people—and FitzGerald was starting to think MacIntyre might be one of them—simply had too much little-tin-god in them to ever make good officers. She was actually a superior technician, and it had shown as she and her skinsuited work party prepped the recon drone in *Copenhagen*'s cavernous cargo hold, however—

"Just hold it a minute, Danziger!" he heard the lieutenant snap suddenly. "I'll *tell* you when I'm ready to kick it loose, damn it! Don't you people *ever* pay attention to what you're doing?"

"Yes, Lieutenant. Sorry about that, Lieutenant," the senior sensor rating replied, and FitzGerald winced. Calling an officer by his rank was certainly proper procedure, but it could also become a backhanded swipe at one as junior as MacIntyre was. Especially when it was used in every single sentence . . . and delivered in the elaborately correct tone Danziger had just employed.

I'm going to have to have a little talk with her once we get back to Hexapuma. *I hope it'll do some good. Although I'm not all that confident it will.*

"All right," MacIntyre said more calmly a few minutes later. "All systems check. Let's get it out of here."

The working party lifted the massive drone—well over a hundred tons—easily in the depressurized cargo hold's micro-gravity. They walked it aft to the gaping hatch, big enough to engulf some destroyers bodily, and used presser-tractor jacks to kick it clear of the ship. MacIntyre kept her eyes on it, which had the effect of holding it in the center of FitzGerald's display, and the commander felt a flicker of relief as the drone's emergency reaction thrusters flared. Its onboard programming obviously had it, and it was adjusting its position to be certain it passed cleanly through the open kilt of *Copenhagen*'s impeller wedge before lighting off its own very low-powered wedge.

"Drone successfully deployed, Sir," MacIntyre announced over the com channel dedicated to her link to Fitz-Gerald.

"Very good, Ms. MacIntyre. Get the hold secured, if you please."

"Aye, aye, Sir."

"Well, Aikawa," FitzGgerald remarked as he returned his attention to the midshipman, "so far, so good. Now all we need to do is recover it again before we leave the system."

"We've been challenged by Monica Astrogation Central, Sir," Lieutenant Kobe announced.

"And about time, too," FitzGerald replied with just a bit more studied calm than he actually felt. "Even a light-speed system should've been asking us who we are before this," he added, and Kobe grinned.

"Shall I respond, Sir?"

"Now, now, Jeff!" FitzGerald shook his head. "This is a merchie, not a Queen's ship, and merchies don't do things the way men-of-war do. Let's not make anyone suspicious by being too on the bounce about all this. Astrogation Central will still be there whenever we get around to answering them."

"Uh, aye, aye, Sir," Kobe replied after only the briefest of pauses, and FitzGerald chuckled.

"At least a third of the freighters in space leave their com watch on auto-record, Jeff," he explained, "and Sollies are even worse about that than most. Generally, there's an alarm set to alert the fellow who's supposed to be keeping an eye on communications that a particular incoming message is important. More often than not, though, the computers aboard a ship like this are too stupid to make that kind of evaluation reliably, so the system simply records anything that comes in and otherwise ignores it until a message has been repeated at least once. At that point, it figures someone really wants to talk to somebody and sounds an alarm to get the com officer's attention. That's why we often have to hail merchantships two or three times."

Kobe nodded, obviously filing away another one of those practical bits of knowledge that places like the Island so often forgot to pass along. FitzGerald nodded back and turned his command chair to glance at the midshipman.

"Anything interesting showing up, Aikawa?"

"Sir, if someone were obliging enough to set off a ten- or twenty-megaton nuke at a range of ninety or a hundred klicks, this ship's passive sensors *might* actually be able to pick it up."

FitzGerald snorted, and Aikawa smiled.

"Actually, Sir," he said more seriously, "I am picking up a few impeller signatures now. Not very many, though, and I can't tell you much more than that someone's moving under power out there. If I had to guess, I'd say four or five of them are LACs, but there's at least a couple acting like bigger warships. Maybe destroyers or light cruisers."

"What do you mean, 'acting like bigger warships'?" FitzGerald asked, curious about the midshipman's logic chain.

"It looks to me as if they're carrying out maneuvers," Aikawa replied. "Two of the ones I think are LACs are moving along under only about two hundred gees with a current velocity of less than twelve thousand KPS. From their vectors, it looks like they're pretending they just crossed the alpha wall and they're heading for Monica. And with that acceleration, they almost have to be playing the roles of merchantmen. Meanwhile, these other impeller signatures over here—" he indicated a pair of unidentified icons on the freighter's deplorably detail-free "tactical plot" "—are chasing after them from astern. Looks to me like *they're* pretending to be commerce raiders, and effective commerce raiders would just about have to be hyper-capable. Which probably makes these two destroyers or cruisers."

"I see." FitzGerald nodded in approval. "Are any of them in a position to pick up our drone?" he asked after a moment.

"I doubt anything in the system has the sensors to spot our bird at anything over five kiloklicks, Sir. And these fellows are so far off the drone's programmed track they couldn't pick it up even with Manticoran sensors that knew exactly where to look."

"I'm glad to hear it," FitzGerald said. "But don't get too confident about the quality of the other side's sensors. If somebody really has been upgrading their naval capabilities, they could have a lot more sensor reach and sensitivity than ONI's estimated."

"Yes, Sir," Aikawa said, just a bit stiffly. FitzGerald only smiled. The youngster's stiffness was directed at his own overconfidence, not at the commander for having pointed it out to him.

FitzGerald tipped back his command chair and glanced at the time display. *Copenhagen* had been in-system for almost thirty-five minutes. Her velocity was up to 14,641 KPS, and she'd reduced the range to the planet Monica by well over twenty-six million kilometers—down to 9.8 LM. And it had been about six minutes since Kobe received Astrogation Central's challenge. So in another three or four minutes, the people who'd sent it would realize *Copenhagen* hadn't replied. Call it five minutes to allow for the usual Verge sloppiness. *Copenhagen* would have traveled about another 4.5 million kilometers during the interval, which would reduce the light-speed transmission time by only fifteen seconds, so it would be roughly another sixteen minutes before the second challenge arrived. The time dilation of *Copenhagen*'s velocity—her *tau* was barely .9974—was so low as to have no effect at all on message turnaround.

Which meant he would enjoy the entire sixteen minutes worrying about whether or not the Captain's stratagem was going to work after all. Taken all in all, that might not be so bad a thing. After all, it meant he'd get to use up sixteen minutes of the six hundred or so he intended to spend in the system worrying about something besides that damned reconnaissance drone.

The reconnaissance array in question proceeded along its preordained path in sublime electronic indifference to any anxiety which might afflict the protoplasmic creatures who'd sent it on its way.

It was a very stealthy array, the hardest to spot, lowest-signature drone the Royal Manticoran Navy was capable of building, which was very hard to spot, indeed. It was equipped with extraordinarily capable active sensors, but those were locked down—as, indeed, they almost always were when the drone or its brethren were deployed. There was very little point in being undetectable if one intended to flounder around shouting at the top of one's lungs. The drone's creators had no intention of allowing their offspring to do anything so gauche, and so they had also equipped it with exquisitely sensitive *passive* sensors, which produced no telltale emissions to give away the drone's position.

Or, in this case, the simple fact of the drone's existence.

It sped onward, under the paltry acceleration (for one such as itself) of a mere 2,000 KPS^2. Because of the profile on which it had been launched, and the need to avoid the fusion-fired furnace of the system's G3 primary, which lay almost directly between it and its intermediate destination, it would find itself forced to travel two light-hours in order to cover a straight-line distance of only a little over forty light-minutes. After that, it would be required to travel an additional thirty-one light minutes in order to rendezvous once more with the plebeian ship which had launched it upon its journey. Thus its pokey rate of acceleration. It had ten hours to kill before it could possibly be collected once again, and its languid acceleration would give it almost twenty-four minutes to look around at its intermediate destination before it had to get back underway if it was going to keep its rendezvous schedule.

The drone didn't care. At such a low rate of acceleration, it had a powered endurance of nearly three T-days, and if it couldn't begin to match the massive acceleration rates of ship-to-ship missiles, unlike those missiles, *its* far lower-powered impeller wedge could be turned on and off at will, extending its endurance almost indefinitely. Besides, the far weaker strength of its wedge, combined with the stealth technology so lovingly built into it, was what made it so difficult to detect in the first place. Let the glamour-hungry attack missiles go slashing across space at eighty or ninety thousand KPS^2, shouting out their presence for all the galaxy to see! They were, at best, kamikazes anyway, doomed to Achilles-like lives of brief, shining martial glory. The recon drone was an Odysseus—clever, wily, and circumspect.

And, in this instance, determined to get home at last to a Penelope named *Copenhagen*.

"Sir, Astrogation Central's repeating its challenge. And, ah, they sound just a touch *testy* about it," Lieutenant Kobe added.

"Well, we certainly can't have that, can we?" FitzGerald replied. "All right, Jeff. Turn on our transponder. Then give it another four minutes—long enough for the com officer to get to his station, turn off the alarm, and get a response from whoever has the watch—and send the message."

"Aye, aye, Sir."

The communications officer pressed the button that activated *Copenhagen*'s transponder, squawking its perfectly legal ID code. Four minutes later, he pressed his transmit key, and the prerecorded message went zipping out at the speed of light.

Aikawa Kagiyama muttered something under his breath, and FitzGerald glanced at him.

"What is it, Aikawa?" the commander asked, and the midshipman looked up with an embarrassed expression

"Nothing, really, Sir. I was just talking to myself." FitzGerald raised an eyebrow, and Aikawa sighed. "I guess I'm just a little worried about how well all of this is going to work out."

"I hope you won't mind me pointing out that this is a hell of a time to be just getting started worrying about that, Aikawa!" Kobe said with a chuckle, and the midshipman smiled wryly.

"I'm not just getting started, Sir," he told the lieutenant. "It's just that the worrying I was already doing has suddenly taken on a certain added emphasis."

Everyone on the bridge chuckled, and FitzGerald smiled back at him. It was good to have something break the tension, he reflected. And, in all honesty, he shared some of Aikawa's trepidation. Not about the message itself, but about who might be receiving it.

Thanks to the manner in which *Hexapuma* had taken possession of *Copenhagen*, all the freighter's computers had been intact and undamaged. True, the secure portions of their databases had been protected by multiple levels of security fences and protocols, but most commercial cybernetics—even Solarian cybernetics—simply weren't up to the standards demanded by governments and military forces. There were exceptions, of course. Without De Chabrol's assistance, for example, it would have been effectively impossible for *Hexapuma*'s technicians to break into *Marianne*'s secure systems. A proper team of ONI specialists could have managed it, in time, but it wasn't something to be lightly undertaken under field conditions.

But a run-of-the-mill, *honest* freighter like *Copenhagen* neither needed nor could afford the same degree of security, and Amal Nagchaudhuri and Guthrie Bagwell had hacked into the ship's computer net with absurd ease. Which meant Lieutenant Kobe had access to Kalokainos Shipping's basic house encryption and authentication codes. With those in hand, he and Nagchaudhuri had crafted a totally legitimate message in the company's encryption format. The message content was just as totally bogus, of course, but there wouldn't be any way for anyone to realize that until it ultimately reached its final destination—which happened to be the office of one Heinrich Kalokainos on Old Earth herself.

When old Heinrich finally opened and read that message, he was likely to be just a little bit irritated, FitzGerald reflected. But the fact that its addressee was Kalokainos Shipping's CEO and largest single stockholder ought to discourage any officious underling from fiddling around with it in the meantime. And that message was *Copenhagen*'s ostensible reason for being here.

The fact that Kalokainos didn't maintain an office of its own on Monica might have been a problem, but there was a gentleman's agreement among the shipping agents of the dozen or so most powerful Solarian shipping lines to act as one another's representatives when circumstances required. Although *Copenhagen*'s message didn't carry any sort of emergency priority (aside from its intended recipient), FitzGerald didn't doubt the Captain was right—the Jessyk Combine agent on Monica would normally accept it and forward it Solward. The only question in the commander's mind was whether or not the Jessyk agent would be feeling equally helpful in light of whatever deviltry Jessyk was up to here.

Well, that, and the question of whether or not he'll ask any questions about it—or us—that we can't answer.

The problem was that while, as nearly as they could determine from *Copenhagen*'s logs, she'd never visited Monica, those logs were unfortunately far from complete. And even if they hadn't been, *Copenhagen* had worked the rest of the Talbott Cluster for over five T-years. The ship herself might never have visited Monica, but that was no guarantee the members of her crew hadn't, or that the Jessyk agent in the system didn't know her legal skipper. Or, at least, what the legal skipper's name was.

Only one way to know, he told himself, and settled back to find out while *Copenhagen* continued toward Monica orbit.

✧ ✧ ✧

"So, of course I'll see to it your message is forwarded, Captain Teach," the man on FitzGerald's com said. "You realize, I hope, though, that it may be some time before I'm able to get it aboard a ship headed for Sol."

"Of course, Mr. Clinton," FitzGerald said. "I never expected anything else. Frankly, it's an unmitigated pain in the ass, but the damned Rembrandters insisted that I relay it to our home offices. And you can guess how often *Copenhagen* sees Sol!"

"About as often as I do," the Jessyk agent agreed with a chuckle.

"If that," FitzGerald replied. "At any rate, Mr. Clinton, let me thank you once again." He paused for a moment, then shrugged. "I'm afraid I'm not familiar with Monican customs procedures. Since we're only passing through, will there be any problem with my sending a shuttle down just long enough to hand over the message chip to you or one of your representatives?"

"As long as you're not landing or transshipping any cargo here, I shouldn't think so," Clinton assured him. "If you'd like, I can have my secretary meet your shuttle at the pad. If your crewman hands it to him through the hatch while the pad Customs agent watches to be sure we're not smuggling any laser heads or nukes back and forth, there's no reason for him to even board it."

"I'd deeply appreciate it if you could do that," FitzGerald said with absolute sincerity.

"No problem. Our offices are right here at the port. My secretary can hop over to the pad in five, ten minutes at most. I'll contact traffic control to get your pad number and have him waiting."

"Thank you again," FitzGerald said. "Kalokainos is going to owe you a pretty sizable return favor someday. I'll instruct Lieutenant Kidd to pass the chip to your man." He paused again, then cocked his head. "Tell me, Mr. Clinton, how do you feel about Terran whiskey?"

"Why, I'm quite partial to it, Captain Teach."

"Well, I just happen to have a case of genuine Daniels-Beam Grand Reserve in my personal cabin stores," Fitz-Gerald told him. "Do you suppose your Customs agent would object to Lieutenant Kidd's passing a bottle of *that* along to you with the chip?"

"Captain," Clinton said with an enormous smile, "if he were so foolish as to object to an innocent little gift like that, he'd be off my payroll in a heartbeat!"

"I thought that might be the case." FitzGerald grinned. "Consider it a small token of my appreciation for your assistance."

It was obvious Clinton found the "small token" eminently acceptable, and no wonder, FitzGerald thought as they completed their conversation with protestations of mutual respect and indebtedness. A bottle of Daniels-Beam Grand Reserve went for about two hundred Manticoran dollars. This particular bottle came from Captain Terekhov's personal supply, and FitzGerald hoped Clinton would enjoy it thoroughly.

Especially in light of what was probably going to happen to the Jessyk agent's career when his employers figured out what *Copenhagen* had really been up to in Monica. It wouldn't exactly be fair of them to blame Clinton for not realizing what was happening, but Mesan-headquartered businesses weren't particularly noted for their passionate attachment to the concept of fairness.

He glanced at the time display again. Right on schedule. In fact, they might be doing just a bit too well, especially if the Customs agent was going to be as obliging as Clinton thought. Well, that was all right. He could always find some reason to spend an extra few minutes in orbit before heading back out for the hyper limit. Or to accelerate just a tad more slowly than he had on the way in.

Copenhagen wouldn't be leaving on a direct reciprocal of her arrival vector. Instead, she would head away from the system primary almost at right angles to her initial approach. There was no reason anyone should be suspicious, since he'd be filing a flight plan for the Howard

System, but it would substantially reduce the total distance the recon drone would be forced to travel to return to the ship which had launched it.

The recon drone continued upon its unhurried way. Its passive sensors quivered like enormously sensitive cat's whiskers, and evasion programs waited patiently to steer it away from any vessel or sensor platform it detected which might have detected it, in turn. No such threats revealed themselves, and the drone brought its forward progress gradually to halt, fifteen light-seconds from the naval shipyard known as Eroica Station.

The tiny, stealthy spy hovered there in the vast emptiness, imitating—with a remarkable degree of success—a hole in space. Passive sensors, including optical ones, peered incuriously but painstakingly at the bustling activity around the space station. Ships and mobile spacedocks were counted, emission signatures (where available) were meticulously recorded. Moving vessels were scanned most closely of all, and careful note was taken of the two enormous repair ships sharing Eroica Station's solar orbit.

The drone spent fifteen of its twenty-four available minutes in silent, intense activity. Then it turned away, activating its impeller wedge once more, and went creeping off towards its scheduled rendezvous with *Copenhagen* with nine precious minutes in reserve against unforeseen contingencies.

Had it been capable of such things, it would undoubtedly have felt a deep sense of satisfaction.

But it wasn't, of course.

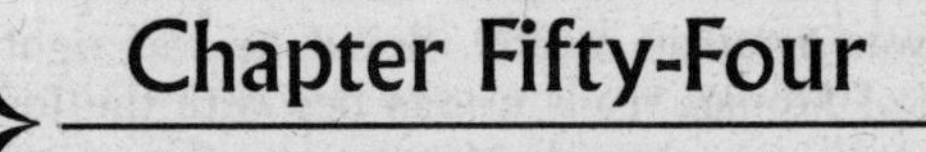

Chapter Fifty-Four

HMS *Hercules* departed Flax orbit exactly eight hours and thirty-six minutes after Rear Admiral Khumalo's meeting with the Provisional Government.

It was unlikely that the elderly superdreadnought had ever taken such precipitous leave of a star system in her entire previous career. Captain Victoria Saunders had certainly never expected to do so, and she felt more than a little out of breath at the sheer whirlwind energy which Khumalo and Loretta Shoupe had brought to the task of getting her ship and every other hyper-capable RMN unit in the Spindle System underway.

Saunders stood beside the captain's chair on her command deck, hands folded behind her, and watched the master plot as *Hercules*, the light cruisers *Devastation* and *Inspired*, and the destroyers *Victorious*, *Ironside*, and *Domino* accelerated steadily away from Flax. *Ericsson*, her sister ship *White*, and the ammunition ships *Petard* and *Holocaust* followed in the warships' wakes, and Khumalo had commandeered five additional dispatch boats. It was, at best, a lopsided and ill-balanced "squadron," although *Hercules* certainly looked impressive as its flagship. Unless, of course, one knew all of the old ship's manifold weaknesses as well as Saunders did.

But she's still a damned superdreadnought, Khumalo's flag captain told herself. *And we're still the Queen's Navy. And I will be damned if* Augustus Khumalo *hasn't actually remembered that*.

She shook her head, bemused and, to her own astonishment, proud of her Admiral. She'd skimmed Terekhov's dispatches—she hadn't had time to actually *read* them—and she couldn't decide whether Terekhov had brilliantly deduced the essentials of a complex plot or whether he was a raving lunatic. But if he was right, if the Republic of Monica really *was* in bed with the Jessyk Combine—which meant with Manpower—then he was probably also in for the fight of his life.

Which is saying quite a bit, given what he went through at Hyacinth.

In fact, it was possible, perhaps even probable, that if his fears were justified, Aivars Terekhov would be dead long before *Hercules* and her mismatched consorts ever got to Monica. For that matter, it was possible Khumalo's relief force might find itself destroyed, as well. But whatever happened to Terekhov, or to them, the Admiralty would have been warned, and the Republic of Monica would *damned* well find out that it should never have screwed with the Star Kingdom of Manticore.

"Excuse me, Ma'am."

Saunders turned towards the voice. It belonged to Commander Richard Gaunt, her executive officer.

"Yes, Dick?"

"The last of the personnel shuttles will be coming aboard in approximately ninety minutes, Ma'am," he said.

"Good, Dick. Good!" She smiled. "Do we have a headcount yet?"

"It looks like the shore patrol managed to round up just about everyone," he replied. "At last count we're about six warm bodies short, but for all I know, they could be aboard one of the other ships, given how frantic this entire departure's being."

"Tell me about it," she said feelingly, looking at the repeater plot that showed the ungainly gaggle of shuttles and pinnaces streaming after the squadron. It was unheard of for a Queen's ship to pull out so abruptly a sizable percentage of her company had to chase after her this way. But at least *Hercules'* acceleration rate was low enough the small craft wouldn't have much trouble overtaking her.

"Ma'am?" Gaunt's voice was much lower, and she looked back at him, one eyebrow arched.

"Do you really think all of this," he continued, still pitching his voice too low for anyone else to hear, and gesturing at the icons moving steadily across the plot, "is necessary?"

"I don't have any idea, Dick," she told him frankly. "But I did have the chance to look over Terekhov's projected ops schedule. If everything's going the way he projected, his kidnapped Solly freighter got to Monica about sixteen hours ago. Terekhov'll be arriving at his rendezvous—this 'Point Midway' of his—in about another seventy-two hours, and the freighter will meet him there about a week later. Call it ten standard days from now. And if he decides on the basis of its report to move directly on Monica, he can be there in another six days or so. We, on the other hand, can't reach Monica for twenty-five days. So, if he goes ahead, whatever he does is going to be over, one way or the other, at least one full T-week before we can possibly get there."

"I can't believe he'd really be crazy enough to pull something like that, Ma'am," Gaunt said, shaking his head. "He must know we're coming—the glory hound didn't leave us any choice about that! Surely he's not so far gone he won't wait one more *week* if it means the difference between going in unsupported and arriving with backup."

Saunders regarded her XO with a slight, rare frown. Gaunt was an efficient executive officer, the sort who always got the details right and developed an almost uncanny ability to anticipate his CO's desires. But he was also a stickler for sometimes petty details, and he had a powerful attachment to doing things by The Book. A certain . . . narrowness, coupled with an aversion to risk taking. He disliked the "glory hounds," a term he used a bit too easily for her taste, and Victoria Saunders had come to question whether or not he had the combination of flexibility and moral courage to wear the white beret of a starship commander. Especially in a war like the present one.

His last comment had just settled the question, and she was guiltily aware that an executive officer was what he would remain. That was what happened when a CO endorsed an officer's evaluation with the fatal words "Not recommended for independent command."

"Perhaps you're right," she said, looking at the man whose career she'd just decided to kill.

He wasn't, of course. But there was no point trying to explain that to someone of his seniority who didn't already understand.

"It's *Copenhagen*, all right, Sir," Naomi Kaplan announced.

"Thank you, Guns," Terekhov said calmly, and Helen glanced sideways at Paulo. The two midshipmen stood beside Lieutenant Commander Wright, where he'd been running through the results of their latest astrogation quiz on one of his secondary plots. Now Paulo met her gaze with no more than the micrometric elevation of one sculpted eyebrow.

It was the tiniest expression shift imaginable, but to Helen, it might as well have been a shout. She'd come more or less to grips with her emotions where he was concerned, although she wasn't positive he'd done the same for her. It didn't really matter. One thing the *Neue-Stil Handgemenge* taught was patience, and she was willing to wait.

She'd get him in the end. Even if she had to use some of that same *Neue-Stil* to beat him into submission.

She pushed that thought aside—or, rather, into a convenient pigeonhole for later consideration—and returned his lifted eyebrow with an abbreviated nod of her own. They were in agreement. The Captain couldn't possibly be as calm as he sounded.

The Squadron (everyone was calling it that now . . . except the Captain) floated in the absolute darkness of interstellar space, over six light-years from the nearest star. Starships seldom visited that abyss of emptiness, for there was nothing there to attract them. But it made a convenient rendezvous, so isolated and lost in the enormity of the universe that even God would have been hard-pressed to find them.

Many of *Hexapuma*'s people had found the visual displays . . . disturbing over the last week or so. The emptiness here was so perfect, the darkness so Stygian, that it could get to even the most hardened spacer. Commander Lewis, for example, made a point of avoiding any of the displays, and Helen had noticed Senior Chief Wanderman watching her every once in a while. There was something going on there, she thought. Something more than the uneasiness some of the ship's company seemed to feel. Whatever it was, Lewis wasn't letting it affect her performance of her duty, but Helen had the peculiar impression that *Hexapuma*'s Engineer would welcome even the prospect of taking on an entire system navy if it only got her away from this lonely spot which the rest of existence had forgotten.

Personally, Helen wasn't bothered a bit. In fact, she rather enjoyed her visits to the observation dome to watch the other ships of the squadron with their lights drifting against the soul-drinking dark like friendly, nearby constellations.

"Lieutenant McGraw."

Terekhov's voice pulled her back out of her reverie.

"Yes, Sir?"

"Please challenge *Copenhagen*."

"Aye, aye, Sir," the com officer of the watch replied,

and Terekhov nodded and settled back in his command chair to wait.

Helen was confident Kaplan had identified the incoming ship correctly. And she felt equally certain Commander FitzGerald was still in command of her. But it was typical of the Captain to make absolutely certain. It was interesting. He took infinite pains, taking nothing for granted, and if she'd seen only that side of him, she'd have written him down as a slave to The Book. One of those fussy martinets who never stuck their necks out, never took a chance.

But that wasn't how the Captain's mind worked. He took such care over the details, whenever he could, because he knew he couldn't always do that. So that when the time came for the risks which must be run, he could be confident of his ship's readiness . . . and his own. Know he'd done everything he possibly could to disaster-proof his position by perfecting his weapon before the screaming chaos of battle struck.

It was a lesson worth taking to heart, she thought, trying to focus her mind on Wright's voice as the Astrogator resumed his analysis of her latest navigational effort.

"Captain on deck!"

Ginger Lewis, still officially Terekhov's acting executive officer, barked the traditional announcement as he and Ansten FitzGerald stepped through the briefing room hatch. It was a tradition Terekhov had dispensed with shortly after taking command of *Hexapuma*, but he wasn't surprised by Ginger's reversion to it. She had an excellent grasp of group dynamics, and she was providing him with every psychological edge she could.

Eleven men and women in that compartment, including himself, wore the white berets of starship commanders, and he saw uncertainty, concern—even fear—on some of those faces. He wondered what *they* saw when they looked at him?

He walked to the head of the table, FitzGerald at his shoulder, and seated himself as the XO moved behind his own chair.

"Be seated, Ladies and Gentlemen," he said.

They sat back down, and he let his eyes sweep silently around the table, looking at each of them in turn.

Anders of the *Warlock*, and his executive officer, George Hibachi. Both of them returned Terekhov's regard steadily. Not without concern, but without flinching. That was important. After Terekhov himself, Ito Anders was the senior officer of the "squadron" he'd assembled.

Eleanor Hope of the *Vigilant*, and her XO, Lieutenant Commander Osborne Diamond. Hope looked acutely unhappy, and her eyes avoided his. Diamond was a cipher, sitting at his captain's left elbow with no more expression than the bulkhead behind him.

Commander Josepha Hewlett and Lieutenant Commander Stephen McDermott of the *Gallant*. Both of them looked uncomfortable; neither looked as unhappy as Hope.

Lieutenant Commander Benjamin Mavundia, *Audacious*' CO, and his exec, Lieutenant Commander Annemarie Atkinson. They were an unlikely looking pair. Mavundia couldn't stand a millimeter over a hundred and fifty-eight centimeters, with dark skin and a shaved head; Atkinson was almost as tall as Terekhov himself, and fair-haired and ivory-complexioned. Yet Mavundia's expression was the closest to eager of anyone's in the compartment, and Atkinson's eyes mirrored his own determination.

Commander Herawati Lignos, CO of HMS *Aegis*, their most modern ship after *Hexapuma*. Only a light cruiser, perhaps, but still a formidable vessel. Much like her skipper, Terekhov thought, looking at Lignos' determined chin and bladelike nose. Her executive officer, Lieutenant Commander Istvan Nemesanyi, sat quietly beside her, his hazel eyes almost vacant and yet, somehow, poised on a hair trigger.

Lieutenant Commander Jeffers of the *Javelin*; Lieutenant Commander Maitland Naysmith of the *Janissary*; Lieutenant Commander Frank Hennessy of the *Rondeau*; and Lieutenant Bianca Rossi of the *Aria* completed his warships' captains. And at the foot of the table sat

Commander Mira Badmachin, CO of HMS *Volcano*, the huge freighter which didn't mount a single offensive weapon of her own and yet was crucial to Terekhov's plans.

A mixed bag, he thought. *Certainly no "band of brothers"! But they're what I have, the best I could shanghai, and they're Queen's officers. That's just going to have to be good enough.*

"All of you know what Commander FitzGerald and *Copenhagen* were tasked to do," he began, and Commander Hope actually twitched as he broke his own silence. "The good news is that the Commander and his people appear to have accomplished their mission flawlessly. The bad news," he smiled mirthlessly at them, "is what they've discovered."

The sound of a pin dropped on the conference table would have been deafening, and he drew a deep, unobtrusive breath.

"*Copenhagen*'s recon drone executed its mission profile to the letter, Ladies and Gentlemen. Its passive sensors swept the volume through which it passed for active impeller wedges and examined the area of Eroica Station very carefully. Its data indicates that the Monica System Navy has been what might be called 'substantially reinforced.' In fact, the drone positively identified eleven *Indefatigable*-class battlecruisers at Eroica Station."

Something very like an audible gasp ran around the table, but he continued speaking calmly.

"So far as the drone was able to determine, all of them are either currently in yard hands or awaiting yard space. I believe they're being refitted in order to disguise their origins as much as possible. Which suggests to me, in turn, that they've been clandestinely provided to Monica. And I can think of only one reason for anyone to do that: to attack the Star Kingdom's interests in the Cluster."

Eleanor Hope shifted in her chair, and Terekhov's blue eyes moved to her.

"You wished to make a comment, Commander?" His

emphasis on her rank title was so slight it was almost imagined.

"Yes, Sir. I suppose I did," she said after a brief hesitation.

He moved his right hand, inviting her to continue, and she looked once around the table and drew a deep breath.

"Captain Terekhov, with all due respect, I see no reason to automatically assume these ships were 'clandestinely provided' to President Tyler's navy. ONI reported months ago that the *Indefatigables* were being retired and replaced by the new *Nevada*-class ships." She shrugged. "We all know about Tyler's cozy relationship with Frontier Security. If the Sollies are disposing of the *Indefatigables*, why shouldn't they sell—or even outright give—some of them to somebody who's been their proxy for the last thirty or forty T-years? And if that's the case, or even if there *is* something 'clandestine' about the way Monica acquired them, it doesn't necessarily follow that they're intended to attack our interests."

Terekhov regarded her mildly, his expression thoughtful, but Anders grimaced.

"If I may, Captain Terekhov?" he asked, and Terekhov nodded.

"Commander FitzGerald," *Warlock*'s CO asked, "are you confident these battlecruisers are being actively refitted at Eroica Station?"

"Yes, Sir, I am," FitzGerald said firmly. "Not all of them are being refitted simultaneously, but those which aren't actively in yard hands are in parking orbits with the space station, and over half have service craft and lighters alongside. There are also two repair ships, each of which is moored alongside one of them. We have optical confirmation that the main broadside sensor arrays on at least three have been removed and are in the process of replacement." It was his turn to shrug slightly. "To me, all of that spells a pattern of mass refits being funneled through limited yard capacity."

"Thank you." Anders looked back at Terekhov, although

it was evident he was actually directing his remarks to Hope. "If those ships had been openly provided by the League Navy to Monica, they wouldn't be being refitted at Eroica Station—not unless the object was to make them *less* capable than they already were. They would've been refitted and brought up to standard in *Solly* shipyards, where all the necessary support infrastructure and personnel would be available to do the job quickly. If they're being refitted in Monica, instead, then the Monicans are deliberately accepting that their limited facilities are going to bottleneck the entire process. And, like you, Sir, I can't think of anything the Monicans could do to *improve* the combat power of an *Indefatigable*-class battlecruiser. Which suggests they're up to something else, and I believe the suggestion that they're trying to hide, or at least confuse, the ships' origins by disguising their emissions signatures and sensor images makes sense.

"Which brings us to Commander Hope's second point, the question of just who the Monicans might intend to employ their new ships against. What Commander FitzGerald's detected is more firepower than Monica could possibly need to deal with any Verge system, or, for that matter, any dozen Verge systems! The only people I can think of in this neck of the woods that they'd need that much firepower against is us."

"Again, with all due respect, Captain," Hope said just a bit impatiently, "even if you're correct about who the ships might be used against, Monica wouldn't necessarily intend to use them offensively. In fact, it would be stupid of them to even contemplate *attacking* us, battlecruisers or no battlecruisers. But it's entirely possible that they could be sufficiently concerned by our presence in the Cluster to feel the need for a force able to deter any designs we might have on Monica."

"I think you're reaching, Eleanor," Commander Hewlett said, and Hope looked at her angrily. Hewlett looked at Terekhov, and he nodded permission for her to continue.

"There's no way those battlecruisers would deter us if

we really wanted Monica," *Gallant*'s CO said. "A couple of pod SDs could turn all of them into scrap in a half-hour. Besides, Monica's not the kind of star nation that worries about what other people are likely to do to it; it's the kind of star nation that spends all its time trying to think of things to do to other people."

"And just what makes you think they're foolish enough to believe they could use those ships to attack us if they believe they're too weak to *deter* us, Josepha?" Hope demanded.

"I think Captain Terekhov already answered that question, Eleanor," Hewlett said in a rather pointed tone. "If they think they can convince the League to intervene on their behalf, they can damned well use those ships to create a situation to justify asking for that intervention."

"Or," Hope said stubbornly, "they could be thinking their new battlecruisers might let them stand off a Manticoran attack long enough for the League to intervene on their behalf. In which case," she kept her eyes on Hewlett's face, but Terekhov knew who she was truly speaking to, "actually attacking their system might be the worst thing we could do. If they're ready to invite the Sollies in to defend them, and if the Sollies have already agreed to do that, then the last thing we want to do is to go right ahead and provide them their pretext."

"Under other circumstances, Commander Hope," Terekhov said coolly, "I might be inclined to accept your analysis. Unfortunately, we also know Monica's been involved, as a staging point, at the very least, in a concerted effort by an outside power to provide weapons and funds to terrorists in the Cluster. *That*, Commander, is indeed an offensive act. Arguably, in fact, an act of war, although the situation's somewhat clouded by the fact that the systems in which they've been aiding and abetting terrorists aren't yet actually Manticoran territory. Based on that fact, I'm disinclined to assume Frontier Security's long-term proxies are forting up in their home system because they anticipate the momentary arrival of Manticoran conquistadors."

Hope's face reddened, and her lips thinned angrily.

"In fact," Terekhov continued, "I assume those ships are part of a strategy aimed at preventing the annexation of the Talbott Cluster by the Star Kingdom. I believe the Jessyk Combine's deeply involved, which, given Jessyk's relationship with Manpower, means *Manpower* is almost certainly the prime mover. And I need hardly remind any officer in this compartment of all the reasons Manpower would have to want to keep the Star Kingdom as far from Mesa as possible. The presence of so many Solarian-built battlecruisers may very well indicate that Frontier Security's openly backing Monica. I'd like to think even Manpower would find it difficult to come up with the cash to simply buy that many ships of that size for someone like the Monicans. Be that as it may, however, I have no doubt whatsoever that those ships are intended to be used against targets in the Cluster for the purpose of preventing the annexation from being carried to a successful conclusion."

He paused, looking around the compartment, then continued unflinchingly.

"Because I believe that to be the case, I intend to advance to Monica. There, I will require the Monican government to cease all work upon their new battlecruisers until such time as they demonstrate to our satisfaction that those vessels pose no threat to the security of the Star Kingdom or to our friends in the region. Should they refuse, or should they employ military forces against us, I intend to attack Eroica Station and to destroy all of the battlecruisers being refitted there."

"Sir," Hope said, "please tell me you're joking."

"I am not in the habit, *Commander*," Terekhov said coldly, "of treating the killing of other human beings as a laughing matter."

"Sir," Hope said almost desperately, "what you're talking about is an act of war. An act of war carried out in time of peace against a sovereign star nation without the direction or approval of our own command authority. Sir, it could be legally construed as an act of *piracy* committed in the

Star Kingdom's name! I can't think of a single thing we could do that would damage our interstellar credibility worse in the eyes of the Solarian public."

"The Solarian public, unfortunately, Commander," Terekhov said, "is in the habit of thinking what the spinmasters who work for Frontier Security and the other Solly bureaucracies tell it to think. And there's no time for us to seek the approval of the Admiralty or the Prime Minister. These ships are being refitted *now*. We have no way of knowing how far advanced the refit process is, how soon some or all of them will become combat-ready. If we delay even a single day longer than we absolutely must, we potentially give the Monicans and their allies in Mesa the time they need to put their plan into operation. Or, at the very least, to kill and wound more of our people when we finally do move to neutralize the threat."

"Sir—" Hope began again.

"My mind is made up, Commander Hope," Terekhov told her flatly in a voice as unyielding as *Hexapuma*'s battle steel bones. "If nothing else, think of it this way. If we move in before those battlecruisers are ready, we'll be in the best possible position to dictate the outcome of the confrontation without *anyone* getting killed. If they can't fight us, they'll have no option but to surrender—under protest, if they will, but still surrender. At which point we can thoroughly investigate the ships and how they came to be there."

"And if it turns out they never were any threat to the Star Kingdom, and that you—and the officers following your orders—have committed an unauthorized act of war with the very real prospect of bringing the Solarian League in against us, Sir?" Hope challenged.

"I don't believe it will. If it does, however, Her Majesty will be able to say with perfect honesty that she never authorized our actions. That we grossly exceeded our authority, and that she disavows everything we've done. In which case, the fact that you'll be following my own formal, written orders to you will absolve you of any blame."

"Sir, with all due respect, your orders cannot absolve any of us of responsibility for knowingly assisting you in committing an illegal act of war, That, at any rate, will undoubtedly be the verdict of the court-martial which convicts any officer who obeys your order of having committed piracy and murder."

The tension in the briefing room could have been carved with a knife. The other officers sat silent, watching the confrontation between Terekhov and Hope, and he leaned forward in his chair, holding her eyes.

"It's entirely possible that you're correct, Commander," he said in a cold, precise voice. "There comes a time in every officer's life, however, when he must confront not simply the possibility of defeat, not even of his own death, but his responsibility to the uniform he wears. To the Crown, and to the oath he swore when he put that uniform on. It's our duty to protect the Star Kingdom of Manticore and its allies and friends from all enemies. That, Commander Hope, is the bottom line of the oath *you* swore. The oath Edward Saganami swore. We're at the end of a very long, very tenuous chain of communication. It's our responsibility to exercise our initiative and judgment in the face of this threat. And it's also our duty to provide the Queen with the means of disavowing our actions—and *us*, if necessary—in order to avoid open warfare with the Solarian League."

"Sir, the fact that you feel it's our responsibility to commit professional suicide in order to deal with a threat which may not even exist doesn't necessarily make it true," Hope said flatly. "And I—and my ship—will not participate in this patently illegal action."

The tension ratcheted even higher, and Terekhov regarded her calmly.

"I don't recall offering you the option of refusing my orders, Commander," he said, almost conversationally.

"Captain Terekhov," she replied harshly, "I don't think you have a choice. You command a single ship. Admittedly, the most powerful single ship present, but only a single unit. And I question, Sir, whether or not your personnel will fire into another Manticoran vessel simply because it declines to join you in an illegal act."

"I wouldn't question that if I were you, Commander." Ansten FitzGerald's voice was colder than ice, and Hope's eyes darted to his face. "This ship and her people will engage whoever the Captain tells us to," the executive officer continued in that same, frozen voice. "Especially a mutinous vessel whose gutless, ass-covering excuse for a captain is refusing the lawful orders of her superior."

"Ansten, that's enough," Terekhov said quietly.

"With all due respect, Captain Terekhov," Ito Anders said, "it isn't. Commander Hope's chosen to suggest she and her vessel would resist your orders with deadly force. She's also observed that you command only a single ship. That is an incorrect statement." He looked directly at Hope, his dark eyes frozen. "If you were so foolish as to attempt to carry through on that threat, Commander, and *if*—as I very much doubt—your people were willing to obey your orders, you would discover that *Hexapuma* wouldn't be the only ship you would face."

"You can't seriously be considering *cooperating* with this!" Hope protested.

"Yes I can," Anders said calmly. He even smiled ever so slightly. "My ship is older even than yours, Commander. And, to be honest, she's always had something of a reputation to live down. She hasn't been fortunate in her commanding officers. I'm not going to add to that reputation. In fact, I'm going to clean it up properly at last. And if I have to begin by blowing your worthless ass out of space, I will."

Hope stared at him, then looked around the other faces around the table, and her mouth tightened as she realized she was alone.

"Skipper," another voice said then, and her head whipped around as Lieutenant Commander Diamond spoke for the first time.

"Skipper," her XO said sadly, "they're right. You're wrong. And our people won't follow you on this one."

"They don't have any choice!" she snapped.

"Commander, you can't have it both ways," Terekhov said. "If they're required to obey you because you're their superior officer, then you're required to obey me, because I'm *your* superior officer. But if you have the right to pick and choose which orders you'll follow, then they have the same right to refuse to follow *your* orders."

"But—"

"This is neither a debating society nor a democratic organization, Commander Hope, and this particular discussion is over. Since you seem to feel unable to carry out my orders, you are hereby relieved from command of *Vigilant*. Lieutenant Commander Diamond will replace you in command, effective immediately."

"You can't do that!" she shouted.

"I just did," he said icily. "And I will tolerate no further disrespect. You have two choices, Commander, neither of which any longer includes command of *Vigilant*. You may, if you so choose, disassociate yourself from the Squadron's—" he allowed himself at last to use the term others had already been using "—future actions and return to Spindle aboard the dispatch boat I intend to send there before proceeding to Monica. Failing that, you will remain aboard *Hexapuma* under quarters arrest until such time as we return to Spindle to account for our actions to our superiors."

He looked into her eyes, and something inside her flinched away from his blue battle steel gaze.

"Which is it going to be, Commander?"

Chapter Fifty-Five

The Crown dispatch boat from Lynx came out of the central terminus of the Manticore Wormhole Junction in a blue lightning flash of transit energy. It seemed small and insignificant, lost amid the stupendous, lumbering freighters and passenger ships, but its imperiously strident transponder had priority over them all. Astro Control juggled arrival and departure queues, clearing a path for it, and it streaked towards Home Fleet's flagship under almost eight hundred gravities of acceleration.

It looked even tinier as it decelerated just as furiously to a zero/zero intercept with the massive SD(P), but appearances were deceiving. Tiny as it was, that dispatch boat carried the message that would set millions upon millions of tons of warships into motion.

"What sort of raw meat do you people *feed* your cruiser captains, Hamish?" Queen Elizabeth III of Manticore inquired acidly.

"With all due respect, Your Majesty," First Lord of Admiralty Hamish Alexander, Admiral of the Green (retired) and thirteenth Earl of White Haven, said with unusual formality to the woman he'd known since she was an infant, "that's not really fair."

"On the contrary, Ham," his brother, William Alexander, Lord Alexander, the recently created Baron of Grantville and Prime Minister of the Star Kingdom of Manticore, said tartly, "I think Elizabeth has an excellent point. We already have one war, and it's not going all that well. Do we really need to provoke another one with the *Solarian League*?"

"Your Majesty, Mr. Prime Minister, I agree the timing could have been better," Sir Thomas Caparelli, First Space Lord and the uniformed commander-in-chief of the Royal Manticoran Navy, rumbled in a deceptively mild tone. "On the other hand, having read Admiral Khumalo's dispatches and gone over Terekhov's report with Pat Givens, I don't think Terekhov had a great deal of choice."

"Possibly—probably—not, but I have to admit I wish he'd at least consulted with Baroness Medusa before he went dashing off to violate Monican territorial space. Someone with his Foreign Office experience has to be aware of the laser heads he's juggling here!" Sir Anthony Langtry, Manticore's Foreign Secretary, had been a highly decorated Marine once upon a time, and he looked like a man caught between his political and military instincts.

"That's certainly true," Baron Grantville agreed grimly. "The political situation in the Talbott Cluster's complex enough without throwing a spanner like this into the works!"

"Fair's fair, Willie," Elizabeth said a trifle unwillingly. She reached up to caress the ears of the treecat stretched across the back of her chair, and her expression eased . . . a little. "The political situation's improved enormously in the last couple of months, and from Dame Estelle's messages, it seems pretty evident Terekhov and Van Dort are responsible for that, as well."

"Despite Augustus Khumalo," Caparelli agreed sourly.

"I'm beginning to think we may've been a bit unfair in our opinion of Khumalo, Thomas," White Haven said.

"He's no genius, and he's never going to be a brilliant combat commander, but it sounds to me as if he's been working his butt off. I question some of his deployment decisions, but all he's got to work with is what was left over after we wrung out the bar rag. And whatever faults he may have, he obviously understands when it's time to back a subordinate's hunch."

"Should I understand from that that you think Terekhov knows what the hell he's doing?" Grantville asked, and his brother cocked his head to one side for a moment, then nodded slowly.

"Yes," he said judiciously, "I think I do. At any rate, I'm not prepared to second-guess him from here. He's the man on the spot, and whether he's right or wrong, he's demonstrated the moral courage to make the hard call."

"Hamish," the Queen said more calmly, but with a worried expression, still stroking the 'cat, "I entirely agree that we have to know, one way or the other, what—if anything—Monica and Mesa are up to. I shudder every time I think of how the League's going to react to Terekhov's little act of piracy, but under the circumstances, I could even condone that. It's the rest of his actions, his willingness to court a shooting incident with a sovereign star nation with such a close client relationship with Frontier Security, that scares hell out of me."

"First of all, Elizabeth," White Haven said, "he's very carefully set this up to give you an out by sacrificing him. Second, if he's right, we've already got a shooting incident with the sovereign star nation in question—it just hasn't happened yet. And, third, there's no way in the universe 'President Tyler' would've signed on to risk something like this without the tacit approval of Frontier Security. So, assuming Terekhov *is* right, the only real change is going to be whose backyard the shooting takes place in. And, possibly, who gets shot."

"Hamish is right, Your Majesty," Langtry said. "And I have to say this, too. There are huge holes in what Terekhov's put together, but just on the basis of what he's already been able to prove, this stinks to high heaven. I pulled the intelligence bio on Lorcan Verrochio, the Frontier Security Commissioner in the region. We don't have as much detail as I'd like, but there's no question that he's inside Mesa's pocket. There were even suggestions in that heap of data Anton Zilwicki dropped on us a few years back that he's directly involved in payoffs to protect the slave trade. If Jessyk is involved, you can be absolutely certain they're operating with Verrochio's knowledge and consent."

"Wonderful," Grantville sighed. "So we probably *are* looking at direct Solarian involvement."

"Yes and no, Willie," White Haven said. "From what Tony's saying, *OFS* is involved. That's not the same thing as the *League's* being involved. It's not even the same as having all of Frontier Security involved. Verrochio has his own little satrapy down on the Cluster's southern frontier. Whether or not he can count on support from his fellow OFS satraps or the SLN's an open question, and it probably depends on how deeply—and publicly—into the cookie jar he has his fingers."

"Either way, Your Majesty, there's nothing we can do to undo what Terekhov's already done," Caparelli observed, pulling the discussion back to its primary focus. "All we can really do is determine how to respond to it."

"What's the Admiralty's serious estimation of how likely we are to see a response from the Solarian Navy to an attack on Monica, Ham?" Grantville asked.

"In the short term, that may well depend on how willing we are to reinforce Lynx and the Cluster. Khumalo's present strength is so low the local SLN forces assigned to support OFS could probably take him without heavy losses. If we reinforce with a squadron or two of modern capital ships, though, we can ensure that Commissioner Verrochio would have to ask for substantial reinforcements to have any hope of taking us out. And, as I say, at that point it comes down to how much Verrochio himself is willing to risk and how likely anyone else is to want to jump into this with him. If we make it obvious that it's going to cost far more than the League can expect to make back off of the Cluster, the odds of his getting any support ought to go down sharply."

"That's true, My Lord," Caparelli said. "On the other hand, I'm not comfortable about the notion of diverting sufficient strength to Talbott to be a realistic deterrent. Not when we're still stretched so tight at the front. We've finally gotten Eighth Fleet reinforced to a level that will let Duchess Harrington shift from a purely defensive stance to a limited offensive one. I'd hate for this to turn into a diversion that would push her entirely back onto the defensive."

"Agreed," White Haven said grimly, remembering the endless months when he'd been the one in command of Eighth Fleet, waiting for reinforcements that never seemed to come. And he had a special, deeply personal reason for ensuring that Eighth Fleet's present commander got everything she needed before she went into battle.

"Nonetheless," he went on, "I think we're going to have to divert at least some strength to Talbott. Suppose we sent a couple of battlecruiser squadrons and a single CLAC squadron to the Cluster proper and moved two SD(P) squadrons and another squadron of CLACs from Home Fleet to the Lynx Terminus?"

"Play a shell game with them through the Junction?" Caparelli said thoughtfully.

"Yes." White Haven grimaced. "I don't really like it. Theoretically, it's elegant enough, I suppose, but if we find ourselves forced to move the Home Fleet detachment further into the Cluster, we lose the ability to recall it quickly in an emergency. And if push came to shove, we could find ourselves in a situation where we'd have to recall the detachment regardless of the exposure for Lynx or the Cluster because of a possible threat to the home system."

"The Lynx Terminus forts will come on-line starting in another few months," Caparelli pointed out. "Once they can take responsibility for protecting the terminus itself, we could withdraw the heavy squadrons and probably make up the combat differential for the Cluster itself with additional cruisers and battlecruisers. And if the annexation does go through—" he glanced at Grantville and the Queen and got matched nods of confidence "—we can begin deploying LAC groups to each of our new systems. That should give us some local defense in depth and free up our hyper-capable units to act as a roving fire brigade."

White Haven nodded slowly, lips pursed as he considered options and scenarios. Caparelli's proposal sounded like their best bet. And, he reminded himself, Caparelli was First *Space* Lord. Operational decisions were properly his, however hard it was for his political superior to keep his own spoon out of the soup.

"It's an operational decision, Your Majesty," he said, looking at the Queen. "As such, it's Admiral Caparelli's bailiwick. For what it's worth, I'd say it sounds like the most workable option, and I'll endorse it officially in my capacity as First Lord."

Caparelli said nothing, but his expression showed his appreciation for how difficult it was for a flag officer of White Haven's experience and stature to refrain from jostling his uniformed subordinate's elbow at a time like this.

"Very well, Sir Thomas," Elizabeth said. "I'll want to send someone senior from the Foreign Office to deal directly with Monica. Who would you suggest, Tony?"

"We could just add it to Terekhov's load," Langtry said with a crooked grin, and the Queen snorted.

"I think his Foreign Office experience is a bit too far in the past for me to feel comfortable with that, Sir Thomas. Besides, having the fellow whose actions we're contemplating disavowing potentially in charge of doing the disavowing in our name might be just a *little* awkward. Next suggestion?"

"My first reaction would be to ask Estelle to take this over, now that the draft Constitution's been voted out," Langtry said much more seriously. "Unfortunately, she's still back in Spindle." He frowned, thinking hard.

"I think we might hand it to Amandine Corvisart. What do you think, Willie?"

"I think it's an excellent idea," Grantville replied. Dame Amandine Corvisart was a second-generation Manticoran whose family had fled the People's Republic of Haven sixty-five T-years earlier. "She's tough-minded as a bull-dog, but she understands the need to control situations instead of exacerbating them."

"And she'd be ready to actively enlist Van Dort in any negotiations," Langtry said with a nod.

"How soon could she be briefed and ready to go?" the Queen asked.

"Unfortunately, Your Majesty," Langtry said wryly, "there isn't a lot of briefing we can do in this instance. I'd say it'll take me forty-five minutes to give her her instructions, and probably another couple of hours for her to pack. Then however long it takes to get her out to join the relief force. She can read up on the situation from Terekhov and Khumalo's raw dispatches *en route*."

"And how soon can we begin redeploying, Sir Thomas?" she asked.

"I can slice one battlecruiser squadron and a CLAC division off Home Fleet with orders for Monica within two hours, Your Majesty. I think I'll ask Admiral Yanakov if I can swap out a division of his BC(P)s for one of our *Redoubtable* divisions. It'll take a little longer to move the heavy squadrons, but I should be able to have them on their way within, say, six hours. I'll send the support elements through over the next day or two."

"In that case," the Queen told him, brown eyes hard, "we'll leave that in your hands. Go ahead and get the lighter forces off as soon as possible. We'll send Dame Amandine after them in a dispatch boat. She'll catch up with them long before they get to Monica."

"Yes, Your Majesty."

"When you give your officers their orders, Admiral," the Queen said, "there's one point I want you to be perfectly clear about. You will inform them that they're to avoid incidents with *Solarian* units if at all possible.

They're authorized to engage Monican units at their own discretion, based on the situation they encounter when they reach that star system, but I would very much prefer to avoid escalating this into a direct, open confrontation between us and the Solarian League. But at the same time, be certain they understand that avoiding incidents with Sollies 'if at all possible' doesn't—I repeat, Admiral, does *not*—include yielding a single centimeter on our claim of sovereignty over the Lynx Terminus or in the defense of the territorial integrity of any star system represented at the Constitutional Convention on Flax. Not a single centimeter."

She glanced at Grantville, who simply nodded his understanding of the policy she'd just announced. Then she looked back at Sir Thomas Caparelli, and the 'cat on the back of her chair yawned at the admiral, showing needle-pointed, snow-white fangs.

"God knows we don't need a war with the League. But we aren't going to let some corrupt Frontier Security bureaucrat connive with leeches like Manpower or the Jessyk Combine to drive us out of the Cluster so they can suck it dry. Not now that the Constitutional Convention's finally voted out an acceptable draft. If that means engaging the SLN, so be it."

"Good afternoon, Ladies and Gentlemen," Aivars Terekhov said.

He sat at the head of the briefing room table, flanked by Ansten FitzGerald to his left, and Ito Anders to his right. The junior-grade captain was his second in command, and FitzGerald was the closest thing the Squadron had to a flag captain. Naomi Kaplan sat beside FitzGerald, and the three of them faced the holographic com display at the far end of the table. That display had been set to its maximum size, stretching from the top of the table to the deckhead above, and it was intricately divided into nineteen quadrants, each occupied by one of the Squadron's commanding officers or XOs.

Despite the efficiency of the electronic conference,

Terekhov would much have preferred for those holographic ghosts to be physically present. But the Squadron was plunging ahead along one of hyper-space's grav waves. Ito had been on board *Hexapuma* since they'd left Point Midway, conferring personally and directly with Terekhov in order to be sure he understood exactly what his superior had in mind. The other officers were stuck aboard their own ships—for now, at least—however, since it was physically impossible for any impeller-drive small craft to transfer personnel in the midst of a gravity wave. And they didn't have time to wait until the Squadron cleared the wave. It was only six days from Point Midway to Monica by the universe's clocks, and *Hexapuma* and her consorts were traveling at seventy percent of the speed of light. That velocity reduced the time available to their crews to only a little over *four* days.

"Commander Kaplan is about to brief you on our ops plan," he continued levelly, facing the com. "Let me emphasize one more time that while I'm prepared to use force, if necessary, I regard that as a last-resort option. I intend to demand that the Monican Navy stand down all its units. And, specifically, that they evacuate all personnel from Eroica Station, leaving all starships in place, pending the arrival of competent Manticoran authority to deal with the situation on a diplomatic basis. I'd like to believe President Tyler's too good a poker player to ride a busted flush down in flames. Failing that, I'd like him to be conniving enough to figure we'll probably be withdrawn from Monica quickly, possibly after a show of force to drive home the point that we're keeping an eye on him. In that case, presumably, he'd get to keep his new toys, and that prospect would have to be attractive to him. The bottom line is that I don't want to kill anyone we don't have to kill, and I'm not interested in destroying starships simply to be destroying them. If we can control the situation without firing a single shot, I'll be delighted."

He let them digest what he'd said, then flicked his right hand.

"Having said that, however, we must be prepared for the possibility that Tyler will opt not to comply with my demand. Perhaps even more to the point, we need to be aware that a government like his, by its very nature, is likely to try to stall. If nothing else, to keep us talking while he brings up his entire navy to confront us. I think he would anticipate that confronting us in that way would cause us to blink and at least hesitate. If we're—I'm—right in my suspicions, there's also the very real threat that still other forces are already in motion, and that if he can stall long enough, still more Solarian, or at least OFS units, will turn up to support his own forces.

"So, eager as I am for a diplomatic solution, I have no intention of allowing this to turn into a long, drawn out standoff. I intend to crowd the senior officer at Eroica Station hard. If at all possible, I want to push him into accepting the stand-down order immediately, on his own authority, then push hard to secure physical control of Eroica as quickly as possible—hopefully before Tyler is able to order him to stall. If there is League involvement in this, I don't intend to give Tyler time to send off to his OFS friends and whistle up an SLN task force to invite us to leave. If he doesn't immediately show clear signs of agreeing to my demands, we *will* destroy his battlecruisers . . . and any other units they send in to oppose us. Which is a very good reason to deny them the time to send those other units in. If nothing else, it will be that many fewer people for us to have to kill."

No one said a word, and he let his eyes move from quadrant to quadrant, meeting their gazes one by one, then nodded slowly.

"Commander Kaplan will now brief you on how I intend to do that, if it becomes necessary. Commander?"

He turned to Naomi Kaplan.

"Yes, Sir." She turned to face the com more squarely and tapped a command into the console in front of her, bringing up a holographic schematic of the Monica System.

"As you can see, Ladies and Gentleman, Eroica Station,

the main shipyard nexus of the Monican Navy, is located in the Eroica asteroid belt, which has an average orbital radius of roughly nineteen and a half light-minutes. The Station is an extensive complex, larger than a Navy this size would normally require, because they took advantage of the proximity of the Eroica Belt to set up a basic heavy industry node for the entire system. All this section here," she superimposed a larger-scale schematic of Eroica Station itself and circled about a third of its total area with a green hairline, "is essentially a commercial civilian operation, servicing the belt's extractive industries."

She moved the superimposed image to the side to clear the schematic of the entire system.

"As you can also see, at this moment, Eroica Station is almost in direct opposition from the planet Monica. They're the next best thing to thirty light-minutes apart, with the primary directly between, so light-speed communications between Eroica Station and the Monican government are going to be slow and ponderous. The need to relay around the primary's going to increase their message lag to just over forty-five minutes. In addition, Eroica Station's less than one-point-two light-minutes inside the hyper limit, where we can get at it quickly."

She gave them a few moments to study the system display, then slid the Eroica Station schematic back to center stage.

"Here's what *Copenhagen*'s recon drone was able to find for us. I've highlighted the *Indefatigables* in red. As you can see, most of them are clustered fairly tightly around the main naval space station, on the far side of the complex from the civilian elements. These two over here," two of the red icons flashed where they nuzzled up against a pair of amber light codes actually in among the civilian platforms, "are being serviced by the repair ships indicated in amber. There are also six cruisers and destroyers, all older ships, in the same area—or, they *were* in the area when the drone dropped by. Frankly, aside from the 'stakes raising' potential the Captain's already referred to, the

Monicans' present naval units don't pose a significant threat to us unless we screw up by the numbers. In addition to the ships, however, there are also remotely deployed missile launchers on these asteroids here, highlighted in yellow, and the naval space station itself mounts thirty-two tubes. We don't know how modern their ordnance is, but the launchers the drone actually saw are big enough to fire current-generation Solarian capital missiles. Under normal circumstances, someone like Monica would only have the export version, with the downgraded seekers and EW systems, but given the *Indefatigables'* presence, that may not be the case here. We don't know that, but we need to keep in mind that they could be extremely bad medicine if we stray into their effective range."

She paused again, waiting to see if there were any questions. There were none, and she resumed.

"In addition to the naval units and repair ships, the drone also picked up half a dozen large freighters. There's no way to know why they were there, but it seems like an excessive concentration of merchant tonnage for a system like Monica, especially that far away from its only inhabited planet. Until we actually secure control of the Station, we can only guess at what they're up to, but my gut feeling is that they're involved in the arrival of all these battlecruisers and, possibly, Jessyk's support for the FAK and MIM. Unless they do something to convince us they represent an immediate threat, however, we intend to treat them as more of the civilian infrastructure and attempt to limit damage to them if it comes to a shootout."

She banished the schematic of Eroica Station back to the borders of the system display and a green line drew itself from a point just outside the system hyper limit to an arrowhead pointed directly at the Station.

"In the broadest possible terms, what we intend to do is make our alpha translation just beyond the hyper limit. As soon as we emerge into normal-space, *Volcano* will begin decelerating, since we have no intention of taking your ship into the path of any missiles, Captain Badmachin."

"That's nice to know, Commander," Commander Badmachin said with a throaty chuckle. "My hull's too thin to react well to sharp pointy objects or lasers."

"That's what the Captain thought, too," Kaplan told her with a grin. "At the same time as you begin decelerating, however, you'll also begin deploying missile pods. We're reverting to older tactics, and we'll go in with heavy loads on tow. Eroica Station may have Solly capital missiles for its tubes, but there's no way they have anything that can match the powered range of our pods or *Hexapuma*'s Mark 16s.

"Once the pods are distributed, we'll continue towards Eroica Station. We'll make turnover to decelerate to rest relative to the Station at approximately eight million kilometers, which should put us a million and a half klicks outside their best range. That will enable us to keep them under our guns while we negotiate. We'll also deploy a shell of sensor remotes to cover our flanks. Frankly, it would be suicidal for the remainder of the Monican Navy to try to engage us, even if it had a chance of sneaking through our sensor coverage, but we don't intend to take any chances.

"If the Captain and Mr. Van Dort achieve a negotiated resolution, we'll also be close enough to get positive sensor confirmation of their evacuation of Eroica Station. Once we're reasonably confident the Station has, in fact, been evacuated, we'll send in the Squadron's Marines in pinnaces to secure it. If, however, the Monicans refuse to stand down and evacuate, we *will* attack.

"Even the most accurate bombardment with laser heads is going to inflict collateral damage," she said, looking up from the system plot to meet their combined gazes squarely. "At eight million klicks, our fire control should give us good accuracy, and we'll do our level best to restrict our fire to the battlecruisers. Our objective is to neutralize those ships, Ladies and Gentlemen, not to kill Monicans and not to wreck Eroica Station. We aren't even interested in destroying their defensive missile launchers or their point defense stations, if we can take out the battlecruisers without engaging those installations. Nonetheless, if it comes down to it and we're required to open fire, we *are* going to inflict serious damage to at least the military component of the Station, and we are going to kill Monican personnel. We'll do our best to avoid that, but we aren't going to take the Squadron into a range at which we suffer avoidable ship losses or casualties just to hold down Monican casualties."

She fell silent again, looking at them while they looked back, then nodded slightly.

"That's the general outline," she said. "Now I'll take you back through it in more detail and discuss individual ship assignments. I'd appreciate it if you'd hold questions till the end, when I'll try to go back and answer them all as fully as possible."

She waited until everyone nodded in understanding, then began.

"As soon as we make our alpha translation, Captain Badmachin, your ship will—"

Chapter Fifty-Six

"Any word on Commodore Horster's little invasion force?" Isidor Hegedusic asked.

"No, Sir." The communications officer half-turned in his comfortable chair on the spacious "flag bridge" of Alpha Prime, Eroica Station's main military component, to face the admiral. "Do you want me to try to raise him, Admiral?"

"No, no." Hegedusic shook his head, smiled, and turned away. He had plenty to do, and fretting over the way Janko Horster played with his new toys was unprofessional, to say the least.

Envy, he told himself with a mental snort. *Pure, dyed-in-the-wool envy. I'd a hell of a lot rather be out there on a real flag bridge than playing senior officer here in this goldplated ration tin. Well, in another couple of weeks I'll have enough of them to justify taking Janko's toybox away from him and playing in it myself.*

He chuckled and stepped through the hatch into his private office. The attention light blinked steadily on his personal com, and he dropped into his desk chair and pressed the acceptance key. Izrok Levakonic's personal wallpaper filled the display, and a courteous computer voice asked Hegedusic to hold briefly.

It couldn't have been more than fifteen seconds before the wallpaper vanished, and Levakonic smiled at him from the screen. Hegedusic smiled back. Although he'd been determined not to like the Technodyne executive—who, after all, was only one more corrupt, overachieving capitalist with a personal avarice on steroids—he'd ended up doing it anyway. He was scarcely blind to Levakonic's manifold character flaws. Most, however, were dismayingly common by the standards of those who surrounded President Roberto Tyler. Levakonic had simply had the advantage of falling into a larger feeding trough than most Monicans ever dreamed of. And, on a personal level, he had a ready sense of humor and a willingness to roll up his shirt sleeves and dig in when the task at hand required.

"Isidor," Levakonic said with a nod.

"Izrok," Hegedusic responded.

"Just thought I'd check and see how Horster's training maneuver is going so far," Levakonic said, and Hegedusic chuckled.

"You, too? I was just out pestering the com staff for any reports. So far, nothing."

"Good! I told you you'd like the EW capabilities."

"And I never doubted it. What I doubted, and still do doubt, for that matter, is whether or not our people will be able to get the same performance out of them that Solarians could."

"Solarian Navy crews aren't ten meters tall, and they don't take shortcuts by hiking across large bodies of water," Levakonic said dryly. "Basic education counts, sure. It counts for a lot. But not as much as hands-on training with good instructors. And you've got *my* people to do the training. I guarantee you that the people who built the systems in the first place know more about what they can do than the uniformed types who actually use them in the field."

"I believe you. In fact, I'm inclined to think Janko's

probably cheating a little right now. I'll bet he's got those same 'instructors' actually operating the systems for him. Otherwise, somebody would've spotted him by now. And, just between you and me, I hope to hell somebody *does* spot him pretty soon."

"Why?" Levakonic furrowed his brow. "Don't get me wrong, Isidor, but if he screws up and lets your people pick him up, that's a pretty bad sign. The Manties' sensors are a lot better than anything you've got—quite a bit better than anything *we've* got, for that matter, despite the opinions of several of our own senior R and D people that ours are the best in the universe, if our field reps' reports are accurate. We haven't been able to get any of those idiots in the SLN's R and D departments to pay any attention to us, of course. They're all locked into the 'Not Invented Here' automatic rejection reflex. Well," he added with a charming little-boy grin, "that and an equally automatic suspicion that we're only telling them all those tall tales about Manty capabilities to scare them into funneling more money into *our* R and D programs. Which there might be just a teeny-tiny bit of truth to.

"But my point is, that if you people can pick him up, then it's for damned sure the Manties could."

"Don't doubt you," Hegedusic said with a grin. "But this is still very early days. Hell, he's only had eighteen days to practice, and one thing about Janko, he's always had a pretty steep learning curve. I'm sure he'll manage to sneak tracelessly up on us soon enough, but there's an expensive dinner and an even more expensive bottle of wine riding on how well he does today. So, if it's all the same to you, I'll settle for his surprising hell out of us tomorrow as long as I don't have to feed his greedy face tonight."

"Ah! I hadn't realized the military stakes in today's exercises were quite that weighty. Now, of course, I fully understand."

"Good. And don't worry, I'll let you know as soon as—"

"Excuse me, Admiral."

Hegedusic turned his head at the interruption. A youthful-looking lieutenant stood in the open office hatch.

"Yes, what is it?" the admiral asked, with a trace of irritation at having someone break in on him in a private conversation.

"Admiral, I'm very sorry to disturb you. But we've just picked up a sizable hyper footprint."

"Hyper footprint? Where?"

For just a moment, Hegedusic wondered if it could be Horster. He was supposed to be "sneaking up" on Eroica Station, but Janko believed The Book had been written solely for him to personally ignore. That was why Hegedusic had chosen him as his first divisional commander. And it was possible he'd decided to try an open approach, pretending to be someone else and using his new EW to disguise his impeller signatures as merchants or something equally silly.

"Celestial azimuth zero-six-three, almost dead on the plane of the ecliptic, and about three-point-eight million klicks outside the hyper limit, Sir," the lieutenant replied.

Then it can't be Janko, was Hegedusic's first thought. *His flight path originated at Monica; there's no way he could have gotten out across the hyper limit, circled around, and come in from the other side like this. Not this soon.*

That was his first thought. His second was, *But if it isn't Janko, who the hell is it?*

"Sorry, Sir," Lieutenant Commander Wright said. "I undershot a bit."

"Stop fishing for compliments, Toby," Terekhov said, never looking away from the astrogation plot. "Five hundred k-klicks off on a thirty-eight light-year jump? Sounds like a bull's-eye to me."

He looked up in time to see Wright's grin. The astrogator remained probably the most private person aboard *Hexapuma*, and he continued to ration words as if someone were levying a surcharge on them. But he did have his own dry sense of humor, and that grin told Terekhov he'd caught the lieutenant commander exercising it.

"I suppose it's *fairly* close, Skipper," Ansten FitzGerald observed over the communications link to Auxiliary Control.

Terekhov had rethought things just a bit, and FitzGerald had Naomi Kaplan with him on the backup command deck. Terekhov had kept Guthrie Bagwell on the bridge, to run *Hexapuma*'s electronic warfare systems for him, but he'd flipped Abigail Hearns and Kaplan. He planned on making his own tactical decisions, anyway, and if something happened to him, Ansten would have the best, most experienced tac officer in the ship to help him deal with it. Paulo d'Arezzo would run the EW console for her, and Aikawa Kagiyama would serve as her junior tac officer. Helen Zilwicki, who Terekhov privately believed was the best tactical specialist among the midshipmen, held the JTO's slot with Abigail, here on the bridge.

"Why, thank you, Sir," Wright said, and Bernardus Van Dort shook his head. The skinsuited Rembrandter—who, when it came right down to it, had no business at all on *Hexapuma*'s bridge—sat to one side of Wright, in one of the jump seats the ship's midshipmen usually used when observing the astrogator. From his expression he was pretty sure there was still a shoe waiting to drop . . . and he was right.

"What I was going to say is five hundred thousand's fairly close . . . for someone who has trouble counting to eleven with his boots on," the XO said, and Terekhov chuckled.

It was a somewhat absent chuckle, and his attention was back on the plot, checking alignments. The Squadron had made its alpha transition in close formation and relatively gradually from a base velocity in hyper of 62,500 KPS. With the inevitable velocity bleed-off, that gave them an n-space velocity of almost exactly 5,000 KPS . . . headed directly for Eroica Station. At the moment, they were decelerating at 350 gravities in order to stay with the ammo ship, which was braking as hard as she could to stay clear of the hyper limit, and their formation looked close to perfect.

"Commander Badmachin reports *Volcano* is rolling pods, Sir," Amal Nagchaudhuri announced.

"I have them on lidar, Sir," Abigail Hearns confirmed from Tactical. "*Warlock*'s picking up her allotment now."

"Very good," Terekhov acknowledged.

"Sir, we're being challenged by the Monicans," Nagchaudhuri said, and Terekhov snorted.

"That was fast," he said dryly. Of course the fact that Eroica Station was so close to the hyper limit meant the transmission lag was only a little over ninety seconds. "No response yet," he continued to the com officer. "We'll let them sweat a little longer."

"Yes, sir."

"Lieutenant Bagwell," Terekhov said, still never looking away from the plot, "let's get the EW platforms deployed."

"Aye, aye, Sir. Deploying now."

"Very good. Ms. Zilwicki."

"Sir?"

"Deploy the recon shell."

"Deploy the recon shell, aye, aye, Sir," Helen acknowledged, and began tapping commands into her console.

Her pulse, she knew, was quicker than usual, yet in almost too many ways, this felt like just another training sim. Which, she supposed, was the point of spending so much time in simulators in the first place.

The first remote sensor arrays launched, spreading out in a vast, hollow sphere around the Squadron. At the same time, she saw the electronic warfare platforms spreading out around the individual ships and settling into a closer, tighter defensive formation than the arrays.

A corner of her mind couldn't help thinking the Skipper was being a little paranoid. The Monicans couldn't possibly have known they were coming, and even the best Solarian missiles had a maximum powered attack envelope of no more than 6.5 million kilometers from rest, even at half-power settings. Not to mention the fact that while Manticoran electronics were the best any navy had ever deployed, the Monicans' basic surveillance systems were obsolescent League crap at least forty T-years out of date. There was no way any threat this system could mount could get through her sensor shell to attack range without plenty of warning.

But only a corner of her mind thought that. The rest of it recognized yet another example of the Skipper's infinite attention to detail. He would dot every "i" and cross every "t" ahead of time, when he had the leisure to be sure it was done right. Who was it, back on Old Earth, who'd said to ask him for anything but time? She rather thought it had been Napoleon. Of course, despite all his strategic genius on land, Napoleon hadn't known how to pour piss out of a boot where navies were concerned, but that particular bit of advice translated quite well across the centuries for any officer.

"*Warlock* has her full pod load, Sir," Nagchaudhuri reported. "Commander Diamond is moving up with *Vigilant*."

"Thank you, Amal," Terekhov said. His tone was courteous and a bit abstracted, but Helen knew better than that. It was a reflection of how intensely he was concentrating, not of absentmindedness.

She thought about Lieutenant Commander Diamond. How did he feel right now? From all she could discover, he'd been with Commander Hope for at least two T-years. Now she'd been hustled off aboard the dispatch boat, returned to Spindle ignominiously with the Captain's dispatches, like so much unwanted freight. If this operation turned into the disaster she'd evidently predicted, she'd probably emerge as the only CO of the Squadron with an intact reputation. But if it succeeded, she'd be known throughout the Navy as the commander of a Queen's ship who'd refused, for whatever reason, to face the enemy when ordered to do so. And whichever way it came out, Diamond would have to live with the fact that he'd elected to succeed her in command rather than follow her into exile.

She watched her own plot as the highly stealthed pods clustered about *Vigilant*'s icon. The latest wrinkle BuWeaps had come up with was to incorporate a small tractor beam into each individual pod. Although their design was maximized for deployment from the new hollow-core SD(P)s and even newer BC(P)s, there were still plenty of old-style ships or smaller vessels—like the ones of Captain Terekhov's small squadron—which could only deploy pods on tow. One limiting factor for those ships had always been the way the number of tractor beams they mounted restricted the numbers of pods they could deploy. By mounting tractors on the pods themselves, that particular problem was overcome, and Captain Terekhov was using that advantage to the maximum. By the time he got done his ships would do well to manage 350 g, but they'd have a devastating long-range punch. Even the destroyers would have ten pods tagging along. Each of the three light cruisers would have fifteen, *Warlock* and *Vigilant* would have twenty-three each, and *Hexapuma* would have no less than forty. Altogether, it added up to a hundred and seventy-one pods for a total of 1,710 missiles. *Capital* missiles of the Royal Manticoran Navy—the longest ranged, most deadly missiles in space.

Somehow, she rather doubted anything Monica had was going to be able to stand up to *that*!

No, not Janko, Isidor Hegedusic thought. *And whoever they are, I don't care for the way they're coming in. They sure as hell aren't merchies, they're completely ignoring our challenges, and approaching from this bearing, the shipyards are their only possible target.*

His expression was grim. There was only one navy he could think of who'd have both an interest in depriving Monica of the *Indefatigables* and the sheer big brass balls to launch some sort of preemptive strike to accomplish that deprivation. And if the reports and rumors Levakonic had shared with him were accurate, those people had the range to turn his entire complex—and the irreplaceable battlecruisers lying helpless in its midst—into drifting debris from beyond the effective range of any weapon he possessed.

The "flag deck" hatch opened, and he glanced over his shoulder as Levakonic came hurrying in, skinsuited like the admiral himself. Technically, the civilian had no business here, but Hegedusic wasn't about to choke on any rules that required him to order a possible source of advice and information off of his command deck.

"No communication from them yet?" Levakonic asked tautly.

"No," Hegedusic replied, "and we've been hailing them for almost ten minutes now. I wonder if they're just going to close to attack range and blow us away without even identifying themselves." Levakonic looked sideways at him, and the admiral shrugged. "Think about it. If they blow the entire Station to bits and then just haul ass out of here without ever claiming responsibility, it'd be our word against theirs if we tried to convince anyone else of what happened."

"They might do that," Levakonic said, setting his helmet down on the seat of an unoccupied bridge chair. His skinsuit was a civilian model, but it was also much better and more capable than Hegedusic's.

"They might," the Solly repeated, "but if they were going to do that, they wouldn't have to come in on us at all. If our reports about how they're pulling off their range increases are correct, they've actually built multiple drive systems into a single missile body."

"What?" Hegedusic looked at him in astonishment, and Levakonic chuckled harshly.

"I know. They have to've developed an entire new generation of superdense fusion bottles, or something of the sort, to pull that off. We know they're fiendishly good at engineering components down, but there are practical limits. Their initial long-range missiles were apparently a lot bigger than their current-generation birds, so they probably went with improved capacitors on those. Hell, you've seen *our* latest-generation birds, and you know how big they are. Well, they still have single-drive systems that just happen to last a little longer before burnout; all the rest of the volume's for the juice they need to take advantage of their drive endurance.

"If our reports from Haven are right, the Peeps are still using stored energy for their birds. It's hurting them in areas like magazine capacity, compared to the Manties, and apparently they only managed that much because they were able to reverse engineer the Manties' late-generation capacitors.

"Of course," his smile was vinegar-tart, "*all* we have since Pierre and Saint-Just got bumped off are rumors and third-party reports. Their new management doesn't seem to like us very much. Which is partly our fault, of course." He grimaced. "They didn't have many samples of the Manties' current hardware after the cease-fire, and we weren't particularly interested in helping them out with their own development programs once the reports on Manty hardware started drying up. They, ah, seem to have long memories out there, and once Erewhon went over to their side with actual working examples of Manty technology, their R and D people pretty much told us to take a hike. So our latest first-hand reports are five T-years out of date, and it's possible all of this is inaccurate as hell.

"But if it isn't, then the Manties are building much smaller long-range missiles than they were. That means they have to've found a better solution than simply using bigger and better superconductor rings. If they're going to cram two—or even three, according to some rumors—complete drive packages into missiles the size of the ones they're supposed to be deploying, they can't have the internal volume to use straight superconductor storage to power the damned things."

"I imagine not," Hegedusic agreed. "But could anybody really build a fusion plant that small?"

"It's theoretically possible. With a powerful enough grav field to do the pinching, it could be done. But the initial power would have to come from a source external to the missile, which would probably mean some tricky modification of the launchers, as well. Anyway," he shook his head, brushing away the speculation, "the point I was going to make is that they have an effectively *unlimited* powered attack range. They could fire the damned things from five or six light-hours out, accelerate the bastards up to speed, and then program the *second* stage drive not to kick in until the birds entered attack range of their targets. If they didn't punch the max velocity too high, they wouldn't suffer significant particle-erosion degradation of their onboard sensor systems during even a very long ballistic flight component."

"Jesus Christ," Hegedusic whispered, and Levakonic snorted.

"No, just damned good engineers," he said sardonically. "And before you get your knickers in as big a twist as I did the first time *I* heard about them, remember this. A missile's only as good as its fire control, and not even Manties can generate good targeting solutions and handle mid-course corrections from half a solar system away. At the moment, they've got a lot more effective range than they can use, and even if they've been able to squeeze their birds down the way some of our sources report they have, they're paying for it with missles which are significantly larger than ours are. That means lower total numbers of birds in the same magazine space, so it's unlikely they'd fire off the thousands of the things it would require to score a significant number of hits at that sort of range in a fleet action.

"But your shipyard here's another kettle of fish. It can't dodge, and it doesn't have sidewalls. So if all they wanted to do was wreck Eroica Station, they could just fire off a saturation salvo of old-fashioned contact nukes to come whipping in here at seventy-five or eighty percent of light-speed. There's no way you could stop enough of them, especially if they seeded the attack wave with their new penetration aids, and they wouldn't really even have to cross the hyper limit to do it."

"But we don't know they are crossing the limit," Hegedusic pointed out.

"I think they are," Levakonic said grimly. The Monican looked a question at him, and he shrugged. "I think that big bastard is a freighter, Isidor—probably an ammunition ship. They won't want to bring her in where anything nasty could happen to her, so they're decelerating to stay with her while they load up with towed pods. Once they have, *she'll* stay out beyond the limit, and they'll come on in."

"What makes you so sure?"

"I'm not *sure*. But they could fire the pods from out there, if they wanted to, and if that is an ammo ship, who the hell cares about onboard magazine space? They've got missiles to burn. They could accept poor targeting solutions if they wanted to this time, so if they're planning on coming on in to a point where they can get better ones, that suggests to me that they want to be sure they hit what they're aiming at rather than simply smashing the entire Station. Which also suggests they'll at least want to talk to you before they kill you, even if they haven't done it yet. And also lends a little extra point to the minor question of just where Commodore Horster is right now."

"All ships report acquisition of all pods, Sir," Nagchaudhuri said.

"Very well. My compliments to Commander Badmachin for a well executed evolution. Remind her to keep an eye on her sensor platforms. If anyone comes at her, we'll meet her at the primary rendezvous."

"Aye, aye, Sir."

"Commander Wright."

"Yes, Sir."

"Resume acceleration and put us on profile for Eroica Station."

"You're right, Izrok; they're coming on in," Hegedusic said. "Which means you've also got a point about

Horster." He turned to the communications section again. "Lieutenant!"

"Yes, Sir?"

"I want a directional broadcast away from these people. Get hold of Captain Simons in CIC. Ask him to define the volumes where Commodore Horster's units are most likely to be and then sweep all of them you can without giving these people anything to pick up. Got it?"

"Yes, Sir!"

"Good. Address it to CO First Division and prepare to record."

"Yes, Sir. Ready to record, Sir."

"Very good. Message begins. 'Janko, unknown but presumably hostile units are approaching Eroica Station. My assumption is that they're here to destroy or take possession of the new units, and I don't expect them to rely solely on sweet reason. I know you're out there somewhere. If you're placed to intervene, this would probably be a good time for a live-fire training exercise. I'll stall as long as I can, but if they're who I think they are, there may not be a lot I can do. Remember the Manties' range advantage. If this is a Manticoran squadron, the trick'll be to get into range of them without getting yourself destroyed in the process. If you receive this message and can confirm without revealing your presence to the enemy, do so. If you *can't* intervene, notify me, regardless of whether or not they can detect your signal. Otherwise, maintain com silence and maneuver at your discretion. Good luck. I think we'll both need it. Isidor, clear and out.'"

He watched the communications officer play the recording back through his earbug. Then the lieutenant nodded.

"Clean recording, Sir."

"Very good. Check with CIC and be sure we append all available tactical information."

"Yes, Sir."

"Skipper, we're coming up on your specified mark," Lieutenant Commander Nagchaudhuri said.

Terekhov glanced at Van Dort, who looked back expressionlessly. There wasn't anything to be said, really, and both of them knew it. This was the entire reason they'd come.

"Very well, Amal. Live mike."

"Aye, aye, Sir."

"—Terekhov, Royal Manticoran Navy. I require you to immediately cease all work on all starships currently undergoing refit, and to evacuate all personnel from the military components of Eroica Station. I have no desire to fire on you or your personnel. My sole concern at this time is to ensure that none of those units enter the service of the Republic of Monica until such time as my government receives satisfactory assurances about the purposes for which you intend to employ them. If, however, my instructions to stand down and evacuate are not obeyed, I *will* fire upon you and destroy those ships. I hereby formally advise you that I am capable of carrying out that bombardment from beyond the effective range of any of Eroica Station's own weapons. You cannot prevent me from destroying those vessels at my convenience, and so I urge you most earnestly to begin evacuation immediately. You have one hour to comply. Terekhov, clear."

Isidor Hegedusic glared at the implacable face of the tall, bearded, fair-haired, blue-eyed man in the white beret and space-black-and-gold uniform. The message lag was only a very little over ninety seconds, and he stamped on his anger hard. At this close a range, he had time to be sure he had a grip on his temper before he responded to the Manticoran's arrogant demand.

"Record for transmission," he said to the pale-faced communications officer after perhaps ten seconds.

"Yes, Sir. Recording . . . now."

"Captain Terekhov," Hegedusic said in a hard, flat voice, "I am Admiral Isidor Hegedusic, Republic of Monica System Navy. What conceivable interpretation of interstellar law gives you the right to sail into my star system and threaten to destroy units of the Monican Navy? Hegedusic, clear."

"Got it, Sir," the lieutenant confirmed.

"Then send it."

The lieutenant obeyed. One hundred and eighty-three seconds later, Terekhov's response came in.

"Admiral Hegedusic, I regret the circumstances which compel me to make such demands, but the 'law' which justifies them is the acknowledged right of any star nation to act in self-defense. We have compelling evidence that the ships being refitted in this system for your Navy are intended for employment against the Star Kingdom and our allies in the Talbott Cluster. I will not permit that. If our information proves to be in error, we will withdraw, and I have no doubt my Star Kingdom will apologize and make suitable restitution. In the meantime, however, I must again insist you obey my instructions. I assure you, however deeply I may regret the inevitable collateral loss of life, I won't hesitate to destroy those vessels if you don't stand down and evacuate within the time limit I've specified. Terekhov, clear."

"Live mike, Lieutenant!" Hegedusic snapped.

"Yes, Sir. Your microphone is live," the lieutenant said, and Hegedusic faced the pickup once again.

"What you're demanding is impossible, Captain," he said harshly. "Even if I were inclined to be dictated to, which I am not, I couldn't possibly contact my government and receive authorization in the time limit you've imposed. Minimum message turnaround between here and the system government is over eighty-three minutes. I assure you messages will be sent immediately, relaying your insulting and arrogant demand and requesting instructions, but I cannot hear back from my government in less than an hour and twenty minutes. Hegedusic, clear."

"I understand your communication problems, Admiral," Terekhov said after the inevitable delay. "Nonetheless, my time limit stands. It isn't negotiable. Terekhov, clear."

"I don't have the authority to give such orders, Captain! I would be . . . strongly disinclined to do so in any case, but as the situation stands, I couldn't even if I wanted to. Hegedusic, clear."

"Admiral, you're a naval officer. As such, you know there are times to observe the legal niceties, and times that isn't possible. This is one of the latter. You may not have the legal authority to evacuate your post, but you do have the *de facto* authority. And you also have the responsibility to preserve the lives of your personnel in a situation in which you literally cannot fight back. I urge you to consider whether your moral responsibility lies in slavish obedience to the law, or in ensuring your people don't die pointlessly. Terekhov, clear."

"If we're going to speak about moral responsibilities, Captain, what about your responsibility not to slaughter people who, by your own statement, can't even threaten your own command, simply because their oaths to their own government require them to remain at their posts until legally relieved by competent authority? Hegedusic, clear."

"You have a point, Admiral," Terekhov conceded. "However, my own duty leaves me no alternative. And honesty compels me to add that neither I nor any other Manticoran officer have conspired with genetic slavers, pirates, terrorists, and mass murderers to commit acts of war on the sovereign territories of at least two independent star nations. Your government has done precisely that. My responsibility to see to it that those unprovoked and murderous assaults end now overrides any responsibility I may have towards your personnel. And I would further add, Sir, that I'm already holding my fire when you're well within my effective range specifically in order to avoid any unnecessary loss of life. That is the only concession I am prepared or able to make. So, I repeat, I require your immediate stand-down and evacuation. You now have fifty-one minutes to comply. Terekhov, clear and out."

The com screen went blank, and when Hegedusic looked at Levakonic, he saw his own amazement in the Solarian's face. How? How could the Manties have figured out what was happening? And what the *hell* was he supposed to do about it?

"Approaching turnover in seven minutes, Sir," Tobias Wright said, and Terekhov nodded.

Some of the sensor remotes speeding out in front of the Squadron had peeled off to put Eroica Station under close-range observation. *Hexapuma* and her consorts had been accelerating in-system for over seventeen minutes. Their initial velocity had dropped to just over 2,175 KPS before they parted company from Volcano, but in another seven minutes, they would reach their peak velocity of 7,190 KPS and begin the thirty-four minutes and fifty-nine seconds of deceleration which would bring them to rest relative to Eroica Station at a range of eight million kilometers.

Admiral Hegedusic had forty-three minutes to begin evacuating.

"Do you think he's going to give in, Skipper?" Ansten FitzGerald asked quietly from the small com screen beside Terekhov's knee.

"I don't know. I hope so."

"He didn't sound very happy about the notion, Sir," FitzGerald observed, and Terekhov surprised himself with a short, sharp laugh.

"You've been practicing understatement with Ms. Zilwicki again, haven't you, Ansten?" he said, then shrugged. "I expected a lot of what he said. Usually, you don't get to be an admiral if you make a habit of caving in easily. And those ships have to represent a dream come true for any admiral in any Verge navy. Not to mention the fact that the Monican government probably has a nasty habit of shooting people it considers guilty of cowardice. He's almost got to stall as long as he can."

"What if he comes back at the last minute with an offer to comply, Captain?" Van Dort asked, careful to observe the military proprieties under the current circumstances.

"If it's accompanied by an immediate start to the

evacuation, I'll grant him an extension. If it isn't, I'll open fire."

Van Dort nodded slowly, and there was a different look in his eyes as he gazed at Terekhov and saw a side of him he hadn't previously met. He'd never made the mistake of imagining Terekhov would flinch from any duty, however grim. But until this moment, he'd never truly realized just how dangerous a killer lurked inside his friend.

But Ansten FitzGerald wasn't surprised. He remembered the Nuncio System.

"Sir! Sir, the Manties have just made turnover!"

Hegedusic's head came up, and he strode quickly over to the officer who had spoken. He leaned over the lieutenant's shoulder, studying his plot.

"Where's his zero-velocity point at current deceleration?"

"Approximately eight million kilometers out, Admiral."

"Oh, is it now?" Hegedusic murmured in a soft, hungry tone, and turned to look at Levakonic. The Technodyne executive looked tense and unhappy, but as he met Hegedusic's eyes, they both smiled slowly.

Abigail Hearns rested her forearms lightly on the arms of her command chair. She could feel Helen's tension beside her, ratcheting steadily higher as the Squadron decelerated towards its attack position. She remembered the question Ragnhild had asked after their firing pass on Bogey Three at Nuncio, the question about how many people they'd just killed, and knew the same thoughts were passing through her surviving midshipwoman's mind at this moment.

If there was a single gram of cowardice in Helen Zilwicki, Abigail Hearns had never seen it. But this was even more cold-blooded and methodical than Captain Terekhov's ambush of the rogue Peeps in Nuncio. At least the Peeps had gotten into a range where they could theoretically have fired back. Eroica Station wouldn't have that option. If this Admiral Hegedusic failed to yield, hundreds, possibly thousands, of his personnel were going to be killed by weapons to which they couldn't even respond. It was a horrifying thought, and she wondered if she should say something to Helen about it.

But what could she say? She wasn't positive how *she* felt about it, so how could she know what to say to someone else?

There were times, as Brother Albert, her old childhood confessor, had warned her there would be, when the teachings of Father Church and the brutal requirements of the profession of arms clashed. When the desire of a loving God for all of His children to live and grow under His gentle Testing collided in a universe of imperfect humans with the unyielding fact that for some of His children to live, others of them must die. That, Brother Albert had told her gently when she first admitted that she hungered for a naval career, would become part of *her* Test if her wish were granted. And, he'd warned her, it was a fortunate warrior indeed—or else a madman—who was never forced to confront the ambiguity of violence. The suspicion that it was expediency, and his own desire to live, and not morality or justice or even the defense of his own nation and family, which truly drove him to kill. The selfish desire to survive, not the noble willingness to risk death for what he believed in.

Brother Albert had been right. And as Abigail had studied her trade, mastered the professional requirements of a tactical officer, she'd come to realize that the highest duty of an officer wasn't to engage in honorable, face-to-face combat. It was to take her opponent by surprise. To ambush him. To shoot him in the back, without warning, without the ability to return her fire. Because if he had that opportunity, some of *her* people would die. And if she gave him that opportunity when she didn't have to, then the responsibility for those deaths would be hers.

It was a bitter lesson, one she'd accepted intellectually

while still at Saganami Island, and one which had been turned into polished steel and hammered home on the surface of a planet called Refuge.

Yet this was different. The disparity in weapon technology meant there could be no possibility of return fire. But wasn't that the essence of successful tactics? Captain Terekhov was doing what every captain wanted to do, using any advantage he had or could create to engage the enemy without risking the lives of his own people. She knew that. And she knew Brother Albert would have told her Father Church and, far more importantly, God Himself would understand. Would forgive her for the blood on her hands, if indeed forgiveness was required.

But God could forgive anything to the truly humble and contrite heart. The question in Abigail Hearns' mind was whether or not she could forgive herself.

"Admiral!"

Hegedusic looked up from the com screen connecting him to Alpha Prime's weapons officer. It was the communications lieutenant again.

"Sir, we just picked up a transmission. I . . . think it's from Commodore Horster."

"You *think*?" Hegedusic frowned, and the lieutenant gave him a helpless look.

"Sir, there's no header and no ID code. Just one word transmitted in clear."

"Well?" Hegedusic demanded when the young man paused.

"Sir, it just says 'Coming.' "

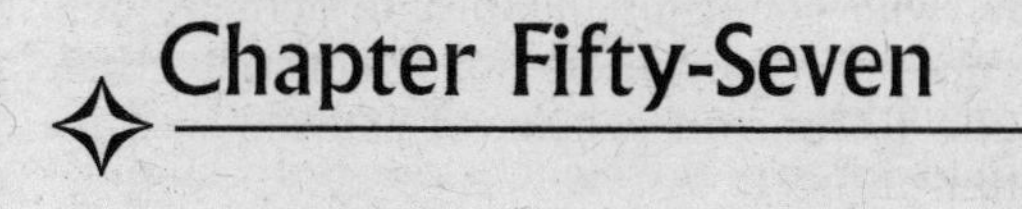

Chapter Fifty-Seven

"Commodore, I just can't guarantee the hard numbers you're asking for," the Solarian technical representative said nervously on the bridge of MNS *Cyclone*. The man was sweating hard, and much as he wanted to, Janko Horster couldn't find it in himself to despise the fellow for it. He was a civilian, after all. He hadn't signed on for a combat mission against a technologically superior opponent.

"I'm not asking you to guarantee it," the commodore said. "I'm just asking for your best estimate."

The civilian fidgeted, pulling at his lower lip and blinking rapidly while he thought.

Horster wanted to shake the answer out of him, but hurrying the man wasn't the way to get a reliable response. So the commodore contented himself with a tight smile, folded his hands behind himself, and took a quick turn around his commodious flag deck.

Under the training mission scenario, the three ships of the First Division—*Cyclone* and her sisters *Typhoon* and *Hurricane*—had been tasked to penetrate Eroica Station's sensor perimeter and get to attack range before they were detected. Given the sensor upgrades the Station had received from the Technodyne people, Horster hadn't been ragingly optimistic about his chances, but he'd been determined to give it the best try he could. Which was why he'd arranged to embark a dozen tech reps aboard each ship for any "emergency adjustments" which might be required. After all, it was less than three weeks since the ships had completed their full-powered engine trials. There was no telling what sort of small things might go wrong. And if the tech reps who just happened to be aboard to deal with them also just *happened* to be qualified EW instructors who could just *happen* to actually take over the systems—purely in order to demonstrate their proper operation to his own people, of course—well, so much the better.

He'd used the marvelously effective stealth systems of his wonderful new toys to cover his relatively low-powered impeller signatures while he accelerated to a velocity of 37,800 KPS. Then he'd shut down to the absolute minimum impeller strength. He would have liked to shut down completely, but even with hot nodes at standby he would have been looking at a significant delay in bringing the wedge back up. So instead he'd held it at the barest possible maintenance level, which would let him bring it back to full power in less than eighty seconds if he needed to.

For the last two hours he'd been barreling through space on a ballistic course. Now he was 48.6 million kilometers short of the Station, which put him just under 58.7 million kilometers from the Manties . . . headed straight for them.

"Commodore," the civilian said finally, "I'm sorry. We just don't know enough about their sensor capabilities. Another *Indefatigable* couldn't see us until we got much closer, probably down to under five million kilometers, given how little emissions signature we're showing. Against Manties, who knows? I hate to say it, but if they've deployed remote arrays, they might be able to see us right this minute."

"No," Horster said. "If they could see us, they'd've already reacted."

"How, Sir?" the civilian asked, and Horster snorted.

"They're still decelerating, and they haven't fired on the Station or, apparently, demanded we break off. Given our closing velocity, they can't avoid us *unless* we break off. So if they're maintaining profile without even mentioning us to the Station, they don't know we're here."

The Solarian nodded slowly, and Horster shrugged.

"At this point, we're going to get to them," he said flatly. "The only way they could prevent that would be to spot us and destroy us first, and I don't think they're going to do that."

"I hope to hell you're right, Commodore," the tech rep said fervently. Which, Horster thought sardonically, wasn't exactly the most reassuring thing one of the people supposed to be teaching him how the ships worked could possibly have said.

He nodded courteously to the civilian and waved him back towards the EW section, then turned to the main plot and puffed out his cheeks as he considered the geometry.

If he'd only started the exercise sooner, he might have been able to intercept the Manties before they attacked the Station. Then again, if the Technodyne people were right about the maximum attack ranges of current-generation Manticoran missiles, they were already in range to attack Eroica. He'd just have to hope this Terekhov was running a bluff, that he wouldn't really inflict the massive casualties an all-out attack on the Station would produce. Surely the thought of how galactic public opinion—and especially *Solarian* public opinion—would react to something like that in time of peace, without even a formal declaration of hostilities, should give the lunatic pause!

"All right!" Hegedusic smacked his palms together and grinned at Levakonic. "The odds seem to be shifting," he observed.

"At least in the direction of having a fighting chance," Levakonic agreed a bit more cautiously.

"But we could shift them even further if we could keep this Captain Terekhov coming in fat, dumb, and happy."

Hegedusic thought a moment longer, then turned back to the communications section.

"Send a message to the Manties. Tell them I've decided to evacuate the Station, but that it's going to take some time. Tell them I estimate a minimum of two and a half to three hours, even using every available vessel from the civilian platforms."

"Yes, Sir."

Hegedusic turned to another staffer.

"Get down to flight ops. Tell them I want a steady stream of lighters and shuttles moving between the Alpha platforms and the Beta platforms. I don't need anybody aboard them but the flight crews; I just need small craft in motion where the Manties can see it."

"Yes, Sir!"

"Well, thank God!" Bernardus Van Dort heaved a huge sigh of relief as the message came in. "Congratulations, Captain. It looks like you've managed it without killing anyone, after all."

"Maybe." Terekhov frowned at the master plot, then glanced at Abigail Hearns. "Any sign of confirming movement?"

"As a matter of fact, Sir, there may be," the Grayson lieutenant said after a moment. "I've got half a dozen—no, a total of nine—small craft impellers moving away from the military portions of the Station."

"You see?" Van Dort's grin grew even broader. "Hegedusic must've realized he didn't have a choice."

"I'd certainly like to think so," Terekhov agreed, his frown beginning to ease at last. "Amal, inform them that as long as they appear to be making a good-faith effort to evacuate the Station, I'll hold my fire. But warn them that restraint on our part is dependent on their continued compliance with our instructions."

✧ ✧ ✧

"How obliging of him," Hegedusic said, and looked back at the tactical officer on his screen. "They're holding profile, correct?"

"Yes, Sir. They're about eighteen minutes from zeroing their velocity relative to the Station. And," the tac officer smiled thinly, "they're just over ten-point-one million kilometers out."

"Patience, patience, Commander," Hegedusic said. "If they're willing to come closer, I'm certainly willing to let them."

"Ms. Zilwicki?"

"Yes, Traynor?" Helen said, turning to the senior sensor rating assisting her with the remote arrays.

"The Alpha-Seven array's picking something up," Traynor said.

"What?" Helen asked. It was scarcely a proper contact report, she reflected. Assuming, of course, that it was an actual contact at all.

"It may be nothing at all, Ma'am. Maybe just a ghost. Look here, Ma'am."

He flicked keys, transferring the data he'd been examining to Helen's secondary plot. She gazed at it herself for several seconds before her eyes narrowed. She input a command sequence, playing with the data, trying to refine it, and frowned.

She considered briefly, then shrugged and sent a request to CIC for the master computers to take a close second look at the suspect datum. Seven seconds later, a scarlet icon flicked into existence on the master plot, strobing with the rapid flicker of an unconfirmed contact.

"Captain," Helen announced, astonished that her own voice sounded so calm, "we have a possible impeller signature, very weak, inbound at three-point-two light-minutes. Apparent closing velocity four-one-five-seven-two kilometers per second."

"Range now ten-point-zero-seven million kilometers," Hegedusic's tac officer said. "Velocity now three-seven-seven-three KPS."

✧ ✧ ✧

"Range to enemy now five-seven-point-six million kilometers," Commodore Horster's tac officer reported. "Closing velocity four-one-five-seven-two KPS."

"CIC, I need confirmation, one way or the other." Terekhov kept his tone as level as possible.

"Yes, Sir. We know. We're doing our best to—"

"Captain, Alpha-Seven has a second possible contact in close company with Bogey-One," Helen announced. She hesitated a moment, then cleared her throat. "Sir, the array's at less than eleven light-seconds from whatever this is."

"Your point, Ms. Zilwicki?"

"Sir, these arrays don't pick up ghosts at that short a range. If they're seeing something that close to them, it's really there. And if they can't see it clearly, it's because whatever it is is doing its damnedest to imitate a hole in space."

"She's right, Skipper," Naomi Kaplan said from Aux-Con. She'd been studying the frustratingly inconclusive data herself. "And if that's what we've got here, Sir," she continued grimly, "whoever it is has got much better EW than any Monican unit ever had."

"Guthrie?" Terekhov looked at his EWO. Bagwell didn't even hesitate.

"Concur, Sir. My guess is that we're looking at a maintenance level impeller wedge covered by some damned good stealth technology. Probably almost as good as our own."

"Understood."

Terekhov leaned back in his command chair, thinking furiously. All eleven of the Solarian battlecruisers *Copenhagen* had discovered were still at Eroica Station.

Which means these people weren't at the Station when the drone made its pass. Battlecruisers they'd already refitted? Possible. Probable, really. They could've been running trials or training missions out-system, where Copenhagen *couldn't see them. Or these may be Solly units that never were intended to be refitted. Either way, I've got a pair of bogeys coming at me that I have to assume are* at least *battlecruisers . . . and there's no way Hegedusic didn't know about it when he sent me that "We're evacuating as quickly* as *we can" message. But—*

"Captain, we've got a *third* possible contact."

He looked up as a third strobing icon appeared in formation with the other two. Helen, a corner of his brain noted, still sounded crisp and professional, but not quite as calm as she'd been with the first two.

And I can't blame her for that! That's three we know *about; God only knows how many we haven't found yet.* He studied projected vectors, and his mouth tightened. At their closing velocity, his squadron's vector intersected almost exactly head-on with the three bogeys' vector in less than twenty-four minutes. *There's no way we can avoid them now, but there's still the units waiting to be refitted. So what do I do? I can hardly even see these probable Sollies. I certainly can't justify wasting missiles on them at this range, not with the miserable hit probabilities we'd have! But if I hold my fire until the range drops and then go for an engagement with them, I could lose everything I've got and leave eleven untouched battlecruisers behind me.*

His jaw tightened.

"Ms. Hearns."

"Yes, Sir."

It was remarkable, he thought, how that soft Grayson accent actually got more musical as the stress mounted.

"We can't leave the battlecruisers in the yard behind us. I want to hold the pods—we may need them against these newcomers. Do you have a good firing solution on the Station?"

"Yes, Sir," she said steadily.

"Very well," he said. "Execute Fire Plan Sierra, broadside launchers only."

"Fire Plan Sierra, aye, aye, Sir," she said, and entered a command sequence.

✧ ✧ ✧

"Missile launch! I have multiple hostile launches! Estimate thirty-plus inbound!"

"God*damn* it!"

Isidor Hegedusic smashed his fist down on his own knee. Missile Defense was tracking the incoming missiles—or *trying* to, at least—and there didn't seem to be many of them. No more than thirty or forty. But the Station's anti-missile defenses hadn't been upgraded. There hadn't been time to do everything, and he and Levakonic had concentrated on giving Eroica Station sharper eyes and longer teeth. Nor had they counted on the fiendishly effective EW platforms scattered among the attack missiles to assist them in penetrating Hegedusic's defenses.

He hesitated, but only for a single heartbeat.

If they take out the battlecruisers, there's no tomorrow, anyway, he thought grimly, and looked at the tactical officer on his screen.

"Engage the enemy, Commander!"

The missile pods provided by Technodyne were very stealthy platforms. In fact, they had even smaller sensor signatures than the RMN's pods did. In virtually every other respect, however, they were inferior to Manticore's weapons. Their single-drive missiles had lower accelerations, less sensitive seekers, poorer EW, and much, much shorter powered attack ranges. But inferior as they might have been in all of those categories, they were far better than anything the SLN had ever had before. They were better than ONI's worst-case estimates. And they were already inside the attack range their improved drives made possible.

To reach their targets with enough time left on their drives for the necessary terminal attack maneuvers, the missiles would have to restrict themselves to half-power, "only" 43,000 gravities and a terminal velocity of "only" .32 *c*. They were big—larger even than a standard capital missile, more like something a ground-based system would have fired—and the designers had been able to squeeze only eight of them into each out-sized pod. But Hegedusic and Levakonic had deployed one hundred and twenty of those pods. Deployed them amid the concealing clutter of Eroica Station's platforms and in the protective radar shadows of handy asteroids.

"Incoming fire! Estimate nine hundred-plus!"

"Point defense free! Case Romeo!" Terekhov snapped.

"Case Romeo, aye, aye, Sir!" Helen Zilwicki responded instantly.

"Fire Plan Omega!"

"Fire Plan Omega!" Abigail responded.

She had assigned Helen responsibility for missile defense while she concentrated on Fire Plan Sierra, targeting her missiles as carefully as possible on the helpless battlecruisers. Now she made the snap decision to leave the midshipwoman in charge. Missile flight times were going to be under a hundred and sixty seconds. This was no time to confuse the situation by interfering. Besides, she had her own priorities.

She'd never really expected Fire Plan Omega to be required. It was the "use-them-or-lose-them" option common to any naval force employing towed pods. Their vulnerability to proximity "soft kills" meant they had to be gotten off before that hurricane of incoming fire arrived, but no one had really expected the Monicans would be able to range on them. Yet the Captain had insisted on planning for even that unlikely eventuality. There was a different, less precise targeting sequence to meet it, one which spared only the two battlecruisers in among the civilians, and Abigail Hearns ignored the missiles screaming in to kill her. She had less than three minutes to completely revise her firing plan and get her birds off before they were destroyed. And so she shut the incoming fire out of her mind, trusting her survival and her ship's to a midshipwoman on her snotty cruise while she called up Fire Plan Omega's targeting hierarchy, handed it to the computers, allocated her pods, and fired.

It never even occurred to Helen that Abigail might have shunted her aside. She was too locked into the job at hand to think about such things, and her fingers flew across her keypads. Her heart seemed to be hammering against the backs of her teeth, yet there was a sort of surrealistic calm to it. A sense almost of floating. If she'd had time to think about it, she would have realized it was almost like the Zen-like state Master Tye had trained into her back on Old Earth, but there was more to it than that. It combined that discipline with the endless hours of drills and simulations. Her hands seemed to know what to do without ever consulting her brain, and yet her brain was whirring with a flashing speed that made even her flying fingers seem slow.

Case Romeo activated the squadron-wide layered defense system Naomi Kaplan had set up on the voyage from Point Midway. *Hexapuma* and *Aegis*, with their superior sensor suites, faster-firing counter-missile tubes, and additional control links, were responsible for the outer counter-missile zone. *Warlock*, *Valiant*, and *Gallant* had the intermediate zone, and *Audacious* and the destroyers had the close-in counter-missile zone.

It was a good plan, and Terekhov's insistence on deploying his full EW assets helped. But there were nine hundred and sixty missiles in that incredible wave. Nine hundred and sixty missiles with penetration aids far superior to anything the Monicans were supposed to have in service, with better seekers and heavier warheads.

Hexapuma and *Aegis*, with their own counter-missiles and enough from the other ships to fill all their redundant control links, destroyed two hundred and nineteen missiles in the outer zone, ripping them apart with precisely directed counter-missile kamikazes.

Seven hundred and forty-one missiles, each fit to blast through a superdreadnought's sidewalls and armor, broke through the outer zone and screamed into the squadron's teeth. *Hexapuma* and *Aegis* continued firing, joined by *Warlock*, *Valiant*, and *Gallant* as the older ships' less acute sensors locked onto the incoming tide of death.

Holes appeared, ripped through the solid-looking tide of incoming warheads, and another two hundred and forty-eight of them died.

But there were still almost four hundred left, and they came howling into the inner counter-missile zone. All the Manticoran ships could see them now, but there was no time for follow-up shots on missiles which evaded the first counter-missiles targeted upon them. The maelstrom of swarming targets and outgoing counter-missiles, the sensor-blinding interference of hundreds of missile impeller wedges, and the jamming, sensor-twisting strobes of the Solarian-built missiles' sophisticated ECM created a whirling confusion no human brain could have sorted out. It was all in the hands of the computers, and *Hexapuma* quivered with the saw-edged vibration of counter-missile tubes in constant, maximum-rate fire.

Two hundred more missiles perished, and "only" two hundred and ninety-three kept coming.

They hit the the perimeter of the final defensive zone, too close for counter-missiles to acquire and intercept in time. Tethered decoys called to them, seducing them away from their assigned targets. Huge bursts of jamming tried to blind them. Laser clusters swiveled and spat, cycling bolts of coherent light in lethal streams, their prediction programs pitted against the best evasion patterns the Solarian League's premier naval shipbuilder could provide. The inner zone was a holocaust of shattering missiles and wreckage, and a hundred and ninety-six more were torn apart in the second and a half it took them to cross it.

It was a phenomenal performance. Ninety percent of that lethal tide was stopped short of attack range. Ninety percent, by only ten warships, none heavier than a heavy cruiser.

But ninety-seven got through.

The Squadron twisted and danced, each captain maneuvering individually, desperately seeking to interpose the shield of his impeller wedge between his crew and the incoming laser heads. But their base velocity was low, and the missiles had plenty of time on their drives. Less than a third of them could be evaded that way. Last-ditch decoys sucked a few of the rest off, and four more strayed too close together and destroyed one other in fratricidal bursts of impeller interference. Two more simply failed to detonate; the rest of them did not.

Hexapuma heaved madly as bomb-pumped lasers designed to shatter the armor of superdreadnoughts slammed into her. Sidewalls did their best, clawing at the beams, bending them. Armor resisted briefly, but the savage bars of X-ray lasers smashed through it. Impeller nodes blew, superconductor capacitors exploded, hull plating shattered. Graser One, Three, and Seven were wiped away as if they had never existed, and despite *Hexapuma*'s manpower-reducing automation, nineteen men and women died with their weapons. Missile tubes were wrecked, ripped and twisted. Frame members shattered. Three sidewall generators went down, and a quarter of her starboard counter-missile tubes and almost half her point defense clusters went with them. Gravitic Array One and Lidar One disintegrated, and a power surge blew into the superconductor ring for Spinal Five, the starboard graser in her after chase armament, like a tornado. The ring exploded, deep inside the ship, like a bomb, and the blast blew back into Auxiliary Control.

Ansten FitzGerald, Naomi Kaplan, and eleven other men and women were caught in the path of the explosion. FitzGerald and Kaplan both survived; most of the others were less fortunate.

Isidor Hegedusic felt a moment of incredible triumph as the missile pods fired.

That tsunami of destruction surpassed anything he'd ever dreamed of commanding, and only ten cruisers and destroyers stood in its path. Whatever happened to Eroica Station, those ships were doomed.

Yet even as he thought that, before the first counter-missile had intercepted the first missile, the *Manticoran* pods fired. He'd sent nine hundred and sixty missiles to crush the Manties; Abigail Hearns sent *seventeen* hundred back into his teeth, and his defenses were nowhere near as good.

Damage reports flooded into the bridge, and Helen cringed.

Javelin, *Rondeau*, and *Gallant* were gone. *Audacious* was savagely damaged and lamed, with less than a quarter of her weapons left. *Vigilant* was little more than a hulk, and *Warlock* was severely damaged. *Hexapuma*'s more modern point defense—and an inordinate share of pure luck—had let her escape with far less damage than her older sisters, but all things were relative. Her maximum acceleration, even without pods, was no better than four hundred gravities. She was down to thirty-five tubes, and a quarter of her broadside grasers—sixty percent of her starboard energy broadside—and one of her after chasers were gone. Thirty-seven of her people were confirmed dead, with at least another seventeen wounded . . . including Surgeon Commander Orban. His sick berth attendants were doing their best, but none of them were fully trained physicians.

It was her fault. She knew that was insane, yet a small, cruel voice deep down inside whispered that she'd been in charge of the missile defenses. *She* was the one who was supposed to stop this from happening.

She stared at the com screen still connected to the badly damaged AuxCon and saw Aikawa working frantically with two uninjured ratings as they applied first-aid to the wounded. But no matter how hard she stared, there was no sign of Paulo.

Aivars Terekhov surveyed the damage, and his jaw clenched painfully.

He'd walked straight into it, and a third of the Squadron's ships had been destroyed because he had. It was all very well to remind himself no battle plan ever survived contact with the enemy. He even knew it was true. But it didn't make him feel one bit better about the dead and maimed who'd counted on him to get it right.

He drew a deep breath and turned his attention to Eroica Station and felt a stab of vengeful satisfaction. Those damned missile pods had savaged his squadron, killed his people, but their own fire had shattered the military components of the Station. The close-in drones made it obvious that at least eight of the nine battlecruisers in the military yard had been wrecked beyond any hope of repair even by a Solarian shipyard, far less Monica's facilities. The other one *might* be repairable, but it would take a fully equipped shipyard months, possibly T-years, to do the job. The two on the civilian side of the installation were still intact, but there wasn't much he could do about that, even using laser heads instead of conventional nukes, without killing hundreds of civilians. He didn't want to do that, and he wouldn't . . . if he had any choice at all. And at least Eroica Station itself had been thoroughly neutralized as a threat.

Which, unfortunately, wasn't true of the oncoming battlecruisers.

Janko Horster's face was white with mingled shock and fury. His sensors couldn't give him as clear a picture of what had happened to Eroica Station as Terekhov's could, but he didn't need details to know the Monican Navy had just been mangled. Most—probably all—of the other battlecruisers were gone, and the same was almost certainly true of the older units which had been laid up at Eroica to provide personnel for his own ships. First Division, by itself, probably had ten times the firepower of the entire Monican Navy before Levakonic had delivered the new ships, but it would be impossible to carry out the operational plan with what was left.

And that didn't include the casualties. The men he'd known and served and trained with for decades. The friends.

Yet the Manties had been hurt, too. Badly. And they must have fired every pod they had to inflict such damage on Eroica Station.

Their long-range missile advantage was gone, and the bastards who'd raped his Navy couldn't get away from him now.

"Get me *Vigilant*," Terekhov grated.

"Aye, aye, Sir," Nagchaudhuri acknowledged, and fifteen seconds later, he found himself facing a lieutenant he'd never seen before.

"Commander Diamond?" he asked.

"Dead, Sir," the lieutenant said hoarsely. "We took a direct hit on the bridge. No survivors, I'm afraid." He coughed on the thin haze of smoke swirling about him, and Terekhov realized he was connected to Damage Control Central.

"Who's in command, Lieutenant?" he asked as gently as he could.

"I guess I am, Sir. Gainsworthy, third engineer. I think I'm the senior officer left."

Dear God, Terekhov thought. *Their casualties must be almost as bad as* Defiant's *were*.

"What's your maximum acceleration, Lieutenant Gainsworthy?"

"I don't know for sure, Sir. It can't be much over a hundred gravs. We've lost the entire after ring, and the forward ring's badly damaged."

"That's what I was afraid of." Terekhov drew a deep breath and squared his shoulders. "You're going to have to abandon, Lieutenant."

"No!" Gainsworthy protested instantly. "We can save her! We can get her home!"

"No, you can't, Lieutenant," Terekhov said, gently but implacably. "Even if she could be repaired, which is doubtful, she can't stay with the rest of the Squadron. Those bogeys will run right over her. So get your people off and set the scuttling charges, Lieutenant Gainsworthy. That's an order."

"But, Sir, we—!" A tear carved a white streak down one dirty cheek, and Terekhov shook his head.

"I'm sorry, son," he said, cutting the lieutenant off quietly. "I know it hurts to lose her—I've done it. But however much you love her, she's only a ship, Lieutenant." *A lie*, his brain shouted. *You know that's a lie!* "She's only alloy and electronics. It's her people that matter. Now get them off."

The final sentence came slowly, measured, and Gainsworthy nodded.

"Yes, Sir."

"Good, Lieutenant. God bless."

Terekhov cut the circuit and turned back to the ships he might still be able to save.

Chapter Fifty-Eight

"They know we're here," Janko Horster muttered.

"What?"

Horster glanced up, irritated by the interruption. But it was the senior tech rep, not one of his officers. The civilian obviously didn't realize he wasn't supposed to interrupt a flag officer's thought processes with questions at a time like this, and Horster decided to answer him.

"They know we're here," he repeated, and gestured at the plot. "Or at least they're afraid *someone*'s out here."

The range was still too great for his passive sensors to provide detailed information, but some things were brutally clear. Four of the Manties' ten impeller signatures had disappeared. Three had vanished with abrupt finality during the vicious missile exchange. Those three, he felt grimly confident, had been hard kills by Eroica Station. The fourth had gone off the display about four minutes after the others. Its strength had dropped precipitously before that, obviously because of battle damage. So either it had finally failed completely because of that damage, or else it had been shut down, which would almost certainly indicate a ship in the process of being abandoned. Whichever it was, the damned Manties had lost forty percent of their strength, and most, if not all, of their surviving units had to have been hurt.

"They've increased their deceleration to four hundred gravities," he told the civilian. "That's an increase of fifty gees over what they were holding it down to on the way in—probably because of their frigging pods—but it's a hell of a lot less than they ought to be capable of. So obviously they have impeller damage. But they've also got a ship out there somewhere that survived the shooting only to have its signature go off the display just a couple of minutes ago. So either its impeller damage was even worse than theirs, and its nodes just packed it in, or they're abandoning her. But they wouldn't be doing that this quickly unless they were afraid someone was in position to engage them."

"How can you be so sure?"

"I can't be *positive*, but they'd have taken longer to reverse course if they weren't. No captain's going to abandon his ship that quickly, not without surveying her damage and being certain he can't save her. And no commodore would leave her behind unless he figured he was going to have a fight on his hands and couldn't afford to be handicapped looking after cripples."

The civilian nodded slowly, and Horster smiled. It was an ugly expression, one that mingled fury over what had happened to his navy with vengeful satisfaction.

"They're dead meat," he said flatly. The civilian stopped nodding and looked at him with undisguised anxiety, and the commodore barked a laugh. "They don't have any of those damned pods left," he said, "and they never had anything bigger than a heavy cruiser to begin with, according to Admiral Hegedusic's tac analysis. At least a hundred of our missiles got into attack range before they detonated, too. They've been hammered—hammered *hard*—and they're going to be up against modern *battlecruisers*. Battlecruisers that can shoot back this time."

The civilian still looked dubious, and Horster could almost hear the thoughts running through the other man's brain. Yes, he had modern battlecruisers to kill them with, but Horster's crews had been aboard their ships for less than three weeks. Their people were still learning how to use their systems, how to master the capabilities, but it wasn't *quite* as bad as it could have been. Their engineering and astrogation departments had been forced to wait until they could actually get aboard the new ships, but the tactical crews had managed to spend over two months in the simulators Levakonic had brought with him. That might not be the same as hands-on training, but it was one hell of a lot better than nothing.

And they *were* battlecruisers, with all the armor and sheer toughness that implied.

"They're definitely battlecruisers, Sir," Helen said.

She was focused on her displays, trying not to think about how many people had just been killed and wounded aboard the Squadron's ships. Aboard *Hexapuma*. She knew Aikawa was still alive, but where was Paulo? Was he even—

She pushed the thought aside again. She had no time for it. Other people were depending on her.

"The arrays are close enough to see them now despite their EW," she continued. "They're definitely running with wedges at maintenance levels, but we're getting enough signature off them to be confident of their tonnage range."

"Can we tell if they're more *Indefatigables*?"

"No, Sir. We're not getting much besides the impeller signatures and some neutrino leakage."

"Skipper," Lieutenant Bagwell said from the electronic warfare station, "until they go active with their sensor suites, we're not going to get any more off of them. From the quality of their stealth technology, though, they've got to be Solly designs."

"Another thing, Sir," Abigail said. "Whoever these people are, they were obviously already on a ballistic course for Eroica Station when we turned up, or we'd have picked up their drives. I suppose it's possible they had their impellers up and their stealth system simply hid it from us, but I don't think so. I think they'd already cut their drives. Which suggests some sort of fleet maneuver."

"And?" Terekhov prompted in an encouraging tone when she paused, although he was fairly certain he knew where she was headed.

"Well, Sir, I suppose it's possible an SLN commander might want to exercise his crews, but it doesn't seem likely he'd have pulled out all the stops that way against typical Verge sensor technology. I think it's more likely these are more of the same—additional ships being turned over to the Monicans, but already through the refit process and working up new crews."

"That's speculative, Skipper," Bagwell said, "but I think it's good speculation."

"So do I." Terekhov smiled approvingly at his youthful tactical officer. And at her even more youthful assistant. Then his expression sobered.

If Abigail was right and those ships were still in the process of working up, there were likely to be weaknesses in their performance, chinks in their armor. But they were still battlecruisers. The three of them outmassed all six of his surviving ships by better than two-to-one, and they were undamaged.

He looked at the plot. Eleven minutes had elapsed from the moment the third battlecruiser was detected. Only eleven minutes, in which hundreds of his people had been killed and the Monicans' casualties had probably run well into the thousands. He was decelerating away from the oncoming battlecruisers at the highest rate the Squadron as a whole could sustain, but nothing he did was going to prevent those ships from engaging him.

The only advantage he still had was the reach of *Hexapuma*'s internal launchers, and the geometry of the looming engagement did much to neutralize even that. The range was down to 30.9 million kilometers, and with the battlecruisers' overtake advantage of 38,985 KPS, *Hexapuma*'s maximum powered envelope at launch was increased to almost thirty-seven million kilometers. Assuming the battlecruisers' shipboard missile performance approximated ONI's estimates, their range would be under fifteen million kilometers, despite their overtake, but at present velocities and accelerations, they would enter that range of him within another 6.3 minutes and enter energy range eleven minutes after that. *Warlock* would also have a slight range advantage over the Monican battlecruisers, but it wasn't great enough to change the tactical equation significantly. Her tubes were simply too small; she couldn't handle even the Mark 14 missiles the *Saganami-B*s had been designed to fire, much less a *Saganami-C*'s Mark 16s, so her advantage would be little more than three million kilometers—barely seventy-five seconds at the Monicans' rate of closure.

The range was still very long, especially against current Solarian ECM and missile defenses . . . and he didn't have all that many missles with which to penetrate them. Each of his Mark 16 missiles came in at over ninety-four tons, and *Hexapuma*'s total designed loadout of attack missiles was 1,200. Fortunately, they'd squeezed in an extra hundred and twenty birds . . . but Abigail had expended most of them in Fire Plan Omega, and fifteen more had been in the feed queues of the five destroyed launchers. Without the redundant manpower *Hexapuma* didn't have, there was no way to manually reclaim those missiles, so his ship was down to an effective total of only 1,155. The cycle time on his launchers at maximum-rate fire was one round every eighteen seconds, twice the time an older ship, like *Warlock*, would have required. Partly because the missiles were simply larger, but even more because of the need to light up the Mark 16's onboard reactor before launch. Still, in theory, each launcher could fire fifty-four times before anyone else on either side was in range to do the same . . . except for the fact that he had only thirty-three rounds per tube.

Yet he had very little time to think about it. Flight time was going to be over three and a half minutes.

"Guns," he said to his youthful acting tactical officer,

"your target is the lead bogey. I want double broadsides at twenty-five-second intervals. You can have four tubes in each salvo for Dazzlers and Dragon's Teeth. Five salvos on Bogey One, then shift to Bogey Two."

"Aye, aye, Sir."

"Ms. Zilwicki, lock the Alpha-Seven array directly to Lieutenant Bagwell." He turned his chair to face the EWO. "These people's defenses are going to be good—very good. We need to hammer them, and to do that we need data on their EW capabilities—fast. The rest of the Squadron will have over ten minutes to engage after they enter their effective powered envelope, but for them to use that time, we need to feed them everything we can pry loose about these people's defensive systems, and our missile range advantage is the only crowbar we have. We need to make them show us their best, people."

"Understood, Sir," Bagwell said.

"Very well, Ms. Hearns—open fire!"

"Missile launch!"

"Wedge up!" Horster snapped instantly, and the division's impeller wedges sprang to full power. It didn't happen instantly, even from a maintenance power level, but there was plenty of time to get them up before the attacking missiles could arrive.

The commodore crossed quickly to the master plot, looking for the incoming fire, and his eyes narrowed as he found it.

The arrow-shaped icons of thirty-five missiles streaked towards his trio of ships, accelerating steadily at 46,000 gravities. Twenty-five seconds later, a second salvo followed. Then a third. A fourth.

"The target is *Typhoon*," CIC announced as the first counter-missiles went out to meet them, and Horster nodded. *Typhoon* was his lead ship. He'd expected her to draw the enemy's fire, assuming they weren't stupid enough to divide it among all of his units.

The Manties had begun firing much sooner than he'd anticipated. For just an instant, he wondered if that meant they were planning on sending them in ballistic. But that would have been a stupid waste of precious ammunition, and they were firing their birds with low-power drive settings. That suggested that they must have the reach to engage under power even at this range, presumably with plenty of time on their clocks for terminal attack maneuvers. Still, there were less than forty in each salvo. They had to be coming from a single ship, so perhaps the Manties actually had at least one battlecruiser of their own out there. Either way, there weren't enough birds to saturate his division's defenses, so—

His eyes narrowed still further as the lead salvo abruptly vanished from the plot. One instant it was there; the next all thirty-plus missiles just disappeared. Five seconds later, they reappeared, but not as the steady, blood-red light codes they'd been before. Now they strobed rapidly, almost flickering, and he jabbed an angry glance at the tech rep.

"I don't know!" the civilian said, correctly interpreting the look. "It must be some sort of jamming platform. That—" he stabbed an index finger at the flickering icons "—indicates we can see them, but we don't have hard locks. And look—look there! *Goddamn* it!"

Horster didn't swear out loud, but his teeth ground together as his division's entire initial salvo of counter-missiles lost lock and went stumbling off into ineffectuality.

Terekhov bared his teeth at the tactical plot. Despite the range, the FTL reports from Helen's recon drones gave him a real-time, close-range picture of what was happening. He hadn't given Abigail specific instructions on how to employ the EW platforms seeded into her attack salvos, but he recognized what she'd done. She'd used all of the available slots in the initial double broadside for Dazzlers but locked them down until they detected the launch of the enemy's first counter-missiles. When the powerful jammers did come on-line, the Monican CMs had already established lock and been cut loose from the launching ships' control links. But the counter-missiles' onboard seekers weren't up to the challenge of that sudden, massive pulse of jamming right in their faces.

The attack salvo jinked and wove, threading through, past, and around the suddenly dazed and clumsy interceptors which were supposed to have stopped it, then drove past the *second* wave of CMs, which had already locked onto Abigail's next attack wave. Four of the first wave's birds abruptly wavered, losing lock, veering away as the Monicans' own EW lured them astray. Then a fifth followed them. But thirty held lock, and their closing velocity was so great the defenders had no time to vector yet another wave of counter-missiles onto them.

Then Bogey One's forward laser clusters opened fire.

This time Janko Horster *did* swear.

Typhoon's shipboard sensors were less affected by the Manties' infernal jammers than the counter-missiles' seekers had been, but it was painfully obvious they hadn't been *un*affected. They fired late, and their solutions were poor. An *Indefatigable*-class battlecruiser's point defense clusters should have been more than equal to a salvo that size, but she stopped only fourteen of them. The other sixteen got through.

Fortunately, three of the leakers must have been EW platforms. But thirteen laser heads detonated in sequence, so rapidly it looked like one, continuous eruption, directly ahead of *Typhoon*. The bomb-pumped lasers stabbed straight down the throat of her wedge, unobstructed by any sidewall.

Typhoon's forward hammerhead was massively armored against just such an attack, but not even her armor could shrug off that staccato thunder of stabbing X-ray lasers. It stopped a dozen of them, but another half-dozen blasted straight through it. They knocked out two of her chase missile tubes, one of her chase energy mounts, two counter-missile tubes and a laser cluster. And, far worse, one shattered her forward radar array. It blinded her, put out the eye of her forward missile defenses, and a second wave of attacking missiles was only twenty-five seconds behind.

Lieutenant Julio Tyler staggered as *Typhoon* shuddered. The engineering officer was in charge of Power One, the battlecruiser's forward fusion plant, and he went pale as damage alarms screamed. Power One was far enough aft and heavily enough armored to make it highly unlikely any cruiser-sized laser head could reach it. But from the sound of the alarms, *these* laser heads were ripping much deeper than they should have.

Tyler swallowed hard and looked around the brightly lit, spacious compartment. He'd been transferred into *Typhoon*'s company three days after the rest of her crew to replace a man who'd managed to fall down an emergency ladder and break his hip, and he knew the rest of the battlecruiser's engineering department wasn't overly impressed with him. He was used to that jealous reaction to his rapid promotion. Relatively few officers made it to senior lieutenant's rank before their twenty-first birthday, but Tyler had always tried to do his job. To actually deserve the fast-track promotions his last name earned.

Yet this time, he was painfully aware of his shortcomings. In the last two weeks he'd begun finding his way around, well enough, at least, that he was pretty sure his ratings and petty officers were no longer laughing behind his back. And he had to admit the Technodyne technicians were right; *Typhoon*'s power rooms really were laid out better, with controls that were easier to use. They just weren't the controls Tyler had spent three and a half T-years learning like the back of his own hand aboard the cruiser *Star Fury*.

As he listened to the alarms howl, he hoped the damage control parties had learned *their* equipment better than he'd learned his.

"Many hits on Bogey One!" Helen Zilwicki announced, half-hunched over her displays. Her eyes were narrowed as she studied the data coming in from her remote arrays. "I think we just took out her forward radar, Sir!"

"Excellent!" Terekhov acknowledged, but he knew that had been the most effective single salvo they were going to get in, and now that they knew for certain he'd seen them, the Monicans were no longer trying to hide. Their wedges were up, and they were accelerating directly towards the Squadron at five hundred gravities. That was going to reduce his missile engagement time, he thought grimly, but it was hardly unexpected. And at least if they were going to chase him, it meant exposing the throats of their wedges to his fire.

And *Indefatigable*-class battlecruisers didn't mount bow walls.

He watched the plot as Abigail's second double broadside roared into the Monicans' outer defense zone. He saw the instant that its Dazzlers came on-line and the counter-missiles which had been speeding to meet them veered aside. But this time there was time for a follow-on wave of CMs to be vectored onto them. Seventeen of them were intercepted and blotted away, and then the laser clusters began to fire. Another twelve were picked off, but six got through, and Bogey One staggered as more stilettos drilled through her armor.

Typhoon shuddered as a second wave of X-ray daggers bored through her armor. She should have stopped more of them—all of them—with her lavish anti-missile defenses, but she couldn't *see* them. Her point defense lasers had become dependent upon relayed tracking reports from *Cyclone* and *Hurricane*, and that simply wasn't adequate against targets coming in so fast. Especially not targets as elusive as Manticoran Mark 16 missiles. Fresh damage reports inundated her bridge, and her acceleration faltered as four of her beta nodes blew.

Power surges cascaded through her systems, starting in Impeller One and Laser Three. Automatic circuit breakers stopped most of them, but three of the breakers themselves had been knocked out. Rampant energy surged past them, and a broadside graser's superconductor ring blew, shattering internal bulkheads and adding its own massive power to the surge.

The surge that came roaring down the graser's main feed trunk and straight into Power One.

The untamed torrent of energy thundered into the compartment, and an already nervous petty officer leapt back as his control panel blew up. He fell to the decksole on the seat of his pants as electrical fires danced through the control runs, and an alarm began to scream.

Aivars Terekhov sat in his command chair, projecting an aura of granite determination. It was all he could do. He'd given his orders; now it was up to others to execute them, and he watched Guthrie Bagwell as the EWO concentrated on the data streaming back from the remote sensor array sitting almost on top of Bogey One. It seemed incredible that the Monicans didn't know Alpha-Seven was there, but surely if they *had* known they'd have destroyed it already!

Bagwell was leaning forward, as if he intended to climb bodily inside his console, and his hands hovered above his keypads. Every few seconds they darted down, stabbing keys, sending another packet of information, another observation on the enemy's ECM, to Abigail Hearns' tactical computers and on to the rest of the Squadron.

Terekhov glanced at the time display. Five minutes into the engagement. Abigail's third salvo was rumbling down on Bogey One, and in a little over seventy seconds everyone on both sides would be in range.

There'd been time—barely—for Abigail's control links to update the third salvo in light of Bagwell's observation of the ECM which had greeted the first salvo, and Terekhov's eyes gleamed. The Monicans' counter-missiles had picked off twenty of the incoming missiles, but only two of the fifteen survivors succumbed to the enemy's EW. Five of the remaining thirteen fell to Bogey One's laser clusters, but three EW birds and five laser heads reached attack range.

They detonated.

"Captain, this is Tyler, in Power One!" the young voice in Captain Schroeder's earbug was raw with terror. "We're losing containment on Fusion One!"

"Shut it down!"

"Sir, I'm *trying*, but—"

Janko Horster's face went white as *Typhoon* blew up.

That shouldn't have happened, a small, stunned corner of his brain insisted. *Not to a* battlecruiser*!*

"*Allah!*" the Technodyne rep whispered. His face glistened with sweat now, and his hands shook. "How—?"

"No telling," Horster said harshly. "A freak hit. Somebody in a fusion room who punched the wrong button. Maybe God just got pissed at us! But it's not going to help them much in another sixty seconds!"

Terekhov stared at his own plot in disbelief. Eight hundred and fifty thousand tons of starship had just disappeared. Just like that.

"Good work, Guns!" he heard his own voice saying even as he tried to come to grips with the reality.

Abigail didn't look up from her console. He didn't know if she'd even heard him. She was oblivious to all distractions, wrapped in a fugue state Terekhov knew from personal experience. Every gram of attention was focused on her displays, her keypads, and the ruby icons of her targets. Anything directly pertaining to their destruction registered instantly, cleanly; everything else was extraneous and supremely unimportant.

Her next two salvos—sixty-two precious laser heads and eight EW platforms—went streaking into nothingness. Their target no longer existed, and there was no time to divert them to Bogey Two; they would continue to the end of their powered run, then detonate harmlessly. But that gave her computers an additional fifty seconds to update the first of Bogey Two's salvos. And she'd taken a different approach with its penetration aides.

It was *Hurricane*'s turn.

Unlike *Typhoon*, there was nothing at all wrong with *Hurricane*'s forward sensors. But the salvo of missiles tearing down upon her seemed totally oblivious to her ECM. They ignored her decoys, brushed aside her jamming. It was ridiculous. No one could respond that quickly to a target's electronic warfare systems!

But somehow the Manties were doing it.

Hurricane's counter-missiles roared out. The Manties' jamming didn't seem quite so intense this time—either that, or *Hurricane*'s tactical officers were getting a better feel for it. Horster smiled as he watched the CMs tear out to meet the Manticoran missiles.

And then, suddenly, there weren't thirty-five incoming birds; there were more than seventy of them.

"Damn them! *Damn* them!" the tech rep muttered. "They can't *do* this shit!"

"What are you talking about?" Horster snarled as the intercepting counter-missiles went berserk trying to maintain lock on their designated targets in the midst of so many abruptly replicated threats.

"They can't have the *power* to confuse our sensors this way!" the civilian said. "They're inside our shipboard sensor envelope. They aren't dealing with remote arrays, or even smaller shipboard suites—these are *battlecruisers*, damn it! We should be burning through that clutter like it wasn't even there!"

"You said they had superdense fusion bottles in their missiles, why not here?" Horster demanded harshly.

"But even if they have the power, the emitters would have to be . . ." The Solarian's voice trailed off, and his eyes narrowed as intense speculation overcame—momentarily, at least—even his fear.

Horster glared at him, but there was more than a little envy in the glare. A part of the commodore wished something could distract *him* from the debacle which had engulfed his Navy. No matter what happened to the Manties in front of him, they'd accomplished their mission. When the smoke cleared, there would *be* no Monican System Navy.

But at least he could make sure they never got to celebrate their triumph.

The bridge lift door opened, and Midshipman Paulo d'Arezzo came through it at a run.

Terekhov saw him; Helen was so tightly focused on the input from her sensor arrays and the looming missile engagement with the oncoming battlecruisers that she never even noticed.

"Sorry, Sir!" Paulo said, as he skidded to a temporary halt beside the captain's command chair. "That explosion knocked me on my ass for a minute or two. I'm afraid it wrecked my EW station, too. So I came up here to see if I could lend Lieutenant Bagwell a hand."

There was blood on the young man's right temple, Terekhov noted, and the entire right side of his face was already beginning to bruise. But he was on his feet, and he was here, and the captain smiled tightly at him and pointed at Bagwell.

"Just don't jostle his elbow, Paulo," he said, and the midshipman bared his teeth in a half-manic grin and dashed across to Bagwell.

The miraculously increased Manticoran missile salvo slammed into *Hurricane*.

Horster wasn't certain how many of the real attack missiles *Hurricane* and *Cyclone* had managed to kill. Some of them, at least. But an entire cluster of them got through, and it was *Hurricane*'s turn to twitch in agony as the X-ray needles stabbed into her. They seemed to be all over her, ripping at her like demons, yet unlike *Typhoon*, she shook the hits off without any apparent effect, and Horster grinned like a punch-drunk fighter. *That* was what it meant to be a battlecruiser fighting heavy cruisers!

"Missile range in twenty seconds, Commodore!"

"Bring the division to starboard. Clear our port broadsides."

"Yes, Sir."

The two surviving battlecruisers swung to starboard, bringing their port broadsides to bear, and Horster kicked himself mentally. He should have done this sooner. He'd been too fixated on pursuing the enemy, accelerating straight after them. He should have let them go ahead and reduce the closure rate in order to bring his broadside sensors and additional point defense to bear. But he'd been confident in the strength of his armor and the effectiveness of his EW . . . until *Typhoon* blew up, at least.

They'd just begun their turn when the second Manty heavy cruiser opened fire, followed seconds later by every surviving Manticoran ship.

Hexapuma and *Aegis* were the only ships in Terekhov's riven Squadron with the off-bore capacity to fire both broadsides at a single target. The light cruiser had twenty tubes. *Warlock* had sixteen in her less damaged broadside. *Janissary* had eight, *Aria* had six, and the severely mauled *Audacious* had three. Altogether, it came to eighty-eight launchers. The minimum cycle time for *Warlock*, *Janissary*, and *Aegis* was eight seconds per launcher; for the older *Aria* and *Audacious*, it was fourteen seconds. But penetrating the battlecruisers' defensive envelope required massed fire, so the controlling factor was the slowest cycle time of the squadron.

Hexapuma had expended four hundred and sixty-five Mark 16s and sixty of her hundred and thirty EW platforms. She had six hundred and thirty attack missiles left—only eighteen double broadsides, but her consorts had full magazines, and the last thing Aivars Terekhov wanted was to let two undamaged battlecruisers into energy range of his mangled ships. The rest of the Squadron had eleven minutes of concentrated missile fire to do something about that, which was the real reason he'd expended so many missiles while only *Hexapuma* had the range to engage, but *Hexapuma* had only another five minutes of fire.

Guthrie Bagwell's analysis of the enemy's electronic warfare capabilities had gone out to the entire Squadron, and if they lacked *Hexapuma*'s reach, even the older destroyers could come close to matching her penetration aids over the range they did have.

If they couldn't stop, or at least severely damage, those oncoming leviathans before the two forces interpenetrated, there would be no tomorrow, and so as the range dropped to 11.4 million kilometers, they went to rapid fire at *Hexapuma*'s maximum rate.

Janko Horster realized he'd made another mistake, one far worse than failing to open his broadsides earlier. Each of his battlecruisers had twenty-nine tubes in her broadside. With *Typhoon* gone, that gave him fifty-eight—two-thirds as many as the Manties had—with a minimum cycle time of thirty-five seconds. Worse, his tactical crews had no information at all on the Manties' electronic warfare capabilities, while it was quickly and dismally apparent the Manticoran CO had learned a great deal about *his* EW during the approach.

His people were doing their best, but seven weeks of combined simulator and hands-on training wasn't enough. It wasn't second nature to them, wasn't instinctive. The slight hesitation in their responses, the friction in the decision loops, might not have been apparent against another Verge navy. But he didn't face another Verge navy. He faced the Royal Manticoran Navy, and that was a mistake few survived.

In the next two hundred and sixteen seconds, Aivars Terekhov's cruisers and destroyers fired nine hundred and ninety attack missiles and one hundred and twenty Dazzlers and Dragon's Teeth. Seven hundred and thirteen missiles and seventy-nine of the electronic warfare birds were in space before the first salvo landed. In the same time period, *Cyclone* and *Hurricane* fired three hundred and thirty-six missiles . . . and *no* dedicated EW platforms at all.

It was a holocaust.

The Manticoran missiles went through the Monicans' electronic defenses like white-hot awls. Counter-missiles managed to kill dozens of them, point defense laser clusters killed dozens more, but for every missile that was stopped, five got through. The battlecruisers' tracking capacity was simply overwhelmed by the Dragon's Teeth's false images of incoming warheads. Their sensors were hashed by blinding bursts of static. They were a third-class navy up against what might well be the premier combat fleet of the explored galaxy, and they were outclassed in every quality but courage.

Janko Horster saw it coming. Realized even Technodyne's "experts" had underestimated the enormous technological edge the Manticoran Navy held over their own hardware. Realized, even more gallingly, how outclassed his crews—and he—were by the crews aboard those Manticoran warships. His ships were battlecruisers, armed and armored on a scale none of his opponents could match. But what use armor when hundreds upon hundreds of laser warheads ripped and tore and gouged? What use massive energy batteries that were shattered and broken, reduced to ruined battle steel and dead and dying crewmen before ever they got into range of an enemy?

Space itself seemed to shudder around the two ships writhing at the heart of the furnace, surrounded by a seething cauldron of nuclear flame as laser head after laser head detonated and hurled its fury at them. Armor and hull plating shattered, atmosphere gushed from gaping wounds like blood, and men died—some instantly, like the switching off of a light, and some screaming in broken agony, alone and trapped in the wreckage of their ships.

By the time *Cyclone* and *Hurricane* reached energy range of the first Manticoran ship, they were little more than hulks, wedges dead, power gone, trailing atmosphere, escape pods, and wreckage.

But they didn't die alone. Outclassed they might have been, with faulty training and poor doctrine, but there was nothing at all wrong with their courage. And however justified Aivars Terekhov's actions might have been, the fury they felt at his attack burned with a clear, white heat. Three hundred of their missiles reached Terekhov's squadron before the blowtorch of his own attack seared them, and the destroyer *Janissary* and the light cruiser *Audacious* died with them. *Hexapuma*, *Warlock*, *Aegis*, and *Aria* survived. Four ships, all that was left of Terekhov's squadron, every one of them severely damaged.

"—and Surgeon Commander Simmons abandoned *Vigilant* successfully with a pinnace full of wounded before she blew. They'll be aboard directly, Sir," Amal Nagchaudhuri said wearily. With Ansten FitzGerald still unconscious and Naomi Kaplan even more badly injured, and with Ginger Lewis working like a titan to deal with *Hexapuma*'s brutal wounds, Nagchaudhuri was Terekhov's acting executive officer. He looked exhausted, out on his feet, and Terekhov sympathized, for he felt exactly the same.

"Good, Amal," he said crisply, and the com officer wondered where the Captain found his energy. No one could look that clear-eyed and alert after what they'd all been through, but somehow, the Captain managed it. "We'll have to find room for the wounded somewhere," he continued. "But thank God we can get a proper doctor in here!"

"Yes, Sir," Nagchaudhuri agreed. He pressed the page key, bringing up his next screen of notes. "We've lost six beta nodes in the forward ring, and eight betas and two alphas out of the after ring. Our best acceleration's about three hundred gravities, but Ginger's working on that. We're down to two grasers in the port broadside—none at all to starboard, although Ginger thinks she may be able to get one of them back eventually.

We've got eight operable tubes to starboard, and eleven to port, but we shot ourselves dry. We're even out of counter-missiles. The after chase armament's pretty much trashed, and I don't think Ginger's going to be able to do anything about that. The forward chasers came through untouched, somehow. And we still have the bow wall. But if it comes to another fight, Skipper, we've got the firepower—maybe—of a destroyer, and we have exactly one starboard sidewall generator."

Terekhov grimaced. They were no unexpected revelations in Nagchaudhuri's report. Indeed, if anything surprised him it was that they had even one broadside energy mount left.

"And our people?" he asked quietly, and Nagchaudhuri winced.

"We're still working on the numbers, and we've still got people unaccounted for who may be alive in the wreckage. But so far, Skipper, it looks like sixty dead and twenty-eight wounded."

Terekhov's jaw clenched. Eighty-eight might not sound like very much compared to what the Monicans had lost. Or the other ships of his own squadron, for that matter. But *Hexapuma*'s total company, including Marines, was only three hundred and fifty *before* her earlier casualties and detachments. Nagchaudhuri's numbers—which still weren't complete, he reminded himself—represented thirty percent of the people he'd taken into battle with him.

And *Hexapuma* was one of the lucky ships.

"What about the rest of the Squadron?"

"*Aegis* is the closest thing we've got to combat-capable, Sir, and she's down to sixty-two missiles and five grasers. *Warlock* doesn't have a single operable weapon left, and *Aria* is almost that bad. Lieutenant Rossi says—"

"Excuse me, Skipper." Terekhov looked up. It was Jefferson Kobe.

"Yes, Jeff? What is it?"

"Sir, Helen's arrays are picking up several Monican warships headed our way. It looks like half a dozen LACs, four destroyers, and a pair of light cruisers. And we've just received a message from an Admiral Bourmont. He demands that we surrender or be destroyed."

Terekhov looked at him, then at Nagchaudhuri. The lieutenant commander's expression was tight, his eyes dark, and Terekhov understood that, too. Obsolete though the regular Monican Navy might be, it was more than adequate to destroy his own shattered survivors.

"How long for their first unit to get here?"

"Toby says four hours for a zero/zero, Sir. Three hours, fifty minutes if they settle for a flyby firing pass."

"Very well." Terekhov strode out of the briefing room onto *Hexapuma*'s bridge and waved for Kobe to resume his station at Communications. He felt his bridge crew's tension, felt them wanting to turn and look at him even as discipline kept them focused on their displays. These people hovered on the ragged brink of exhaustion, and they knew as well as he that they couldn't fight the Monicans.

"First, Jeff," Terekhov said calmly, "get Commander Badmachin on the FTL."

"Aye, aye, Sir."

It took less than a minute to make the connection. *Hexapuma* and her three battered consorts floated in space, less than nine million kilometers from Eroica Station with zero relative motion. That put the ammunition ship, still hovering at the hyper limit, 12.2 million kilometers further out.

"Yes, Captain?" Badmachin's expression was eloquent with concern.

"Captain Badmachin, I want you to join the rest of the Squadron here at your best speed."

"*There*, Sir?"

"Yes. You should have time to join us, drop off a couple of hundred more pods, and still return across the hyper limit before any Monican unit is in range to fire on you. Please get underway immediately."

"Yes, Sir. Immediately!" she said.

"Good. Terekhov, clear." He looked back at Kobe. "Now record for Admiral Bourmont, please."

"Yes, Sir. Standing by to record."

"Admiral Bourmont," Terekhov faced the visual pickup, his shoulders square, his expression confident, and his voice was icy. "You've called upon my Squadron to surrender. Unfortunately, I can't do that. I came here to do a job—to neutralize the battlecruisers your star nation has been assembling to attack mine. I have not yet completed that task. Two of your battlecruisers remain undamaged, because I refrained from firing upon them in light of their proximity to the civilian portions of your Eroica Station complex. Should any of your armed vessels continue to approach my own command—and we have all of them under surveillance as I speak—I will have no option but to complete my task before withdrawing into hyper *before any of your warships can reach me*. I regret to say it, but this will require a bombardment of the battlecruisers in question with contact nuclear warheads, and it will be impossible for me to permit the evacuation of your civilian workforce first."

He heard someone inhale sharply behind him, but his own expression never wavered.

"Should you choose to stand down your warships, and to maintain the present *status quo* unchanged pending the arrival of the approaching Manticoran relief force, I will be spared that unpleasant necessity. Should you choose not to stand down your warships and maintain the *status quo*, I will proceed with the bombardment. And under no circumstances will I permit the evacuation of your civilians. The choice is yours, Sir. You have two hours in which to make it and get your decision to me. Terekhov, clear."

He stopped and looked at Kobe. The lieutenant looked severely shaken, but he nodded.

"Good copy, Sir," he said with only the slightest tremor in his voice.

"Very well. Attach the latest tactical summary, including the positions of all of their units we currently have under observation. Then send it, please."

"Aye, aye, Sir."

"Now, Amal," Terekhov said calmly, turning back to Nagchaudhuri, "I believe you have a report to complete. We'll have time for that before *Volcano* arrives. If you please."

He walked back across the deathly silent bridge to the briefing room, his boot heels sounding clearly on the decksole, and Nagchaudhuri followed after only a brief hesitation. So did Van Dort. He hadn't been invited, but Terekhov wasn't surprised at all to see him after the hatch closed and he turned back to Nagchaudhuri.

"Yes, Bernardus?" he asked in that same, calm voice.

"Aivars, you *are* bluffing, aren't you? You wouldn't really massacre all those civilians?"

"Bernardus, we can't leave. Monica's squarely in the middle of a hyper-space grav wave. The only two ships we have left who can still generate Warshawski sails are *Aegis* and *Volcano*, and they don't begin to have the life-support to take all our survivors with them. And what do you think will happen to my people if I allow them to fall into Monican hands before the relief force gets here?"

Van Dort didn't answer the question. He didn't have to.

"But what if there *isn't* a relief force?" he asked instead.

"There will be," Terekhov said, with the certitude of God's own prophet. "And when it arrives, my people will be alive to see it."

"But you won't really bombard the battlecruisers?"

"On the contrary, Bernardus," Captain Aivars Alexsovitch Terekhov, Royal Manticoran Navy, said coldly. "If these bastards call my 'bluff,' I will blow their goddamned battlecruisers, and every civilian around them, to hell."

Epilogue

"So you're finally ready, Captain," Vice Admiral Quentin O'Malley observed.

"Yes, Sir," Aivars Terekhov replied.

"I imagine you'll be glad to get home," O'Malley said.

"Yes, Sir," Terekhov repeated. "Very glad. *Ericsson* and the other repair ships have done a remarkable job, but she really needs a full-scale shipyard."

O'Malley nodded. In the three T-months since Rear Admiral Khumalo's arrival in Monica, the Talbott Station support ships had patched HMS *Hexapuma* up enough to at least get her home. Which had been just as remarkable a job as Terekhov had implied. They hadn't had much to work with, after all.

Of Terekhov's impromptu squadron, only *Aegis* and *Hexapuma* would ever return to service. *Aria* and *Warlock* were simply too old, too obsolescent, to be worth repairing, even if they hadn't been so severely mangled in the Battle of Monica. *Warlock*, at least, would be returning to the Star Kingdom under Commnder George Hibachi's command and her own power in company with *Hexapuma*, but only because repairing her alpha nodes had cost less than the Navy would be able to reclaim from her hull when she was broken up.

Yet the name *Warlock* would not disappear from the Royal Manticoran Navy. As Ito Anders had once said, HMS *Warlock* had not been fortunate in her commanding officers or her reputation. But Anders had repaired that fault. It had cost him his life, but his ship had redeemed herself. Like every unit of Terekhov's "Squadron," her name had been added to the List of Honor. Those names would be kept in commission in perpetuity in recognition of what they and their people had accomplished at such dreadful cost.

Fifty-one percent of Terekhov's personnel had died in Monica; another twenty-six percent had been wounded. Manticore's total casualties had been far lower than those of the Monican Navy. Probably, O'Malley reflected, even proportionately, but certainly in absolute terms. Which didn't change the fact that sixty percent of his ships had been destroyed outright, that the remaining forty percent had been brutally crippled, and that less than a quarter of their personnel were fit for duty. Yet somehow, with the missile pods from *Volcano* as their only remaining hole card, Aivars Terekhov's surviving, broken, air-bleeding wrecks had managed to hold an entire star system captive for seven standard days. One entire T-week. All by themselves, with no assurance Augustus Khumalo was really coming. With no way of knowing when a Solarian League task force might come over the alpha wall with blood in its eye.

No, O'Malley corrected himself. *They had one other card, beside the pods. They had Terekhov.*

He looked at the broad-shouldered, bearded captain whose blue eyes looked steadily back from under the band of his white beret. He looked so . . . ordinary in so many ways. A bit taller than average, perhaps. But there were only those unflinching eyes to give the lie to his ordinary appearance. And they were enough, O'Malley decided. Enough to explain why this man was already being compared by some to Honor Harrington or Ellen D'Orville. Perhaps even to Edward Saganami himself.

O'Malley wondered what Terekhov had thought when *Hercules* finally arrived. Had he been relieved? Or had he anticipated that Khumalo would order his arrest? Have him charged, court-martialed? From what O'Malley had seen of Terekhov since his own arrival in Monica with the Home Fleet relief force and Dame Amandine Corvisart, he suspected that the thought of court-martial and disgrace had held no terror for this man. No officer with the moral courage to do what he'd done, to risk—and suffer—the casualties his people had taken, after having already survived the Battle of Hyacinth, would hesitate to pay the price he'd known his decision might carry. Which was not to say he would have found the destruction of his own naval career any less agonizing simply because his own sense of duty had required that sacrifice of him.

Yet whatever Terekhov might have feared, Augustus Khumalo had turned out to possess hidden depths of his own. Depths Quentin O'Malley, for one, would never have suspected. Whatever Khumalo might have thought during his long voyage from Spindle to Monica, he had never hesitated or wavered a single millimeter after his arrival. He'd backed Terekhov's actions to the hilt. When Roberto Tyler demanded that he withdraw immediately from Monican territory, Khumalo had flatly refused. Perhaps the evidence of the two remaining *Indefatigable*-class battlecruisers at Eroica Station helped explain that. Yet O'Malley felt oddly certain that Khumalo would have supported Terekhov's actions anyway. The man would never be a brilliant officer, perhaps, but he'd demonstrated an astonishing depth of moral courage of his own, and his undamaged superdreadnought flagship and her consorts had been more than sufficient to transform the tense stalemate in Monica into a complete Monican surrender. Especially when he endorsed Terekhov's threat to destroy the remaining battlecruisers by bombardment.

There might still be a little hell to pay over that, O'Malley reflected. Under the letter of interstellar law,

Terekhov and Khumalo would have been within the legitimate rights of a belligerent had they done precisely what they threatened, but that wasn't the sort of tactic the Royal Manticoran Navy normally embraced. Especially not when the Navy had invaded another sovereign star system without benefit of the minor formality of a declaration of war. Not to mention the fact that destroying the remaining battlecruisers might very well also have destroyed all supporting evidence for Terekhov's interpretation of the Monicans intentions if Tyler had chosen to stonewall.

Yet circumstances sometimes required draconian measures, and O'Malley's own report had fully endorsed Khumalo's and Terekhov's actions. And, unlike some, Vice Admiral O'Malley had no doubt whatsoever that Terekhov, at least, would have done exactly what he'd said he would do.

More importantly, perhaps, Roberto Tyler had believed it. When Dame Amandine finally arrived aboard O'Malley's flagship, over a month after the battle, Tyler had been a broken man, desperate to save what he could from the wreckage. Some of his subordinates, like Admiral Bourmont, had clearly clung to the hope that Frontier Security and the League might yet ride to their rescue. Tyler had cherished no such illusion. Or, at least, no hope that they would do so in time to make any difference to him personally. And so, rather than defy Dame Amandine's demands, he'd capitulated promptly in return for her promise that O'Malley would not complete the destruction of his military forces or forcibly topple his regime.

The bargain had been a simple one. In return for its continued existence, the Republic of Monica had signed a permanent nonaggression pact with the Star Kingdom of Manticore . . . and surrendered to Manticore the two surviving battlecruisers and all documentary evidence of the involvement of Manpower, Technodyne Industries, and the Jessyk Combine in its projected seizure of the Lynx Terminus.

Dame Amandine had proven fiendishly devious, too.

She'd actually arranged for her own diplomatic and intelligence teams to be accompanied every step of the way by representatives of the Sollies' own interstellar news services. The League's reporters had observed every bit of evidence as it was handed over by the Monicans, and they'd been allowed to examine it themselves. O'Malley had seen their reportage, and in his opinion, no unbiased observer could possibly doubt the validity of that evidence. Of course, that probably wouldn't make a great deal of difference to Manpower or Jessyk. They were both headquartered in Mesa, not the League. As such, the League had no responsibility for or jurisdiction over their actions, however reprehensible the League might—officially—consider those actions.

Technodyne, though. Technodyne was another matter entirely. Izrok Levakonic hadn't survived the destruction of the military component of Eroica Station, but his body had been positively identified, and his personal computer files had been recovered from the wreckage. Coupled with the evidence Tyler had provided as the price for continued political survival, Technodyne's guilt could not be denied. In the face of such evidence not even the League's bureaucracies could protect the enormous corporation, and it had already collapsed, the value of its stock plummeting, a third of its board of directors already under indictment, and half of those not indicted—yet—turning state's evidence in an effort to save their own skins.

No doubt Technodyne would survive. It was too big, too important to the League—both to its economy and its military—to be allowed to fail completely. So one day it would reemerge, phoenixlike, from the flames of reorganization, but not quickly or soon. And at least some of those responsible for what had happened here would probably actually spend time in prison, which was more than O'Malley had ever believed might happen.

Dame Amandine had already announced the Star Kingdom's intention of seeking the extradition from Mesa of Aldona Anisimovna and Isabel Bardasano on charges of complicity in murder, terrorism, and illegal weapons trafficking. No one believed for an instant that the extradition request would be granted, but at least Anisimovna and Bardasano would know what was waiting for them if Manticore ever did get its hands on them.

The one thing which had unfortunately avoided Dame Amandine was positive proof of *Frontier Security's* involvement. Anisimovna and Bardasano had gotten off Monica aboard their private ship before Khumalo arrived. With his own ships so badly damaged, Terekhov would have been unable to prevent their escape even if he'd known about it in time, and all indications were that certain Gendarmerie officers had disappeared with them. Tyler and Alfonso Higgins, the head of his intelligence services, both claimed the Gendarmes—and, so, by extension, Frontier Security itself—had provided Anisimovna with significant support. But there was no concrete evidence to support that contention, and so Dame Amandine had opted to make no charges against OFS.

O'Malley didn't like that, but he understood it. Even with absolute, irrefutable proof such charges would have been extremely dangerous. They would have backed Lorcan Verrochio into a corner, and there was no way of knowing how he and his fellow Frontier Security satraps would have responded. Given the powerful Solarian bureaucracies' *de facto* control of League policy, it was entirely possible that accusing OFS of complicity would have resulted in outright hostilities with the Sollies. And so, reluctantly, O'Malley found himself forced to agree with Dame Amandine's decision. It left a sour taste, but sour tastes sometimes had to be swallowed.

And no amount of pulser dart-dodging on Frontier Security's part could detract one iota from what Terekhov and his people had accomplished in Monica.

"Well, Captain," the vice admiral said, holding out his hand, "I'm sure the yard will put her back to rights quickly. We need her—and you—back in service. Godspeed, Captain."

"Thank you, Sir." Terekhov gripped his hand firmly.

Then he stepped back and saluted. Electronic bosun's pipes wailed and the side party came to attention, and Terekhov turned and swung himself across the interface into the zero-gravity of his waiting pinnace's boarding tube. Then he was gone, and Vice Admiral Quentin O'Malley discovered that the boat bay gallery was a smaller, poorer place without that ordinary-looking man.

HMS *Hexapuma* and HMS *Warlock* emerged from the central terminus of the Manticoran Wormhole Junction, exactly one T-year from the day Midshipwoman Helen Zilwicki, Midshipman Aikawa Kagiyama, and Midshipwoman Ragnhild Pavletic had reported aboard her. Now Ensign Zilwicki sat beside Lieutenant Senior Grade Abigail Hearns at Tactical. Naomi Kaplan would live, and return to duty, but her injuries had been so severe that she'd been returned to Manticore for treatment months ago. Abigail was undoubtedly too junior for permanent duty as a *Saganami-C*-class heavy cruiser's tactical officer, but Captain Terekhov had flatly refused to allow anyone to replace her before *Hexapuma*'s return to Manticore.

Helen was glad. And she was glad some other people were still aboard, as well.

She glanced over her shoulder and hid a broad mental smile as her eye met Paulo's. Ansten FitzGerald had been less severely wounded than Kaplan, but although he'd been permitted to return to active duty for *Hexapuma*'s voyage back to Manticore, he was still in obvious pain and more than a little shaky. That wasn't especially amusing to anyone who knew and respected the Exec, but watching Aikawa Kagiyama hovering—unobtrusively, he undoubtedly imagined—in the background while he kept an anxious eye on FitzGerald certainly was.

"Message from *Invictus*, Sir," Amal Nagchaudhuri announced.

"Yes?" Terekhov turned his command chair to face the communications officer. HMS *Invictus* was the flagship of Home Fleet, no doubt in orbit about the planet of Manticore.

"Message begins," Nagchaudhuri began, and something in his tone made Helen look at him sharply.

"'To Captain Aivars Terekhov and the men and women of HMS *Hexapuma* and HMS *Warlock*, from Admiral of the Green Sebastian D'Orville, Commanding Officer, Home Fleet. Well done.' Message ends."

Helen frowned, but before the message had time to sink in, the main tactical display changed abruptly. In one perfectly synchronized moment, forty-two superdreadnoughts, sixteen CLACs, twelve battlecruisers, thirty-six heavy and light cruisers, thirty-two destroyers, and over a thousand LACs, activated their impeller wedges. They appeared on the display like lightning flickering outward from a common center, a stupendous globe thousands of kilometers in diameter, and *Hexapuma* and *Warlock* were at its exact center.

Helen recognized that formation. She'd seen it before. Every man and woman in Navy uniform had seen it, once every year, on Coronation Day, when Home Fleet passed in review before the Queen . . . with its flagship in exactly the position *Hexapuma* and *Warlock* now held.

Even as she stared at the display, another icon appeared upon it. The crowned, golden icon of HMS *Duke of Cromarty*, the ship which had replaced the murdered HMS *Queen Adrienne* as the royal yacht, sitting just beyond the threshold of the Junction. A Junction, Helen sudden realized, which had been cleared of shipping—*all* shipping—except for Home Fleet itself.

The vast globe accelerated towards *Cromarty*, matching its acceleration rate exactly to *Hexapuma*'s, holding formation on the heavy cruiser and her single escort, and the raised wedge of every ship in that huge formation flashed off and then on again in the traditional underway salute to a fleet flagship.

"Additional message, Sir," Nagchaudhuri said. He stopped and cleared his throat, then continued, and despite his throat clearing, his voice seemed to waver about the edges.

"Message begins. 'Yours is the honor.'" He looked up from his display, meeting Aivars Terekhov's eyes.

"Message ends, Sir," he said softly.

Character List for The Shadow of Saganami:

Adolfsson, George—Planetary President of Pontifex.

Agnelli, Joanna—Captain Aivars Terekhov's personal steward.

Alexander, Hamish—Earl White Haven; Admiral, Royal Manticoran Navy (ret.). First Lord of Admiralty, Star Kingdom of Manticore.

Alexander, William—Baron Grantville and Lord Alexander. Prime Minister of Manticore.

Alquezar, Joachim—Senior delegate to the Talbott Constitutional Convention from San Miguel, major stockholder Rembrandt Trade Union, leader of the Constitutional Union Party in the Convention.

Anders, Ito—Captain, Royal Manticoran Navy. CO, HMS *Warlock*.

Anhier, Franz—Engineer, Jessyk Combine freighter *Marianne*.

Anisimovna, Aldona—Board member, Manpower, Inc.

Antrim, George—Platoon Sergeant, Royal Manticoran Marines. Senior NCO, 1st Platoon, Marine Detachment, HMS *Hexapuma*.

Atkinson, Annemarie—Lieutenant Commander, Royal Manticoran Navy. XO, HMS *Audacious*.

Badmachin, Mira—Commander, Royal Manticoran Navy. CO, HMS *Volcano*.

Bagwell, Guthrie—Lieutenant, Royal Manticoran Navy. Electronics Warfare Officer, HMS *Hexapuma*.

Bannister, Trevor—Chief Marshal, CO, Montana Marshals Service.

Bardasano, Isabel—Cadet board member and chief of covert operations, Jessyk Combine.

Basaricek, Brigita—Colonel, CO, Kornatian National Police Force.

Binyan, Duan—CO, Jessyk Combine freighter *Marianne*.

Bjornstad, Alvin—Vice-President, Union of Monica.

Bourmont, Gregoire—Admiral, Monican Navy. Chief of Naval Operations.

Budak, Aranka—Lieutenant, Kornatian National Police.

Burke, Kathleen—Lieutenant, Royal Manticoran Navy. XO, HMS *Aria*.

Caparelli, Sir Thomas—Admiral, Royal Manticoran Navy. First Space Lord, Manticoran Admiralty.

Chandler, Ambrose—Commander, Royal Manticoran Navy. Rear Admiral Augustus Khumalo's staff intelligence officer.

Clary, Jeanette—Senior Chief Petty Officer, Royal Manticoran Navy. Senior helmswoman, HMS *Hexapuma*.

Corvisart, Amandine—Special representative from the Manticoran Foreign Office assigned to negotiate settlement with Republic of Monica.

Crites, David—Platoon Sergeant, Royal Manticoran Marines. Senior NCO, 3rd Platoon, Marine Detachment, HMS *Hexapuma*.

D'Arezzo, Paulo—Midshipman, Royal Manticoran Navy, assigned HMS *Hexapuma*.

Debevic, Judita—Leader, Kornatian Social Moderate Party.

De Chabrol, Annette—XO, Jessyk Combine freighter *Marianne*.

Dekker, Hieronymus—Chief factor, Rembrandt Trade Union, Montana System.

Divkovic, Drazen—Cell leader, Freedom Alliance of Kornati.

Divkovic, Juras—Cell leader, Freedom Alliance of Kornati.

Djerdja, Darinka—Vuk Rajkovic's personal assistant.

Diamond, Osborne—Lieutenant Commander, Royal Manticoran Navy. XO, HMS *Vigilant*.

Dunblane, Arnold—Rembrandt Trade Union employee on Montana.

Duncan, Andrea—Lieutenant, Royal Manticoran Navy. Logistics Officer, HMS *Hexapuma*.

Egervary, Zeno—Security Officer/Tactical Officer, Jessyk Combine freighter *Marianne*.

Eichbauer, Ulrike—Major, Solarian Gendarmerie. Brigadier Yucel's chief intelligence officer.

Einarsson, Magnus—Captain, Nuncio Space Force. CO, NSS *Wolverine*.

FitzGerald, Ansten—Commander, Royal Manticoran Navy. XO, HMS *Hexapuma*.

Gaunt, Richard—Commander, Royal Manticoran Navy. XO, HMS *Hercules*.

Gazi, Andrija—Chairman, Kornatian parliamentary Special Committee on Annexation.

Grabovac, Vesna—Kornatian Secretary of the Treasury.

Grantville, Baron of—see William Alexander, above.

Gray, Oliver—Colonel, Royal Manticoran Marines. CO, Marine battalion assigned to Dame Estelle Matsuko.

Groenhuijen, Arjan—Captain, Rembrandt System Navy.

Gutierrez, Mateo—Lieutenant, Owens Steadholder's Guard. Abigail Hearns' personal armsman.

Harahap, Damien—Captain, Solarian Gendarmerie. Ulrike Eichbauer's assistant and contact point for Talbott Cluster terrorist organizations.

Harrington, Lady Dame Honor Stephanie—Duchess Harrington; Steadholder Harrington; Admiral, Royal Manticoran Navy; Fleet Admiral, Grayson Space Navy; CO Protector's Own; CO Eighth Fleet; CO HMS *Unconquered*.

Hearns, Abigail—Lieutenant, Grayson Space Navy. Assistant Tactical Officer (acting), HMS *Hexapuma*. Daughter of Steadholder Owens.

Hedges, William—Lieutenant, Royal Manticoran Marines. CO, 2nd Platoon, Marine Detachment, HMS *Hexapuma*.

Hegedusic, Isidor—Admiral, Monican Navy. CO Eroica Station and designated CO battlecruiser strike force.

Hennessy, Frank—Lieutenant Commander, Royal Manticoran Navy. CO, HMS *Rondeau*.

Hewlett, Josepha—Commander, Royal Manticoran Navy. CO, HMS *Resolute*.

Hibachi, George—Commander, Royal Manticoran Navy. XO, HMS *Warlock*.

Higgins, Alfonzo—Director, Monican Intelligence.

Hollister, Jeff—Member, Montana Independence Movement.

Hongbo, Junyan—Vice-Commissioner, Office of Frontier Security, Solarian League. Lorcan Verrochio's senior subordinate.

Hope, Eleanor—Commander, Royal Manticoran Navy. CO, HMS *Vigilant*.

Jeffers, Bruce—Lieutenant Commander, Royal Manticoran Navy. CO, HMS *Javelin*.

Jezic, Barto—Captain, Kornatian National Police Force. SWAT specialist.

Johnson, Liam—Sensor Technician 1/c, Royal Manticoran Navy, HMS *Hexapuma*.

Kaczmarczyk, Tadislaw—Captain, Royal Manticoran Marines. CO, Marine Detachment, HMS *Hexapuma*.

Kagiyama, Aikawa—Midshipman, Royal Manticoran Navy, assigned HMS *Hexapuma*.

Kalokainos, Volkhart—Senior vice-president, Kalokainos Shipping. Son of Heinrich Kalokainos, CEO and Board Chairman.

Kanjer, Mavro—Kornatian Secretary of Justice.

Karlberg, Emil—Commodore, Nuncio Space Force. CO, NSF.

Kaplan, Naomi—Lieutenant Commander, Royal Manticoran Navy. Tactical Officer, HMS *Hexapuma*.

Kelso, Angelique—Lieutenant, Royal Manticoran Marines.

CO, 1st Platoon, Marine Detachment, HMS *Hexapuma*.

Khumalo, Augustus—Rear Admiral, Royal Manticoran Navy. CO, Talbott Station.

Kienholtz, Gunda—Lieutenant Commander, Royal Manticoran Navy. Tactical Officer, HMS *Vigilant*.

Kobe, Jefferson—Lieutenant, Royal Manticoran Navy. Assistant Communications Officer, HMS *Hexapuma*.

Krietzmann, Henri—President, Talbott Constitutional Convention.

Krizanic, Cuiejeta—Chairwoman, Kornatian parliamentary Standing Committee on Constitutional Law.

Kubota, Joshua—Lieutenant, Royal Manticoran Navy. XO, HMS *Rondeau*.

Kulinac, Amelia—Lieutenant, Royal Manticoran Navy. XO, HMS *Javelin*.

Lababibi, Samiha—President of the Spindle System and its senior delegate to the Talbott Constitutional Convention.

Langtry, Sir Anthony—Foreign Secretary, Star Kingdom of Manticore.

Lewis, Ginger—Commander, Royal Manticoran Navy. Chief Engineer, HMS *Hexapuma*.

Levakonic, Izrok—Technodyne Industries of Yildun's representative to the Republic of Monica.

Lignos, Herawati—Commander, Royal Manticoran Navy. CO, HMS *Aegis*.

MacIntyre, Freda—Lieutenant (junior grade), Royal Manticoran Navy. Engineering department, HMS *Hexapuma*.

Maguire, Alberta—Platoon Sergeant, Royal Manticoran

Marines. Senior NCO, 2nd Platoon, Marine Detachment, HMS *Hexapuma*.

Majoli, Goran—Kornatian Secretary of Commerce.

Maksimovac, Slavko—Sergeant, Kornatian National Police Force.

Mann, Bill—Lieutenant, Royal Manticoran Marines. CO, 3rd Platoon, Marine Detachment, HMS *Hexapuma*.

Matsuko, Dame Estelle—Baroness Medusa, Provisional Governor of the Talbott Cluster for the Star Kingdom of Manticore.

Mavundia, Benjamin—Lieutenant Commander, Royal Manticoran Navy. CO, HMS *Audacious*.

McCollum, Wendell—Lance Corporal, Royal Manticoran Marines. Squad leader, 3rd Platoon, Marine Detachment, HMS *Hexapuma*.

McDermott, Dame Beatrice—Baroness Alb, Vice Admiral Royal Manticoran Navy, CO Saganami Island Naval Academy.

McDermott, Stephen—Lieutenant Commander, Royal Manticoran Navy. XO, HMS *Resolute*.

McGraw, Hansen—Lieutenant, Royal Manticoran Navy. Communications Department, HMS *Hexapuma*.

Medusa, Baroness—see Dame Estelle Matsuko, above.

Melville, Janet—Lieutenant, Royal Manticoran Navy. XO, HMS *Janissary*.

Mestrovic, Alenka—Kornatian Secretary of Education.

Mrsic, Eldijana—Member Kornatian parliamentary Standing Committee on Constitutional Law.

Nagchaudhuri, Amal—Lieutenant Commander, Royal Manticoran Navy. Communications Officer, HMS *Hexapuma*.

Naysmith, Maitland—Commander, Royal Manticoran Navy. CO, HMS *Janissary*.

Nemesanyi, Istvan—Lieutenant Commander, Royal Manticoran Navy. XO, HMS *Aegis*.

Nimitz—Honor Harrington's treecat companion.

Nordbrandt, Agnes—Leader of the Kornati National Redemption Party; organizer and leader of the Freedom Alliance of Kornati.

Olivetti, Frances—Lieutenant, Royal Manticoran Navy. Assistant Engineer, HMS *Hexapuma*.

O'Malley, Quentin—Vice Admiral, Royal Manticoran Navy.

Orban, Lajos—Surgeon Commander, Royal Manticoran Navy. Ship's doctor, HMS *Hexapuma*.

O'Shaughnessy, Gregor—Baroness Medusa's civilian senior intelligence analyst.

Ottweiler, Valery—Diplomatic representative, Mesa System.

Palacios, Luis—Stephen Westman's ranch foreman and second-in-command, Montana Independence Movement.

Pavletic, Ragnhild—Midshipwoman, Royal Manticoran Navy, assigned HMS *Hexapuma*.

Rajkovic, Vuk—Planetary Vice President of Kornati, leader of Kornatian Reconciliation Party.

Ranjina, Tamara—Senior Reconciliation Party member, Kornatian Special Committee on Annexation.

Rossi, Bianca—Lieutenant, Royal Manticoran Navy. CO, HMS *Aria*.

Saunders, Victoria—Captain, Royal Manticoran Navy. CO HMS *Hercules*. Rear Admiral Augustus Khumalo's flag captain.

Sedgwick, Lewis—Captain, Royal Manticoran Navy. CO, HMS *Ericsson*.

Sheets, Jensen—Lieutenant, Royal Manticoran Navy. Assistant Astrogator, HMS *Hexapuma*.

Shirafkin, Azadeh—Purser, Jessyk Combine freighter *Marianne*.

Shoupe, Loretta—Captain, Royal Manticoran Navy. Chief of staff for Rear Admiral Augustus Khumalo.

Stiles, Jasper—Treasury Secretary, Montana System.

Stottmeister, Leopold—Midshipman, Royal Manticoran Navy, assigned HMS *Hexapuma*.

Suka, Vlacic—General, CO, Kornatian Defense Forces.

Suttles, Warren—System President of Montana.

Terekhov, Aivars Aleksovitch—Captain, Royal Manticoran Navy. CO, HMS *Hexapuma*.

Terekhov, Sinead Patricia O'Daley—wife of Captain Aivars Terekhov.

Tinkhof, Jacomina—System President, Rembrandt System.

Toboc, Adrian—Major, Kornatian Defense Forces.

Tonkovic, Aleksandra—Planetary President of Kornati, Split System. Split System's senior delegate to the Talbott Constitutional Convention. Leader of the Liberal Constitutional Party in the Convention.

Tyler, Roberto—President, Union of Monica.

Urizar, Hermelinda—Sergeant Major, Royal Manticoran Marines. Company sergeant major, HMS *Hexapuma*.

Vaandrager, Ineka—Chairwoman, Rembrandt Trade Union.

Van Der Wildt, Bernadette—Admiral and commander-in-chief, Rembrandt System Navy.

Van Dort, Bernardus—Founder and ex-chairman of the Rembrandt Trade Union.

Verrochio, Lorcan—Commissioner, Office of Frontier Security, Solarian League. OFS administrator for the Madras Sector, which borders on the Talbott Cluster.

Wanderman, Aubrey—Senior Chief Petty Officer, Royal Manticoran Navy. Engineering department, HMS *Hexapuma*.

Westman, Stephen—organizer and leader of the Montana Independence Movement.

Wexler, Alberto—Personal assistant to Planetary President George Adolfsson.

White Haven, Earl of—see Hamish Alexander, above.

Wright, Tobias—Lieutenant Commander, Royal Manticoran Navy. Astrogator, HMS *Hexapuma*.

Yucel, Francisca—Brigadier General, Solarian Gendarmerie. Senior Gendarmerie officer, Madras Sector.

Yvernau, Andrieaux—Chairman, New Tuscany delegation, Talbott Constitutional Convention.

Zilwicki, Helen—Midshipwoman, Royal Manticoran Navy, assigned HMS *Hexapuma*.

Zovan, Tomaz—Kornatian parliamentary deputy.

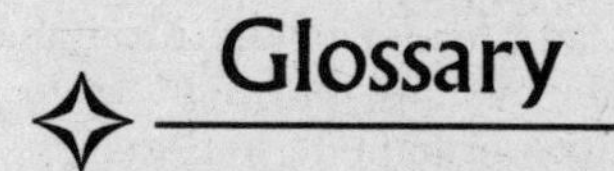

Glossary

Alpha nodes—The impeller nodes of a starship which both generate its normal-space impeller wedge and reconfigure to generate Warshawski sails in hyper-space.

Alpha translation—The translation into or out of the alpha (lowest) bands of hyper-space.

Andermani Empire—Empire founded by mercenary Gustav Anderman. The Empire lies to the "west" of the Star Kingdom, has an excellent navy, and is the Star Kingdom's primary competitor for trade and influence in the Silesian Confederacy.

Andies—Slang term for citizens and (especially) the military personnel and forces of the Andermani Empire.

Apollo—A Manticoran development utilizing forward-deployed FTL communications links to provide real-time fire control for long-range missile fire.

BB—Battleship. At one time, the heaviest capital ship but now considered too small to "lie in the wall." Average tonnage is from 2,000,000 to 4,000,000 tons. Employed by some navies for rear area system security but no longer considered an effective warship type.

BC—Battlecruiser. The lightest unit considered a "capital ship." Designed to destroy anything it can catch and to outrun anything that can destroy it. Average tonnage is from 500,000–1,200,000 tons.

Beta node—Secondary generating nodes of a spacecraft's impeller wedge. They contribute only to the impeller wedge used for normal-space movement. Less powerful and less expensive than alpha nodes.

BLS—Basic Living Stipend. The welfare payment from the PRH government to its permanent underclass. Essentially, the BLS was a straight exchange of government services for a permanent block vote supporting the Legislaturalists who controlled the government.

DD—Destroyer. The smallest hyper-capable warship currently being built by most navies. Average tonnage is from 65,000–80,000 tons.

"Down the throat shot"—An attack launched from directly ahead of an impeller-drive spacecraft in order to fire lengthwise down its impeller wedge. Due to the geometry of the impeller wedge, this is a warship's most vulnerable single aspect.

DN—Dreadnought. A class of warship lying midway between battleships and superdreadnoughts. No major navy is currently building this type. Average tonnage is from 4,000,000 to 6,000,000 tons.

CA—Heavy cruiser (from Cruiser, Armored). Designed for commerce protection and long-endurance system pickets. Designed to stand in for capital ships against moderate level threats. Average tonnage is from 160,000–350,000 tons, although that has begun to creep upward towards traditional battlecruiser tonnage ranges in some navies.

Centrists—A Manticoran political party typified by pragmatism and moderation on most issues but very tightly focused on the Havenite threat and how to defeat it. The party supported by Honor Harrington.

CIC—Combat Information Center. The "nerve center" of a warship, responsible for gathering and organizing sensor data and the tactical situation.

CL—Light cruiser. The primary scouting unit of most navies. Also used for both commerce protection and raiding. Average tonnage is from 90,000–150,000 tons.

CLAC—LAC carrier. A starship of dreadnought or superdreadnought size configured to transport LACs through hyper-space and to service and arm them for combat.

COLAC—Commanding Officer, Light Attack Craft. The commander of the entire group of LACs carried by a CLAC.

Committee of Public Safety—The committee established by Rob S. Pierre after his overthrow of the Legislaturalists to control the PRH. It instituted a reign of terror and systematic purges of surviving Legislaturalists and prosecuted the war against the Star Kingdom.

Confederation Navy—Organized naval forces of the Silesian Confederacy.

Confeds—Slang term for citizens of the Silesian Confederacy and (especially) for members of the Confederation Navy.

Conservative Association—A generally reactionary Manticoran political party whose primary consti-tuency is the extremely conservative aristocracy.

Coup de Vitesse—A primarily offensive, "hard style" martial art preferred by the RMN and RMMC. Main emphasis is on weaponless combat.

Crown Loyalists—A Manticoran political party united around the concept that the Star Kingdom requires a strong monarchy, largely as a counter balance to the power of the conservative element in the aristocracy. Despite this, the Star Kingdom's more progressive aristocracy is heavily represented in the Crown Loyalists.

Dolist—One of a class of Havenite citizens totally dependent on the government-provided Basic Living Stipend. As a group, undereducated and underskilled.

"Donkey," The—The popular name given by Havenite crews to the tractor-equipped platforms developed by Shannon Foraker to increase the number of missile pods the Republic's warships can tow.

Keyhole—A Manticoran-developed deployable platform mounting control links and telemetry channels for offensive and defensive missiles.

ECM—Electronic counter measures.

EW—Electronic warfare.

FIA—Federal Investigative Agency. The national police force of the restored Republic of Haven.

FIS—Federal Intelligence Service. The primary espionage agency of the restored Republic of Haven.

Ghostrider, Project—A Manticoran research project dedicated to the development of the multi-drive missile and associated technology. The original Ghostrider blossomed into a large number of sub-projects which emphasized electronic warfare and decoys as well as offensive missiles.

Gravity waves—A naturally occurring phenomenon in hyperspace consisting of permanent, very powerful regions of focused gravitic stress which remain motionless but for a (relatively) slow side-slipping or drifting. Vessels with Warshawski sails are capable of using such waves to attain very high levels of acceleration; vessels under impeller drive are destroyed upon entering them.

Grav pulse com—A communication device using gravitic pulses to achieve FTL communications over intrasystem ranges.

Grayson—Habitable planet of Yeltsin's Star. Star Kingdom of Manticore's most important single ally.

Hyper limit—The critical distance from a given star at which starships may enter or leave hyper-space. The limit varies with the mass of the star. Very large planets have hyper limits of their own.

Hyper-space—Multiple layers of associated but discrete dimensions which bring points in normal-space into closer congruence, thus permitting effectively faster than light travel between them. Layers are divided into "bands" of closely associated dimensions. The barriers between such bands are the sites of turbulence and instability which become increasingly powerful and dangerous as a vessel moves "higher" in hyper-space.

IAN—Imperial Andermani Navy.

Impeller drive—The standard reactionless normal-space drive of the Honor Harrington universe, employing artificially generated bands (or "wedges") of gravitic energy to provide very high rates of acceleration. It is also used in hyper-space outside gravity waves.

Impeller wedge—The inclined planes of gravitic stress formed above and below a spacecraft by its impeller drive. A military impeller wedge's "floor" and "roof" are impenetrable by any known weapon.

Inertial compensator—A device which creates an "inertial sump," diverting the inertial forces associated with acceleration into a starship's impeller wedge or a naturally occurring gravity wave, thus negating the g-force the ship's crew would otherwise experience. Smaller vessels enjoy a higher compensator efficiency for a given strength of wedge or gravity wave and thus can achieve higher accelerations than larger vessels.

InSec—Internal Security. The secret police and espionage service of the PRH under the Legislaturalists. Charged with security functions and suppression of dissent.

Keyhole II—A successor to the original Keyhole platform which is configured with FTL communications links instead of light-speed telemetry.

LAC—Light Attack Craft. A sublight warship type, incapable of entering hyper, which masses between 40,000 and 60,000 tons. Until recently, considered an obsolete and ineffective warship good for little but customs duty and light patrol work. Advances in technology have changed that view of it.

Laser clusters—Last-ditch, close-range anti-missile point defense systems.

Liberal Party—A Manticoran political party typified by a belief in isolationism and the need for social intervention and the use of the power of the state to "level" economic and political inequities within the Star Kingdom.

Legislaturalists—The hereditary ruling class of the PRH. The descendants of the politicians who created the Dolist System more than two hundred years before the beginning of the current war.

Manties—Slang term for citizens of and (especially) military personnel/forces of the Star Kingdom of Manticore.

Mark 31 Counter-missile—A new, longer-range counter-missile developed by Manticore and deployed by the Alliance to give greater stand off engagement range against MDMs. The Mark 31 also provides the platform and missile drive for the Viper (see below).

MDM—Multi-drive missile. A new Manticoran weapon development which enormously enhances the range of missile combat by providing additional drive endurance.

Mistletoe—Codename assigned by Sonja Hemphill to weapon-equipped "reconnaissance drones" used to creep into attack range of critical system defense infrastructure.

Moriarty—Codename assigned by Shannon Foraker to a specially developed centralized fire control node deployed to coordinate MDMs used in the system defense role.

NavInt—Shortened version of Naval Intelligence. The naval intelligence agency of the Republic of Haven.

New Men—A Manticoran political party headed by Sheridan Wallace. Small and opportunistic.

Office of Naval Intelligence (ONI)—The RMN's naval intelligence service, directed by the Second Space Lord.

Peeps—Slang term for citizens and (especially) military personnel of the Peoples' Republic of Haven.

Penaids—Electronic systems carried by missiles to assist them in penetrating their targets' active and passive defenses.

Pinnace—A general purpose military small craft capable of lifting approximately 100 personnel. Equipped with its own impeller wedge, capable of high acceleration, and normally armed. May be configured for ground support.

Powered Armor—Battle armor combining a vac suit with protection proof against most man-portable projectile weapons, very powerful exoskeletal "muscles," sophisticated on-board sensors, and maneuvering thrusters for use in vacuum.

Progressive Parught—The largest and most powerful hyper-capable warship. Average tonnage is from 6,000,000–8,500,000 tons.

Shuttles—Small craft employed by starships for personnel and cargo movement from ship to ship or ship to surface. Cargo shuttles are configured primarily as freight haulers, with limited personnel capacity. Assault shuttles are heavily armed and armored and typically are capable of lifting at least a full company of ground troops.

Sidewalls—Protective barriers of gravitic stress projected to either side of a warship to protect its flanks from hostile fire. Not as difficult to penetrate as an impeller wedge, but still a very powerful defense.

Silesian Confederacy—A large, chaotic political entity lying between the Star Kingdom of Manticore and the Andermani Empire. Its central government is both weak and extremely corrupt and the region is plagued by pirates. Despite this, the Confederacy is a large and very important foreign market for the Star Kingdom.

Sillies—Slang term for Silesian citizens and/or military personnel.

Solarian League—Largest, wealthiest star nation of the explored galaxy, with decentralized government managed by extremely powerful bureaucracies.

Sollies—Slang term for citizens or military personnel of the Solarian League.

StateSec—Also "SS." Office of State Security. The successor to Internal Security under the Committee of Public Safety. Even more powerful than InSec. Headed by Oscar Saint-Just, originally second-in-command of InSec, who betrayed the Legislaturalists to aid Rob Pierre in overthrowing them.

Star Kingdom of Manticore—A small, wealthy star nation consisting of two star systems: the Manticore System and the Basilisk System.

Treecats—The native sentient species of the planet Sphinx. Six-limbed, telempathic arboreal predators which average between 1.5 and 2 meters in length (including prehensile tail). A small percentage of them bond with "adopted" humans in a near symbiotic relationship. Although incapable of speech, treecats have recently learned to communicate with humans using sign language.

Triple Ripple—A Havenite defensive technique utilizing heavy concentrations of nuclear warheads to blind and disable enemy missile seekers and electronic warfare platforms.

"Up the kilt shot"—An attack launched from directly astern of a starship in order to fire down the length of its impeller wedge. Due to the geometry of the impeller drive, this is a warship's second most vulnerable aspect.

Viper—A Grayson-Manticoran-developed missile with shorter range but higher acceleration rates and better seeker systems and onboard AI to create a "launch and forget" weapon for use in the anti-LAC role. Vipers can also be used as standard counter-missiles.

Warshawski—Name applied to all gravitic detectors in honor of the inventor of the first such device.

Warshawski, Adrienne—The greatest hyper-physicist in human history.

Warshawski sail—The circular gravity "grab fields" devised by Adrienne Warshawski to permit starships to "sail" along gravity waves in hyper-space.

The following is an excerpt from:

AT ALL COSTS

An Honor Harrington Novel

by David Weber

Available in hardcover November 2005
from Baen Books

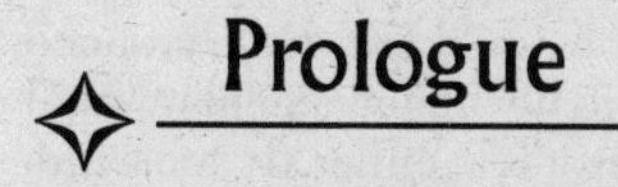

Prologue

The big *Aviary*-class CLACs and their escorting battlecruisers crossed the Alpha wall into normal-space just outside the hyper limit. There were only two of the superdreadnought-sized vessels, but their LAC bays spat out almost six hundred light attack craft, and if the Republic of Haven's *Cimeterre*-class LACs were shorter-legged, more lightly armed, and nowhere near so capable as the Star Kingdom of Manticore's *Shrikes* and *Ferrets*, they were more than adequate for their current assignment.

They accelerated in-system, building vectors towards the industrial infrastructure of the Alizon System, and discovered an unanticipated bit of good fortune. A pair of lumbering freighters, both squawking Manticoran IDs and bumbling along on the same general flight plan, found themselves squarely in the path of the incoming storm and already within extreme missile range. They accelerated desperately, but the LACs had an overtake velocity of over a thousand KPS at the moment they were first detected, and the freighters' maximum acceleration rate was little more than two hundred gravities. The *Cimeterres* were capable of very nearly *seven* hundred, and they were armed . . . which the merchantmen weren't.

"Manticoran freighters, this is Captain Javits of the Republican Navy," a harsh, Haven-accented voice said over the civilian guard frequency. "You are instructed to kill your impellers and abandon ship immediately. Under the terms of applicable interstellar law, I formally inform you that we do not have the capacity to board and search your vessels or to take them as prizes. Therefore, I will open fire upon them and destroy them in twenty standard minutes from . . . now. Get your people off immediately. Javits, clear."

One of the two freighters killed her impellers immediately. The other skipper was more stubborn. He continued to accelerate, as if he thought he might somehow still save his ship, but he wasn't an idiot, either. It took him all of five minutes to realize—or, at least, to *accept*—that he had no chance, and his impellers, too, went abruptly cold.

Shuttles spilled from the two merchant ships, scuttling away from them at their maximum acceleration as if they expected the Havenite LACs to open fire upon them. But the Republic hewed scrupulously to the requirements of interstellar law. Its warships meticulously waited out the time limit Javits had stipulated, then, precisely on the tick, launched a single pair of missiles at each drifting freighter.

The old-fashioned nuclear warheads did the job just fine.

The *Cimeterres* sped onward, ignoring the dissipating balls of plasma which had once been somewhere in the vicinity of fourteen million tons of merchant shipping. Their destruction, after all, was a mere sideshow. Ahead of the Havenite units, a half-dozen destroyers and a division of RMN *Star Knight*-class CAs accelerated to meet them. The range was still too long for the *Cimeterres* to actually see the defenders, but the remote reconnaissance platforms spreading out ahead of the LACs were another matter, and Captain Bertram Javits grimaced as he took note of the drones' relayed report of the defenders' acceleration rates.

"They're not killing themselves to come out and meet us, are they, Skip?" Lieutenant Constanza Sheffield, his executive officer observed.

"No, they aren't," Javits said, and gestured at the cramped, utilitarian LAC's bare-bones plot. "Which probably means Intelligence is right about what they've got covering the inner system," he told her.

"In that case, this is gonna hurt," she said.

"Yes, it is. If not quite as much as they *hope* it will," Javits agreed. Then he punched a new combination into his com panel. "All Wolverines, this is Wolverine One. From their acceleration rate, it looks like they've got to be towing pods. And from the fact that there's so few of them, I have to assume Intelligence is right about their defensive stance. So instead of walking obligingly into the inner system, we're shifting to Sierra Three. We'll change course at Point Victor-Able on my command in another forty-five minutes. Review your Sierra Three targeting queues and stand by for a defensive missile engagement. Wolverine One, clear."

The range continued to fall, and the recon platforms began to report widespread active sensor emissions. Some were probably search systems, but the primary search platforms for any star system were passive, not active. So the odds were high that most of those active emitters were tied into fire control systems of one sort or another.

Javits watched his own platforms' telemetry as it streamed across his plot's sidebars. The far more capable computer support aboard the CLACs and battlecruisers which had launched the platforms could undoubtedly do more with the data they were acquiring, and he knew how the tech teams back at Bolthole would salivate when they got a look at it. All that was rather secondary to his own calculations, however, since those calculations were mostly concerned with how to keep as many as possible of his people alive through the next few hours.

"Looks like we've got four main nets of platforms on this side of the primary, Skipper," his XO said finally. "Two of them spread to cover the ecliptic, and one high and one low. Gives them pretty fair coverage of the entire sphere of the limit, but they're obviously concentrating on the ecliptic."

"The question, of course, Constanza," he replied dryly, "is how many pods each of those 'clusters' of yours represent."

"Well, that and how many pods they want us to *think* they have, Sir," Lieutenant Joseph Cook, Javits' tactical officer pointed out.

"That, too," Javits conceded. "Under the circumstances, though, I'm prepared to be fairly pessimistic on that particular point, Joe. And they've clearly gone ahead and deployed the sensor platforms to *control* the pods. Those're probably at least as expensive as the pods themselves would be, so I'd say there's a good chance they wouldn't have deployed them if they hadn't also deployed the pods for them to control."

"Yes, Sir."

Lieutenant Cook's expression and manner couldn't have been more respectful, but Javits knew what he was thinking. Given the totality of the surprise Operation Thunderbolt had achieved, and the equally total incompetence of the previous Manticoran government, it was entirely possible—even likely—that Alizon's defenses had not been significantly upgraded in the immediate run up to the resumption of hostilities. In which case the defenders might, indeed, be attempting to bluff Javits into believing they had more to work with than they really did. On the other hand, there'd been time since Thunderbolt for the Manties to ship a couple of freighter loads of their multi-drive missile pods out here. And however incompetent Prime Minister High Ridge might have been, the new Alexander Government knew its ass from a hole in the ground. If those additional missiles hadn't been shipped out and deployed, the recon platforms would have been reporting a far heavier system picket than they were actually seeing.

"We're coming up on course change, Skipper," Sheffield told him several minutes later, and he nodded.

"Range to the nearest active sensor platforms?" he asked.

"Closest approach, twelve seconds after we alter course, will be about sixty-four million kilometers," she replied.

"A million inside their maximum effective range from rest," Javits observed, and grimaced. "I wish there was another way to find out if Intelligence knows what it's talking about."

"You and me both, Skip," Sheffield agreed, but she also shrugged. "At least we're the ones calling the tune for the dance this time."

Javits nodded and watched the icon representing his massive flight of LACs sweeping closer and closer to the blinking green crosshair which represented Point Victor-Able. By this time, the *Cimeterres* had traveled almost thirty-three million kilometers and were up to a velocity of over twenty thousand kilometers per second. The Manty picket ships were still accelerating to meet them, but it was obvious that they had no intention of entering standard missile range of that many LACs. Well, Javits wouldn't have either, if he'd been towing pods stuffed full of multi-drive missiles with a standoff range of over three light-minutes. However good Manticoran combat systems might have been, six hundred-plus LACs would have swarmed over that handful of ships like hungry pseudo-piranha if they could get into range of their own weapons. If there'd been heavy defending units in-system, things might have been different, but in that case, Javits would never have come close enough for them to get a shot at him in the first place.

"Victor-Able, Sir," his astrogator reported suddenly.

"Very well. Order the course change, Constanza."

"Aye, Sir," Sheffield said in far more formal tones, and he heard the order go out.

The green beads representing friendly units on his display shifted course abruptly, arcing back out and away from the inner system on a course which would take them right through one of the more heavily developed and mined portions of the Alizon System's asteroid belt. For several seconds, nothing else changed on the display.

And then, like a cascading eruption of scarlet curses, dozens—scores—of previously deployed MDM pods began to fire all along the outer edge of the inner system.

The range was incredibly long, even for Manticoran fire control, and one thing Thunderbolt had taught the Republican Navy was that as good as Manty technology was, it wasn't perfect. Hits at such extreme range, even against all-up, hyper-capable starships would have been hard come by. Against such small, elusive targets as LACs, they would be even harder to achieve.

But of course, Javits thought, *hyper-capable units could take a lot more damage than we can. Anybody they* do *hit, is going to get reamed.*

The missiles streaked outward at well over forty thousand gravities. Even at that stupendous rate of acceleration, it would take them the next best thing to nine minutes to reach his ships, and his missile defense crews began to track the incoming threat. It was hard—Manty ECM had always been hellishly good, and it had gotten even better since the last war—but Admiral Foraker's teams at Bolthole had compensated for that as much as they could. The *Cimeterres'* point defense and EW weren't in the same league as Manty LACs' systems, but they were much better than any previous Havenite LAC had ever possessed, and the extreme range worked in their favor.

At least three-quarters of the total Manticoran launch simply lost lock and wandered off course. The recon platforms reported the sudden spiteful flashes as the lost missiles detonated early, before they could become a threat to navigation here in the system. But the rest of the pursuing missiles continued to charge after his units.

"Approximately nine hundred still inbound," Lieutenant Cook announced in a voice which struck Javits as entirely too calm. "Allocating outer zone counter-missiles."

He paused for perhaps a pair of heart beats, then said one more word.

"Engaging."

The command *Cimeterre* quivered as the first counter-missiles blasted away from her. They were woefully outclassed by the missiles racing to kill her, but there were almost two thirds as many LACs as there were attack missiles, and each LAC was firing dozens of counter-missiles.

Not all of them simultaneously. Admiral Foraker's staff, and especially Captain Clapp, her resident LAC tactical genius, had worked long and hard to develop improved missile defense doctrine for the *Cimeterres*, especially because of their small size and the technological imbalance between their capabilities and those of their opponents. They'd come up with a variant on the "layered defense" Admiral Foraker had devised for the wall of battle, a doctrine which relied less on sophistication than on sheer numbers and recognized that counter-missiles were far less expensive than LACs full of trained Navy personnel.

Now Javits watched the first waves of counter-missiles sweeping towards the incoming Manticoran fire. EW platforms seeded throughout the MDMs came on-line, using huge bursts of jamming in efforts to blind the counter-missiles' seekers. Other platforms produced entire shoals of false images, saturating the LACs' tracking systems with threats. But that had been accepted when the missile defense doctrine was evolved, and in some ways, the very inferiority of Havenite technology worked for Javits at this moment. His counter-missiles' onboard seekers were almost too simpleminded to be properly confused. They could "see" only the very strongest of targeting sources at the best of times, and they had been launched in such huge numbers that they could afford to waste much of their effort killing harmless decoys.

A second, almost equally heavy wave of counter-missiles followed the first one. Again, a Manticoran fleet wouldn't have fired the salvos that closely together. They would have waited, lest the second wave's impeller wedges interrupt their telemetry control links to the first wave's CMs. But Javits' crews knew that at this range, the relatively less capable onboard fire control systems of their LACs had nowhere near the reach and sensitivity of their Manticoran counterparts, anyway. Which didn't even consider the effectiveness of the Manty missiles' penetration aids and EW. Since they could barely see the damned things in the first place, they were giving up far less in terms of enhanced accuracy than a Manticoran formation would have sacrificed, and the larger number of counter-missiles they were putting into space more than compensated for any target discrimination they lost.

The *Cimeterres'* own EW did what it could, as well. The first-wave counter-missiles took out over three hundred of the Manticoran missiles. The second wave killed another two hundred. Perhaps another hundred fell prey to the LACs' electronic warfare systems, lost lock, and went wandering harmlessly astray. Another fifty or sixty lost lock initially, but managed to reacquire their targets or to find new ones, yet their need to quest for fresh victims delayed them, kicked them slightly behind the rest of the stream to make them easier point defense targets.

The third and final wave of counter-missiles killed over a hundred more of the incoming missiles, but over two hundred, in what were now effectively two slightly staggered salvos, burst through the inner counter-missile zone and charged down upon Javits' LACs.

The agile little craft opened fire with every point defense laser cluster that would bear. Dozens of lasers stabbed at each incoming laser head, and as the attack missiles rolled in on their final approaches, the targeted *Cimeterres* rotated sharply, presenting only the bellies and roofs of their impenetrable impeller wedges to them. The targeted LACs' consorts continued to slam bolts of coherent light into the teeth of the Manticoran missiles. Over half of those missiles disappeared, torn apart by the defensive fire, but many of the others swerved at the last moment, either because they'd been executing deceptive attack runs to mask their true targets or else because they'd lost their initial targets and had to acquire new ones. Most of those got through; only a handful of the others did.

Vacuum blazed as the powerful Manticoran laser heads detonated in vicious, fusion-fueled chain-lightning, and immensely powerful x-ray lasers stabbed out of the explosions. Many of those lasers wasted their fury on the interposed wedges of their targets, but others ripped through the LACs' sidewalls as if they had not existed. These were capital missiles of the Royal Manticoran Navy, designed to blast through the almost inconceivably tough sidewalls and armor of ships of the wall. What one of them did to a tiny, completely unarmored light attack craft was cataclysmic.

More explosions speckled space as *Cimeterres'* fusion bottles failed. Almost three dozen of Javits' LACs were destroyed outright. Another four survived long enough for their remaining crewpeople to abandon ship.

"Wolverine Red Three, Wolverine One," he said harshly into his microphone. "You've got lifeguard. Pick up everyone you can. One, clear."

"Aye, Wolverine One. Red Three copies. Decelerating now."

Javits watched the designated squadron decelerate slightly—just enough to match vectors with the skinsuited crewmen who could no longer accelerate—and his eyes were hard. Under other circumstances, delaying to pick those people up would have represented an unacceptable risk. But at this range, and with the range already opening to the very edge of even Manticoran missiles' reach, it was a chance well worth taking.

And not just because of the "asset" those people represent, he thought. *We left too many people too many places under the People's Republic. Not again—not on* my *watch. Not if there's any option at all.*

He watched the plot's sidebars silently update themselves, listing his losses. They hurt. Thirty-eight ships represented over six percent of his total strength, and he'd known most of the four hundred people who'd been aboard them personally. But in the unforgiving calculus of war, that loss rate was not merely acceptable, it was low. Especially for LAC operations.

And we're outside their reach, now. We've confirmed what they're deploying for system defense, but they're not going to waste more missiles on us. Not at this range . . . and not when they can't be certain what else *may be waiting to pounce if they fire off all their birds.*

"Sir," Lieutenant Cook said. "We're beginning to pick up active emissions ahead of us." Javits looked across at him, and the lieutenant looked up from his own display to meet his CO's eyes. "The computers assess them as primarily point defense radar and lidar, Sir. There don't seem to be very many of them."

"Good," Javits grunted. "All Wolverines, Wolverine One. Stand by to launch on Sierra targets on my command."

He switched channels again, back to the civilian guard frequency.

"Alizon System Central, this is Captain Javits. I will be bringing your Tregarth Alpha facilities into my extreme missile range in twenty-seven minutes from . . . now. My vector will make it impossible for me to match velocity with the facilities or send across boarding parties, and I hereby inform you that I will open fire on them, and on any extraction vessels within my missile envelope, in twenty-nine minutes."

He looked down at his plot once more with a hard, fierce grin. Then keyed his mike once more.

"I advise you to begin evacuation procedures now," he said. "Javits, clear."

"So what's the best estimate of the results, Admiral?" President Eloise Pritchart asked.

The beautiful, platinum-haired President had come across to the Octagon, the Republic of Haven's military nerve center, for this meeting, and aside from one bodyguard, she was the single civilian in the enormous conference room. All eyes were on the huge holo display above the conference table, where the reproduced imagery from Bertrand Javits' tactical plot hovered in midair.

"Our best estimate from the recon platforms' data is that Captain Javits' raid destroyed about eight percent—

probably a little less—of Alizon's total resource extraction capability, Madam President," Rear Admiral Victor Lewis, Director of Operational Research replied. Thanks to venerable traditions of uncertain origin, Naval Intelligence reported to Op Research, which, in turn, reported to Vice Admiral Linda Trenis' Bureau of Planning.

"And was that an acceptable return in light of our own losses?" the President asked.

"Yes," another voice said, and the President looked at the stocky, brown-haired admiral at the head of the table who'd spoken. Admiral Thomas Theisman, Secretary of War and Chief of Naval Operations, looked back at her steadily. "We lost about a third of the people we'd have lost aboard a single old-style cruiser, Madam President," he continued, speaking very formally in the presence of their subordinates. "In return, we confirmed NavInt's estimate of the system-defense doctrine the Manties appear to be adopting and acquired additional information on their fire control systems and current pod deployment patterns; destroyed eight million tons of hyper-capable merchant shipping, better than five times the combined tonnage of all the LACs Javits lost; and put a small but significant dent into the productivity of Alizon. More to the point, we hit one of the Manticoran Alliance's member's home system for what everyone will recognize as negligible losses, and this isn't the first time Alizon's been hit. That has to have an effect on the entire Alliance's morale, and it's almost certain to increase the pressure on the White Haven Admiralty to detach additional picket forces to cover the Star Kingdom's allies against similar attacks."

"I see." The spectacularly beautiful, platinum-haired President's topaz-colored eyes didn't look especially happy, but they didn't flinch away from Theisman's logic, either. She looked at him for a moment longer, then returned her attention to Rear Admiral Lewis.

"Please pardon the interruption, Admiral," she said. "Continue, if you would."

"Of course, Madam President." The rear admiral cleared his throat and punched a new command sequence into his terminal. The holo display shifted, and Javits' plot disappeared, replaced by a series of bar graphs.

"If you'll look at the first red column, Madam President," he began, "you'll see our losses to date in ships of the wall. The green column beside it represents SD(P)s currently undergoing trials or completing construction. The amber column—"

"Well, that was all extremely interesting, Tom," Eloise Pritchart said some hours later. "Unfortunately, I think we're into information overkill. In some ways, I think I know less about what's going on now than I did before I came over here!"

She made a face, and Theisman chuckled. He sat behind his desk, tipped back comfortably in his chair, and the Republic's President sat on the comfortable couch facing the desk. Her personal security detail was camped outside the door, giving her at least the illusion of privacy, her shoes lay on the carpet in front of her, and she had both bare feet tucked up under her while she nursed a steaming cup of coffee in slender hands. Theisman's own cup sat on his desk's blotter.

"You spent long enough as Javier's people's commissioner to have a better grasp of military realities than that, Eloise," he told her now.

"In a general sense, certainly." She shrugged. "On the other hand, I was never actually trained for the realities of the Navy, and there've been so many changes in such a short time that what I did know feels hopelessly out of date. I suppose what matters is that *you're* current. And confident."

Her tone was ever so slightly questioning on the last two words, and it was his turn to shrug.

"'Confident' is a slippery word. You know I was never happy about going back to war against the Manties." He raised one hand in a placating gesture. "I understand your logic, and I can't disagree with it. Besides, you're the President. But I have to admit that I never liked the idea. And that Thunderbolt's success has exceeded my own expectations. So far, at least."

"Even after what happened—or didn't happen—at Trevor's Star?"

"Javier made the right decision on the basis of everything we knew," Theisman said firmly. "None of us fully appreciated just how tough Shannon's 'layered defense' was going to be against long-range Manticoran missile fire. If we'd been able to project probable losses during the approach phase as accurately then as we could now, then, yes, he should have gone ahead and pressed the attack. But he didn't know that at the time any more than the rest of us did."

"I see." Pritchart sipped coffee, and Theisman watched her with a carefully hidden smile. That was about as close as the President was ever going to allow herself to come to "pulling strings" on Javier Giscard's behalf, lover or no lover.

"And Lewis' projections?" she continued after a moment. "Do you feel confident about them, too?"

"As far as the numbers from our own side go, absolutely," he said. "Manpower's going to be a problem for about the next seven months. After that, the training programs Linda and Shannon have in place should be producing most of the personnel we need. And a few months after that, we'll begin steadily mothballing the old-style wallers to crew the new construction as it comes out of the yards. We're still going to be stretched to come up with the officers we need—especially flag officers with experience—but we were able to build up a solid base between the Saint-Just cease-fire and Thunderbolt. I think we'll be all right on that side, too.

"As far as the industrial side goes, I realize the economic strain of our present building plans is going to be heavy. Rachel Hanriot's made that clear enough on behalf of Treasury, but I didn't need her to tell me, and I deeply regret having to impose it. Especially given the high price we've all paid to start turning the economy around. But we don't have a lot of choice, unless we end up successfully negotiating a peace settlement."

He raised his eyebrows questioningly, and she gave her head a quick, irritable shake.

"I don't know where we are on that," she admitted, manifestly unhappily. "I'd have thought even Elizabeth Winton would be willing to sit down and talk after you, Javier, and the rest of the Navy finished kicking *her* navy's ass so thoroughly! So far, though, nothing. I'm becoming more and more convinced that Arnold's been right about the Manties' new taste for imperialism from the very beginning . . . damn him."

Theisman started to say something, then stopped. This wasn't the time to suggest that the Queen of Manticore might have very good reasons to not see things exactly as Eloise Pritchart did. Or to reiterate his own deep distrust and suspicion of anything emerging from the mouth of Secretary of State Arnold Giancola.

"Well," he said instead, "in the absence of a negotiated settlement, we don't really have any choice but to press for an outright military victory."

"And you genuinely believe we can achieve that?"

Theisman snorted in harsh amusement at her tone.

"I wish you wouldn't sound quite so . . . dubious," he said. "You're the commander-in-chief, after all. Does terrible things for the uniformed personnel's morale when you sound like you can't quite believe we can win."

"After what they did to us in the last war, and especially Buttercup, it's hard not to feel a little doubtful, Tom," she said a bit apologetically.

"I suppose it is," he conceded. "But in this case, yes, I do believe we can defeat the Star Kingdom and its allies if we have to. I really need to take you out to Bolthole to actually see what we're doing there, and discuss everything Shannon Foraker is up to. The short version, though, is that we hurt the Manties badly in Thunderbolt. Not just in the ships we destroyed, but in the unfinished construction Admiral Griffith took out at Grendelsbane. We gutted their entire second-generation podnought building program, Eloise. They're basically having to lay down new vessels from scratch, and while their building rates are still faster than ours are, even at Bolthole, they aren't fast enough to offset the jump we've gotten in ships already under construction and nearing completion. Our technology still isn't as good as theirs is, but the tech information Erewhon handed over, and the sensor data we recorded during Thunderbolt—plus the captured hardware we've been able to take apart and examine—is helping a lot in that regard, as well."

"Erewhon." Pritchart shook her head with a sigh, her expression unhappy. "I really regret the position we put Erewhon in with Thunderbolt."

"Frankly, I don't think the Erewhonese are exactly ecstatic over it, themselves," Theisman said dryly. "And I know they didn't anticipate that they were going to hand over their tech manuals on Alliance hardware just in time for us to go back to war. On the other hand, they know why we did it," *why* you *did it, actually*, *Eloise*, he carefully did not say aloud, "and they wouldn't have broken with Manticore in the first place if they hadn't had some pretty serious reservations of their own about the Manties' new foreign policy. And since the shooting started, we've been scrupulous about respecting the limitations built into the terms of our treaty relationship."

Pritchart nodded. The Republic's treaty with the Republic of Erewhon was one of mutual defense, and her administration had very carefully informed Erewhon—and the Manticorans—that since Haven had elected to resume open hostilities without being physically attacked by Manticore, she had no intention of attempting to invoke the military terms of the treaty.

"In any case," Theisman continued, "they at least gave us a look inside the Manties' military hardware. What they had was dated, and I could wish it were more current, but it's been extraordinarily useful to Shannon, anyway.

"The upshot is that Shannon's already working out new doctrine and some new pieces of hardware, especially in the LAC programs and out system-defense control systems, based on the combination of our information from Erewhon, examination of captured and wrecked Manticoran hardware, and analysis of operations to date. At the beginning of Thunderbolt, we'd estimated that one of our pod superdreadnoughts probably had about forty percent as much combat power as a Manticoran or Grayson SD(P). That estimate looks like it was fairly accurate at the time, but I believe we're steadily moving the ratio in our favor."

"But the Manties have as much operational data as we do, don't they? Aren't they going to be improving their capabilities right along with ours?"

"Yes and no. Actually, except for what happened to Lester at Marsh, they didn't retain possession of a single star system where we engaged them, and none of Lester's modern hyper-capable types were taken intact. We, on the other hand, effectively destroyed virtually every one of their pickets we hit, so those pickets didn't have much opportunity to pass on any observations they might have made.

"In addition, we captured examples of a lot of their hardware. Their security protocols worked damned effectively on most of their classified mollycircs, and quite a bit of what we did get we can't really use yet. Shannon says it's a case of basic differences in the capabilities of our infrastructure. For all intents and purposes, we've got to build the tools, to build the tools, to build the tools we need to reproduce a lot of Manticore's cutting edge technology. But we've still picked up a lot, and, frankly, our starting point was so far behind theirs that our *relative* capabilities are climbing more rapidly than theirs are.

"As I say, we'd estimated pre-Thunderbolt that each of their modern wallers was about two and a half times as combat-effective as one of ours. On the basis of changes we've already made in doctrine and tactics, and allowing for how much more capable our missile defenses turned out to be, we've upped that estimate to set one of their SD(P)s as equal to about two of our podnoughts. On the basis of the current rate of change in our basic capabilities, within another eight months or a year, the ratio should drop from its original two-point-five-to-one to about one-and-a-half-to-one, or even one-point-three-to-one. Given the difference in the numbers of ships of the wall we can anticipate commissioning over the next T-year and a half or so, and especially bearing in mind how much more strategic depth we have, that equates to a solid military superiority on our part."

"But the Legislaturalists had a solid military superiority when they started this entire cycle of war," Pritchart pointed out. "And, like the one you're talking about, it depended on 'strategic depth' and offsetting the Manties' tech edge with numbers."

"Granted." Theisman acknowledged. "And I'll also grant you that the Manties aren't going to be letting any grass grow under them. They know as well as we do that their big equalizer has always been their superior technology, so they're going to be doing whatever they can do increase their tech edge. And as someone who had far more experience than I ever wanted working with the bits and pieces of assistance we were able to get from the Solarian League back in the bad old days under Pierre and Saint-Just, I sometimes suspect that even the Manties don't realize just how good their hardware really is. It's certainly better than anything the Sollies actually have deployed. Or *had* deployed as of two or three T-years ago, at least. And if NavInt's right, they haven't done a thing to change that situation since.

"But the bottom line, Eloise, is that they simply can't match or overcome our building edge over the next two T-years or so. Even then, the sheer numbers of hulls we can lay down and man—assuming the economy holds—should be great enough to allow us to more than maintain parity in newly commissioned units. But for those two years, at a bare minimum, they simply won't have the platforms to mount whatever new weapons or defenses they introduce. And one thing both we and the Manties learned the last time around is that strategic hesitation is deadly."

"What do you mean?"

"Eloise, no one else in the history of the galaxy has ever fought a war on the scale on which we and the Manties are operating. The Solarian League never had to; it was simply so big no one *could* fight it, and everyone knew it. But we and the Manties have hammered away at each other with naviess with literally hundreds of ships of the wall for most of the last twenty T-years now. And the one thing the Manties made perfectly clear in the last war is that wars like this *can* be fought to a successful *military* conclusion. They couldn't do it until they managed to assemble their Eighth Fleet for 'Operation Buttercup,' but once they did, they drove us to the brink of military collapse in just a few months. So, if they won't negotiate, and if we have a time window of, say, two T-years in which *we* enjoy a potentially decisive advantage, then this is no time to be dancing around the edges."

He looked her straight in the eye, and his voice was deep and hard.

"If we can't achieve our war objectives and an acceptable peace before our advantage in combat power erodes out from under us, then it's time for us to use that advantage while we still have it and *force* them to admit defeat. Even if that requires us to dictate peace terms in Mount Royal Palace on Manticore itself."

Chapter One

The nursery was extraordinarily full.

Two of the three older girls—Rachel and Jeanette—were downstairs, hovering on the brink of adulthood, and Theresa was at boarding school on Manticore, but the remaining five Mayhew children, their nannies, and their personal armsmen made a respectable mob. Then there was Faith Katherine Honor Stephanie Miranda Harrington, Miss Harrington, heir to Harrington Steading, and her younger twin brother, James Andrew Benjamin, and *their* personal armsmen. And lest that not be enough bodies to crowd even a nursery this large, there was her own modest person—Admiral Lady Dame Honor Harrington, Steadholder and Duchess Harrington, and *her* personal armsman. Not to mention one obviously amused treecat.

Given the presence of seven children, the oldest barely twelve, four nannies, nine armsmen (Honor herself had gotten off with only Andrew LaFollet, but Faith was accompanied by two of her three personal armsmen), and one Steadholder, the decibel level was actually remarkably low, she reflected. Of course, all things were relative.

"Now, that is *enough!*" Gena Smith, the senior member of Protector Palace's child-care staff, said firmly in the no-nonsense voice which had thwarted—more or less—the determination of the elder Mayhew daughters to grow up as cheerful barbarians. "What is Lady Harrington going to think of you?"

"It's too late to try to fool her about that now, Gigi," Honor Mayhew, one of Honor's godchildren, said cheerfully. "She's known all of us since we were born!"

"But you can at least pretend you've been exposed to the rudiments of proper behavior," Gena said firmly, although the glare she bestowed upon her unrepentant charge was somewhat undermined by the twinkle which went with it. At twelve, the girl had her own bedroom, but she'd offered to spend the night with the littles under the circumstances, which was typical of her.

"Oh, she knows that," the younger Honor said soothingly now. "I'm sure she knows we're not *your* fault."

"Which is probably the best I can hope for," Gena sighed.

"I'm not exactly unaware of the . . . challenge you face with this lot," Honor assured her. "These two, particularly," she added, giving her much younger twin siblings a very old-fashioned look. They only grinned back at her, at least as unrepentant as young Honor. "On the other hand," she continued, "I think between us we have them outnumbered. And they actually seem a bit less rowdy tonight."

"Well, of course—" Gena began, then stopped and shook her head. A flash of irritation showed briefly in the backs of her gray-blue eyes. "What I meant, My Lady, is that they're usually on their better behavior—they don't actually have a *best* behavior, you understand—when you're here."

Honor nodded in response to both the interrupted comment, and the one Gena had actually made. Her eyes met the younger woman's—at forty-eight T-years, Gena Smith was well into middle age for a pre-prolong Grayson woman, but that still made her over twelve T-years younger than Honor—for just a moment, and then the two of them returned their attention to the pajama-clad children.

Despite Gena's and Honor's comments, the three assistant nannies had sorted out their charges with the efficiency of long practice. Faith and James were out from under the eye of their own regular nanny, but they were remarkably obedient to the Palace's substitutes. No doubt because they were only too well aware that their armsmen would be reporting back to "Aunt Miranda," Honor thought dryly. Teeth had already been brushed, faces had already been washed, and all seven of them had been tucked into their beds while she and Gena were talking. Somehow they made it all seem much easier than Honor's own childhood memories of the handful *she'd* been.

"All right," she said to the room at large. "Who votes for what?"

"The Phoenix!" six-year-old Faith said immediately. "The Phoenix!"

"Yeah! I mean, yes, please!" seven-year-old Alexandra Mayhew seconded.

"But you've already heard that one," Honor pointed out. "Some of you," she glanced at her namesake, "more often than others."

The twelve-year-old Honor smiled. She really was an extraordinarily beautiful child, and for that matter, it probably wasn't fair to be thinking of her as a "child" these days, really, Honor reminded herself.

"I don't mind, Aunt Honor," she said. "You know you got me stuck on it early. Besides, Lawrence and Arabella haven't heard it yet."

She nodded at her two youngest siblings. At four and three, respectively, their graduation to the "big kids" section of the nursery was still relatively recent.

"I'd like to hear it again, too, Aunt Honor. Please," Bernard Raoul said quietly. He was a serious little boy, not surprisingly, perhaps, since he was also Heir Apparent to the Protectorship of the entire planet of Grayson, but his smile, when it appeared, could have lit up an auditorium. Now she saw just a flash of it as she looked down at him.

"Well, the vote seems fairly solid," she said after a moment. "Mistress Smith?"

"I suppose they've behaved themselves *fairly* well, all things considered. *This* time, at least," Gena said as she bestowed an ominous glower upon her charges, most of whom giggled.

"In that case," Honor said, and crossed to the old-fashioned bookcase between the two window seats on the nursery's eastern wall. Nimitz shifted his weight for balance on her shoulder as she leaned forward slightly, running a fingertip across the spines of the archaic books to the one she wanted, and took it from the shelf. That book was at least twice her own age, a gift from her to the Mayhew children, as the copy of it on her own shelf at home had been a gift from her Uncle Jacques when *she* was a child. Of course, the story itself was far older even than that. She had two electronic copies of it as well—including one with the original Raysor illustrations—but there was something especially *right* about having it in printed form, and somehow it just kept turning up periodically in the small, specialty press houses that catered to people like her uncle and his SCA friends.

She crossed to the reclining armchair, as old-fashioned and anachronistic as the printed book in her hands itself, and Nimitz leapt lightly from her shoulder to the top of the padded chair back. He sank his claws into the upholstery, arranging himself comfortably, as Honor settled into the chair which had sat in the Mayhew nursery—reupholstered and even rebuilt at need—for almost seven hundred T-years.

The attentive eyes of the children watched her while she adjusted the chair to exactly the right angle, and she and the 'cat savored the bright, clean emotions washing out from them. No wonder treecats had always loved children, she thought. There was something so . . . marvelously whole about them. When they welcomed, they welcomed with all their hearts, and they loved as they trusted, without stint or limit. That was always a gift to be treasured.

Especially now.

She looked up as the veritable horde of armsmen withdrew. Colonel LaFollet, as the senior armsman present, watched with a faint twinkle of his own as the heavily armed, lethally trained bodyguards more or less tiptoed out of the nursery. He watched the nannies follow them, then held the door courteously for Gena and bowed her through it before he came briefly to attention, nodded to Honor, and stepped through it himself. She knew he would be standing outside it when she left, however long she stayed. It was his job, even here, at the very heart of Protector's Palace, where it seemed unlikely any desperate assassins lurked.

The door closed behind him, and she looked around at her audience in the big, suddenly much calmer and quieter room.

"Lawrence, Arabella," she said to the youngest Mayhews, "you haven't heard this book before, but I think you're old enough to enjoy it. It's a very special book. It was written long, long ago, before anyone had ever left Old Earth itself."

Lawrence's eyes widened just a bit. He was a precocious child, and he loved tales about the history of humankind's ancient homeworld.

"It's called *David and the Phoenix*," she went on, "and it's always been one of my very favorite stories. And my mother loved it when she was a little girl, too. You'll have to listen carefully. It's in Standard English, but some of the words have changed since it was written. If you hear one you don't understand, stop and ask me what it means. All right?"

Both toddlers nodded solemnly, and she nodded back. Then she opened the cover.

The smell of ancient ink and paper, so utterly out of place in the modern world, rose from the pages like some secret incense. She inhaled, drawing it deeply into her nostrils, remembering and treasuring memories of rainy Sphinx afternoons, cold Sphinx evenings, and the sense of utter security and peacefulness that was the monopoly of childhood.

"*David and the Phoenix*, by Edward Ormondroyd," she read. "Chapter One, In Which David Goes Mountain Climbing and a Mysterious Voice Is Overheard."

She glanced up, and her chocolate-dark, almond-shaped eyes smiled as the children settled more comfortably into their beds, watching her raptly.

"All the way there David had saved this moment for himself," she began, "struggling not to peek until the proper time came. When the car finally stopped, the rest of them got out stiffly and went into the new house. But David walked slowly into the back yard with his eyes fixed on the ground. For a whole minute he stood there, not daring to look up. Then he took a deep breath, clenched his hands tightly, and lifted his head.

"There it was!—as Dad had described it, but infinitely more grand. It swept upward from the valley floor, beautifully shaped and soaring, so tall that its misty blue peak could surely talk face-to-face with the stars. To David, who had never seen a mountain before, the sight was almost too much to bear. He felt so tight and shivery inside that he didn't know whether he wanted to laugh, or cry, or both. And the really wonderful thing about the Mountain was the way it *looked* at him. He was certain that it was smiling at him, like an old friend who had been waiting for years to see him again. And when he closed his eyes, he seemed to hear a voice which whispered, 'Come along, then, and climb.'"

She glanced up again, feeling the children folding themselves more closely about her as the ancient words rolled over them. She felt Nimitz, as well, sharing her own memories of her mother's voice reading the same story to her and memories of other mountains, even grander than the ancient David's, and rambles through them—memories he'd been there for—and savoring the new ones.

"It would be so easy to go!" she continued. "The back yard was hedged in (with part of the hedge growing right across the toes of the Mountain), but . . ."

"I imagine it's too much to hope they were all asleep?"

"You imagine correctly," Honor said dryly, stepping through the massive, inlaid doors of polished oak into the palatial chamber which the Palace guides modestly referred to as "the Library." "Not that you really expected them to be, now did you?"

"Of course not, but we neo-barbarian planetary despots get used to demanding the impossible. And when we don't get it, we behead the unfortunate soul who disappointed us."

Benjamin IX, Planetary Protector of Grayson, grinned at her, standing with his back to the log fire crackling on the hearth behind him, and she shook her head.

"I knew that eventually all this absolute power would go to your head," she told him in a display of *lesse majeste* which would have horrified a third of the planet's steadholders and infuriated another third.

"Oh, between us, Elaine and I keep him trimmed down to size, Honor," Katherine Mayhew, Benjamin's senior wife said.

"Well, us and the kids," Elaine Mayhew, Benjamin's junior wife corrected. "I understand," she continued with a cheerful smile, "that young children help keep parents younger."

"That which does not kill us makes us younger?" Benjamin misquoted.

"Something like that," Elaine replied. At thirty-seven T-years, she was almost twelve years younger than her husband and almost six years younger than her senior wife. Of course, she was almost a quarter T-century younger than Honor . . . who was one of the youngest looking people in the room. Only the third and most junior of her personal armsmen, Spencer Hawke, and the towering young lieutenant commander in Grayson

Navy uniform, looked younger than she did. Prolong did that for a person.

Her mouth tightened as the thought reminded her why they were all here, and Nimitz pressed his cheek against the side of her face with a soft, comforting croon. Benjamin's eyes narrowed, and she tasted his spike of recognition. Well, he'd always been an extraordinarily sharp fellow, and spending eight T-years as the father of a daughter who'd been adopted by a treecat had undoubtedly sensitized him.

She gave him another smile, then crossed to the young man in the naval uniform. He was a veritable giant for a Grayson—indeed, he was actually taller than Honor was—and although she was in civilian attire, he came to attention and bowed respectfully. She ignored the bow and enfolded him in a firm embrace. He stiffened for an instant—in surprise, not resistance—and then hugged her back, a bit awkwardly.

"Is there any new word, Carson?" she asked quietly, stepping back a half-pace and letting her hands slide down to rest on his forearms.

"No, My Lady," he said sadly. "Your Lady Mother is at the hospital right now." He smiled faintly. "I told her it wasn't necessary. It's not as if this falls into her area of specialization, and we all know there's really nothing to be done now except to wait. But she insisted."

"Howard's her friend, too," Honor said. She glanced at Andrew LaFollet. "Is Daddy with her, Andrew?"

"Yes, My Lady. Since Faith and James are safely tucked away here in the nursery, I sent Jeremiah to keep an eye on them." Honor cocked her head, and he shrugged slightly. "He wanted to go, My Lady."

"I see." She looked back at Carson Clinkscales and gave his forearms another little squeeze, then released them. "She knows there's nothing she can really do, Carson," she said. "But she'd never forgive herself if she weren't there for your aunts. By rights, I ought to be there, too."

"Honor," Benjamin said gently, "Howard is ninety-two years old, and he's touched a lot of lives in that much time—including mine. If everyone who 'ought to be there' really *were* there, there'd be no room for the patients. And he's been in the coma for almost three days now. If you were there, and if he knew you were there, he'd read you the riot act for neglecting everything else you ought to be doing."

"I know," she sighed. "I know. It's just—"

She stopped and shook her head with a slight grimace, and he nodded understandingly. But he didn't really understand, not completely, she thought. Despite the changes which had come to Grayson, his own thought processes and attitudes had been evolved in a pre-prolong society. To him, Howard Clinkscales was *old*; for Honor, Howard should have been less than middle-aged. Her own mother, who looked considerably younger than Katherine Mayhew, or even Elaine, and who'd carried Faith and James to term naturally, was twelve T-years years *older* than Howard. And if he was the first of her Grayson friends she was losing to old age so preposterously young, he wouldn't be the last. Gregory Paxton's health was failing steadily, as well. And even Benjamin and his wives showed the signs of premature aging she'd come to dread.

Her mind flashed back to the nursery and the book she'd been reading, with its tale of the immortal, ever-renewed Phoenix, and the memory was more bittersweet than usual as she saw the silver lightly threading the Protector's still-thick, dark hair.

"Your offspring and my beloved siblings did quite well, actually," she said, deliberately seeking a change of subject. "I'm always a bit surprised by how they settle down for reading. Especially with all the other more interactive avenues of amusement they have."

"It's not the same, Aunt Honor," one of the two young women sitting at the big refectory-style table to one side of the cavernous fireplace said. Honor looked at her, and the dark-haired young woman, who looked remarkably like a taller, more muscular version of Katherine Mayhew, reached up to rub the ears of the treecat stretched across the back of her chair.

"What do you mean, not the same, Rachel?" Honor asked.

"Listening to you read," Benjamin's oldest daughter replied. "I guess it's mostly because you're involved—we don't get to see enough of you here on Grayson—and you're, well, sort of larger than life for all the kids." No one else would have noticed the way the young woman colored very slightly, but Honor hid a smile as she tasted Rachel's own spike of adolescent admiration and embarrassment. "I know when Jeanette and I—" she nodded sideways at the slightly younger woman sitting beside her "—were younger, we always looked forward to seeing you. And Nimitz, of course."

The treecat on Honor's shoulder elevated his nose and flirted his tail in satisfaction at Rachel's acknowledgment of his own importance in the social hierarchy, and several people chuckled. Rachel's companion, Hipper, only heaved a sigh of longsuffering patience and closed his eyes wearily.

"She may be right, Honor," Elaine said. "Young Honor certainly volunteered suspiciously quickly to 'help keep an eye on the littles' this evening."

"Besides, Aunt Honor," Jeanette said in a softer voice (she was considerably shyer than her older sister), "you really do read awfully well." Honor raised an eyebrow, and Jeanette blushed far more obviously than Rachel had. But she also continued with stubborn diffidence. "I know I always really enjoyed listening to you. The characters all even sounded different from each other. Besides, there's more challenge in a book. No body just *gives* you the way the people and places look; you have to imagine them for yourselves, and you make that *fun*."

"Well, I'm glad you think so," Honor said after a moment, and Katherine snorted.

"She's not the only one who thinks so," she said,

when Honor looked at her. "Most of the nannies have told me what a wonderful mother you'd make, if you weren't so busy off blowing up starships and planets and things."

"Me?" Honor blinked at her in surprise, and Katherine shook her head.

"You, Lady Harrington. In fact," she went on a bit more intently, "there's been some, um, discussion of your responsibility in that direction. Faith is a perfectly satisfactory heir for the moment, you understand, but no one in the Conclave of Steadholders really expects her to *remain* your heir."

"Cat," Benjamin said in an ever so slightly quelling tone.

"Oh, hush, Ben!" his wife replied tartly. "Everyone's been pussyfooting around the issue for a long time now, and you know it. Politically, it would be far better in almost every respect for Honor to produce an heir of her own."

"That's not going to be happening any time soon," Honor said firmly. "Not with everything I already have on my plate at the moment!"

"Time's slipping away, Honor," Katherine said with stubborn persistence. "And you're going back out into another war. Tester knows we'll all be praying for you to come back safely, but—"

She shrugged, and Honor was forced to concede her point. Still. . . .

"As you say, Faith is a perfectly acceptable heir," she said. "And while I suppose I ought to be thinking in dynastic terms, it doesn't really come naturally to me."

"I hate to say it, Honor, but Cat may have a point from another perspective, as well," Benjamin said slowly. "Oh, there's no legal reason you need to produce an heir of your own body right this minute. Especially with, as you say, Faith acknowledged as your heir by everyone. But you're a prolong recipient. You say you're not used to thinking in dynastic terms, but what happens if you wait another twenty or thirty years and *then* have a child? Under Grayson law, that child would automatically supplant Faith, whatever special provisions the Conclave may have made in her favor when everyone thought you were dead. So there's Faith . . . who's spent thirty or forty years thinking of herself as the Harrington Heir Apparent and suddenly finds her nose put out of joint by a brand new infant nephew or niece."

Honor looked at him, and he sighed.

"I know Faith is a wonderful child and she loves you dearly, Honor. But this is Grayson. We've seen a thousand years of those dynastic politics you don't think in terms of, and there have been some really ugly incidents. And the ugliest ones of all have usually happened because the people they happened to were so sure they couldn't arise in *their* families. Besides, even if no overt problem crops up, would it really be fair to Faith to yank the succession out from under her like that? Unless you produce a child fairly soon, she's got to grow up thinking of herself as Miss Harrington, with all the trappings and importance of the job. You didn't do that, but she's in a totally different position, and it's going to be fairly central to her self-image, you know."

"Maybe so, but—"

"No buts, Honor. Not on this one," Benjamin said gently. "It *will* be. It has to be. I know it was a lot harder for Michael than he ever let on, and he never wanted the Protector's job in the first place. But he was in exactly the same position Faith is, and when Bernard Raoul came along and pushed him out of the succession, he was almost . . . lost for a while. He needed to redefine who he was and what he was doing with his life when he was suddenly no longer Lord Mayhew." The Protector shook his head. "I was discussing this with Howard just last month, and he said—"

It was Benjamin's turn to break off suddenly as Honor's face tightened in remembered pain.

"I'm sorry," he said after a moment, even more gently. "And I don't mean to be exerting any unfair pressure. But he was concerned about it. He loves Faith almost as much as he loves you, and he was worried about how she'd react. And," he smiled crookedly, "I think he was sort of hoping he'd have a chance to see your child."

"Benjamin, I . . ." Honor blinked rapidly, and Nimitz crooned soothingly in her ear.

End excerpt from *At All Costs*, by David Weber
available in hardcover November 2005 from Baen Books